The Stones of Summer

THE STONES OF SUMMER

DOW MOSSMAN

THE OVERLOOK PRESS
Woodstock & New York

This edition first published in paperback in the United States in 2004 by
The Overlook Press, Peter Mayer Publishers, Inc.
Woodstock & New York
in association with the Lost Books Club, Inc.

WOODSTOCK:
One Overlook Drive
Woodstock, NY 12498
www.overlookpress.com
[for individual orders, bulk and special sales, contact our Woodstock office]

NEW YORK:
141 Wooster Street
New York, NY 10012

Cataloging-in-Publication Data is available from the Library of Congress

ISBN 1-58567-517-2
Manufactured in the United States of America
1 3 5 7 9 8 6 4 2

For John T. Frederick and William Cotter Murray, who wrote things down And for Net, Cliff, Jus & Sandy, who didn't.

For Mark Moskowitz: & also because you made this happen in The Real World / 1998–2003

& The Author wishes to thank Betty Kelly, Carl Brandt, Laura Nolan, & Steve Riggio for helps, even empathies, in the short & long life-weathers involved in this book —

My characters, though resembling real people in many ways, are not responsible for themselves in this novel. This dream is my fiction entirely.

— Dow Mossman

INTRODUCTION

I am the guy who in 1972 wrote an enthusiastic review of a novel by Dow Mossman called *The Stones of Summer* for the *New York Times Book Review*, which had no immediate effect except for a letter of thanks from the author informing me that he was then driving a truck for a living. About thirty years later, I got a phone call from a filmmaker named Mark Moskowitz who had read my review at the time and later bought a paperback edition of Mossman's book and had finally gotten around to reading it. He agreed that *Stones* was a work of pure genius and wanted to interview me for a movie he was making about the book and its author.

Well, sure, and even though Alice and I were just then leaving Florida for our summer house in Maine, Mark was so all-fired curious about Dow and his marvelous book that he traveled from Pennsylvania with a five-man crew and his wife, Clare, to the easternmost town in the United States. (When the sun rises over Campobello Island it shines through our bedroom window.) He shot a week's worth of film, recording a lot of breathless scenery and sundry picturesque Yankee types who like myself were mostly "from Away," a place generally identified with the other forty-nine.

Well, it was great fun giving my opinions about literature in general and Mossman's book in particular, but the most pertinent question Mark asked me I could not answer, which was what had happened to the author since 1972. Of course, if I had kept up with Dow after receiving that letter about his driving a truck for a living and had known that he was still in Cedar Rapids, Iowa, and had worked as a welder for eighteen of the intervening thirty years, having suffered a writer's block the size of King Tut's tomb, then Moskowitz would have had no movie—much as if, had the Prince of Denmark had obeyed his father's ghost, *Hamlet* would have been a one-act play, which was not the fashion at the time. No, for Mark's quest to have duration and meaning it had to continue, and so Stephen Dedalus and Leopold Bloom wander around Dublin for a whole Joycean day and many hundreds of Joycean pages and the namesake of Joyce's book is continually blown off course by adverse winds, and the Joads take forever to get to California; for what is an epic but an interminable and fascinating quest?

I am glad to have played my part, which began with the review of Dow's book in 1972. The early '70s was an exciting time for popular culture and experimental literature, publishers being open to innovative forms and styles, thanks to the influence of novels like Kerouac's *On the Road,* Pynchon's *V,* Heller's *Catch-22* and Gaddis's *The Recognitions.* Tom Wolfe was responsible for a newfound journalistic freedom, a pyrotechnical non-prosaic prose, and when I began my book-reviewing career in 1970, starting with *The New Republic,* I benefited from that tangerine-colored dandified style.

The poet Reed Whittemore was then literary editor of *The National Review,* and allowed me to write what I called "galactical" reviews, which surrounded the book in question with digressively spiraling nebulae. John Leonard was then in charge at the *New York Times Book Review* and my contact there was Charles Simmons, who wrote the quiff classics *Powdered Eggs* and *An Old-Fashioned Darling.* It was Charles who asked me to review *The Stones of Summer,* and the result was typical of the thing I did, stylistic fireworks that managed to catch Mark Moskowitz's attention at the time, resulting (after a thirty-year delay) in *Stone Reader* and the eventual—whiz!—reissue of Dow Mossman's— bang!—brilliant novel—aahh!

"*The Stones of Summer,*" I wrote, "is a whole river of words fed by a torrential imagination," and something like that might be said of my review, which obviously got carried along by the same force of the book I had read that was "not a novel in the classic sense, not as merely a *novella narratio,* a new kind of story, a news event, material to be shredded in the chattering machines of journalists"—by which I meant typewriters, still then in general use—"but as something more solid, more closely approaching that other (not etymologically related) 'novel,' that legal term in Roman law pertaining to a new order, a new way of regulating things."

Sticking to the imperial mode, I said that reading Dow's book was "like crossing another Rubicon, discovering a different sensibility, a brave new world of consciousness. *The Stones of Summer* is a holy book and it burns with a sacred Byzantine fire, a generational fire, moon-fire, stone-fire." What I was holding in my hands bore "the evident impress of an entire generation's experience on the ordering of form, the fashioning of style, the entire business of putting so complex a novel as *The Stones of Summer* together." Mossman's manner reminded me of "the Faulknerian swarm miasmic, given order not by the baroque turbulence of Jacobean Gothic, but by the whining rise and fall of a ceaseless sitar." As you can see, I preferred to write about style stylistically, and not according to the Associated Press's tight-crease format. In sum, "You ain't alive if you ain't got that jive."

The autobiographical antihero of Mossman's novel is Dawes Oldham Williams (D.O.W.) and much of the book is that standard device of first novels, the chronicle of a youth's coming of age, but with a number of differences. Thus I compared Mossman as a surregionalist of adolescent sex to Larry McMurtry, "the Grace Metalious of the Plains," who in *The Last Picture Show* "comes on with the specious realism of soap operatics, a flat style evoking mostly flat women with boys on top of them, [whereas] the ebullience of Mossman's acrobatics succeeds in conveying the rebellious energies of youth, the essential madness of adolescent reality. As in real life, no generous, but defeated, yet kindly and still rather pretty, if tearful wives offer their bodies to the boys" in Mossman's novel: "Most older women here are mothers, and they always come into the room at the wrong time, and are universally a pain." As a woman in the '70s was overhead by *The Village Voice* saying in Max's Kansas City, "The Fifties? Oh yeah, that was when no one got laid," and that truth is demonstrated at length by the unrequited yearnings of Dawes Oldham Williams.

He has a companionable gang of friends with "a taste for outlandish episodes and violent pranks," and in the final third of the book the hero increasingly resembles a literary character he greatly admires, the original American picaresque saint, Huckleberry Finn: "Ragged, dirty, unkempt, eternally rebellious, battered from pool cues and fists, a sort of WASP Schlemihl, Dawes persists in imposing his self-denied role of saintly malcontent upon the world, which rewards him as all truthtellers are rewarded, by grinding him slowly to bits." As Dawes comes apart, so does the last third of the book, the structure of which is "discontinuous, circumambient, lost in time and space, an eternal bummer to Mexico and death." In sum, *On the Road* meets *Easy Rider* head on.

"Is there a moral to this story," I asked, "this magical tale of rolling stones and singing stones, stone tongues and stone lights, this stone fishing in America? I don't know, and even if I did, I wouldn't say. Let me conclude, rather, with something by way of tribute to this very talented writer, an invocation of that moment of absolute silence that follows when you have finished the last chapter, paragraph and word of a book which you greatly admire, and set it aside so as to hear your own inner echoes, the dying chord of sympathetic response." Let me interrupt my own silence by adding that I hope that nothing I once said by way of sympathetic response dissuades you from reading Dow Mossman's book for the first time, an experience that I myself can never have again, an unrecoverable moment like the one Jay Gatsby sought in vain to retrieve, like the home to which Thomas Wolfe told us we cannot return.

John Seelye
July 2003

CONTENTS

THE
STONES
OF
SUMMER

BOOK ONE

A Stone of Day
1949—1950

"History's the maddest hat. I'm doin' fine . . . ."

"That's what you think, Bronco . . .

tell it to Saxon angels.

The walls have eyes."

—Dawes Williams and Abigail Winas
colloquying conversing airs.

1

When August came, thick as a dream of falling timbers, Dawes Williams and his mother would pick Simpson up at his office, and then they would all drive west, all evening, the sun before them dying like the insides of a stone melon, split and watery, halving with blood. August was always an endless day, he felt, white as wood, slow as light. Dawes shifted about in his seat, uncomfortable, watching the land slide past. It was late, a steady progression of night; the conversations inside the car were like great wood eyes and, driving west over Iowa, the evening was always air vague with towns, blue fences, and crossroads vacant of cars. He watched the deserted country porches slide by like lonely pickets guarding the gray, outbreaking storm of sky; like juts of rock.

They were going to the farm again, like all those other summers, he thought. He grew restless, like something stuck to his seat in a movie theatre; like something being made only to watch everything at once, and his mother, Leone, Arthur's daughter, would feed him crackers and Coke and tell him they couldn't possibly stop at another service station because her parents, Arthur and especially Gin, were growing older now so they must reach the farm before midnight. The new '50 Chevy was silent and green, smelling almost of iron linen, as they rode down the last of day, and the boy would ask about the greyhounds again, and why his grandfather didn't simply raise corn like the other farmers. Simpson would take the cold cigar from his mouth and say:

"Yes sir, old boy. Art still grows some corn for the science of it, but Arthur's a smart man for a farmer, and knows that greyhounds are the best crop that can be taken from Iowa."

"Is that the way it is, is it?" Dawes said.

"It certainly is, old boy. I wouldn't lie to you," Simpson said, smiling. "It's taken him forty years, but Art's got most of a half million dollars in the bank off those dogs."

"Thank you for telling me that."

"That's quite all right," Simpson would say. "Arthur's a pretty sharp man, old boy."

"Really," Leone said, "what are you two talking about?"

The car would grow periodically quiet. Dawes Williams sat utterly silent now, trying to piece together a picture of a half million dollars all in one pile and in a bank, and Simpson continued driving down strings of impossibly green fields, a single corn leaf blowing south, broken only by the dark and sightless country roads running, like masts, away with the eye, over the backs of the hills like ridges of dark bone, and Simpson continued to chew his black cigar driving through the still chains of towns—the one they were in looking exactly like the last, and the next—sleeping on the prairie like windless, land-hung schooners now beginning to lie down in night.

"What's this town?" the boy finally asked.

"This is State Center, Dawes," Simpson would say.

"Well, if it's that, how come it's so small? You'd think if it's the real center of the state it'd have more people than this."

"It does, old boy. They're all hiding out."

"Yes, Dawes," Leone, said, smiling, "this is also the cultural hub of the state."

"They're hiding out, playing their pianos," Simpson said.

"No, I mean it," Dawes said.

"In Iowa," Simpson said, "the people like to live on the edges."

"As if they were about to spring off at any moment," Leone said.

"I see," Dawes Williams said.

"I doubt that very much, old boy," Simpson said, blowing his thin, asthmatic smoke from the window.

"I see anyway," Dawes Williams said.

The brown crossroads ticked past like posts. Dawes sat watching Simpson's smoke drift in the air like blue, ringless angels, shapeless as the country evening. He was growing restless with leaving home. Before him lay the farm, Arthur. He could see Arthur standing by his gate, calling the grey-hounds in to feed. Slowly at sunset the packs of hounds, of Blacks and Fawns, Brindles and Grays, all mixed together, would be moving up the lane where the quiet walnuts hung on trees, casting up green stains on the wind. They were lean, howling everywhere. They were Arthur's greyhounds, and the dust clouds of walking, earthbound, laced within their step, left dying swirls in the wind as they moved up Arthur's lane to the swinging, rusted gate. There Arthur would be standing, as always, tall, thin and nearly aristocratic, even in his khaki, calling them in to feed. And soon, man high, still partly furious from the day spent nosing through the scrub, the fields, in the ditches of the Lesser Bovine

River, they would be jumping against him. In the dark now, as he was driving toward them, they would be all around him, Arthur, who was bent against them, on the long edge of their motion, within their dense and furious dog sounds, their whimperings and frantic invocations. Arthur, he knew, was bent within them, calling, Sis! Here Sissy. You sassy-sissy. Atta girl. RED JACK! Red dog. You old winner. You come home to feed finally? Gray-bearded. Cantankerous. Son of a bitch. Whatsamatter, fella? Like me. Mean again today. Too old? You mean old tracker. Red, atta boy. Sassy-sissy. RED-JACK-GET-THE-HELL-OFF-OF-LADY-MARY, calling, now, into the herding packs around him . . .

Only the car was quiet. Behind him lay the city, Ronnie Crown. And Dawes was restless because it was August, and August wasn't a month, it was a short afternoon, an executioner leading directly, without jury, and finally toward school where they chained him to dull rooms . . . where he sat all year watching the moth swarm, and where nice old ladies in flower-printed dresses and impeccable backgrounds complicated it further by parading past all day making him memorize cards, with stupidly large-block numbers, that passed for mathematics and that never talked back. Yes, Dawes Williams thought, rolling west, watching the moth swarm, dreading only September, dreading August, I am only eight years old and Ronnie Crown is right. Crown is always right. I am wasting my life. I am being forced to. The bastards. The mothers are robbing me and calling it good.

Dawes sat thinking of home, of kick-the-can, of summer nights like eyes, and of Ronnie Crown. He could still see him, Crown, slitting bicycle tires or, cursing, laughing, peter out, peeing on a bonfire of stick matches, night itself; like cans gone dead and swollen in alleys. Ronnie Crown, who was peerless, he knew, and who stole money from sheriff's pants to buy candy, fresh butts and stick matches for Dawes and the whole neighborhood. Crown, whose father's pants were fourth deputy sheriff of Thomas County, Iowa; Crown, whose mother owned a huge yellow shell of a nursing home, full to the walls of peacefully rotting bodies and who, himself, therefore, he thought, seemed always nervous, about to run off somewhere unnamed at any moment, and who smelled always like a dark spiral of old flesh, the well of a staircase, himself. In fact, Dawes could still see him moving down those rotting stairs, pausing only to spit into the huge yellow bowl of butter in the kitchen, before he, Ronnie Crown, ran cursing into the summer dust sleeping in the curve of his back drive. He saw Ronnie's old man, Elvin Crown, the fourth deputy, standing in the dark doorway, his belt off, calling Crown home.

"Why don't you wait for awhile?" Dawes Williams would say. "He'll cool down and hit you less."

"No," Crown would say, "if I come in now he'll only hit me once. If I come home in five minutes, the bastard'll hit me twice."

The great Crown, Dawes thought, who, when he could not steal or scrounge the necessary change, his father's silver, would steal instead the stick matches and cigarets from the new Hoinky-Toinky supermarket parked between Wadlove and Main Avenue . . . and who even smoked old cigars off the streets themselves when he couldn't buy them from the F Street Flyers, and who even succeeded in shooting damn Catty Byers, who was cute but who was a known snotass at age seven

> Catty Byers Catty Byers
> your old man's a damn mechanic
> but he's got no pliers

right between the eyes with the new, super Sears and Roebuck B-B gun which his father had given him for good grades exactly two days before he was expelled forever from The James Knox Polk Grade School . . .

The Chevy was silent. Dawes Williams thought only, next to his mother, riding west over Iowa, that Ronnie Crown was a great one. Not only had Crown managed completely to end his school days in the third grade, but what had amazed Dawes even more was that Ronnie had spent the rest of that last, selfless spring merely scuffing the indolent, nearly sacred dust of the A Avenue Alley, and throwing the wetted and smoke-tailing stick matches (like German-mother-fighter planes, Crown said) down in arcs from Dunchee's wall, all as if he truly had no second thoughts.

"Hello-mother-school," Ronnie Crown had said all that spring. "What'd you manage to fuck up in that dippy-assed James Knox Polk today, Dawes Williams-huncher?" Crown had asked innocently.

He could still see him, Crown, sitting on Dunchee's wall, high up, throned, looking down and inquiring, waiting, using—as Leone said—his usual "overkill" of language. Dawes was stopped below, looking up. Crown was intent, hiding it, busying himself by arching another smoking trail of a German fighter over Dawes' head. It crashed without real flames in a pile of others behind him.

"Nothing much," Dawes Williams had finally said. "Hit two homers in recess, though."

"Big screwy deal, Dawes."

"Ya. One was only a grounder-homer. What'd you do?"

"Screwed off some. Screwed off plenty."

"Oh ya?"

"Oh-humping-ya. What the hell is this, Truth and Answers forchristsake?"

"You mess around all day?"

"I messed plenty. I messed right through that old house on C Avenue finally. Broke every window in it, thought of burning the goddamn place down for awhile. —You tell anybody and I'll kill ya. Anyway, Dawes-dude, you should have been there. I missed you about three curve balls worth. That was about the time I was considering burning the frigging place down to the fugging ground."

"Oh ya?"

"Oh ya, Dawes," Crown said patiently. "Neat-screwy-neat-man. Finally met this dippy-assed, flunky kid name of Jip Reed from Chester A. Arthur down by Ben Franklin Field. We fixed our bikes some, putting balloon-bombs in our spokes."

"Oh-ya?"

"Oh-ya!" Crown said. "Oh ya! ya! frigging ya! —What the hell is this, my name's Dawes, I'm an idiot-silly-mother, and it's oh-ya time forchristsake!?!"

"Don't get nervous on me," Dawes Williams said. "What'd you do, put pinstripe decals on the fenders?"

"You know, Dawes," Crown said, "for being one of the smarter mothers I know you sure are dumb. I don't have any silly-assed fenders on my bike. Fenders are for pussies."

"You reverse your bars then?"

"Hell-yes. Then we put more cards and big-assed balloon-bombs in our spokes and buzzed the hell out of my old man's jail all afternoon. Neat man. He's going to-kill-piss-out-of-me when he gets home."

"What's so neat about it then?" Dawes said, jumping in.

"Beats school, doesn't it, mother-school?" Ronnie said finally.

"Guess so," Dawes said indefinitely.

"You bet your sweet ass," the great Crown said, even more forcefully, hopping the other side of Dunchee's wall. Dawes had stood watching him beating it off into the bush, disappearing like a small, neurotic, burrowing animal with watery eyes vanishing down a thin hole of light in the woods. And it didn't seem to Dawes that Ronnie Crown could have cared less if they ever let him back in again. He was free.

Because, he knew riding west to Arthur's, they never had said that. Usually they would let you crawl back, grateful, saved, to James Knox Polk in a week, two at the most. Even Dawes had done that. But to be told—short of moving to another state or outlying territory, to Texas or Alaska maybe—that you were through in the third grade, beyond forgiveness or pardon, could never come back for forever (for as long as Miss Wilma Spent continued to teach in the Thomas County school system) was an unusual thing. Only Ronnie Crown could have managed something as final and clean as that; no one else.

Simpson took out another cigar, rolling west in his Chevy . . . . But damn, Dawes thought, kicked out of the third grade, drummed out of school, was serious business in the end. From the window that day Dawes had watched Ronnie Crown giving the whole school, the whole class, mainly the third-grade window of Miss Wilma Spent, *the finger* as he headed up the long hill homeward. He was a worn shadow, pathetic, proud. He had only his thin cast-off spelling book to keep him warm. Dawes could see him punting his lunch pail before him, into the late fall wind. It was hopeless, of course. The great Crown was a goner for sure. But he had stood there a long time giving them, all of them—the teachers, the buildings, the school, the sky itself—the *finger* before he turned. He was a furious stone, Dawes Williams thought, and Ronnie Crown would always be standing around alone on sidewalks, swearing at people in general; at anyone who would pass by and listen. Most people, Dawes believed, they made go to school; Ronnie Crown, a kind of genius, had found a way so they thought they weren't even letting him in the door. Simpson, however, said Ronnie Crown would end up leading a life of petty crime; it was too bad, he said, but there it was.

Dawes sat silent, remembering it; that instant. The class that day still sat in the death hush Crown had brought down upon them like breath stuck in their throats. Crown had gone over the back of the hill. The teacher, Miss Wilma Spent, was just then coming back into the room. Because when pressed in the middle of a lesson, mathematics hour, for the answer to nine times six, Ronnie Crown had merely stood calmly against the furious glance of that vague old lady in the flower-printed dress and said:

"What kind of shit is this anyway? What the hell do you know about it? You probably ain't even been fucked on any good yet?"

There was a silence like Dawes Williams knew he'd never hear again, a silence like screaming roses growing in glass houses.

"WHAT did I hear you say?" Miss Wilma Spent finally managed, choking.

"Here I'm standin, ain't I, bitch?" Ronnie Crown said.

There was a grand, impeccable silence on that one. As soon as Miss Wilma was able to rise back from her knees, where Crown seemed to have put her with an invisible blow, she tried to rub the redness out of her face with a handkerchief, failed, turned calmly to Crown and said:

"I am afraid this cannot be tolerated."

Then she fell very silent. Then she chased Crown around the room with a paddle and a ruler for twenty-five minutes.

"So what?" Crown screamed, running. "Who cares? Fuck off."

"You leave this room before I'm done with you, Crown," Miss Wilma screamed behind him, "and I'll see you'll be sorry forever!"

"Doesn't follow. Shut up your goddamn trap," Crown said, squirming, maneuvering, moving about in and under the desks like the fastest-muscled worm in the world. "You're making me pee my pants with fear," he said laughing, filling the room.

"You despicable little boy!" Miss Wilma said. "You *trash!?!*"

"Help," Ronnie Crown said, "this old woman's trying to *kill* me."

Crown was trapped there, perched on the highest level of the book racks, moving about, back and forth, agile and fast on his knees, as Miss Wilma stood below, poking her ruler slightly below and behind him.

"Come down," she said.

"Shoot me if you want," Crown said, "but don't give me any more of your horseshit bullshit." But he was too fast for them all, Dawes Williams sat there thinking, and the paddle which she had already thrown had broken a window, raining down glass on kindergarten children, and that'll get the old bat back, he thought, and you can't be going around breaking windows and showering glass on kids if you are a teacher, American, responsible, and be getting away with it for long. That'll get her fired in the end, he thought, and Crown is taking her down with him for all of them. Only as it all turned out, Dawes knew now, he was wrong, and Crown was still perched up there saying:

"Why? Why?" he said. "Oh goddamn ball-less mother's milk why? Why did this goddamn goddamn thing have to happen to goddamn me? My old man's going to-kill-piss-out-of-me when I get home."

Miss Wilma, however, was not feeling mercy. She crossed the room, returned. She got Crown down finally by running him in the ass with the end of a long geography pointer. She shook him until she smiled and took him out by the ear, beating on him all the way, but Crown was really furious then, swearing in earnest, and soon Dawes—still locked to his chair locked to the floor—could hear him, Crown, free—two flights up through halls, stairwells and doors left ajar—cussing, cursing—and screaming straight in the principal Taft's face for justice, law and mercy in the world. There was, however, none to be had, and next he appeared, almost out of nowhere, outside in front of the window, giving them all the finger, swearing silently through glass, against the distance, across the space he had traveled. Then he turned, went up the dark spine of the hill, and was gone.

Then Miss Wilma Spent came back into the room, smiling as if she had just eaten cats that had eaten mice. Dawes Williams sat at his desk, picturing old movies he had seen on Simpson's new TV. It's one of those Ronald Colman's perhaps, he thought.

He sat watching, there, in the rain dark as spies falling, watching the real scene, the ideal one that was taking place in his head: There, stripped of his tassels and braids, Crown paraded before them. They were drumming him out, but he remained dignified. The whole school had fallen out in a thin formation of fists and hands saluting the air. Bugles blew in the distances. Morning was a perfect warning bell in a tower. Stillness. Then Miss Wilma Spent had advanced from behind softball diamonds and begun stripping Crown of his gear. His spelling books, his arithmetic cards, finally his pencils and notebooks fell by the wayside and blew noiselessly in the wind. Then Crown turned on his heel, a slight smile caught on the corners of his mouth, and headed for his mother's nursing home. He was finished but glad. Then, at the last moment, the last possible opportunity, with the whole school watching, Dawes Williams himself fell out of line and spit on the ground and walked arm in arm with Crown up that hill. . . .

"What are you thinking so seriously about, Dawes?" Leone said beside him in the car.

"Oh, nothing much," Dawes said.

His father said nothing. He was intent, driving the Chevy. The land was still sailing by, deeper with night and locust. Dawes settled in and began thinking about the great Crown again. He was unhappy over his mother's interruption. She was always doing that, watching him for signs. He knew she thought he might be crazy; or end up going to jail with Ronnie Crown. She wanted to sell the house and find another neighborhood. Simpson would laugh at her and call her polite, legal-sounding names. Thinking about it, Dawes finally relaxed. He was sure he would get kicked out of school many times before he was through; that he would eventually show them what he was made of, but somehow too, he knew, he had missed his day . . . . God, I love that ole Ronnie Crown, he thought. I should have defended him. I should have spoke up.

Later, in that spring and summer, in the evenings when his mother mis-placed him long enough to sneak outside, he met with Crown. They sat, hud-dled on the wall, talking. Crown lobbed nervous stick matches into the dust. They still had a secret—Mrs. Lowbus' exploded horse barn full of gasoline fire—that kept them together. The summer air unpaved the alley, leaving it open; a rutted mule tied to one place. The trees were air. Recalling the word, dark, deeper and more full of sin than the roots of Indian fires, than his grand-mother Gin's Methodist radio on Sunday morning, Dawes said:

"C'mon, Ronnie, you can tell me. What's 'fuck' mean?"

"Don'no, Dawes," Crown said. "Don't really fucking know. I just got Roger Casey to tell it to me once, though!"

"Doesn't seem they can kick ya out of school for a word if you don't know what it means."

"Roger Casey said they could, I asked'm—Hell of a mother that Roger Casey," Crown said.

They sat quietly on the wall for a long time, shadowed, deserted in the summer, only their skins keeping them warm. Crown lobbed slicked Ohio Blue-Tips. Dawes thought of the word again. It seemed full of curiosity, knowl-edge, a maze spreading through pale moonlight and green glass from nothing outward, ever-expanding beyond a point which wasn't known either. In

Crown's silence Dawes watched the old vine-choked wall open onto a lawn; the rear of Dunchee's nearly fallen mansion full of crannies, statues of wood like birds and witches' eyes. Just beside it, facing Main Avenue, sat another mansion just as shapeless; the one remade into a Catholic mortuary. Crown looked out over that lawn and visibly shivered.

"C'mon, Ronnie, you're holding out on me."

Crown wouldn't answer. Instead he sat silently eyeing the long distances down to Dunchee's mansion, the shorter space over to Mrs. Lowbus' fallen horse barn on the other side.

"Going to be Halloween soon enough, Dawes Williams," he said, nearly winking. "My favorite-favorite day of the year."

"Yep," Dawes Williams said, refusing to feel guilty. "C'mon, Ronnie, what's it all mean?"

Crown wouldn't answer. He was thinking about something else entirely. From that lost, dreaming look Dawes knew he was thinking about last Halloween. He looked finally, almost softly, at Dawes and said:

"Didn't we do it, Dawes? Didn't we show'em all? Didn't we explode that old bitch Lowbus' wood last Halloween, Dawes? And didn't we get away with it? And wasn't it beautiful, Dawes?" he said.

Dawes didn't answer. He sat, looking off at Dunchee's garage. He and Ronnie Crown were the smartest bastards in the world for their ages, but sad. The shadows moved on Dunchee's walls again, sad, like always. In Dunchee's second story, his garage, which was only another barn vacant of horses, was an old pool table. Sounds came from the walls and, lying hidden within, the light was dark as mirrors. The early August shadows, the low angle of afternoon sun, red as faces, would bloom through the high trellis, bursting with wishes, leaving only caged sounds like shades moving about within the softened walls. "There's old, rotting people in these walls I tell ya," Crown had once said.

In the dusk like dark milk the old pool table sat ruined forever on three legs; an overgrown stool not rolling and caught with spider webbings and lacings. In the late afternoons earlier that summer, after they had finished hitting stones with old rock bats and brooms, Dawes and Ronnie watched, like periscopes lost below the line of the brick wall, for old man Dunchee to leave his yard and enter his house; down the long, tended edge of driveway. It took him forever. Then, playing Indian in the brown summer overgrowth, they would crawl their way to the rear of the garage and, going up the back of the trellis, prying at the window, the dead and broken hole in the wall, they finally made it into the black loft. There they would whisper excitedly, covered with only the evening shadows, themselves, their red design. They lay low, listening to only the walls move, shift out from under them now in a light wind of noises as the old people were trapped in the windows now. Finally, they would shine matchlight at the old man, at Dunchee, from the dusty and reflectionless windows. They would move it about in the dim interior cracks, the walls of thin wood, until he would finally see it and begin picking his listing way up his driveway, waving his cane, threatening lawsuits, and they would begin retreating again, exploding with laughter, down the back of the trellis and over the brick wall like rabbits, to the safety of the unpaved alley; the long summer grass and hidden weeds of the vacant lot beyond. Soon, a half hour later, the old man's cane could be seen waving just over the rise of his wall. Loud lamenting curses lay beyond; his cane was coughing.

"He's a mean ole bastard's heart," Ronnie Crown had said.

Dawes knew different; he knew they were keeping Dunchee alive; that it was the same act, but different feelings . . . .

"But c'mon, Ronnie," Dawes Williams was saying later that summer, "what *does* 'fuck' mean, do you suppose?"

"Hell, Dawes, I tell you I just don't know," Ronnie said.

He sat on the wall, smoking a butt. The sun, low and dancing, moved off his thoughtful face like the red membranes of locust wing shredding with noise. He still spoke with a hushed, careful tone that implied always, of course, he really did know, exactly, what 'fuck' meant, but for vague and personal reasons he wasn't talking about it just then.

"How should I know, Dawes? But ole Roger Casey has a damn neat way of saying it, rolls it off his tongue like, you know, like he's about to pounce on you and bite off yer goddamn head with it, and I got'em to tell it to me. It was a long time ago, before I can even remember."

There was a silence.

"Hell of a mother that Roger Casey," Ronnie Crown said.

"I still can't figure how they could expel you for a word if you didn't know what it meant," Dawes said.

"You're goddamn obsessed with that problem, Dawes," Crown said finally. "That's what I like about you, Dawes. You're about as cowshit smart as I am. You're the only one comes close."

"Thanks, Ronnie," Dawes said, grinning. "That means a whole lot to me."

"Fuck off," Crown said. "Anyway, it was a little-horseshit-fucking confused at first, but it all worked out fine for me in the end. I got all the peehole time in the world now."

"Simpson says you'll never be a lawyer for General Motors at this rate," Dawes said. "That's the only thing about it."

"What the fuck does Simpson know about it? He's not a lawyer for General Motors himself I notice."

"That's true," Dawes said.

In the silence, the vine shadows moving in moonlight, Crown sat smoking and lobbing chewed stick matches into the alley. Dawes felt a sudden chill, the night wind going through his skin like it was actually true he was only dressed in his bones; the stalks of summer flowers. He sat watching blackbirds flying in the trees, the sails of near night sky for awhile. Finally he offered:

"Well, I'm going to Arthur's farm again soon."

"Big screwy deal, Dawes."

"What's a big screwy deal about it?"

"You idiot-mother," Crown started out. "Stand around and milk some fat old cows. Stand around with your finger in your ear all morning counting dippy-ass chickens. Big screwy deal, Dawes. By Farm-All Jesus, that is."

"You want to go?" Dawes Williams said.

In the stillness Crown was incredulous.

"Hell no, I don't want to go. How in pisspoorsake does it sound like I want to go, you dipshit? Besides, your mother hates me," Crown'd said. "She won't even let me on her sidewalk. How's she gonna let me ride in her damn car? I'm not walkin', and I'm not sleepin' in *those* woods. Now I ask you. What a fan-friggingtastic leap."

"Ya," Dawes said, "but sometimes too she says you have 'native intelligence' and can be salvaged."

"Big deal of her. So your mother's an ass. So goddamn what?"

"I keep thinkin' maybe that will help one of these days."

"You keep doin' that, Dawes. Oh-goddamn-surefire."

"She says you may have musical talent, too. Sometimes she wants to give you piano lessons."

"Well tell'r she's goddamn right," Ronnie said. "I can dance. I know more motherless swearing combinations than any other crazy sonofafugging bitches you ever seen in *your* frigging life."

"Language is a good thing, all right," Dawes said.

"Fuckin'-A," Crown said.

"I'll go in and ask her anyway. I'd like to have you along."

"Thanks, mother, that's big of you," Crown finally said. "Dawes, you are one dumb beautiful kid. You're the only goddamn friend I got."

Dawes said nothing more. Silent, he got down off the wall. He went inside to find his mother. She was upstairs packing, humming Schumann, nearly singing in Dawes' grandmother Gin's high, measured, Methodist soprano. He noticed she was putting his clothes into her suitcase.

"What?" she said, dropping Schumann like a dish. "*Have* you gone mad? I should say not. You're not even supposed to speak with Ronnie Crown. Is that . . . *criminal* outside?"

"But he's my buddy," Dawes Williams said.

Leone went to the window and began peering round corners of her grandmother Dawes' lace Victorian curtains. She assumed nearly the pose and posturing of an excited wren, knocked nearly senseless with the fear of climbing cats, but peeking round sunlit leaves heavy with edges and shadings. She seemed somehow too young to be that nervous.

"I can see you lurking behind that tree, Ronnie Crown," she said finally. "Go directly home if you please."

"There's too many goddamn people dying there," Ronnie called back from the street.

"I'm sorry about that," Leone said, "but I'm afraid I'll have to ask you to go home anyway."

"Thanks for the feelin's, Mrs. Williams," Crown called up, moving out from behind the moon shadows of his tree now. "But while yer at it— why don't you go fuck off with'em?"

"GO DIRECTLY HOME! " she screamed.

"I got rights," Crown said. "Who are you, Mrs. Williams, the queen of ice cream, forchristsake?"

"GO DIRECTLY HOME THIS MINUTE IF YOU PLEASE!"

"That's damn silly," Crown said. "I don't please at all. You must have figured that out by now, Mrs. Williams."

"GO!?! YOU . . . GO!?!"

"It's a free damn country, Mrs. Williams. I got rights. This sidewalk's public to me as if it was George Washington himself, the silly dip-ass, who was standing here. Who do you think you are, Mrs. Williams—the queen of France forchristsake? I got rights and I know it."

"SO WHAT!?!"

"So that's what makes me dangerous," Ronnie Crown said.

"*Mister* Crown," she said, "leave. Or so help me I'm coming down there and spanking you within one inch of your dubious life. I only wish my husband were here to hear about this!"

"My red ass you will," Crown said. "My old man's a deputy of the court and you're crossin' his line now, by God. He'll come over here and bust your ass backwards with a damn board, by God."

"THIS IS INCREDIBLE!?!" Leone screamed. "I'M CALLING THE POLICE ABOUT THIS!?!"

"You got no sense, Mrs. Williams. My old man *is* the frigging law. I just got done telling you that!"

"GET OUT!?! I . . . I THINK YOU NEED TO BE BEATEN!" Leone said breaking down.

"Who are you bluffin'? Bloodless-Jesus, I'll call a damn sheriff and have you stuck in a hole. Bread and water, you witch!"

She was repressing a scream by then, falling away from the window, and

Dawes could see she was about to cry. She was always crying, he thought. Still, standing there, something went out of him, flowing like dead rivers from the edges of his hands. Suddenly going to the window and hanging out, he called down to Crown:

"You leave my mother alone, you bastard!"

"God's body," Crown said. "You fuck off too, Dawes."

"Listen, you asslick," Dawes Williams said, "you leave my mother alone or I'm coming down there with a bat and feedin' you your ass!"

"DAWES!?!" she said behind him. "Dawes!?!" Leone said, nearly fainting, staggering backwards, recognizing him.

She revived, however, to spank him violently with her hairbrush. She shook him like rags.

"What'd I do? What'd I do?" Dawes Williams said.

"Ohhhhhhhhhhhhhhhhhhhhhhhhh," Leone said, recognizing him again, breaking down, lying out on her bed. "I just don't know!"

In the silence he went back to the window. Hanging out, he could see that Crown was gone; vanished in the darkening, swirling evening light like air twirled through a sieve.

"How comes he always wins?" Dawes Williams said finally.

"Leave me," she said, murmuring, reclining close to her early evening pillows.

"I guess it just wouldn't have worked out," Dawes said.

But now they were riding west in the car, she had forgiven him (not that he ever knew exactly what it was she was forgiving) and they were going to the "kennels," as she called them; and now she was wiping the fine hair away from his face and he began wondering what she was really like. Dark-skinned, like Arthur, she was more of a mystery to him than Simpson, who was open and blond. She seemed to be two things at once to him; she was both soft and hard, fierce and quiet, sincere and ridiculous. Still, flying beyond the blur of the slower, western river bottoms, the gullies of corn, he thought things must remain one at once, not two. Things are whole, not-half-times-two-divided-by-one. He thought, finally, mathematics was mad; as aimless as nine times six.

He thought he would put thinking about Ronnie Crown away for awhile now; perhaps forever. The car was too quiet for thinking. Still, it was a mystery how Crown had ever done it. He could see Crown's thin form, nose to nose with Miss Wilma Spent. It was like standing in front of a mirror and telling yourself, Dawes Williams thought, that you would eventually starve, or only dig ditches, or walk in the big snows without shoes, or something damning like that. Yes, he thought, Simpson Williams—taking the cold cigar from his mouth—had told him early about the importance of an advanced pragmatic education, and, in his early wonderment, Dawes Williams felt himself trapped within a necessary unbelief. . . .

"Lemme time you again, Simpson. Gotta go sixty miles an hour. One every minute. Give me your watch!"

"Big deal, old boy," Simpson said.

"You've done that fifty times, Dawes," Leone said.

"One more won't kill anything," Dawes said. "Nothin' else to do."

He took his father's watch. It was a thin pocket watch, old and worn, the crystal was smoked and yellow as the faint gold around the rim. His father's father—Ceril Percil Williams, the Midwestern lawyer who had died before Dawes was born, who was always therefore, to Dawes, a gray picture dressed in flannel vests, gold watch fobs, and pale asthmatic spectacles—had given the watch to Simpson when he died of a disease rare for Nebraska, and which sounded always to Dawes as if it could have only been invented in some exotic place, like Europe, and Simpson said that Dawes could have it (the watch, not the disease, Dawes hoped) when he died, but, to Dawes again, that seemed too far off to count on, and a lot of dying for only one watch anyway and, besides, Dawes said he wanted a wristwatch—that he didn't think of old, pale, ticking pocket watches in the first place.

"Did Hyoot John Williams himself give you that watch fob?" Dawes Williams asked. "Is it the bronzed Mexican bullet that was taken out of him, that was put in him by the famous bandit Charcon?"

"No," Simpson said, "no, old John gave me other things, though."

"What kind of things?"

"Oh, just things, old boy."

"Cowboy things?"

"No. Guess not."

"I see," Dawes Williams said.

"No, I doubt that, old boy," Simpson Williams said.

"Who cares? I'll be a monkey's uncle, if you'll be a Hyoot John Williams' nephew," Dawes said, laughing out loud.

Simpson threw a match out the window, saying nothing. He looked at Dawes strangely. Dawes knew he had missed on that one; that he would have to control himself or Simpson would be wondering next if he was all there as a boy. Anyway, Dawes thought, Simpson didn't know much; he only liked very old things, to begin with; he was a conservative man and he wore vests, deep, impossible linen smelling of yellow tobacco, years after everyone else in Rapid Cedar had given it up. Usually in the mornings this made Leone irritated and she would eye Simpson coming round the edge of the dining room arch, descend, and say: "Simpson, when are you going to break down and get a new pair of pants!?! Honestly. You look like two walking potato sacks with shoes on. Oh well," she would say, bending over bacon, the stove, gazing at a magazine, the morning paper, a cookbook or, perhaps, a stray piece of piano music, "no one pays any attention to what *I* think anymore," she would say, "but I guess I came by it honestly." "I don't need this sort of thing in the morning, Leone," Simpson would say. "Yes, well," she would say, "why, when Dad's dogs were doing well at the tracks round the country he'd spend over two hundred dollars for suits in the thirties." "Your father had a lot of faith in the future, Leone," Simpson would say. "Perhaps that's what it takes after all," she would say, "anyway he was such a striking-*looking* man. I'm sure he would have succeeded at something." "Yes, God bless him," Simpson would say, snatching his coffee off the stove. "Even my brother Dawes dressed that way. Oh well," she would say, turning her bacon. "Yes, yes, I've just heard all about your family, Leone," Simpson would say, walking out into the morning. Dawes would watch him go; an armload of company mail, a thin bemused smile, an old hat were keeping him warm. He sat watching him walk under an arch again; this time the front door, under the technicolor, Walt Disney–bright reproduction of the Williams coat of arms (a tattered mantle surrounding an open book; an extended hand, holding the book, rising cuffed in clouds straight and vertical from the top of a knight's helmet, he knew, ME MELIORA MANEUT; things lost, drawn and quartered in Elizabeth's search for crown jewelers, for Mary Queen of Scottish Williams' crown jewels) on his way to the post office to drop off and pick up more company mail . . . .

"One minute! Hang on here," Dawes Williams said, not listening to his mother, who had been chattering again. "One minute! Did we go a damn mile exactly?"

"Dawes, don't say 'damn.'"

"Who cares?"

"Pretty close, old boy," Simpson murmured.

He looked down at Dawes and smiled warmly. Still, Dawes thought, it was as if he were about to take out a cloth and begin absently polishing one of the more prized fossils in his accountant's wonderland of geological artifacts. His shiny, bright, prized, possessed, scrubbed rocks.

"Not exactly. I knew it. Do it again just right this time."

"Yes," Simpson said, "but by the time you tell me it's a minute, it's not a minute anymore, is it?"

"Yes, but it's pretty close."

"Yes, but if it's pretty close, it's not exactly, is it?"

"Oh-ya," Dawes Williams said. "You got me there. Who cares?"

"Simpson!" Leone said. "*Why* don't you tell him it's a mile a minute or whatever and let it go at that?"

"Well, Mother," he said, looking over at her, "if it's not a mile, it's something else, isn't it?"

"Really, Simpson," she said quietly, beginning to ignore him.

It was late now; they were beginning to approach, rhythmic, ritualistic, a dance of summers, the town that was drying, a melodrama, a simple mass of broken pots against the hills. Dawes City, Iowa, population three hundred sixty-two, some picked-over red chickens, and Abigail Winas.

"West Iowa is different from east Iowa," Dawes Williams said. "It's full of old hills and roads running in the river bluffs. The sky is different."

"How's that, old boy?" Simpson said.

"It's deeper, stranger."

"A glacier did it," Simpson said through his black cigar.

"How's that?" Dawes Williams said.

"Well, the last glacier kind of wound around like a snake, missing eastern Iowa, but digging up the west."

"I'll bet that's true," Dawes Williams said.

"Of course it is. A scientific fact."

"I'll bet that's true anyway," Dawes said. "Like Hyoot John Williams almost."

In the silence Simpson sensed something had gone out of Dawes' voice:

"Hyoot John what, old boy?" he said, almost tentatively.

"Hyoot John was a cowboy's ass," Dawes said. "He never was."

"Dawes," Leone said, "don't say 'ass.'"

It was late. Simpson said nothing more. Soon they would reach the last gravel road, Dawes knew, the one he had been watching for, waiting to come up surprising him, a sudden door not open. Then they would turn off the concrete highway, a last cold evening ribbon behind them, they would clatter over the twin sets of railroad trackings running just west to Omaha, and a long way east now to Chicago, and they would cross the thin, summer mudhole, the Bovine River. It wasn't much of a river, he knew, and he began thinking how he could jump the whole thing with a short run late in the summer. It would be a slow road then, closing behind them all and, in his silence, coasting before itself, watching the moon skim the black, almost vacant river, he thought he was nearly dreaming. He could already see himself there, running on the banks in other summers . . . .

Because he often came down here to the river with the greyhounds. They all ran in the late afternoon sun; blurred with brilliance, dark ghosts made of flesh. And he had sat on the banks and watched them. At evening they would bow their heads, nosing under the sill of the river. And sometimes he and the dogs would get by Arthur's fences and, roaming wild here, they would bark, sing, celebrate, slide down mud banks and splash in what was left of the water. Dawes would be almost naked. And sometimes, late at night even, Dawes would come with his grandfather, with Arthur, down there to the moon of the river to fetch in loose, running-away greyhounds; to chase them and fool them back to their huts on the hill. Then the night would spring alive; the dogwoods; the blackness; a wash of moon and fire and water. And walking, in the late fields, in the hut of dark behind Arthur's deep gait, moving, running to keep up with his step, his speechless walkings striding through the clover ends, Dawes Williams would suddenly be afraid the world would go out. He was afraid of the night, of even the black wind flying like blind birds through the edges of corn leaf. Then it was as if Gin's thundering God were out and walking, too; were summering in an Iowa barn and about to sound; to come forth and collapse the air with shouting; to sally about in his own turned droppings of night. It was as if something furious and unnamed, some illusion, were waiting for him, out, breaking off whole, exploding in on him from within the fields of black, waving corn, the deep night, the eyes like sheep sleeping in a field of darkened teeth, there, gazing at him, something only blowing itself up to rise soundlessly through him; through Arthur's walking footsteps. There. In that moon. By that river. And within that wind and summer. Like notes of dead music.

Now it was night too. They would be crossing soon, and he knew the Lesser Bovine River was named for a cow, or for all cows at once. He never could understand that. Still, without having to look, Dawes could see that around the banks, like open earth ditches, the ground was swollen, it heaved and caved at once, like roots without trunks; and always, year to year, there were bits of trash—old papers yellow with sun, cast-away cans and wire, even an old bathtub or two-covering the banks. Simpson said it was like a marching band of wrecked tin lizzies which nobody cared to explain. Dawes wondered why there was so much junk and his father said it was because the people had all given up and didn't care anymore.

"Yes, there's certainly a fine lot of degenerates left around here," Simpson said.

"How come it's Dawes City? Like me," Dawes Williams said, riding south on gravel now.

"You know very well why, Dawes," Leone said quietly. "Because your great-great-grandfather, S. J. K. Dawes himself, came out here in the 1840s, and because he settled it, and because they finally named the town after him."

"No, I mean *why*? Not how much great work it was."

"Well, because," she said.

"Do you think America will ever be understood by the D.A.R., Leone?" Simpson said, chewing on his black cigar. "Or saved from itself by the Junior League? I'd like to have your opinion on that."

"Oh, be quiet," she said.

"Is that your opinion?"

"That's my opinion as it stands today."

"Single-handed, I bet," Dawes said. "Like Hyoot John Williams almost, I bet."

"Who, Dawes?" Leone said.

"S. J. K. Dawes."

"No," she said. "I don't think he had any six-guns on."

"Big screwy deal," Dawes Williams said, "it's not much of even a town. Looks like nobody but some stray goats lives round here in the first place."

"Less than four hundred now," Leone said defensively.

"That's all right," Simpson said. "Dawes and I mostly like stray goats better than we like fenced ones anyway. Don't we, Dawes?"

"Anything you say," Dawes said.

"But in the day of the small town, in my day," Leone said, looking from the window, "there were many fine people living here in Dawes City. Then the roads came and they all moved to Davis Groves and farther on."

"Well, that was their first mistake," Simpson said. "We'll all look back on that someday."

"I agree," Dawes said.

"That's right, old boy," Simpson said, sensing openings, "after taking all the trouble to make the long road in, they found suddenly they had to turn about and take the long road out. A lot of bother to wind up eventually where you started at."

"Where's that?" Dawes said.

"Europe," Simpson said. "Damn ironic if you ask me."

"Sometimes I just could sit and marvel at the way you have of visualizing history," Leone said.

"Do you think she means that, Dawes?" Simpson said.

"Nope," Dawes said.

"You happen to be right. And you couldn't prove it by me. Is that it, Leone? Hell, why don't you tell the boy about the time you single-handedly won the Crawdor County Music Contest on your clarinet, the Crawdor County Poultry Festival's Foot Races, perhaps?"

"Oh, be quiet, Father," she said so slowly Dawes could hardly hear her. "But once we did belong to all of this and—"

"Owns she means," Simpson said.

"All right. Once we owned all of this and then the old house, the stone house, and finally only the hotel and then that was gone, too."

"It's a sad, sad tale," Simpson said.

"It sure is," Dawes added.

"Oh, be quiet," she said. "You two."

"Christ," Simpson said.

The dark car ran easily through the constant ticking-razz of gravel. Leone watched them, not really thinking, the fields which have always been there, lying below.

In 1916 she had been born here, in her grandfather's last hotel. Gin was her mother; that must mean something, too. The roads were dirt and mud, and salesmen stopped from the train and stayed the night. The old folks lived in the old stone house, three miles out beyond town. And there had been people here then; Sunday afternoons like swings in gardens. And on Saturdays, late at night, in the tall wooden hotel, she helped her Aunt Dode whip the buckwheat batter into standing, cream-colored bowls. She liked that. And everything was named Dawes, like her mother Gin was— the bank, the grain mill, the silos, although they had all burned to the ground; even parts of the land. At least once it had been that way, and the name was left. Her name was Leone Oldham but her brother's name, the given one if not the other, was Dawes. And Arthur was young, only twenty-three, having only ten acres and as many dogs.

On the weekends he left to play baseball, amazing the small prairie towns with his curve and spitter and slider, but during the week his huge voice filled the house worrying about money to buy new dogs, and even about how the ones he already had might run.

Arthur was tall, dark as his shadow, and hard to live with. In the mornings he woke her forcefully, filling her with a deep, deathlike, forgotten voice; filling her with a fright nearly as complete, big and destroyed, as the land under storm. But on weekends, when she would help Dode with the batter, her Uncle Tomilson would sit in his red whiskers, tapping his foot on the floor, rocking his straw chair, telling her stories of the valley. In August, in the nights so hot she couldn't sleep, her Aunt Dode, dark and tall and beautiful, would come down the long hallway, she could hear her coming, and sit in the rooms tall as wood men, with ceilings as high as whiskers, and fan her for hours with cool, leaf fans. Then she would sleep. Once, she had won a foot race and Arthur had smiled. She was slender and fleet. The hotel had a swing, a porch with a trellis as white as a Protestant God. . . .

"Then what happened to all this?" Dawes asked, nearly interested.

"My Great-uncle Clarence by marriage happened," she said, still looking from the window.

"I knew it," Dawes said.

"He was a Harvard graduate but he traveled a lot, Dawes," Simpson said.

"Well," she said, "I'm skeptical myself."

"Me, too," Simpson said, winking at Dawes, "but then anyone serious enough to be carrying paper proving he was a Harvard graduate—but not changing his name from Clarence—couldn't be a complete liar."

"Well, everyone certainly respected education in those days," Leone said, "so when he 'stopped forth' from the train in Dawes City, he didn't have any trouble marrying my Aunt Julia."

"From what Art says about it," Simpson said, "no one would have had any trouble marrying your Aunt Julia—Harvard diploma or not."

"Anyway," she said, "he took her directly to Mexico with him."

"Some say he only took her to Arizona to murder her, Dawes," Simpson said. "And that he buried her, eventually, in New Mexico."

"Neat," Dawes Williams said.

"Well, no one ever *did* hear from her again, you know."

"Well," Simpson said, "according to Art—that was the reason exactly why no one would marry her in the first place . . . she didn't say much. In fact, some say she didn't have a 'personality' at all, not that she was dumb, but she was a furious knitter."

The car exploded with laughter. Simpson almost missed a turn on the gravel and moonlight.

"Anyway," Leone said, "suddenly there he was again. Clarence. He just got back off a train one day, Julia wasn't there, but he still talked S. K. Dawes into mortgaging all of his land to buy Mexican copper, a mine of it, and . . ."

"There wasn't any copper," Simpson said, "not even enough to make a small sword to fall on."

"My, aren't we melodramatic tonight?" she said, looking past him at his father.

"Well, for God's sake, Leone," he said, "it's a melodramatic, poorly operated family. How many times do I have to tell you that?"

"Anyway, Dawes," she said, ignoring Simpson, "what was left, which wasn't much, finally all burned down. First the bank, then all of the silos, finally even the old stone house."

"Yes, I know," Simpson said. He was perfectly calm, chewing furiously. "Either it was God himself, or one of his helpers, an evil witch perhaps, the same thing I suppose—even the devil is determined—either that, or there was simply an extraordinary amount of barn burners running around in one place at one time."

"Same thing," Dawes said, "but you better not let Gin hear you talking about Jesus that way."

"Figure of speech, old boy, excuse me," Simpson said.

"It's not me you have to worry about. It's Gin."

"I'll watch it," Simpson said.

"Well, anyway," Leone was saying, "someone certainly had it in for us. Some*thing.*"

"Someone hell. Dawes," Simpson said lighting the cold cigar, "some say— I've heard Abigail Winas say it myself—that it was S. J. K. Dawes himself who went mad one summer and burned it all down. I guess that proves he was stupid . . . . Apparently he hadn't even heard property insurance hadn't been invented yet."

"Simpson!" Leone said. "That's a lie! What a perfectly horrible thing to say."

"I take it back, Mother," he said. "Figure of speech."

"You'd better," she said. "You'd better or you know what."

"What?" Dawes said.

"I do. I do," Simpson said, amused. "I just don't happen to think it was all that mysterious myself. I think things like that are mostly practical in nature. I think there just didn't happen to be a Dawes who ever happened to know the first thing about money. That's all."

"Is that all?" she said.

"That's all. There just didn't happen to be a Dawes around at the time who happened to know that it's usually harder to hold on to it for any length of time than it is to make it in the first place."

"Anyway, Dawes," she said, still trying to ignore Simpson, "Mother didn't have a penny. It was all made and gone in sixty years."

"You couldn't call that made along the order of the Hapsburg empire all right, Leone," Simpson said.

"You should have owned a fourth of this whole valley, Dawes, because the Daweses are all dying out."

"Yes," Simpson said, throwing the tired cigar from the window, "the blood was too inbred to support any more financial wizards. As Art himself said—they just weren't ever too terrifically prolific either."

And they were finally laughing. Only Dawes didn't know what it was they were laughing about. It didn't seem to matter. They were only moving on the sleeping road, toward home and night, his small summer dream of walking yellow water, and he had finally gotten her to laugh, Dawes thought . . . .

"That's why you named me Dawes?" he said.

"I've got some theories on that one, too," Simpson said, still laughing.

"I'll bet you do."

Biting into the ends of another cigar, Simpson said, "I believe you could call this one splendid decline. The whole damn country's full of it. Great sport, about to be practiced by all. I could go into a long bit of business here, but I wouldn't want to bore your mother."

"The damage has already been done," she said.

"Yes, well, this town of yours gets me to feeling that way."

In the dark the land was a perfect sill to look over. He sat listening to his sound, their noise turn to stones, rain, drifting the roads into fields.

"Go on then," she said, smiling at Simpson. "Be an ass."

"Well, then," he said quietly, "think I will. It's all based on the great idea, like poetry I guess, that a lost town is better somehow than no town at all. And twice the fun. And three times the story. That must be it, old boy," Simpson Williams said. "Think of all the Americans with a lost nineteenth-century farm town that got left somehow like pots of feudal castles two generations back."

"That's a pretty speech," Leone said. "You read that somewhere."

"Damn," Simpson said, "it boggles the mind. There must be tens of thousands of them loose by now."

"Do I need you to tell me that?" Dawes said. "Do I?"

"No. But after all, a town like that generally turns out to be more trouble than it's worth."

"You're only extemporizing," she said.

"Well, it's like a damn rose bed, isn't it? You tend it, water it, even when you own it you're the only farmer in town who has to put on a stiff collar every morning and dance it around its own square."

"Do I need you to tell me that?" Dawes Williams said. "I got a mind. I could have figured that out for myself, you know."

"Yes. So, if you don't have the town, you have at least the children—which you'd have had anyway, of course, town or no town, so that's all right—which are named after the town. And that's nice, I guess. So in the end, like old posters in a yellow antique book, you have something that turns out to be finer, better in every way than the town was. You have a comfortable myth."

"Oh-ya," Dawes Williams said. "It never happened."

"Why's that?" Leone said.

"Why!?!" Simson said. "Why, because all lost, past things can be made over more easily, with less bother, than present, physical things, which only remain, embarrassing you. And which can only get in the way."

"Don't be so cynical," Leone said.

"What were you trying to call me?" Dawes Williams said.

"Formless, maybe," Simpson said.

"I don't think that's a very nice thing to tell him, Simpson," Leone said. "At this point and all."

"Why not?" Dawes said.

"Good for you, old boy," Simpson said.

"What's so good about it?" Leone said.

"So you named me Dawes. Is that it? Is that what you want me to know?"

"I don't see anything particularly good about it," Leone said.

"Besides," Simpson said, looking sheepishly into his new cigar, "your mother did most of the work. She insisted she had rights. What could I say?"

"You could have told her to guess again. That's what you could have said," Dawes Williams said. "They say, 'Dawes-Caws Dawes-Caws,' at that goddamn Polk School."

Simpson looked over at him. Often, to Dawes, it seemed his father had moments when he suddenly should have flashed forth a head of gold, leering teeth like operas when he smiled. He never did, and Dawes was always slightly disappointed.

"What can a fella say?" he finally said. "They used to say 'Simpson the winsome' to me. We just happen to have sprung from a long line of eccentric mothers, old boy."

"What are you talking about?" Leone said. "You're just making it sound ridiculous somehow."

She was looking out of the window again, somehow slightly behind the motion of the road.

"Dawes is a nice name for a boy," she said. "My brother never minded it."

Dawes and Simpson exploded with laughter.

"Oh ya," Dawes said, "well, I mind it."

"We could have named him simple old Mike, you know, Leone."

"But that's so common. Besides," she said, "simple-old-Mike is a perfectly ridiculous name for a boy."

"There's worse things than common."

"There is and there isn't."

"Yes, well, as long as we're just sitting around in limbo anyway, Leone, my uncle's name was Homer Williams. I liked old Homer Williams. We could have named him Homer Williams."

"Maybe we're making too much of this," Dawes said.

"Or Edmund Gaston," Leone said calmly. "Maybe we could take him back and name him Byron Bertram."

"Don't think you like uppity-sounding English names, Leone."

"I think you're only trying to make me see how lucky I really am. Being only partially screwed and all," Dawes said.

"Don't say 'screwed,' Dawes."

"I can't just say 'being only partially and all.'"

"I think you're being overly clever now, old boy."

"Who cares what you think?" Dawes said.

"Yes, well, what's in a name?" Simpson Williams said. "Let's name him Shakespeare Williams and be done with it."

"Leave me alone," Dawes said. "What'd I ever do to you?"

"No," she said. "Shakespeare Williams would be stretching a point."

"Hell, nobody asks me anything."

"Well, make your point, old boy."

"I am. I am. I'm making my point as well as you are. It's just that nothing is happening."

"Maybe you need a lawyer, old boy."

"I don't have any money."

"You could get that paper route," Simpson said, smiling.

"Seems like a lot of unneeded bother to me," Dawes said. "But I could get some money from Gin if she thinks I been keeping my Bible studies up. Hell, Gin's got more money than both of you."

"That's an idea," Simpson said. "I didn't know you were so concerned."

"I'm not really," Dawes said. "I'm just talkin'."

"Well, I don't know, old boy," Simpson said, almost sighing.

"I know you don't," Dawes said. "Hell, Ronnie Crown says the only answer is start kickin' a few girls who say 'Dawes-Caws' where it hurts the most."

"Ronnie Crown would say something like that," she said softly, watching the distance the moon made moving within the glass. "Don't say 'hell,' Dawes."

It was late, and they were approaching the farm and Arthur's hill, and nothing ever changes, he thought. The night was only sleeping, breathing with insects.

"What's in a name?" Simpson said, tired now.

"Hell," Dawes said, "Ronnie Crown's the only one with any answers for it all."

"Don't say 'hell,' Dawes."

"Hell. How come every time I say 'hell,' you say 'hell'?"

"Now, Mother," Simpson said.

"Listen," Dawes said, "the only thing I want to know here is—how come every time Ronnie Crown says 'mother,' you call it a dirty word?"

And then he heard his grandfather's hounds. They sang on a mysterious drumlin, a perfectly oval and unexplaining thing. They moved closer to it. They were nearly being pulled along by the sound. Gin would be lying asleep, tired, too broken almost to move down the hill, but waiting for him. They pulled slowly along the lane, under the hill. He saw again the two houses sitting on the middle, sloping level scooped out of the mound. They hung flat, peering light from their windows. One was the larger, stucco ranch-style house where Gin lived among the clutter of Arthur's trophies; the other was the gray frame house where Jake Skout lived with his wife and sprawling collection of farm-machinery magazines. It was late, the same. Dawes watched, and he began hearing the long pens, the greyhounds stirring, and in his listening Dawes could see the hills fold themselves together. Looking up, Dawes could see Arthur standing within a corner of his porch. He was like a watchtower, coming on guard after midnight, surveying the hill. He stood, smoking, looking back at them. Watching Arthur's watching on the porch, Dawes could suddenly feel the naked locust grow quiet in the lane. The eyes of the houses were bored out hearts.

Ya, he thought, it must be that time again. Here comes Leone and that kid of hers again. Ya, hell, here's Simpson and his damn poet again. I'm damned if that one's ever going to be run for President. That's sure. That kid doesn't understand anything. Not him. He's moon-eyed as bitches.

"Awwwww Criminy," Arthur said to himself, laughing deeply, softly, standing back in his dark.

He remembered a poet of a dog he had which acted something like that'n. Reminded him of that'n some. A bitch. Named Blackey Jane. She was still 'round, past bitching of course, still running in the rain all night long every chance. *Likes it. Going to build her a theatre one of these days. Used to scream at the moon till it'd go back behind clouds and be dark. Then she'd feel real pleased with herself. Go back to sleep. But soon's that moon flashed back out again, there she was, tearing furious as races through that door of her hut. You could still hear her in town. Frozen there like knives on that hill, screaming at the moon. And screaming at the rain comin' up south. Like it was insults. Jaaeesus Criminy, was she somethin' . . .*

"Criminy," Arthur said to himself. Embarrassed, he noted he was practically talking to himself. *They must be getting to me already this year,* he thought.

. . . but he's somethin', too. That one. That Dawes Williams. Criminy. Too close to Leone and he still takes after his old man. Makes you wonder. Too smart, I guess, in a backwards way to be sharp. Smooth. Sure of it now. Thought I'd hold back for awhile, see, give'm a chance, when he was smaller. Too late now. It's midnight. I'm up at five. You'd think they'd lost the road, couldn't even find the place. Criminy. That Simpson's a bright enough man, full of humanity, tax information, like him, but I can't figure what Leone figures she's got herself in for. Jaaeeesus Criminy, send'em to college and they come home loaded with preachers, poets, rock collectors, all of'em. What's it coming to? Man works all his life and he gets poets, Jaaaeeesus Christ.

Not in my day, he thought. *Had a poet dog like him. Moon-eyed as mother's bitch's milk. Had a lot of dogs.*

Hell, he thought, *I looked at my brother Burt that day in high school in Nebraska flat as ruined spoons and I said, "I'm getting the hell out. I'm either playing pro ball or doing something else, but I'm making it big, see?" But hell no. Burt didn't see. Not him. Not that one. But I did. Old Tom saw it, too, I know he did. He wished me well. It was understood between us. Christ. How do you tell a rock-collecting kid about that? Christ. How did Tom ever hang onto his simple sanity out there in the middle of the devil's flat grass? New Leeds, Nebraska. Christ. Knowing what he knew. Coming from what he came from . . . you could see it with mother, being from Liverpool. She was coming up. Funny-as-hell world. Not Tom. He had lost everything. Hell, Tom was halfway to being the king's own aristocrat before they kicked him out. Sent him packing. Before they drummed him out of his own country. My father said they called him in one day, his own people, the parlor full of maids and things, and they gave him a steamship ticket and fifteen pounds, and they kicked him out. To America. Just for hitting a schoolmaster. My father, Tom. So, I guess, that's how I came to turning to Burt, twins after all, that day in old man Emmit's pasture with some whippets, and I said again, "I'm making it big, see? You had any sense, or simple pride for what you really are and come from, and you'd do it, too."*

So I did.

Christ, he thought, *old Tom must have wanted a litter. Maybe even Mother did. My sister Leone, dead. Buried out there somewhere still. Hell, in England Mother would have been Tom's maid, if she had come across him at all.*

Sometimes he couldn't stand any of them, not even Gin. Don't even want'em around the place. Sometimes he just wondered. Tom never left. It was 1872 he came to Nebraska. Then, the end, just nothing I could ever see. Just jailor and traffic cop to a town which possessed six hard-core drunks and eleven Fords near the end. Christ.

"Ya," Arthur said to himself, watching the Chevy pull in under the lane. "They're here, Gin," he said louder.

The next time, he thought suddenly, I told Burt I was leaving to be making it big, we were clerking in a damn dry-goods store on the prairie. Christ. Believed me, maybe, I'd never left. Good thing maybe he didn't. Maybe we did it together then. Nearly hit him at the time, though. Hard to tell about things poetical. Maaan oh man, dropping the apron, not saying a word, walking over to the house, small as clean boxes, packing six shirts, three pair of pants, my glove and spikes in a canvas bag, and hitting the road. I must have never looked back for a long time. When I did, I don't remember thinking they were even there. I was scared, being a kid, that day. I must have been. Went over to the jail, I remember, telling old Tom goodbye, leaving, and he says, "Arthur, you just remember it isn't all the money in it now. You go home and kiss your dear sweet old Mater goodbye." That must have been old Tom after all, all right. Always wonder what he meant. As if the times hadn't passed him up. As if the things that really happened to him hadn't really happened.

Maybe I'll ask that one. He's a poet. He's generally got opinions on the moon.

Remember I already took that Dawes down to the fence, one night after supper, and I began explaining it all to him. He's moon-eyed. He never understood anything about me. Not that one. Makes me uneasy. Don't even want'em around. But there he is, standing over by the near fencerow, where I keep my best pups, and from his eyes he looks like he can't understand a word of it. I don't know. Maybe he's innocent. He's got his finger in his mouth. He can't talk to me. Maybe Leone's whelped herself an idiot after all. The blood's too thin. I don't know. Either that, I think to myself, or he understands it better than I do. I can't tell which, and it makes me uneasy.

He's been living too long already with that Simpson.

Mostly, though, I'm talking about the dogs. About blood. That's what I talk about best, that's what I know better than anyone living, I guess. Anyway. Whatever. I'm telling him how, I wasn't much older than him, I once knew bloodlines going back to the middle of the fourteenth century in my head. Used to study notes all day scrawled in my arithmetic books, I remember. And he's impressed. I can see it in his eyes. He better be. But then the town, Leeds, was full of English and Irish too afraid, I thought, to go to America, even after they got there, but it was good for me, I guess, as it all turned out, as they ran the dogs, the greyhounds and even whippets, every weekend. So it was natural, I guess, knowing blood like I did. . . .

Not that damn Dawes Williams. He doesn't know anything yet.

So I told him how it was, picking up six bits or a dollar in a ball game, and he looks like he's listening real hard. Oh, maaan oh man, he's a listener, all right. I'll give him that. So I told him how it was, getting off the back of a train when you could find one, looking for a ball game on Sunday afternoon. One that'd pay ya to pitch. Finally I got to the important part.

Poor Doc Mahoney. Dying, drinking to forget it, not caring about anything. 1910. No, actually, I guess he still cared about good blooded greyhounds. I guess he cared about me some. Who knows? Not me, I guess. But he did know blood nearly as well as I did. Know that now. Knew it then. Always knew that about a dog man big enough not to be jealous about it, I guess. We got on fine. Two months and I was in charge of his kennels. A year and he was giving me some picks on his litters. Doc and I that summer, we got on fine, I guess, travelin', bettin', racin' those dogs of his. Cratin' those dogs and traveling out by train. High summer. High times, me and the Doc, before he went broke and died. I guess he was about the most important man I ever met, as it all turned out. Yes sir, the Doc. Tubered and dying. Lucky for me but a hellauva thing to see. Then that second year, worse, having some big ideas, a small stake, time killing you like poison, knowing some dog men worth knowing, some not. But I had that line on a string of small tracks out west that needed dogs. From then on I knew it was only a question of time.

I was right, but the time involved was poisoning me.

Then one day I saw this bitch named Marry Meadowlane running in an open field. Gin often says it must have been love at first sight.

"Let's buy'er, Doc," I remember saying real calm, cutting on a stick. "Hell no, Art," Doc said at first. "That old dog? You buy'er if you want, but she's blinded in one eye. All the old-timers know'er, Art. She's flashy but blinded in one eye." "She's better'n flashy," I said, cutting on that stick. "Don't know," the Doc said. "I know, Doc," I said. "I know all about the eye taint in that cross, but I want to try'er with this imported sire I have a line on. I got Royce Dobbs even to cut back on his stud fees for me on that sire. They'd be perfect together, Doc." "Could be," the Doc said. "She's plenty good. Especially intelligence. We could split the first litter even up," I said, letting it lie for the time.

I knew all about her taint. I knew, but I had faith. I had faith, but I didn't have the capital to swing it on my own. And Doc coming finally off a bottle and saying only, "Arthur. Why the hell not? Never overlook completely the chance to bring two good hounds together. You can't go on breedin'em forever, you know, Art." So that was it. The rest was easy time. More or less. Then, when it came time to be splitting up that litter, knowing suddenly even a man or boy smooth as oil needs a hand up. Because I can still see him, Doc Mahoney looking at me, like he's known for months what I been thinking, worrying to death about, and he says, calm and easy, but not just deadlike like a tuber, "You go ahead, Art. You got more time than me. You take first picks. All three of'em. I like to see a fella get ahead, and I hope you make a pile."

So I did.

And forty years later I find myself down by my own fences, trying to explain to that one how I picked two bitches and a male. And how the bitches weren't worth damning, but the *male, first choice, was Traffic Judge, who was also the greatest coursing, racing sire who ever ran in American air, and that's by general knowledge and given opinion. We spend half the year in the house in Miami now but, late at night sometimes, in the summers, back at the farm, I lay in my bed just thinking "Well, by God Art, what the hell do you think of that?"*

And I lay listenin' to that crazy poet of a dog, screamin' at the moon.

Guess I'm just not contented. There must be something missing. Must be getting soft. Don't know, I guess that's what it is. What old Tom meant that afternoon I spent leaving. I guess he'd be the one to know. About those things. About missing, unrealized things. Don't know. Wish'd I'd got back to Nebraska to see old Tom once more, though. I sure wish that. I don't know. Ya. So, anyway, I guess, after Doc finally died on me one day, I tell him, I took the dogs he left me, the dogs he didn't, more of a care for him than anything else, and I moved to Dawes City 'cause the land was black and cheap in those days, fertile, and I met Gin in what they used to call the City Park, an old piece of common cow ground, and married her one day. She's a good woman, but tiring on me. God, but she brutalizes me something terrible with that tongue of hers anymore. I don't know. But I've got a half million in the bank, half that much in land, equipment and dogs, setups in Miami, I haven't got enough yet to buy the estate and Victorian starch works, as Tom used to call'em, back in England yet, but I'm minding my own business and working on it. I've got everything I want, I guess, and forty years this Dawes Williams comes along. It's just a simple curse, I guess. It's tolerable but irritating.

He doesn't understand anything about me. Hell.

Gin began moving about, lighting more lamps in the house, returning to bed. Dawes got out of the Chevy and stood on the edges of Arthur's fields. Arthur began coming down his hill. His strides were strong, even. Dawes watched him. His nose was sharp; his eyes were deeply set, narrowed by years spent squinting into the sun. He was hawkish, physical, immediate.

"What's the matter with you!?!" Arthur called to Dawes. "You too proud to carry something for your mother!"

Dawes said nothing, not even turning. He felt suddenly flooded with shame and guilt. His blood felt hot and weak at once. He was glad to get into the house. The house was a shell, fragile, but possible as Arthur lived mostly in the fields. Arthur was gone all day, doing something else. He told himself he was glad to get in the house. The house was generally safe.

Entering it, he was flooded with the clean smell of mothballs and linen; of polished, antique wood. Gin had made the couch down for him as she always had. He slept in the den alone. He was grateful to Gin for giving him a place to go; for excusing him without even appearing or saying so. Gin and he were partners sometimes. But Arthur, who was still behind him, didn't know. Or, if he did, there was nothing he could do about it against Gin. He was grateful for Gin, except on Sundays, and he was naked and feigning sleep before he even hit the doorway to the den, leaving only a trail of clothing behind him.

He lay down, closing his eyes tightly. If Arthur came close to him, he would snore. It was late.

"Now, Dad," he heard Leone saying faintly, moving through the living room. "He's just tired, that's all."

"Awwww Criminy, Leone," Arthur said.

"Now, Art," Simpson said.

Their voices moved on into the bedrooms beyond him. He ignored them. The greyhounds were still singing an arch of sound. He lay within it, seeing them with his ears, hearing them with his eyes. Then the last night train moving on Omaha rose and fell, a second, a late final stone fusing it all, a wall, sound, with the far-moving song of a last bitch dog, dark bones and ridges, fixed to the high spine of the hill. The beginning. The high note. The single arcing. The stopping. The end. *Dawes* . . .

And the land was best when a storm came, and the wind and the small rain blew the shadow and gown of the grown pillow against the window; a hurt, whispering thing growing on glass. Then sometimes Arthur got up, and passed through the living room, the den where the boy lay sleeping within the sprawl of gold trophies and old, dustless stud-books which were cloistered in the walls, nestled like birds, like so many scattered but well-kept tombstones. The wind then was an easy hand; a furious wood of night. It was an eye lying beyond easily, drifting, something full of smoky listing water. And Arthur would pass on, stopping on the back stoop, standing into the wind, the thin strands of light, the tents of water, the retching and heaving face of storm. For a long time, it seemed, his etched water-form flew in the wind; became the frozen statue of a general eyeing angrily the chaos being wreaked on his hill.

Later Dawes would think he could hear the sudden voice of Gin rolling easily across the dark house, low floor, the distance of his dream, saying:

"Art! Arthur, you get that boy down to the storm cellar."

"Awww, Gin," he answered.

"I'm coming, now. Now I'm coming. We're all coming."

"Nawww, Gin," he said. "Go back to sleep. It's not even a storm yet. The wind is barely up. Good show, but it's passing over north."

The land was best when a storm came . . . and the wind and the small rain . . . and the dogs safe and near destruction in their huts . . . and the locusts and green train a single hill, a blowing up into sound . . . and he was away from them now, far beyond, dreaming easily within his land of yellow walking water . . . and in his dream the yellow, the unbelievable journey to be found in plumage, he dreamed only of the dark passings of airless noises . . . wings . . . red eyes . . . the effortless, the strainless . . . the soft birds of night . . .

2

The mornings through the curtains were a line of gray August clouds. Waking, he knew it was Thursday, the first day at the farm, and Arthur was up and marching about the house in his boots and yelling in his dream:

"Get up!" he was screaming. "Get the hell out of that bed! The sun's nearly going down the damn-well other side!"

"So what?" Dawes Williams said.

"So you're not going to be laying round that bed all day. Get out and get doing. That's what. You're not worth the powder to wake you up," Arthur said, walking away.

Dawes sat up in bed, feeling worthless, shaking the sand, the early and desolate hill of dog yips from his head. Arthur turned. He stood, leaning against the wooden jamb of the double glass doorway, looking back, and his eyes seemed almost dull, flatter than last year, muted somehow like reptiles not swimming in open water anymore. The doorway was wide and swinging apart and blowing the farm inward like morning fans; hot seepings of dogwood and fertile, silent manure. Arthur stood as if, even slightly slouching, he was holding up the house. A carefully weathered, twenty-five-dollar straw hat was on his head. Dawes decided suddenly that this would be, this must be, this might be the summer he would tell Arthur what a son of a bitch he really was . . .

"You leave that boy alone, Mister," Gin was saying from the kitchen. "He didn't come out here to plow. He came out here to see his grandma. Didn't ya, Dawes?"

"Awww God, Gin," Arthur said.

Dawes said nothing. He sat listening to Gin, who was still sightless behind her kitchen and behind her stove and behind her white piles of flour, waiting for him to answer by affirming what she had said. He didn't, as Arthur was still staring back, freezing his voice.

"It's only seven, Arthur," Gin was saying again. "And the grass is still wet. We don't want that boy out yet, anyway. Where's your sense? He's not the hired man. You want him to become the hired man, you start paying him wages to put up with you. What's the matter with you, Art? You bent on losing all your sense so early in the morning?"

"Awww God, Gin," Arthur said, withdrawing.

Dawes still said nothing. He knew Simpson and Leone were sleeping too, sprawled and unfastened in country sheets, but Arthur wasn't stomping around, bothering them.

"Awww, Gin," Arthur said through the kitchen screen, moving across the back hill. "He can't spend his whole life in bed. Jaaaeeesus, is he lazy."

"Go feed your dogs, Mister Industry," Gin said, laughing now with real, catching humor.

"Awww Criminy, Gin," Arthur called back near the barn.

Dawes got up feeling confused. It was as if another year had passed—a long, impossible string, a time untying them all—but the others had refused to admit it. He walked around the edges of the room, trying to shake even the early August sun from his head, putting his pants on carefully before he went into the kitchen.

" 'Lo, Grandma," he said.

"Dawes!" she screamed, sitting down and pulling him against her, nearly within her legs.

" 'Lo, Grandma," Dawes said again, "how are you doing?"

He stood before her, pulling slightly away, looking into her eyes as green as vague, washed clouds drifting indefinitely within her large, oval face; like farms of watching, he thought, thinking he saw disappointment there in his final lack of feeling; talking; love. He knew that the summers refused to change; that she was somehow wide, and bent over, and indefinitely crippled even sitting down. He remembered again she had been operated on over thirty times; that everything, as Leone said, that could be taken out of her with a knife had already been taken; that she drove up with Arthur every year in his new Lincoln or Cadillac to Mayo's, a special hospital huge and vague as cities up north, to have something else checked, or repaired, or stripped away. He stood before her, confronting her, waiting, suddenly surprised that her mysterious parts, missing and unnamed, did not somehow spring from her body like in an old, half-ticking clock still registering time.

She walked under invisible weights, and yet she seemed also more alert and active than Arthur. Leone said it was "will." Dawes thought perhaps it was only a trick; some near secret that she managed. He remembered she was always the last to come down the hill when they were going anywhere; to Davis Groves even. She would come from the house finally, emerge, bent, nearly unable to rise up to look over the level of her own eyes. And they sat below, waiting, trying to catch her, thinking the hill might sway out from beneath her. Arthur would always go up finally to help her and she would always refuse, telling him to mind his own business; shooing him away with a perfumed handkerchief. Then he would pace slowly behind her, laughing quietly in his well-made trousers, spry and aristocratic, dutiful as forgetful sons, thinking of catching her. The air was always full of waiting; evening; the country; falling; things fragile with other designs entirely. Gin would ignore them. It took her forever even to make the steps. Simpson would smoke patiently, and Dawes would drift off to the near pens to pet the year-old pups which had promise, and which therefore needed to be near for studying.

Leone and Arthur would grow finally impatient, pacing furiously, but containing themselves. The Cow River whispered, wandering, out, incredibly brown. Often when Gin got finally through the thick air to the bottom of the hill she would spy Simpson's cigar, turn and go back toward the house, insisting to check it herself for possible fires. This was the moment Dawes waited for; the moment Arthur would finally break, saying, "Jaaeeesus Criminy, Gin," as he ran up before her, clearing the way. Dawes would sit down in the tall grass near the pens listening to the brown smell of the river wind, laughing, watching them go as they climbed the back of the shadowy husks of the hill like spines of dry but willful stalks. Leaving was a possible thing, he would think, but horribly slow.

"Dawes!" Gin was saying, almost startling him with the vagueness of her direct intentions. "My, my."

"Ya," Dawes said, "guess so."

"Another year. . . . I can scarcely believe it. You've gotten so big."

"I'm growin' all right, I guess."

"How's my good-lookin' boyfriend?" she said.

"Awww, Grandma," Dawes said.

"Well, now," she said. "Com'ere and let me feel you. Year's a long time, you know."

She hugged him, smelling of flour and cold cream and rouge and linen ghosts. He avoided her slightly and she looked disappointed again.

"I only get to see you once a year, you know," she said.

"I know."

"Miss me?" she said accusingly.

"Sure."

"What did you do this year?"

"Oh, you know, messed around and stuff. Lots."

"Well, that's good to hear, I guess," she said.

"Keep busy, did you?"

"Ya."

"Miss your old grandma?"

"Sure I did."

"Keep up on your Bible reading?"

"Ya. Every night. Simpson gets mad, though, and says I'm going to be a fanatic at something or other when I grow up."

"Well now, you know," she said, "Simpson's a kind man, but he doesn't know everything yet. He's got a few surprises in store, too, you know. We all do. He's kind, but he's got just a real funny streak when it comes to serious Bible reading."

"Guess so, Grandma."

"You betcha," she said, still touching his bare arm. "You may even make a good preacher some day."

"Can't tell."

"I know I marvel at your knowledge, and have often wished I could stick with something like that myself."

"You never can tell. Simpson says if there's one thing I can do, it's stick to things."

"Well now, you know," she said, ignoring him, "that may be, but I told some of the ladies—'course I don't get to town too much anymore—how you read one chapter a night *without* fail, and how you're only eight, and already nearly three-fourths through the Old Testament, nearly understanding every word, memorizing verses even, and they marvel, too."

"Ya," Dawes said, "it's a hell of a thing, all right."

"Dawes!" she said, nearly laughing.

"Well, you know, sounds like a lot of marveling to me."

"Well, it is. Those ladies don't have anything better to do. Do you want bacon and eggs and cinamon rolls?" she said, releasing him, giving him three dollar bills.

"Sure, Grandma," Dawes Williams said.

He sat in the corner of the kitchen eating silently. The country morning was cool, filling with screens and windy leaf shadows like black spiders. Finally he got up and ran into the yard.

The sun went through him, surprising him with red seams, sudden blood, things. On the road, below, red tractors and black trucks went past all morning. Dawes walked the fence down to the road and sat baking on a high, solitary rock. In the distance he could see Arthur leading strings of dogs near the river; others were unseen but howling behind the tree line, a thin and vertical net of wood filling with brown light.

Looking up, squinting east and south into bright, uncertain directions, he saw the farm was bent and twisted; pushed out and mounted before old glacia- tions. The high pastures, lying up from even the house, hadn't been planted in decades and were deserted with a house of tangled flowers, a weave of mad grass, and an old greyhound track complete with a homemade electric rabbit which had sat for years decomposing on its metal casters and rain-gray wooden railings. Nothing, he knew, followed that stuffed cotton rabbit; and only by accident, not design, would curious dogs come to sniff the edges of that track. Only an easy herd of milk cows sat up on that hill, year after year, chewing their silky, flowery cud. Arthur believed only in coursing his dogs now on live jacks in an open field. Nothing moved up there, he knew, but wind in the dark trees and green snakes weaving the grasses together.

Getting down from his high rock, he turned into the low front field. He wandered out into its carved shell, its lake bed deserted with boulders, its nest of green leaf, blowing over his head, full of shadow and a too early interior, rustling evening. The brown wind blew the fences, bulging with leaf, out to the Bovine. He sat for awhile, thinking hard about nothing, digging for rich earthworms in the dirt. Rising again, turning through stalks, he saw the hill behind was long as a mountain, dark and thick with trees of all kinds throwing their roots into the sky. At the far end was the row of houses and pens for the dogs running out east and west for over half a mile; and, a half-mile away, sightless, through the sea of corn leaves, he could hear Arthur going in the opposite direction, leading a string of twenty dogs back to the ridge. He would, he knew, be leading them down the worn path torn with dog sign, scratched and dug at with paws . . .

Dawes began moving toward the river. Arthur was going in the opposite direction, encamping this batch of hounds back on their hill. Just a summer before he had found a pile of nearly organized stones. Digging beneath them, he had found a skull, a broken pile of missing bones. High on the trunk of a nearby oak he had had to climb with ropes, he found some words he couldn't understand. Hiding the skull in an old, deserted Packard that had been made even before the war, Dawes had finally memorized the letters. He took them back to Leone. Leone studied them over and finally said they meant: JACQUES GRILLEAU DIED HERE OF FEVER, 1820, WHILE PRAYING ON THE TERRACE. Dawes didn't believe her. He had gone back once to look at the Frenchman's skull, almost afraid, thinking already in his absence it had probably become a nest for either birds or rats. It hadn't and, still lost under the seat of the Packard, it seemed almost innocent; a hollow pot to grow flowers in. He had thought for awhile of sneaking it into his mother's suitcase, and taking it back to show Ronnie Crown, who would think of something useful to do with it, but he settled finally on stashing it for a year under the seat again. He had wrapped it in old newspaper, and worried about it somehow off and on all winter, but now, returning, it was gone. He could already see, even just breaking through the last of the corn, that both the Packard and the Frenchman's skull were gone. Dawes felt suddenly it was sinful to be returning, looking again for that skull. He was glad it was gone. Then he began to miss it, thinking of how innocently he could have brought it to Miss Wilma Spent in a brown paper sack. Then he began to feel guilty. He thought perhaps it was truly unholy to be mixed up in separating a Frenchman's skull from his bones quite this permanently. After all, he had half-decided, too, to replace it first thing back at the farm. Perhaps the Frenchman was Catholic, and blessed in water, and haunted, and full of taboos. Perhaps he was somehow watching, or crying for the flower pot of his deserted skull; or perhaps, more scientifically, he had caught him like some germ because he had been sinful and his guard was down. Dawes was worried. Something seemed violated. Perhaps God would get him. Perhaps he would just die into blackness, suddenly, without remembering it, and never feel anything again. Perhaps he wouldn't even remember leaving. Dawes threw rocks at the far bank for a long time and decided finally that it couldn't be helped. Perhaps the Frenchman was Catholic and would somehow forgive him anyway . . .

He walked down the snaking river for awhile, exploring it for signs of larger life. Finally he circled back through the ring of woods, breaking onto the open coursing field and heading back toward the house. He wandered into the pens, through the huts and caves where the greyhounds lay in the shade. He wrestled them, his sweatshirt limp and tied off and hanging loosely down to his knees like a rag. He stopped in to run wild around the windmill with Blackey Jane and Steel Count's Folly. Blackey Jane sang rivers, even at noon. Steel Count's Folly trailed, intimidated, behind. He loved the dogs, and noon was a sun so high the shadows of the red trees were skies drawn so straight up, out of themselves, they seemed to stand without breath in the light. An aura of green stains, curious house spiders, dog ticks full of bloody glands and hot, seeping eyes blew across the spinning, blighted leaves.

Noon and the red tractors and black trucks broke off for lunch.

Coming back, he sat silently in Gin's kitchen again, eating tomato soup and crackers. Arthur eyed him quietly, a school of manners, watching intently for sign as Dawes stirred his heap of crackers into a thickened mush. The boy ignored him:

"Criminy," Arthur said finally, laughing deeply without humor. "I'll bet a horse thief wouldn't eat that mess."

"What's wrong now?" Dawes said.

"You sure have enough crackers in that soup," Arthur said.

"Ya."

"Now, Dad," Leone said, coming in already tanned, smiling at both of them, dressed in halter and shorts.

Simpson was sitting out on the back stoop, looking up the back of the hill at the sky as if it were a long weed stuck in his mouth.

"Why don't you take some of those damn crackers out of your soup?" Arthur said, not even looking away yet.

"Honestly," Leone said.

"Well, they're in here now," Dawes said. "Wouldn't you say so?"

"Don't talk back to me," Arthur said.

Dawes ignored him, waiting, afraid his soup would suddenly fill with tears and give him away. Gin remained silent. Finally she began prodding Arthur, whipping him from a distance with a wooden spoon. Arthur looked away from her and said:

"Going to course them today. Me and Jake. You might as well come along and watch."

Gin had made him say it. Arthur didn't want him along, he knew, and later, as they walked in the wormy lane, Dawes stepped in a fresh pile of damp cow manure lying neatly covered in fine coats of afternoon dust.

"God, are you clumsy," Arthur said, not breaking stride.

Dawes said nothing. He kicked off his shoe and managed to step in another pile of warm cow droppings with the same motion.

"Ja-eeesus Christmus," Arthur said turning back. "Do you have to dance in it? You must be a damn city kid all right."

The huge straw hat that shielded Arthur's head from the August sun threw a round and perfect circle of black, inverted sun on his face. Dawes remained silent and began trailing farther behind.

"Maaan oh man, you're slow," Arthur finally said. "Get the hell up here, Dawes. You're going damn wobbly on me."

He was turning at the gate, rubbing the brown leather sides of his face, laughing deeply to himself, contented even while angry. Dawes watched him staring back; a lost, reversed moon of dark judging; a hat.

Then Arthur went through the second gate, the one opening onto the open coursing field, but he was stopped again, yahooing at Jake Skout, who was furiously chasing jackrabbits into the distance. Skout was busy waving rags at strays popping into every direction from the grass like animated corks. He was trying to drive any loose ones into and through the cornstalk blind, into the short field fenced behind, where they could be captured again and put into burlap bags.

"KEY-RIST, SKOUT!" Arthur was yelling down to him. "THE FIRST DOG DOWN'LL TAKE CARE OF THAT!"

"JUST TRYING TO HELP, ART!" Jake called back, not looking up, continuing to chase jackrabbits behind and before him.

"Key-rist," Arthur said again, softly this time, spitting, lighting a cigaret, bracing his foot through the gate and squinting down the distances of his field. "I'll be lucky if he doesn't manage to set the river on fire," he said finally, laughing to himself as if he knew something Dawes couldn't.

Dawes, however, came up and stood beside Arthur near the fence. Arthur wasn't looking at him, and he followed Arthur's gaze down the field as it studied Skout, who was now walking back, stomping the grass, carrying back two jacks under his arms and two more huge, limp ones out in front by the ears. Skout's hat was half-turned absently on his head, and he spit tiny explosions of chewing tobacco before him like exclamations.

"Trapped and netted these here four in the corners for ya, Art," Skout said proudly, approaching. "Betcha can use'em."

"Real fine," Arthur said vaguely, laughing.

"Yep. Betcha can use these here four doggers, Arthur," Jake said, dropping and kicking the jacks into the hutch.

"Yep," Arthur said, running his hands through the pockets of his well-made jacket, nearly mocking Jake openly Dawes thought.

"Good goddamn afternoon for it, Arthur, if you ask me," Jake said.

"You feel like runnin', do you, Jake?" Arthur said.

Then there was a long silence. Dawes almost wondered why, but finally he only stood watching Arthur; watching his slowly burning cigaret; watching the field which was flat and green, and which drifted, glazed and sloping, for over five hundred yards, down to the elm woods ringing the river.

It was a dog field, Arthur's field, lying within its own four posts, falling easily with the incline of its own plain, and everything except the river, which snaked completely around it on three sides and headed back south and west into the Missouri, had a purpose. The blind, freeing the jacks from the long field, trapping them in the short field behind, was set at the far end; just in front of the dry backdrop of the woods and the invisible river. The blind was a construction of old cornstalks two lengths high; a dead twenty-foot weave in the air strung through heavy chicken wire. The wire itself was strung before high posts and mounted tightly over small, open-ended boxes that were really a single horizontal ladder; a network of plankings, two hundred yards wide, parallel and fitted with short vertical partitions only ten inches high and apart. Narrow, nailed and wired and ground flush within the very bottom of the blind, the open-ended boxes were the single escape, sightless holes of expiring light, and the short field, a funnel fenced with rapidly triangulating wire, lay behind. The short field was a lie, a false-bottomed escape, a net meant to catch flying jackrabbits, ruins trapped just short of the woods and the river. The jacks, he knew, escaped through the boxes; but not for long. Arthur lit a cigaret and said:

"Bring in the first two dogs, Jake—Lady Mary there and The Big Policeman."

"Can't," Jake said almost proudly. "They're up running in the high pasture those two this afternoon, Arthur."

Arthur looked out suddenly from beneath his dark hat. The near fence, where he was standing, was lined with implements, but Dawes stood watching the field quilting itself with afternoon light. It covered itself with a clover sun, shadows like blackbirds with seeds in their mouths moving across the bright pennies of grass and the small snails of flowers. For the first time he looked behind himself, and he saw that Lady Mary and The Big Policeman were indeed not in their pens; that they were long gone and running for themselves in the high pastures. His eyes seemed fierce, contained but beyond his face, and turning this way he always reminded Dawes of Gary Cooper halfway through a slow draw; it was as if, Dawes thought, even on the verge of sudden murder and death both remembered mostly they were somehow wrapped in darker, finer English skin. Arthur rubbed his well-made hands slowly over the quick sides of his face and said:

"Key-rist, Skout. I thought I told you 'to run that pair down here sometime this morning. Early. Without fail.'"

Then Arthur threw his smoking cigaret into the grass, stomped it and began running his hands through the pockets and seams of his jacket, which was graceful with weather. He took off his circular straw field hat. He began putting on his Irish four-square cap with one hand, taking it out of an inside pocket, running down his black, straight hair with the same motion.

"That a fact, Arthur?" Jake Skout said.

"Ya. That's a fact," Arthur said.

Jake began pacing, spitting the chewing tobacco's nervous brown crud down on the ground; the tops of his shoes; the hems of his bib overalls.

"That a fact, Arthur?" he finally repeated. "I thought you told me 'to run that pair up there sometime this morning. Early. Without fail.' And that's exactly what I did. I ran'em up there."

Dawes watched, waiting for Arthur to rise up and cross the field, walking straight out of his cap like a herd of furious Indians, leaving Jake Skout finally murdered and behind him forever. Instead, however, Arthur only scuffled some nearby dirt with his hand-stitched walking shoes. Dawes felt disappointed, vaguely disillusioned that nothing had happened when he had thought it would. Arthur ignored everything and stared out into his open field.

"Almighty Key-riminy," he said behind him. "I knew if I wanted those two down here to tell you to run'em up there. I *knew it,*" he said under his breath, spitting thinly.

Then he took his foot out of the fence and crossed over to the bell pole. He set off a bell, like boxes going off at electric racetracks, and dogs began coming out all over the hill, as if by order. They were curious stones. They bent and stretched, shaking out their tails like canes, in ones and twos, in bands and stringing-out lines. Then they moved down from the higher shade trees; their insulated huts which, lining the rim, were nearly exploding with an orderly whiteness in the afternoon glare looking up. They flexed themselves in the grass. They looked for only a moment like old men taking the air; talking socially in select groups, howling madly by turns in informal arrangements, and the huts, he knew, were warm in winter and cool in summer. He knew because he had often hid out, crawled through their wormy straw basements when he was younger than now . . .

Dawes sat on the fence watching Arthur. Jake ran up and down the lane, opening gates, shooing the pens, and the dogs moved easily down the lane like slick athletes not committing themselves. Soon nearly sixty of them were grouped before the gate to the coursing field. They seemed to be strangely quiet, milling about, walking in circles known only to themselves. Arthur and Jake began moving among them, selecting out, roping them into groupings known only to Arthur, leashing them and tying them off to posts. Jake seemed

to be untying Arthur's shoes behind him. Arthur seemed to have rhythms and
ceremonies, like Methodist churches only at Christmastime. Dawes laughed
and Arthur looked up at him darkly.

Then Arthur came back into the inner field. He moved along the railings,
checking the chaos of slip ropes, leashes, extra halter strappings; stray muzzles
meant only for greyhounds which, lost in their own heat like dreamers, snap at
and fight with their coursing mates, which are also greyhounds; the general
tangle of leather goods that drapes the fences for the first ten yards.

"Damnit," he said abstractedly, "that pair haven't been run all month."

Arthur opened the door to the rabbit hutch. And even anticipating his movement into the doorway, the greyhounds went suddenly mad and began splitting
the shreds of air. The air filled with their single voice, the catch and drawl of their
dry, furious teeth, and Arthur soon made it stop suddenly deathly still for a
moment, by merely emerging again from the dark hutch of his jack house. Then,
after a moment, it erupted again. The sixty greyhounds exploded, jumping over
themselves with conviction. It went higher, distant, over itself, because behind
him Arthur, on a long leather strapping, was dragging a crated dozen—twelve—
giant jacks shipped up to Iowa on a train with the legend ANDERSON'S JUMBO JACKS
CO. INC. OF TEEPEE FALLS KANSAS still stamped in ink on the side.

"All right, Jake," Arthur said, "since everything else seems to be running
loose up in the pasture today anyway, we'll run the two-year-olds."

"You betcha, Art," Jake Skout said, smiling.

Dawes moved down from his fence to be closer.

"When you gonna run that old red dog, Arthur?" Jake said. "He's dyin'
fer't, you ask me about it."

"Didn't ask," Arthur said, checking slip ropes. "He's retired past stud even."

"Kinda cruel to keep him penned so though, ain't it, Arthur?"

Arthur went suddenly still. Without a word he turned against Jake with a
soundless look that made even Dawes, who was only standing there, want to
crawl under the ground, and pull it over; or that made him wish the house was
good-and-on-fire, or that he was even in a house, so that he might have a good
excuse for running immediately outside. Then, drawing up the long, willowy
muscles in his neck, Arthur said:

"Listen, Skout, you shut up your damn dribble in front of the boy. You
know I walk Red Jack every morning. Like always. You also know he's sixteen
years old and one more good run would burst his heart like rotten strings."

In the silence Dawes could hear blackbirds crying, too close, like a river of
shadows. Looking down slightly, respectfully, yet still spitting a fine spray of
tobacco, Jake said:

"That so? For a fact, Arthur? You still walkin' that old red dog every morning?
Damn me," he said.

"Listen, damn you," Arthur said, moving in on him, tense and wound as rope, "I'll damn you all right. You start runnin' those dogs in here by twos, just like dancing, without getting the pairings all mixed backwards this morning, or I'll damn you, I'll damn you all right, I'll run your behind all the way off this farm and into lesser Nebraska!"

"Okay, okay, Arthur. Anything you say. No need to get nervous. You're the fella," Jake said, moving away toward the pens.

Arthur stared after him for a moment. Then, turning away, he began checking releases on all the slip ropes again. The slip rope was made of two collars wed in tandem to a metal joint resting on the backs of the greyhounds' necks; the joint was further lashed to ten feet of strapping running up to a wooden handle, a heavy string line tied off within a leather bracelet buckled to Arthur's arm. The slip rope locked two dogs together, releasing them evenly and against and within each other with a backwards jerk they never noticed. The collars slipped off like whips twelve feet from Arthur's wrist. Dawes got up on the busted gate again to watch. He sat, swinging his legs, chewing on a long weed, finally saying:

"You got any new dogs this summer, Granddad?"

"I've got new dogs every summer," Arthur said absently.

"I know. But I mean you got any really *good* new dogs you're happy with this summer? You know, I mean promising like."

"Oh, don't know. Got a dog named Maryella Jones who's running in Miama who isn't too bad. She's fast and bright, but she's small. Flies the turns a little and gets muscled a lot. But when she breaks inside right, she wins."

"That's a good deal, I guess."

"What are you talking about?"

"I mean . . . you don't like track racin' much still, do you?"

"Nope. Open field and coursing's the sport. Live jacks. Dog's got to have more than muscle and speed for that. He's got to have brains and agility and timing. Also got to have a heart and nose for killing. Track racing's like croquet."

"What are you talking about?"

"You know. I mean like something like croquet would be to a great golfer. It's nothing but turtle watching. At the track ninety percent of the race's finished three yards out of the boxes. It's flim-flam and two turns."

"Why do you do it, then?"

"Money, I guess. All I get out of the Nationals, the coursing meet is cups. Can't live off cups. I sure wish people'd find out something about greyhounds one of these years."

"Ya," Dawes said. "Open fields are better."

"What do you mean?"

"I mean why would you ever name a greyhound Maryella Jones?"

"Why not?" Arthur said. "I named her after one of my mother's aunts."

"Why? Did you like her or something?"

"Don't know. I never met her. She lived in Liverpool, England. You run out of names after the first thousand greyhounds, you know. I've got things to do, Dawes."

"Can I name one of them then? You know, if you're hard up or something?"

"Be quiet, Dawes," Arthur said.

"What the hell are you doing now, Jake!?!" Arthur said turning again.

"Well, I'm leading these dogs, these greyhounds up here, Arthur."

Jake was a ridiculous cartoon man with leashes sticking out of pockets everywhere, roping him off from further movements.

"Get out!" Arthur said.

"Figured you'd be wanting these dogs, Arthur," Jake said.

"Well, don't figure then. I don't want those dogs in here."

"Where do you want'em?" Jake said.

"Does it matter?" Arthur said.

"Well, I can't stand here holdin'em up with my teeth, Art."

"Well, tie'em off on the damn fence then."

"Hokay, Arthur," Jake said, almost saluting the bill of his Oshkosh railroad cap by running his thumbs through his bibs.

"*Pairs,* Jake," Arthur said finally, quickly.

"Which two, Arthur?" Jake said slowly.

"Key-rist," Arthur said, moving into the posted dogs with a slip rope. "I'll do it. Get the hell out of the way."

For a moment, embarrassed, nearly intimidated by Arthur's thrust, Jake pulled away, caught himself and stood leaning on the fence. Arthur stared against him, like something leaning into a faceless wind.

"Your granddaddy's an old cusser, ain't he, Dawes?" Jake said, winking at Dawes with conspiracy. "You want me to go plow something or other under, Arthur?" he said finally.

Arthur scowled at Dawes, ignoring them both. He led the first two greyhounds through the gate. They seemed like dancers, tentative, overdelicate athletes putting the paw down as if skating thin water. They raised their heads, sniffing the air for sign. Finally, trying to nose under the ground, they found they were attached and moving only as far as Arthur would release them. They sat for a moment, licking their wormless tails. Finally they began pulling Arthur like determined mules, in one organic direction, drawing him out toward the box of thumping jacks; the wires and wood crates, like hearts, already making small, rapid drums in the air. The two hounds moaned, raising their heads again, nosing under themselves. Yanking them back by the throat, Arthur said:

"Heeeeeeyyyyyaaaaawwwwww, Sissy. Get out of there! Here, Sis!" He made clicking, sucking noises with his tongue and cheek.

"That's Jasper Judge and Mayflower's Rain, isn't it, Granddad?" Dawes said, recognizing them from other summers.

"That's right, Dawes," Arthur said, not looking at him. "You have a head for names all right. Take these two out, Jake," Arthur said. "I don't think they are ready."

"What have we got here, Arthur?" Jake said. "A couple of yer regular red brindles? They look like Traffic Judge hisself, eh Arthur?"

"The hell they do," Arthur said. "They don't even look crossbred. They look so primitive they look sired by Wandering Tom."

"Just makin' talk then, I guess, Arthur."

"If you only knew," Arthur said, laughing only to himself. "Look at the way that back arches, look at those sunk withers, they don't even look bright."

"Sorry, Arthur," Jake said.

"My line's going to hell and you're sorry about it."

"Well, don't know what I can do about it, Art," Jake said, laughing, spitting in the grass. "You wouldn't want me to try sirin' one of those greyhounds for ya, would ya, Arthur?"

"Christ," Arthur said flatly. "You're not worth powder, Skout. You know that?"

"Reckon if I didn't I'm supposed to now," Jake said.

In the silence that followed, Jake spitting, Arthur rubbing his face quickly, Dawes sat on the fence wondering suddenly if even the dogs would break out into actual fighting.

"When you about to get that English import bitch over here you're always talkin', Arthur?" Jake finally said.

"I'm not," Arthur said, still staring, watching Jake look away finally. "After what you managed to do last winter, I'm quitting, retiring to Miami. Guess you're quitting, too, eh Skout?"

In another long silence, Jake cut easily on his plug.

"I'm sorry, Arthur," he said finally. "You know I truly am. I didn't mean it. It was an accident like all right."

"It sure was all right," Arthur said.

"I couldn't help it them six pups got frozen to death, Arthur. How was I to know they was hooked out'a their hut and all?"

"You could have looked. That's what you're paid for when I'm down south, you know."

Jake began quietly kicking at dirt, looking away.

"Hell, Dawes," he said finally, smiling, "I thought yer old granddad was going to *kill* me fer that one."

"Best litter I had in fifteen years," Arthur said quietly.

"Now, you don't *know* that fer sure. Positively, do you, Art?"

"I know it because I knew that blood," Arthur said quickly, clenching his teeth so tightly Dawes could see the anger along the seams of his neck muscles like tiny flecks.

"I was snowbound in town, Art. Couldn't be helped so to speak, I guess," Jake said.

"People have been known to walk three miles in the snow for less reason that that," Arthur said.

"But I was snowbound. A real blizzard, Arthur."

"You were drunk, the way I heard tell it," Arthur said. "You were probably to busy shakin' and being cozy, too."

"It was a tired snow all right," Jake said, smiling warmly.

Arthur, however, refused to respond. He looked, instead, as if he were thinking of whipping Jake with twenty feet of leather strapping. Jake looked as if he were not afraid of that but were still about to melt away, crumble like the air in old, bloodless clothes, under Arthur's glare. He looked finally at Dawes, angrily. Then, real slow, he said:

"Well, like I say, awful sorry, Art. I know it could have cost you a lot of money. 'Course, I guess you got plenty of that."

"That's right," Arthur said quietly. "It was those six pups. I'll never know how they might have turned out now."

"Sorry, Art," Jake said. "So you selling out, huh?"

"That's right. Got a breeder in Georgia interested."

"Well, Arthur, I tell ya," Jake said, something new yet planned coming into his voice, something cutting on an invisible stick, "do you think this new breeder could use a good hand knows something about greyhounds?"

"Christ," Arthur said.

"You go over there and get those next two dogs ready to come in, Jake," he said, leading in a pairing, "that fawn female, Mrs. Micawber, and Burt's Shoe."

"Check, Arthur," Jake said, moving slowly away.

Dawes watched him, still inverted, swinging on the tying posts which were upstanding, weathered, full of dead nails and worm tracings. Behind him the two dogs Arthur already had were on the pads. They clawed the worn strip of ground wormed with markings and tracings no one could read. Bending down, talking low circles in his throat, Arthur began again rubbing rapid, oval demands into the nearly loosened and hanging ribskin of the two greyhounds. He talked close to their ear. Dawes had already recognized the gray male from another summer, remembering his name was The Jailor's Badge, but he didn't know the red female.

She pranced on glaring air and danced on deep grasses. Softly, beside her,

The Jailor's Badge began rubbing up against her, quieting her down. And the dogs, Dawes knew, worked the rabbits in pairs. Instinct. No one could teach them. Arthur only let them practice, develop their skill and desire for murder and success. Even he could only let them improve on what they already knew from a secret heart, and often, he knew, it was the slower of the pair who got the jack; because the faster dog would only use his speed to outcircle the jack, to startle the flying rabbit, turning him into the determined path of the slower hound, which was coming up behind.

"Dawes," Arthur said, "you get down in here from that damn worthless fence and work the slips on the jacks."

"Sic them bunnies, Dawes," Jake Skout said, laughing deeply.

Getting down, Dawes tried to ignore them. Passing before Arthur, feeling as if he were crossing a stage full of others' eyes, he sat on the crate of jacks. He crouched over the opening, peering in, and the jacks were already filling the air with a thudding red wind. He looked down into them and they refused to come out. Sliding out, Dawes could see that the lead jack was only sitting on his huge haunches, thudding his drumming wood, staring back blankly. Jake Skout's laughter rolled in the air. Arthur lit a cigaret, staring through Dawes, looking for an invisible sign. They were his jacks and Arthur's hounds, and they refused to come out. It was war.

"What's needed here are larger carrots," Dawes Williams said, already biting his tongue.

Jake Skout's laughter stopped short, drifting and still. Arthur dropped his cigaret in the grass. It lay smoking, and Arthur stood looking down at Dawes, staring out queerly from behind the black house of his hat.

"Where did you learn to talk like that? So funny. Like some damn dude accounting in kneesocks," he finally said.

Dawes said nothing, watching him back, feeling like screaming suddenly at jackrabbits refusing to run out and be known. Nothing, however, no jacks, no hounds, no boxes or electric bells went off in the air.

"Now, Art," Simpson said quietly, "I guess the boy, like anyone else, is not really responsible for his diction."

Startled, looking around, for the first time everyone noticed Simpson standing there.

"I thought you were coursing dogs down here, Art," he said, smiling now. "I haven't heard anything really howl for an hour."

"Key-rist," Arthur said.

"You seem to be doing that badly, old boy," Simpson said.

"He won't come out, the mother!" Dawes Williams said.

" 'Course he won't come out," Arthur answered. "He's no dummy—he's been here before. Well, damn it, get a damn stick and poke him hard in the ribs."

"He sure is big."

"Oh ya, some of them Kansas jacks get to be forty pound 'er more," Jake said. "Get a stick, Dawes Williams, and stick him one up his ass."

The day was hotter, and walking up along the fencerow, looking for a stick, Dawes could feel the insects screaming up through the wires from beneath their pilings and stakes. Coming back he squatted once more over the opening of the jack crates:

"Well," Arthur said. "Damn it, MOVE! Don't just sit there. Poke him one!"

"I'm poking him," Dawes Williams said, "I'm poking him plenty."

" 'At's it, Dawes Williams," Jake said, "poke him one in his ass fer me."

Even Simpson was laughing now. And sitting over his crate Dawes continued poking. And soon, poking at it, he drew meat, blood almost, and the marble eye of the first jack broke from the opening, was gone in five bounds, and Dawes was about to call over to Arthur that he was gone, vanished, that it was too late, that he (Arthur) had been startled and missed this one, a joke, when quicker than flies' wings Arthur flicked his wrist—and both neck straps fell away at once, and those two dogs, the red female and The Jailor's Badge now, took off down the field like perfectly matched cannonballs going off, smoking, in the same wind and symmetry with an instant velocity, so that they, all two, all three, all four, all six and others moved down field in the same circle of air; a low-flying machine, a tight muscle, a flickering wrist and outgoing eye all straining like joints of bones and earth, things bo-jangling, and spots on noiseless dice.

And when they were finished, spent, Arthur waited for his dogs to pick their way home to the hill; down the path that was worn and curling easily, like a nesting snake, under the west fence. He stood, etched, the afternoon blazing like leaves, waiting for them to come home at a trot, proud as unlanded kings, holding their heads like crowns resting upon muscle, yet slow and methodical as only a trickle of past, half-excited water. Dawes watched them. Arthur smoked, looking for sign.

"You ask me," Jake finally said, "these dogs run faster'n niggers."

"They're agile and lean and fast," Arthur said.

"Damn graceful," Simpson said, finally speaking, throwing his cigar into the grass. "Certainly not a race of thick-thighed axe fighters all right."

Arthur looked at him queerly for a moment. His gaze was broken, carried back to the field unfinished by the noise of a pair of young pups which were fighting, jumping over themselves on their way back up the field.

"HEEEEEEYYYYYYAAAAAAAAAWWWWWWWWWWW!" he said, glaring into the sun, standing in the blowing, cooling grass.

The others, the mass of greyhounds both run and unrun, both winding up and undone, sat outside the fences on their haunches, furious, watching Arthur's every movement. The few which seemed to be occasionally bored were caught by Arthur's glance, which danced everywhere, and sent back to the hill with Jake to repent their sins. Most, however, paid fierce attention to what was happening on the field. The closer the course, the flight and cutting of the hounds and jacks, the longer and higher the cries near the gate. They were like players almost; animals warming the bench, attentive with envy, but watching every move. And sometimes something that even could be called sarcasm was howled down from the hill by the outcasts—it drifted down, swaying with despair, onto the hung head of a slow-running bitch, a gimpy male or a slacker which hadn't done well and which was, just then, jogging back down the side of the west fence.

But after the last trace of the jack had died off, and the two dogs were returned to their posts, there was a moment of silence. The howls wound down into next to nothing, breaking out quickly, absolutely again, at the second the new jack appeared from Dawes' crate; his magic box and blinking eye of noise. And soon they became a well-oiled machine: Jake led them in, two in and two out, and Dawes poked a jack in the ribs, and Arthur gauged the distance against the known capacity of the two greyhounds he had in the ropes and let them slip. Simpson watched, smoking easily, his foot still through the fence, taking nearly complicated and immediately forgettable notes with his eyes.

"Arthur," Dawes Williams said late in the afternoon, "how come they always come down the west fence that way? How come never the east, or just mess around in the middle?"

"You know," Arthur said, "I've wondered that myself. Once old Emile Peck had his dogs out here from Davis Groves, and they never came back the fence that way."

"It's strange," Dawes Williams said. "I don't think I'll ever forget that."

"What the hell's so strange about it? That's just the way it happens to be. More pairs, Jake!" Arthur said.

And when Jake led them in, the lean, well-bred muscle mounted only by a pointed, turning head, strained and nearly convulsed. The eyes distended, went slightly wild and then settled down into nothing. The heads of the pack, the hordes still outside, still beating the gates, were a thousand painted compass hands, reaching, pointed at all possible degrees into an otherwise open sky.

They jumped against the old gray boards and went periodically crazy over one another, like fools.

But the evolution of their bodies was perfectly overwrought. They were flawless and nervous, all at once, and they tensed against it. Sometimes, for the younger dogs, Arthur crossed over and plucked a dazzled jack from the crates with one hand, working the slip ropes with the other, and he shoveled the smell of the rabbit under the noses of the (by now) almost fainting dogs. Their nostrils fanned out, sails slack and reaching for a thicker air, and the two hounds snapped and pulled like violent executioners at their leashes. The jack, high as a low knee, sat frozen with ceremony yet twitching spasmodically. He was small, dazed in sunlight. His eyes were perfect black marbles, too close, too soft, too cowlike to look at for long.

Then Arthur let the jack loose. He jagged yips up the field, side to side, even though there was nothing in front and everything behind, and he zigged the air, leaving stripes through a field of scattered daylight, moving toward the wall of broken stalks. And the dogs, furious, left behind, crying as if someone had stepped on their feet, lifted their mad heads and answered the outgoing motion with begs and invocations until the instant Arthur let them slip.

Dawes knew he was fixed by the scene, the fields of grass stalks and jacks' ears running before him. He sat watching the rhythms; the jacks' comings and goings propelling the late afternoon through a mirror, like a motion of himself.

Toward evening the heat of the tall standing grasses and the shadowy trees of earth crossed, contrasted, merged again with a small movement. But the greyhounds moving about the open field were still an unbroken series. Now two females, young ones, were jostling each other madly, turning sharply, running down and overrunning the headlong flight of the jack. Arthur ran his hands into his pockets and seams as if he were looking for old tobacco, and said:

"Look at her, Dawes. That's Ella's Whiskers. She's a high-flying bitch all right."

"She's a damn good bitch, Art," Jake put in.

"You got another winner there, Art?" Simpson said.

"Don't know yet. She may be a good one all right, hell, good as sin if she doesn't fly those turns. I believe I'll take that bitch south with me to Miami next spring. But she flies out a little. Look't her, Dawes," Arthur said. "Look at that big grey bitch hip and go!"

He did and Ella's Whiskers, the single great greyhound which was out in front, all by herself, flying in a purer dream, seemed to be perfect with motion. Only the space around her seemed to be suddenly imperfect, filling in the low-lying gray light like a flickering movie. Ella's Whiskers, however, was by herself, outrunning her mate, overrunning the jack four times in only five hundred yards, nearly spilling herself over in rolling circles.

"Beautiful!" Arthur yelled down to Ella's Whiskers.

She was absolutely still, nosing under the corn, confused, disappointed, standing straight into the perplexed hole; a knife of frozen light, deranged, stolen from within her own impulse, she seemed to be trying to peer down low, within her own shadow, into and under the ground. She seemed to be waiting, illogically, for the next jack to bound forth from the other end and be known; to be chased among cheers and cut down at the pass.

"Beautiful!" Arthur said again, waving his red blanket of rags at the long edges of distance. "She may be a honey. Good speed."

"Good speed on that'un, Art, if you ask me," Jake said behind him, spitting again. "She may fly the turns though."

"All my great pups start out fast and green the first two seasons," Arthur said to himself.

Then he settled into an utter and contented silence. He lit another cigaret and leaned against the railing, watching the blue, sun-hung smoke curl around him.

The afternoon, smooth and even, was beginning to tail into evening like a river flowing into a glass of dead light. The first four batches of jacks at least had all made it through the boards, into the open boxes and short field trapped behind. With the crates empty, Arthur motioned and they, all four, began taking the gunnysacks down the long field. They entered the gate in the blind, going through a door of corn. They began picking the jacks out of the short field fenced behind. The jacks seemed somehow carnivorous, but their quivering made them give in easily. Dawes tried to ignore them, but he could see their eyes sticking out from within nets of grass like polished marbles of fearful glass. He chased them into corners and picked them up by the ears; stuffed them into his jumping sack. Arthur, however, picked them up as neatly and practiced as silver forks; Jake waded through them like kicking shucks; and Simpson seemed to be missing every motion, but hiding it better than Dawes. Then, moving back up the field, some of the old jacks began to come alive in their bags; some weighed over twenty-five pounds, and they were kicking out straight and strong as young mules. Art and Jake had two bags full, even Simpson did, and Dawes was struggling back with both hands knotted to only one; a sled, behind, running hoarsely on the grass. He was ridiculous, holding on for life as if the jumping sack were about to spring apart like a wheel, and sprout wings, and thump beyond him, and Arthur and Jake, even Simpson, were almost rolling on the ground, laughing at his fury, his tuggings, laughing at that and the fact that already one jack had already stuck his head through the sack and was spitting at him; and their single voice was rolling lightly through the wind when Arthur finally got out:

"Some hand you are, Dawes! That damn silly jack . . . that jack's bigger'n you are, Dawes . . . he's just about ready to turn on you and chew off your arm!"

Then Simpson laughed, and they all laughed, and Jake Skout laughed so hard he dropped his sack and half his jacks broke back up toward the dogs. The dogs erupted near the gate, nearly tearing loose, dying over one another, and the jacks ran in confused circles and then tore back up the field, behind them, skirting them all, disappearing once more through the blind. Then Dawes Williams began laughing.

"Sorry, Art," Jake said finally. "I guess you surprised me with your sense of humor. I guess that's about the funniest thing I heard you say in twenty years."

Arthur, however, didn't answer. In the failing light the men's moving shadows, walking the center of the field like a highway, were speechless again. And, returning, the boy sat again on the jacks' crates, which were like reloaded shell casings, and watched. He was tired, something gone out of him now, and he sat transfixed, alone within full evening forms this time.

Then one of the dogs won. The sun was already a low, burned-out stub end, and it was a pair, surprised, overrunning even themselves; a pure fawn, Brittle Snows, and a wild-looking brindle that Dawes had just named. And then, watching, he could see both dogs becoming wild as practiced axe murderers and, without turning, feeling the whole hill breaking loose from its earth, something flying, something humming under the ground in a long cavern, he sensed a dense, detached, throated silence, like vacant, dripping cave water, just before all the dogs began straining their fences. He watched the forms, one broken, two whole, two frantic, one calm, turn into the sun, high, silhouetted in red blood-stone, and all three tore open the finished and softened ritual of the jack's guts, shucking it out, spreading it all over the ground like a purse with a zippered flap to be examined by cold-eyed judges . . . whipping the rabbit into all directions of opening, organic dreaming. They shucked its form and pranced on its shadow. They threw it high in the air and carried it off in their jaws like lions. They ripped the jack into instinctively opposite directions; into pieces of stringy viscera that draped like rags from their noses; into gray balls of slick, nearly fluffy sky that fell to the ground, slapping like dead eyes and rain.

Arthur broke just as suddenly from his railing. Giving networks of leashes to Jake, telling him to tie them, and others, off on the railing, to shut the damn gate behind himself, Arthur ran lightly out toward the center of his field. He was still calling behind:

"Tie them off good, Jake. I've got to tear them off 'fore the others break their necks trying to get in here. Hear me, Jake!?! I guess they got the idea," he said.

But Jake didn't hear him or, if he did, he tied the ropes and leashes off badly, not well. Anyway, Dawes could see something was going wrong. Because in his excitement to join Arthur, to help him out, Jake let all of what was left of the leashes and ropes slip loose, the damn gate was open, not closed at all, and all of the dogs on the place, the whole string lucky enough to be caught up in Iowa, began breaking their necks running over each other's backs, trying to be the first out into the center of the field.

It was as if the jacks were drowning and in need of more help.

It was as if Jake, instead of holding off the parade, had chosen to lead it.

It was as if Arthur, instead of turning to see that his farm and English garden had been safely secured, pinned down behind him, saw only that his whole hill, his barracks, led by Jake Skout himself, was in the act of filing unbugled onto his parade ground and charging him down from the rear.

Dawes Williams began to roar with compulsive laughter. Simpson took his hand:

"Well, Dawes," he said, "this is just a game of sergeants and colonels any more. What do you say you and me go to dinner?"

It had been a long afternoon, he thought. The shadowy voices of the men were still running behind them to tear the dogs away. He and Simpson had turned from it and were walking to the house. The green hang of the walnuts left an eave, a stain, on the red and ballooning rib of sky. The trees spread, grew outward, leaving a roof behind as they threw the low angle of the sun, the thin shadow of the long hill, all the way down to the river. The moon would be out soon.

It was my planning that did it. It was the wild brindle greyhound that got him first, the boy thought. The only one all afternoon after all. The one he had let me name. Even before. The only one that came by, unnamed, that way because he has only two brindles that wild-looking left on the place. It was my fault. My planning that did it. It had, too. It makes sense that way.

Jake Skout had led him out and in.

"That's a wild-looking brindle, Arthur," Simpson said.

"Yep. That's right," Arthur said. "Only got two like that on the place anymore. He's just the pup of a nameless throwback. That's why I got some hope for him."

"Nameless!" Dawes Williams said.

"That's what I said."

"Let me name him!"

"What makes you think you have that right?"

"Why not? I'm your grandson, aren't I?"

"I guess so."

"He needs a name, doesn't he?"

"Ya. He needs a name."

"You're running out of names, aren't you? You said so yourself. Well? Can I? Can I name him?"

"You can name him," Arthur said.

"For real? Will it stick? No matter what I say?"

"All right," Arthur said. "What do you name him?"

"I don't know," Dawes Williams said finally, "I hadn't thought of it."

Arthur was looking down, kicking at dirt.

"Name that dog, Dawes," he said quietly. "Right now."

"Yes sir," Dawes said. "I name him . . . I name him . . ."

"Yes?"

"Damn it all," Dawes Williams said, "I can't think . . . I forget . . . I name him . . . hold on . . . all right then all right . . . I name the son of a bitch . . . MR. NORTON-THE-MAD-NORMAN-CELT!?!"

"MR. NORTON-WHATEVER!!??!!" *Arthur screamed.*

"All right," Dawes said, "I name him MR. NORTON-WHATEVER THEN!!??!!"

"What is that!?!" Arthur said. "What the hell kind of a name for a greyhound is that!?!"

"I don't care then," Dawes said. "I gave you your chance to back out on it. I name the nameless son of a bitch Mr. Norton-The-Mad-Norman-Celt."

"Don't say 'nameless son of a bitch' to me," Arthur said. "You can't do that. Where'd you ever get a foolish name like that?"

"Abigail Winas, I suppose," Dawes Williams said. "Where else? And I betcha it wouldn't be foolish if ya asked her about it. Matter of opinion, you know."

"Ya," Arthur said, turning away, "I only hope this one never makes it to the track."

But it was my fault, he thought, my planning that did it. I have named him, like Death, a greyhound brindled; wild with eyes; easy lucky mistakes almost. And the jacks, they are the only bones, the fish of thin light dancing through it, the stone branches running within it, holding it together in one place for a second at a time . . . and things can be even more than twice, at once, and usually are . . . .

They walked up the lane. Simpson was beside him. He was humming a tune, and soon they were back on the porch. Simpson went back easily, directly into the house. Turning, Dawes could see that the country lay open again below him. The air was without words but close. The heavens were a sill; a window; a sail. They looked back in, over his great-great's land, thinking of rain. There was a dream walking by in that window; a sail looking back in from that sill; a reflected ancestor's light. It promised to rain, filling this soil with tiny, fishless rivers; with green pools like eyes. The sky is blooms. Dead branches weave the air of the trellis, wounding the house, speechless, beyond the hedges, whispering. But these fields, he knew without words, were his blood. This sky, looking back in with dreams of rain and ancestors, his bulb of flesh. In their sills lay the seeds of his waking; in this waking were the bulbs of his loss, his sleep. These trees were his tiny jackbones of light. He was heavy with rivers; with coming. In his coming he was left behind. In these stones, he thought, lie the dreams of my waking; in these dreams lie the stones of my sleep . . . . Behind him, caught within the screens, Leone was saying something:

"Where have you been, honey?" she said.

"Just watchin' the dogs. Arthur's dogs."

"Was it fun? Was it interesting?" she wondered. "—Dawes?"

But he was beyond them already, and wasn't listening. People didn't feel the way he did. No person ever could. He was learning to ignore all of them except, perhaps, Abigail Winas. She knew something, too. Picturing her to himself, he stood there thinking it would be fine, just then, to escape again with some of Arthur's hounds; to run wild and risen and screaming within the stone sun, flat evening glare of the Lesser Cow River. But all of the hounds were locked on the hill; or soon would be as already Arthur and Jake were leading them back up the lane, shutting the carnival down. Soon, locked up on the hill, sleeping, quiet, they would be once more like the long, whispering edges to be found rising within the shadowy rain; they would be again within themselves, mysterious, howling quietly.

Looking back down over the lane, Dawes could see Arthur's near shadow pause by the end pen. Easily, like a player, he hurled what was left of the single dead jack over the wire. For a moment, standing under porch light, staring outward, Dawes watched the pups nestle around it like hungry birds. Then he entered the house. Soon it would be deep evening again, time to dream.

3

Leaving the kitchen light behind, Dawes went out on the hill. The early dark was a magician's air, another evening entirely, a sieve and sill, faint with forms, waiting for the first bones of the moon to come rolling home. The others, he knew, were still eating inside the house, bright corpses hunched over opened shells, in the swelling bones of yellow light and layers of frying chicken parts. Soon, he knew, the dishes done, Gin would be leading them all to Davis Groves.

The early moon, flat and luminous, obscure as wings and eyes, was a dance of naked fish scales propelling white, staring weather through the reeds of driven storm clouds. The west wind off the river was rising. The evening was going to rain. Lightning flashed in the far tree lines, illuminating dark ridges for seconds with electric nets. Off, distant, the thunder collapsed the blue bluffs like puffs of Indian smoke instantly dead. The hill shifted in the air, positioning itself, waiting.

Other summers blew before and behind him in the broken clouds. On another hill, only four miles away to the west, he knew, Abigail Winas would be driving her wild flocks of chickens from the tall grass into denser shelter. Her head would be terrible, lean, sensing the storm. He could see her then. The early wind ravaged her, untying her ends, moistening her skirts with delicate, unfastening leaves, unmasking her naked legs, lying beneath, like unguarded stalks gone limp in the folds of yards and yards of dead ribbon. The bright heads of the flowers, a confusion of late summer sparrows swimming on black hillsides, exploded into sleep around her. She would be locking her eye on the horizon. The bone and feathers of far trees would be climbing white distances, superseding the lightning like spines, rounding the darkened ridges like Indian bonnets catching fish light. The grass would be a smooth stone, far out, gray, merging the clouds, the horizon, the air and water, leaving no lower edge to the sky. She would shift her weight delicately against it, the air, the light, deliberate, uncomprehending sin. The huge white flues of moon and the black, horse-faced shadows of the leaves which moved about her, dancing, consuming themselves quickly, would seem to be untying her, toying with her hair, lighting tiny, glistening jewels of fire along her edges, before they flared out in the blackness again. She was light's water, its prism, its only river. She moved against the air, a following face, something locked to the season. The sudden motion of the ash tree, rattling, unhinging the boards and glass of her house, startled her out of her dreaming. Turning, she watched the separate, murdering limbs trying to be strainless, to graft themselves onto the cut and structured timbers, to grow on the scratching, incredible glass. They fell away, bloomless, an airy ghost, riders of older ruins. She was hard as diamonds, a closer, more possible carbon horizon. She shifted the basket of eggs back to her shoulder and turned back, into the deserted house. Moving back, onto the porch, she knew again that her humor had saved her only for larger destructions; that the mad and the murdered, the living, must learn to hold their chemical breath . . . .

"Yes sir, Dawes," Abigail Winas said in other summers, sitting alone within her thick hennery of fox grass, carving on chickens, "it's exactly like that French skull you dug near the river with that old set of junked spoons. It's mostly dead and not swarming beyond itself is what it is. This valley is. It's damn history, and not much of that, is what it is. It's dire is what it is," she said, laughing, "just dire's hell."

"What's dire about it?" Dawes Williams said.

"Oh, just everything was dire, Dawes. Take the winters, for example. They were dire. They were choked so badly with blizzard snows at the center you'd pro'bly choked."

"You're probably right," Dawes said, acceding already.

"Take Joseph P. Ahart, for example," Abigail said, "the first white Englishman into this valley from Council Bluffs. He was dire as hell. If you'd check the map on't, you'd see right off he was westering by coming east!"

Her sharp chicken knife glowed like lightning on the insides of dead chickens. Her shrill laughter, cackling, rolled off clouds, textures, piercing the air. She paused only to search his eyes carefully, poking him in the ribs with the butt of her skinning knife to make sure he was listening.

"Not only that," she continued, "Joseph P. Ahart strapped his babe, his seed and plowings, to the back of an old gray wheelbarrow and he came wheelin' 'em in here on the wind. Like he was goddamn Johnny Appleseed or something!" she said, laughing. "Christ, that's dire."

"Sounds all right to me."

"Shows what you know about it. Sounds like banjos to me. —Or, take Cornelius Durham driving everything he owned, his whole herd of hogs, his red felt hat, his stocking that rolled past his knees, out here from Boston in 1830, westering west at least, with nothing more to guide him, I bet, than a water stick. They, his hogs and then him, only stopped here because they liked the acorns growing in the groves of the Lesser Cow River so well. Christ, that's dire."

"What's so dire about it?"

"What isn't?" she said. *"Who can say? People talked that way in the old days. A bunch of jawers. A regular vale of tears. They didn't know anything about what was coming or they'd have had better sense."*

"That so?"

"It certainly is if I have anything to say about it. After all, why the hell do you suppose a comedy of a man, a tin pot of a man named Cornelius Durham, a founder—a man who had a name, after all, which either sounded as if he owned the only bank in Onion, Iowa, either that, or which sounded like he slept with a red felt hat on his head, and two-way knee stockings that rolled past his unmentionables—a man, no doubt, who never paid any attention to his own mind, let alone to anything else's in the first place— yes, why, I ask you, would a man like that pay any attention to a herd of swine to begin with? It's dire I tell ya," Abigail Winas said, laughing, opening another chicken like bloody shuckings, spilling the insides out onto ground like the tiny, shivering hearts of other summers; the insides of knowing . . . .

The rain, a full moonspout now, was driving the wind up higher on the hill. Dawes had drawn back to the porch. Behind him, standing at her screen, Gin was watching him. She was nearly a shadow, unaware, netted within buildings and wire. Soon they would leave for Davis Groves. Across the river a train was moving along the horizon. The lane was drowning, slick with voices, caught in breathless layers of water.

"I don't know," Dawes Williams said. *"Why?"*

"Why indeed? That's what I have always wanted to know. The answer is, of course, he didn't but the question becomes—why even would a herd of swine pay that much attention to a man like that, moreover, why would a herd of swine, in fact, pay that much attention to a herd of swine?"

"I knew that was coming."

"I knew you knew."

"I knew that, too."

"It doesn't matter," Abigail said. *"What does matter is this: why stop here? Why not keep movin'? Why this particular place? In fact, makes ya feel just damn near anointed to be just living here, doesn't it? It's more'n just acorns an' hay if you ask the preacher, you know."*

"I don't know."

"What don't you know?"

"I don't know."

"Well," she said, "that's a start. Listen here, Dawes, have I been telling you these damn-fool histories of the valley since you were three or haven't I? Don't you believe me?"

"Sure. Why not? You're my friend, aren't you?"

"Oh, that's too damn bad. That's terrible," she said, nearly snapping at him. "I had hoped you'd have outgrown all damn-fool believing by now."

"Believing in what?"

"Why, believing in all this trashy true history is what."

"Why?"

"I had better hopes for you, Dawes. I truly did in my day."

"Well, what do you want me to do? Why don't you just say it?"

"All right, I will. What I want you to do is just promise me not to believe anything anybody tells ya as long as you live."

"What'll I get out of that?"

"You'll get my respect, my undying gratitude, and my love from the grave is what you'll get."

"I guess I could use that."

"History comes mighty dear all right," she said, laughing.

There was a silence. Abigail finished off a chicken with an axe and turned back against him.

"We aren't getting back into these prime movers again already this summer, are we?" Dawes said, knowing she expected him to speak.

"That's right," Abigail said. "Look at it this way: maybe none of this ever happened to begin with."

"None of what?"

"Why, none of this history. What else?"

"I don't think that is true."

"I do. Shows a lot you happen to know about it. I keep looking for improvement and what do I find? —Jaspers!"

"Maybe so then. I hate to let you down."

"And don't go 'maybe-soin'' me now. You've only been here a day. Look at it this way: if Cornelius Durham's hogs hadn't stopped here, Cornelius Durham himself wouldn't have, either. If Cornelius Durham hadn't spent those six winters living under a tree, making friends with the Indians, the Mormons wouldn't have stopped here. If the Mormons hadn't cleared the place so well in the name of passing through, your great-great-grand-daddy, S. J. K. Dawes himself, couldn't have stepped in here like the already fashioned dude he was and bought the place. If your great-great hadn't have bought the place out from under itself, your grandmother Gin couldn't have afforded the luxury of going broke and being forced to more or less hang around here all these years. So that's *why you happen to find yourself here, washed up on this particular hill. Did you ever think of that?"*

"No."

"Well, I did. I happen to think of things like that all the time. You think I'm crazy, Dawes. I value your opinion."

"No. It sounds sensible to me. Is that the end of it?"

"No. That's just the beginning. No telling where it'll lead you from here. For example: if you hadn't happened to be washed up on this particular hill with me, how could I have formed on ya any?"

"I don't know."

"We are still to be married soon's you sprout wings, aren't we?"

"Sure," Dawes Williams said. "Why not?"

"Good," Abigail said. "My life is finally worked out for me. Help me shuck this corn. I'll meet you at the Outlander Hotel in Tucson in 1959, Dawes. Until then, we'll just have to dream about one another."

"I see," Dawes Williams said.

"That's what I like about you, Dawes," Abigail said. "You don't stifle a person by being overly witty. You're just the most earnest damn kid I ever saw."

"I can't help it."

"I know you can't, honey," she said, hugging him. "We're workin' on that. It doesn't make a damn really. Not any of it. Down with Kaiser Bill, eh, Dawes?"

In another sleeping silence near her stoop Abigail opened another rich pullet with her knife.

"So, you see, Dawes," she said, "that was really why and why is only like counting up numbers forever."

"Why what?"

"You show me more'n just rhythm in counting from one to two, and I'll put in with you. There's no proper religion in just counting up to why."

"Why what?"

"Why, why Cornelius Durham's hogs were the prime movers and no-account propagators of your piece," she had said. "If your grandma Gin hadn't gone broke and married Arthur and gotten rich again, how could she have managed to hang around that particular hill all this time? How would you have made this particular trek every summer? I ask ya?"

"How indeed," Dawes Williams said.

"Sass me if you want, you little bugger," Abigail said, "but it'll take more than that to save you from this world of believers. And don't you forget it. Here, help me shell these bloody peas. You're talking too much."

In the stillness, close to Abigail like others exploding, the peas flew into the steel pot, steadily, huge and loud and regular as shell casings, not seeds.

"Yes," Abigail said finally, "all so that your great-great could wander all over him-

self, through the blizzard of '53, over the ridge road to the mill to grind up settlement wheat, and be named hero, banker, landowner, founder of towns. That's dire, too. History's mad as a hat. It's an opera for cowboys. It's just dire as hell."

"I don't buy it," Dawes Williams said, overly serious.

"'I don't buy it. I don't buy it,' he says," she said. "Here, peel back this potato and don't cut off your head."

Out before the porch the rain was driving harder. That was to be expected, he thought. The second train had died off finally, a yellow smoky light ticking off beyond the hills. Behind him, the screen was wet as netting, black and sleeping with watching. The problem here, Dawes Williams thought suddenly, is that I am constantly expected to act like a child; and I don't know what that is.

"It's an opera all right," Abigail said, rinsing off chicken parts. Then she got partly up, on her haunches almost, and something strange and plucked came into her voice: "History's like baroque, monosyllabic librettos; Indian Love Calls echoing back."

"What the hell is that?" Dawes Williams said.

"Don't you ever say that as long as you live!" Abigail said, nearly snapping at him again.

She took off her shirt, got up and lay down in a circle of sun. She had been nearly forty that summer, lean and tan as a man. She was crazy, he knew, beautiful. She sprawled out, a lazy coil in the grass, looking back at him vaguely, a piece of dry straw in her teeth, nearly clenched, her mouth partly open, and she had said:

"Picture this, Dawes: in the winter the land was white and unbroken as an animal's back. Picture this, Dawes," she said. A small theatre came quietly into her voice: "The river froze, thin at first, and then you could see the hard brown water form blue circles in the ice."

"A single Indian pony!" Dawes Williams said.

"That's right, Dawes," she said easily. "Picture this: a single Indian pony, nearly riderless, pranced loudly within the powdered confusion of cold and singing birds; within the chalk and stone and snow of the river's crossing. His nostrils steamed like God. It was nearly perfect then; there was nobody. There was silence. His nostrils rose perfect tombs and smoked the air. He threw his tail in the wind."

"It's a fairy tale," Dawes Williams said.

"That's it, Dawes," she said. "It never happened. Only Jacques Grilleau just up and damn died here of fever, 1820. That's all."

"What did happen then?" Dawes said.

"Nothing at all happened," she said. "That's the only thing that saved it. That's the only thing that helps."

"I don't get it. Something must have happened."

"All right," she said. "Picture this: spring, an old cuckoo bursting its ticker. Civilization came. The flowers fell over themselves into pots. Your great-great-granddaddy rode up swinging his cane."

"That's not a story," he said.

"All right then," she said. "Picture this: a thin day in March. An Indian fire. The ashes rise out of the pot like sound. The sound rises over the river like smoke. The smoke is their voices, tired, moving through the wind like nothing ever heard; like horses throwing their tails out to thunder."

"That's crazy," he said laughing.

"Yes," she said quietly. "And then what happens?"

"I don't know."

"I do. I'm making it up. Besides, it's written out in a county history."

"Written out?"

"Well, partly written out. Anyway," she said, "those Indians got up that morning, apparently for the sole purpose of stealing your great-great's feather ticking from his first winter's cabin's bed, and him still sleeping in New England probably, and them taking the ticking, not the springs, and not the bed, and also as hindsight I suppose taking a few horses, leaving only the feathers to float like quiet notes in the opera and kitchen of Mrs. S. J. K. Dawes, who had probably never wanted to leave New Hampshire in the first place."

"And that's it?"

"Yes," she said, "and all of this in only the mistimed, first act of a comic opera of the air, you know, Dawes, people running wildly about, into and through each other on a wooden stage, almost dancing, screaming over each other in foreign languages in which incidentally, Dawes, just before the final curtain, they are all seen chasing themselves, each other and Indians into upper Minnesota, oh ya, where their caps and leaden balls cut harps through the grass with the sound of broken pi-ana strings, for hours, days, hitting no one."

"Did they get their horses back?" Dawes Williams said.

"History doesn't say," Abigail said. "Who cares? Who wants to know?"

"Maybe I do."

"Well, maybe I don't want to tell you," she said. "Maybe that's the end right there."

"That can't be the end. The 7th Cavalry hasn't even charged down anything yet."

Abigail laughed. She lit her pipe and her blue smoke drifted over the fox grass.

"Yes, well, maybe the end was already in the beginning," she said. "So maybe it never occurred to any of them—the prime movers, the heroes of the piece and the propagators of the plot—nor to any of their children— their hog-children still living back easily within the same dim provinces of the same thin hog-minds—that there was any need of ever moving again. Unless, of course, the acorns ran out. Which they haven't. So they all just sit. And chew on oak trees. Hearts. They all just sat there on that hill and grunted to the moon and each other."

"You're just telling me stories," Dawes Williams said.

"'Course I am. It's history," she said, "popular history. It's an American tradition."

Before him, the rain was driving harder. It was sheet and hammer, driving the fields below themselves. A third train, going east toward Chicago, moved through it, the sound obscured. Beside him, only her howling etched in the rain, Blackey Jane was screaming along the ridge of the hill. She was running, happy, weaving the wind with her delirious tail. She was out of her mind, crazy, barking at the rain, and the hill was for tall, shadowy hunters. The valley was for jacks and clovers of sun, free, blowing bright pennies in the light and wind. The valley had escaped from the hill. The hill only watched, waveless, penned up, black and wooden with eyes, trapping the valley. Behind him, at her screen, Gin was speaking:

"Dawes," she said, "you'd better come in now. It's going to be a terrible storm."

"Naww, Grandma," he said, "I'm not even wet yet."

"Well, you may be."

"But I'm not."

"Well, you might be."

"Awww, Grandma," Dawes Williams said, "I can tell which way the rain's blowing. It's blowing out, the same direction as the wind."

"Well, the wind can shift, you know," she said. "You never know."

Then she didn't say any more. She stood behind her silent screen, watching. They never left him alone, he thought, Leone and Gin. They fluttered about, waving and beating him to death with the shadows of their invisible wings, like Abigail's hens. They never left him alone. He sat staring out into the torn wind, refusing to turn and notice her. Before him the night's voice, tearing the trees like faces of stone, rose even higher than Blackey Jane's.

And sitting on Arthur's black, sightless witch's hill, he felt suddenly he could see it all: the single Indian pony's crossing; Joseph P. Ahart loading up his wife, his babe and all his goods and wheeling his barrow across Iowa . . . going west by coming east; Cornelius Durham, rolling up his Boston socks, beating his herds of unruly hogs through the underbrush with walking sticks; S. J. K. Dawes and his bank and houses, his hotel and silos, his mills and land and saddled horses. He could see it all; in the clouded nightwind, forming itself within Abigail's strange, broken voice; in the strange notes that went out on her fingered air. Because the hill sits here, he thought, not Dawes Williams, not me. A red felt hat, with a feather in it . . . Words . . . like ashes of Indian Fires, like I-o-wa he knew, nearly saying it suddenly within the storm; within his wondering at its long and rooted and hidden meanings.

"Yes sir, old boy," Simpson said once, crossing the state just outside of Tama, "'Iowa' means 'a beautiful land' in Indian talk. The Iowa Indians named the place after themselves and it stuck apparently. Must have thought themselves a beautiful people in a special land. Got wiped out though in the end. The Iowas did. Clubbed 'em all.

The Sac-Fox did. It must have been a regular Sabine rape. You see, the Sac-Fox invited the Iowas to a horse race—don't know who won the racing—but the Sac-Fox were low on women and clubbed'em right after. The Sac-Fox kept clubs under their blankets and they seemed to be the only ones holding a small war after the races. Didn't miss a one. Took all of the women and children into the tribe and clubbed the rest. That was the end of the Iowas, old boy," he said. "But they left names. Words. Sometimes words are the longest things there are."

"No, Simpson," Dawes Williams said quietly, "that's wrong. 'Iowa' is Indian talk for 'The Sleeping Ones.' That's what it means. Even Wilma Spent knows that."

"A Methodist, a Baptist," Leone said, "what's the difference?"

"Ya, Simpson," Dawes said, "what's a Methodist after all?"

"Well," Simpson said, "after all a Methodist is a Baptist who has gotten a better job and refuses therefore to get dunked anymore in the river with his suit and tie on."

And they laughed at that, riding west over Iowa.

And he laughed, remembering it, sitting on the hill and saying the name, but he could see that words were only vessels for defining place, not time, because time had no vessels for defining itself, even in shadows, the way water forms itself in a jar. Words. Inside, Arthur was sitting in his den reading over his accounts and stud books, *Winning Strains 1880–1911,* in two volumes.

"Not now, Dawes," Arthur said. He was in his study, his den carved and polished from the inside of the wood, and he was bent over a mound of stud books, a pile of light, reading: Maid of Dorset out of Commercial Traveler and Ebony's Babe; Miss Ann by Clansman and Lady Mary (out of Buckshorn and Misery's Melody); Strange Singer by Strawberry Girl and Wandering Tom; Bridgeport Bill by Sal o' The Mill and Rio Carlos; War Lord out of Dancing Polly and Money's Eye; Flower of Shannon out of Fluttering Flyaway and Fife the Fluteman; Ellen Tree by Tom and Elastic Fawn; May Morning by Beacon and Minnehaha by King Lear out of Ballad Singer and May Knot (May Moon III's line, Erston T. McPhillip's cross); Mediatrix (r.b.) 1897 by Fortunate Future and Faithful Fanny from Ned Needleham's line crossed to Wild Norwood Annie.

"Not now, Dawes," Arthur had said. "I'm reading . . ."

Outside, the hill remained, a thunderhead of rain, a bag of magician's air slipping over the slick horizon toward Omaha with the trains, the lighted, warm compartments of sleep. Gin was gone from the screen for a moment. Blackey Jane, whose track name was simply The Queen of England, maybe, was still singing high songs from the broken hill. Soon they would be going to Davis Groves to see Grandma-great, Arthur's mother. History was mad. He sat, waiting for other trains to break it, its surface, the night and the hill. Often he and his mother had rolled west on the train, rolling like bright stone strangers carved together from her sleeping air, rolling past evening toward night, but that was impossible, history, 1949 . . .

"Honestly," Leone said during the tenth hour, "there simply isn't a name for this railroad. I'm writing a letter."

It had already taken them ten hours to cross, almost cross, they hadn't made it yet, the two hundred and fifty-odd miles of Iowa. They were going from east to west, even slower than the sun. The sun was a stone on the fields, for hours. They were pilgrims, but no one had told them. He had forgotten his Bible, one chapter a night, and wanted to go home. Leone rode, warm and perfumed, beside him and told him it was nonsense. Waking, he stared from the windows for hours. Arthur would be waiting in the dark country depot shadows at the other end. At least they would stop at Dawes City. That was something to wait for. Simpson had stayed home. The red, beet-faced conductor with too-washed hands, Dawes had decided somewhere in the sixth hour with nothing better to do, was a khaki priest. He would eventually pass, swinging his invisible and holy flower pot of a lantern, saying "Dawes City, Dawes City, Iowa, everyone out that's headed for Dawes City, Iowa"—the way he had religiously for every other town along the line. And there, at Dawes City, a mass of brightly colored people like balloons going up in sunny skies on Sunday afternoons would exit as if to foreign places with a gay laughter echoing slightly from brass fittings. He knew they wouldn't, of course, these particular people weren't even on board yet, but he believed it.

"Dawes," Leone said, "this train doesn't even stop at Dawes City any more. We have to go past it and get off at Dunsmoor."

Dawes stared from his window again. He settled himself and watched the fat, shapeless land stroll by his window frames. Arthur was at the other end. His Cadillac was so quiet it was a speech, a perfectly combed horse roped to the dusty evening shadows. It was a spittoon not usable, but only a spittoon bought because it had happened to be the finest, the only piece of quality brass available in the county and said, therefore, in effect, HEY, I'M A FINE SHINY BRASS SPITTOON WITH KNOBS STICKING OUT EVERYWHERE, EVEN WHERE I DON'T NEED THEM, BUT I'M ALSO CLEAN AND WELL GROOMED SO DON'T SIT IN ME, OR TOUCH ME, OR FOLD ME OR OTHERWISE SPOIL ME FOR OTHERS' EYES.

"Here, Dawes," Leone said touching him, "it's peanut butter and jelly."

"Awww, damn," Dawes said, "I've had four of those."

But he took it and sat chewing. The land was red, split by a shaft of fire and blood for awhile, in the middle, and dull and shadowy on the edges. Her eyes were distant. The train held a gray, side-to-side sound below it. She was thinking of her father, of Arthur. The land was framed and made sense by the window. He had slept two hours in her warm, foreign lap. He had not touched her for years. Waking, he had seen that quiet, distant look in her eye. He never knew what she was thinking when she was thinking of Arthur. She was dark like Arthur, somehow lean and swift like Arthur, not Gin. But he knew, by some instinct, by some strange animal seed, left over, cold as a staring fish's eye, he must not even ask her until it was time; until he was called; and it was never time, and you are never called. And the rails rowed side to side, forever, going out into the illusions of distance, never touching, narrowing but never moving together.

"Honestly," Leone said, "I am writing this railroad a letter if they ever let us off."

And once, late in the afternoon, he remembered a large red, beet-faced man with muscles that defined his shirt had come on the train and sat looking at his mother in an unexplainable way until Leone began to glance up in his direction. Then the man had looked quickly down at his hands, between his legs or out of the window. It went on beyond her. When Dawes watched the man he was oblivious to the boy's stare. Just once, just short of Boone, the man's fierce yellow eyes, like dog water, yes, cold and uneasy in a morning ditch, the boy thought, watched Dawes Williams watching him back. But that was hours back. The man got off the train at Vann's and was forgotten. The rails only ballooned with a rib of evening then.

"Dawes," Leone said, "Dawes, look in the road there. It's Granddad and Gin! See the car there. They must be going to meet the train."

Arthur's white Cadillac was raising the dust below on the road. He almost heard it gliding, hushing, ticking its own sides like a cuckoo bursting its clock. And through the window, opposite, the farm lay below for awhile. A few late greyhounds were running in the fields below. They seemed almost slippery, smoke, bound like loose chemicals to the earth; dark, shadowy, they seemed to slip the grass, weave the woods, the corn, the open space. They rose to howl and continued to glide everywhere. They seemed incapable of grazing. They knitted the lower air with dreams, running forms more dense and lonely. They snaked and bound the wind. They were perfect. They sensed the moon. The iron railings boomed beneath him.

The storm was and wasn't easing. It flashed and withdrew. Gin had come back to the screen.

"Come on in and listen to the radio or the television for awhile, Dawes," Gin said, standing behind him. "I'll give ya some ice cream. Homemade, now. Can't pass it up."

"Nawww, Grandma. Not now."

"Only get to see you once a year."

"Ya. I know. Maybe later. It's neat out here."

The screen was black and moist. Gin stood within it, as if she were trying to warm muffins by keeping them bunched in her dresses and away from the rain. The air was a river, thick, outside and around its own throat, breathing with gills.

It was Gin's radio, her Word actually. On Sunday mornings she got him up. She came across the heavy floor by herself, slowly, the house seemed otherwise deserted, and she finally reached him, shook him, woke him gently. He was still with a wall of sleep, but he was nevertheless led out, sat down and made to listen carefully to the church services that bloomed hell all over the kitchen walls like fiery paint. Her radio was a Methodist radio, and it only worked best when plugged in in the country.

He sat sleeping backwards over the edge of a chair.

"Wake up, Dawes," Gin would say, "help the Lord put some life in ya."

"Aww," Dawes would say, nodding, "he doesn't mind."

"How ya talk, Dawes," she would say, "Dawes, how ya talk."

But she stood at her bread board, her hands already unnaturally white and dipping into the dough, laughing at whatever he said. She was just glad to have him cornered, it was her kitchen, huge, new, full of polished porcelain ovens, old wood bowls, wrought-iron skillets, and expensive China pitchers and serving dishes perched and hung from the walls, all of it looking, generally, as if it were a spoon which could, at any moment, lick itself clean and fly itself out the door; a partly old, partly new airplane which dreamed secretly of doing other, more acrobatic, work. And it was also her radio, her God actually, and she always filled the house with it. God was an airplane, too . . . he buzzed through the beams and the roof. No one slept for long on Sundays; usually the second, the beginnings of the third, sermon would get to them and finish them for sure. Arthur would get up and walk around the dazed kitchen for a minute in his underwear and look as if he were being invaded, and then go back to bed:

"Key-rist," he'd say. "A little peace and quiet, Gin."

"Mind your own business, bub," she would say.

Then she'd stand over her bread, humming the hymns loudly, stopping only to turn the eggs or bacon she was feeding Dawes, or to reaffirm the truth or beauty of what was being sung or simply said. Usually, however, the preacher was a Baptist and the sermon was proportionally full of sin, fire, and just general hell. Then God was an acrobat, an airplane of electric radio tubes buzzing in the walls. And the preacher, who barked at carnivals in the off season, Dawes thought, brought all of hell's color, glory, logical sequence of descent and interlocking stage movement upon arrival into the dazzled kitchen.

"It appears to me, Dawes," Gin said, "that those Baptists own twice as many radio stations as anybody else."

Dawes said nothing at all, trying to sleep. But after the first service was over (with Gin already moving to the radio to begin the search for other services, soon to be wrought through the kitchen like nets and veins of iron—this time by Presbyterians, or Lutherans, or perhaps even a stray Latter-Day Saint) for awhile, at least, Dawes would hear the sudden shift of the freed people as they left the sanctuary, and Gin would say:

"Well, Dawes, he's no Methodist today, like we are, but he's the only Protestant at hand, so he'll have to do."

"Ya. Guess so. He was a corker all right."

"But, Dawes," she would say, "if you could only know the Goodness of the Father. My word, it's not all that burning and ravaging that he's saying. Like it was all a troop of crazy cavalry. No, it's softer and quieter I tell you. I think the man may be touched, Dawes. Why, it's more like a good fine Father, Dawes, that makes the world so fine and green. No, he's no Methodist like we are, Dawes, but even if he's a Baptist, it would behoove us to forgive him for it and, besides, he may even have some fine points if you listen close."

"Seems to me," Dawes Williams made the mistake of saying, "you heard one, you heard them all."

"You listen to him, Dawes, and you just remember what I said was different."

Then she turned against him, looked down, and smiled in exactly the way the early and hooded councils must have looked upon the misguided, the unconfessed but guilty heretic. After that Dawes said nothing at all. He sat, trying to keep his eyes open. Gin found another station. Strangely almost it was an Episcopalian, straying into the country. Dawes only listened, drooping, becoming uneasy within the endless rhythms spinning, rising up, riding over the kitchen and dying under the roofs like black-slate cocoons spun from an electric eye; from the radio perched like precious centerpieces on the oblivious table:

"God then," the second, only nine-thirty, preacher said, "is in us all. Do we need any more proof? Perhaps. Perhaps not. We are, after all, not children any more. The problem remains basically this: God, then, must apparently remain, forever, an abstraction we can never really penetrate, or know, or touch, or perhaps even fathom but WHO, nevertheless, reveals himself fully to us through his works of 'suas naturas.' That is, through his creation, through the aspects of his own nature of which we are paramount. Can we not see him working, BEING, in the simple tree? I can. Is it not so that he is in the act of evening? The land? In the boundless nature around and IN us? I think so. How else could, therefore, this Nature have happened, come about so to speak without a Former; a Maker; a Prime Mover and Personal God of Creation? I ask YOU to search your own souls and find the truth of these whispers . . . . God then," said the second, Episcopal preacher, his voice now running together, a full tilt of strings and dry, happy, cloud-fearing rain dancers, "is therefore a benevolent Creator of a benevolent Universe. Is that not so? I think so. Man's Goodness, then, is but an exten- sion, and conversely a PROOF, of God's Goodness. Are we not, therefore, OF his Image and Likeness? Are we not, therefore once again, 'God'!?! I ask you. I implore you. I tell you it is so. Also then, God's basic Goodness IS mirrored in his Word, his Chris- tian Creation, in Us, and in Nature which is God's sign and his token to Western Man. AFTER GOD DESTROYED THE WORLD DID HE NOT SEND A RAINBOW . . ."

"Wait a minute," Dawes Williams said, waking, "just hold it right there. If this Lord's so good, why did he destroy the whole world? That's what I want to know."

"Shhhhhhhht. This one's pretty good. Don't be silly, Dawes," Gin said, "it was his to do with, wasn't it?"

"Gin!" Arthur called.

"Mind your own business, bub," she said.

" . . . any guilt then," the second preacher said over Sunday morning static coming in from Omaha, "or sin, or impurity, or just plain negative reality that can be empirically and inductively perceived by the merely SUBJECTIVE viewer of Man's filthy existence MUST, therefore, be assumed (by us, the objective, the rational) to be the mere fury of lunatics, a misconception of the misguided and the misinformed, OF WHICH

GOD, *The Good Father, The Absolute Sovereign, can obviously take no responsibility. Am 'I' saying then,"* the second preacher said, *"that evil does not exist at all? Hardly. To say that, obviously, would be to be severely derelict in my duty to you. What I am saying, however, is this:* EVIL DOES NOT POSSIBLY EXIST IN GOD. *Are you with me on this? Do you see it? It is, of course, perfectly obvious . . ."*

"You see, Dawes," Gin said, "The Good Father. I told you so. Oh, it's beautiful."

"Yes," Dawes Williams said, "I like the land, too."

" . . . in short," the second preacher said, summing up, *"*EVIL EXISTS IN ONLY MAN, THAT IS, IN THE PRECISE DISTANCE HE STANDS AWAY IN HIS OWN NAKEDNESS FROM GOD. *Or,"* he said, *"that is: one: God is Good. The World is God. The World is Good. And two: Man's Guilt must be his own. Does not exist in God. Does not even, therefore perhaps, exist in Man. And three: if this is not the best of all possible worlds in your opinion,"* he said, *"A., your opinion is theologically untenable and, B., none of it is God's fault in the first place."*

"Isn't that marvelous, Dawes!"

Dawes Williams, however, said nothing at all.

"Turn that damn thing off, Gin!" Arthur said from the bedroom.

"Go read your funny papers, Art!"

"You're driving me nuts I tell you!"

"Faith," the second preacher in Omaha said. *"One simple word. Ultimately we must accept all I have said on* FAITH. *And faith,"* he said, withdrawing, *"must and will always remain the exact, reasonable center of Christian belief. Because,"* he said, *"God we can never really know directly. 'God' we can only deduce . . ."*

In the momentary, freed silence that settled over the kitchen, like a rainbow almost, Gin was already moving the dial, searching for a ten-thirty service. She was moving before Dawes could.

"Well," she said, "what do you think?"

"That one wasn't bad," Dawes said.

"Oh, how you talk," she said.

"He wasn't bad, but I think he may have gotten mixed up at the end there and was, you know, walking circles over his own tracks."

"Maybe he was just nervous talking in front of so many people."

"Maybe."

"Oh, how you talk," she said. "Wait'll you hear this next one. Maybe we can catch a Methodist this time."

"They're some a the best all right," he said.

He wanted to leave but she always held him. Without words. Without anything at all. There was just nothing he could defy. There was just never anything particularly wrong with her. She was always like having to pass through something already unobstructed.

Even during August afternoons, when he would rather be loose outside, she somehow kept him longer in the kitchen. Her hands were white as Protestant walls in the *flour. They only formed things, forming only the grazing, cowlike dough. But she was obsessive, too. Her house, he remembered later, in winters, always smelled of closets, cedar, linen, mothballs all fresh in their combined summer of cooler, hiding-out darkness.*

But in the kitchen, in August, the afternoon light always fell off the long hill, skimming the walls with pepper and cinnamon as it swam through a sieve of willow trees. The locusts droned. The light always went skinning along the wood and the paint, carving it, leaving only deep, violent shadows on the walls; the sides of her face. And sometimes, out of that, the sudden richness of her voice, the thick choir of her soprano that caught itself through the listless screens as it rose in the yard, would surprise and startle him with its quality and unlikeness to her. It always seemed impossible that it had risen out of her tired body. The locusts droned. Her voice moved for awhile easily in the white flour. It always puzzled him. The attic light and shadow off the hill made her large oval face seem even more sullen and withdrawn. He couldn't not believe her. Gin, it always seemed to him, must have once sung in a Methodist choir and then never managed to get over it.

"You can help Arthur feed those dogs any day," she always said.

She looked at him with a warmth muted, even dull; the stones of summer rain running patterns down green windows. He wanted to be away from her suddenly. She lived in linen houses, he knew, one chapter a night . . . he checked himself. She touched his face with flour; white and Protestant wheat. He moved slightly away to the door.

"You can help Granddad any day," she said. "Why, heavens, I only get ahold of you once a summer, once a year, you know. Arthur doesn't want you with those dogs, Dawes, you'd just be in the way down there. You stay here by me today and let Jake and Granddad handle those dogs."

So he stayed, suppressing his desire to leave screaming and breaking for the corn, and the kitchen was a sudden box. He could only remember her wordless oppression.

The radio was droning on.

"GOD THEN," said the third preacher, a Witness, summing up, "HAS DAMNED US IN THE FLESH, HAS DAMNED US IN OUR SIN, HAS DAMNED US IN OUR MOTHER'S WOMB, HAS DAMNED US IN THE GARDEN (YOU DON'T THINK EVE, OUR DAUGHTER OF RIB FLESH, COULD HAVE E'T THAT APPLE HAD HE NOT WANTED HER TO, DO YOU, BROTHERS AND SISTERS?) AND I JUST SAY, I'M JUST HERE TO TELL YA THAT'S A LOT OF DAMNIN' FOR NO GOOD REASON. THAT HE MUST HAVE HAD A GOOD REASON FOR AS MUCH DAMNING AS THAT. AND I'M HERE TO TELL YA WHAT THAT REASON IS. AND THAT REASON IS THIS: YOU SEE WE WERE DAMNED IN THE START TO BEGIN WITH AND THAT'S REASON ENOUGH . . . ."

"Turn the damn thing off, Gin!" Arthur said.

"Well," she said, "you happen to be right on this one, but it's only an accident! Don't let it ruin your head!"

"Maaaan oh man," Arthur said from another room, "you're gifted today."

Gin ignored him, but was moving to her radio anyway. Dawes got up to leave:

"No," she said, "it's not even noon yet. We'll get something worth listening to on here yet. Maybe some hymns."

Then Arthur reappeared in the doorway.

"By God, Gin," he said, "I thought you had invited the whole church, organ and old ladies' societies and all, up to the house for breakfast. Key-rist, Gin, it sounds like a wake in here."

Gin ignored him this time by scowling through him. But he laughed to himself; as if he were the only one, certainly the only one in that room full up to bursting with old women and even smaller children, who was even remotely capable of seeing the humor he saw in it. Then, without further comment, he crossed right through it, the kitchen, striding with three steps into the dark sunroom, where he sat, laughing quietly again, rubbing the sides of his face, reading his papers, his comics and sports pages come in a week late in wrappers and mailboxes from Omaha, too.

The radio, however, was undaunted and spoke on (and on) and was a bowl of electric fruit, perched on a table, a cracked sill of God, a chorus of angels was singing now and yes, that's it, Dawes Williams thought, you have to be a dumb airplane of a radio with cracked electric tubes to ignore the simple point of view, the wrath of Arthur Oldham . . . .

The kitchen was an opera then at last. Then Simpson came in, robed, yawning, still tying off his strings, and rubbing his head, and he said:

"Gin? Do you really think we need this sort of thing on Sunday morning? Day of rest, Gin, not war."

"That's asinine!" Gin said. "That may be the most asinine thing I ever heard in my life."

"Don't know," Simpson said, "maybe so."

"Gin!" Arthur said.

"Maybe!" Gin said, ignoring him. "There's no maybe about it. This boy needs his religion, and you know he needs it, and I certainly know he needs it if you don't, and while he's in my kitchen he's going to get it I can tell you that," she said. "The rest is nonsense."

"He certainly is," Simpson said gently.

"Gin!" Arthur said.

"Now, Simpson," Gin said, "you're a kind man and I, for one, am forever glad to think Leone was wise enough to settle for someone like you, but you get out of my kitchen on Sunday morning! Because you just happen to be a little confused in the mind when it comes to this boy's religion," she said.

Then she stood, looking across at Dawes, encompassing him within her virtuous circle; her outright, holy war. Dawes Williams said nothing at all.

"Maaaaan oh man," Arthur said from the other room. "Who put kerosene in her motor this morning?"

"Did the Red Sox win again, Art!?!" she said. "Mind your own business!"

"Oh, I am," Simpson said mildly, ignoring them. *"I am confused, am I?"*

"You are," Gin said, trying not to ruin it all by laughing.

"Now, Gin," Simpson said, beginning again, *"sometimes I think even the unbounded mercy of Jesus can be just a bit overdone on occasions like this, I . . ."*

"Well, I don't," Gin said. *"I don't think I've ever heard of that!"*

"Gin!" Arthur said from his sunroom. *"Leave that kid alone!"*

"Go read your funny papers, Mister!" Gin said. *"You prattle about, but I notice you don't manage to say a lot."*

"Awwwwwww Criminy, Gin," Arthur said.

"Leave us alone," she said, *"we're doing fine."*

"That's all right, Art," Simpson said, *"I'll handle this . . ."*

"You'll handle that one all right. Maaaan oh man," Arthur said.

"Now, Gin," Simpson said, *"I really feel one or two services a day is certainly enough for . . ."*

"What is this?" Leone said, coming through the door.

Dawes sat watching them all. His mother, still heavy with sleep, seemed younger, fresher than the rest, a girl, a curtain still thick and not awake in the August morning, but that was not strange, not startling somehow, because the farm, and Arthur, at certain moments made her seem more like a sister than a woman all grown . . .

"Now, Leone," Simpson was saying.

"Do we really need all of this on Sunday morning, Mother?" she was saying, ignoring them all. *"Granddad sounds like an angry railroad man or something in here and . . ."*

"That wasn't Arthur. That was the choir," Dawes Williams said.

"You see, Art!" Gin said. *"You woke her up!"*

"I didn't say a damn thing," Arthur said from his den.

"You did! Why can't you see that the whole world does not necessarily get up with you, fool!"

"You're nuts! You're all nuts," Arthur said, rising, taking his papers out behind him to the hill.

He stopped on the back stoop; began reading again. Gin had followed him part way out.

"Now everybody's up!" she said. *"You see. You see what you did this time, Art!"*

"Honestly," Leone said.

"Call me when the opera's through," Simpson said. *"I'm going back to bed."*

"Awwwwww, Gin," Arthur said.

Dawes Williams began roaring with laughter.

"You see, Art!" she said. *"The boy's not even serious any more! Out. Out, out. Everybody's 'out!,' Art! That's what I say."*

Then, pretty soon, everyone but Gin laughed.

"Well," she said, *"that's all right, too, but Dawes and I were getting along just fine*

without you, weren't we, Dawes? And we'll still continue to do that just as soon as you all get out of my kitchen."

"Let us all now turn to five hundred and seven in our hymnals and sing the praises of the Lord," the fifth preacher was saying.

"This boy needs his religion," Gin said.

"Nobody needs anything this much," Arthur said.

"But, Mother . . ." Leone said, laughing through tears.

"Out," Gin said, "that's the last word I have."

Then the whole congregation began to sing. One voice, caught in the radio's kitchen, they bloomed out and fried the whole filling house.

The storm was trying to finish itself.

"Dawes!" Arthur called out from inside the house. "Get the hell off the porch!"

Dawes ignored him by obeying him and moved down into the lane. There the night was a thicker throat of wood. The rain was only blowing off the motion of the trees now. The clouds were a high, vacant howl moving over. He could hear them. The horizon was black and still again there, under the lane, behind the moonless mass, the wet clouds of trees . . .

"Dawes," Simpson had said, calling up his stairwell, the midnight banisters in Rapid Cedar, "that's all very well, but put that flashlight away. Don't you think you could read two chapters of that tomorrow night with equal grace or impunity?"

No. One chapter a night. But he is my friend (I know it) because I am only six, seven, eight, nine (don't step on a crack) years old and because I have read all of the Old Testament, and some of the new, every Word, one chapter, each and every night, and also because I know the books of Gospel, Matthew Mark Luke John, one chapter a night, by flashlight, Word by Word.

"Hey, Dawes," Simpson said, "it's late. Damn it, turn off that flashlight and read two chapters tomorrow!"

Nope. One a night. By flashlight, under the sheets then. From Mark, not Luke John, not Matthew tonight. Soon I'll be on Paul's histories, not Gospel but Word. One a night. From it all. In order that you could read it in order it started at the beginning and continued by number. Everything was numbered. Impossible to get lost. Even in the dark I'll be done when I'm twelve. Done. At last. Finished forever. Thank God. No. One a night. I'll be able to put my flashlight back on my bicycle. Or sell it for scrap. Or trade it to Ronnie Crown for fireworks. No, not done. When I am twelve I will begin again. Help. Save Us. Mercy. More damn thunderbolts on the Tribes. Oh my God. I'll enter a Methodist's Monk's Place, a holy wood when I'm thirteen. Yes, like that. Gin had a plan. O God, Our Father, oh crap, help, protect us, keep us (from thy mercy), save us (from ourselves . . . you). One chapter a night and say your prayers. And do your first-base plays. O. O, our Father, Far Father, Who art, Who art . . .

ON THE ROOF NEARBY.

No. That's wrong. That's dangerous. That may be sin. Stay in line. Say your prayers. Read one chapter a night. Hit Home Runs in recess. Be alert and good.

AND LIVING IN THE RUNNING RAIN PIPES, THE CROSS OF SKY.

Because, that night, that night Simpson spanked me for defying him and reading by flashlight a cross, THE CROSS OF GOD, *an opening in the far and nearsighted trees appeared. It was nearly perfectly carved (Bless Me) as a bush and nearly certain. It was positive sign. It rose. In the far trees over Dunchee's,* IN IOWA YET, *through trees and screens a cross of sky. Either omens or chewing birds.*

"You got trouble there, Dawes Williams," Crown said. Yes. I got trouble. Nobody knows the trouble I see. Responsibility. If I slept then, too soon, the world would go out. One chapter a night. And God said don't step on that crack, and scuff your shoe (and pass the hat) and look at the sun, and smile, NO THREE TIMES, and hit a homer, and look at the sun, and smile, no three times, and don't step on a crack, no that one, and smile, no, over your LEFT shoulder and, jesus, I got to stop this some day.

"Spanked your ass, did he?" Ronnie Crown said.

"Yes, my ass, but you see God is higher than Simpson, who spanked my ass, and he sent a cross in the trees to prove it."

There was a moment of utter silence. Dawes had never heard anything like it. Crown was thinking. Dawes said:

"It's positive sign."

"My ass, my red ass," said Ronnie Crown.

But Crown or no Crown, he read one a night. And watched the sky, the far cross, for shifts in sign. For further messages and prayed for mercy (because he loves us with thunderbolts), no, it's three times three times three; that's twenty-seven. TWENTY-SEVEN IS THE NUMBER. My Father, My Father, My Father, etc., etc., until you got to twenty-seven . . .

"No, Dawes," Simpson once said, "it's Catholics who do that. We Protestants take it easier."

My Father, My Father, My Father (27) Who Art, Who Art, Who Art in a roof in heaven, no heaven, Who Art nearby IN A ROOF OF HEAVEN, WHOSE NAME IS TWENTY-SEVEN . . . Living. Dead. Living and Dead. Flesh and Ghost. Dead and Living. Renting all space. Throwing thunderbolts. Flying around. Three times three (times three) times just farther than that farther star. Just over the county line. There. In Iowa. In the center exactly of the cross of sky.

"You're just fevered, honey," Leone said. "You're probably only having a nightmare. They pass in the morning."

Sleep. Sleep now. No. Nope. Couldn't. DO THE FIRST-BASE PLAYS FIRST. And (Jesus, *sir) if you could find the time, you think you could talk to your Father about me hitting some homers? I can catch 'em anywhere. Over my head. In the dirt. Beside me. Your Father, The Blower Of Winds. But I can't hit homers. Too far inside, to the baseline side and you use your head you*

TAGGED THE RUNNER

who was coming down the line. Good play. Now, look yonder, look into the sky and smile three times. Thanks. Once, twice, three. Times three that. No. Yes. Total: TWENTY-SEVEN TIMES! A fever. No. A good bet. Sleep. No. Do the first-base plays: men on first and third, one out, or none out, GO for the double. The old double play. Throw'er down to second, TURN FIRST, and cover the bag. Swivel on the ball of your RIGHT foot and don't look back until you've reached the sack.

"What the hell are you doing, Dawes?" Crown said. "I'm practicin'," Dawes said, "just practicin'."

"You're dancin' around in the air you ask me," Crown said.

But I'm a fine glove man. Modest. One of the finest glove men for nine years old in the block. If you're not modest, your talents vanish and all your work's for nothing. Work. Three hours a day (three times on Saturdays) I throw the ball against the wall. The wall. The wall. The wall. The wall's a perfect stone, not the ball, not me. I'm hopeless but improving through modesty. Work. The ball returning. Forever. Crown above. Stuck to the wall, sitting, watching. He said nothing. He laughed on the hour. He smoked cigarets and fired wetted smoking stick matches in arcs, never burning, over my head all morning. It's a dream.

The ball returning. Worse than Yo-Yos. It sounded always like chickens walking, recurring back over their own feathers, their own steps, stomping on their own eggs. Forever. Crown or no Crown. Crown may have even been the devil.

But I'll be good. But (Jesus, sir) I can't throw so hot either. Must be a curse. Can't see any other reason for it, for going Over their heads. in the dirt. Beside them. Can't throw or hit either. Can only catch. Jesus, sir, your Father is The Blower Of Winds . . . I was just wondering: could you see your way clear to . . . O. Our Father Who Art, one out, or two out, or in heaven and the bases are loaded, or even none out, GO TO THE PLATE AND GET THE SURE ONE. Cut off the lead run, or the tying run, or any run at all, GO to the plate, the old green plate, and spit in your glove, and wipe it off, twenty-seven times, and look yonder in the sky . . . .

"Hell yes, Dawes," Crown said, "get the mother-green-fucking sure one. Often go around saying that to myself myself. What the hay, I say, get the fucking-green-mother sure one. Hell, I'm just not happy a day goes by, you know, and I haven't said that. What the hell are you doing, Dawes!?!!!?!!?"

Crown did not believe it.

Threetimesthreetimesthree times. And get the old green Sure One, and Hallowed by Thy old gray Head, no, Thy Name, and Hallowed be Thy Name because, because

ONE SUNDAY CHRISTMAS THE PREACHER TOLD AN ANTIDOTE

about the poor poor kids in the orphan's home. And how they'd got there. We have wicked hearts. Because we have wicked hearts. But outside it was snowing, easily, gently, cleanly as a newly shaped beard. Outside, even dreaming, it's white as a Protestant fence.

"Well look at this," Simpson said out loud in his pew, louder than whispers. "The reverend is outdoing even himself today."

Some of the others nodded in agreement. Some scowled at Simpson, turning, twisting their ugly heads. Like snakes.

The Reverend continued, unnoticing, unmoved, over the top. Amen. Amen. Right there in the church he told it. Was telling it still. The antidote to wicked living. The message. His eyes were black and chewing as hearts. The message for Christmas morning. Amen. Amen. O, Our Father Who Art One Out And a Runner on First, a ground ball, these were the tough ones, the ground skimmers, the tricky hoppers shot from cannons

CATCH IT FIRST, YOU DUMMY

then *run the runner back to third. Then* get the hitter. Then *hope the shortstop from the orphan's home has covered a sack, and has remembered to own a glove, and can catch in the first place and, poor poor kids from the orphan's home, never had any socks for their shoes. But they were lucky, the preacher said, they had a Methodist orphan's home. O, Our Father Who Art on the roof in heaven, forgive us, give us this day our daily bread, and forgive us our trespasses because*

THEY NEARLY BIT THROUGH HIS THIGH
"YOU SEE THEY ATE HIS LEG!" THE REVEREND SAID.
BECAUSE WE ALL OF US ATE HIS LEG

because we all of us, drunk and happy as Saturday night, were his parents, but the cupboard was bare so we carved on his leg. It was tragic and warped, the preacher said. It had only been last Thanksgiving but pondered a month well, now, the preacher said. They were only symbols of us all, celebrating but damned anyway in the first place, the preacher said. And "the cupboard was bare," but that's no excuse, the preacher said. Because we caught'em in the act of trying to bring him into the Methodist hospital, the preacher said, had tooth marks on his thigh so we had to send them to jail, send him to the orphan's home, the preacher said. On Christmas morning. He told the antidote to wicked living. Fear. Said we ought to fear our monsters. Said we ought to be thankful for our blessings. Said it was just lucky and To Be Forever Grateful the devil hadn't tempted US *into eating our chil-*

dren's legs. Said the story had its point. On Christmas morning. Only the snow was ever clean.

"*YOU SONOFA BITCH!*"

First and second and no one out. Go to third, to second, back to first and cover the sack. Triple play! One chapter a night . . .

"*What did you say?*" *the reverend said.*

"*I SAID: YOU MAY EVEN BE A SON OF A BITCH,*" *Simpson Williams said, rising calmly in church.* "*I SAY SOMEONE, AND I GUESS IT IS ME, SHOULD INDICT YOU FOR BEING THE ABSOLUTELY CONSISTENT, MORONIC JACKASS YOU REGULARLY HAVE PROVEN YOURSELF TO BE.*"

The reverend said nothing at all. Leone gasped.

"*Are there any questions?*" *Simpson said.*

Said it, leaving the church. The sanctuary. The fold. Said it calmly standing back, parting the aisle like an usher without platters, for Leone and Dawes. Leone was nervous. Dawes felt suddenly relieved. Said it before he'd even gotten a good chance to underline the Christian moral for the second time. Dawes felt like dancing out. Like flapping the ears to his snow cap at them like tap shoes. Leone was still surprised, surprised she had gotten up, surprised she was walking out, surprised at where she suddenly found herself, surprised she had even come. Simpson was sure. Dawes was sure; sure he had never heard Simpson curse before, not once; sure it was the right time for it; sure that he must have just been saving it; sure that Simpson had been one beautiful bastard, for a minute there; sure that the amazed Methodists turning with his outgoing motion were still there, in place, like the zoo of a single wave . . .

> "*Here is the church,*
> *Here is the steeple,*
> *Just open the doors wide*
> *And see all of the fundamental people,*

Simpson said, laughing, bouncing his knees. Dawes was three. He squealed with delight. He nearly fell through to the floor, expecting it, surprised, horsie and rider. Simpson's hands were laced, invested and opened. The people were fingers, expected, surprised. Simpson caught him. He trusted him. The hands were white and soft as if they had never worked. He wore funny glasses, yellow and forgiving and easily blind; looking through . . .

"*Turn off the lights and go to sleep, Dawes. You can surely read two chapters with equal grace tomorrow night,*" *Simpson said.*

The words came up the quiet stairs. The stairs were sleeping. Softly, and like a father's words. No. Yes. No. Read one chapter a night. Review Genesis. Strange. God kept a stud book. "*And Bashemath Ishmael's daughter, sister of Nebajoth. And Adah bare to Esau Eliphaz; and Bashemath bare Reuel; and Aholibamah bare Jeush, and Jaalam, and Korah: and these are the sons of Esau . . . . And these are the generations of Esau the father of the Edomites in Mount Seir."*

And God's real name was twenty-seven . . . Raz-a-ma-taz.

And the wind and sharp rain were still driving into the lane, the living hill, the chicken stump of sky, fresh, pure as cuttings, but nothing responds . . . .

That Simpson, he thought, was quiet and faceless as a snow-white beard, a gentleman who kept books, Arthur was thunder, one out, men on first and third, and the batter bunts . . .

"Dawes!" Gin was saying, standing on the porch. "What are you doing down in that lane?"

"You'd better come in now, Dawes," Leone said behind her.

He ignored them, however, and moved farther into the lane. The rain was dead and nearly still then. The moon was a round white reptile's stone hung in a sightless wood and leering over. All the dogs were coming out, sniffing as if they might fall through the wet ground, and moving along the brighter ridge of the hill. The night sky was too close with sudden stars. The two women, higher up, recessive in the yellow light of the porch, seemed to be clearly defined in the new air. The greyhounds began moving down, testing the lean grass, putting the paw down lightly and looking for positive sign; a fire of sudden jacks in the houses of grass. They seemed disappointed; already informed. Blackey Jane, The Queen of England, and Zippy Tommy moved down, shadows, outcircling themselves, howling over each other's tracings, whispering like galloping snakes through the fine, pure cuttings of grass; the shoots of hanging air smelling freshly tended as hay. The wind had stopped then, and the trees were rhythms vanished and sleeping in still awnings, dead canvas. The light only reflected the pool of the heavens. The light was an illusion, the trees a voice, impossible to touch. The fields were cool and black but impossible to enter. The stalks were upstanding and bare, the naked white bones of moon, rustling shadowy, trying to knit the universe together under a sea. Their leaves were long with edges, sharp, like knives and slight bracelets on the breeze. Vanished Indians and grazers hid out in their silky rows. The evening, a ghost of rain . . . he thought it was time he should be leaving and striking out on his own.

"Come on in for awhile, Dawes," Gin called down from the porch. "It's late, but we still may be going to Davis Groves anyway."

"I'm doin' fine," Dawes finally said, climbing over the ten-foot gate into the inner lane. "Leave me alone."

"Where are you going, honey?" Leone said.

"I'm just going down along the pens for awhile. You call me when you're ready to go."

"Stop this nonsense, Dawes," Gin said.

"What's nonsense about it?"

"It's nonsense," Gin said. "You've seen that lane a million times before. Come on up and be with people for awhile."

"I've never seen it at night."

"Well, I bet it's the same thing only darker," Gin said, laughing.

"How would I know? I've never seen it before."

"Oh, Mother," Leone finally said, "I guess it'll be all right."

Big deal, Dawes thought, goddamn people. But the porch did seem like distances you had to call across, and higher up, and across the spaces of more than blocks in the yellow light. It seemed hooded and closed. Then Arthur came out onto it, and his laugh was heavy but understated, quiet but clear, and it dominated the rolling night.

"Don't get mauled by a dairy cow," he said.

Simpson came out and stood behind them. He seemed peaceful within a hallway of porchlight and swarming life. He seemed to be the only one watching it all, behind, safe, and Dawes watched him back. The katydids and locusts went up higher and wider than a wet wing of a river after the rain. Dawes slipped over the fence.

"It's raining," Gin said.

"For God's sake," Dawes Williams said, "it's not. It's stopped."

He slipped into the lane. The row of pens was a frontpiece on the lane, a net of wire. It seemed a mile long, immense and sleeping. The dogs were snaked quietly under the grass and moonshadows now like hearts of hidden wood; the eyes and dreaming memory existed only in the long bone of their noses. He could see Old Traffic Cop—son of Traffic Judge, son of Traffic Jester, son of Traffic Elder, son of Traffic Light, son of Traffic Car, son of Traffic Joker's Dam, daughter extraordinary of the great Traffic Court himself, dog of the twentieth century, stud of America—moving down the slow light of the hill beyond. Dawes went down to meet him, climbing the fence.

"Hey, Traffic Cop," he said, "how have you been?"

Traffic Cop jumped feebly against him, sniffing, putting both paws over his shoulders, licking his face. The wind remembered him. It was faint, dull, but there was a remembering air, a boat of it drifting in Traffic Cop's nose. His red jaws were graying with age; his muscles were lean but still somehow soft and withered up like an infirm old man's, but he remembered him, whimpering gently, as if only his eyes were gone. He remembered him, a suppressed and furious howl rising and forced through his throat now, and he rubbed the deep, cold night of his nose against Dawes' face. He got down and began leading Dawes up the hill toward his hut. It was almost formal, shadows dressed in tails, moving up the hill to have some tea, and Traffic Cop continued on ahead but stopping often to check the shadow behind him. Dawes followed. At the ridge they sat by the hut watching the moonlight move below. Dawes wondered suddenly if Traffic Cop's memory of first meeting Dawes Williams was more vague than his. He wondered if he really remembered meeting Traffic Cop, or only the picture Simpson had taken of the occasion; but in it, the picture, Dawes was dressed in a cowboy suit, and smiling with glee, and standing holding onto Traffic Cop's thick leash as if tied to a mountain that could fly. Traffic Cop's tail seemed higher than Dawes Williams. In the second picture, Dawes Williams did have a hold on Traffic Cop's tail; but Traffic Cop, whose head was turned and looking back in this one, still seemed unworried, quiet, gentle, even protective and dreaming though he was being attacked by a monkey. Dawes had been two, and Traffic Cop had been twelve, but the dog had seemed wiser, more bemused, and with more distance than that . . . . Dawes laughed thinking of that, and he thought of Arthur talking; of him moving down, onto his fences, waiting for Gin to make her way down the hill so they could start for Davis Groves; of him lighting another cigaret, putting his foot through the low rungs, talking about his thirty generations of half-blinded—the outside eye, you could predict it almost, but I was all right on that one—fast-running dogs. Arthur was one fine human when talking about greyhounds . . . . Dawes laughed suddenly, thinking of that, and he buried his head in Traffic Cop's warm fur smelling still of winter wood and worms and the wet flower ends of grass, hugging him with a quiet fury, and this seemed to rouse Traffic Cop, who lived alone in one of the far pens now, enough for at least sitting up on his haunches. Then the two shadowy forms, like old friends without any need of talking, sat on the ridge for a long time, side by side, staring down into the fixated light . . . .

Soon, he knew, rolling back over the bridge, the gully water, the Frenchman's skull of a river, they would be going to Davis Groves to see Burt and Ella and Grandma-great. They would be talking but he wouldn't listen. The summer light, a family, another August storm of familiar air, cloudy blood walking over the bones of fields, would move with them along the road. He would sit, watching it, away from them. Perhaps S. J. K. Dawes, founder, benefactor, good pioneer, indulger of his daughter's fancies, had crossed this part of the land, still fleshed and walking blood . . . and the oval whiteness was stuck in the windless sky like a sail not moving or even recognizing its sea. He would be away from them and moving beyond already. They would be talking, but he wasn't listening . . . .

"Art," Simpson'd say, "how's your mother holding up this year?"

"Oh," Arthur'd say, "she's ninety-one this year."

"That a fact, Art?" Simpson'd say.

"Ya," Arthur'd say, "that's a fact all right, I guess."

The others always thought Simpson was bright enough, but dull sometimes. He often seemed to talk more to himself, in circles, for the sake only of conversation:

"Well, ninety-one," he'd be saying, "she seems always incredibly lucid for a woman of her age."

"Well," Arthur'd say, "she is. She's always been very awake."

"Now, take my family," Simpson'd say, "the Williamses all go completely senile, completely bugo, around fifty-five."

"Is that so?" Leone'd say. "Do tell."

"Ya, that's so, Mother," Simpson'd say.

"Do tell," she'd say.

"Well, I will," he'd say. "But speaking of relatives, my great-uncle old T. Tom Williams always said he was potent at ninety."

"He was, was he?" she'd say.

"Hell no, of course he wasn't," Simpson would say. "When he said it, he was completely bugo at the time. Didn't know potent from chickens."

"Really?" Leone would say.

"Oh ya," Simpson would say.

"Ya," Arthur'd say, laughing slightly, "that's a joke all right."

Simpson, however, would be enjoying himself, laughing widely, surrounded by Daweses and Oldhams and Williamses, and going to Davis Groves. Arthur would be driving the car. Out the window Dawes would be able to see the summer lights of Davis Groves flare in the hills. The streets approaching hang out into the corn. The yards were thick, close with bushes within; a fortress of stifling lilac folding the houses like prisoners. And the streets near Ella and Burt's were unpaved, slim dirt clouds too small for Arthur's car. Finally they would go up a steep hill, almost a perpendicular in the air, and stop.

Ella would snap the porch light on. Burt wouldn't say a word. Burt never said a word. Ella did all the talking. Arriving, Dawes would be able to hear Arthur close the door behind him. The air in Davis Groves always carried sound. It drifted the notes of dark night birds through the thick, English throats of the bushes; it waffled the tiny street noises, and made them louder, and carried them through the long choke of the yards to the houses dug like eyes into the black hillsides. There were no lamps in the streets. The summer there was darker than the country. Burt, however, he knew, wouldn't say a word. Burt, in fact, never said anything at all. He was Arthur's twin brother.

To get to the porch, he knew, they must cross a yard black with flowers and bees, thick, sweet air. Ella, who nearly had whiskers and was Burt's wife, would be on the porch, snapping on the yellow light like a curtain and ceremony of swarming gnats. Even the street sounds rising behind bushes, passing cars rattling themselves to death like rocks in passing cans, or like Indian chiefs shaking out the gourds of the bluffs, reek of decaying plant life, black grass, dying flowers, and forms drawing themselves inward.

"Lord, it's Leone, Simpson, Gin and Arthur, Burt! Hi there, Dawes!" Ella would say from the porch.

Ella would speak a great deal but say nothing at all.

Finally Ella's laughter and greeting would die away over the sweet, dead lilac, the yard. Within its stoppings he would be able to hear Grandma-great's rocking chair begin, rowing the dark of the porch over with the motion of her rocker. She always seemed cracked and splitting, interior, a pillar of wood, and Dawes would sit on the steps below her, just close enough so she could reach out and touch him to make sure he was still there. The others would be already drifting away, forming their own gossiping circles across the porch. They were away and not listening, but he could see Grandma-great didn't mind; she knew about the others, and the only one she had left to be curious about was Dawes Williams. She had great faith in curiosity, and she was incredibly old. Dawes had never seen anything that old before. In Ronnie Crown's nursing home the people were that old, but you didn't look at them; you looked instead at the walls beyond. Crown looked at them. Crown cursed at them, and laughed, and moved through the kitchen spitting in the huge bowl of common butter before he broke through the back screen and ran screaming into the yard. Not Dawes. He could never look them in the eye. They weren't people; they didn't exist. They only sat in their own falling-apart shadows, watching the fat sky pass the tub of their window. But Grandma-great existed. He would have to look her in the eye. And the veins climbing in her face and arms were thick as ropes. Her soft skin, pale as the light passing through it, hung on her bones, which were sticks. Her eyes had clouds in them. Leone called them cataracts, which sounded like rivers, and he knew she had already been nearly blind when she came to Nebraska from the slums of Liverpool as, as Leone said, already a seventeen-year-old girl's idea of an old woman. Abigail Winas said she was probably another tough old Celt. But she would be on ninety-one now, and she was already so old the light went through her, a sieve coming out the other side, and he couldn't even imagine her as being in any other state now; and her eyes were yellow and held shadows, veneers, dead houses, thin, unwaking clouds before . . .

She was Arthur's and Burt's mother, and others he had never met. He knew she still lived by herself, except when people were bothering her, in her small house two blocks down the hill from Ella's. It was much like the one she had raised her children in in Nebraska. Arthur was the only one with any money and he wanted her placed in a nursing home. She didn't want it, and wouldn't hear of it, but thought it was only a mild conspiracy. She said she thought she would only consent to die in her own (and God's, too, of course) good time. She said she didn't believe in nurses anyway. Leone said she had taken out a five-year subscription to The Saturday Evening Post *and was feeling rather good about it, all in all. She was in good shape, they all said, for a ninety-one-year-old woman who was dying of age. They all liked to remark on her. Abigail Winas had once said she thought, in most ways, Grandma-great was in better shape than Dawes, but still, he knew, her eyes threw the light back; and what she couldn't make out in her Saturday Evening Post she would have read to her, and her Bible too, of course, one chapter a day, and her eyes still remained utterly soft and*

*looked as if the yellow clouds were measuring themselves, growing out to the edges, and
when they finally reached there she would die . . . and she would be smaller this year.
She seemed to shrink more every year, a core, as if she were slowly withdrawing into a
center. She seemed to shrink three inches a year, like a dike, and he knew she had never
been five feet on a high day to begin with. And Thomas Oldham, whom she never
would have met in England, and whom she married in Hipple, Nebraska, was six feet
six. They were a sight, Leone said, and it was a comic and ironic marriage in more
"tangible" terms than class. Thomas Oldham's people owned a starch works, but
hadn't worked in it for generations, when he had gotten kicked out to America.
Grandma-great had come to America by a different route, but eventually came to
believe in the "idea of open geography." It was said that Anna Sewell, an English
woman who had written* Black Beauty, *a story told through the eye of a horse, had
given her £100 to make the trip though no one remembered any more quite why.
Dawes knew he didn't. He asked once, but the others were always too busy talking
about other things. And in the new town, Hipple, Nebraska, she had married Thomas
Oldham, who wasn't inheriting a starch works any more, who had fallen from grace to
the status of sheriff, jailor and traffic cop, which must be also, he thought, why generations of greyhounds wound up by being named from the recurring ideas of Traffic,
Court, Judge, Jailer, Cop and Officer. So that was it, he thought, history, that was why
. . . Grandma-great, Gin and Leone said, had "will power," but Dawes knew better.
Dawes knew Grandma-great had just willed them all.*

*And the others would be drifting off. They were talking, but he wouldn't be lis-
tening. He would be listening to Grandma-great, to her flat words, still sleeping, lying
out easily with the porch's air, waking slightly with the stones of yellow clouds within
them. But her words were also strange and foreign, with letters dropping off everywhere, and she still had some of the old ways and thought, for example, that tomatoes
were poison. "Don't ever eat a tomato," she once told Dawes. "They'll kill you dead,"
she said. But he didn't answer her. He had already eaten plenty of tomatoes, and none
of them had killed him yet. He only sat watching her, and she was very present when
she would come out onto the porch, feeling more the light, smelling the sound, the
summer of drying flowers and thickened locusts in the yard, and once she had said to
him: "'Umming the locusts die, Dawes," she said. "it's a good a way as any. Better'n
some. They make me see England when I was a girl taken to the country once. England was a wonderful place, except for the people, th' geography of the thing and, yes,
I'm considerably glad I 'ave left," she said. Then she sat, rocking under the light, quivering to herself with a soundless delight. The others were listening to Ella's gossip, but
Dawes watched her, fearful almost, as her knotted hand left its cane and reached for
his head.*

"Are you 'ere, are you, Dawes?" she said.

"Ya, Grandma-great," he said.

"Oh, that's so good t'know, don't ya know."

He didn't answer.

"'Ow are you?" she said.

"Just fine. I feel fine."

"Oh, that's too bad," she said.

"Bad?"

"Oh, Dawes, the 'ealthy 'uns die young. They go fast," she said, laughing almost deeply. "Why, 'en we planted Tom he 'us almost still tap-dancin' in e's boots awl mornin'!"

"How's that."

"'Ow isn't 't?" she said. "Av never known myself, but I was never a bit 'ealthy, Dawes, and I outlived'em all. You'll do th' same if you don't make the mistake of bein' too 'ealthy."

"How'd you manage all that?"

"Don't know, but well," she said, laughing again, "fer one thing I never ate a tomato."

"I'll try and be ill then."

"Well," she said, "not too ill a course, but some. An' you remember what I told ya, Dawes. 'Cause I've seen'em all come and go. Seems like most a th' time 'ey been going though. Seems t'me now I spent most of th' time plantin'em. You are not 'ere long enough, I can tell you that."

In the silence the still, blackened, burned wing of the locust whined its dying spiral. The lawn was a wet bowl stirred and thickened, a lilac's throat. A car passed down the hill, breaking its surface. That was 1949, too. History. Time mad with hats. A cuckoo bursting its ticking.

"Oh, what a line of memories I 'ave 'ad," she said.

Only Dawes was listening. The others were talking of rheumatism and baseball scores and crops and weather. Burt wasn't saying much but smiling pleasantly at the air. He looked like an Arthur from which a cloud had suddenly passed like a hat of sunlight on the ground. Perhaps, Dawes thought, it was because the others had heard it before, but then so had he . . . .

"It's prob'bly sen'imental," she said, "but six generations I 'ave seen. They come and go like doors, Dawes. My grandfather was 'orn even before Victoria was a girl, ya know, I can tell 'e 'at, and now we 'ave Dawes 'ere on my porch in Iowa now, is it? A long 'ay from 'ere we 'ave been, I can tell 'e that."

But she seemed tired last summer, not quite as not dying as the other summers he had known her. And she was already dead, before he could get back and see her. In the winter. Grandma-great, he knew, had crossed the Atlantic to Nebraska in '78, and was married in '88, and had given him a copy of Oliver Twist to read, after having read it by having taught herself to read it herself, once, and had died in her house late in the winter of 1950.

" . . . yes," she said again, "a long way from 'hat. An' I've seen'em all in the

ground, but me, and I guess I'll see that 'ery thing pretty soon. I guess it's my turn now," she said, laughing, gripping softly her ivory cane.

He sat only studying it for awhile. The cane's head was nearly alive, ornate with carvings, still moving with turning knife cuttings. It was old as sign. And it had arrived, he knew, in Nebraska, just out of the sky and the mail and nowhere else, with only the note "Emma is dead" scratched on cheap paper; and with the signature simply "Bessie"; and with the postmark "Liverpool, England." . . . And after she died, last winter, Gin had sent the cane in the mail to Leone and Leone had put it, he knew, her grandmother's cane, carefully away in the attic.

But he sat, nearly tired with traveling, studying its design of ivory lions' eyes. And her voice had stopped for awhile; broke off short with sleeping. Her chair creaked loudly under the still air. A smile, destroyed with veins, caught itself openly on her quiet face. He thought somehow he understood her, the rooms she had moved in. He thought it must be that she reminded him of the people in Oliver Twist, but different, and the storm was riding up higher, opening the air, out somewhere, over the Missouri like a tiny Indian gourd of thunder in the west when she came out of a shallow, momentary sleep to say:

"What kind of a gent will ya be, Dawes?"

In the silence he knew he hadn't thought of it. It never occurred to him he might have to live that long. He had never been asked a question like that. He didn't know. He hadn't thought of it and, in his silence, beginning to watch himself think about it, he didn't answer. He forgot she was blind and couldn't see he was thinking.

"Dawes?" she said finally. "Are you still with me, boy? Am I going too fast for yer?" she said, laughing.

"No. I'm keeping up, I guess."

"Well? What kind 'en?"

"I don't know, I guess, exactly."

"You should. The sooner the better. If you don't, 'ow's anyone else expected to, I ask yer?"

"I guess they just wouldn't."

"You bet they wouldn't. If you know nothing, 'ere's nothing to know. You'd just be faceless as the rest, maybe even something else. Maybe a faker."

"Yes. I follow that," Dawes Williams said.

"Oh I 'ope so," she said.

In the silence the trees were rowing the distances over, whispering in a single glass net. The sky was funneling itself through another August sieve; a light like water. They were, he thought, they must have been. The trees were curtains, flowing, inverted through rivers of ghosts. And suddenly, stopping the rocker, she said:

"There's a part a me left over in you, Dawes. I'm almost sure of it." And her voice tailed off, died softly, a fire in the wind, a wood wet in the bones of her rocker.

"I'm old and tired as a board this summer, Dawes," she said, "but I 'ope you don't *waste it. What's left. Don't like talkin' this way as a rule, but I 'ope, I'm not too dead to 'ope you'll be big enough to be good. And take care of the land. Good men are scarc'r 'an good animals, Dawes, mules an' dogs. I'm not all 'at far gone 'et. Not me . . . . Set out, Dawes," she said. " 'Ere's a part a me an' someday you'll remember 'bout setting out. Go while th' getting's still good, Dawes, and don't look back, and don't you ever think of living in a small set of 'ills. Not for a minute. Not you. 'Cause I'll tell 'e, fool or prince, good or bad, any man's all there was, or ever is, made like'em. 'At's all I 'ope you get from me, Dawes, and don't think behind yerself, Dawes," she said. " 'At's all I 'ave to say."*

She stopped completely that time. He waited for her to go on. She only rocked; her eyes closed, her voice broke off like a stem going deep into shallow water, sleep. The others had gotten up and were waiting for him in the yard. Setting out, her rocker said, setting out. Burt hadn't said anything. He stood in the yellow light, smiling, almost mindless. Arthur came back from the near yard. He seemed almost out of place, prodding himself, as if he were drawn along by remembering his manners. He stood by the rocker for a moment, almost a son again, dutiful, wondering if he should wake her near sleep. He was uneasy, almost protective, with her weakness and infirmity. He seemed to hover about her edges, afraid, for a moment something too close for him coming into his formal eyes.

"Goodbye, Mother," he said finally, too loudly, shaking her hand.

And they left, driving down the same vertical streets. It was still. The close leaf blew on the window leaving shadows pure as cuttings. Only Burt, he knew, didn't have any words. Burt lived in a shoe shop. Once, in other summers before even that, Arthur had dropped him off there on his way to play golf. He had sat there all afternoon, watching Burt, watching Arthur's twin, watching the line of nails that had left Burt's mouth and went into the shoes, straight and regular as lines of cannon shot. The shot held always an instant, clean smell; the smell of old hideouts defining themselves at once within the huge piles of houses and leather cuttings; the forgotten tracings of his knife. Burt lived in a shoe. The nails from Burt's hammer went in fast and regular, all afternoon. Sitting on grooved benches Dawes watched the passing street sounds, and only they were drawn, disjointed, jangled cuttings. The walking women rustled like sacks. The rumbling, prewar Fords and Chryslers sounded like black 'gators eating stones on the white, wafting sills of day.

The women's step was cold. The brown sacks burst the passing window, white with sun, with red flags of bread labels sticking out everywhere. Burt was Arthur's brother. They had nothing in common.

Burt reached rhythmically for the endless series of seamless nails that went, with one stroke, into the shoes.

Nearby the yards were fortresses built with bushes. The wind blowing through was laced. The air was red with white stones of lilac and dog dung. The birds were black. Burt was Arthur's twin brother because they had nothing in common.

But it had been cool there, interior, that day watching Burt's gentle, mute eyes flick easily through his rimless glasses with each fixed thud of his hammer. He was making shoes.

Interiors were cool. The room was thin and long; an impossible room; a made-over poolroom, or a barbershop, and when the pairs of shoes were finished and fixed forever together, Dawes ran the trolley ladder down the endless hallway of a wall and placed them, new soles of fresh leather outward, into the ceiling-high library of racks and the brilliant window. There they baked, like bread, like bright candles nearly burning; like labels or tags or flags nearly catching themselves up with fire.

But the sun was high, and almost over the roof, and the shop was shaded. It moved through a swell, like a church, or the inside of a large boat that was carved but not formed. Everything merged, flowed together except for the line of light and shadow dancing along the inside of the window; as if the sun had stopped short there, pulled up, or as if a line had been bit-punched between day and night.

The town's summer sounds, insects flying together in a canopy, a flame, a sweat of leather droned black, epileptic suns in Burt's screens; his rimless glasses; his rhythmic hammer.

And the farmers, not really wanting any discourse with anyone, dry, sullen in the eyes as hearts of wood, would come in all afternoon, fishing in their bibs for change as Burt sailed his ladder built on castings and trolleys down the clanking racks. He was searching the afternoon of hanging tags and labels only for names.

And the wives, wanting even less talk, smelling brown and like bread sacks bursting with red labels, would hang back, just inside the hang of the door, saying even less than their husbands weren't saying. And Burt was Arthur's brother because they had nothing in common.

And it had been very cool shuffling in the knee-high piles of dead leather, old nails and stitchings all day; and Dawes Williams thought suddenly that Burt was a humble man, a quiet one who only sewed things up, and that he liked him very much because his shop was cool as hell and blowing flies, had a ladder that rolled on wheels along walls smelling of fresh rotting leather, doors of sun and air, nails and old stitchings; because he was a quiet man; because of the fact he said nothing at all; because of the way his cannon of a hammer moved, into the black forms of the shoes, within the glaring mirrors of his rimless glasses, through the streets of burned leather, August lilac, and nearly wet dog dung, and because he was as much unlike his brother Arthur as he could be . . .

Dawes Williams and Traffic Cop still stared down into the round stone moon of the lane. Traffic Cop seemed to be nearly sleeping but Dawes felt like moving. The night was motionless, utterly still now, moving off, drying itself like a bone caught in a drift of trees. The old hound groaned slightly in his dreams beside him. He could hear Gin's voice move along the ridge, calling him in. He wanted to be moving anyway, so he followed her voice down toward the lane. The night, too clear, shadowy with throated stones, mooned in the huts on the hill, remained behind. The greyhounds were moving down with him, around him. He could hear them. They split the grass. They left no sign. It was a dream. It was two dreams; ten; time and place and crystal light unwound through glass bent with prisms. Only the dogs were not nervous at all. The dogs ate grain and meat from tin pans, and wore only leather bracelets round their necks, and ran wild in the woods. They were softer raiders. They raised their curious heads and forgot it. They howled at the furious moon and went on home to sleep it off. The roof of the sky was a stuck clock, moving across, frozen on its hinges of air. The light in that prism spread out softly only so that it might converge again. Something was always missing. Just as you thought you had it it halved apart again in the crumbling wind. Time had no sequence. Time had no time. Place was a walking hill. They were the longest shadows of heaven. They rode beyond themselves, dreaming of light. All others died. She was dead. Grandma-great had died that winter, alone in her house, while he was away. All form withers and withdraws, becomes black in a trellis heavy with locusts, lost in a window of moon, a sieve of water funneling the sky, broken and trapped in a disintegrating wheel of the fields: black, lost, broken . . . .

Climbing the fence, he was tired. Traffic Cop turned and went back up to his hut. Gin was calling from the hill. She was his kind. He recognized her, returning. *Not even a sparrow can fall and lie forgotten, she had said*. It was late in the lane. He felt too tired to walk; but Big Red Mike and Lady's Babe hung their long snouts through the fence. They were still wondering at Dawes. *Are you really going to fall for that crap, Ronnie Crown had said, you shit, you dumb shit, you mother, you sonofabitch are you are you? he had said*. He didn't know. Perhaps Abigail Winas could tell him. Big Red Mike and Lady's Babe had dreaming eyes. The soundless flutes like moonlit shadows still danced on the perpendicular green inversions of the fence posts, the planted iron bones of trees and standing men, running away with the eye, the distance, the distance, and time, that had no eye; the distances that collapsed themselves whenever you weren't looking along edges of strung wire. He didn't know. It didn't matter. It was a dream of pots. The water wove itself within a moon and trellis, a stone of grass, and disintegrated. The locusts spun between two separate wheels at once. The night was mad; his only brother. His blood was the voices of other summers, always another, never now, calling back; the flutes of water bodies and underrivers like wandering spoons. He didn't want to go to Davis Groves. The thin moon was hanging lower now, nearly within the river woods, far, upstanding bones, the sill of the Great Cow River. The house was a dreaming place, laced with light, high on the hill. And crossing the second fence, to get back on the hill, he heard Gin calling:

"Dawes," she said easily, "what have you been up to? Come in now, Dawes," she said, "we've decided not to go to Davis Groves this year after all. It's too late. The rain has washed us out."

Dawes Williams roared with laughter. He saw the dogs moving up with him along the long edge of the hill. He saw the grass was sleeping. He knew it didn't matter, it was a dream, an illusion whispering the trees like ashes and wood smoke, the body of God, and *IamaliveIamalive* in the locust whine, and the hot stone fields, and the torn gut moon, and the quiet porches so it didn't matter . . . he went up the hill and entered the house.

4

In the morning after the storm the yard was strewn with branches. The early light was quieter, grayer, and stray, glistening leaves were everywhere. The farm's hill was torn and littered, nearly opened and uprooted, covered with twigs and blackened, netlike ends of larger, untied things still standing.

It was Friday morning. Dawes was sleeping, feeling worthless and uneasy already as he heard the sudden slap of the screen door announcing Arthur's coming. Waking, turning, he could see the green hill lift its shucked light, its dull patterns and strewn arabesques, up vertically over the back stoop like an army of dazed yellow cobs, stunned and flattened after the rain,

It was only the second full day at the farm. Arthur, just finished with the morning feeding and walking several strings of dogs, crossed from the screen. Even near sleep his strides were huge, measured, as if he were still walking over his furrows, and they shook Dawes firmly. It was still early. Arthur hung his field hat on a wooden peg like a regiment of officers, and said:

"We're going to town."

Waking, Dawes was relieved to hear that this was all that had happened, that he had willed only this, because Arthur's resolute and burned sheriff's face always seemed to say, "And you get your worthless sleeping carcass out of my bed, my town (by eight-fifteen pronto) or I'll use you to wipe up my streets, your head for a brush to whitewash my walls."

So getting up, he sat in Gin's kitchen for a while eating bacon and cinnamon rolls. He stared grimly at her Methodist radio. Its bald face, vacant with plastic silence, seemed about to be exploding with an oncoming Sunday.

"Have a nice fresh egg this morning, Dawes," Gin said.

"Nope. Don't like eggs," Dawes Williams said. "Don't even seem to like chickens much any more."

"Have a nice ice-cream cone then this morning," Gin said.

"All right. Sure," Dawes said.

"Awww God Almighty, Gin," Arthur said.

Leone and Simpson were still sleeping again, lost in their sheets, once-a-year travelers to the country, he thought, and soon he and Arthur were out, and down the hill without a word, and driving toward town. Dawes sat, braced against the fine linen leather that smelled clean as minted coins and looking from the window. He was fearful of even glancing across the wide, opening spaces of the vast Cadillac. The car's insides were an expensive country and, just across, Arthur sat steering it over the constant gravel-razz, the thud of gnats like rocks ticking the sides of his tailored paint. Looking finally across, Dawes could see Arthur's glare was hawkish, fixed forward on the road as if it were nearly an obstacle, not a road at all, and as if his will, and not the interworkings of the car's logical fixings, were dissolving the spaces before them. Dawes thought they would probably roll on into town, even if the car quit running. But he was fascinated, watching Arthur. He even thought, for a moment, in a burst that withdrew before it even took hold, he even understood him. *"And, whatever you do to me, don't you ever tell Granddad I told you that story,"* Leone had said. And Arthur was still bent forward, intense, relaxed only within the joint made by his calmly smoking cigaret and his easily well-made hands. And Dawes thought suddenly that must have been the exact way he looked, nearly fifteen years ago, that day in 1937, that day in the story Leone once told him, that day Arthur had sat in the dugout of the Boston Red Sox, watching his son try out for the major leagues. *"What's that kid's name at short?"* he had heard that coach say. *"Oldham, Dawes Oldham,"* Arthur had heard the other's vague reply. Then there had been a kind of scruffing laughter. And Dawes' uncle Dawes, who had also been named for Gin's town going dead as a mule behind hills, who had just returned from the Berlin Olympics, was taking infield. The afternoon must have deepened. The shadows must have thickened in center field. Then: *"God, that kid's got lead in his arm. Never make it past C Ball if he had a broom to take him."* In Berlin, Dawes thought, where my uncle, the other Dawes, at least got to see Hitler exit the stadium, the story, the twentieth century; so much for him. At least he said he did; he swears he at least saw that, the commotion for sure. *And then finally: "Ya, well, he happens to hit like he's got that broom."* And Arthur had heard it all, by mistake. It just happened, like everything else, an accident, but that is the way he must have looked, forward, intent, covering spaces, nothing crossing his face, his feelings. Arthur Oldham. He only stands there, watching his son whom he has sired just miss the starting boxes. He, Arthur, is bent slightly over the cement uprise of that Red Sox dugout, now, that's all, wrapped in that calm of his, like a flow. And when he looked around, even those coaches were talking about something else. *"And whatever you choose to do to me,"* Leone had said, *"don't you ever tell Granddad I told you that story."* And he had only heard that story one day, like old yellow posters from old family books, after he had completely worn down his mother with his endless talk about how he was going to play one day for the great Brooklyn Dodgers. She had only been trying to do her washing. She had been flushed, startled as a cat when she turned against him, accusing him before the fact. And then, remembering just as quickly that she wasn't a girl any more, that she had grown up and moved away, that she hadn't even lived in Arthur's house for over ten years, she had given him an embarrassed quarter and he had gone to the store with Ronnie Crown . . . .

The automobile was running, steadily ticking the gravel.

Dawes Williams sat apart, nervous, eating the ice-cream cone Gin had given him for dessert. He felt hot words rise in his throat only to be choked there, and fall, accusing, and rise back again, and suddenly he saw the great Crown sitting there, in that same seat, with that same sneer caught over the endless side of his face like an honest mask. Yes, he thought, that old Ronnie would know what to do, how to handle this. He'd just look'em in the eye, square as God, and tell him, damn calmly, to stick one of his damn running corncobs where it'd do him the most good. Hell yes, he thought, this is the summer when I finally tell him what a bastard he really is, must have always been. Hell, that even his own daughter thinks it, too, only she doesn't know it, only she won't admit it, not even to herself. Certainly never to him. Not her. Not to him. He'd kill her. I mean he's capable of that, of murder, Dawes Williams thought, I mean he'd probably kill us all if the spirit of Ronnie Crown ever said that to him. I mean he wouldn't even give'em a fair chance to explain himself . . . .

Then, turning sharply toward Arthur, surprised by his own sudden design, Dawes watched closely to see if somehow the sound of this thought had escaped him; his body. But no, his skull was all right, tight as bone, a perfect seam that hadn't betrayed him. And morning was nearly up. The ditches were huge as rising bones, a heat red and drying with blooms. A gray truck, limp and dappled, passed them, throwing a cloud of fine road dust and gravel all over the side of Arthur's white Cadillac.

"Jaeeesus Keyrist," he said. "You don't have to go to Texas to see cowboys. We got'em here. I didn't know Jake was ever up this early."

Then he busied himself flicking the sides of his face and laughing slowly. Then the stillness returned; it was twice as quiet in there now, Dawes thought, until finally Arthur said:

"God damn it, you throw that mess Gin helped you make away."

"You mean me?" Dawes Williams said blankly.

"What are you talking about?" Arthur said, nearly stopped with a sudden embarrassment.

"Why?" Dawes said.

"You look about as bright as Jake Skout eating that thing."

"It's just frozen cream."

"We'd had a lot of things like that as kids, we'd have come off as soft as you are going to be."

"It's pretty degenerate all right," Dawes said.

Arthur only looked at him.

"All right," Dawes said. "I mean cream's supposed to be good as anything for you. Builds your bones. Got to support your local cows," he said lamely.

"Awwwww," Arthur said.

"All right," Dawes said, throwing it away.

It would rot in the ditch, he thought, or the dogs might get it, hope it rots their bones, their teeth, serves him right, but now it's getting three times as quiet in here, he thought, and already we have used up all of the things we have to talk about.

"Awwwwwwwwwwwwwwwww," Arthur finally said. "Criminy."

So, done with speech, Dawes began to slouch more into his seat, on his side of the car, and he began only watching the red grasses slip by in the dry ditches toward town. The Cadillac rolled over the bridge, the gully river, the tracks, and Dawes began seriously watching that same bathtub, the one with the stain as yellow as flowers of wood, the one that perennially sank, three inches a season, into the mud of the bank; the one, he thought, that was a landmark of summers, that would eventually weave itself under the river and be swept out to sea. And he was still metaphysically trying to piece that bathtub together, trying to wonder why someone didn't come along and claim it, or move it, or use it for a wheelbarrow to haul expeditions in, or at least try and sell it because, uncracked, still able to catch rain, it would hold water, and was still perfectly good for its original purpose, when he noticed Arthur had already reached town and was parking his car.

"You're sure not much of a talker, are you?" Arthur said.

"You think you might be dumping me off at Abigail's this afternoon?" Dawes said suddenly, thinking it was four times as quiet now.

"Might be. If you don't give me any more trouble," Arthur said. "In fact, I think I might be dumping you out there this morning even . . . .Com'on."

Dawes got out of the car.

Men sat sunburned, gristled and cracking, drying in their bibs and tossing cigaret butts or spitting the muley tobacco into the streets. They sat in a row on the sill of the post office and, walking past, a review within Arthur's shadow, Dawes could see them staring at him queerly. He watched them tense slightly, look down between their feet and then, just as they were passing, look up shyly and nod politely at Art. Arthur always answered the greeting with a near hitch of his handsome brow. He was a regular social democrat, Abigail had said. Arthur was a magnanimous man.

"Look at these lazy dudes," Dawes said under his breath, smiling up hopefully at Arthur.

"Awww, be quiet, Dawes," Arthur said, "I still have to live here in the summers."

"What the hell," Dawes said, "I mean hasn't anybody got a damn field to milk? A cow to plow?"

Arthur responded only by scowling. Dawes began to trail farther behind. Scuffing the dust, he began drawing a line with his foot: it ran past The Duck's Bill, a tavern, a sign, owned by Elmer T. Jones. It was the only one in town and, as Abigail once said, it was also the only one run by the only thinking Methodist in town, Elmer T. Jones, who usually had a lot to say worth laughing at on Wednesdays during pheasant season. Once, just last summer, Dawes had strayed quietly in to talk it all over with Elmer T., but before he had even gotten a good start, Arthur had come furiously in and chased him back down the street with a long, invisible stick. But the street hadn't changed. He continued drawing a line down it, scuffing the dust. Besides, he thought, he probably hadn't missed much; Elmer T. Jones' Duck Bill was probably only another tinny place of brassy night where the women said, *Hey, baby, hey, baby, gotta dime for the juke?* all the time letting their cigarets hang smoking from their mouths, like in this movie he once saw, and nobody had a sword. It was very dull, and the line stretched farther, never breaking once, concentrated upon like trances carving totem poles: it ran past the post office, full of locks and keys and antique pigeonholes, full of old-time and worn-thin flooring and daylight blowing through the back door; and it ran past the movie theatre with the fifty folding chairs that only ran on Saturdays, that was showing Buster Crabbe and Tim Holt on the same bill for the remainder of August; and it ran past the only gas station with only the cardboard sign, STANDARD OIL OF DAWES CITY, wedged in the shattered window, and with the last part added in ink by the owner, A. T. Riley. And it ran finally up to the near edge of Brogan's red, white and blue twirling barber pole, and he knew suddenly why Arthur had brought him into town. Squatting down, breaking the line, he edged under the line of the window and sneaked into Willis Creamer's general store smelling suddenly cool and dark and generally of cleanly baked bread a hundred years old. He clutched at the four dollars Gin had given him and began edging toward the comic-book rack.

" 'Lo there, Dawes Williams," Willis Creamer said. "Have a good winter?"

"Hi ya, Mr. Creamer," Dawes said.

He circled the rack. With a little luck, he thought, Arthur would never miss him until it was too late to get his hair cut. Because as soon as eleven o'clock on Fridays rolled around it would be time for Arthur to go to Davis Groves. There, with one of the few Catholic priests left in western Iowa, who came the same distance from the other side and Carroway, Iowa, to meet him, he would play golf all afternoon. That was western Iowa, Dawes knew. In Carroway there were nothing but Catholics; in Dawes City there were nothing but Baptists and Methodists. Davis Groves lay exactly between because, in Iowa at least, the great religious wars had been mostly solved and gone to seed and other occupations. Mostly, as Simpson said, in Iowa the Catholics and the Baptists and the Methodists and the others had just chosen up their own corners and bred on their own sides of the room, and called that the end of culture and progress.

So, walking gently in an abstract silence around the edges of the comic-book racks, Dawes thought suddenly with a little luck that bastard Arthur would leave him alone; he would never know he was gone till it was too late to remember to notice he was missing. It was great to be smaller and have hiding out for your only defense, he thought, putting it out of his mind for luck. Looking at Mr. Creamer, Dawes said:

"Hey, Willis! What is this? Where's the Classics?"

"The what?" Willis Creamer said, counting his loaves of bread.

"The Classic Comic Books. You know: *The Iron Mask,* Dumas and Robert Louis Stevenson, and Nathaniel Hawthorne and Poe, and Sir Walter Scott and William Shakespeare and *A Midsummer Night's Dream* and all of that."

"We don't have none."

"Well, what do you have?"

"Well, we don't have none of those."

"This town has no magazine racks, no culture," Dawes Williams said.

"How are you this summer, Dawes?"

"I'm fine, Willis, but I have nothing to read. I have four dollars though."

"Gin came through for you again, did she?"

"Oh ya. If you don't even have the Classics, Mr. Creamer, what do you have?"

"Well, Dawes, this summer we have the latest selection," Mr. Creamer said. "We have both back and forward issues of Superman and Batman, the entire Jet-Fantasy Series, Dunkirk the Invisible Soldier, all of the Hell-War Series and Donald Duck, Plasticman the Elasticman, and Flashman the Fastestman and . . . say, Dawes, I just read that one this morning. The August issue—you probably haven't seen it yet—is called only *Flashman the Fastman, the Silver Streak of Light and Fastest Human Man, Goes to Australia.* I believe it begins to go like this . . ."

"Are you sure about this?" Dawes said.

"Yes, lemme just tell ya this one. You see there's this tidal wave that's going to *inundate the entire subcontinent of Australia*. But you also see that Tom Wells, this Flashman the Fastestman, who also happens to be a great all-time track star at U.C.L.A., he gets the call from the President, Harry Tubmann, and right away he runs across the Pacific Ocean. There ain't no damn ocean going to slow him down: he runs on water. Yes, well, and when he gets there he immediately runs around the entire subcontinent of Australia so fast he sets up *a parabolic force field of magnetic light* with his body. He's so fast nothing fazes him and he screens the whole island *within a whirl of contradictory force lines*. 'Course, this is only a story, but the tidal wave's real enough, and it's coming in from the north, from *the diabolical underground laboratory of a famous Japanese submarine scientist* located somewhere in the Lesser China Sea. I figure that part is nonsense, Dawes. If this thing's coming in from only the north thataway . . . why's he running around the whole island? That's what I want to know."

"Maybe turning around slows him down," Dawes said.

"Could be. I never thought of that. Anyway, in the end, he runs around the entire subcontinent of Australia every two point three seconds. He keeps this up for five and one-half hours, until the famous Japanese scientist—you ought to see this guy, Dawes, he's strange and evil-looking and has Manchu fingernails and all—anyway, until he gets tired out working the buttons to his infernal wave machine and gives up, and calls it quits, and then the F.B.I. moves in—Stars and Stripes into the Lesser China Sea—to pick him up for good. So that does that. Then, in the epilogue, this Flash, whose real name happens to be Tom Wells, goes back to U.C.L.A. just in time to win the season's track meet. He competes in every event at once. *Simultaneous* he's so fast. You can just see the announcer's going crazy trying to follow him. He's got seven heads suddenly. No one can believe it yet. He's an American athlete, see. In the last frame ole Tom Wells is seen standing proud with his girl, name of Mary, receiving the President's Medallion of Liberty—you want to buy that one, Dawes?"

"Oh, damn me," Dawes Williams said, "that sounds terrible. Do you have *The House of Seven Gables* by Nathaniel Hawthorne? Besides, Mr. Creamer, you just told me the whole thing and . . ."

Just then, however, Arthur stalked into the store and said:

"I think you could use a haircut, Dawes. You look like hell."

"I knew it," Dawes said.

"You knew nothing," Arthur said.

"I had one two months ago. I'm doin' fine. Leave me alone."

"You look like two girls fighting over a jack ball in May," Arthur said. His eyes were darker than ever, muted but piercing. They gave the old air of the cool store a sudden feeling of explosion. Willis Creamer laughed. "Let's go," Arthur said, exiting him out, nearly picking him up by the neck.

"Let go'f me!" Dawes Williams said. "I can walk."

And he sat there, all morning it seemed, in Jacob Brogan's barber shop watching again the summer catfish nailed to the wall. Its jaws were open and a baited hook with a stuffed minnow was tacked on the yellow board two inches from the outstretched, varnished fish.

"I got'em with just worms up on the cutback on Shadywillow, Arthur," Brogan said, blowing through his clippers.

"Ya, you and Ted Williams," Arthur said, laughing.

"What's that, Art?"

"Never mind. Just shave him good, Brogan," Arthur said. "Want him to look like a ballplayer. Want him ready to go."

"I keep this clipper work up much longer he's going to look like a damn German is what he's going to look like, Arthur," Brogan said.

"Where are we going?" Dawes Williams said.

"Nowhere," Arthur said. "You're going out to Abigail's hen ranch. That's where you're going."

"Big deal," Dawes said. "I don't need a haircut for that."

"Why not?"

"Because she likes me the way I am. That's why."

"You need a shave. You look like hell," Arthur said.

"Thought you had this boy better trained, Art," Brogan said.

"Ya, well," Arthur said, laughing, looking about abstractedly for some open place to spit, "*if he gives you any trouble, just hang a notch in his ear.*"

He sat quietly watching the fish eye, cat's eye, yellow marble; the laughless, sheenless glint. A shaft of light fell through the old poolroom shades, cutting it into two parts, dancing on the solid eye; it seemed to squint at him with the motion of the clouds, and Brogan's fat head peeked around the corner to adjust the evenness on one spot of his head. The gaps in Brogan's teeth seemed bottomless, as mysterious as a boneless mouth; the waterbody of a fish swimming, peeking, turning about for a moment in the leafy underlight.

"*Never mind playing the violin, Jake, just cut it all off.*"

"But this kid's going to be bald as snakes, Art," Jake said winking.

"*Never mind that. Use your razor.*"

Stuffed and boarded, it looked alive and somehow strangely bloated. Looking at it he could see the violet mud rise on its body, form itself into green pools of light, scales, as the fin flicked, as the shaft of the waterbody, the fish, moved out, up, through various levels of ignorant water; and as the parted mouth closed on the surface, a strange place feeling like two worlds, sinking the sullen form again to the cardboard bottom. It seemed somehow bloated, strangely dead with satisfied food.

"You sonofabitch, Arthur," Dawes Williams said under his breath.

"Yes, I stuffed that fish myself, Arthur," Jake said.

"Do tell," Arthur said.

"Oh ya, Art. The other side I pretty much butchered up. I tore the eye socket out somethin' terrible trying to fix him up there so I had to settle for a ferocious side pose. There, is that enough, Arthur?"

"Hell no. You never were any good with a razor, Jacob," Arthur said.

And then the line was there, holding it fast, swirling like curtains, there were violent clouds in the underrivers, mud rising, stirred shafts of sunlight, and the falls like ceremonies of light coming finally through the sunken shades and the fat, peeping windows, in Brogan's shop, casting green, sleeping prayers, drunken and leering morning vespers almost, in the varnished scales, the softened speeches to be found in the yellow eye, cat's eye, fish's marble.

"Hear about all the excitement last night, Arthur?" Brogan was saying.

"I'll bet," Arthur said.

"Oh ya, they were up in arms, had the constable out and everything last night, Art."

Brogan stood, confidently blowing air through his shears.

"Constable, hell," Arthur said, laughing. "Old Weeters couldn't pee into the wind on a good day."

The laugh came from a deep place, recognized itself, and passed over everything, leaving Dawes feeling warm and cold at once. It died finally on the peaceful walls, a pronouncement from another county entirely, shadowy and moving about within the morning glare.

"Oh ya, Art," Jacob Brogan said, "Weeter's no Harry Truman all right. But you know that new yellow line the state's been painting down S. J. K. Street?"

"Are they thinking of making it into a war museum?" Dawes Williams said.

"Yes," Arthur was saying, "what about that yellow line?"

There was a silence. Jacob Brogan's mother, Dawes knew, had been a famous Jewish manicurist who had been on her way to Hollywood when she stopped off the train at Dawes City and never left. She was mostly famous because she remained all those years the only Jew in Crawdor County, even perhaps, it was thought, west of Des Moines and east of Omaha, and because she had married Brogan's father, who was a quiet Irish farmer who only liked to play poker on Thursday night and who never did again, not once in forty years, Abigail Winas had said.

"Well, Art," Jake Brogan continued, "that's just it. It's ruined, that line is. It's ruined because this drunk pool-shooter type from Davis Groves went through here last night knocking the pylons over. Said he was a bowler. Said he couldn't quit until he got 'em all at one time. Hell, they all thought he was a fine sonofabitch for awhile. Then, around midnight, they got tired settin' 'em up for him, so they told him to quit it. Said he couldn't. Said he was a bowler. Said he had to knock'em all over at once and yell strike. They didn't like it, so pretty soon a fight broke out. Well, this pool shooter was getting the worst of it so he got in his car and ran it straight into the out-of-town mailbox. Knocked it down . . ."

"So the F.B.I. got'em!" Dawes Williams said. "This is the part where the F.B.I. steps in and cuffs this pool shooter."

"No," Brogan said credulously. "That didn't happen."

"Anyway," Dawes said, "I'll bet it was J. Edgar himself who put the cuffs on him."

"No, the Highway Patrol came and took him away, though."

"I'll bet it's all a great lie," Dawes Williams said.

"What for? Running over the out-of-town mailbox? Federal crime or something?" Arthur said vaguely.

"No. On his way to run over the post office, you might say, he knocked Harriet Tubb over instead. Nearly killed her. So, instead, you might say, while he missed the mail, he hit his Tubb."

"What the hell are you talking about?" Arthur said seriously.

Jake Brogan stood there before him, nearly chuckling out loud. Dawes, at this point, was only sure that Jacob Brogan had once sorted mail before he became a barber. Arthur was almost scratching his head, obsessed by the need for order and logic and sense in it all.

"Eh, Art!?!" Brogan said, nearly elbowing Arthur with his humming clippers and clicking his tongue in his cheek.

There was another silence. Arthur began pacing, saying nothing at all, and looking out of the window.

"Just a little joke, eh, Art?" Brogan said. "Thought I'd throw it in. Free of charge. Been sitting here all morning, thinking about it."

"How did it end up?" Arthur said suddenly.

"What do you mean?" Brogan said.

"What happened?"

"Oh. Well. That then," Brogan said real slow, "they took him off to Davis Groves to jail, I guess. Like he's robbed the bank, only we don't have one. Then, this morning, Dexter Thomas came by and said they were thinking of trying him for attempted manslaughter."

"How's Harriet?" Arthur said seriously.

It was then that Dawes broke out in gales and fits of laughter.

"Attempted manslaughter!" he said. "I'll bet it's all a made-up lie and fiction."

Then Jacob Brogan began laughing, too. He nearly slapped his knee in Arthur's face.

"That's true," he said. "It's all a lie! I been standing here by this window all morning just waiting for some fool to come in here and listen to that yarn."

Then, just as suddenly, light vanishing from stone, Arthur's face changed. Brogan, instinctively, lightly, reached for another razor. But not Dawes Williams; he only kept laughing with a broad humanity. He didn't give a damn; he was feeling too well. Finally Arthur looked at him squarely and said:

"How'd you know?"

"Hell, Arthur, I knew before we ever came in here."

"You didn't," he said. But his voice had the black ring of dogma in it, something forced from stone, an untrue process.

"I did, too," Dawes Williams said. "We walked cross that street twice this morning. And nobody's painted a line on it I could see."

"Ya. He's got you there, Arthur. That's why I thought you were looking out the window," Brogan said, cutting again on Dawes' head.

And Dawes Williams felt the naked wind blowing off his completely hairless head, and he watched the open door, and he eyed it for sign, and he thought of The Fastest Human Man, and he began laughing blindly and uncontrollably, in large waves and small fits, and he looked into the blacker, inverted eyes, Arthur Oldham's eyes, and he broke off suddenly and quit without a sound.

"What the hell is so funny?" they seemed to ask him.

"History is mad," Dawes Williams seemed to say.

"What's so funny about that?" they seemed to answer. "You gone nuts on me?"

"This town," Dawes Williams said quickly, "this town is so funny it isn't here."

The frog's head rose and fell under the surface of green water; the plate of earth. It was afternoon. Dawes threw his last brown stone.

The air near Abigail's farm was a soft, decomposing fish. The sky was a belly, an underside; a drifting boat. Dragonflies had flown by for an hour; and the sun had grown white, ballooning with a trellis of veins, with the image of their wing.

He threw his last brown stone at the snake.

He missed. The green water was a ditch of hot dog water, small and circular, lying in the northeast corner of Abigail Winas' field. The pond was behind the first hill near the road. Arthur was gone.

He turned and began walking in the wild grass. The tall wind, drawn and knotted, was a madhouse blowing too closely over his head. Arthur had let him off, left him on the road near Abigail's house while he was off to follow golf balls flying over the hills in Davis Groves.

"Tell her we want three fryers," he had said, closing the door, receding in a cloud of white dust.

Over the top of her weeds now, he saw the house. Walking over the last hill, he saw her small stone chicken coop, her house and barn rise planted in the clearing carved out of her round grass in a mad, ragged pattern. The clearing, a perfect box of shade, lay nearly devoured within the heave of her trees leaking splintered knives of light onto her dark, hidden patch of ground. The afternoon light was a quilt, and the house's stone was a snail fixed heavily to the ground, surrounded by growth. Dawes studied it again for a moment, caught on the hill. The yard was strewn with chicken feathers, a fine coating of snowy down like a factory, a chaos of meat-packing, a thousand nights of delirious pillow fights. The hills beyond were thick with the whine of crows, and hardshelled insects.

In the long grass, just the other side of the small stone coop, Dawes could hear Abigail Winas cackling quietly to her flocks of hidden chickens. The darkened hollow below stilled. It was, suddenly, as if he could, with one step, walk from openness into a blanket of black droppings, silence, as if, almost, he could cross from heat into quietness, from day into night and the shadowy blue wings of locusts expired in fallen caves.

"She's really something this year," Arthur had said, steering his Cadillac out, delicately, through the ruts on the road.

"She's really something every year I can remember," Dawes had said easily.

"Ya. But she never even goes to town any more. She's in bad shape, I guess. She just sits out there in that grove of grass of hers. In the dark. Jaeeesus Criminy. It's so chicken-cloudy and overcast out there you can't even make her out half the time. And there she sits, cutting up and selling her damn chickens. Hell," Arthur had said, "and she never cuts that stuff. Bet she loses most of her damn eggs in the weeds every summer. She must. And there's more wild-eyed chickens out there per square yard of knotted grass than anywhere else in the world, but she never mows it. Hell no, not her, she likes foxes and she likes living in that house half-full of chicken shit all winter long. Hell. I ask ya?"

"Ask me what?" Dawes Williams said.

"So," Arthur continued, driving out, "when someone offers to cut it, or hack it all down, or build her a damn chicken coop proper, so's she could move some of her damn chickens out of her house one of these years but no, not her—what's she do, I ask you?"

"What's she do?" Dawes Williams said.

"Well," Arthur said, laughing within himself, rubbing down his chin, "I'll tell ya. She just screws herself up and laughs that damn chicken laugh of hers, like she was forty years older than she really is, and tells them *they're* crazy. I ask you. As if they are the ones who are crazy. Not her. Oh maaan oh man, is she something. Hell no, not her. Hell there's enough furious fox out there, I bet, hell, there's enough wild-eyed, happy fox out there per square chicken, I bet, to populate the world with natural slaughter forever. But when Skout and his crew tried to hunt them off one summer, what did she do? Why, she spent the whole damn summer sneaking around her woods, hunting *them* off with a Civil War breechloader. It must have been old Duncan Winas'. It'd have killed her, of course, if she ever would have shot it off. She didn't, but she sure stirred the woods up. Skout didn't see a fox all summer. Some of them decided finally she must have been hiding them out in her closets to begin with. The rest was just a ruse. Maaan oh man, Jaeeesus Criminy, is she something," he said, his eyes nearly glowing with happiness, as he pulled the car up short into the long beginnings of her roadless grass. "She sure could use a driveway, though," Arthur Oldham said.

"I forgot where the house is from here," Dawes had said.

"It's just over that first hill. You can't miss it. Past that pond of hers where she still breeds all the mosquitoes who live in the county."

And, turning, Dawes had become immediately lost under her net and tent of grass.

"And don't step on any of her eggs, she may be feeling overly motherly this afternoon and decide to be slitting on you, instead. And don't take her opinions too seriously, and don't get snakebit," Arthur had laughed after.

He sat down for a moment and studied the terrain. Abigail was nowhere to be seen.

"Abigail," he called. "Are you out there?"

Only shadowy bees danced like light along the buzzing line of waving grasses. Then, shortly, as if by order, he saw her nesting weeds bend and finally part, and Abigail stepped through into the clearing, trailing the chickens behind her.

"Gracious!" she said. "Why, it's Dawes."

Coming from the grass, she was followed by a slow parade, colored roosters and hens like flags and drums in the breeze. She was draped in dull clothing, and she should have had a pot on her head, he thought, like Johnny Appleseed; that is all she needs.

"Honey, how have you been? I've changed my mind: history is legal if you read it backwards."

"Fine, Abigail."

"You just come let your old friend and Platonist see ya, Dawes," she said approaching. She encircled him, full of deceptively offensive design, like a circle of covered wagons, crushing him softly within her arms. She smelled of chicken feathers and moist summer dust; and she felt close, both knit and drawn. Then she stood back, held him at arm's length and searched him deeply, scanning his face for possible sign. Finally she began pulling at his vacant hair, slowly, and poking and pinching him some to see if he had fattened any.

"Your hair," she questioned, "what's happened to all your damn curls? Why, Dawes, I say you're bald as gizzers."

"Granddad told Brogan to shave me good."

"That Arthur always was part ass," she said. "And 'course, that beanbag Brogan's always wandering around, a complete nit doing what he's told, long as you're there writing it out for'm."

"Grandma wants three good fryers," Dawes finally said.

"Why, we'll have plenty of time for that, Dawes," she said curiously. "You can help me pull feathers, honey, and then I'll gut'em and cut'em up for you."

She stood looking vaguely over her yard, casting her eyes into the sporous blobs of white and red dullnesses scratching in the dirt for seeds and grain. Her eyes stared and squinted into the drifting sun and shadow, and she began softly to stroke the back of his neck.

"How about those three over there, Dawes?" she asked. "They're young and not too tough. George Armstrong Custer, Florence Nightingale and General Patton. In fact, I can recommend them highly. They could use some slaughtering."

Her slight cackle wiffled on the wind, shadowy and understated. She ran her hands into the pockets of her jeans.

"You go herd them around back to the stump, and I'll get the axe from the house," she said.

And he thought the forms of the three dead chickens almost comic, sprawling in the dust by her killing stump. The white feathers were grooved, stained with dark blood, like the strange carvings fixed and worn into the woodblock itself. The axe had fallen like clocks. The three heads watched the separated sky rising on the other side of the stump. One horny beak rose supported from the small pile of heads. For awhile he sat trying to fit which head had gone onto which body but, forgetting, hearing only the mosquito trance rising in the naked green water droning behind her hill, Dawes became fascinated by the shallow explosions of feathers dancing in sudden spirals of wind.

"Say cluck, cluck cluck," he whispered quickly, below his breath.

"What's that ya say, Dawes? Can't hear ya. Speak up like a dude," she said.

Their two shadows bent over the chickens. He didn't answer her. She was bent, mindlessly almost, smiling over her work. Her knife rode under. The sun was dazed and over its roof; her tree line. The sky was unstrung with cords, shafted and drifting, and the white floats of the feathers flew up, rhythmic, darkening her clearing with mirrors, dancing along the line of the ground for a moment, and covering her yard. Soon there was only goose skin and a laughable, foreign nakedness hung about the flesh-colored husks.

"Now I'll gut them for you, honey," she said. "Here, you hold him down firm, so he doesn't get any ideas of flying away, and old Abigail will cut off his legs and slit up his middle."

Pretending to look away, he watched. The cold ivory edge of the knife slit the bag of the chicken with a tiny, letting sound. The steaming balloons of gut spilled out onto the porcelain pan. Then her hands were red and darkly stained with carvings, signs impossible to look at for long, to read, and they reached back deeply into the chicken, steady with rhythm, and then in the middle of it, his head, he thought he could hear something breaking off, tearing loose from its casing, its flesh, its shell of black, whining locust. The other chickens blew in from the yard, circling, curious, in flocks pecking abstractedly at the piles of insides like slick balloons, or stray droppings of grain. The afternoon was thickening. She held him fast with her gaze. Taking his face in her hands, amused, she began painting him with the thick blood of chickens . . .

When things began to run low, to wind down, they used to sit talking of history. In the early afternoons she always talked about a man named Spencer who had been shot in Italy only four, five, now six years before. She was only approaching and leaving forty then, in all those summers, but she looked both younger and older. She was thriving with death.

He always asked her, year to year, why she had never married. He never remembered when it was he had first asked her, or why, but it came to be expected of him, and she was usually disappointed if he didn't ask about it. It was when he first asked her why she had never married that she had, eventually, begun talking about Spencer. First, however, she gave other reasons. She said it was because no one around there had any sense; that they were all scared of her, for one reason or another; that she was obviously too smart and experienced for them, although what it really was, she admitted, she wasn't sure. Once, she said, she had caught Skout, late at night, in her woods; hunting, she said he had said, though he didn't have a gun, nor any dogs, nor a light, nor anything else you need to hunt coon at night. But Skout was married anyway, she said winking curiously, so that didn't matter much one way or the other. Dawes thought the reason she had been winking curiously was just general confusion, perhaps, and he was about to ask her if that was it when she spoke: The real reason, she said, getting to the point, was because she lost interest in that sort of thing once she had been informed that Spencer was buried in Italy. At least the pieces, what they had been able to scrape off of the mountain at Monte Cassino, were buried there, she said. She had a short letter to prove it, she said. The light was thinning near evening. Perhaps that was the reason, he thought, she always liked to read letters at evening, because once, walking back from the broken doorway, she had brought the letter out into the light of the thin porch and read it to Dawes:

Dear Miss Abigail Winas,
   I am taking the liberty of writing to you as old "Spence," I know, would have wanted it that way. I understand he always spoke of you highly. One doesn't, of course, ever know what to say at times like these . . . . Perhaps all I can really do is offer to you my sincerest condolences, and to let you know that Pvt.

Spencer Durham Riley, who was so highly regarded and liked by everyone who knew him well, did not die in vain. I'm sure, as an American of our times, you know full well the worth and necessity of the great cause he died in, as did and will, I suppose, if it's any consolation, so many others. Let me only hasten to add that Spencer Riley was always unfailing in his duty to his God and his Country, and that he went most bravely, if not gloriously, to his end.

Most Sincerely Yours,
Capt. Jackson S. Thompson

I am enclosing and sending on Pvt. Riley's medals and commendations as I know he would have wanted you to have them could he present them in person. Let us pray for a quick and sure end to all of this.

"I believe you," Dawes said. "You didn't have to prove it to me."

"I know. I know it, Dawes," she said, "but this makes it backwards and legal. This makes it history."

But those weren't the only reasons. Another reason, a big one in her mind now, she said brightening, was that she was still waiting for a well-bred, educated city man, like himself, to grow up into dudeship, and pass by, and marry her finally off. And in the dark standing porch shadows her slow laugh rilled up when she got to this part; from a well, reeds bending back over river flowers; from a secret place, a house and sleeping lumber heart, dreaming through yellow, wooden eyes at its center's falling stone: and he looked at her, puzzled at first, then laughing too. But, already, he could see she had shifted out from under him and her eyes were filling with a mocking, self-conscious sadness.

"But Dawes," she said, almost prodding him, "I can tell that you will grow up and still be a boy. I can see it in your face. You will always be innocent, no matter what, and you will forget about this place and never think about me any more."

"No," he said. "That isn't a fact. That's just more of your stupid history."

But he knew he had risen to say this too quickly. He could not look at her any more, but only at something that had been away from her, within, behind. Even not looking, however, he could see the brown skin, the fullness of her mouth, the defined bones of her face, and the patterns the taut veins made rising from her temples and the backs of her hands. She became a soft blur to him, impossible to reach in the winter, unavoidable in the summer, an impression of an image that still held within it, sharply, the fierce blue eyes and the calm fall of her hair. Also, however, he saw always the tough quality in her flannel shirt, her faded jeans; in the quick knife, her working, gutted laughter. But she was more than that, and her softness, warm hands stained with eggs of blood, the quiet sadness nearly torn within her eye, would remain with him longer.

In town, they said she was working hard at becoming a witch.

And the longer shadows of late afternoon began to rift the yard. Abigail always got down, eventually, from the porch. Sitting near her killing stump she washed vegetables torn, like roots, from her broken dirt; her open patch of black ground. The split, unhinged earth was blacker and richer than God. She dipped her hands in the bright water, and her rotten aluminum bucket nearly rattled with onions.

"It's all a damn ceremony," she said finally, "like a ritual of looking over your shoulder to step on the cracks you have already missed again. Like washing your hands. —Don't you ever apologize, Dawes."

He didn't answer her. He only lay on her short lawn in a patchwork of quilted sun, broken light, with his shirt beside him, listening to her telling him again about the man, Spencer, whose name she would never say, coming just short, saying simply "he," and sometimes slurring over even the pronoun to the idea she was carefully walking the edges of, never quite falling in, the idea she was about to put in quick and quiet phrases, like her knife, he thought, yes, sharp and quick, and used before like her chicken knife, he thought, cold and self-sharpening and cleaned in blood.

And he lay on her short lawn, hacked out, stolen with a sickle, listening more to the sounds and rhythms of her voice than to the meanings of her words. The long edges of words about the "he" who had been, she said, different and finer, in his way, than anyone else around there at least, not much, she said, only she hadn't quite managed to make him over enough. But she was working on that. Who had been stronger (except in some ways and those, as it all turned out, as it all ended up as legal history, had been the important ways), she said, than even she had been; who had not been too bright, ever, but whom she would have formed, she said, and molded into something finer, something better than even she had expected and more set apart than it had been to begin with. Yes, she said, into something so quietly apart that no one would have noticed it, like Midwestern dirt. Because he was, she said, a somewhat finer clay. (And what are you going to do about that now? she said.) Because he had had the absence, the perfect absence of soul for it, as if not a damn bit of him had been cooked on any yet; it had only been just buried a little, he had been starting, he was even trying to read the books, at least the newspapers, she had gone all the way to Davis Groves for, and they were going to get married too, any day, any month at all, only every time, the hour, minute, it came around to do it the big bastard was too drunk to walk. For ten years it had gone on that way, before the war; but hell, Dawes, she said, almost puzzled by it now, I never trusted a man who didn't drink too much, did you?, especially in this damn place and neck-of-the-woods because otherwise, she said, they were just damn shepherds and nothing more unpredictable or exciting than moonlight. Only he had been more than that and, even if he wasn't, she said, she'd have seen to it herself; yes, just as soon as she'd succeeded in releasing him from free-bondage, from all those countless gen-erations of mute thinking, and bread begging, and thankyouing for nothing, and just generally downright serflike ass licking he'd be fine, as good as new, she said. Only he didn't. Yes, she said, I was busy making on him when that damn war came along *again, out of nowhere, regular as planned and necessary clockwork, spoiling it all. I don't know, she said, maybe I'd just made on him too much by that time. Anyway I know he was all fed up, she said, because all he seemed good for after that was walking round town, preening, spouting damn-fool war slogans, over and over, again and again, I think all wars start in barbershops, she said, over and over, until I thought all I'd ever be good for again was screaming on street corners at which point (the goddamn ass) all he was good for was to enlist. A damn knight in goose's clothing, she said, he got drunk one morning and drove Wilbur Ahart's new tractor over to Davis Groves, and signed the lists and came back twice as drunk, and snorting in the nose, and proud of his papers with his shiny name writ all over'em, and of course forgetting Wilbur Ahart's tractor, the bastard. I would have taken him back as a serf. I should have polished his nose that morning and been finished with it, she said. Maybe, she said very low in her throat, it was just to get away from all of my making, I don't know, but then pretty soon he was in Africa and Sicily and north Italy, seeing the world, he was all over hell in a box all right, she said, in more ways than one in the end, and all I ever got out of it was letters to prove it with. To make it history and noble sacrifice. Listen, Dawes, she said, he was forty if he was a day, older'n me, I was still young then, I'm sure of it now, old enough to know better, the damn kid, but hell, he was enjoying himself; and all those letters, papers full of praise, praise for the kids he was fighting with, praise for himself, praise for the enemy, praise for the damn noble sky, praise for the release of boredom, and making, and praise for how they were busy saving me and every other ass in the world from all of those black-shirted, baby-devouring FascistCommunists.*

"Listen, Dawes," she said, "you want me to go in and get those letters now? It's no trouble. I will. How about this summer, Dawes? You want me to show them to you?"

"No. You don't have to do that," Dawes Williams said, "I know. I believe you. You don't have to prove it to me."

So anyway I just wrote him back, she said, I sent him a book telling him how Fascists and Communists were two different things, even if they were riding an ass of the same color, eating the same babies, and him, he just wrote back more slogans, then he didn't write for awhile at all, not a word, he must have been fighting Rommel by then I figured later; then, finally, more slogans, which remained asinine enough, even if they were true, and I just hadn't made him enough, she said, that's all, but it still wasn't over, no, not yet, Dawes, because in his last letter even he remembered all those nights, ten years' worth, I had brought the blanket, Christ, Indian style, down the sides of the vines—Jesus, thirty years old, older, and I was still living with old Duncan, my father, and having to sneak it down the side of the porch, in the fields like cows, which was nice, or like some damn schoolgirl that wasn't even housebroke, which I wasn't—and I would have done it, too, she said, I would have done it yet, made him over, it all just would have set me back some, that's all, but now, she said, now the damn fool is not even a shadow in the ground,

*a rotting corpse any more . . . . And now I've got nothing to make on, she said,
looking away.*

*"And you, Dawes Will-i-ams," she said finally, looking back. "What are you going
to do about all of this?"*

*There was a long silence, as if she were expecting an answer by return mail. He
could remember opening his mouth, about to say, "What can I do? Can I change it?
Any of it?" when already, she'd got up, come across the short distance, the space of her
furious lawn separating them.*

*"That's right," she said, "because, in the end, he wasn't fighting anyone. None of
them were. That's right. It was newspaper history. They were just passing through each
other's headlines. It was an opera, a play. It never happened."*

*"I know, I know. You don't have to prove it to me," Dawes Williams said, fixed,
looking up furiously against her.*

*"That's right. He had no stake. None of 'em did. Hell, Dawes," she said, pen-
etrating him, moving back a step but only to get closer to him, "none of 'em did.
Only Roosevelt and Stalin and Hitler and Tojo and that Italian Railroad Bastard
had anything in it. Everyone else was only putting up and taking down fences.
That's oversimple, but you know what I mean. You're a smart boy. Well don't
you!?! You look at me!" she said. "HELL, THAT'S ONLY FIVE PEOPLE IN THE WHOLE
WORLD! You look at me when I'm talking to you!" she said. "Because everybody
else, the flat old people of this world of ours, who never had a stake whatever in it
at all, from the first to the last, we should have locked those five little dudes in a
closet— with one light bulb, two rifles and four bullets—on the first day and let
them figure it out for themselves. Then, after they finally managed that, we should
have shot the winner upon emergence. What's one measly corpse compared to millions? I ask ya?"*

*In the long silence she watched him closely for sign, not letting him move away, or
even look down. Then slowly she said:*

*"Private Williams, I'm doing you the honor of promoting you this summer. Come
to attention. Corporal Williams, I am taking the liberty of informing you that this
world's composed of the following composition: peasants; peasants following themselves; peasants following other peasants; and peasants without leaders but looking for
some. And don't you ever make the mistake of becoming one of 'em, of joining. They
deserve themselves. Don't you even come close. Dismissed, Blessèd Anarchist
Williams!"*

*Then she had released him, laughing suddenly, high as kites, the air still,
breaking out all over, unstrung and twining and making him go cold as blood for a
moment as she began moving against him again, nearly attacking, playfully
touching him, head down, almost butting him, coming at him, again and again
until he began fighting back, laughing, trying to tackle the hard shift of her
breathing, her sun-hard muscle, the riddle of her skin. And going down, giving up,*

he knew she was too strong for him, knew also that she had only wanted to make him feel her, see her, know her presence, remember. He couldn't, and she pinned him to the ground, slightly beneath her, under a common tent letting the fall of her hair drape downward, over his face. She looked at him for a long time, not moving. The air was deep and black, droning with a single wing. She froze him to her center, to the long edges of her eyes, the glint and sudden, shifting sunlight drifting her hair, the knives of light and grass looking directly through him with missing glass. Her eyes were openings, nearly missing windows staring through him, not letting him move, pinning him to her insect board, her farm of sky, saying, not demanding, only Look at me, now you look at me damn you when I'm not talking at you, now you look at me, *for a long time, until he thought he had become frozen forever, caught deep as a stone in his own throat by some terrible knowledge and a question she was trying to give him.*

Then, just as suddenly, she released him completely, rolling slightly away beside him on the hot ground. He thought it had been an illusion, black water, bluebirds' voices swaying gently in the swelling river trees, the distance.

The place was a stone wood, torn with eyes. He lay in the rounded grass, dead with motion, watching her sharp face: it was darkened, heavy with sun. It was a mask again, afternoon, all image stopped in the jewelry of her eyes. Her lips and mouth were full of hollow bloomings. There was something he could never give her.

He felt trapped in something, soft, a snare and impression of sky, the tactile release of grass beneath him. He felt caught in a rise, the oval swirl of something swelling around him. She was always a tent of common dreaming. And suddenly she moved, taking his mood with her, out from under itself, undermining their design by slapping his stomach, rolling away silently and, sitting up, he had watched only a late-afternoon oil of light halo in the pale, reflectionless skin of the three other chickens hung up lost in the rising wooden dust near her porch.

"You're not much of a talker," *she said finally.* "That's what I like about you, Dawes Williams. You're quiet a lot, and you have such suffering eyes . . ."

He was beside her again, now, this summer, watching her, held fast to her furious gaze, her sign. In the long silences he had wanted to run but couldn't. Arthur would be coming before long, striding over the hill with the ends of other seasons. They would be thrust out before him in the pace of his walking, a lance, separating them. Forever this time, he thought. She set the last dead and opened hen down like a husk, still looking at him.

"Here, honey," she said easily. "Are you still my good-looking boyfriend?"

He didn't answer. She laughed, saying this. She tilted his face higher, up into the light, still holding it fast. He was surprised that her hands were nearly smooth. He laughed, feeling strange and warm all over. Her hair blew in wisps round her forehead and shoulders. She sat, smiling at him, wiping his drawn face with the blood of her chickens.

"Here, Dawes," she said finally, "here, I'll paint you up like an Indian and you can hunt fox for me with pointed sticks."

For a moment, convinced of something, he wanted to sharpen a long wood stick and run wild in her woods. He wanted to tear away and run stalking quietly within the low houses and red turning networks of her high, mad grass.

He didn't. She held him in place with her sudden laugh; like the dusty air fixed within one of his grandma-great's doilies, smelling mysterious and old, about to jump out and explode, yet pinned and bleaching the back of dull cloth rockers in Davis Groves. And Abigail had two laughs, he thought. She had the shrill idiot whine of her cackle, and also the other, that unexpected, unusual and natural rinse of golden afternoon wind that would rise through her as she sat talking, abstracted as whittling on rocks, stroking what was left of his vacant hair with her hands. But when she laughed like this, rarely any more, he would want to look away. He didn't. He saw somehow those far, destroyed eyes, and he was held by the passionate haze he saw lying behind.

"Those curls," he could almost hear her say. "All those damn, unruly curls," she would finally say out loud, "someone's trying too hard to unmake ya."

Afternoon slowly drew off, crossed easily into other light. The stones of early evening, brindled, changing forms easily, the ripples of a great loping hound, were already growing around the porch. The stillness of his thought had killed the hours of early afternoon. He had gone off into her high grass with pointed sticks, and messed through her fields looking for signs of fox until early evening, when she called him back to the porch. These, the two shadows, the woman's and the boy's, sat in the recessive spaces. Like two childhood friends who had pressed bloody thumbs, or sworn to never part, or at least to meet on the same spot, with the same thought, twenty years later, but who knew, also without words, that they would do neither, they sat passing near-whispers between them, like telegrams before they were needed, like valentines with bloodied hearts. They sat in the deeper country shadows, conversing still over disjointed history, a ritual, a ceremony of summers, and meanwhile only the trees were busy streaking orange and red and going stiff as feathers standing on the graying canvas night behind. The boy, lulled once near sleep by the rhythms of her words, saw a goose and chose to call it a witch, as it climbed crossing the massing cloud of the western sky. She had begun to talk about the old time still pressed in the ridges and hills now. Perhaps, he thought, waking slightly, it was only another damn airplane going to Omaha after all. It was time for that, his history as spelling lesson again, he knew.

"Joseph P. Ahart, down the bluffs he came, Dawes," she began.

"I know. That's so," Dawes Williams said.

"Strapped his wife, his babe and all his goods on an old gray barrow, and westering east he came from Council Bluffs."

"I know that's a fact. You don't have to tell me that."

"Crazy banjos and whistling jars all over again if you ask me," she said.

"I know."

"Nothing here then, Dawes. Only a bunch of nearly wild-eyed Mormons, the Bovine River, tall oak groves and Cornelius Durham's hogs."

It was a history, like running over water to Australia, he knew, she had gathered slowly, nurturing it carefully and tending it regularly, like a bowl of roses risen from the dust of an old county history. He had seen it. The county history was a book collected, conceived, written and published (eventually peddled door to door) by a man with rimless glasses from Chicago, 1910. Abigail had shown the book to him only once, but he could remember the man's picture in the frontispiece looking pale as schoolmasters and bloodless as scholars, and generally exactly like his grandfather Ceril Percil Williams in a similar picture Simpson had once given him. Dawes was nearly certain at times that Abigail absolutely believed none of it, however, but he still listened to the sounds her words made dying off, stone bells and slips of grass sailing in her hush of tanglewood. The light steadily thickened. Arthur had not returned. Night, a great dog nearly black, began squatting on the land.

"You want to look at what I found, in the old stone house, this winter while you were gone, Dawes? I been at my research, all right. You want to see it? I been saving it for you. I'll go in the house and get it," she said, standing, paying no attention, leaving for her door.

Coming back, sitting again slowly, she began reading it off in the air. "This makes it legal. This makes it backwards," she said continuing:

" 'S.J.K. DAWES

MORTUARY NOTICE

Born April 17th, 1819
At Hopkinson, New Hampshire

Died October 30th, 1907
An Esteemed and Christian Gentleman
At Dawes City, Iowa

FUNERAL AT METHODIST EPISCOPAL CHURCH
DAWES CITY, THURSDAY, NOV. 4TH, AT 3:00 P.M.

Father, lead me to Thy heavenly abode
Where with Thou, face to face, I will meet
Where we can through all eternity dwell
With friends, loved ones and Jesus;
O! 'twill be a happy day,
A peace that passeth all human understanding.

Jesus, plot me the entire way
From Dawes City to the Pearly Gates,
Of Thy Golden City far away.'"

Dawes laughed slightly. Abigail's voice stopped, tailed off, looking at him intently, and she put the yellowing piece of quality cardboard away in her jeans. She spit on the ground with a clouded contempt. She flipped her knife and stuck it in a tree. It stared back, wafting slightly, twanging the breeze.

"If that notice doesn't steal the preacher's pious cake," she said, "nothing will."

"What's an 'Esteemed and Christian Gentleman'?" Dawes said.

Her laughter went up high in the air like a shoot.

"That's the question of the ages all right," she said. "What gets me is the timing involved in the thing, you know Dawes—Born At, Died, Esteemed and Christian Gentleman, Buried At, Soon To Be Ascending and In Residence . . ."

She sat chuckling to herself in the evening. Dawes sat, remembering their pictures which he had often seen, propped rigidly into Gin's combination catchall, four-foot-high Methodist Bible. The woman, Mrs. S. J. K., was small and wrenlike, afraid of Indians, well dressed in sacks and curtains of dresses, nearly lost within mountains of clothing and yet a clear, unhappy distance hung about in her tiny, overcomposed face. And also the one of the man, S. J. K. himself, fearful-looking, even mad, dressed mostly in a gray, daguerreotype of a beard he could still easily make out as flaming red, nearly wild-eyed, composed into a stiffened, stuffed and bloated turkey of a suit and staring out of the flat, faded light behind him; both, he knew, foreign-looking, the man red-faced and moon-eyed, more than the woman, more self-conscious, aware, all of them dead now, for yellow centuries it seemed, dead, but still pressed and staring back and drifting from within the heavy pages.

"Well, which do you want to get into first this year, Dawes?" Abigail was saying. "The most famous, the exciting or the legal parts first?"

"I don't care. Whichever you want," Dawes said.

"Yes, sir," she said, "after Joseph Ahart came here with his family, the Aharts, who are still here, eighty miles in from the Missouri, going west by coming east, with everything he owned tied into an old hand barrow on wheels, yes, after that all of the comedy and excitement of the thing seemed to be gone and done . . ."

"I know that part."

"Do you?"

"How could I forget it?"

"How indeed?"

"Anyway, you don't know that. Not for sure," Dawes Williams said. "It could have been a wagon, with a regular mule."

"No, it was a wheelbarrow. Had his firstborn strapped to it like a pot and pan . . . . Gonna plant some more children among the corn tracings soon as the plowin' was done."

"And so S. J. K. came riding in on a big red wind," Dawes Williams said. "Is that it? I suppose that's true. He already had a hotel in his pocket. I suppose that's what I'm supposed to suppose out of that one."

"No. I don't give a damn what you make of it. You know me. It's a free country if you've got the head for it."

"Ya. I know you all right."

"He did have plenty of money though," she said. "He came dressed in style. On a horse, and he spent most of his time the first ten years just buying it all up for a dollar an acre."

"I don't see what we have to do with any of this."

"That's the question everyone was asking all right," she said. "But, anyway, he met Noah Winas in Illinois one day and then later, by some forks near the Missouri, your great-great turned to mine and he said: 'Noah Winas,' he says (he was always an orderly, punctilious man, Dawes, S. J. K. Dawes was), 'you go set this stick in the forks of the road, and whichever it falls we'll go.' So Noah set that stick up real straight, and a wind came up in about an hour, and it blew backwards—so they turned around and headed back into Iowa."

Dawes felt suddenly he was losing his patience already.

"Damn it!" he screamed.

"Good for you, Dawes," she said. "My aren't we enjoying ourselves!— But what are you talking about specifically?"

"A big wind came up and blew it backwards! I suppose that's what you really said! I suppose that's what you are trying to tell me! Is that it? I suppose that makes it 'legal.' I suppose that's supposed to mean some damn thing! Is that it? Well, what does it mean!?!"

"I don't know, Dawes. 'Course, there was only about fifty lost Mormons in the Groves here then. Them and old Cornelius' eccentric hogs. So I suppose it doesn't mean too much of anything, even if it does."

"I don't understand it," he said. "Just what the hell *do* eccentric hogs have to do with all this? That's what I have always wanted to know."

"Have you?"

"I have."

"Well, why didn't you just say so? Ask? My land, Dawes, you know very well why. They were the first to stop, next to Indians, who were civilized and didn't stop anyway, so I guess that doesn't matter either way."

"I see. The moral is only hogs stop in one place."

"Hogs and swineherds, not shepherds," she said.

"So they stopped. So they quit going. So what?"

"So everything!" she said. "You know very well my whole theory begins with that. That my whole point of view on it, at least, is built upon those stopping hogs."

There was a silence.

"So which came first, Dawes," she said, "the acorn or the hog?"

"I don't know. Has this theory of yours got any bigger than it was last year?"

" 'Bout a year bigger," she said, "like an oak. But answer my riddle."

"All right—I'll take the acorn."

"You'd be right," she said.

"So what's the point of that?"

"That's the point all right," she said, "that there is a point. That mostly too much is made of these things, Dawes, except, of course, for entertainment. You can't hatch a hog from an acorn, you know."

"Maybe to a point."

"You mean you still have questions about the wisdom of it?"

"Some."

"That's good to hear," she said. "I hope they drive you nuts, you little bugger."

There was another silence. Abigail sat studying him.

"So what else happened that first year that S. J. K. Dawes came?" he finally said, uneasy and forcing himself. "Eighteen forty-seven, wasn't it?"

"No, 1846."

"What's the difference!?!"

"About a year, give or take a bit," she said, running more peas through her bright bucket of water. "But, you're right, there's not much reason for difference there. Who needed national newspapers in those days anyway?"

"I don't know. But if this theory of yours is like last year, I suppose the fifty lost Mormons, camped in the Groves in 1846, are still lookin' for heaven and for their souls and for the Promised Land."

"That's right, Dawes. The City of God in The City of Man. They were all after land! Those Mormons and Daweses were crazier than hell. But, like I say, the only reason anybody stopped here in 1846, or any time else, was because the hogs liked the place. One thing generally has a way of leading to another without changing much once the character'f the thing's set down."

"But Indians didn't have hogs, and didn't make it a practice of stopping anywhere, and generally didn't lead from one thing to another that way."

"That's right, Dawes," she said. "Indians are circles. I sure like the idea of Indians . . . . I see you've been remembering your ideas of history."

"That's right . . . I been remembering."

"So what's bothering ya?"

"So what's bothering me is that once I was telling Miss Wilma Spent, this third-grade teacher, all of this, about this Cornelius Durham and these Indians, and she got red in the face, said I was lying or crazy, called me a lot of names, and made me stay after school for a week."

"That a fact, Dawes?"

"Oh ya, that's a regular history."

"What kind of names?"

"Well, she called me a Communist Bullshevicky for one."

"Why, that woman should be drawn and quartered and maybe whipped to death if you ask me," Abigail said.

"Ya, she doesn't like Ronnie Crown much, either."

"Well, that's all right, I like him fine."

"You don't even know him."

"Ya, well, that's all right, I like him just fine anyway."

There was another silence.

"So anyway, you see," Abigail said, "it was precisely 1830 that this vague, strange man named Cornelius Durham, from just west of Boston, began driving his herd of hogs across the country. Lookin' for a place they liked. So, when he stopped here, he invented it all you might say. Time and creation. He invented history you might say. Otherwise we wouldn't even *be* here."

"I guess we should be grateful to him."

"Not at all, Dawes."

"I see," Dawes Williams said.

"He lived in a hollow tree the first winter. To get closer to his hogs, no doubt. Creators are like that. It's a plot."

"And that's a history, I suppose?"

"It's a pure-dee fact at least. —You want me to get that book and show you where it's written again, Dawes? I will. I'll go in the house and get it."

"No. I know. That's not necessary."

"That's good," she said, "because I was being ironical. You know how I feel about books—they were invented by mere Germans with a need for things like that. You wouldn't ever catch an old Celt reading a book or, at least, believing it."

"I believe you."

"No, you don't, Dawes. I can feel it. But, anyway, just because you don't believe it doesn't mean it happened any other way. That's how Dawes City got its start. It was Cornelius Durham's pigs that did it. Not the Mormons, nor Dawes, nor Noah Winas, nor even the Indians. He was the real pioneer, the first degenerate . . . ."

"Yes," Dawes Williams said, "but Cornelius Durham always sounded like a man who was lost in the woods most of the time to me."

"That's true. Sounded like the name of a man who had a red felt hat on his head, stockings that rolled past his knees, and went crazy finding a bank of acorns in the end."

"Is that a history? A pure-dee fact?"

"No, that's probably slipping into what you call an 'interpretation' just there," she said.

"Well, I'd like to stick to pure-dee facts if you don't mind," Dawes Williams said.

"I don't mind. I've got plenty of them. So they liked those acorns raining from the Groves so well they never moved again. They never took another step. And that's a pure-dee fact. Want another?"

"I don't mind. I have all evening looks like."

"Well," she said, "it's also a fact and logical extension that you'd have owned this whole thing today, Dawes, every damn naturally falling acorn in the place . . . . Except for the fact that none of your ancestors ever had the least bit of sense, nothing was holding you back. You were lucky."

"That so?" Dawes Williams said.

"That's so," she said. "Like my granddad Tom Winas always said: 'It's been fifty years or more I been watchin' these damn Daweses dying off, falling over themselves, going down hill, and they ain't got and never had a lick of sense about anything; especially money. They're just a greedy lot pure and simple.'"

"Pure and simple!?!" Dawes Williams said. "What's so pure and simple about it all of a sudden? It's all a made-up lie. A damn slander if you ask me."

"No," she said, "it's a history all right. A pure-dee fact if we can believe our reason, which, incidentally, we can't."

"It's not."

"Anyway," she said, sensing his inattention, "we had other things besides Daweses; we had wolves, bad weather, righteous and revengeful Indians, blizzards, and things like that, Dawes. 'Course, the whole thing started with only a bunch of acorn-happy hogs who had spotted their chance . . ."

"That's wrong," Dawes Williams said, "that's when you think it ended. It goes back farther than that."

"Maybe," she said. "I like the idea of Indians better myself. Some called it progress though. But we know about them, don't we, Dawes?"

"I guess we do now."

"Forgive them," she said, "but beware. While they can't help it they're simple, they are dangerous nevertheless . . . . Don't argue with me now."

"Not me," Dawes Williams said. "I wouldn't think of it. Not with the kind of pure-dee facts you happen to have."

"But anyway," she said, "about the money. That's the part I have been working toward."

"That's the part I should hear, is it?"

"Maybe so," she said, "because they always said it was only your great-great's wife's to begin with. That he forced her to marry him for it. That it was his start, crooked you might say, in life and that, incidentally, this Mrs. Dawes was descended directly from the great and furious, single-minded Hannah Dustin—a famous New England lady back east most remembered for killing and scalping sixteen Iroquois braves single-handed one night by firelight."

"Wait a minute here," Dawes said, "it's a lie."

"No," she said, "they had, previous to their own scalpings, murdered her babies and committed other unnatural acts on her own body."

"I can't believe that!" Dawes Williams said.

"You can't even understand it," she said.

"Besides, I thought all this history definitely started in 1846. Isn't there a line under that?"

"Anglo-Saxons draw lines under things," she said. "That's flat-footed, don't you see? Celts, and everyone else in this world, draw uncoiling coils. Besides, 1846, which never existed either incidentally, was only a line under 'here.' The Anglo-Saxons, and Normans like Arthur, have been going around ripping everything apart in the name of order for a long time, you know. But, anyway, about the money," she said. "They say that old S. J. K. just married her for it. The money. Picture it, Dawes, he must have pulled himself together for six months of gay deceiving at one point. And they were doing pretty good for awhile, forty years or so . . . . They came out west and had land, a grain mill, silos, a hotel, the bank and a huge house with high ceilings and long corridors mounted on a hill even bigger than Arthur's. Too bad, because they also had a copper mine in Mexico with no copper in it. Because . . ."

"Wait a minute! Hang on here!" Dawes Williams said. "What's all this 'because' about!?! You're the only one I know who's always saying their becauses after they're already past!"

"Hang on here, Dawes. Bear with me," she said. "It was because your great-great's daughter, Niomi, who married this no-account Harvard horseshoe pitcher from the east . . ."

"Wait a minute here," Dawes Williams said. "I thought it was Julia who married this traveling Harvard graduate named Clarence."

There was a long silence. Abigail Winas was scanning the insides of her eyes.

"You may even be right on that, Dawes," she said. "Wait right here. I'll go get the book where it's written."

"That's not necessary," Dawes said.

"I'll be right back," she said. "This is ironical."

Coming back, sitting down on her slow porch, she said:

"You're right, Dawes, it was Julia who married this no-account Harvard graduate passing through town on a train. Anyway," she said, "in the end there was nothing."

"Oh, God," Dawes Williams said.

"I never heard you swear over history before, Dawes."

"I never heard you take history serious before. Besides, in the end there was me. That's not much, but it's somethin'."

"You're the butt'f all this, all right, but I keep makin' on ya enough maybe it's the beginning too," she said. "But anyway it all ended one summer in the nineties in the first place."

"Oh, God," Dawes said. "Which ninety?"

"Eighteen ninety-three," she said, not batting an eye. "You want me to go on or not?"

"Yes," Dawes Williams said, "I guess that's all straightened out and taken care of."

"Yes, well then, it was very simple. The silos burned down. The mill burned down. The bank went broke. And the upper story of the house collapsed, killing the serving girl in a storm, and nobody could live there any more. Then news came up there was nothing but rock in that Mexican mine. Clarence, the Harvard graduate, left Julia in Arizona and ran away to California—Julia was a famously homely girl, Dawes—and was never seen again. Rumors—it's a fact, therefore, poetical—had it he died a black, lonely death, Dawes."

"All right. I'm game," Dawes Williams said. "How did he die?"

"Well," she said, "it's a long story, but the short of it was they said he got himself caught robbing a stagecoach—no money, only a U. S. marshal in it in the first place, on vacation, Dawes—and he spent ten years in Yuma prison, got out, went mad and died sticking a shotgun in his mouth. It was one of those melodramas and they buried his bones on Boot Hill."

"I'll be damn," Dawes Williams said. "You think that's true? A pure-dee history? Fact? Who's these 'they say' anyway?"

"Hard to tell, Dawes."

"Doesn't sound much like Hyoot John Williams to me. No, sir, it doesn't at all."

"Who was this Hyoot John Williams, Dawes? How'd he get crossed up in this simple county history of ours?"

"He was my *father's* great-uncle or something," Dawes said. "He was a cowboy."

"I'd almost forgotten we were only talking about half your problem, Dawes," she said. "What was this Hyoot character famous for?"

"He was mostly famous, I guess, for lynching cow thieves. And for carrying on border wars. And for killing the famous Mexican bandit Charcon in a duel in a place called Durango."

"Is that a fact?" she said. "I'm fascinated."

"That's a fact," Dawes Williams said. "Simpson showed me a book on it once."

"Well, Dawes," she said, "books are less good than genuine letters, but poetical rumors are better than both."

"Yes, well, Simpson's got some of those, too."

"Well then," she said, "it sounds like history to me."

"The hell," Dawes Williams said. "It sounds like a pack of lies to me. I don't believe in any of it. It never really happened. Not a bit of it."

There was another silence; the moon was nearly rising.

"That's just fine," she said, "that's hopeful, that's good, but don't you want to know about these dying-out Daweses anyway? Don't you want to know why it all burned down? In the same year? In the same summer?"

"All right," Dawes Williams said. "Why did it all burn down in the same summer?"

"I'm glad you asked me about that, Dawes," Abigail said seriously, "because I have a theory on that."

"I thought you might."

"Well, you see, some say it was witches."

"Not me," Dawes said, "all of a sudden I don't say it was witches."

"Not me either, though," she said. "I believe in the witch's spirit all right, but I just think it was a lot of hard luck and coincidence all at once. On the other hand, however, I still think it was a curse. In other words, I think you are your own worst witch."

"Oh you do, do you?"

"Yes, I do. For Christ's sake, Dawes, that's just good ole Free Will in reverse. And like my granddad Tom Winas always said: 'Those Daweses— you get just damn tired watchin' 'em, they're just meant to be plagued. Always were. Always will be. Their blood runs all right until it reaches their head, at which time it promptly sours on'em and turns to vinegar and sand. You ought to see'em dance when the moon is out.'"

"Is that what he said?"

"That's what he said."

"Well, I don't believe it."

"Well, I do. I heard him say it."

"Say," Dawes Williams said, "what the hell was your granddad doing when he wasn't watching and commenting on Daweses? What else did he have to say for himself?"

"Well, he was a quiet man mostly," she said, "but he did say: 'Those Daweses just don't know what's worth real value, and never did, and never will, 'cause only the land's worth anything real, and always was, and that's just a sad lot for a people who are basically that damn greedy.'"

"Are you through now? For today?" Dawes said, nearly angry. "Do you have anything else you want to tell me?"

"Now, don't go peein' your drawers on me, Dawes," she said, "I'm not through yet. Because now you take Arthur—he may be part ass, but that man knows how to turn a dollar. He may not know much else, but he's a damn successful breeder, Dawes! Hell, in fact, he may be the most successful breeder in this whole damn country! You may be rich again yet, Dawes, if he keeps on breeding that way. Wouldn't that be fine," she said running over her own question, "because then maybe you could buy this whole place back someday and sit on the hill like a dude, watching, waiting so's you could have the pleasure of noticing it was all burning back down around your head again. That would be just swell! By God, Dawes, that would make a pretty circle of it all at that," she said, laughing furiously, pushing him roughly away.

He sat, watching outward, saying nothing at all. The great black hound, night, was moving in more now, squatting on the day like leavings, squeezing its life, its heat, out from under the bottom. Yes, Dawes Williams thought, history is an impossible thing, like being almost able to count backwards forever from nothing but one.

"Now, we had Indians, too, Dawes," she was saying, sensing what she mistook for boredom. "We had a lot of those things. In the winter wolves roamed in packs down the bluffs, the edges, and through the snowheart of the valley. Picture that, Dawes! Hell, that must have been fine. Once some Indians stole your great-great's feather ticking, his bed—spring was an opera—taking the cloth tick to use as a blanket, and leaving the rest, the thousands of feathers to float like notes in her kitchen, leaving the house with pots and pans on their heads to drum fierce shouts of victory in the yard, and stealing some horses, too . . ."

"But not stealing the land, leaving that, too," Dawes Williams said, "because as Tom Winas said: 'The land's the only thing that's worth real value.'"

"That's right," she said, "you've got it now, all that, just so your great-great and Noah Winas and some others could chase themselves, each other, and the Indians too, clear up into the lake country in Minnesota, where they could all hold a big opera and ceremony of a gun battle, harps in the grass hitting no one, nothing but the tops of trees and the sky . . . Hell, it must have been fine."

"Yes," Dawes Williams said slowly, looking at her, "that's true. It must have been fine."

There was a long silence. The two bent shadows, the woman's and the boy's, sat staring out into the open yard.

"But the most fabulous story my grandfather Tom ever told me," she said finally, "was the one about the famous drunk who got himself lost in the big snow of '78. Well, Dawes, it seems he was a traveling man, drinking in the tavern, the snows came up, but that didn't bother him. Hell no, not him. He said he was going to California anyway. Well, three days later they found him just a few feet away; just outside the tavern door in Davis Groves. He'd been there all that time, sleepin' in his swill, and they only found that bastard—a few feet lost from being found—three days later, because his feet were sticking out of the snow mound! Saved by a foot! Why, he was famous for years. Used to walk around the county on two hand-carved sticks, Dawes! Why, except for the fact they had to cut off both his feet to save his life, he was perfectly all right."

"I think, I know," Dawes Williams said. "'Of course, his travelin' days were done, but you should have seen him dance!'"

"That's right, Dawes," she said, "you're catching onto this history business all right. Nothing wrong with him! Damned and saved by liquor—eh, Dawes? Settled him right down. What a crazy son of a bitch *he* must have been—eh, Dawes? He became a dancer in the end," she said, laughing uproariously, poking his ribs.

But he moved away, wasn't listening. Then it came out, surprising him, and he said:

"Abigail, what do you think? What was Dawes really?"

"Really? You want to know what I think? Exactly?"

"Yes."

"Are you ready for that, do you think? In a word? Do you think you will understand? You'll listen at least?"

"Yes. I don't know. You're my teacher, aren't you?"

"Well then," she said, "I think it's almost pure-dee simple finally. I think he was just another mad, run-of-the-mill old Celt, like me, like you I suppose, looking for a place, another deserted wood to stone himself off from them for awhile. For another hill to make walls on. The Celts you know," she said, "were the Indians and weed smokers of Europe for centuries."

"Awww, you never tell me anything," Dawes Williams said, " 'Them.' Who's all these 'they' at least? Tell me about 'them.' "

"Why, Dawes, they're the Anglo-Saxons and the Normans," she said, "and the Greeks and the Romans, and they haven't even got the shit off their shoes yet for thinking about government and concrete hats all the time. You'll find out about them all right, you won't be able to help yourself, but when you do, just remember—just go about your business and pretend they was only passing through."

In the weave of silence, a basket of tall blowing grass, her voice had stopped; but she was still looking at him so intently he had for a moment the illusion that she was still speaking. It was soft, nearly recognized, going through him cold as a knife.

"Is that what you think?" Dawes finally said.

"That, in a word, is what I think."

"That sounds fine, that doesn't sound like any word I ever heard," he said, "but what does it mean?"

"You're the best student I ever had, in fact the only," she said, "but I can't explain that. Fact is, if I had to, you wouldn't be. You sense it, that's enough. It's blood thinking. It's what they call intuitive, *a priori* thinking."

"I don't understand that either."

"That's all right, too," she said, "no need to, ever, and you sense it, and you'll figure it out some day and remember me by it. That's enough."

"Has any of this got anything to do with why this place is named Dawes City? Is that the point?"

"No. Nothing at all," she said. "All that was another accident that only happened along the way."

"But everything has a purpose!" Dawes found himself saying, almost defiantly.

"Not at the time," she said, "only after it ended and is just sitting there and has to be explained."

"Awww," Dawes Williams said.

"Well, he owned it, didn't he, in the end? It was natural, wasn't it?"

"Is it?" Dawes said. "What's so natural about it all of a sudden? I never saw anything natural about it before."

"What isn't?" she said, almost winking. "It all seemed natural enough to me. Just another opera in the air. You can't be hanging round me, Dawes, if you don't think things are just mostly natural," she said. "I absolutely won't hear of that."

"But how about all those people he rode out to save in the big winter of '78? When nobody would . . ."

"When nobody else did," she said, "happened to come along."

"Ya, well, what about that?"

"Pure-dee shucks," she said studiously, "there was only five of 'em."

"Ya," he said, "but the ones he found by the frozen sled when no one else would go out and look? The half-dead ones and the baby he found lying under the only half-warm, pure-dee dead horses!?! How about the orphanage and school he built? Wasn't that a part of it?"

"Yes," she said, "provided you need orphanages or schools in places you live, provided you live in a place that doesn't take in people and teach them, I guess some good along the way was a necessary accident, too."

"Thanks at least for that," Dawes Williams said. "You are all heart, Abigail."

"Well," she said, "I'm glad you brought that up. As old Tom Winas always said: 'It's not the size of the heart that counts, it's the quality of blood that's going through it that makes it dreams or merely nightmares and operas for everybody around.' "

"Tom Winas never said that in his life," Dawes Williams said.

"You're right, Dawes," she said. "Tom Winas was mostly a quiet man. Fact is, that was what was the matter with him. He never said a damn thing as long as he lived. None of 'em did. It was a goddamn shame."

"I don't believe any of it ever happened," he said.

"Good for you," she said.

He sat watching her. It was true. He knew it. She was dying. It was all true. It was full night now, still early, her face was drawn and fleshed and outlined with moon; her raw edges, her loose hair merged gently, were cast against the perfect black shadow of a tree, the gray vertical light of a porch pole as naked as photographs. She was dying. He knew it because Arthur had told him on the way out. And he could only watch her, the way her profile shook slightly in the sudden, weaving wing of moonlight. The locust rowed over windgrass, foreign, strange and unrecognized, and constantly exploding with bursting summer frogs, sound as rhythmic as blood, dark blood, voices even higher than themselves. All moon was a clear water of light in her elm. Because Arthur had said it, it was so. Something was wrong with her blood, her head, they said. "You be real polite to her now, Dawes, this year," he had said driving out. "Very polite and respectful or I'll whip you good. She wants to see you, and you be real good to her now. You hear me?" The elm was a dead shadow of water in the moon. The land was closed, and Abigail's words still hung near the wind. Arthur was coming soon, scheduled like a train going toward Omaha. He would rise out of the crazy windgrass, tall, dark as whispering, unexplored houses. He would ruffle the night, a pond, closing behind him without notice. The weather in his face was beardless and sane. Dawes would watch him. And she, Abigail, would remain behind. She was getting tired now, winding down, wanted to go in and sleep. He felt it, across her porch.

"A valley, a stone grave by the river," she was saying. "A mountain, a stone grave by an Italian mountain . . ."

"Stone markers," he said.

"Of wind . . ."

"Markers of stone wind."

"History is a drunk in the snow . . . his feet sticking out," she said.

"Mrs. S. J. K. Dawes' feather ticking," he said.

"Joseph P. Ahart and Cornelius Durham . . . there in the walking moon . . . their babes in a barrow," she said.

"A frozen sled, the gristmill in wintertime," he said.

"History is an early fire, a stone horse breathing steam . . . an Indian prancing on the blue ice of the river . . ." she said.

There was a silence. She drifted out before herself, without moving. It was pure-dee night, he thought.

"Joseph P. Ahart, down the east bluffs westering he came, Dawes," she said.

"Yes, I know."

"Yes, I know you know," she said.

"Well, I know it."

"Yes," she said, "I know it because your greatest was probably just another wood-eyed, stone-hefting old Celt, Dawes," she said, "like me. A burrower."

"I don't know."

"I can see it. Round your eyes on Friday afternoons."

"Arthur's a Norman. You said so. Simpson's no Celt."

"Well, don't take it too seriously whatever you do."

"Anyway, it's all only a legal, pure-dee fact, don't ya suppose?" Dawes Williams said. "It's backwards."

"No way to tell," she said, "no true Celt ever wrote a history. Did you know, however, that some Dawes and some Winas intermarried somewhere finally? Dawes? Did you? I like to think we are almost distant."

"No," Dawes said turning into her. "I never knew that."

"It's a pure-dee fact," she said. "Some of 'em even work out frontways."

"I don't believe that."

"Good for you."

"Awww," he said, "you never tell me anything."

She laughed, then drifted off, and stopped utterly. He sat watching her and, after she had stopped, he wanted her to go on. He waited, easily, expecting. She must go on. She would. Then she almost surprised him and, taking her chair up, carrying it in behind her, she only got up and said, "Excuse me now, Dawes, but I have to sleep. Arthur will be along," and entered her house.

"Goodbye, Dawes," she said.

He sat for a long time on the porch, silent, watching now only the moon of night move through the trees. He sat waiting for Arthur. Then, in the flat, dead motion he saw the rise part slightly, as if by order, give in with rustling white light, and Arthur stepped through and came walking over the hill. Moving swiftly he was a distanced, nearly remembered ghost of afternoon; a stern motion moving in the pale light closing the grasses behind him. Dawes listened to the slight sound of his walking whipping the air. The form, nearly sightless, began coming near him and he shifted quietly on Abigail's porch.

"Dawes?" Arthur finally said, coming through to the yard.

"I'm here, Granddad," he said.

"Let's get goin'," he said, moving across into the open light. "I'm late. Where's Abigail?"

"She's in the house. She's sleeping."

"Oh," Arthur said, moving directly across the porch and straight through the door.

Dawes felt something had been nearly invaded. He waited for Arthur to emerge again with the same loud stride, like swinging around a pole, but Arthur was inside longer. He could hear his voice moving about in the dark house, but could not make out the words. Finally, after Arthur was through looking in on Abigail, and apparently had paid her for the chickens, he came out without a word and they began walking back. Dawes followed. They collected the three dead husks hanging on hooks near the porch and walked out into the tall, whispering grass. The sky was a white trestle space through the trees. The air was an erosion of green apples, thick, a throat full of flying insects and birds feeding on motion. Arthur moved on ahead, parting it. The moon was a globe of far walkers. They headed up, moving around until they found the path to the pond. Higher, turning, Abigail's house was black, receding into the vale, a net of light, below. He tried to remember it. Her old hut, nearly kicked out and eaten with shadowy feelers, neighed silently behind. He stood watching the wind blow the shadows across it, its face. Then Arthur called out hoarsely to him in the darkness, way in front, laughing, telling him to keep up and that the snakes were larger at night.

They moved down together, around the pond, careful of stepping through the ground. Arthur said they were late, but cursing nearly pleasantly. The pond stretched out, a white bucket full of dank and singing frogs. But the whole earth was still, an ear vacant of people, a lonely wing breaking loose except for Arthur, who rowed before him parting it like an aisle.

He thought he heard foxes sweep by, unseen, dressed to kill in silent tails, and hogs grunting, a larger machine of dark, lumbering about, moving in the underbrush, rubbing their coarse hair together like sandpaper. They were all passing, eating small birds of darkness which had already eaten smaller eggs of daylight. The thick, white moon ran like a round, naked rain through the dry spines of the trees. And he, Dawes Williams, was the smallest, most losable dark of all. Hell, he thought, everything else is eating everything else around here. Hell, this whole place is breathing with death. A whole country of it. Hell, maybe me and that sonofabitch Arthur, who is related to me by blood if by nothing else, will just give it all up and pitch tents out here and spend our lives being Indians. I want to be an Indian. Ronnie Crown is the head council of war, the avenger, who scavenges the woods for signs of rabbits. This is only 1950.

Hell, we're not too far from that yet. We can visit Abigail, all of us, every day and she can cast spells from her black pot, and burn people's barns down and run naked around the fire. Simpson wouldn't want to. He works in an office and doesn't understand these things. But I do, Dawes Williams, and the ghost of trees, my greatest grandfather, a far-walker, moon-driven naked man who wasn't much for banks and offices either, after all, is out here, too. Somewhere. Now. Watching me. Not really, of course, but he is. Out there now watching. There in this night, the white spines of trees round and worn and torn like stone eyes, heavy, unspun, twisted with all of it, because this is an old land and already tired and full of stories, white graves, black houses and people who tell stories in the evenings so old, older than paper, funny as operas, so broken with light you can hardly see them, any of them, but you know they are here—they are pure-dee here in your singing blood. . . .

"Dawes," Arthur said, "get in the damn car."

And in the car, driving, it was harder again, still. The road was dark, a funnel of things flicking by in the light, either just bugs or tiny stone hearts smashing the glass without noise or comment. Arthur had stopped to drink beer with the priest he chased the golf balls over the hills with in Davis Groves, and was late for his dogs' feeding. Swaying his white boat of a Cadillac down the deserted ruts and wakes of the road, hurrying, he seemed changed from the morning, stranger, out of place, like a Texas cowboy in Iowa who had put on a new hat and changed his name. His outline, sharp with edges, lost within the dark interior hood of the car, flared up regularly across spaces within the flash of his lighter.

"Well," he said finally, "what did the green witch have to say for herself this year?"

"She's not a witch."

" 'Course not. But she could pass."

"I like her."

"So do I, but that doesn't mean she isn't a witch."

"What's green about her?" Dawes Williams said defiantly.

"Well, she's not a black witch. And she's certainly not a white one, either. I guess she's a garden witch," Arthur said, laughing easily, blowing out his smoke slowly as decisions.

"You just think she's different and strange. You just don't know her well. That's all. Those are the reasons you don't like her."

"What are you talking about now?" Arthur said, genuinely confused. "I like her fine. I always liked her. I don't care if she's different. And, Jaeesus Keyrist, I've known her thirty more years than you've been around. Old Duncan used to work for me when she was a girl, you know. Hell, don't talk to me about knowing Abigail, because you don't know what you are talking about. Hell, Duncan was working for me, and she grew up next door . . ."

"In Skout's house!"

"That's right. Except it's *my* house."

"I'll be damned . . ."

"You talk like a cowboy all right," Arthur said, laughing, drawing on his cigaret.

"I mean I take it back. I didn't know all that," Dawes said. "But then maybe you don't know everything, either, maybe."

"Could be," Arthur said, "but then I don't talk as much as you. You just jump at things too quick, Dawes. You judge people. There's just a whole lot of happenings went on around here you never knew about, nor ever will."

"That's me all right, I guess," Dawes Williams said.

In the silence Dawes sat feeling embarrassed and angry. He didn't know why. He never did. He only knew Arthur made him feel impossible, like something caught in his own throat, as if he had said something completely foolish before he even spoke, as if, even, he had been born under someone else's rock. Leone said Arthur had been always that way with everyone, and not to take it too seriously, that soon they would be home in Rapid Cedar and it wasn't important, only something one had to learn to live with, a feeling, so it didn't matter. Simpson said nothing at all. Gin said Arthur was mostly noted for being very good with greyhounds and other dogs. And Ronnie Crown, who had never met him, said Arthur was only a prick. Suddenly, however, riding back toward town, Dawes knew Arthur made him feel that way only because he was always judging him, every minute, as if the only thing he was even curious about any more was if it was even possible Dawes might grow up into something he might even recognize. Dawes knew he had given up the possibility of eventually being proud long ago, that that was past, that Dawes Williams was easily a commonplace mistake in the sheer luck of the breeding. There was nothing anybody could do about it now; it was finished; the wheel had spun and been read for that one, and now he was only waiting for others. In the quick dark of another match, Arthur was saying:

"She's dying anyway. So I guess it doesn't matter what she is."

Even knowing about Abigail now, Dawes felt something cold flinch through him and, just as suddenly, relax.

"It does matter!" he said. "Someone should organize a damn collection so she could go to the hospital."

"There you go jumping at air again, not knowing, with nothing to start with," Arthur said. "I wrote her out a check for a thousand last spring myself. She wouldn't take it. She won't even take twenty dollars for a chicken. She won't take anything and she's not just proud. Dawes, she doesn't want to crawl off and die. She wants to be where she is."

"But she's got no one to check her."

"To check what?" Arthur said. "To check if she's still pumping blood every hour? What the hell are you talking about, Dawes? We check her."

"But something could be done. Something can always be done!"

"It can't. I took her to be X-rayed in Omaha myself."

"But she's got no one to watch her out there."

"Hell," Arthur said. "She wanted to see you, and what do you think you were doing out there today? It was you baby-sitting her, I guess. Someone goes out there every day now. We take care of her."

"But how long can that go on?"

"A year. Two. As long as it has to," Arthur said.

Then Arthur lapsed into silence. Dawes knew when Arthur was done with a subject, and he was finished with this one. He rubbed his hands, thinking, against his face in his usual five-part motion that never changed. Then he said:

"Strange? Strange, hell. You couldn't move around this country as much as I have in the last forty years and think anything is strange any more. It's all getting worse, too."

"Mother said it was strange all right," Dawes Williams said, not thinking, trying to bite his tongue.

"What!" Arthur said, looking down in the flaring dark. "Did Leone really say that?"

"Sure," Dawes said, eyeing him back, "why not?"

"Awwww," Arthur said, backing down.

"She said you lived like a bunch of Gypsies. With tents and caravans of dogs and things like that. Said once at home in the summers you wouldn't let her go to *The Hunchback of Notre Dame* when it came to Charlie Smith's Silent Theatre, or play near the river."

"Awwww," Arthur said, "it was probably only after I sent her to college she thought like that. I never used tents, and I never asked my daughter to sleep in one if I did."

"Why not?" Dawes asked. "Was she too good to sleep on the ground? Would she break?"

"Of course she was. But not even in the thirties, which were hard times but overrated," Arthur said ignoring him now, "not even then when it might have been a good idea did I use tents. 'Course, three of the trailers were always screaming full of dogs—made it a little hectic in the mornings, and stopping to walk them five times a day, going all the way east to Boston, south to Miami, or west to California or Mexico that way—but we never had to camp exactly. If we'd had to have done that, I believe I'd either gone myself or not gone at all. And we were never damn Gypsies and don't you damn forget it."

"But I don't mind Gypsies. In fact, I like 'em. I even think they're probably neat as hell if you knew some."

"Awwww," Arthur said, "you're nuts."

"What's nuts about it?"

"All right, you're not nuts, and Gypsies have rights, but if you ever grow up to be a Gypsy, I'll break your neck."

"Why would you want to do that?" Dawes Williams said easily.

Then he broke off. The car was swaying gently, headed out onto the concrete now, and he sat studying Arthur polishing, erasing his face with the five separate, thinking motions, as if he were already at the end of something working backwards toward the beginning and end again.

Soon they were pulling up the black hill to the farm. Gin was standing in her kitchen. He was nearly startled to find her there, and that she had never left it. The light was harsh, sudden, unusual, a yellow bone swelling after the long dark. Dinner was over but she waited it nevertheless, stirring it with a wooden spoon. Arthur came in after feeding the dogs. He and Dawes sat across from each other, eating in silence. The table seemed long and vague and overbright. Arthur's thin, nearly aristocratic frame was still somehow muscular as it bent with a dirty khaki shirt. His bibs, also slipped on for the feeding, were off and hanging on hooks on the stoop and the shirt looked incongruous above his pants, which were still his expensive golf pants. Looking up from his plate, Arthur said nothing at all. He didn't recognize Dawes. Leone didn't, either. She came through the door and began to wipe the nonexistent hair away from his face.

"What did you do today? Did Granddad take you golfing?" she said. Then her hand made the sudden start at the involuntary recognition that all of his hair was missing. Looking at Arthur, catching herself up, she said only: "Really, Fa-ther. It's a little short, wouldn't you say? I hate to be critical, but why didn't you just have that idiot Brogan peel his entire scalp back and be done with it?"

Arthur looked up, laughing his dark laugh to himself.

"Now why would I do a thing like that, Leone?" he said. "He may grow up to be a tap dancer some day and want to grow a pompadour."

They were both dark, staring against each other, the same. The light in the kitchen was suddenly washed out, too pale to understand them. Gin's radio stared out at him, about to blare, something, looking over the yellow country kitchen, about to run off, and switch itself on, and hatch at any time like an electric feather of genesis.

"I think he looks pretty good that way, Leone," Arthur finally said. "Looks all set to go. Looks healthier. Looks like a ballplayer. Looks pretty damn good that way if you ask me."

"Well, nobody asked you," Gin said.

"He looks freakish," Leone said.

"He looks like a Nazi is what he looks like," Gin said.

She laughed with contempt. It was a perfect, practiced contempt that hung over Arthur's head and filled the kitchen like stoves. It was the laugh she used, had developed over the years, to counter his excesses, to pit them and put them in their place. It was the laugh that always signaled that she was ready to speak, to begin:

"Arthur," she said, "you may have really done it this time. Sometimes, Mister, I don't think you are possessed with the sense you were born with. Sometimes I think you misplaced your wits early in life—the sense the Good Lord gave those dogs of yours. You are bereft, brother. Why didn't you just take him over to Dooley's and have him sheared for a quarter, Art? Well? I'm waiting, Art? Why didn't you bring him home earlier, Art— while we were still doing the floors—and I could have had Alma Skout wax his head! Why didn't you think of that one, Art? Why didn't you just think of bringing him home earlier so we could've had a fair opportunity to wax his head? Because that boy, Arthur," she said, pointing at Dawes, "that boy is as bald as the inside of your vision!"

"Awwwwwwwwwwwww, Criminy, Gin," Arthur said.

But Gin was laughing too hard to continue now. Her large oval face was open and merry.

"Awwwww heck, Gin, I thought the boy and I had a pretty good day. Didn't we, Dawes?" Arthur said, suddenly warming to him, including him in a vague conspiracy.

"Yes, sir, we did, I guess," Dawes Williams heard himself say, and not only say, but mean it, believe it, at least for the time it took him to say it thinking suddenly, yes, it was a good day, that is true, as Simpson Williams came finally through the door with a book tucked under his arm, making the kitchen's opera complete by saying:

"All right, what's the crisis this time? Sounds like Lum and Abner out here. Can't you people take it easy for awhile? This is a weekend in the country, isn't it?" he said.

But now Leone and Arthur were laughing too hard to continue. Dawes began studying Simpson, who only stood there, forcing confusion, partly naked in a robe, a copy of *Abraham Lincoln: The Prairie Years,* Volume Two, in his hand. He was too blond for this conversation. He smiled like a devious sheep, a grazer, out of his water. Dawes was suddenly tired. Getting up from the table, he went into the den to sleep. It was late, well past dusk, and time to dream, to watch the pale moons of trains steam past all night toward Omaha, to see the greyhounds sail by like dreamers of possible sanity, a release into deeper seams, a water of vines and trellises growing, taking root on the glass, because this was the day he had gone to town with Arthur, because the night was a bell, safe, beyond the house, because Abigail Winas was dying, because history was a personal hat, because beyond the house, the night, the river, the locusts sang in sleeves of grass.

5

I*t was not the dream; it was what he thought about the dream that mattered; standing, watching it unroll itself again like a piece of yellow, nearly transparent tape sliding gently from its silent, splitting reel. He lay in the moon of Arthur's sunroom, all night, twisting again, guilty, nearly waking hearing the upstanding willows, black and sweet, sweep up the sides of the blowing hill forever. It was a dream, a thing without words describing itself, speaking with pictures, knowledge, feeling, a soft, coherent thing, a dream that really happened, a space of real cohabitation, knowledge and guilt. And, walking within slight red fogs, he and Ronnie Crown and Johnny B. Harper were waking once again like standing water. The eye of the Catholic mortuary next door, a neon sign blinking, on and off, was saying:*

SPECIAL TONIGHT—RONNIE CROWN'S HALLOWEEN.
FOR BUCKAROOS ONLY.

Because he and Crown and Johnny B. Harper were watching again. Crown was hawk-eyed, flicking about with every motion in the street. Dawes was softer. Johnny B. Harper was not looking at anything. In fact, Johnny B. Harper was crying.

"Shut your goddamn face, Harper," Crown was saying.

Crown was talking quickly. His words were fast snakes spit from the side of his mouth. He was intense, staring into the street, about to sweep down upon any motion, any surprise, any opportunity, any counterplan. Johnny B. Harper began whimpering. Crown was stone; unmovable.

"SHUT THE FUCK UP OR GET OFF MY WALLS!" he screamed within whispers. He rose up, leaping over the bushes, searching for sign.

The deeper edge of the wind ran in the long yards, bowed the trees, slept on the houses, and wove itself on the lantern-hung and shattered windows.

The windows made moaning sounds in the night. The Catholics were holding another wake, behind them, in one of the old brick mansions that lined Main Avenue, black windows, sleeping eyes, a line of old stables far back from the street. Simpson's house was before them, a great gray tent of stucco, blowing vines and elm leaves, the light a yellow cocoon trapped inside. The windows howled, lost, a village of wood framings.

The air was a strange pipe, an organ moving back over itself in opposite directions, sightless, autumnal, black air in black rooms, moving, dreaming, breathing, as if someone were dying, coming back to life, breathing, dying again.

The wooden shutters flapped together in the loose, releasing breeze like dead, flying-together ancestors.

The trees of dark were standing back, screaming gently at the tops, swaying, noiseless as recessions. The houses were black and naked as the bones of hotel windows filling with voiceless, humming spirits.

The wood shutters blew together. And Mrs. Lowbus, whose house was next to Simpson's, was out in the night. She was dressed in a sheet and playing ghost. Crown would get her. She was Dawes Williams' nearest neighbor lady. She held the hollows of her cruel eyes before her like candles refusing to burn or ignite in the wind and be whole. She popped forth, into the knotted together groups of smaller children that approached her porch. She was a mask, a suddenly sprung jack-in-the-box. She cackled horribly and returned behind her elm, hiding again. The children clutched at themselves, one circle, one spark drawing together into tighter knots. They broke screaming down the hill, into the halo of the larger street. There, under the lights of the avenue, they looked risen, still painted, a history of costumes and tiny clowns. They were a jumping ring of excited bandits, mummers tramping together, beyond. Crown sat on the wall watching, a match in his teeth, studying the dark. His face was lonely, intense, bent forward with motion. The children's footsteps going down the hill still sounded like a ring of cannon exploding with feathers and sticks and popping cloth.

"Shut up, Harper," Crown said.

"But I didn't say nothin' lately, Ronnie," Johnny B. said.

"Shut up anyway," Crown said.

Dawes watched Crown. Crown was a genius. The Catholics, however, he knew, were witches who were always holding wakes. At night sometimes he sat in his room and watched the dark souls fly over the cross in the trees, the hide of the moon.

It was Halloween. Ronnie Crown's favorite day of the year. Ronnie Crown and Dawes Williams, and even Johnny B. Harper, were Indians free. Johnny B. Harper was not much of an Indian. Crown was a chief. Dawes was a Winnebago, and they had already sneaked down the back wall of the alley, crouched with cunning and belief, escaping, leaving the early night's warm-up behind. They had already finished dumping the garbage of sixteen straight cans on the corrugated alley two blocks away and running, running down the rattling wind behind them. They had already wrecked four bikes, a trike and three red wagons; soaped twenty-seven cars closed; broken sixteen windows; and Ronnie Crown himself had even succeeded in dumping a burning bag of dog shit on the surprised rug of a man who had promptly beat it all to death with a stocking still attached to his foot. Crown was plotting. He sat on the wall; the man still cursing behind them on 16th Street was too busy wiping the shit off his foot to follow.

The pumpkins burned their hollow, carved-out, fire-black eyes within the dark of the porches. The air was fall, chilled, as cold as if the hanging apples were wine.

Ronnie Crown and Dawes Williams, and Johnny B. Harper especially, were trying to get warmed up for the big one.

They had got a late start on Halloween because Johnny B. Harper's mother had made him stay in until he had finished her dishes. Johnny B. Harper washed dishes for nine.

Crown got down from his wall. The others followed. Johnny B. Harper was last. Johnny B.'s eyes were tired, trailing behind, covering everything. They were as wide as quarters and wonder. Crown snaked into the vacant lot and sneaked through the lean grass to get a better eye and angle on Mrs. Lowbus' garage. The grass was cold and wet. Dawes lay low in the covering, listening to himself hearing Ronnie Crown talking. Because he was talking directly to Johnny B., Dawes knew Crown was speaking to only himself:

"But Johnny B.," he said, "I've got to get that miserable old excuse for a twat this year for sure. Now or never. Besides, I swore to her I would. Besides, you never know where they might send ya next."

They were still bent low into grass, whispering shadows, barely visible in the deep cover of the vacant lot. Across the kittycorner alley lay Dawes' house. The alley was broken and distorted suddenly with terrible lines. Simpson had come out onto his back porch, switching himself on with light.

A crowd of children came up the alley, moving past, knocking the door. Simpson asked nothing. He stood laughing, doing the tricks. His high laugh, full of real delight, spun on the air, went over October, the moon. He did a soft tap dance on his boards and shoveled candy and dime suckers within the sound of their running feet and thousand bursting sacks. They were hooded and happy. They left screaming with glee, promising to soap his screens with lard. Simpson was delighted, unforgotten.

"I guess I made a bad job of insurance," he called after, laughing and happy.

His voice waffled over the still air of the alley for a moment and was gone. He went back into his house and closed the door. His voice and his image were snapped up by nothing, disappeared, and gone. The light went off. The porch was silent.

Dawes lay in the lean, snaking grass, watching. The screen was black and vacant and cold. The alley was impossible to walk across. At least the moon was conscious, a stone rowing over, blown by the wind through the trees, naked and white. Only Crown was whispering. Then even the alley was still. Yes, he thought, *that is Simpson, my father. He lives in that house. No, not mine. I do not live there. Not my father. I live out here with Ronnie Crown, and even Johnny B. Harper. I have never looked at him before. Who does live in that house? That place? Those rooms? That quiet man. Not me. No. Who is that—Simpson?—his ghost gone moving across that porch, who is laughing, good, too close, tap-dancing, handing out candy to children dressed up in rags and painted masks. No. Thou shalt not know thy father's nakedness, it said, his goodness, I guess. Too close. No. I do not know them. Live there. No. Those are Simpson's quietly polite children who run dancing down into lights and the ends of streets happy and full. I live out here. In a dark corner of air, a stand of night, an eye.*

I am the wildest man in the world. I live out here, safe, hiding, beyond them in the night as lean as grass. Except for Ronnie Crown, I am the wildest. Johnny B. Harper is third.

"Shut up, Johnny B. Harper," Crown was whispering again. "Goddamn-yournervousasstohellshutupshutup. JUST SHUT THE HELL UP! I'm going to do this! Sweet Jesus I am," he said, calming.

He was bent again forward, staring out furiously into the dark, intensely watching Mrs. Lowbus' horse stable of a garage as if it might sprout wings and gallop away. His eyes were round and hooded, crouched on walls still, peering just over the small flare of his cigaret. The high, blowing grass was still an autumn fire and wind of Catholic wakes.

When he stood, the stick of dynamite stuck out of his hip pocket as limp and nervous as chewed-on rags. *It bobbed in the wind behind him as he bounced up and down on his haunches, just over the level of the grass. He clutched at it from time to time. He made sure it was still there.* It was the stick of dynamite. *The one that blared out at Dawes every time it was looked at. The one Crown had stolen last spring, and then cherished and chewed on all summer,* Thou shalt cherish Thy stick of dynamite, *from the construction shed down on Ben Franklin Field. The detonator caps were in his hands and he was holding them like hot, sun-clammy pennies which might be counterfeit, which might not work and unspring the machine.*

"HOW, Ronnie!?!" Johnny B. Harper was saying. "But HOW!?! HOW in the holy hell're you ever going to set it off!?!" Johnny B. Harper was saying.

"I don't know. I think you need some goddamn electricity or some damn thing," Crown said. "Ask Dawes here. He's a mother-school."

"You got me," Dawes said.

"Nobody knows, nobody knows, nobody knows," Johnny B. said.

"Oh, for Christ's sake," Crown said, "just shut up about it. I got to think. I don't know how these asshole caps work, Johnny B. Harper, and I got to get me a couple of good ideas. That's all. Any fool could see that."

Crown was unmoved. He stood, staring back directly, not even batting an eye, trying only to shake his mind out into the night.

"Don't fail me now mother-mind," he said.

"What ideas, what ideas, what ideas," Johnny B. was whispering frantically, under his breath.

"What are you!?! A Jesus train!?!" Crown said.

"What ideas," Johnny B. began saying lower and slower and with more conviction.

Just then, interrupting him almost, the moon boomed out blooming through clouds and thicker layers of cold air. Johnny B. was striped and carved with sudden light. He was standing, casting his eyes down and away from Crown's, round and cloaked in a blanket his mother said he could wear for Halloween, and he was quivering slightly in the wind. He was like a tiny Friar Tuck saying frantic prayers, sad and hopeless penance, to the silent grass. His eyes were immense. Yellow and round, larger than his head.

"Goddamn-goddamn thing," Crown said. "This prick-stick will never explode. Or, if it does, it may finish us off instead."

"Shit, shit, shit," Johnny B. said. "What ideas!?!"

"Well, I'll just tell ya," Ronnie Crown said, "I once thought of taping about fifteen goddamn cherrybombs' fusings together (that was all I goddamn had, fifteen), you see, and then just fusing the goddamn thing ass-over-tail downthemiddle sure as a burning rope in a straw-fucking-berry sundae you see, mother-school, and that was 0-god-damn-K as far as it went, I suppose, only it didn't go far enough, you see, because I didn't know (for Jesus-one) if you could set dynamite off with cherrybombing fusing or, even if you could (for Jesus-two), I wasn't sure-for-Mary-mother-certain when or even if it'd blow. And I didn't want to waste it— not this mother. And besides," he said, "for Jesus-three I didn't want to waste fifteen cherrybombs, either. What goddamn good does it do ya to set off a stick of dynamite and then wind up with fifteen- airy-cherry-bombs that don't even work? I ask ya? Iaskya-laskya-Iaskya, Johnny B. Harp-per!?!" Ronnie Crown said.

"I don't know," Johnny B. Harper said, calming some.

"You-goddamn-right-as-clean-jaybirds-shit you don't. That's why you'll always be a kid, Harper," Crown said. "Not like my buddy Dawes Williams here. I love'm. He's going to grow up to be a goddamn tall dwarf."

Dawes could feel himself again not answering.

"So what?" Johnny B. Harper was saying.

"So," Crown said, "I gave it all up and went fishing for Lent. My first idea of fusing it, that is. But don't you go screwy-worry-ass on me now, 'cause I got another'n coming right up the flute. One of my better ones, too. I can feel it now."

Dawes could see Crown pause to light another cigaret in the silence. It flared up nervous and shaky in the wind. Crown seemed thoughtful, dreamy, lost within himself as if he were a theatre of thought, self-conscious, intense, still about to stalk outward into the grass without having to move.

"Hell," he said finally, "I wasn't even sure whether the motherless thing'd blow my goddamn head off or not!"

"That's all, that's all then. Bull's shit is what I say then," Johnny B. Harper was whispering fanatically into the round, cold moon of the grass. "I'm not going into that garage with you, not me, by GOD I'm not," he said.

Crown was lost in another thoughtful silence

"Ya well, fuck-ya-then, I'll do it myself," he said. "Ya well pee-on-ya then," he said still looking at Dawes. "Me and my buddy Dawes'll do it then. Won't we, Dawes-you-mother?"

Dawes Williams was lost in another thoughtful silence.

"What's your other idea, Ronnie?" he heard himself saying.

"Well," Ronnie Crown said slowly, "the second idea is even trickier than the first, but it's goddamn nifty…"

"That's it," Johnny B. Harper said, "that's all I need to hear about it . . ."

"Shut your clanking ass, Johnny B. Harper," Ronnie Crown said. "it's trickier, but then it's also a-fug-of-a-lot safer than fusing it and that's nobody's lie. It took me a whole damn week to figure this one, and it's just now starting to come around the bend."

"Well, let's hear that one," Dawes Williams said.

The night collapsed with stillness now. Crown was its core; its clock on the verge of hatching. His mastermind was clicking over, about to tick, revealing itself. The earth was long, pounding, red. Crown's brow was furrowed. Then:

"Well, Halloween-motherfuckers," the great Crown began, "do you think you are ready for this one? Can you take it?"

"Com'on, Crown," Johnny B. Harper said.

"All right," he said, "it's those motherless rafters."

"What rafters?" Johnny B. Harper said.

"Those old rafter beams up in bitty-lady's-Lowbus' garage. They started me thinkin' and gave me the idea. You see, Halloween-ding-dongs," Crown said, taking his last warm-up before it all came gushing out; before it all became a flow, a flood of brilliant Halloween genius; before it all came gushing out of a fountainhead at once. "You see, you asses," he said, "it's obvious—we just tape ourselves about fifty of these damn-special-detonator caps to the stick, the dynamite-mother, at all angles, sticking out, you see, and then we get ourselves about seventy-five pounds of mother-load-rock, and a rope, you see, and we put it, the rock, on a two-by-four-which-we-have-also-gotten, you see doncha, and we put it all—the rope around the rock, the rock on the two-by-four, and the two-by-four just barely loose's hell on the edge of the rafter, you see—square as grease in her garage . . . . It's what ya call an 'apparatus,' you see, a spring an' a hinge an' a bang," he said . . . His voice tailed off for a moment, resumed again:

"Then we just graft ourselves onto our long-huncher-of-a-rope, you see," he said, "and we just get the hell out, we draw off some at our leisure, back in her damn bushes and . . ."

"You mean we tie the rope off on the two-by-four, don't ya?" Dawes Williams said.

"Ya. Right. Good idea, Dawes," Crown said. "Are you with me? It's like Dawes here says, Johnny B., it's the old-damn-trapdoor-bastard-trick, you see, but only we got the key this time, the pope's own rope you might say . . . and so then, frigging-nifty man," he said, his voice tailing off into nearly nothing, "the whole thing just goes bang, mother," he said, rising up, screaming, uprising over the general din of Halloween, "then BANG-MOTHER," he said, "BANG-MOTHER, BANG-BANG-MOTHER, AND DOUBLE BANGBANGMOTHER'S ASS!" he screamed.

The alley resolved finally like a gun of echoing silence.

"Geeeezzzz, is that something," Johnny B. Harper said.

And he, Johnny B. Harper, could barely contain himself. He rolled and clutched at his straining sides like whispers of laughter. He dove into the lean, October mats of grass. He came up, bobbing, trying not to yell with joy.

"Don't go fruity on me," Crown said, studying him.

The grasses blew spasmodically, back against themselves, off and on, against their cold grain like the faucets of Catholic wakes and dead-flying Protestant witches.

"You in this, Dawes?" Ronnie Crown finally said.

Dawes could see he was studying him. His, Crown's, eyes were black and searching and quiet at last and hard to find in the hoods and shadows of his head. He was finally confident.

"You in this, Dawes?" he said again.

"You think I'm a dink or something?" Dawes Williams said.

"I know that. I know you're a dink," Ronnie said. "What I want to know is—are you a mother's dink who is in this, or are you a mother's dink who is not?"

"How would you like me to knock your head off with this old ashcan lid?" Dawes Williams said.

"Oh-fucking-ya?" Ronnie said. "I'd like it fine. How would you like me to stick my dynamite up your ass and pull yer trigger?"

"Com'on, you guys," Johnny B. Harper said, "we haven't got time for two things."

The night returned, blooming around them, twisting in the turning lot. And still in his dream of falling timbers, crawling without noise in Simpson's garage, they found the long ropes (the ropes to his summer awnings) and the two-by-four. And the rock (it must be the most absolutely perfect rock, Ronnie said, hard as a motherless stone) was found two blocks in the very bottom of someone's unraveling wall. Then, just as suddenly, they were walking back. Johnny B. Harper was carrying it or, rather, the rock was carrying Johnny B. Harper. And Crown was alert, not talking anymore though, and busy taping carefully, lovingly, the detonator caps onto the stick (at every possible angle, like a flag unfolding in the wind). Taking the large roll of genuine electrician's tape (stolen from J. T. Sandrool's Hardware Store), his eyes narrowed, but he was quiet and wondering suddenly (perhaps for the first time) would it really happen, was it a dream, would it really go bang at all? Would—it—go—BANG?

Then they were in the bushes behind Mrs. Lowbus' horseless stable and they sat, buried in curtains of leaves, searching the nightwood for possible sign. Crown was nearly coming apart with calmness. He crouched in a branched heart of wood, whispering, staring out at the lay of the air. He was waiting for Mrs. Lowbus to make her final thrust, into and through the last group of bewildered children, and to take her sheet off, away from her head, and to ascend her deserted, husbandless porch, to go back into her dark house, turning her lights off further, leaving the night quiet again and possible at last. His eyes were camouflaged with expectation and the leafy moon-shadows moving across with the wind. He seemed nearly painted. His face was more real than a hood.

"Well, you-commando-mothers," he said, "we may pull this off."

But it seemed hours before all that, the other, happened, finally began to move. And there, next to his own breathing, twined completely into the sodden bushes, eyes looking out from within leaf, he listened steadily to Johnny B. Harper's heavy expiring, and he heard Crown say:

"The bitch. The dried-up, cow-faced, snake-hearted teat. I'll get'em all. She nearly scared holy crap out of me last year. She loves it. I'll get'er ass. I told her I'd get'er ass. Who does she think she is? I got rights. It's natural. And I been brownin'er-up all winter, too. I'm gettin' goddamn away with this. She thinks I forgot. But I didn't. Not me. She thinks I like her ass. I never forget. She's nuts. Not me. Not ever. I don't like'er at all. I'm happy. I'm in heaven. Boooy, is she set up good. I told her, and now I'm goin' through with ma plan. I'm retribusing her ass good. I'm lettin' her damn ole cow-hearted, snake-sheeted ass have it tonight. I never forget. Not me. I feel great. I'm in heaven. She shouldn't have been jumping at me that way. She had no right . . ."

"Were you afraid?" Johnny B. Harper said, biting his tongue.

Ronnie Crown said, "She made me a little mad is all. I'm an easy guy. It's a debt is all. I told her. I'll get'em all before I'm done. By God, I will. How'd you like this B-B sonofabitch-dynamite stuck up yer ass and set on fire, Harper?"

Ronnie's third and last cigaret flared up in the dark.

"Damn," he said, "I been savin' these dude-cigarets for this special occasion and now I'm out."

The bushes were still again. In his dream of staring at the old stable he knew somehow he felt hours had passed. Then, just as suddenly, they were moving out of the bushes, watching, beside themselves, fearful of dreaming, low as Indians, hugging the ground, afraid of laughing or crying or peeing in their pants. Ronnie had the stick of dynamite thrust before him like a war lance. Dawes Williams had the long system of ropes draped round his shoulders and fixed in his teeth. They were nets already catching themselves. And Johnny B. Harper was dragging the two-by-four behind him.

"Keep yer ass low, Harper," Crown whispered after.

The grass smelled of musk, earthworms and rocks. It was rich and strange. Soon they were climbing in the high rafters of the horse barn. Crown was below, lining up the shot. He moved up, crawling over them, whispering orders, and went down again to inspect the work. It took hours. Finally it was perfect. The trap was in place. The rock was in place. The line was tied off to a nail and ready. Johnny B. Harper said suddenly he was wetting his pants. Crown ignored him by telling him to sneak outside and be ready to string back the rope. Johnny B. got down, leaving Dawes alone in the rafters. It was cold and old and smelled of spiders and ghosts wearing harness and riding horses. Crown was below and sure-handed. Dawes was climbing out and down now, that moment, that moment in the dream that flinched at itself, and Crown was busy feeding the line out of the hole in the window (he had made silently with rock and tape) to Johnny B. when Harper pulled too quickly on the whole damn thing and the *thin, placed board tottered, waved, began to sit back, rocked on its haunches, and then it collapsed, fell, and*

it

took

forever

for

the

rock

to

fall,

killing him of course, he was already dead in his own water watching, staring at his own dream, almost waking even now, watching an exploding feather of light, a puff, killing him dead, even just then, except for the basic fact that even now Ronnie Crown had the simple wit, tact, presence of mind to merely kick the stick of dynamite deftly aside, at the last possible junction, just before it fell far enough to go BANG BANG MOTHER MOTHER, *saying simply:*

"*Okay, Dawes, you mother-breed-idiot-hunch, I just saved yer goddamn worthless life. I didn't care about me. Now go up there and set that boom-boom-screwing rock right this time.*"

And this time he was relaxed, seeing he set the board more firmly before he came down sliding like a mad fireman on his rafter of a pole. The rock was sitting above, smiling, staring with eyes like naked potatoes. The rock was rehinged.

"*Betcha ya caught splinters up the crotch on that one, didn't ya, Dawes?*" *Crown says.* "*Let's beat it.*"

And this time they made it out of the horse barn. They dove noiselessly back into the dark hedges, feeling suddenly warm and loving themselves, safe. The horse barn sat, staring back, lonely, deserted, loaded and ready. It was finally ready like a destructive egg that was hinged. And the great Crown was crouched low. He was so calm he was coming apart with nerves; and the rope, the rope was caught in his hand, almost sweetly, an offering made in a pew. And Johnny B. Harper was moaning then, clutching his balls, reaching for the line, but already Ronnie had slipped his rope and it all went finally

bang!

not BANG-BANG-MOTHER-MOTHER, *not even* BANG-BANG-MOTHER *or* BANG-MOTHER-MOTHER, *but then, as it all turned puttering out,* "*bang!*" *seemed to turn out just fine, it worked real well, because the garage gave up easily, collapsed, the entire right side shot gently from under itself. Then, after a moment's pause, its accordion, its voice box expelled air and a ball of fire. It was a dragon. It was a bonfire for honest Celts to dance around, the biggest in the history of civilized man living in houses on A Avenue and Wood Street in Rapid Cedar, Iowa. A fire, yes, but only because the great Crown had, as an afterthought almost, remembered to douse Mrs. Lowbus' ten-gallon-guaranteed-fireproof-gasoline-can where it would do her the most good.*

Only already, he could see, they couldn't stay around. Already he could see they were fearful as animals trapped without plans. They were running. Dawes had what was left of the rope in his hand. They were flying mindlessly back over themselves, their own footsteps. They climbed Dunchee's inside wall and, not knowing where, trapped in the surprising light and openness of the alley, jumped back over again. At least it was darker in the yards. They ran back over themselves in opposite directions. They laughed fitfully, knocking each other down, and crossing each other even trying to pull apart. They were clowns in a funny movie. The film was broken and tricky and over fast.

"Small world, huh?" Crown said, knocking over Johnny B. Harper, picking him up and dusting him off. "Who asked ya to come?"

"Nobody," Harper said.

"Well, keep it to yerself," Crown said, "and nobody'll notice."

They skirted the lights. They were lost in the backs of the long yards. They moved on the edges, screaming with whispers, and their voices were swallowed up in the thicker wailing of the Catholic wake, a dim, interior light wafting from partly open curtains and a single back door. They tried to shift for themselves in the outskirts but, giving it up, they began moving in closer like sniffing a yellow bone. The wake was still being held in the grotesque house. It was in full swing as if nothing serious had happened. Moving closer, however, something escaped them. A thought slipped through their fingers and they began running again, completely mindless, until Ronnie Crown tackled Dawes Williams and Dawes Williams tackled Johnny B. Harper, laughing uncontrollably until, finally, through windless lungs the great Crown got out:

"I got it! This idea is unusual even fer me!! But it's been comin' round the bend now fer five minutes now. It's a hot one!!!! We got to hide out!!!!!"

"Good!" Johnny B. Harper said. "Where!"

"In the damn Catholic garage!! In their damn rows of coffins!!! By God, it's perfect! Who'd ever look there in those damn pearly boxes? By God!!!!" he said, so unusually happy he nearly slapped his knee.

In the moments of utter silence that followed, the idea collapsed into being. They slipped through a crack in the mortuary's garage.

"But what if we get one that's already full, Ronnie?" Johnny B. said, crying again.

Crown didn't answer. He only stood there staring back. He too seemed easily caught up in his own design and partial ruin.

And it was dark and safe, lying there on the soft felt, silent. There was a small breathing crack left open for shutting down noiselessly in sudden emergencies. Just lying there waiting for someone to come in and bury you by mistake. For hours. Days. To his right, Dawes could hear Crown pretending to play submarine. To his left, Dawes could hear Johnny B. Harper crying softly, all spent out now like a monk whispering vespers in another hall. They were far away.

"Dive! Dive!" Crown was whispering. "Goddamn-dive!"

No one answered. Sirens were going up and down the street. Even the thin wake had *stopped. People rushed out on the lawn. They stood around on the crushed-stone driveway, talking, smoking, watching the fire. He could hear them standing under the trees.*

When he talked, Crown screamed through his whispers.

"Dawes!?! Dawes!?!" he was saying. "Do you think we could have got lucky? Do you think we got her house, too? Dawes!?! Do you think we could have got her, Dawes? Dawes!?! Dawes, are you listening?"

When he cried, Johnny B. Harper seemed lost in the woods.

Inside, it was almost warm. Outside, he could hear the police and their cop shoes galloping up and down the alley and through the yards. He could hear them flashing their lights through the high leaves and the trees. The whole sky was filled and blowing with the music. They shone their lights through it, inquired and left. They were moving about on the crushed stone of the driveway, asking questions under the trees. No one at the wake knew anything at all. Suddenly, however, the beam, the flashlight, the fish's yellow eye was filling the doorway. It began moving along the row of coffins, respectful, tipping its hat. Thin clinks of it began filling the breathing crack in his coffin. The lid fell noiselessly shut.

Dawes Williams lay low on his soundless felt. It's goddamn black in here all right, Dawes Williams knew. But it's just a good damn thing I guess Ronnie Crown knew a secret way through a hole in the wall in here. I guess God just takes care of his own. He gives them the luck. And shows them the way.

But even through the walls he could hear the cop's shoes leave. He opened the chink in his lid, holding it up and open with his feet, like prying a ceiling slightly open; and he was glad thinking backwards that no unexpected lock had clicked shut around him. He could hear Crown breathing again, thinking of talking. Johnny B. Harper was laughing now. He was either well and over it, or mad and lost forever. And they, all the others outside, were standing around the lawn still asking excited, Catholic questions. In the distance he could hear more red engines wailing up the broken alley. The fire department was only warming up! They went on by, up, and he could see them turn right at the corner. In the blackness as they passed their aluminum ladders clanked shut together. They were like lids, passing Crown's head, leaving pennies and dark noises for Johnny B.'s eyes. It was a dream only of voices now. In the stillness only Crown was speaking again:

"Damn it. Damn me to hell anyway," he said, "but I never planned on that! Not this. Not dumb ass me. Jesus H. Bohemie, I swear to God I never planned on any of this. This is Hell, I tell ya . . . . Shut up, Johnny B. Harper. You shut up, too, Dawes. DO NOT SAY ANY ONE DAMN THING. Even if they take us alive. Not on your screw-honker, mother. We got rights! You just keep damned buttoned, no matter WHO comes through that motherless door and opens these coffins . . . . I mean it," he was saying, "and it was all a damn accident anyway. THAT'S IT. We didn't mean it. Hell no, not us. Not really and besides, you see . . . you see, BESIDES, WE DIDN'T EVEN DO IT. God, I'm smart. Deny it, see. That's it, you see, hoooo-weeeee-dogies-fuck, we just always happen to

hang out here . . .That's it, you see. Every Halloween we just happen to come down here and sleep in these damn fine coffins. We're weird, see. Hell, sure, we have a real deal for it. We're a little strange, BUT WE'RE INNOCENT, SEE, *and we just happen to belong to a three-man club who goes in for this sort of thing, sleepin' in caskets on Halloween . . . . How's that sound, Dawes? Johnny B.? Hell, that's natural and all. King's X anyway.* IT'S HALLOWEEN, ISN'T IT!?!" *he said. "I mean we're innocent, aren't we!?! Well, aren't we? Doesn't anyone out there have a sense of humor any more!?!* SAY— WHY MARYINHELL ISN'T ANYONE ANSWERING ME!?!" *he said. "Hell, we just happen to go in for this sort of thing is all. Sleeping in coffins. Shitin' around. We're just crazy for it. We wouldn't be without it on Halloween. Not us. Not them. They love it, too, you know. Gives'em somethin' to do . . . You think they'll buy that, Dawes? I'd like to have your opinion on that. What's your opinion on that? (Are you there, mother?) . . . that we didn't do it . . . that even if we did, we didn't mean it . . . that even if we did, we're innocent . . . that even if we aren't we're just weird anyway and wouldn't be without sleepin' in these coffins on Halloween. How's that sound? Johnny B.? Dawes Williams? You think they'll forgive us?" Ronnie Crown said. "Because we were innocent in the first place, aren't we? Well, aren't we?* SAY—WHY THE HELL ISN'T ANYONE ANSWERIN' ME?"

His voice hadn't once risen over a whisper.

"Well, I think . . ." Dawes Williams began.

"Shhhhhhhhht! Don't say a damn thing, Dawes. Don't make a sound or they'll take us alive," Ronnie said, lapsing back into the silence of his enameled box. "They'll catch us for sure."

The night, a lonely dream, collapsed then. It had no center. Dawes could only lie there, at peace, listening to invisible water running through invisible seams on invisible walls, a dream of cold stone lilies. He could spend his time only trying to piece together who the WHO who Ronnie Crown had mentioned WAS or could possibly BE. Because Ronnie Crown had caved in in the end. In the end all he could hear was Johnny B. Harper's crying, something remembered gratefully, something placing them again exactly in the universe, something as small as soft rain falling, there, in the next elaborate box over from the left.

The wake resumed. It picked itself up on a high, reaching note and continued inside. It was perfectly still, germinating with black air; suitable only for night-growing things. And it was then Dawes could hear Ronnie Crown's coffin clank open like a pod. Crown laughed to himself for a moment. Then he rose, lit a stick match and swore.

"Well, Halloween-mother fuckers," he said, "that was a close one. Nearly had me worried there for a second. You might have noticed that if you're a sissy yourself."

He laughed again, lighting more matches. But something had gone out of his voice now. He was unsure and shaken, even feverish. He was self-conscious suddenly. He laughed nervously, for the first time recognizing himself and not knowing what to do with his hands. He lit more matches and hooded himself with light in the darkness. He *made ghoulish faces. He stepped forth, made the rounds, said he was looking for his buddies and, for the hell of it, he began tapping All Clear in Morse Code on the hollow backs of all of the coffins. He was using the bones of some keys that fit no doors and that he had stolen from the pockets of his mother's patients who didn't need them any more either. Crown's mother, Dawes knew suddenly, was a nurse. . . .*

It's just his way of having fun. Being funny, Dawes Williams knew, lying out cold and horizontal and flush with the engraving and walking out from the door.

He could see them. They didn't rise and stretch fully, yawning and looking around sheepishly at one another, until they were safe in the fuller dark of the open yard. Ronnie Crown found a single cigaret butt left on the driveway and lit it. He sighed for the heaven in it and blew himself out easily with the trees. They finally departed, not looking back, walking in the net of streets, making their way down into the quiet shadows of Ben Franklin's Track and Football Field where Crown said they planned on hiding out further. They sat for a long time watching the moon curl in the light ice of the water. It was later, fall, cold. The drainage ditch flowed pointlessly by, urine brown, naked, eventually swallowed too easily into the ten-foot standing hole of the culvert. Crown studied it:

"Nifty, you assholes," he said suddenly, brightening. "Let's hide out in the culvert tonight!"

"Go to hell," Dawes Williams said.

"Ya," Johnny B. Harper said.

"Why's ma gang pissin' and moanin' on me now?" Crown said.

In the utter silence that followed, the summer of ghosts of tree frogs came out of the drainage ditch, singing and fading far away like lights. Crown sat holding his head in his hands.

Soon they all felt that way. They sat on the banks, still following his lead. There were images in the water. Throwing the smooth stones into what was almost frozen, thinking they could see the dark, they watched the passing shells of drowned dogs and other things.

Still it is only sometime after eleven, early really, he thought, when they found themselves chased out, running again, this time chased, and fair game, all of them, for bands of older gangs of Halloweeners . . . Running. Running. And who eventually were only catching the slower Crown, who was screaming already for mercy, grinning pleasantly and cursing and spitting by turns, all within a rather real opera composed of parts, the accused and the accuser, the barn burners and the witch burners who burned the burners of the barns . . . yes, and who were, still in his dream he supposed even at the time, nevertheless paying no attention to the great Crown whatsoever, as they were simply

> *de-pantsing the great Crown*
> *and hanging him naked and*
> *screaming for reason*
> *and by the heels from a tall*

pine tree at the end of the field. They danced beneath him for a moment, dreaming of capture and joy. Then they set his tree afire with gasoline and matches. It ignited barely, burning slowly round the bottom and edges. Crown was alternately screaming and laughing his swinging, naked ass.

And Dawes Williams and Johnny B. Harper, who had circled back, helpless, outnumbered and alone, sat watching it all. They were at a discreet distance and behind a bush.

It was then, as Ronnie was swinging by his heels, for a moment looking as if he might really burn, that Johnny B. turned directly to Dawes: "I'm going home now, Dawes," he said. "I believe I've had enough of this Halloweenin' for one year. I believe I'm done and moving along now, Dawes."

"Me, too. I believe that's right, Johnny B.," Dawes said.

They were turning off, making their way through the faint, quiet, malevolent nets of streets, too close, bowed and distorted with lamp poles already. A row of houses slept in the darkness beyond, unafraid, waiting only for the news and the scores of the end. Crown is finished at nine, not me; Johnny B. was never begun. And it was then, just turning off, they could hear Crown behind. He was still swinging naked from his naked tree, screaming at the others:

"I'll get you!!! I'll get you all!!!! I'll get'em all 'fore I'm done! So help me God, you lousy BASTARDS ARE LOUSY . . ." he was saying.

"See ya, Dawes. Don't let your meat loaf," Johnny B. Harper said.

"Oh-ya," Dawes Williams said, "I feel fine. I guess the cops'll come pretty soon and free Ronnie Crown's ass . . . . I suppose the neighbors will call in and save him."

"I guess," Johnny B. Harper said, turning off. "It sure has been a funny night."

"God, what an end to it."

"See ya, Dawes."

"See ya, Johnny B."

And when he got there, still in his dream, home, he could only find his mother, who was flying around the living room before him, screaming, too:

"Dawes! Blew up! It just blew up, Dawes! Old—well, she really isn't 'old'—Mrs. Lowbus' horse barn just bleeeeeeew up mysteriously! Hadn't you heard!?! I was frantic. And I didn't know where you were," she was saying, hugging him, with rising syllables and a laughable concern.

But Simpson was also standing before him. His eyes. He was trying to pin him down and focus him in with his eyes. The eyes which still had, to Dawes, the look of someone who had, already, discovered he was missing the ropes to his summer awnings, but which also had the look of someone who knew he didn't know and knew only he would never talk about it or even mention it once. But who doesn't have to. He knows I know. He knows he has got me. Yes, Simpson, who was trying to pin Leone to the sofa like an excited moth too near her only flame, who was trying to calm her down into her own slow cocoon again, except within his vague, nearsighted eyes Dawes could see that he had been worried, too.

So without saying a word, too, he could see he was making his way upstairs to his room.

For Christ's sake. Damn it, he thought in his dream still looking directly back into his father's eyes, you can't even have a fine time blowing up some damn old horse barn without feeling guilty and mixed-up about it . . . It's a plot . . . and he'll never say anything about it . . . not him . . . he's too smart for that, to let me off that way . . . he'll let it lie for years . . . he knows I know he thinks he knows . . . he's silent . . . he's never making a way out of this one for me . . . never letting loose of anything by never grabbing it . . . just silent and accusing as a wall, smiling, making me feel worse and worse . . . he's tricky . . . not him, he's too smart for that . . . I'll pay . . . that's not Simpson, my father . . . it is, he'll never let me have a way out of this one . . . not him, he's too damn clever for that . . . he's sneaky and mean.

He could see himself. He was a dream of being a space. He stood looking out from his high, cold window. It was overlooking Mrs. Lowbus' side lot. The side lot was newly opened and vacant, it was frosted with moonlight and early signs of snow. The window was freezing, hard to touch for long. Deep fall was in the air. It would be good for sleeping. Her ground was heavy and draped with firemen's icicles, a wonderland of white and broken, naked shapes, shadows of earth that already broke through like thaw. But it was prettier than before. Hell, he thought at his window, that Ronnie Crown knew how to set off that dynamite. We did a good job. That's something. Hell, she never had any horses in the first place. He felt very good. But somehow below there was still the moon inverted and trapped in ice, a layer of it, a thin rink without children or lights, utterly deserted, and covered over gently with night; and there within the frosted ground, the soft and decomposing water, stood the burned-out crater, the pile of blackened wood, boards, glass and old nailings like moonstatues and rounded stone and deserted, pagan eyes. A vacated piece of firemen's hosing was frozen within circles of ice. But the horse barn was gone. The ground was more beautiful in the round eye of the moonlight. It was alive, a white carnival of thawing shapes. It was getting colder. It had been a good Halloween. It would be winter soon. And everywhere the fall, the shades of past insects drooping downward on the brown, deep waters, was dead and gone. Only the Catholic wake was trying to resume itself again, completely vacant of superstition and dead-flying witches now, now that it had been entered and seen. It tried only to find its voice again on the sustaining, mirror of the wind—and the great Crown . . . he is safe, and lost, and swinging and still hanging, ass-end up, and naked and strung from the heels, and smiling back from a high pine tree, and laughing, and higher, and screaming, "EVERYBODY'S ALWAYS TRYING TO KILL PISS OUT'F ME!?! WHAT IS THIS SHIT ANYWAY!?!??!!" and even wondering how in the hell will I ever get down?

6

Saturday. After breakfast, therefore, he stumbled out onto the lawn behind Arthur's taller shadow. They were going out to play another game of catch-it-or-die, but he knew, already, he was only getting up to play croquet.

"What is this? Spring training in August?" Dawes Williams said.

He went down to take his place in front of the oak. The tree was wider than walls and guarded the lane in case he missed. Arthur said nothing at all. Walking a foot back from where he had warmed up, Arthur began throwing the low-breaking fast balls down the pipe.

"You're losing your stuff, Arthur," Dawes Williams said.

"I'm just not full warm yet," Arthur said.

Dawes braced himself before the oak tree; beside it lay the big and genuine puttin' green Arthur had laid out for himself in the shady hollow between his two houses. Slightly below lay the most diabolical croquet course ever devised. It had countless twists, existed on many shadowy levels and went in seven rolling directions. It was carved into the terraces of Arthur's terminal hill; and Gin had ordered the set of hoops and mallets and painted balls for Dawes, on one of his first summers at the farm, from the thick, religious catalogue she kept tied with string to her kitchen.

"Lay that dude in here, Arthur," Dawes Williams said.

His manner was strangely defiant, but his eyes were watering. The hard ball moved in fast with motion and weight. It made quicker, dancing movements, up and in, down and out, on the wet morning air.

"Don't you worry about me," Arthur said. "You just worry about you. I'm going to burn your hand off this morning. I feel good. I feel right."

"Lay that dude on me, Arthur," Dawes Williams said.

Arthur scowled back, struck and wondering at his attitude. The ball kept moving in faster and harder. Dawes felt suddenly good. He knew suddenly he wouldn't break or be the least bit chicken this year. He wouldn't cry. He knew he'd got Arthur this year. He wouldn't quit. He knew, in fact, he wouldn't even betray himself by flinching.

"Don't let your arm drop off trying, Arthur," Dawes Williams said.

Arthur was throwing in earnest now. He was rearing back, reaching and following through. His face was straining with calm.

"That's a near sizzler, Arthur," Dawes Williams said. "Let's have the fast one."

"Maaan oh man," Arthur said quietly.

But he wasn't laughing at all now. He stood, hat off in his hand, wiping the sweat from his forehead with the forearm of his shirt. Dawes wasn't worried. He knew he'd got him this year.

"Well, get the leather on't. It's not a gun," Arthur had said. "Wake up, Dawes! You can do it. Do it *every* time then! You're some slugger, you are," he had said.

"Good catch," Arthur had said. "I thought I had you on that one. I thought you'd had it for sure."

"You mean son of a bitch," Dawes Williams had said, under his breath, where not even the whispering locust and blowing-by house flies could hear him.

But that was other summers. Now he wasn't flinching. Arthur, however, refused to notice it.

"What'd ya think of that one?" Dawes Williams said.

"Ya," Arthur said.

"Lay that dude-spitter on me, Arthur," Dawes Williams said. "I think you're losing your stuff."

"Ya," Arthur said.

It was a duel of silent rhythms. The sun wove itself overhead. Arthur refused to notice Dawes was winning. Dawes smiled, ignoring everything, trying to overlook the pain in his hand. The fast balls kept moving in, slower but heavier now, all morning, forever it seemed. Nothing was proved. The ball moved back and forth. Dawes could feel himself nearly losing control, exploding, not even biting his lip this year, obsessed with the lunacy of it all, but containing himself. Finally, Arthur quit. He was sweating, breathing heavily, but refused to notice it. Dawes found suddenly it didn't matter; that, strangely, he didn't want Arthur to admit he had lost anyway. But he felt safe, relieved, let out of school. Eventually, however, as the game of catch-it-or-die was over the game of croquet began.

Dawes followed Arthur over. It was a ceremony of pieces, and they began making their ritualistic way past the putting green still glazed with rain, storm and the black droppings of the oak tree from two days before. Arriving at the steep croquet course where he had left the wild grasses to their own devices all winter, Arthur was studied and morose. He paced the ground around the mallet rack. He was about to launch upon one of his famous and drawn-out lessons entitled: The Elementary Need and the Universal Import of the Competitive Drive in Man, saying nothing, saying by way of preface only:

"It's only an old ladies' game when it's being played by old ladies."

Dawes thought that tended to add in a way, but he was ready for Arthur this year. He had looked "Croquet" up in the encyclopedia over the winter and had memorized something. Stepping up, almost formally near the mallet rack, he intoned:

" 'Croquet gained its great fame and popularity in Victorian England as a family game played for relaxation and social amusement. It is often best when played for fun.'"

Arthur said nothing. He looked at Dawes queerly. Then the game began to begin. All other things went still. Arthur, The Black Fox of the Mallet Blade, began stalking the racks. He was careful. He studied himself, the wood. Finally, satisfied with something, he chose one in terms of balance and harmony. Dawes felt suddenly plotted against. He thought he knew suddenly that Arthur had perhaps taken his mallets to Florida with him, and spent all winter looking them over like bats, things to be recarved, rebalanced in the mind out of hickory and ash.

Dawes, The Green Enchanted Knave of the Blue Mallet's handle, felt beaten already. But then he had clues. He had, over a five-year period, already lost one hundred and seventy-four straight matches. Nevertheless, still mad, talking a good game, searching the implosive sky for positive sign, feeling strangely defiant, and breaking into the still church of air near the mallets' rack, he said:

"You can't have that one, Arthur."

"Why not? Is it hexed?" he said with a quiet anger.

"It's blue."

"Of course it's blue. Do I need you to tell me it's blue?"

"Blue's my color," Dawes Williams said.

The silence in Arthur's eyes was now deeper than stone, more infinite and complex than light in a problematic painting. Finally he said:

"What the hell has that got to do with it?"

"Everything," Dawes Williams said defensively. "What are you trying to do—mess me up? I would be hexed with any other color. I never won a game except with that blue mallet and that yellow ball."

"You never won a game from me any time."

"That's because you're fifty years older than I am."

"I'm an old man nearly, and you still never won a game from me."

"Yes, that's true, but I'm about to win this one if you'd just give me that blue mallet and that yellow ball."

"Bull," Arthur said pointedly.

"Them's ma colors," Dawes Williams said, smiling.

"That's the dumbest thing I ever heard," Arthur said finally.

"I don't care," Dawes said. "If I can't have that blue mallet and that yellow ball, I quit."

"No quittin'," Arthur said. "I think maybe we should just take this blue mallet out of competition and use it for the tosser."

"Maybe," Dawes said, "but why don't you just break down and give it to me anyway?"

"No," Arthur said.

"I didn't hear anybody elect you the umpire," Dawes said. "Who made you the omni-potent around here?"

"Awwww," Arthur said. "What are you talking about? I did."

"Big deal," Dawes Williams said. "That's nifty."

"Maybe," Arthur said. "But are you ready to quit this talkin' and begin this playin'?"

"Why not?" Dawes said. "I got ya easy."

"Awwww, I never heard anything so foolish in my life," Arthur said.

Dawes could feel himself going silent, but it was obviously another match in which he was up against it.

Arthur threw the blue mallet high in the air like a bat, and Dawes caught it, and they went hand over hand (no topsies) for the first shot. Dawes lost. The sky was black. Arthur's larger hand spread itself easily out, higher on the mallet. The sky grew dim at its core; white angels fell.

"Why don't you spot me the first shot anyway, Arthur?" Dawes Williams said.

"Hell no. Fair's fair."

"Why don't you decide to be big about it?"

"Hell no. Why don't you?" Arthur said.

In the stillness Dawes figured he had him there; he also thought this was where The Great Crown would tell him to go take a big flying buttkiss for himself and play all alone. He didn't, however, and he spoke only to cloak his thoughts:

"Seems to me," Dawes said slowly, "that anyone who has managed to win one hundred and seventy-four . . ."

"One hundred and eighty-four," Arthur said.

"Excuse me. I lost my head . . ."

"You lost count is what you did."

"All right. I lost the count. But it seems to me," Dawes said, "on a deal like that that anyone who has managed it could at least afford to spot first shots."

"Hell no," Arthur said. "That's not how it works."

So the game began without them. Arthur placed his black-striped ball down and neatly cleared the first two hoops. Dawes swore to himself softly and leaned against the maple tree, watching. Arthur stalked the third hoop. He was a finely tuned, grotesque golfer risen and marching on the screens of his own green, and he played the ball finally, up, carefully beyond number three. He had one shot left. He paused, stalked number four, then came back through the third hoop at an angle. The ball rolled neatly with the contour of his hill to the far edges of the fourth hoop and stopped dead as a perfect gull.

"Nice shootin'," Dawes said casually.

"This is a game of far edges," Arthur said.

"Damn it," Dawes said, "you been practicin' on me all winter."

Arthur laughed to himself, not looking up from the ground. He was stalking number five. With the extra shot he had gained by navigating the third hoop, Arthur stroked the ball cleanly through the fourth hoop, leaving perfect shape, leaving it directly in front of the fifth hoop, across the growing distance of the hillside. Dawes thought, if anything, Arthur was doing too well, but Arthur was impatient, even cross with the shot and he said:

"Damn me . . . I told you it was a game of far edges. I left that shot on the short side. You see that one, Dawes?"

"I'm standin' here, aren't I? I got eyes, don't I?"

"Yes, well, I got a little careless with that one. I got it too straight on the number five hoop. I should've been on the far side so's I could have set up shape on the number six and seven hoops with my next shot going through number five here. But I didn't. I can't. So I played that shot poorly, poorly, and it's all a waste."

"Don't pull your hair out," Dawes Williams said. "You seem to be doing all right to me."

"Ya," Arthur said. "Shows ya what you know about it."

Dawes felt he had nothing to do. He stood alone, under the maple tree, cinching and recinching his Roy Rogers belt, only watching, but knowing his chance at playing would come. Besides, he wasn't really worried, not yet, because he was vaguely certain a rather huge thunderbolt would break out of an otherwise cloudless sky, hitting Arthur, striking him cold, and thereby saving the game.

Nothing responded.

Arthur, however, seemed unconcerned. He was seemingly unaware even that a bolt of sky was about to light up and pay him off by knocking him cold on his hoops. He paced, unmoved, studying only the lay of the ground. Finally he stroked his black-striped ball through the fifth hoop, laying up close to six and seven, the terminal hoops, saying:

"Now it's your shot."

Dawes set his yellow-striped ball down, completely aware. The yard was a trance. He set himself too near the stake, caught his backswing, and drove his ball squarely into the second hoop. It bounced off, back again, wooden, a spent duck with stripes for eyes.

"It's a bad start," Dawes mumbled quietly. "No fair."

"Ya," Arthur said, watching him abstractedly with growing humor.

"No fair!" Dawes Williams cried. "Overs! I can't beat you with a shot like that. I claim overs!"

"The hell you do," Arthur said.

The yard was a growing distance, breathing with the dark motion of leaves, dancing with splinters of shadow. Arthur was standing under the brim of his hat again, studying him, his eyes hooded with shade and narrowed with uncontained laughter.

"I got rights," Dawes Williams said.

"I'd let you, but you'd never learn anything that way."

"Who said I want to learn anything? How does that manage to sneak into this?"

"Just does, I guess," Arthur said.

"The name of this game is extra-shots anyway," Dawes Williams said.

"Shoot," Arthur said.

"Big deal," Dawes said, "I just want to get off to a good start, you know. So I can beat you. That's all I want to do. I don't know how any of this other got into this."

"I haven't got all day to lollygag, Dawes. You've got one legal shot. Shoot!"

He shot, but he didn't like it. It went like a marble through the second hoop, and he laid up toward the third. Then Arthur went through the sixth and seventh and came back out again.

"I have three shots left," he said quietly.

"THREE SHOTS!" Dawes Williams said, gasping like a fish for thicker air. "THE STAKE WIPES IT OFF! YOU ONLY HAVE TWO!"

"Just seein' if you're paying attention," Arthur Oldham said.

"I bet," Dawes Williams said. "I don't believe that. I think you were trying to cob one off me."

Arthur said nothing at all, but was planning revenge. He made it through the eighth level with the two shots he got for passing the sixth and seventh. Now, by making the eighth, he had one shot left.

"Oh damn," Dawes Williams said, "what a game. Every time you start running out of shots you get another. You're drivin' me nuts."

"Don't know," Arthur said, intently pacing, "I've got no shot at the center hoop."

"You're breakin' my heart," Dawes Williams said.

Arthur ignored him, pacing, eyeing the rises of ground, concentrating, a putter on a green. Dawes sat on the far end of the lawn, watching him. Then Arthur began pacing the distance off between his own black-striped ball and Dawes' naked, insecure yellow-striped one.

"What the hell do you think you are doing?" Dawes Williams said.

"Thinking. Just thinking," Arthur said.

The mallet was held at his side as he walked with even strides, eyeing the ground like a hawk. He was bent in rapt concentration.

"You're not going to do what I think you are going to do, are you?" Dawes Williams finally said.

"I have no other reasonable shot," Arthur said. "I am going to roquet-cro-quet you good."

"Oh damn," Dawes Williams said. "Haven't you got anything better to do? I knew it would come to this."

Arthur said nothing at all. The black-striped ball rolled silently, like a putt, once right, once left, in two large parabolas of the same hanging motion across the lawn, coming, rolling, moving suddenly across an infinitely complex distance he thought he would have had to have raised his voice to be even heard over, a cricket of distance, coming, swaying, stopping finally with one fertile roll and heave against the side of Dawes' yellow-striped ball. . . . He couldn't believe it. Sitting there, watching its comings, its long black strings of fated rollings, its broken snakes weaving the yard, watching them clink together, he could only let out some air and turn away.

"DID YOU SEE THAT DAMN SHOT!" Arthur said in utter fulfillment. Catching himself up he said: "That's got to be one of the finest roquet-croquets in the history of the game."

"I don't see how you could have missed it," Dawes Williams said. But he knew he had given up scanning the sky for vague bolts of God, for sign. He said: "Of course I saw it. I'm squatting right over it, aren't I? It's my ball you hit, isn't it? If you're that good, why didn't you just make your hoop? Why don't you leave me alone?"

"I've got you now. Booooooy," Arthur said, drawing the word like weeds caught through the dark flower of his laugh, "boooooy, have I got you now."

"I wasn't bothering you none."

"Dawes," Leone said, hanging from the window, shaking out a quilt and watching the game, smiling, "don't say 'wasn't none.' It's a double-negative form."

"Awwwww, you're all nuts," Dawes Williams said.

"What are you talking about?" Arthur said. "I'm just practicing my rover game."

"Why don't you just go about your business down there and leave me alone?" Dawes said to Arthur. "I'll compromise. I'll give you your shot back."

"Don't need it back. Boooooy, have I got you now. Maaaaan oh man," Arthur said, "am I going to roquet-croquet you good now."

He put his high-top shoe over his black-striped ball. Dawes could see only that it was an evil, unnatural act.

"Wait a minute," Dawes said, "maybe we can still negotiate this."

Without another word he got up, walked straight into the house and rifled Gin's kitchen. In one of her drawers he found what he was looking for, *Routledge's Handbook of Advanced Croquet,* and, emerging again, standing before Arthur, he read off a footnote on page forty-three:

" 'The rover game, in civilized countries,' " he said, " 'is only played in partners croquet. It takes place, transpires, only when one partner is so in advance of the field that, rather than strive for the Start/Home stake and thereby win his end of the game, he selects, instead, the option of spending his time and energies roving the field of combat, generally disrupting the business of the opposing team . . .' "

"So what?" Arthur said.

"So I have the legal part on my side, don't I?" Dawes said.

"Don't know," Arthur said, "but I still have to practice my rover game."

"Why!?!" Dawes Williams said. "What the hell for? You're already six hoops ahead of me. What the hell'd I ever do to you!?!"

"Well, it's part of my game," Arthur said. "Watch this one, Dawes," he said, following through, roquet-croqueting the stuffings out of the yellow-striped ball, sending it like air mail twenty-five yards up the hill and behind the oak.

There was a silence as utter as bugles as it came to rest.

"DAMN IT ALL," Dawes Williams said, "IT'S NOT EVEN ON THE DAMN COURSE ANY MORE!"

"Nothing's out of bounds," Arthur said.

"We'll have no more 'damns,' Dawes," Leone said, hung still from her quilt and her window.

"You're all nuts," Dawes Williams said.

Arthur laughed. Dawes was red with anger. He trailed his mallet behind him, like wringing a limp duck's neck, as he trudged up the hill. Soon he was buried squarely behind the oak, broiled with rage. He was netted in the mulberry bushes, fighting for swinging room; and the oak's shade was a black pot, dropping endlessly down into the center of an even darker pit, and Dawes had given up looking even for rain. He was resolved, however. Set upon the gathering of destiny by means of his own making, Dawes Williams screwed up his will and swung, driving the yellow-striped ball into the utter solidness of the tree. It was all a mistake. The ball ricocheted off the tree and finished spinning sullenly in the thick bushes near the house. Arthur was standing, bent, watching it all with an abstract and growing humor.

"Well," he said finally, rubbing his face, watching Dawes' ball spin itself out, "my shot. I guess I'm going to have to just roquet-croquet you again."

"What?" Dawes said, lifting his head into the open sky.

"That's what I say. This is definitely a roquet-croquet opportunity," Arthur said, stroking his ball.

Dawes was silent. Arthur's black shot caromed itself neatly off a flagstone and then finished itself by quietly ticking the side of the yellow-striped ball and rolling by. Arthur crossed over the field behind it, stalking his swing.

"Well," he said, "not bad. Looks like one of those shoeless roquet-croquets to me."

"WHAT!" Dawes said.

"That's what I say."

Dawes began pounding the ground with his mallet. Arthur's form nestled itself easily into the outskirts of the bushes. He groped for swinging room, found just what he needed, and finally set Dawes' wooden ball farther up the whacking hillside. Dawes stood helpless, watching it go. It was like watching a marble shot forth from an invincible underground cannon. It perched at its top, looked for a moment saved, as if it were going to roll back down, and then came to rest forever on a twig. And to top even that, Dawes Williams thought, the damn shoeless shot also just happened, at the same time, to send Arthur's own black-striped ball softly back onto the playing field. Arthur was nearly resting where he had been to begin with:

"Maaaaan oh man," he said. "I'm having some game."

"Arthur, you big fool," Gin said from the back stoop, "you leave that boy alone."

"Can't, or couldn't," he said. "It was a roquet-croquet opportunity. Definitely was."

Leone was still hanging from the opera of the bedroom window; Simpson was sitting under the single sag of the willow, smoking quietly on his cigaret like a transcendental poet of a bookkeeper who worked in an office all year, who only got to the country on weekends and therefore enjoyed it; and Dawes was making his way up the long hill with his mallet clutched firmly in his hand. He was lost in a clear preface of a moment. Speaking finally, he turned:

"WHAT IS THIS SHIT ANYWAY!?!?!?!" Dawes Williams said. "ROQUET-CROQUET HELL!?! WHY DON'T YOU TAKE A BIG FLYING BUTTKISS FOR YOURSELF AND CALL IT A DAY!"

Then it became absolutely still. Everyone was frozen. Then Arthur turned on him. Coming up the hill, a great and gray-faced God with terribilita drenched in his turning beard, Arthur stomped himself forth behind strides approaching thunderclaps.

More out of self-defense than fear now, Dawes brought the mallet down with a swing furious as blind tears. The outgoing, yellow-striped ball, like an exploding divot, sailed past Arthur's head and split itself quietly as a shredding bomb against the side of the house. Suddenly everything—Simpson, Gin, Dawes, Leone, Arthur, the locusts again—was in motion. And over it all, rising, was his mother's screaming falling from the house's window, as she clutched at the distances of Arthur's walking shadow, calling:

"Arthur!?! Dad!?! Don't kill him. Don't you *dare* kill him! Please, oh my God, leave him alone, he didn't mean it. I know he didn't!"

It was an English opera. The words were foreign, caught and jumbled in her cold hysteria, drawn within her scream, and she was crying now, almost out of her head. Even Simpson was moving now, against the falling diagonal of the hill, and he could hear Gin too, carried away too, screaming, nearly singing in her high, natural soprano:

"Arthur Oldham! You leave that child alone, you big fool, he's not yours to judge. You let Simpson handle this or I'm packing my bags!"

But Arthur was having none of it. He was almost running. He was ahead of mere words, ahead of everything but his own design. And even Simpson was running now, all things in motion; even the dogs were things unloosened with tension, howling in the higher air, jumping like fanatics into their wire fences. They were caught up, too. All things were merging, running against, into and through each other without moving in the red sleeping air, the high August noon, back and forth, passing without touching themselves like tricks with mirrors.

Then Arthur brushed Simpson aside, almost knocking him down with his simple desire to be somewhere else, somewhere he wasn't, somewhere more slightly forward in time and in space, and he reached for Dawes, for the only frozen thing in a sea of motion. He caught him up by the shoulders and shook him until he could feel the bones of his brain rattle on the stones of his skull, until he felt his nose was about to fly from the wheel of his face. He shook him like a rag in the wind. He departed down the hill, dragging one of Dawes' arms behind him like an afterthought of sacked leaves. Dawes Williams followed.

Brushing aside Simpson's reasoned analysis of what was actually happening, and also the more furious and impractical arguments of the two women, Arthur carted Dawes off to the back stoop, where he broke a not-too-small board over his ass. Then Arthur Oldham retreated with absolute dignity into the stone peace and silence of his house.

"YOU BIG SONOFABITCH!" Dawes Williams cried after.

Simpson followed. He was completely angered now, perhaps for the first time Dawes had ever seen him that way.

"Damn it, Art," he said with a rising quietness, "you had absolutely no right to do that. Absolutely. Categorically. Whatsoever. The boy may have been wrong, we all know that, we all may even freely admit that, but that gives you no right to break a board over him. If there was any board busting to be done, and I seriously doubt it, I would have been the one to do it. . . ."

And by this time everyone was beginning quietly to enjoy themselves, even Dawes. His mother was bent, holding his dazed head in her lap, and he knew he didn't give a damn what Arthur thought any more. He wasn't the least fearful of him now; and he was free, almost feeling good about it all, when he looked suddenly into Gin's tremendous eyes and he thought he could hear her saying:

"I'd rather have a grandson of mine dead, six foot under and buried, than ever once in his lifetime hear him talk to his grandfather like that. Do you hear me, Dawes? Six foot under and gone," she said. And for a moment her voice was a radio, something real and present and horrible working within the lines and tight veins roping her face. She had turned on him out of nowhere.

She got up and entered the house, moving slowly. Leone was embarrassed. Dawes felt betrayed and ashamed.

"Now, Mother," Leone said after her, "it's not that bad. It simply isn't *that* important. Besides, it's finished now. It's all over and let's just forget it. It would be better forgotten . . . ."

He spent all that remained of that day wandering in the fields. They were all gone, behind him now; and after they left, he had lit out from that hill as though it were burning down.

He moved back and forth. The earth was soundless and warm. He hid out, lay low in the thick rows and black furrows. It was dark, cool, green as a house. The tall stalks blew over his head, vining. The light moved across the tops of hills, down into the green, quilt-crazy fields of weaving corn. Occasionally he startled huge jacks, running outside the bounds of Arthur's fences. The fields were nets to catch him. He moved for hours, escaping, living wild in the world. He followed tracks left in the soft earth, the rainy ground by a clubfooted jack. He was a tracker.

His name was Jackrabbit Davis and he lived in a hole in the woods.

He was a tracker in the low fields and the tracings took him across fences, but hardly ever near roads, and he heard red tractors steaming in the distances all afternoon. They glistened in the sunlight like metal shells. They were casings without hearts, chewing the land. Coughing kerosene, they spit it back. They were caterpillars with smoking stacks, gliding down to the river without needing the water. He watched them all afternoon, and once he lay hidden under a fencerow listening to himself watching a man cross his barnyard and enter a house. He was unknown, hidden. Near evening he broke out of the woods near the river. . . .

The river was the evening and he was Jackrabbit Davis. He came across some hounds. Red Man, Fawn Cop and Blue Hat's Lady had slipped their fences and were nosing the last light from the water. They were great stone dogs, turned in the sun. He sat in the rushes and waited for dark. The river was a great drifting cow. The insects whined higher than racing clocks. The high grasses blew over themselves, a dream of weeds blackening the banks. The stone dogs pranced on the water. They kicked holes in the surfaces. They were crazy, dancing together. He sat watching them. Their bodies were flutes, magic, snakes growing legs and weaving the tracing wind. They were crazy, waiting for the bones of moon in the water to come rolling home. He would miss them.

High trees tall as dark poles of wind rowed over. Taking off his shoes, he ran naked-footed for awhile with the dogs in the river. They were mad with splashing. They recognized him. It was early evening, the heat a rising mirror, and more dogs came down from the corn and the woods. The moon was thin, transparent as tape. Soon they were all running wildly. The dogs were his brothers, rattling pans, opening the night like playhouses and calling him in.

On the far bank, near the junkyard of hanging sun, was a pile of rocks. Higher on a nearby tree, partly translated, it was written: JACQUES GRILLEAU DIED HERE OF FEVER, 1820, EN PRIÈRE SUR LA TERRASSE. He had dug a summer ago for three afternoons. It was buried directly under the pile of stones all the time. It had been hiding out. He had dug up the skull. It was a moon, faint with light; only a rotten pot for growing hollow seeds and flowers. He decided it was really an Indian. He had wrapped it in some old rags and pieces of blankets and hid it in the elm at first. It was treasure. But last summer it was gone; and now, again, he crossed the river to see if perhaps it had somehow returned. It hadn't. The dogs, he thought, have got it and carried it off in the corn to chew it into black pieces of wind, earth, fire and moon . . . .

He seemed to have been moving for hours, but it was effortless and gliding. The dogs around him were running in the same direction. If they were dancing in circles, they seemed to be sightless, and swaying. Once he almost lay down in the tanglewood to sleep, but then he saw it, the single hill, a black rose rising and vined in the dull light.

Standing below, the ends of the thin branches were like hair in the moon. The house was fallen. He hurried up the banks, climbing with his hands. He fell over a large section of porch. It was propped into the hill; buried like a monumental nesting, a sculpture of wild, flying birds. The house seemed to be slipping down into the erosion before it, splitting the hill. Pushing the dirt away, he saw the wood was paintless but ornately carved; a piece of window framing rested against it. There was an oak door, carved on too, and a piece of knob as fat as the top of a cane. The light shredded the wood. He threw it into the darkness. His pants were torn and he could feel cold blood drying on his legs. He slipped, tearing furiously at the ground. Large sections came loose as hinges and made small earth slides behind him.

He broke into a sea of grass and he tripped on a chicken. He stood cursing in the clearing. It was nested easily in a hollow carved in the fat grass and suddenly the field was soft against him, alive almost, after the climb through the brush of the hillside. The hen broke into the low surface of night, fleeing, screaming for justice and murdered eggs. Her high, mad cackle followed behind. The night closed again. Then, turning, he could see it was still again across the flats of grass and he began moving toward the long shadow of the house.

The owls ticking, haunting the clock . . .

Stopping, he sat under a blowing hickory, watching it move. Now at the top he could see it wasn't a hill at all; it continued out, a new level, a cliff of black dirt, flowers and weeds, and a stretch of level ground lying back evenly into the distance before him.

He saw it in the burned ends of wind—the old stone house made of brick, standing and risen with falling. It was a shell without the vital parts, beatless, without muscle or organs. It was large, three-storied, with a flat roof and an ornate cornice, and it seemed to have windows stuck to it everywhere, strange windows, nearly six feet tall and a foot wide.

Dawes, it said. The door said, Dawes.

He began moving around it and then crossed the rotting boards of the porch. It was a piece of toy house, a piece of broken glass, torn apart in a fit of anger. He moved through the doorless entry, began wandering the dark rooms, where sightless yellow figures were trapped in walls, staring back from the lilies of speechless stones. The faces of the old people hung in the gray, open grates of the fireplaces. The wind wailed easily, breathing, making complete circuits through the walls. He moved before himself on plankings, watching his blood run through his ears.

He kicked a pig in the darkness. It was a pig in a sleeping kitchen and, exploding with noise, filling the night, the distance with a large wing and key of squeals as the dark, unknown pig broke across the hollow flooring and out into the grass. And it was then, in the kitchen listening to him go, that Dawes was sure his heart had exited his mouth, and bounced for awhile on the ceiling, and jumped over the roof.

He stood there, wanting to move. Something was rowing above. The window was a moon, nested, fanned with thick, dark edges, hats of straw and cooing chickens. Finally, back in the long central hallway, he followed the drift of the walls. Bumping the sides, he listened to the conversations, the deep stone Indians and whispering animals within. He was completely sightless now, the white bloom of the moon vanished. He went down, hand by hand, the long echo of hallway air until he found the cold stairwell with broken railings and he began going up. The well was ascending, soundless, cracking black at the center. For awhile he thought he was dead. He was full of a violence that had no noise. He felt he was watching himself being watched, but people lived here. They must have. He was almost sure of it now. It was a real dream. They had walked here, the same rooms, he knew it. He was their sound. . . .

Dawes, it said. Spelled in stone, wrought in leafy moonlight like rainy horsemen. The door was a gate.

Upstairs he wandered the bedrooms and the small deserted parlors. And in one last, vacant parlor, before the circular attic window, near the open door leading like a thin keyhole to a tiny porch, he found the one chair, the only piece of furniture in the house. It sat blowing in the deserted light. He was behind it, and a white shaft of naked light split it in halves. It was a rocker, placed directly into the oval opening of the window, and it seemed to row itself with flat, steady rhythms in the wind.

He looked suddenly to his left. The night, its sound, its beat and heart went suddenly still. The wind was a rush of blood. His heart exploded in his mouth. It was dry, tasted of salt and green walnut shells fried in the sunlight.

To his left Abigail Winas was slumped in the sleeping rocker . . . .

He thought he had died and was gone already into some deep hole in the woods.

Instinctively he crouched low, froze, caught himself up under the muscle of the flooring and within the corner's wall. He could hear himself holding his breathing inside.

From his corner he could see her form bend like a weed into the bowing rocker. The moon was twisted, a streaked wood moving across her face making it seem pitted with holes, dark holes, running into a deep, uncertain surface, and he could see she was wrapped tightly in an old blanket. She seemed dead and, watching her harmless form make no motion, he thought she was fixed safely beyond sleeping, when suddenly, with the quick alarm and motion of a startled cat, *she moved.*

It was then he knew his heart hadn't jumped over the roof. It had jumped over the moon, because her head revolved, quick on a swivel almost, separate from her body almost. Separate even, he thought, from her mind. And her ears seemed to sense him, stand away from the sides of her head, out, like the ruffled fur of a small, frightened animal's. . . . as her face turned, violently almost, into the light leaving only white shadows in the hollows of her eyes and nose and lips. He knew suddenly that she was retribution, that she was going to take out her chicken knife and cut out his throat, his heart, that she was going to murder him and run through the naked, thinning woods . . . . Then she sighed and relaxed. She went back into the easy sway of her chair. And he knew that she wouldn't have ever murdered him anyway, not her; that it had been only a sudden trick, a reflex of his mind.

He lay waiting, watching her. She broke the air with the stroke of her chair. She cackled again. And in the dark she began beating time on the wood, the flooring, tapping her foot in a violent, disconnected, idiot's version of 1/1 time . . . . She was humming.

Dawes wanted to run. He figured, flying the fields, he could be at Arthur's in six point two seconds easy. He figured, if he could only be permitted to move, he would be the cleanest angel-sonofabitch who ever lived. He figured if he ever got started, he'd be gone so fast he'd never look back. And, sitting there in his blood, he could still hear her cackle. Her laugh, he thought, was mad as history.

He nearly relaxed, slumped in his corner. He knew he was finished, finally leaving all of this behind and forgetting it once and for all. But then, just as he was feeling better about it all, just as his blood quit singing so loud he could begin to hear himself thinking again, just as he settled easily into the nest of his corner, she went and spoiled it all. She spoke, breaking the wheel of air, his dreaming, startling even the round light in the window.

"Abigail," she said, "there must be an old rabbit moving in the house. I heard him breathing like a dude. Well, maybe we'll just have to get out our knife and skin him out. That is, if we can git'm. . . ."

She hummed a low, organed sound. He could feel it again running high wheels, pins of light in his blood. He said nothing at all. He thought perhaps it was another game. He sat watching her rock. Her sound was deeper now, and he lay listening, scanning her vague face for positive sign. He wondered why he didn't speak, but knew he wouldn't. Seemingly for hours he lay, checked, still as stone untying its own ends in the corner of his great-great's flooring. Once, stopping, almost waking, she said:

"We mustn't forget a chicken on our way home, Abigail . . . . I do hope that Dawes Williams will come and see us sometime . . . . We must keep our strength up . . . . Our blood is turning . . . . He may be a good one, mad as a hat, sane . . . . Oh, I hope so . . . . I guess we are dead . . . . Sunday dinner though . . . . Yes, Captain Jackson S. Thompson Fifteen is a rooster who is ready to go . . . . I hope he'll remember someday . . . a few months more . . . . Our blood is starting to turn . . . . Those needles were never for knitting, they're sign . . ." she said, breaking off, rocking quietly.

She drifted off again. He thought she might be sleeping, dead even. It was then he could feel all of the blood left in his body running in one spot, over the ends of his windpipe. He wasn't frightened any more; he was only finished. He was somewhere else, dreaming with her.

He wanted to cross that space and touch her. But he didn't, couldn't; something was holding him to his single board, a rotten sway of immaculate flooring.

Then, suddenly, she moved again. She got up slowly from her chair. With an old length of rope she tied the rocker to her back and began moving across the room in the attic shadows.

"Well," she said, "we'll take our chair now. We'll not need it here any more. We'll not be coming here any more. It's been a lot of damn, foolish years . . ." she said.

It was then Dawes Williams could feel all of the blood in his body spring back, alive again. He followed her step with his eyes. Her heavy slide cracked stray pieces of glass, wood-sounding, dead. Her chair moved side to side in the stairwell. He could hear her wandering below in the house and he thought: She is moving in the house, the old stone, in all of the rooms, as if she were saying goodbye to them all, the spaces themselves; as if she were leaving on a train for somewhere, never coming back. She is moving in the house as if she were decorating herself, pausing awkwardly before mirrors, putting on a red felt hat with naked chicken feathers pasted to the edges, and rolling the stockings finally up past her knees. . . .

Finally she began crossing out onto the porch. And when Dawes Williams finally moved, he didn't move, he merely collapsed on his flooring. Then he let out a sail of air, and moved to the window, replacing her there. She paused below and stomped the night from her foot. The sound was clean and died over the bluff; the moonlit sway of the clearing, the open trees and black mooncorn beyond.

The old blanket was wrapped around her. The chair was tied off backwards with ropes to her shoulders and hanging down. She seemed a circus departing in hats.

Then suddenly, letting the chair slip loose with a sound shattering the surface of the night, she broke from the plankings and began chasing a chicken through the squawking woods.

The night burst open, higher than airplanes. Caught through his railings, he could see her form rise and drop back, running, chasing the noise into holes of light in the woods, coming out again, her sound running behind the whiter form of the frantic chicken. And in the end she rearose for the last time, with the bleating whiteness held high over her head. It was a victory of circles. The chicken was a bleeding heart of light, a squawking baton. She stood, holding it high in the air, and she began whipping it around in quick, unfastening circles until the neck broke and the heavier body fell to the ground.

Quietly she began plucking it in a clearing of light. The limp feathers fell like a chaos of small rain, leaving only a circular patch of whiteness around her. Continuing to pluck, she took a knife from beneath her blanket and gutted the bird. It held the amazed sound of warm air being let from a knotted sacking. She flung hunks of gut to the ground, and finally cast the fleshed husk onto the seat of the rocker with a hollow sound.

Retying the chair to her back, she began to sink downward into the shallow ravine seaming the side of the house. She seemed to slink off into shadows. She was laughing her idiot cackle that rode high in the air. Suddenly it seemed a meaningless effort. Stopping short, she turned back along the edge of the house, into the high night of Dawes Williams' circular railings and, crying into the already shredding fabric, she said:

"Dawes Williams! —And this has been all brought to you by the legendary generosity of Captain Jackson S Thompson, Propagator and Primemover of Pieces. Dawes Williams! Why didn't you speak to me? You don't fool me for a minute," she said, "and I don't bite! —Dawes Williams, TAG, you are in that window now, and you happen to be it," she said laughing.

Her voice was a root, sailing, dusted, hollowed. He was its vase.

And, turning, she was gone.

And, turning, he lay on his back and watched the mad clouds sail patterns across the moon.

He was tired, finally giving in, and wanted only to rest on the destroyed balcony. He shinnied down the pipes and vines, onto the falling overhang. He wanted to forget, to lie back again and sleep.

It's this place, not me, Dawes Williams thought, I'm doin' fine.

Tomorrow he would find his way through the sun-drab rooms, down the black and slipping hill, and back into the brilliant grasses. Tomorrow he would pick his way over the slack hill facings and, coming to the dog pens, he would find them there, and he would pause, perhaps for the last time, to watch them rise, clean as unsaved things, and move down from their huts, scrubbed and faceless as ticking clocks. They would be everywhere, bursting their springs. The static from Gin's kitchen, her Sunday morning radio, would be coming over the hill, and the dogs would all be jumping frantically into the long wire of their fences as they saw him break over the last black rim of grass. No, he wouldn't show up till well past noon. Later, the greyhounds would be lying in the higher light, sunning themselves. A farm truck would be moving down the bright dust, swinging its cane of a cloud toward town. Perhaps a train would be moving before him on a flattened horizon. If it wasn't, he would invent one that did. But it would be Sunday morning and very still.

Coming down the last steep hill, he would circle Arthur's house. A few old golf balls, like eggs, would be deserted on the putting green. He would finally slide the diagonal of the black hill and enter the house. He didn't want to. But sooner or later, he knew it, he must enter that house. He didn't want to; he wanted to live out here forever in the real country with Arthur's wild jacks. But there would be that inevitable, frantic scene. Mixed with Gin's and Leone's joyous and damning questions, there would also be Arthur's stony withdrawal, Simpson's eyes. Arthur would never completely forgive him, not him. He knew you really only sin against Arthur Oldham once; you never get another chance. It didn't matter. He would not, of course, ever tell them about Abigail Winas. He would keep that part locked quietly inside himself, a wet seed, a black pit in the exact heart of bulbs never quite managing to mature or grow, locked deeply in speechless rock.

The day itself would eventually settle down, within the wall of Arthur's paper. And in the afternoon it would be time to start again for the city and Simpson's office. It would be a silent ride with none of them, not even Dawes, completely yet at ease with the fact of returning. They would drive through the dusky Iowa towns, rolling east. The rain, off behind in the west, would be darker and closing. It would have been silent, leaving in the lane. Gin would have forgiven him, not Arthur. And Arthur would be staring back down the line of his hill at his hounds, withdrawn into his stone, covered over and not even looking, once. Only the dogs would be frantic with the car's outgoing motion; nothing else. Perhaps, for the last time, they would be jumping into their wire fences, dreaming of motion everywhere on the hunting hill. And it would be the last time, because Arthur was thinking of finally retiring this winter, to Florida. It would be the last, because Arthur would be selling the farm out from under all of them. Things end quietly without notice, Dawes Williams thought; they just wind down without happening . . . because Arthur was selling the farm, what was left of his great-great's land, and they wouldn't be coming back this way, ever, none of them would . . . . The string was dying off, after fifty good years, becoming too inbred. One last promising litter of yearlings, seven pups in all, had been found frozen on the farm. Jake Skout had done it. He had had a red felt hat on his head and stockings that rolled past his knees, and was drunk in town. They had been frozen, tiny, furless, quivering hearts hooked out of huts in the winter. They were history, the final thing. But Arthur would never have lost a dog like that, never in fifty years, not once in a lifetime. Dawes knew that. Arthur would have fired Jake, or killed him, but what was the use? It was over and he'd just have gotten another just like him. He'd been putting up with men like Jake all his life; they sprang out of the ground like teeth. Arthur was bad, he knew, but provided for his living things; Abigail was good and butchered hers.

He didn't know.

The moon blew like mad reeds through rivers of clouds, moving off south without rain, and Arthur was pulling out and moving to Miami. What the hell is a place like Florida to me? Dawes Williams thought. It was vague, unimportant geography. One night late Dawes had heard Arthur and Simpson talking it over. Simpson was an accountant and would set it all up. He would handle the money, the papers, the liquidation. Dawes wouldn't be coming back here any more; no one would. It was the last summer for them all. Even Abigail Winas was dying. Tomorrow she would be moving in her dark coop of grass, the same circles, like always for awhile, lost in her fox-hung field and cooking her chicken in a deep Sunday pot. She would be roasting again the late Captain Jackson S. Thompson the Fifteenth. This place, Dawes Williams thought, has reeked with death. But they would be moving away. History was a hat, a pot to grow flowers in. And she would be moving here, in her own circles, walking the floor of her coop, talking to her heavily drying body. And it would never fuse; it had no greenness, no stem. It was only memory, a loose screen flapping in the wind, swinging on hinges of sound, something thinner than a singing; memory, finally only words, tricks to be pulled like red felt hats from stockings that rolled past your knees, a lie of halves, whole, not whole, impossible to touch, two things once and, soon, they would be pulling into the driveway again, and parking Simpson's car, behind the shadow of the Catholic's witchery, and Ronnie Crown, who had never left, would be sitting once again, mounted on Dunchee's wall, looking longingly already at Mrs. Lowbus' newly remade garage, thinking fondly of Halloween, of the only day in the year when you could be who you really were . . . and he would be throwing the wetted stick matches down in thin tails of German fighters, in fictive trails of smoking planes that would never really burn . . . and everything would be as it was, real, the same, changed, safe, and it would be late, on just another August evening smelling of rust and old nails and flowers and garages which had already burned, and somewhere, across a state, Abigail Winas would be sitting, too . . . watching it all move . . . watching her children of murdered chickens move onto the last red light, the wind becoming orange spinners of sleep and August becoming, finally, nothing, over and done. But that would be tomorrow, he thought, because now Dawes Williams was only lying on his back, watching the mad reeds of moon slip across the yellow clouds, in a thousand unnamed patterns of faceless sleep, and he would sleep, sleep in the old stone house sinking into the black farm, a worm of earth, and it would not be until dawn, until tomorrow, that he would have to be awake and moving again. Now he was only lying low, hiding out, missing already the dead voices of other summers calling behind pilings and leaving just the next county over, in Iowa, seeing the mad reeds slip the moon and thinking, yes, only the living could find a dream that fit as well as this . . .

BOOK TWO
Stones of Night
1956—1961

"Well, I tell ya—I think we're probably so goddamn beautiful out here, with nothing to do, that if we hadn't learned to effectively say screw it early in life, we'd probably be 'bout as crazy as Dawes Williams here."

—Travis Thomas in conversation with Eddie and Dunker.

"Oh-ya. I am a spy in the house all right."

—Dawes Williams' reply.

1

"Hell of a sweetmother universe," Dunker was saying drawing easily on his beer. "How can you think of something that hasn't got an end?"

"Everything has an end," Dawes Williams said.

"What do you know, Willy?" Eddie Welsh was saying. "You look mighty pissed-over to me."

Dawes didn't answer. He was eighteen then and very drunk, moving along with others, not thinking about himself because he hadn't done that in years. Turning, he saw that Dunker was sprawled like a moose over the bonnet of his six-thousand-dollar Ford, opening sloe gin, and watching him back; and that Eddie was suddenly up and running the footballs of empty beer cans along the dark edges of the quarry, and that Travis Thomas had pulled himself up against a tree and was resting quietly.

The air was soft, full of curtains of dung, warm udders, the undersides of cows, and it was August again.

The night, he thought, is my brother, a dwarf who rustles open the forest before me, calls me home, closes a center full of violet moon within me. I do not know him. Cars have started and died; begun again. Some were leaving to find girls, others were just driving around in the trees for the hell of it. Travis, Eddie, and Dunker were his truer brothers, brothers in the blood because they had nothing in common but experience. He did not know them. He knew he did not. The cold fish eyes of light out front of cars moved, rose, mowed down the stillness, fell away in the underbrush. Only I think this, he thought. Dawes Williams was very drunk.

A radio bloomed. Someone, B. J. Reedy perhaps, was tuning in *She Cried* by Jay and The Americans. Dawes stood, watching for minutes, as the rhythmic sweep of beer cans, bottles of sloe gin, Scotch and whiskey pints sailed into the small wash of the quarry water. Then turning to B. J. Reedy, Dawes Williams broke his long silence by saying:

"I hate that goddamn song. Turn that thing down. It sounds like sodomized burro droppings. If I hear that goddamn Jay and his Americans sing that goddamn *She Cried* once more, I'm going straight up that tree."

There were small patches of laughter over the water.

"Ya, Jay and his Americans can sing those songs," Dunker said slowly, those eyes watching him, that long edge of his giant's arm reaching out to fire an old sloe gin bottle into the black surface of inverted moon.

"Oh, Christ," Dawes Williams said, "I'm going out in the woods and pee on a log."

"Attttts Dawes," Travis Thomas said.

"Piss one for me, Willy," Eddie said.

B. J. Reedy said nothing at all. He only looked up through the heavy underlids of his eyes and smiled quietly. Dawes Williams lit a Lucky Strike and thought suddenly it was all grand. He walked higher in the woods, and watched some of the older, college guys like Hake Cutty, Dino Ravenelli, Flip Smith and Mike Cooper drive off in Dino's old green '50 Chevy to buy more whiskey and beer, and he thought they probably wouldn't be back. Some of the younger guys were fruiting around, talking about going over to Mike Hanna's garage where they had set up The Black Rabbit Casino Gaming Room to play cards and shoot dice all night. Barney Ingersoll and Jim Inge were hanging around and talking about hanging around and watching the game, and Danny Deeder, the best natural gambler in Rapid Cedar, was already angling for banking a session of black jack. Dawes stood listening to his pleasant, incessant con operating through the trees, the small hooded wash of the moon, the night, the water, the flaring lights moving in the trees. Eventually Danny Deeder and Mike Hanna and Peter Wolsey and Jim Inge and Barney Ingersoll and T. T. Calders and B. J. Reedy and Jasper Hally all moved off in B. T. Saus' father's convertible. B. T. Saus just turned round from his second bottle of Old Crow and said:

"O ma Gawd, they're stealing Four-Square's car."

Four-Square Saus was B. T.'s old man, a rich lumber dealer, and from his hill Dawes saw that B. T. had already turned back to the quarry and picked up the uninterrupted thread of his conversation with B. R. Bush, who was a foot and a half shorter than B. T. but built solid as oak. B. T. Saus, they all said, could drink that whiskey, and he had just sat there all night with a bucket of ice cubes, a canteen of water, and two bottles of Old Crow, smoking Camels, and talking hard and furious to B. R. Bush. Dawes Williams had sat nearby, but he and B. T. were always uneasy around each other as they had spent the last two and a half years both dancing like alternating yo-yos on Summer Letch's string. They never fought over her, however, and this was what made them uneasy, as they always wondered why they hadn't and if they should. Dawes Williams thought all of that was probably all right anyway, as B. T. Saus had six inches or better on him and probably thirty-five pounds; besides, Dawes thought, he wasn't going to lose himself over a damn cunt like Summer Letch, whom he still loved, nevertheless, with a pure and abiding passion, as clean as Dante's almost, no, sir, not if he could help it . . .

The night began winding over the moon. It was deeper out in the fields now. Dawes' three best buddies—Dunker Nadlacek, Eddie Welsh, and Travis Thomas himself—called him over in the drawn-in dark of the far trees to talk over their plans. Tonight was one of their last nights together as soon they would be moving off, in opposite directions, to college. Tonight was the night they would spring it on that damn sonofabitch farmer Cotter for sure.

"Git yer ass over here, Dawes!" Eddie yelled.

"Ya, Willy," Dunker added, "we got to have some plans and serious hatchings laid on us over here."

"Atttttsssssss Dawes Williams," Travis said.

Dawes got up and moved to the other side of the quarry. He walked over the cold stones in his canvas shoes, stopped to throw rocks in the water, acting casual, thinking that this was the first place they had gotten drunk together, three years before. Approaching the small fire, he saw the rest of the guys his age—Ratshit Rawlings, Terry Murray, Mike Eagle, Tom Olsen, the all-state basketball player, Turk O'Hara, the others, even Barney Redwood carrying his bottle of apricot brandy—were moving off in groups, back to the party on the lawn of the Woods twins' house.

"Aren't you guys coming?" Tom Olsen said.

"Fuck no," Eddie said, "you pussy-whipped assholes go ahead."

"Com'on Tray," Mike Eagle said.

"No," Travis said, "I think I'll hang around here for awhile. Me and the fellas have something to do tonight."

"We'll see ya, Willy," Barney Redwood said, moving to his Ford, wrapping his brandy in his jacket.

"See ya, Barney," Dawes Williams said, moving away from him.

"Okay, see ya," everybody said.

"Ya, see yer ass," Eddie said.

As soon as they left, Dunker turned to Eddie and said:

"Now how can you call those pussy-whipped assholes pussy-whipped assholes, when you happen to be the biggest pussy-whipped asshole in town?"

"Kiss my ass, Dunker," Eddie said.

"Kiss my ass, Eddie," Dunker said.

"Why the hell would Dunker want to kiss your ass, Eddie?" Dawes Williams said.

"Atttttssssss Dawes," Travis Thomas said. "Why don't you all shut up. We have other things to do tonight you know than just sitting here bitching at each other."

So they all shut up for awhile and began thinking of other things. They began looking over the motion of the flat water and the dark stones. Dunker went for another case of beer and three sacks of ice from the trunk of his Ford. Dawes settled in against a gray outcropping of cold rock and thought the night was just another field of silence; lying beyond.

"Tonight we get that Cotter for sure, right Travis?" Dunker said.

"That's right," Travis Thomas said, "nobody shoots at Travis Thomas and gets away with it for long."

"That was two years ago," Dawes Williams said.

"Hell, Dawes," Travis said, "we might be splitting up tonight. I like a sense of completeness about the things I do."

"That's so," Eddie said. "Travis is right."

"Fuck me," Dunker said, "Travis is always right."

They laughed quietly over that for a while, and drifted off. Dawes sat watching the blue water, the pure washing stone in Coachman's Quarry.

Dunker was watching him again. He handed him another beer, hooking empties into the water, and said:

"Not the universe, you ignorant bastard, Dawes. The universe hasn't got end or beginning. Everybody knows that. Jesus."

"That's dogma both ways," Travis said. "Neither of you know either side of it for sure."

"That's absurd," Dawes Williams said.

"What's absurd about it?" Eddie said. "That sounds fucking reasonable to me."

They were still talking, off somewhere, but Dawes decided he wasn't listening any more. He only drifted back, hearing a train making passes on high gray trestles to the south, making it all whole again for awhile. He was an old man then, he decided, nearly nineteen.

"It's absurd," he said again, sensing something was waiting on him, "because either it does or it doesn't or it doesn't matter. In any case, if there's one thing Absolute left, it's the universe."

"What are you talking about, Dawes?" Travis said.

"I don't know. But I'm drunk as hell I tell ya."

"That's what I said," Eddie said. "Let's blow this Cotter's farm out from under him by midnight and get some ass."

"That's what I said," Dawes said. "It's absurd. It's absurd because it sounds like something reasonable, like something Simpson would say. I think he's been reading a lot of William James lately."

"Christ," Eddie said, looking away.

"Shut up, Dawes," Travis said. "You're wrecking the drunk."

"God, I'm drunk," Dawes Williams said. "I'm so drunk I'm dying of lung cancer. It's going all wrong on me."

Looking up, over his beer, Dawes could see Dunker was watching him again, nearly leaning into him, so he continued by saying:

"Dunker, it was my mother that showed me how. She's been dying of lung cancer now for twenty-five years. She taught me how. Everytime something goes wrong she goes to the exact center of her bedroom and says, 'Leave me alone. I'm dying of lung cancer.' She showed me how to die of lung cancer without even fainting."

Dunker stared back, laughing, nearly choking on his beer, and Dawes Williams looked away at the water. His eyes were very nearsighted and his hair was cropped close to his skull. He stared into the heavy water and thought it would be winter soon; another summer stone evaporated into dustless cold. He thought, looking back on it from a century of time, that he must have been born in a manger of poor but simple Midwestern yeoman stock; that Arthur was still loose and aloof in his roof somewhere, waiting, grayfaced, Nordic, thundering; that his mother was a virgin and his father a C.P.A.; that he loved Summer Letch still with a pure and abiding passion, like oil on a surface of fire, and that he was very drunk and moving on.

"This is not prologue. I'm finished. It's dogma," Dawes said to Dunker, but Dunker was dribbling cans over the water and wasn't listening.

"God's box," Eddie said. "What's dogma?"

"Dogma's a great mama dog with warm nipples, sitting on your head," Dawes said.

"No, dogma's something you believe in when you don't know any better," Travis said. "Like Catholics."

"That's what I said," Dawes said. "And it sure beats trying to arrive at dogmatic pragmatism."

"You asshole," Travis said.

"Frogs screw underwater and hatch on rocks," Eddie said. "So what?"

Dunker said nothing at all. He only sat watching Dawes Williams with a small amazement. The water swayed, leafless with summer, off with the moon. Small fish ran after . . .

"What's the matter?" Dunker said, hooking another can. "Doesn't anyone believe in Science any more?"

"Science can take care of itself," Dawes Williams said.

"I didn't come out here to talk about Science and Religion," Eddie said. "I came out here to get drunk on my ass."

"The universe is now a Mr. Wizard saysitsso," Dawes said.

"Mr. Wizard, hell," Dunker said. "Haven't you got any respect left for progress? For immensity?"

"I got respect for me," Dawes Williams said. "I made the universe, didn't I? If I died, it would vanish wouldn't it?"

There was a silence on that one. Dunker, whose father was a surgeon and a scientist, drew down half a beer without ever taking his eyes off Dawes, without ever raising them over the frozen lid of the can, watching him as if he were studying something, as if he were thinly impressed, generally bored, and suddenly struck by the heavy, dull edges of time come upon only cornered in rooms watching wet Wednesday afternoons wash white windows gray as skies. Dawes ignored himself, studying his own watching.

"Mr. Wizard," Eddie said, sensing a lapse, "never knew his ass from steelies."

Laughter, a dark field of it, rose softly against the windcorn. Small mites and water fish, bodies of air, shuttled off in the black turnings of earth; approaching rain, inverted wind and undersky. Dawes sat listening to cow sounds, a thousand wet herds, climb over the quiet roads which ran immediately, nowhere, over the hill and down the pike, into the King's Road, into only the next county over in Iowa, where it was probably already winter, snowing on barns, raining wind on drenched and ruined hounds, on cold and foreign things, running forms, animals swimming over living bluffs. In just twenty-seven counties over, he thinks, someone is still mocking drama.

"Hey Travis," Dunker was saying, "I hear Dawes Williams here lives in a room."

"I hear he never comes out except to pee in his hat," Eddie said.

"That's so," Travis said.

"Can't you ever think of something besides the sordid act of me going off somewhere to wizz, Welsh?" Dawes Williams said.

"Kiss my ass," Eddie said.

"That Dawes Williams," Dunker said slowly, musing it over, "he just sits out there in the dark thinking about nothing."

"You can't tell about him any more," Travis said, warming up to it, "you just can't. He has his good days, but he's changed. All different."

"I hear you're sneaking books out of the library and reading them by flashlight at night in your room, Willy," Eddie said.

"Hell," Dunker said, "the other afternoon I spent most of my valuable time listening to Dawes Williams here trying to tell me all about some broad named Gertrude Stein who used to live over in Paris."

"He's nuts all right," Eddie said.

"Jesus. I said: 'What's that all about?' He couldn't tell me. He just walks around all day trying to scribble things onto paper, like he was an accountant or some damn thing. So I say—'Let's get some beer and go down by the river and get tan.' He says, 'No.' I say—'Let's go over to Diana Joyce's house, there's girls over there,' He says, 'No.' I say—'Let's get out our pistols and pot some squirrels.' He says, 'No.' I say—'Let's shoot pool then.' I knew that would get him. He says, 'No.'"

"Shut up, Dunker," Travis said, smiling, "and let Dawes Williams here get on with this damn dreaming of his that's messing him up."

"It's yours, too," Dawes said.

"Like hell," Travis said, "it's got nothing to do with me."

"Like hell," Dawes Williams said.

"You can't tell about him any more," Dunker was saying. "He's changed. He just walks around all day scribbling things onto paper. I say— 'Dawes, can I read what you have messed on that paper today?' He says, 'No.' I say—'Why not? Is it dirty stuff?'—but he doesn't answer."

"It's yours, too," Dawes said. "God, I'm drunk."

"The hell," Travis said, "not mine. It's yours and nobody else's."

"It is," Dawes Williams said.

"The hell," Travis said, "I wouldn't step into that room of yours on a bet— even if I *had* the damn moongoggles for it."

"Like I say," Dunker said, "his pockets are full of crumpled paper. The windowsills in his room are full of blowing paper. I say—'Why the hell would you do something like that?' He doesn't answer me. What the hell. He's my friend, I've known him a long time, but he's nuts as hell. Right now he's just sitting over there in the dark thinking about nothing."

"Shut up, you assholes," Dawes Williams said dramatically. "I think I am breaking down again."

"I think Dawes Williams is crying," Travis said.

"I think Dawes Williams is a dink," Eddie said. "I think it's time we forgot about Cotter, and started stamping out crazy Willy Williams."

There was a long silence on that one. Everyone began looking at Dawes Williams. Even Dawes began doing that, and it made him uneasy.

"Oh, Christ," he said. "I believe the Huns have me cornered on this one."

"That's it," Travis said, "I'll kill him! Where's the sonofabitch trying to escape this time! I'll kill him!"

And as soon Dunker and Eddie and Travis Thomas had Dawes down on the ground and were pounding him around quietly, and Eddie was stealing scribble paper out of his pockets, and Travis and Dunker were heaving him into the quarry like the bowing ribs of old sacks. Soon he was standing hunched over in the water, calling for a cigaret, watching as Dunker and Travis threw Eddie in after him; and as Dunker and Travis finally succeeded in throwing each other in behind Eddie; and as Dunker waded out with large strides to get dry matches so that they could all stand in the exact middle of the pond reading the crumpled paper Eddie had swiped from Dawes' pocket. As it all turned out it was only a letter from Summer Letch, but that was enough:

"Christ," Dawes Williams stood dripping, saying, "I think I've been raped and had at the same time . . . Who got my fly?"

"Shut up, Willy," Travis said, "I'm trying to hold matches for Dunker here, so he can read your mail . . ."

Dunker was bent over in the water, using Eddie for a reading desk as Eddie was standing erect between Dunker's slumped arms, reading furiously, facing the same direction, as Travis stood nearby lighting matches in the wind. Dawes Williams moved slightly off and sat down in the water. He felt suddenly like pissing his pants, and the place went absolutely still as Dunker read:

My own Dawes,

Hi! O, Dawes, guess what, honey? I got my hair cut today! I hope it will please you. (Big man!) Probably won't tho. Dawes, do you realize we still won't see each other for *two more weeks!!!?!?????!!!!!* How can I last? Can you sweetie? I hope not. Even if you can, you better not tell me. You'd make your Summer mad at her Dawes!?!

My grandmother said for me to tell you 'hello.' Hello, Dawes. Isn't that sweet? O 'damn' this place anyway. I miss you.

Dawes, have you been 'good'?

Mother and Dad are impossible. They still don't know what they want to do. Dad wants to go to Wisconsin, and Mother wants to stay in Minnesota. O Dawes, what am I going to do!? I may be going 'mad'!!!???!!!

"O Dawes! O Dawes! What am I going to do! What am I going to do!" Eddie was screaming, running wildly through the shallow water, flailing his arms, howling at the moon, slightly drunk and wobbling off center— "I'm going mad! Mad! Mad!" he said.

"Dawes," Travis said, "I believe you've found yourself a simple one here for sure."

Dunker continued reading:

Dawes, I miss you, and I don't (*absolutely*) want to stay in Minnesota. All there is is fish, (Ick!), leeches, beer and baseball!!! O fudge.

Dawes I feel I really miss you. You're my honey and I love ya. The other night my grandmother heard me talking in my sleep. All she could make out was "Darling Darling." Well, well. What could I have been dreaming about there?

I love you, Dawes, see you soon (I hope),

Summer

P.S.

"P.S.! P.S.!" Dunker yelled, laughing, spinning furiously in the water. "P.S.! P.S.! P.S.! Christ! This is out of control!?! How does Dawes Williams here always wind up with some space-headed girl like Summer Letch!"

Then he continued to read on, through a broken and breaking voice, into the final P.S.:

P.S. Dawes!
("Dawes!! Dawes!! Dawes!!Dawes!!Dawes!!" Eddie was screaming three blocks out in a field.)

P.S. Dawes!! Let's make a deal—I'll be a good girl and you be a good boy, but the minute you're a bad boy, I'll automatically know, long distance, then you'll know (automatically) I'm already being a bad girl.

Only a silence, the fall of Dunker's last words, still as death itself, remained hanging over the quarry. Dawes Williams, still off at a slight distance, sat in the water, holding his head. Eddie had wandered back in from the field. Travis had already emerged and was sitting on a rock. Dunker stood in the exact middle of the pond, hand dropped, the letter still draped in his fingers, like an oratorical statue of a Confederate General beset with pigeon dropping and wind. Finally Dawes Williams roused himself from the sudden stupor and said:

"Well, it's a con, of course, so how do you figure this one: Christ, I love that girl."

Then it all broke loose again flying its hinges, as Dunker had already dissolved with laughter into the small surface of the water; and Eddie sat straight down in the mud; and Travis had nearly fallen off his rock. Then Dunker waded out of the water, green and dripping and looking around, tall as a house, and, walking straight to the hood of his six-thousand-dollar, flame-jobbed Ford, he was just as suddenly out of control and rolling right off its side. Travis and Eddie began throwing mud balls at Dawes, who was still in the water and catching half of them and throwing them back at the dark and the voices, and he was still trying to bend down into the shallow water, feeling in the soft green mosses for his glasses, not finding them, swearing, when Dunker got on his knees and managed:

"That's it! I'm a dead man. A goner. Shovel dirt on my head, Travis. I'm a goner! Swear to God, Travis, Dawes just broke my mind. Swear to God. Just shovel me over. I'm callin' it quits!"

"I believe you got yourself another real simple one there, Dawes," Travis said abstractedly, still throwing mud balls at the water.

"Git'm. Git'm, the silly sonofabitch," Eddie was saying.

"Leave him alone," Dunker said.

"All right. That's it!" Dawes Williams said, moving from the water, thinking seriously of trying to punch Eddie, not Travis, in the teeth. "That's it! Who the hell hit me with a rock!"

"Who hit Dawes Williams in the head with a rock!" Dunker said, throwing a beer can at a tree.

"Maybe I did," Travis said.

"Fucking-A," Eddie said, "you want to fight about it?"

"Fucking-A-Huey-Longfellow's ass, ya maybe," Dunker said.

There was another silence on that one.

"Dawes," Dunker said, "go over there and punch Eddie out."

"How would you like a piece of lumber on your head, Dawes?" Eddie said.

"How's he coming through here to Eddie?" Travis said.

"That won't be any problem, Travis," Dunker said, turning against him.

There was another silence, and Dunker and Travis began looking at one another curiously. Dawes knew Eddie could outpunch him, but that he could wrestle him down and break his head with a rock anyway. Travis and Dunker, however, didn't know what to make of each other, and had stayed clear of each other since two summers ago when Dunker grew six inches in three months. Before that, Travis Thomas could have ended the whole thing by taking sides with anyone at all. Dunker and Travis shuffled quiet marks in the dirt before them for a long time, not looking away, and then Dunker said:

"What do you think, Dawes?"

"Well," Dawes Williams began, "I think a lot of things."

"What!?!"

"Well, one, I think this is a lot of crappy John Wayne stuff. Two, friends don't kick themselves around this way. And three, who gives a shit?"

Then, without ever taking his eyes off Travis Thomas, Dunker began looking at Dawes Williams with a very contorted and pained look on his face.

"Dawes," he said, "that's about the dumbest thing I've ever heard."

"Could be," Dawes said.

"No 'could' about it," Travis said.

"Kiss my ass, Travis," Dawes Williams said.

"Kiss my ass, Dawes," Travis Thomas said.

"Let's have another goddamn beer," Eddie said.

"Oh help," Dunker said, walking away, "I need a drink."

Soon they were sitting around the small fire, drying out, watching the black water wash over the stone, and Travis was saying:

"Hell, guys should fight their enemies, not their buddies. Besides, I didn't want to bust you up, Dunker. You're my friend."

"I'd have broken you like a stick, Thomas," Dunker said, not looking up from the fire.

"Bullshit!" Eddie said.

"How would you know?" Dawes Williams said, staring straight across at him.

Dunker had gotten out a bottle of wine, a dry Anjou Rosa he had swiped from his father, and everyone was feeling very warm except for Dawes Williams, who was sitting hunched and shivering in an old horse blanket. They scuffed around in the dirt and threw stones in the water and smoked cigars for awhile. Then Dawes Williams began studying the sky and said:

"Looks like rain off to the north."

"What are you—a pioneer forchristsake?" Eddie said.

"Go to hell, Eddie," Dunker said.

"I'll follow you down, you big freak," Eddie said.

They sat silently again, washing their wine down with beer, and after awhile Travis began stirring the fire with a stick, looking around the circle, saying:

"Yep, you should fight with your enemies, not with your friends."

"Think of Winston Churchill," Dawes Williams said.

"How can I make peace if you persist in talking like a damn fool?" Travis said, spitting into the fire.

"Here, Dawes," Dunker said, digging around in the sand, "here's your damn letter."

"Big deal," Eddie said, "fuck Dawes."

"Hmmmmm," Dawes said, not listening, musing over his dark papers in the firelight. "Her passion does seem to be strangely ambiguous in places. It's damn suspicious."

Dunker hooked another beer can into the quarry, refusing to pay any attention.

"That's fifteen," he said. "God, Dawes Williams is drunk."

"I can't help it I love Summer Letch," Dawes Williams said.

"What is this," Travis said, "a damn baseball game?"

"Fifteen," Eddie said.

"P.S.," Dunker said, "that was about the most piss-poor, half-assed P.S. I ever heard in my life."

"How'd you meet that girl Summer, Dawes?" Travis said.

"You remember, Travis," Dawes says, "it was that night just after Dunker finished telling us how he lost his virginity."

"Hell, yes," Dunker said, "I was talking about the buttons of the universe."

There was a silence as portentous as hung stone strung over the air of the quarry.

"I remember," Eddie said.

"Big frigging deal," Dunker said.

"I still don't know how you managed it," Dawes said. "I mean six foot nine, and in the front seat of a convertible, and in a drive-in movie—no experience or anything."

"Oh, Christ," Travis said, "that was two summers ago."

"So was Cotter," Dawes Williams said. "Everything happened that night."

"That's different," Travis said.

"Hell, yes," Eddie said, remembering, "that was the night Dunker said: 'Her cunt was the center of the known universe.' I remember that well."

"He said it was a button," Dawes said.

"Jesus H. Christ," Eddie said.

"Well, it was," Dunker said. "It was like a tight button of light locked in the exact center of the known, scientific universe."

"Oh, my god," Dawes Williams said, "now I know why there is a bulldozer parked in Ratshit Rawlings' front yard."

"That's right, Willy," Dunker said. "I put it there. I can now inductively hot-wire anything that moves at will."

"A button?" Travis Thomas said.

"A clit, for Christsake," Dawes Williams said.

"And that was Cotter's fifth mistake," Dunker said.

"Hell, yea," Travis said, "he cut Dunker off in midsentence, in the greatest sentence he had ever made in his life, when he fired that shotgun of his."

"What were his other four mistakes?" Eddie said.

"What is this, a damn black catechism?" Dawes said.

"Hell, yes," Dunker said, "I was talking about the button of the universe."

"After we get through running him around his own tree," Travis said, "his first mistake tonight was even getting born in the first place."

"This is our last night all right," Dawes said.

"Ya," Eddie said, "tomorrow we're off to college."

"What are you going finally, Tray?" Dunker said.

"Think I'm going Phi Delt," Travis Thomas said.

"That'll be nice," Dawes Williams said. "I think I'm going to hell."

"That's no shit, Dawes," Travis said, "you're all shot through."

"I'm a dead man all right," Dawes Williams said.

"What is this," Dunker said, "you never looked any particularly worse than you do right now."

"That's right," Dawes Williams said, "I'm doing fine."

The night drifted off again, big and formless as the coming rain. The beer was cold, a perfect sound, and it foamed up springlike whenever the opener snapped the tin, clearly reminding Dawes, suddenly, that he had nearly not graduated from high school.

"All sound" (Dawes remembered Mr. Peter Beaker, the physics teacher, saying) *"is a mere physical wave, a concussion that rolls in the air. In this sense, then,"* Mr. Peter

continued, boring hell out of Dawes Williams, who was trapped in his forgettable room, "sound is a tangible. Physical! Attainable! Realizable! Energy, you see, is not lost, only lost in the sense that it is transformed, but not lost. So. So," he said, busting his suspenders, twirling his bow tie, "so if you could only invent a machine that would possess the capability of rescrambling transmutated energy, you could, theoretically, mind you, in principle, listen to, say, Lincoln's Gettysburg Address as pronounced by Lincoln himself."

"Excuse me," Dawes Williams said, raising his hand, "but what has this to do with Walt Whitman?"

"This is Science class, Williams. You seem to refuse to get it through your head," Mr. Beaker said, kicking him out.

Just later, as Dawes Williams was walking down the hall of the brick and glass edifice they had named William Wadlove High after an old beaver trapper who had left parks to the city, he thought: Yes, hell yes, and maybe, with a big enough breakthrough, you could invent a primitive radio set capable of listening into the small, screaming silence of Jesus himself, dying, nailed to the Cross. What a real success that would be. Soon, down in the office again, he was facing Principal Wilson, who was folding his handkerchief again in loose, organic pinafores, saying:

"Well, Williams," Dr. Wilson said, twirling circles in the air with his swivel chair, "what are we to do with you this time?"

"Well," Dawes Williams said, surprising himself for a change, "I've been thinking that over myself, and do you suppose you could expel me for a couple of weeks? I've got some reading I want to do."

"You'll have to do your reading on your own time, not ours," he said. Then, looking down at his dark papers come in from the files, Wilson continued: "Dawes, my boy," he said, drawing an invisible cigar from the air, "I see here from your profiles your grades aren't up to your capacities."

"Whose are?" Dawes Williams said, biting his tongue.

"Don't you like it here?" Wilson said pensively, studying him.

"It's not that, sir," Dawes Williams said, "it's just that I'd like to go somewhere where I could get an education."

"Perhaps your folks could send you to a private school," Wilson said. "That's not our responsibility, you know."

"No. Don't think so," Dawes Williams said. "My father, Simpson Williams, is a regular social democrat and believes in public education."

"I see," Wilson said.

"No. I don't think so," Dawes Williams said, "because the real reason here is the fact that Simpson Williams is only a secretary-treasurer, and not even the boss's kids go to private school. How would it look?"

"We mustn't judge our parents too harshly," Wilson said. "I'm sure they're doing their best."

"With all due respect, Mr. Wilson," Dawes Williams said, "I don't think you should judge whether or not I am judging my father."

"You're on one of the lesser units of the basketball team, aren't you, Williams?" Wilson said.

"Absolutely," Dawes Williams said, "great experience."

"Well," Wilson said, "let's see that your conduct straightens up around here, or I'll have to write our Coach Red Jarvis about this. For now . . . for now, I'll just write Mr. Beaker a note that should get you back into Science class. All right?"

"Fine," Dawes Williams said, "if you think that's all you can do about this."

"It is, for now. You may go now, Williams," Mr. Wilson said.

But, turning at the door, Dawes Williams felt suddenly that Mr. Wilson looked a little too smug, so he said:

"Excuse me, sir. But as long as we are on the subject, do you suppose you could answer a question that's been bothering me for some time?"

"Yes, of course," Wilson said.

"Is it true, Mr. Wilson," Dawes said, warming up to it, "that Red Jarvis makes more money than you do? And that he has been asked to join the Country Club?"

"Good day, Williams," Wilson said. "That will be all."

Dawes Williams closed the door behind him. He felt suddenly he had vindicated his old friend and companion Ronnie Crown, who was already, he had heard, in the pen for trying to pass bad checks in a tavern. All the way down the hall he did a tap dance like Fred Astaire brushing up his top hat, fixing up his tails. He got back to Beaker in time to present him with the note before the class was dismissed, which was his real intention in the first place.

Dunker was opening another case of Schlitz he had gotten from his trunk. The bitch dog hadn't come to drink from the white quarry water yet, but Dawes Williams sat, very drunk, listening for only the hound.

"Hell yes," Dunker was saying, watching him, startling him some, "some day we'll be able to invent machines that can unravel sound."

"We've been able to do that for a year now," Dawes Williams said, not batting an eye, "ever since Peter Beaker and you first thought of it in Physics class."

"You two shut up," Travis said. "I want to talk about Cotter."

"Open up," Eddie said. "Peter Beaker is a faggot."

"Nobody," Travis Thomas said, "shoots Travis Thomas in the head with a shotgun and gets away with it for long."

"That was two years ago," Dawes said.

"Two hundred, it doesn't matter," Travis said.

Dunker sat drinking a second bottle of wine. He passed it wordlessly. Two faint streams of red ran easily as water down Travis' chin and then Travis got up, began kicking cans light as empty rocks into the flat pond, lit up a thin cigarillo, and said:

"Hell yes, the way I figure it is this: that first night we came past, old Cotter was loving her up. He works all day, tired as hell, but why take it out on us? We didn't make his miserable world—so there he is, finally getting his miserable time in, plowing a damn furrow in the ground all day, all night, back and forth, and so he's finally there, putting his poor, misused wife and we, all four of us remember, pull into his driveway, so what's he do? Does he pull a civilized and continue pumping? Hell, no, he doesn't, not him, he just pulls on his pajama tops—Jesus, with red polka dots and flowers on'em—and he gets out of bed and whips the shotgun on us innocent as lambs. And that was his first mistake."

"And that was two years ago," Dawes Williams said.

"That's right. Red polka dots and flowers on'em. I got a memory for things like that," Dunker said.

"That's not what I meant," Dawes said.

"Shut up, Dawes," Eddie says, "he wasn't getting any at all. The sour bastard never gets any. So he's a miserable motherfuck and he just naturally pulls his peehole shotgun on anyone and everybody who happens to wander in out of the rain and onto his peehole driveway."

"And that was his second mistake," Dunker said. "He wore pajamas with red polka dots and flowers on'em. I can't tolerate that."

"But that was three years ago."

"Shut up Dawes," Travis says. "I choose to agree with Eddie: day or night he shoots innocent people down; he's funny that way, straps a gun to his tractor, like he was in Texas or some damn place, and plays Bronco Jim Cotter all day potting people who come past his fields. To hell with the bastard. This is Iowa. Civilized forchristsake. He's got it coming. This is it. I don't feel bad at all."

"I'm for killing him outright," Eddie said.

Huge laughter.

"This is our last night," Travis said. "I like a sense of completeness about the things I do."

"You're a real poet, Travis," Dawes Williams said.

"And that was his third mistake," Dunker says. "He underestimated our sense of vengeance."

"I believe in just war," Travis Thomas said.

"Two years?"

"Two hundred years," Eddie said. "Makes no difference to me. Have you forgotten it was your trunk he riddled with his double-barrel? You could have fainted you were swearing so hard by the time you hit town."

"I hate a man who resorts to violence," Travis said. "Have you forgotten I caught a BB in the head?"

"It's rough growing up here on the frontier," Dawes said.

"Have you forgot that?" Travis said, accusing.

"How could I? You've been wearing it around your neck on a silver chain three years, haven't you?"

"It's cool," Eddie said.

"Listen," Travis Thomas said, "you're damn right I have."

"Wasn't I the one who picked it out of your head with a fork?"

"Damn right, Dawes. And don't think I wasn't grateful."

"And that, Dawes," Dunker said, "was his fourth mistake."

"Damn right. Nobody shoots Travis Thomas," Travis Thomas said, "and gets away with it for long."

Dawes drifted off again. And in his distance he heard a dog breaking for home. The water went off with the whiteness. The earth remained. And he thought: And I watch those two fragile eyes of Dunker's, not mine, look out into the evening, immense, sane, fragile as rain, very drunk, as obsolete as the lily growing on stone.

And I say: Where? When? Will it ever be over? Will I always be mad? Locked in my trellis of stone?

And they say: There is really no need of any of this. We have already absolved each other.

And I say: We can't.

And they say: There's no need. Absolution is only construct. It's your madness that's not. It's here. In this room you have made for us all.

And I say: It isn't. It can't be.

And they say without ever looking: It is.

And they say: Who has made this room? I do not live here.

And I look out on the evening. And I watch those two fragile eyes look out into the evening without ever looking, immense, as fragile as the lily growing on stone, as obsolete as the rain.

2

The white dreaming rock drifted off. Sitting over the quarry, Travis Thomas shuffled the dirt through his hand, smoked a long, casual cigaret, and watched the pleasant motion of his own ashes sail the water. He thought only: When I was fourteen and saw those three assholes coming up the hill that day on their bicycles, I knew it was trouble.

He shifted himself into the light and watched Dawes Williams move around in the stones. He was only busy overturning the earth, the old useless smoke, the worms of runes you get with a sifting spade. He thought Dawes Williams was mad as a hat and only half as dangerous. He claimed none of him. But turning back suddenly, it struck him that at least Dawes Williams was not a midget any more, not four foot eleven like that first day he saw him; that at least he looked like a taller version of the same thin, nervous, bespectacled and burrowing animal that had come, pushing that busted machine of his bicycle, puffing in the wind, loose chain wacking the side of it all, up that hill five years before.

Dunker and Eddie were riding on both sides, like cussing outriders. They were kicking at his slowness and swearing in Midwestern Anglo-Saxon; and Dunker was bending down and removing the ace of spades from his spokes. Eddie still used balloons. No, Dawes Williams is larger than that now, still running out loose in the quarry, in the thinly thatched woods of his kinky hair, alone, ready at any moment to howl at the moon. Yes, Travis Thomas thought lying out comfortably in the moon, Dunker still had cards in his spokes; Eddie balloons; and Dawes Williams had had a busted bike . . .

"This simple sonofabitch never works right," Dawes said, moving up that hill on Greenwater Drive S.E. "I swear if Simpson doesn't come through with a new-motherless-Schwinn pretty soon, I'm leaving home."

"You dinks still ride fenders on your side of town?" Travis Thomas said.

"That's right," Dunker said, stopping dead, cold in his tracings, staring straight over his cherry and reversed handlebars. "Want to make something out of it?"

"Maybe," Travis Thomas said, turning, punting his football fifty yards onto his porch.

"Nice kick," Eddie said.

"Yep," Travis said, spitting on the grass.

"Shut up, Eddie," Dunker said.

"What is this?" Dawes Williams said. "Penrod and Sam, forchristsake?"

There was a long silence on that one. Dunker was already six feet three, and his knees bowed out of his small machine like reversed hinges, or like something trailing on the ground behind the tracings of a small burro. Eddie was sharp, quick: Travis could see it in the way he darted his used and fenderless American Racer up beside Dunker. Dawes Williams had already dropped his bike on the pavement and was staring straight into abstract space. He was working hard at developing the notion that his immediate destiny was being threatened. He kicked rocks at the street for awhile; then, deciding that he was ready, Dawes turned into it all dramatically and said:

"Thomas?" he said. "I hear you are a pussy-whipped sonofabitch pee-hole bastard."

"Good job, Dawes," Dunker said.

"Thanks, Dunker," Dawes Williams said.

Dawes Williams had only been swearing in earnest for a year then, but he was *nearly as good at it as anyone else. The veins on Thomas' face, however, had already begun to thicken. He began looking straight into Dawes Williams and throwing rocks at his tires. Soon Dawes was winding his bike up and backing off; he was getting ready to run Travis Thomas over, so naturally Travis couldn't take that and began throwing larger rocks, higher on the rims of his tires, and Dawes Williams could only sit there, drenched in the flooding emotion of his own blood, saying:*

"Big deal. This damn thing doesn't work anyway. You can't hurt it."

"Oh ya?" Travis Thomas said.

"Oh ya," Dawes Williams said.

Then Dawes threw the bike to the ground again, and borrowed Eddie's cherry, pin-striped fender with the plastic rat tails draping from his bars, and he pedaled it down the block. Stopping, turning, he wound up on it and prepared to run Travis Thomas down. Coming down the block, he decided suddenly he was going to lock his wheels and spin out around Travis Thomas' outer foot.

"What's this guy all about?" Travis said, watching him come.

"Who knows?" Dunker said, just then becoming a lifelong friend of Travis Thomas. "I never say. I think he's mostly about himself—you know, whatever-it-is-happens-to-be-passing-through-his-head-at-the-time type of crap."

"Ya," Travis said, "I've noticed that type before."

But Dawes Williams was still coming. He pedaled into the wind. He was moving down that hill, thinking more about the moving than the ending, so naturally, when he got there, Travis Thomas just stepped aside and busted him along side the head.

Dawes Williams was out for a couple of minutes. Travis had just given him one of the blackest eyes he had ever had, so naturally Dunker and Eddie ran Travis down, kicked him a couple times, and by the time they got back up the hill Dawes was awake, looking flatly at the sky, the trees, the faint rise of the moon, and he slowly opened his other eye with his fingers, saying only:

"Did I get'm? Did I get the sonofabitch?"

So they picked him up and dusted him off. Then they all shook hands and Dunker rode Travis over to Dawes' house on his handlebars to steal some cigarets.

"Dawes' mother isn't home. She went to her pimpy bridge club," Eddie said, riding along.

"Leone plays a mean game of bridge, and reads a lot of biographies of Frenchmen," Dawes Williams said.

"What's he talking about?" Travis Thomas said.

"Dawes doesn't smoke," Dunker said. "He trains so he can play sixth man on A-Squad. Don't you, Dawes?"

"Ratshit Rawlings is sixth man," Eddie said. "Dawes is seventh."

"Nobody shoots better'n me, keek-seekie," Dawes Williams mimed, pedaling along.

"That's true. I'd back Dawes in a Horse game any day," Dunker said.

"That's true," Eddie said. "Dawes is only seventh man, though."

"I been screwed, Eddie," Dawes Williams said, looking over at Dunker, running a curb.

Getting up, swearing to the air, Dawes Williams set his chain again, kicked his tire and continued down the road behind them now.

"Quit forcing me off the road," he said.

"Atttttsssss Willy!" Dunker yelled behind.

Dawes caught up to Eddie. Eddie, Dawes thought, looking over at him, flying past, always reminded him of a movie he had once seen that was set in a Welshman's pub. The whole of it never got out of the place. Eddie was short and very quick. He caddied at the Country Club. He played guard, halfback and shortstop. He also played catcher and outfield. He golfed, ran track, swam and shot marbles for money. Eddie Welsh was one of the few natural athletes Dawes Williams had ever known who was four feet six.

They rode over to Dawes' and hitched their bikes by the porch. Entering the house, Dunker bumped his head on the door frame.

"Why don't you buy yourself a white man's house, Dawes?" he said. "I feel like I'm walkin' around in a goddamn dollhouse."

"Leone can sure keep herself a pretty house all right," Dawes Williams said, spitting out the window.

"I think I like nonfilters better," Travis was saying, smoking slowly on Dawes' mother's Kents. "They're more a man's smoke."

"Kents are fags for fags all right," Eddie said.

Travis handled the cigaret deliberately, as if the stem were made of glass and breakable, as if he were in a movie or some damn thing. He thumbed it, blew the smoke through his nose.

"Hell, yes," Eddie said, "I think I'll have another."

"I only like to light up every five or ten minutes," Travis said.

"Atttttssss Travis," Dawes Williams said.

"What's this 'aaaaaatttttttttsssss' shit?" Travis said, opening a bottle of Seven-Up on the woodwork.

"Well," Dawes Williams began, "whenever you say some particularly bright thing, or some particular dumb, asshole thing you get an 'atttttssss' laid on ya."

"How do you know which it is?"

"Atttttssss Travis," they said, "you don't."

Travis had joined.

"Whenever you reveal yourself is when you get an 'atttttssss' laid on ya," Dawes Williams said.

There was a silence on that one. Dawes Williams was already beginning to feel directly responsible for all of the great, pregnant silences in the world; and he wanted to do something about them because everyone in the room began looking at him as if he were made of more curious air, and breakable.

Finally Travis shifted himself in the sunlit, leaf-filtered kitchen, and he began exploring Dawes Williams' house as if it were to be the new home of his deeper cave of prowling around. Leone, Dawes' old mother from another of his lives, had decorated the inside air with taste and some expense. Simpson wasn't an accountant any more; he was a secretary-treasurer. Dawes Williams wasn't a singing cowboy any more, riding down thin horse trails between the shadows of arrows; he was a baseball player. He was a first-baseman, only he didn't think like one. He still thought like one of Arthur's greyhounds, Blackey Jane singing, running in the rain, the shadows, screaming all over the summer of the living hill, and it was making him nervous to see it all happen in this way. Dunker and Eddie, now Travis Thomas himself, were helping him through: they were straightening him out.

"I'm showing Dawes Williams here the skinny," Dunker had once said, introducing him into a pickup basketball game in Shandlin's driveway.

But Travis was still walking around in the house, examining the walls. Dawes went to a back window and began looking out at Dunchee's old wall. Ronnie Crown was gone, fled with the law. All the old things dissolve, change, pass away, Dawes Williams thought at the window. He was an old man now, nearly fourteen. The outside of the house hung in the late summer air like a great and gray, old and disused tent. It was a vaguely grotesque wall of stucco, heavy with black climbing vines and the past, an edifice to be collapsed by the transparent weight of memory itself, rooms breaking apart with silences, walls full of oracles without speech or even noise. It was an English house; a place full of function, and people who passed through each other in the halls, like water bodies, slender light, speechless, saying nothing at all. Often, sitting in his room at night, alone, looking out at Dunchee's wall, Dawes Williams wished his father were an Italian, wild-eyed, close, a Latin who could pull a knife on his mother or do something equally exciting as that.

Travis was still moving around the house. Dawes sat watching the yard behind. Dunchee's mansion, the brown open yard, the pool-tabled garage had been sold to the Catholic mortuary, breathing, expanding over the lawns. They were moving in closer, a circle of coal-eyed souls flying the moon. But the sky was vacant of a cross in the trees, personal sign; the wind full of portentous deities was gone, disappeared, fled with his neurotic God.

The neighborhood, Crown, was gone. Sometimes at night Dawes could hear the faint sounds of Catholic wakes come through his walls, the two opens lawns separating the houses. Then he could hear the night; they had given it sound, and it sounded like huddled cats, tails raised in the heat, crouching low in an alley against winter. Sometimes, late at night, sitting breathlessly at his high window watching the moonfall in the two open yards before him, it was almost as if his soul had fled, escaped with them; and he would have to walk out, across the distance of that window, the rose and myrtle ruffling the walls, the leafy waterspouts and horsemen of the stoned rain, the things calling him out to thunder, to walk around within their dark, their turning droppings of night, yes, to find it again . . . to put his soul back on again, like a hat.

"Not a bad little house you got yourself here," Travis said.

"It's all right if you like wakes," Dawes Williams said.

"Fish eaters," Eddie'd said knowingly, nodding across the two open lawns. "Hell, yes. It's those fish eaters burying one another every night that's about to drive Dawes Williams here nuts as birds."

"Dawes already is nuts," Dunker said.

"Kiss my ass," Dawes Williams said.

Then he shifted himself back on the windowsill and began scanning the street. Two doctors' clinics—gray and looming—had moved onto the corners of Main Avenue. They were like underwater animals, shells, efficiently trying to move closer to the Catholic mortuary to form the rudiments of a feeding chain, an underwater thing that was beautiful, tenuous, flowery, and poisonous. Looking down the hill, he could also see that the Crown Nursing Home stood half-demolished, closed down by the law, and waiting for an insurance company. It was a yellow husk, knee-bent and falling. Ronnie Crown had fallen, abdicated, gone over the hill on the arm of a cop, and Travis was running his hand over one of Leone's satin chairs, smiling. Travis seemed wrapped in a finer skin. Dunker and Eddie were sitting in a circle, talking. And at night, in his room, Dawes Williams could listen to only the high sounds of the organs and singing, the wailing, funerals of wind. Yes, they're air-mailing the soul to heaven, he thought, high in the coal-eyed sky, over the moon, across the cross in the vacant trees, like white-robed witches sailing the black broom of sky.

God damn me, he thought.

He roused himself from the window and turned back. The room seemed the same as when he had left it. It always did.

Things were beginning to wind down, like a slow afternoon watching the rain now; Travis had come back and already gone out in the back hallway to rummage around in Dawes' icebox. He wanted to show these guys something, so he turned back in the doorway and with the hook of his arm he reached out a large, raw rump roast. He held it out for awhile, letting it tail in the air. Finally, without looking away from the room before him, he raised the meat and took a huge bite off the raw hanging rear of the roast. He stood there for a moment with the red, watery and bloody meat draped from his chin:

"Christ," Dawes Williams said, "why didn't you at least wait until my mother has had a chance to cook on that some?"

But Travis Thomas had his answer ready. The juicy meat stuck nicely in the round pouch of his cheek and he just stood there, staring back, looking exactly like a full-grown, muscled Tab Hunter. He wasn't worried about anything; he knew he would live forever. He had his answer ready:

"I like mine rare," he said.

"Attttttsssss Travis," Dawes Williams said weakly.

"Hell, Travis," Eddie said, "you look like a coon with a watermelon."

"I'm happy all right," he said, not even smiling, as cool as a selfless stud.

"That's too easy," Dawes Williams said, "I don't believe any of this."

No one, however, was paying any attention at all to Dawes Williams; the shadows were growing longer in the back hallway, which meant Mrs. Williams would be home from bridge club and soon they would be invaded, and Travis had moved off again and was eyeing a bottle stuck in the back of the icebox. In it was some bad homemade beer one of the workers at Simpson's office had given him; but Travis didn't know it. It was deep, rancid yellow, the color of ginger ale, and it was in a clear, unlabeled Canada Dry bottle. Dawes, Eddie and Dunker knew it was bad beer, and if Travis drank any of it he would puke it all over himself like a girl. Travis began circling around it with his mind and finally, after long seconds of indecision, he picked it up to the light. He began, pulling the cork. Eddie and Dunker and Dawes looked at each other. Travis began watching the other three watch him. He sensed, down in some naturally dark and remote animal region of his, that something was wrong. Without the eye looking at the bottle, the arm wavered and fell. Dawes could see that Dunker was about to fall apart, and one thin crack in the cement mask would do it. The arm wavered and the eye watched them intently for a sign. But the mind still thought ginger ale. It wasn't too late. There still was time. Dawes Williams thought the tension was terrific.

"Don't drink any of that ginger ale of my father's, God damn you, Travis," Dawes said quietly.

And that must have done it, because instantly the arm rose with a reflexive contempt as Dawes thought it would. Travis took a long, thoughtless pull. There was a sudden reptile recognition, and then—but strangely, calmly, walking around like he was a portable fountain, a planned thing supposed to be there—Travis spit the homemade brew all over the kitchen, in fine sprays, and controlled liquid convulsions, and without even batting an eye. He was nonchalant almost; he spit, stood there spitting, nonchalant as hell. He spit over the walls, the neatly pressed window curtains, as if they weren't really there. Then he turned and said:

"It's just that that's about the worst beer I've ever drank. It tastes like dung."

Then Eddie and Travis and Dunker and Dawes lay there speechless on the floor and laughed. The late-afternoon sun came into the kitchen in arabesques and thin, vanishing patterns of sun-filtered dust. It would grow quiet and then someone would see something new in it and it would break out all over again. Finally, much later, Travis arose from the wooden chair, crossed the shadow, the long edge of the room, and stood tall as Napoleon before the mirror in the back hallway. Turning, posing into the long edge of the glass, Travis looked at himself and said:

"Don't you ever die. Oh, don't you ever die."

A long, slow movement of silence had settled over the kitchen. Travis had joined.

3

Not much was moving out in the dark light now. The moon had settled itself in a pale house of clouds. Soon rain would be blowing in, and the air was heavy, and Dawes Williams felt he was alone and swimming, somewhere under the sky. He had moved off farther from the quarry and was stretched out flat with the August ground, drunk, blowing thin smoke at the patterns of wind, thinking about nothing at all. He watched the single light on Cotter's barn flare into nothing. He shifted himself around, feeling quietly relieved that he had finally made it out of himself, and realized his criminal heart.

"Atttttsssss Willy," Travis called at him, somewhere beyond the pond, the soft rise of locust wing tearing August.

For awhile he almost thought he was back at Arthur's farm; that he had finally, once again, managed to be captured by time, the burn of fireflies trapped in small jars, glass, his mind. Blowing the blue smoke out on the wind, he waited for its sound. . . .

Coming back from the farm that day, the last time, Dawes had watched as Simpson steered the Chevy onto the dead gravel behind the house. Ronnie Crown had been risen again, sitting on Dunchee's wall, a thin, nervous inquisitor throwing the matchsticks of fighter pilots up at the sun, watching them abstractedly as they parked the car. He'd been risen, Dawes Williams knew. He'd been waiting, Dawes knew, for Williams to come tell him about the farm.

Later, after dinner, Dawes went outside and hopped the wall and sat down beside Crown:

"Well," he said, "I just got back from the farm."

"No shit."

"Yes," he said, "it was beautiful as hell."

"Listen, Dawes," Crown said, "just shut up about it, would ya?"

Then, in the long silence, Crown looked over with those eyes of his, those eyes too old for his head almost, like he thought Dawes Williams was his idiot brother, and finally he broke the still evening by saying:

"And so you think you are the only one who can think like that now. Is that what you think? You silly ass," he said.

"No, I don't think I think that."

"You idiot," Crown said, "ten years old and already you are a dip-shit."

"I'm only nine."

Crown looked at him. He saw those wet eyes, like a doe or some damn thing in a book of pictures, and they were looking back at him from another part of the wall as if they were watching witches flying from hats.

"Okay, you're nine. Big deal, Dawes, you are nine and you are a dipshit. What'll you be like when you're an old sonofabitch? Twenty-fucking-A-or-so. What kind of a horse's ass'll you be like then I wonder?"

"I'm doing fine," Dawes Williams said. "You just don't understand about it all is all."

"That's a good one. I don't understand about it all is all. That's a good one all right."

So then Dawes hopped down, just standing below Crown in the alley and not saying anything more.

"Fuck off, Dawes," Crown said, "you just don't happen to know your ass from a bug's. You look like the dumbest thing around. You look like secret stone you gotta send out for with box tops."

"You just don't understand me is all."

"So you saw yer big-mother witch, huh?" Crown said.

"Yes."

"Was she flying her big-assed broom over the teat of the moon? Is that it, Dawes?"

"No. She was just sitting there in a rocking chair with a shawl. Not moving. Dying."

"Jesus. So you saw another jack get shredded on a little again this year. Is that it?"

"No," Dawes Williams said, "I don't think that is it."

"What do you think it is? Listen, Dawes Williams, I'm talking at ya . . ."

"I don't know what it is. Maybe it's nothing at all."

"That's what I think it is," Crown said. "But, on the other frigging hand, maybe there's really something here after all."

"Could be," Dawes Williams said. "Maybe not."

"Shut up, Dawes," Crown said. "Listen, maybe it's your damn grandfather that's screwing you up so much each summer."

"Yes," Dawes Williams said, "but I don't think so. He was only like looking at the shadow in the hallway of a dark building. You know what I mean?"

"Sure," Crown said. "I gotcha. I gotcha. Listen, Dawes," he said, beginning to chew on a small twig still attached to its tree, "listen, I think maybe you ought to move north to the Arctic Circle. Then you wouldn't have no more summers to worry about."

There was a long silence.

"Jesus," Ronnie Crown said.

Then he looked Dawes Williams in the eye some more:

"So you found yourself watching some damn hounds running on a hill!"

"Yes," Dawes said finally, "only they were the hill."

"Jesus, Dawes, you're nuts as hell," Ronnie Crown said, hopping his wall. . . .

Later, in another summer, he remembered . . . there were shadows in the street.

Running children. Forms. Ronnie Crown was up another high pine tree. Dawes Williams couldn't see him but he could hear his breathing. It was like listening to air escape gratefully from an attic. Faintly, in the moon, Dawes could see Johnny B. Harper wrapped around one of the old chimneys on Dunchee's roof. Down the block, at the ends of the long shadows of alleys, big Roger Casey was kicking the can on one of the younger kids. Tin rattled the air and was gone, evaporating the wind. Caught! A huge bus, higher than buildings, passed on the avenue a block away. It was so still Dawes noticed himself listening to people speaking together in the bright, passing windows. Lying under a blanket of musty leaves, hiding out, he could feel Mary Louis' hot breath in his ear. She was older, thirteen, he thought. . . .

Suddenly it sounded like rain in the leaf, over his head. . . .

Mary Louis was smooth and perfect against him. Thirteen, he thought. She unbuttoned her blouse. She made him bury his hand, then his mouth, on her small hot nipples barely starting to grow.

"Touch them," she said. "Rub me," she said. "Kiss them. Don't be afraid. I like you to do that. It's nice. It's nice to do that," she said. "I like you, Dawes."

For a long time they lay hidden under a perfect house of leaves.

Suddenly it sounded like rain in the pines growing near Dunchee's wall.

"Roger Casey will never find us. We will never be caught. Kiss them some more, Dawes. You're so warm. So small," she said. "Roger Casey will never find us here."

She was so warm and the leaf was dark with fall. Winter was near; in the air, just beyond the edge of the wall. The pines were already ominous with the suggestion of snow. . . .

"Touch me some more."

"Yes."

"It's like a dark house, or being in an attic."

"Yes."

"Now me. Let me."

"What do you want?"

"Let me touch."

"Touch?"

"Yes, your things for awhile, Dawes. It's my turn now."

"I don't think I have any."

"What!?"

"Any things!?!"

"Yes, you do. Let me touch. Let me show you."

"I don't. I don't."

"You do. You do."

"Listen, Mary Louis, what the hell kind of things are you talking about!?!"

"Your things, Dawes."

"Listen, Mary Louis, I don't think I have any things."

"You do. You do too. Yes. I'll show you," she said.

Her hand was soft against him. He wondered what it was she did. It was like listening to yourself move through a glass.

"Ronnie Crown!!" Mary Louis was screaming, suddenly, into the dry rise of smoking evening.

Her voice was round, still, had a center, but soon it became a tin can, rattling the wind, and she said:

"Ronnie Crown!! What are you doing up there!"

Crown was laughing, nearly falling out of the tree, and he said:

"Easy, Mary Louis. I'm just tak'n' a pee."

So one day, the end of Crown, he thought—after Crown had finished hopping down, out of all of his pine trees for awhile—he came across Dawes Williams shooting baskets in the yard and he said:

"Dawes? How about you and me goin' down some fucking place and bustin' some windows?"

"No. I don't think so," Dawes William said.

"I got a new pocket knife, we could slit some tires?"

"No. Not today," he said.

"We can't hang around this wall forever," Ronnie Crown said.

"That's true, I'm nearly eleven now," Dawes said.

"For whatever that means," Crown said. "Go frog stabbin' maybe?"

"No. I don't think so."

"It's Saturday for Christsake. What are you—a goddamn saint?"

"That's right. It's Saturday. I got up knowing that."

"Dawes, you simple sonofabitch," Crown said, "I love ya. You are the dumbest thing around."

"Yes," Dawes Williams said, "you just don't understand about these things."

For whatever that means, Crown thought, mounting the wall.

"Dawes," he said, lighting a butt he drew from under his shirt. "What do I have to do—be my own Tom Sawyer, my own dreamer, forchristsake? Maybe you're just pissed because of those few stray seven hundred marbles of yours I won last week. But fair's square, isn't it?"

"Best set of antique cat's-eye marbles Simpson ever gave me," Dawes Williams said, standing below, shooting jumpers.

"Yep. They're pretty all right," Crown said. "Listen. I'll give'm back. Then we can go and bust us some windows."

He knew he had Dawes there, so he just sat on the wall, looking down, smoking, throwing stick matches at the wind. But Dawes Williams said:

"No. Not today. I've got two thousand more baskets to sink."

"Dawes," Crown said, "quit being so pissy athletic all the time and I'll tell you about how I managed to have stuck a stick up Mary Louis Loomis' greasy thing."

"What thing?" Dawes Williams said, potting a set shot, not even interested.

Then there was a long silence in which Crown looked down from his wall. Finally he'd shot his butt and said:

"Jesus Christ, Dawes. There just ain' no hope fer you."

So then Dawes Williams sank a hook shot, and Crown hopped down off his wall, and they started walkin' anyway.

After they had been walking awhile, they came upon Fat Albert Romeo, the fattest cabdriver in town. Before that, however, they passed Mrs. Lowbus' porch, her new garage, her side lot full as fields with rotting stones of apples. Crown stopped to load his pockets. Dawes Williams even thought Mrs. Lowbus had been a dull old woman ever since her stable burned down. She rarely went out in sheets any more. Her life, he remembered, was spent picking newspapers off her lawn at five in the afternoon. Mrs. Lowbus had only a pewter cat which Dawes Williams liked to kick on his way to school. It was the one outright act of meanness he allowed himself at this time, but it made him feel a whole lot better just to do it. It was war, and Mrs. Lowbus used to arrange her days so she would have plenty of time in the afternoons to sit on her porch and complain when a long football pass would find its way into her yard. She had given him a cookie once. It was pewter. It was like chewing on the bowl itself. Ronnie Crown used to dump her rocking chair on its back like an inverted shroud every night before he went to bed. For him it was like saying a catechism. Why not, Dawes Williams thought; it was a middle-class neighborhood, wasn't it? Anything goes. But in the evenings in summer, he remembered, the old women on his block hoed the black dirt over like reverting serfs.

They were still walking down the hill and Crown, of course, had been already plotting with the rotting apples lining his pockets. They passed down, into the three wide cement avenues of the small city—Rapid Cedar, gem of the prairies, seventy thousand now and bursting with progress—which flowed endlessly over the black dirt and waving cornstalks, all the way out toward exotic places like New York City and beyond. There, he knew, at New York City, the cement avenue merged, dropped off mysteriously, went under the sea like lost gopher tracings, subterranean, quiet, vague, foreign to the touch, and there the world began.

As they walked, Crown broke out singing his own version of Gonna Beat My Meat on the Mississippi Mud in broken English. His pockets were full of apples; his thoughts of chaos and larceny to be wrecked off whole upon an unsuspecting world.

On Second Avenue, shadowy in leaves of sunlight, the yellow cab of Fat Albert Romeo was parked. It was obviously a challenge; even Dawes Williams could see that.

"That dumb mother can't park there," Crown said. "I won't let'm."

Away, in a target of slight distance now, the cab lay glistening in the terrible August heat. A metal sun, round, inverted, it was a mirage, belly-up and fixed to the light and, inside, Fat Albert Romeo's head lay snoring soundly; the perfectly bald, red top skin was mooned over the sill, round as a beckoning spheroid. In the winding-

down, sleeping air the dispatcher's broken static hung shredded and forgotten as locust wings. It must have been a hundred and six in the shade.

"Dawes," Crown said, reverently approaching the front at twenty-five yards, "that mother's one beautiful target and a fifth."

And so, with that, they just moved in some, to about seventy-five feet, to where it all was just across the street, and Crown began eyeing the target with hawk's eyes, checking the day for windage, loosening up the old arm about three or four times, and then he just let Fat Albert Romeo have it. He hit him with six straight-shooter humming apples before he ever woke up.

"THEM ROTTEN APPLES SOUNDED LIKE HORIZONTAL BOMBS ON HIS FAT RED HEAD, I TELL YA!" Crown screamed as they tore back up the hill, running away.

And they had seemed to fly through the white, dreaming stone, August, the still and vacant water of his illusion, the sleeping quarry, and Dawes Williams could still see the face of Fat Albert Romeo, rotund, puffing like dead blowing window curtains bowed to the wind, as it chased itself and Crown, and himself, and everything awake in that August down the alley, across Dunchee's wall, through the brown side lot frying summer in the pans of the trees where it all, the race, the soft fall of old light again, slackened for awhile until, once again, Fat Albert Romeo flushed them like quail flying mindlessly once more through Mrs. Lowbus' washing (the sheet wet and cool in the sun against his face) until it all ended, once and for all, as Fat Albert Romeo trapped them, a full mile away, on the open, defenseless grass of Ben Franklin Field. It was a strange place, a place named for some obscure American Dawes Williams had never even heard of for the moment. The light deepened beyond the goalposts, and Fat Albert was trying to kick the great Crown through to the other end. Dawes Williams stood around and watched, winded, nearly fainting. Coughing, wordless, Fat Albert Romeo seemed just to stand there, spitting apple seeds into the ground. Fat Albert Romeo was determined. He picked Crown up by the ears, and he fed him a rotten apple out of his own pockets nearly whole. Crown stood spitting the seeds; and Dawes Williams was safe, uninitiated, alone, as Fat Albert Romeo was only capable of catching one of them at a time, and he wanted Crown worse, and then Fat Albert Romeo looked Crown square in the eyes, and Crown looked him square back, and Dawes Williams became obsessed by only the squareness of it all, and Crown said finally:

"You son of a bitch! You son of a bitch! I didn't mean it! I didn't mean it! it was all a goddamn accident like."

Then, in the end, Ronnie Crown went over the hill, the end of the world on the arm of a cop and was never heard of again.

Dawes Williams shifted himself against the white, dreaming rock of the quarry and stared into water.

4

A thin bush of an apple tree grew over in a corner of Ben Franklin Field where Fat Albert Romeo and Ronnie Crown had once stood, spitting their seeds. Dawes Williams, fourteen, playing tackle, stood in his pads and helmet, alone in his bone and naked blood, figuring he would get to the parts where he was Byronic later. . . .

Across from him, on the line of scrimmage, stood Ratshit Rawlings in his horn-rimmed glasses. Mrs. Rawlings, Dawes remembered, once told him that Harrison "Ratshit" Rawlings was directly descended from an obscure New England Transcendentalist of another name entirely. Looking at him, bent low over scrimmage, Dawes Williams told himself it was all true because Harrison "Ratshit" Rawlings looked exactly like a long, nervous version of Ichabod Crane in tennis shoes. Travis was calling signals, and soon, on the command of hut-hut, Dawes Williams—descendant of eleventh-century Celtic pig rustlers; turned fourteenth-century Scottish keepers of the English border; turned fifteenth-century Edinburgh goldsmiths and court jewelers to the Stuarts turned drawn and quartered, and embarrassed, and strung on a post by the Tudors; turned exiles in Northern Ireland for the duration; turned American farmers, and cowboys, and accountants—lunged into Ratshit Rawlings, clipped him and cut him off at the knees. Soon they were back in the huddle, and Travis Thomas—who claimed on occasion to be part Seminole—was saying:

"Dunker—you go down about ten yards, fake to the out, cut to the in, behind that apple tree, I'll fake to Eddie off-tackle and hit you with the pass. Dawes—you block out."

"We only have one lineman—how the hell can Eddie go off-tackle?" Dawes Williams said.

"Never mind," Travis said, slapping his hands and breaking the huddle.

It was Saturday morning in midville. Everyone Dawes Williams seemed to know in the world was fourteen years old. Dunker was already six and a half feet high while Dawes and Eddie were trailing more than a foot behind. Travis was blonde, six feet and muscular, filled out completely and looking to everyone as if he should leave immediately for Hollywood. He always said it was his Seminole Indian blood, an out-cross, that made him so cool and wonderful to behold. No one, however, really believed him—which was why he said it, Dawes Williams thought—because Travis' father was a lawyer, and lawyers are not part Seminole.

Standing over the line of scrimmage, waiting, Ratshit Rawlings knew Dunker would eventually cut past that damn apple tree: he knew it because they'd been trying variations of the same play now for five straight hours. It was high noon; nearly time, Ratshit knew, to be thinking about going over and stealing his parents' car for the afternoon. Dunker dropped the pass. It didn't matter, however, because they had been playing since seven o'clock—the score was 276 to 249—and everybody was getting very half-assed about it all anyway.

"You idiot-mother, Dunker," Travis Thomas said.

In the huddle again the others listened to Travis saying:

"Dawes, you take the next one."

"Go catch it yourself, Travis," Dawes Williams heard himself saying. "I'm so tired I couldn't walk over to the creek and pee in the water."

"Shut up, Dawes," Travis said.

"I catch better'n Dawes anyway," Eddie said.

"Nobody catches better'n me, cocksucker," Dawes said.

"You block for me, Dunker," Travis said.

"Block for yourself, asshole," Dunker said.

"Bitch bitch bitch," Dawes Williams said.

"Atttttsssss Dunker," they all said with harmony finally. The first part of *Atttssssss* was always ceremoniously pushed from the stomach like a blow; the second part was slid and drawn through the teeth slowly, like a long-dead weed not meant somehow to grow.

Then the noon whistle went off and the game was over. The huddle dissolved and they began stringing their way up the hill. Dunker was for going over to Dawes' and having lunch, but Travis and Eddie were for getting over to Ratshit's in time to steal the car as soon as possible. Travis said:

"Mrs. Williams can't cook anyway. We can stop at Jiffy Burgers once we get the wheels."

"Wait a minute," Dawes Williams said. "What do you mean? My mother can cook like a sonofabitch."

"That's true," Eddie said, laughing, "Mrs. Williams makes a mean peanut butter sandwich."

"Christ," Dunker said, "why don't all you guys just shut up."

"Hey," Ratshit Rawlings said, "there goes Willis Skokes in his neat old Ford round that corner. Looks like Dixie Kakes's with him again today. Must be knockin' some off."

"Ya," Travis said quietly, "what a neat guy. Damn good quarterback."

"Quarterbacks get a lot of ass," Eddie said.

"Neat neat neat," Dawes Williams said.

"Shut up, Willy," Dunker said. "You're startin' to repeat yourself. It's a bad sign."

"Ya, Dawes," Ratshit offered, "don't pimp around about Willis Skokes. He happens to be one of the neater guys who ever lived."

"Hell," Dawes Williams said finally, "that dumb mother'll probably wind up in a factory someday tying the ends off wieners he's so neat."

"Attttsssss Willy," they all said.

"Shut up," Ratshit Rawlings added.

So Dawes Williams fell quiet for awhile, and they continued stringing up the hill. It was the same hill Crown had disappeared over years before, dancing with Fat Albert Romeo, Dawes Williams thought.

But that was all behind him, and Dawes Williams was walking up the hill with the guys. Because on football Saturday afternoons, when the fighting Hawks were playing down at Iowa City, and before they were sixteen and had their own cars, they would go over to Ratshit Rawlings' house. From noon on they would quietly sit around the Rawlings' living room and eye Ratshit's parents. When would they leave? Sitting there, Dawes remembered it was Eddie who first renamed Harrison Rawlings, Ratshit Rawlings. It was also Eddie who was quietly determined to drive Ratshit to the point of suicide. Dawes Williams sat back and watched him almost make it over the course of the years.

Ratshit Rawlings was the same Ratshit who was sixth man, one ahead of Dawes Williams, on the ninth grade basketball team. But because Ratshit rationalized better than anyone he had ever known, and because Dawes Williams was so struck and interested in absolute forms, Dawes nevertheless genuinely liked Ratshit. Besides, Dawes Williams thought, Ratshit Rawlings had the naïve instinct, perhaps courage, to actually explore what it was they all thought they'd become—an all-American fuckoff.

Sitting on the living-room floor, playing the latest chic game—composed mostly of a single wooden frame and some Newtonian steelies swinging together on strings—flown in from New York with Mrs. Harrison Rawlings, Sr., Dawes Williams suddenly felt if he ever wanted to describe the perfect circle of Ratshit's life, he would need an example. And sitting there, watching the steel balls describe perfectly inert actions against one another as they spun perfectly retraced parabolas in the air, Dawes Williams suddenly figured it this way: Ratshit Rawlings idolized, much too openly, the older athletes; and the side that Ratshit idolized was the blatant fuck-up side. In the eyes of Ratshit Rawlings, to be an all-American, clean-cut, crew-cut fuck-up was a sophisticated thing. Throwing it all away in the end was the epitome of style. And, still sitting there watching the steel balls rebound against one another with a perfect, repeating, waning symmetry, Dawes Williams felt even that he had found the example to prove it all:

One night they had all sat in the gym that was also the auditorium watching the varsity practice. A stage set for Booth Tarkington's *Seventeen* was set against the far wall like a pink summer cloud, nature-given; an archaic vision of near innocence the moment it was painted, a hollow log of a stage just waiting for the players, waiting for the sophisticated kid from Chicago to come rolling into town in his gay, hopelessly affluent yet somehow rustic, yellow, open-air road-ster meant for stopping at illicit roadhouses just over the county line. The bas-ketball court lay its naked four-square reality in front.

The late, gray winter shadows had come from the chicken-wire windows leaving only cages of shade to overlay a painted-on-cardboard summer gazebo. Dawes Williams thought he had been sitting there, trapped only in his skin, in Iowa which was really the same as Indiana, in the exact middle of the twentieth century. Coach Orville Boggs watched, whistle-mouthed, the late practice like a Florentine prince who was unaware except for the fact that he was vaguely conscious of being asleep. Everyone was tense, because the team was miracu-lously in the finals of the sectionals. Willis Skokes began a slow, deliberate, rhythmic dribble down the floor. He was bringing the ball down, right hand raised in signal, a screaming banshee without a sound, the middle finger extended, and the yellow-shirted second string eyed him with the stare of a single animal. The gym hushed itself and became a closed box. Dawes Williams thought the tension was terrific. Willis Skokes was approaching midcourt. The stars came out. What would he do? Drive it? Fade softly as night into the lane, past a screen, and jump-shoot it? Drive in like a furious cat and then, at the last moment, with great grace and magnanimity, bounce-pass it off? The sun wavered in the west; then decided to fall in again. Suddenly—with feeling— Willis Skokes merely tucked the ball under his arm like a movie of Goose Tatum, did a small bunny-hop, a Chaplin walk three times round the center circle, he swiveled his butt in two cutely contradictory movements and he . . . he fired the ball from midcourt. Good God, Dawes Williams thought, sitting there, there is no precedent for this. Good God, Dawes Williams thought, it rose, rises, in a speechless arc and then falls against the back wall of the gym with the sound of a small fish being hammered to death on a flat, dry rock.

HE HAD DRAWN NO IRON.

He had drawn no iron, and Coach Orville Boggs slumped to the floor, his life over. A life once dedicated quietly to example and youth, the American way, was now over and lost in the deep winter shadows of an unpretentious gym. He was finished. He had failed. With nearly his last breath he ordered Skokes from the gym, the entire building. Orville Boggs' arm extended baroquely toward the door, offering nothing, saying simply:

"Willis, leave us please," with some last dignity.

And with that, Willis Skokes turned on his heel, like a French clown, to an audience deathly shocked with pity and adoration that approached self-recog-nition and horror, he bowed, smiled like a faggot, and walked to the door on his hands.

When Ratshit Rawlings saw that happen, he knew there was God.

Willis Skokes would never play again, but then it didn't matter: he had become a legend and, besides, Eddie said he would probably be banging his girl Dixie Kakes again in a mere matter of hours anyway.

Only Ratshit died. He never recovered. He lay broken-backed over two auditorium chairs and laughed a high, echoing rill for nearly an hour. In the end, Dawes Williams carried him home and left him on his mother's stoop, like carrying a drunk with one separated arm and shoulder. He didn't come to school; and he didn't eat. He just lay in his room and became periodically hysterical. From the day he arose, Ratshit Rawlings believed firmly in Willis Skokes. He emulated him; studied him in the halls; talked about him incessantly. Finally, Ratshit even analyzed him. He discussed him, frankly, some years later, in terms of Christ-like salvation. It grew. It became mythic; and at the center remained always the image of Willis Skokes; Willis T. Skokes as the personification of— "I could have done it all right, if I had so chosen: but fortunately for me and my being I did not so choose."

Because you weren't a fuck-off if you chose to become one. Anyone in Rapid Cedar could tell you that. Even Travis Thomas almost understood that. And so, from an early age, Ratshit Rawlings had chosen an unclassical variation on a court-jester theme in which, by merely choosing to play the fool, he thought he would be able eventually to mock, enlighten, finally even rise above the king; the entire system of the king, his father, Mr. Harrison "Ratshit" Rawlings, Sr. Dawes Williams understood it. He watched it grow; he watched it all flower like a manure-headed weed until finally, breaking through, festering into a field of only sun after all of those years of rising through soil, it became suddenly self-conscious and merely eccentric. And that was ironic, or maybe it wasn't, because Ratshit Rawlings claimed some obscure New England Transcendentalist as ancestor and because, Dawes Williams thought finally, Ratshit must have inherited Willis Skokes like some brilliant seed of a gene that never quite bloomed; that refused to hatch back over in this dreaming, more technical air; that had somehow got choked, blackened, inverted and reversed somewhere along the way. In the end, Dawes Williams could remember Ratshit Rawlings talking of Willis Skokes in terms of being some kind of a secular oversoul. . . .

Soon Dawes Williams, who was not really playing with Mrs. Rawlings' Newtonian steelies anyway, roused himself from his dreaming and began to watch Eddie, who was sitting over in the corner, watching him back. Eddie was looking back over at him, and they were beginning to watch each other think. Eddie, Dawes Williams knew without asking, was sitting over there thinking that Dawes Williams was dreaming up another of about the biggest batches of crap he had ever heard. Eddie knew that Dawes Williams liked to distort things, to make them complicated for the hell of it. He knew that Ratshit Rawlings was often a whipped-out bastard that couldn't cut it. He knew that there was just a lot of Ratshit Rawlings in Dawes Williams too, by God. He knew mostly that Ratshit Rawlings was only good for games when things got dull. And that he, Eddie himself, had a Welshman's liver and a limited explanation for things; and that although Dawes Williams was one of his best friends, he hated his guts. . . .

It was still Saturday afternoon, and everyone was waiting, waiting for the Rawlingses to leave for Iowa City. Just then, however, everyone was watching as Mr. Harrison Rawlings, Sr., busily and drunkenly threw Ratshit's entire allowance, a crisp ten-dollar bill, on the exact center of the carpet. Then Mr. Rawlings sat back, into the bemused distance of his chair, and watched as Harrison, Jr., went over, bent down, and picked it up.

Coming back into the circle of Newtonian steelies, sitting down Indian-style, Dawes could see Ratshit's face was bright red, glassy and stoned over. But soon even that passed because it was a football afternoon, the Evashevski era, and because everything was filtering into the grander design of stealing the car. Around twelve-thirty *the* Country Club set began coming past, and drifting in. They stopped in small, select caravans of Cadillacs, Lincolns and an occasional Mercedes convertible. There was a quiet parade of tasteful straw baskets with neatly checkered cloths, tweed coats and sleeveless V-necked sweaters, brown wing tips and an occasional lawyer's pipe. Silver flasks flashed in the Midwestern sun. The sun sank beyond noon, the fighting Hawkeyes had already kicked off, and everyone who was fourteen wished suddenly that the whole world would get its ass on the road.

But Dawes Williams thought Ratshit's mother, who was sitting in a chair near the window, who was obviously not leaving for anywhere at the moment, was one of the most striking older women he'd ever seen. The dense fall light fell through her premature platinum hair. Dawes remembered talking to her one Saturday about Martin Luther. He had sat back, judging her ideas about Martin Luther, becoming the real snob in the piece by deciding she was really quite intelligent, but in the middle she had destroyed the whole mood anyway by pausing and intoning:

"Dawes, you sound like such a nice, reasonable boy. Is there any way you could . . . that is, is there any way you could use your influence to see that Harrison is not called Rat's . . . Rat's '*shit*' any more do you suppose?"

Dawes Williams promised he would try his best, but nothing had come of it.

Later, after stealing the car and making long circles through the town and returning, reparking the whole thing on its chalk marks in the driveway long after the Rawlingses had left, they sat in the kitchen and drank straight warm bourbon from wine glasses and tried not to wince. Travis and Dunker took theirs down in two large gulps and then looked out of the window for a long time. When they looked back, their eyes were still slightly flushed. They all drank two apiece and sat on the kitchen floor talking in the late, drifting shadows. Dawes Williams said:

"By God, I think I'm drunk," and they all began laughing, and looking at each other closely as if they were supposed to see something they had never seen before. The early fall evening began wafting the walls of Mrs. Rawlings' kitchen without even a voice. The Rawlingses would be home soon. It was time to roll the underground up and call it a day. They got up and headed for the porch. They hung around for awhile and said goodbye to Ratshit. Travis turned the other way. Eddie, Dunker and Dawes walked to the corner. They turned. The pale light grayed in the bare trees, drifted off like a boat in the cold autumn limbs. Travis was already down the block.

"Hey, Travis," they said, "we'll be seeing ya."

"That's right, you will," he said, turning. "Damn right. I'll be seeing ya. And don't let your meat loaf," he called after them down the quiet street.

It had been a good day, a day already slipping into memory, gone down the long edges of boulevards full as houses with dark elm and white cedar.

"What's up tonight?" Dunker was saying.

"I'm taking Georgia down by the hedges on Ben Franklin Field and wrestlin' her for it," Eddie said.

"Wrestle her for what?" Dawes Williams said, turning off, calling behind himself, moving up the hill for home, drunk on the air.

5

One evening, when they were still fourteen, when Eddie was at football practice and Dunker was home reading comic books, Ratshit and Dawes finished shooting baskets early and went over to The East End Drugstore. Ratshit sat dropping peanuts in his Coke. They fizzed and went dead. A wet-faced, linoleum-looking woman approached the druggist. He handed her a bluish box, she trudged out of the store and Ratshit began laughing so hard that soon he was nearly spilling the peanuts in his Coke.

"Did you see that!?!" he said.

"Sure," Dawes Williams said. "What?"

"She bought her some Molly Rags!"

"Some Molly who?"

"Some Kotex!"

"Sure," Dawes Williams said easily. "What's that?"

"Oh, my God," Ratshit Rawlings said.

"Hell, yes," Dawes Williams said, sensing some trouble, "she bought her some Molly Ragging."

They left the store walking toward Ratshit's house. The street, a boulevard once shaded in summer by a completely twined canopy of cedar trees, was a sleeping mass, a rustle of leaves. It was late autumn. Fall. The leaves were raked in piles and were drying from yellow to brown and dying.

Dawes sensed something was about to happen. It was more than winter. It was memory come home; something he had no conception of, yet knew. It was something to be completely unrelated to his life.

"Hey, Ratshit?" he said, "what's a Molly Rag exactly, would you say?"

Ratshit looked at him in disbelief and he said:

"That's pretty damn funny, Dawes. That's a good one."

So Dawes Williams stared back, without even batting an eye, and to Ratshit it was as if he wanted him to tell him something he already knew. Then, after another long silence, a shift in the wind, Dawes said:

"What's so funny about it would you say offhand, Ratshit?"

"You mean . . ."

"Mean what . . ."

"THAT'S EXACTLY WHAT I MEAN," Ratshit Rawlings said, "THAT YOU DON'T KNOW THE FACTS OF LIFE!"

Silence. Dawes Williams was watching the trees for sign.

"Hell, yes," he finally said. "What facts exactly?"

Silence. Pretty soon Ratshit was watching the trees with him. It was as if, perhaps, they were both searching for a hole in the sky.

"The facts the facts the facts!" Ratshit Rawlings said.

"Hell, yes," Dawes Williams said, "the facts."

"Whadaya mean what facts!" Ratshit Rawlings said suddenly. "There's only one facts I know about, man. A woman bleeds once a month. That's what the facts are!"

"That's the facts?"

"Hell, yes, that's the facts," Ratshit Rawlings said. "You got any other kind we're not aware of yet, Dawes?"

"She bleeds, huh?"

"Hell, yes, she bleeds."

Silence. Ratshit could tell Dawes Williams was thinking it over.

"Hey, Ratshit," he said.

"Ya," Ratshit said, biting his lip.

"Why exactly is it, would you say, that's a fact?" he said. "You know, I mean among all other facts, for example?"

Silence. By this time Ratshit Rawlings was beginning to worry about himself. To hell with Dawes Williams, he thought.

"You know, I mean, why exactly would you say *that's* a fact and some others aren't?" Dawes Williams was saying very low in his throat, over and over, walking abstractedly along with himself, as if no one else were listening any more.

Hell, Ratshit thought, I know I am listening. I know I am here. It is Dawes Williams who is losing his way.

"What the hell," Ratshit said. "Dawes, get ahold of yourself."

"I mean," Dawes Williams said, walking alone, continuing to pace in a garden, "why exactly is it she bleeds?"

"Well, she damn well better bleed, Dawes, or she's pregnant! Then you've got trouble, by God!"

Silence. Ratshit was nearly certain he had Dawes Williams there. He could tell Dawes was thinking that one over for sure.

"You mean *those* facts?"

"Hell, yes. You got some others, Dawes?"

"Of life?"

"Yep," Ratshit said, trying to draw a line under the conversation, once and for all.

"I'll be damned," Dawes Williams said, striding along, not even batting an eye. "Hell, yes, those facts of life."

"The Birds and The Bees," Ratshit Rawlings said, smiling, at ease now because it was finally over.

Silence.

Silence. But something was missing. Ratshit became uneasy, doubtful, disturbed. He could see Dawes Williams was ticking over, about to hatch again.

"Hey, Ratshit," Dawes finally said not looking over at him any more. "Pregnant?"

"Oh, my God," Ratshit said, biting his lip again. "Where am I? Heavy with child, Dawes. Going to have a baby. Fat, for Christsake," he said.

In the silence Ratshit thought that one must have got him for sure, pierced his heart and shut him up for good. But it didn't. Instead, Dawes Williams screwed himself up and he said:

"Ratshit, old man, whyd'ya suppose it is she gets pregnant? Do you have any ideas on that subject?"

"WHY *HELL!!!???!!!*" Ratshit screamed in the open air.

"God damn it," Dawes Williams said. "You don't have to get so excited about it."

"Listen," Ratshit said, " . . . because a little black elf comes down the chimney once a year and sprinkles magic gold dust on her head. Because a great white bird works for the post office. Because the old man didn't pay his income taxes!!! Why the hell do you think WHY, you silly bastard," Ratshit said, developing an eye twitch. "Listen," he said, "where exactly in the hell would you say you are right now, Dawes? Would you say you are even here?" he said.

"That sounds pretty goofy to me, Harrison," Dawes Williams said.

"Thank God for something, Dawes. Do you want to go on?"

"I think so. Yes, why not? I think I am up to that."

"Jesus H. God," Ratshit Rawlings said.

In the silence Dawes paused, began shooting baskets against a tree.

"Well, you know, Ratshit," he said finally, busy not batting an eye again. "I mean exactly."

"Listen," Ratshit said, "I think I am making a bad job of this one."

"Com'on," Dawes said. "Tell me about it."

"All right," Ratshit said, giving up, "this is the way it goes for ya, Dawes. EXACTLY because," he said, "EXACTLY because the man gets hard and sticks it up the woman."

"Oh, Christ," Dawes Williams said. "That's incredible."

Then there was another long silence.

"His what?" Dawes Williams said, quietly, not even caring any more.

"His 'WHAT'!!!???" Ratshit Rawlings said, stamping his foot nervously, not caring any more either.

"Sure," Dawes Williams said. "Why not? His 'what'?"

"Listen," Ratshit Rawlings said. "His cock. What else? Dawes," he said. "I don't think you have this thing quite down yet."

"IN HER!" Dawes Williams exploded.

"Where else?" Ratshit said quietly, giving in. "Out the window for Christsake? This thing *has* a certain logic, you know, Dawes."

In a silence deeper, more flecked than the afternoon Ratshit *knew* he had him there for sure. It was that simple. It was over. Then Dawes Williams said:

"Hell, yes," he said seriously, not even batting an eye again, "those facts. For a minute there I thought you were talking about some new kind of facts."

"Oh, for Christsake, Dawes," Ratshit said. "Where the hell are you at?"

In the stillness Ratshit could see that Dawes was still chewing it all over in his mind, trying to figure it out. It worried him.

"Take it easy, Dawes," he offered. "I won't tell the guys what a stupid sonofabitch you are."

"Thanks, Ratshit," Dawes Williams said. "I believe you."

They began walking the boulevard again. That damn Dawes, Ratshit thought, he's still thinking about it. He may go about thinking about it for the rest of his motherless life for all I know. A guy does too much of that and he goes nuts in the end. I guess I made a bad job of that one all right, he thought, striding along, dribbling his ball.

"But it isn't natural somehow," Dawes Williams finally began saying. "It just isn't natural."

"Besides, Dawes," Ratshit said, ignoring him, "I was the same way once. Ignorant. Give it time, it'll grow on ya."

"I guess it'll have to," Dawes Williams said.

"Last summer," Ratshit said, continuing to ignore him, "my dad let me drive the car out into the country. I knew something was up—he usually doesn't let me drive that car anywhere. Anyway, we were just driving along there, high as the king of France, and pretty soon he starts to talking about fish swimming up the damn river once a year. I thought the crazy sonofabitch was nuts. I never saw any fish swimming up the damn river once a year, did you Dawes? Anyway, pretty soon he's talking about apes and people. He's calling it progress or something. Finally I can see he's getting to the point, and he says something about a man sticking it up a damn woman—only he doesn't say 'sticking' exactly."

"What is it exactly it is he is saying?" Dawes Williams was saying, looking for words to hold on to.

"Well," Ratshit said, having to wind up all over again, "he said something about 'coipussy' or some damn thing. Anyway, at that point, I drove straight off the road and put the car down a ditch, and just sat there looking at him. I put two hundred dollars' damage in the front end, Dawes! But he—he's just saying nothing at all, sitting there mindlessly in the ditch like he's been caught out in the rain, that eye twitch of his going like sixty now, you know—and then finally he just turns to me, looks me in the eye quietly, like I'm not even there, and he says: 'Well, Harrison, I guess I made a bad job of that one.' Imagine that, Dawes. Two hundred dollars' damage!"

"Then what happened?"

"Happened! Why I just looked him square in the eye, and I said: 'You actually mean to sit there and tell me he PISSES in her!!!???'"

"PISSES IN HER!!!!" Dawes Williams exploded.

"Easy, Dawes. Hell, no, he doesn't piss in her exactly."

"Well, what is it he does would you say exactly?"

"He comes in her," Ratshit Rawlings said.

"Comes where?"

"In her box."

"What box?"

"Her cunt. Between her legs."

"My God," Dawes Williams said. "With what?"

"His nuts," Ratshit said. "What else?"

"MY GOD, RATSHIT," Dawes Williams said quietly. "YOU MUST BE OUT OF YOUR MIND!"

In the silence, chewing on his tongue now because he could see Dawes Williams was losing it for sure, was beat down to nothing on that one, Ratshit let out a single heavy breath and seemed to be searching the sky for nervous rain.

"It's not natural. It's just not natural," Dawes Williams was saying. "I know it isn't."

"I know. Kinda cherry, isn't it?"

"So that's what 'cherry' means."

"Hell, yes."

"By God," Dawes said, almost furious about the eyes now, realizing something that had been lost. "So that's what 'fuck,' itself, means."

"Hell, yes," Ratshit said.

"Well I'll be damned," Dawes said. "I never knew that."

It seemed suddenly to Ratshit that Dawes was becoming more interested in the language of the thing than in the thing itself. Then Dawes Williams spoke again:

"Ratshit," he said almost formally, nearly shaking hands, "I sure want to thank you for tellin' me all this damn fact-of-life crap. It sure straightens a lot of things out."

"You're welcome, Dawes," Ratshit said.

"I never would have figured all that out. I just never would."

"You're welcome, Dawes."

Dawes half expected Ratshit to go on with even greater mysteries, but just then Mrs. Rawlings (they had gotten to Ratshit's house by that time), who had been standing on the porch, eyeing them, said:

"Harrison! Whatever are you boys talking about out there?"

Ratshit leaned back on a tree, and he felt that was an opening for something if he'd ever heard one, but he restrained himself. He didn't want to set Dawes Williams off again if he could help it, and he didn't say a word. The air was leafless, and all three of them then just stood hanging around for awhile in the same circles of dreaming air, listening to the same silence until it got so bad Dawes Williams turned round dramatically to her, Ratshit's mother, and he addressed her and said:

"Mrs. Rawlings, Martin Luther must have been out of his mind. I never thought of that before!"

And with that, he turned again and dribbled down the street.

Dawes went straight home and got down the thin black book his parents had gotten him two years before from the back of his closet. It began at "amoeba," progressed through "worms" and other various fishes and flying reptiles, and eventually wound its way toward the "primate." By the time he was finished, Dawes was sure he was one again with Blackey Jane, a guttable jack, and he wanted only to go downstairs and discuss his bodily functions with the family cat. The book had anti-Michelangelo line drawings and it was the first time in his life that Dawes didn't believe the printed word. On the dull brown surface of his mind he had somehow always managed to confuse anything printed with the true, gold-leafed, parchment-papered, musky yellow wind of the old family Bible. The Word was law. Something printed was old and polished and worked on, and shredded and falling apart, but true. Why should anyone take the trouble to print something unless they were sure it was true? After finishing *Facts for the Young Man or Woman Coming of Age*, however, Dawes Williams never believed another printed word as long as he lived.

Besides, Dawes was still interested in the Rover Boys and Robin Hood—both brought to life in worn, dog-eared volumes handed down long corridors of English-American fathers. He believed in clean violence that left only dead numbers and living civilization standing behind; in Ethan Allen, Mad Anthony Wayne and Marion the Swamp Fox. Dawes even believed in the military tactics of the fall of Byzantium, but not in the simple tedium, the natural phenomenon of fish swimming up the damn river once a year. The Rover Boys raced neat Anglo-Saxon ice boats not long after the turn of the century. They outwitted schoolmasters and various other assorted villainous rogues and outright scoundrels through Yankee ingenuity, forthrightness and American perseverance in the right to triumph. Dawes' early politics could best be described as "benevolent fascism"—nonsexually somewhere just to the right of the Marquis de Sade. That was the American myth Dawes Williams lived in innocently, peanut Walter Mitty, exactly fifty or so odd years after it never even happened. It was a land full of guiltless heroes and monosexually celibate skyscapes. The psychoanalytic explication of the *Nancy Drew Mystery Series* in terms of sapphic "butch" hadn't been published yet. Or, if it had, Dawes hadn't seen it yet. Dawes thought things were getting a little Gothic, but he mulled it over and began going to parties. . . .

He went back downstairs. He buried himself in Little League. He didn't know what Gothic really was yet and wouldn't for years; but he did know how to hook slide. Ty Cobb, in fact, the Georgia Peach, invented the hook slide, Coach Otto Volkavitch said, hosing down a long patch of summer dust and ball field until it was fine mud. Sliding practice. Little League. Ratshit Rawlings' fable slipped into memory for awhile. Robin Hood rode past on a great gray ass. Robin Hood was dead. Robin-Hood-on-the-last-page of the book lay quietly sprawled on the ground; his head was supported by Little John. You could smell their leather jerkins, a blending, musty as pine wood and smoke, rise over the nettled lilac at the forest edge. Robin shot an arrow into the air. It flew straight as a goose's edge, up, over England; became a fine, red-tipped swan graying in the far western sky. Robin Hood turned to Little John—"Bury me," he said, "where the last shot comes to earth." Silence. His last clean shot. . . .

6

Travis Thomas paced the mound for William McKinley. Dawes Williams was hitting lead-off for Benjamin Franklin. The veins on Travis' neck stood out in the lengthening sun and shadows like perfect ropes, and Dawes began watching him, staring him down, from the other end of a long tunnel. Knocking the dirt off his spikes, stepping back in for the 2-2 pitch, Dawes noticed it was the first time he had ever really looked at Travis Thomas. . . . The long, sleeping edge of day was drifting off, and the stands were full of girls, sweaters, bright splotches of color, the slow, self-consuming chatter of wrens. . . .

That spring Dawes was hitting lead-off. He wasn't hitting well that year, but he was usually able to get on base somehow. Eddie had once hit lead-off, and the worse he hit, the more Eddie sensed an advantage. Dawes can't hit the fast one this year, he said. In fact, Dawes can't hit shit. And the more Eddie said it, the worse Dawes hit. Baseball was a simple thing, too simple, in fact, to master for long.

But Dawes Williams, trying to put everything away from himself now and failing, stepped back into the box. On the next pitch of the game Dawes watched fiercely chicken-eyed as Travis wound up with a slow curve ball: he watched the thing begin to sail in and curve away with an unbelievably slow arc. It was as if the ball had made a life of its own and was dreaming of only the sound its own wind left on passing afterthoughts of air. As it sailed in by itself, Dawes Williams began thinking of a plan—by merely putting his head down and letting the pitch bounce softly from his four-ply Wilson's batting helmet, he was on first base. . . .

"That's using your head, Willy," Eddie called out.

Travis was so mad at it all he took too long with his wind-up and Dawes stole second. Then Travis began throwing so hard—standing on the exact top of second, Dawes could see the blue ropes of veins on Travis' neck stick out like muscles before he turned his head to the plate—that he got wild and walked the next two hitters. With the bases loaded, Travis was forced to let up on a 3-2 pitch to Dunker, it was another slow one, and Dunker took his time and nearly guillotined him with it. The returning white streak was a recoiled cannon, a yo-yo with the recoil being twice as fast as the pitch, and it knocked Travis off the mound and, when the dust settled, Dawes had scored. Travis didn't settle himself down any, but he struck out the side. He walked from the mound like a retired America matador, and the game a 1-0 pitcher's duel— Travis Thomas versus Ben Franklin's own Mike Eagle. The late afternoon darkened around home plate, and the girls began talking in increasingly self-understood chatter, in self-appointed groups, the sound of wind-blown paper, deep sun and rustling leaves. They began trading ballplayer's rings in the stands. It was all like a flesh market conducted by celibates.

They only played seven innings. Soon it was the top of the fifth, and McKinley was going to lose. Travis sat on the bench watching. He had walked Dawes twice, and so Dawes, counting the time he'd been struck on the head, had been on base the three times he was up. In the third Travis had hit a ground ball to Eddie, who had made a good backhand play on it and made the long throw from short toward Dawes at first. In a remote animal ear Dawes heard the ground thunder, the illusion of hooves that Travis made coming down the base path. Travis was running on the inside of the base line, Dawes could hear it, and as Dawes did a ballet split (something he practiced religiously at night in his living room), Travis came down hard on his Achilles' tendon, opening up a nice, two-inch-deep bloody gash. It was a close play— "You're oooot!" screamed the black, peanut-hatted umpire.

Then Dawes got off the ground and took off his glove with the ball still in it and threw it in Travis' face. Then Travis picked up Dawes Williams and threw him in the air about six feet. Then the umpire came down the line like a renegade humanist and broke it up.

"What is this shit?" Eddie called over from short.

"You sonofabitch, Travis," Dunker said, coming in from right field to ass-end him and knock him in a pile over Dawes. "You spiked Dawes on purpose, you miserable excuse for a cocksucker!"

Both benches began milling around; a few were carrying bats.

"Did not," Travis said. "So what? He had his damn foot over the bag."

"Bullshit. Dawes is a regular toe dancer at that. I saw it!"

"The hell you did, Dunker."

"Kiss off, Travis," Dawes said.

"Kiss off, Dawes," Travis said.

"Now, boys," the old white-haired gentleman volunteer umpire said, "play like men or we'll not play at all. The next cuss word is out of the game and sent home."

"This is how men play. I seen'em on television," Dawes said.

Then they all settled down and began drifting back to the benches. The essence of law and penalty is the loss of position and sexual standing, Dawes thought, standing newly risen at first base. No one wanted to be thrown from the game.

But now it was the fifth, and Travis had just hit a sharp single to left. He was on first, proud, feeling justified by fate. Dawes went over to the mound: he stuck the ball in his belt, under the robe of his bulky woolen shirt; it was all illegal, but then the umpire hadn't seen him. The pitcher, Mike Eagle, began kicking dirt from the mound, stalling.

"Travis, you're a cheat'n' sonofabitch," Dawes said after coming back to the bag. "You spiked me on purpose, mother."

"The hell. Besides, you'd have spiked me if I gave you the chance."

He would have. Dawes Williams was stumped for a minute. Then he said: "Yes, and I stole second off ya, too. You said I'd never do that—remember?"

Travis began remembering.

"I'm going to steal second and third right now," he said.

"Bet you a buck."

Travis began thinking—second was easy, third was much harder. "I'll take fifty cents on second," he said.

"Hell," Dawes Williams said, "I'll bet you the buck on second."

"You must have the ball in your glove then."

"Hell, no, look."

"Lemme see the inside palm."

"Here, I wouldn't lie to you," Dawes said, "we're friends."

"You're a dumb bastard then, because I could steal second on a trike."

"You won't even get a good lead-off off the Eagle," Dawes Williams said.

"The hell. You just come down and pay me," Travis said, edging off first.

Dawes was becoming quietly hysterical. He had already won, it was over, but nobody else knew it yet. He had Travis cold. He waited until the umpire and Travis were both looking away, then he slipped the ball from under his shirt and saying, "Hey, Ump," he walked over deliberately and tagged Travis out.

"You're oooot!" said the old white umpire.

Travis froze. He turned red and fumed. He kicked at some dirt and didn't believe it. It was the oldest trick in the game. Even the bored stands had come alive again for a moment. The veins stood out from his face. He kicked at some more dirt. Dunker sat down in right field laughing. Eddie was rolling on the ground at short; he couldn't contain himself. He thought beautiful old Dawes Williams could sneak himself in anywhere and steal anything at all. Then Travis pulled back to throw a punch, and Dawes began to feint backwards so that when it came, he could duck forward, thinking vaguely, only, God this is going to hurt. He's going to kill me this time. I almost don't blame him. I'm going to need a place to duck real soon. Christ this is going to hurt. Then, just as suddenly, Travis straightened up, threw his powerful shoulders back and walked with black dignity off the field. Dawes relaxed and threw the ball around the horn. Arthur had taught him that one. One night at the farm. Talking, down by the dog pens. In August. In one of his other lives. A thousand years ago. The fifth inning was over. . . .

In the seventh McKinley managed to tie the score. The third sacker had hit a homer over Dunker's head. In the bottom of the seventh the first Ben Franklin man, Ratshit Rawlings, managed to get around to third. Two others were put out. Dawes was up. "You can do'er," said Mr. Stebs, a senile coach. Like hell I can, Dawes thought. "Bring in the old winning-run slugger," Eddie said, laughing. Flustered, Dawes Williams then brought larger guffaws by turning back to the bench, to Eddie, and saying:

"Is it my fault I am up? I can't help it."

Then he turned back and headed out, like Jesse James mounting up and stringing toward town, for the old rubber plate. Soon he was in the box again. He knew only that everybody was eyeing him, and that he clearly lacked all ability to eye them back. It was a terrible moment. But just maybe this could all turn out all right, into the finest tradition of American finishes he thought; like hell, Dawes thought back, against his own grain. LIKE HELL , he thought, why me, there's eight others who just as easily could be up right now. "Let's have a hitter up here, getting late," the umpire said. Like hell, Dawes thought, I'm no hitter. He stepped into the box but he didn't like it. He thought the tension was terrific.

The first two pitches were straight down the heart of the plate. Like hell, Dawes thought, this umpire's a volunteer. He stepped back out of the box. He looked the old gentleman square in the face. It looked suddenly to Dawes as if the umpire needed cornea transplants in both eyes. He felt as though he wanted to wet his pants. He stepped back farther, rubbed some dirt on his hands. He spit on the handle of his bat. He didn't want to fight. He didn't want to do anything at all. He thought he had wet his pants slightly. Then he hitched up his crotch and knocked some imaginary dirt from his spikes.

"Never mind that," Travis said from the mound, "you're not runnin' anywhere, Dawes."

"What a fantastic breach of etiquette, Thomas," Dawes heard himself say, absentmindedly blowing his cool, bringing laughter from everyone involved.

"Hit it a fur, fur piece, Dawes," Eddie yelled from the bench, laughing hysterically.

Everyone looked around at Eddie, and most of them were laughing. The coach ignored it, and only fumed slightly. Dawes Williams was his boy. Dawes stepped back into the box. WHAT the hell, he thought. I haven't got a chance. My own team's laughing at me. I'm going to swing. Travis began a wind-up that went on for years. He did (swing).

He swung like the lost sonofabitch he was. He caught it ignobly on the handle, three inches higher than the top of his hand. It flew as high, straight, far as a water-logged duck. Wet and shot-at-the-top-before-it-took-wing, it made a low deathlike arc, sputtered in the wind and began going dead. It flew like a magnificent bit of Halloween genius, a plot of air, and it metamorphosized finally, became a white swan, and fell safely to earth exactly two feet past the shortstop's death plunge. Travis convulsed slightly, and Ratshit Rawlings scored. Dawes Williams had hit a blooper. A dying gull. A sad watermelon. A fat bat. A ladies' aid. A Texas leaguer. A clean scratch hit. *Le roi le vent.* DAWES WILLIAMS HAD WON THE GAME.

"Dawes," they all said for the next couple of days, whenever it came up, "you was one lucky sonofbitch that day."

Only the great sky remained vacant of naked God. A sign . . .

7

After that, Dawes thought over Ratshit Rawlings' fable for awhile and began going to parties. There he developed a purer passion for a girl named Becky Thatcher. The irony was terrific, but he didn't care, that was her name. She smelt of dancing cinnamon moving about on the burned edge of dark rooms. They waltzed in the long, innocent cavern together. She watched him play baseball. He walked her home, along the wet cement, in the rain. He didn't care. He loved her like God and the Angels. He recognized himself to be Andy Hardy, Henry Aldridge, Beaver Cleaver. He didn't care. He was out of his mind. They talked, he thought. At the end of two endless months he kissed her quietly.

Eddie had said, "Ya, and Dawes hasn't even kissed on her any yet." And the more Eddie said it, the harder it became. Eddie said it at the end of the First week, Second, Third, Fourth. He was keeping a running score.

It was hell. Dawes was still in the ninth grade and slightly backward. Travis and Eddie had kissed so many girls in so many black and tactile corners they said they'd lost count. Dunker hadn't done anything yet, but he would be the first to lose his virginity. Bare Teat was an ultimate, a consummate, an absolute value. It was as if, walking in an abstract wilderness, a barren reach of snow, you could come quietly upon a trader's post, and merely sashay up to the bar, and use—"Hey, I've known someone once who has gotten Bare Teat"—in direct trade for canned goods and furs to keep you warm.

They all said they had known someone vaguely who "had gotten Bare Teat."

Bare Teat was a noble thing; dark labyrinths streaking beyond red mirrors. An American experience. Like having a mother. Apple pie. The Fourth. And so throughout that furious spring and summer they all spent their time trying to politely rape girls of their Bare Teat. They took them under trees and begged; chased them quietly down alleys; took them into dark corners where they couldn't scream and wrestled them for it; tried to buy them with rings and promises of eternal faithfulness. They raised up idealized images in heat and cast them down again in futile curses. It was hell.

So Dawes Williams hung his baseball spikes part way up the wall and began going to parties held always by girls with newly remodeled basements. Dawes quickly learned that only through social standing in the womb could one be assured of it in preschool, in grade school, in junior high, senior high, could one find it in college, in life, which didn't necessarily take care of the Hereafter, but it all helped. In the end Dawes arrived at the conclusion that it was all a Puritan Eventualism crossed impossibly with the Romance of an American movie.

"You dance with her," they all said.

"No, you," they all said, passing the buck, standing quietly in the corners of a room.

"It seems to me," Dawes Williams said, "that everyone around here is standing on the outskirts of something or other."

"Jesus," Travis said, turning away.

"What the hell, if I wanted to dance with her, I would," Terry Murray said.

"Well, why don't you just damn well dance with her then?" Mike Eagle said.

"Don't want to."

"Oh."

Silence.

"What the hell, dance with her," T. T. Calders said.

"Don't want to, what the hell," Barney Ingersoll said.

"The bitch," Eddie said.

Silence.

"Lookit'em over there," B. T. Saus said.

"What about'em?" B. R. Bush said. "Saus, I don't believe I'm with you on this one."

"Oh, ma Gawd," B. T. said, "I don't believe these girls are ma brand. They're just sitting over there."

"Have another Coke, Saus," B. R. said, laughing. "This is a strain. You better rest up for awhile."

"I'm a busy man all right," said B. T. Saus, drinking from the bottle. "Oh, ma Gawd, what is this piss!?!" he said a moment later, nearly spitting it on the floor.

"Saus," B. R. said finally, "I think you need a drink."

Just then, over there, Carol Smith turned to Nancy Jones and she whispered:

"Just look at those boys over there. They're just *standing* there."

Silence.

"What the hell," Mike Hanna said, "they're only flesh."

"Okay, let's go," they all said, hitching their ties, stringing out for town.

"No," Barney Ingersoll said, stopping them, "I mean, what in the hell do they think they're good for?"

"They aren't good for anything," Eddie said.

"Not you, too," Dunker said. "Dawes just had that all explained to him the other day and. . ."

"Good, Dunker," Eddie said, "real fine. . ."

Just then, however, a nice-looking woman with a smile on her face and a daughter who was giving the party came in with a fresh bowl of pink dip.

"Thanks a lot, Mrs. Prescott," they all said.

After she had left, B. T. Saus took a bite, turned straight to the wall, and pronounced brokenly:

"Christ. What is this stuff? I think I'm poisoned."

"Hell, Saus," Eddie said, "it's probably nothing at all. Looks to me like purified sheep come. Can't hurt you at all."

Silence. Everyone was looking at Eddie and smiling.

"Yep," Travis Thomas was saying, resting against the basement wall and rubbing abstractedly at the muscle of his right arm with his left hand, "they aren't good for much all right."

"Hell, yes," Ratshit Rawlings said.

"Damn straight," they all said.

"Why not dance with one of them?" Dawes Williams said. "You've got nothing to lose."

"Attttttttsssss Dawes," Dunker said. "Why don't you?"

"Oh ya?" Dawes Williams said.

Silence. Everyone was looking at Dawes Williams and smiling.

"Hell, yes," they all said.

"Damn straight," they said.

Silence.

"Hell," Eddie said, laughing, "if Dunker was to dance with a girl right now, she'd be making out with his knee."

Silence. Everyone was looking at Dunker and smiling.

"Why do they just sit there like stone?" Ratshit said.

"I'm not sure," Dawes Williams said. "I believe their damn mothers told them to."

"Oh."

"I believe we've already covered that ground," B. T. Saus said, turning away, lighting a cigaret in a corner of the wall.

Silence. Carol Otis, with a pure passion that transcended guilt or innocence, with eyes fixed and even fused on Travis, crossed through the center of the longest room of her life and asked him to dance.

"Lookit Travis turn that one down," Barney Ingersoll said, half-whispering. "He's a cold one by God."

"Damn straight. Travis knows what he's doing," Eddie said. "I think I'll go ask that one to dance."

"To *dance?*" Ratshit said.

"Hell, yes," they all said.

Silence.

"You pussy-whipped sonofabitch, Welsh," Dunker said.

Silence. Everyone was looking at Eddie Welsh look at himself.

"Ya," Eddie said, backing away, "she's a bitch anyway."

"Yeah. Yeah. Right. Right," B. T. Saus said.

Silence. Crossing the room to grab another bag of potato chips, Dunker bumped his head on a piece of fake ceiling.

"By God," Ratshit Rawlings said.

"Who's playing B-ball tomorrow?" Tom Olsen asked.

"Everybody," Dawes said.

"Over at Shandlin's?"

"Yep."

"Dunker and Eddie and Travis coming?"

"Sure, the guys are coming," Dawes Williams said.

Silence. Over in another corner others were talking.

"Say," Terry Murray said, "what the hell is Dawes doing here anyway? Thought Dawes doesn't believe in parties."

"Doesn't. Believes in shooting baskets mostly," Dunker said.

"At night?" Mike Eagle said.

"No," Eddie said, "sleeps at night, shoots baskets at dawn or some damn thing."

"Jesus," Turk O'Hara said.

"He only came because Eddie said he'd sneak over and bust up his bicycle if he didn't."

"Ya," Eddie said, leaving for the other side of the room, "I'm doin' Dawes a favor."

"Nobody rides bicycles," Terry Murray said.

"Dawes does," Dunker said. "Says it builds up his legs or some damn thing."

"Jesus," Travis said.

"Oh, ma Gawd," B. T. Saus said.

In the silence Eddie was dancing.

"Hey," Dunker said, "lookit Eddie out there dancing with Cathy. He must be a horny one, by God."

"What a sell-out," Travis said.

"What a romantic dink," Dawes Williams added.

"That's it, Dawes," Dunker said, "I think you've got it."

"Oh, ma Gawd," B. T. Saus said, "these girls are just not ma brand."

"Why not, let's dance," they all said finally across those dark rooms of single file.

It was then Dawes Williams asked Becky Thatcher to dance. He walked right up to her, sort of waltzed and whistled around her for awhile, like she was made of a purer sugar candy and breakable, and said only:

"Hey—you wanna dance?"

After that, they said nothing for hours on end. They strolled on the long edges of the room, moved quietly without strain beyond red mirrors and walls. The place grew darker; a deeper night fell. Everyone began looking for a corner to hide in; but the purer girls remained in the exact center of the flooring and remained relative virgins for weeks on end. Becky and Dawes grew completely together without ever touching. He knew he loved her. It was hell. They danced on, beyond themselves, beyond the room and the windows which were dreams. He knew he loved her, but he didn't know how to proceed. He knew if he kissed her, he would dissolve and pass through to the other side. She moved her fresh blouse against him and hugged him to her with both arms. He felt there was something pathetic about it. They danced on. Mrs. Prescott came in and turned on the lights seven times. No one spoke. The lights went out. Mrs. Prescott came in and told her daughter, Debora, she would be severely punished if this kept up. Everyone stared at Mrs. Prescott for minutes on end. No one spoke. The lights went off again. Mrs. Prescott gave up and went to bed. They danced on to the sounds of I Want You, I Need You, I Love You; Blue-Suede Shoes; The Twelfth of Never; Be-Bop-Alula; I'll Walk the Line; Silhouettes; Heartbreak Hotel; and especially But It's Only Make Believe by Conway Twitty. . . .

Once, on a Saturday, she came past Shandlin's to get him. The ball thudded the cement and went silent. The dull wood of the back board still hung in the air. The bright orange hoop was full of late winter sun. His ring was around her neck. He felt suddenly proud of her. He grabbed the ball, hit a shot from the corner, way out in the yard, and felt good. Soon it would be spring, time to play baseball again. She stood silently as a demanding fawn, small as perfect light, at the corner of the tall wood fence and waited for him.

"Whose ring has Becky got on?" Dunker said.

"Dawes'," Travis said.

"You've got to be shittin' me," Dunker said under his breath, "that's not possible."

"Hell, yes," Eddie said. "Dawes never does anything halfway. Now he's made himself into the biggest P. W. sonofabitch in town."

"Kiss off, Eddie," Dawes said.

"Kiss off, Dawes," Eddie said.

And Becky just stood there quietly, at the end of the fence, probably knowing she was being talked about. It was nearly spring and blooming red. She seemed small and somehow damn cute, not yet grown; just standing there in the wind and early flowers, across the closable distance of the yard. She was looking straight at Dawes and smiling.

"Good God, Dawes," Dunker said.

Dawes crossed the distance to the fence. He and Becky began walking down the shadowy, slap-quiet streets of elm and cedar. Dawes Williams felt whole again. Dunker called after:

"Hey! I think you two are right out of a bad Walt Disney movie. *The Lady and The Tramp.*"

"No," Eddie said, "*Bambi Meets the Dwarf.*"

"Hell, no," Travis said, "I think it is *Tom Thumb Meets the Virgin Mary, Mother of God.*"

Huge laughter went off behind him, but Dawes Williams didn't care; he was proud of her.

They walked along alone together. Walt Disney himself smiled after in the heavens, with unbelievably pearly teeth, with red dancing angels and green flying fairies, with hair as slick as a riverboat gambler's, with a deific head bigger than all the oil money in Texas . . . he was their patron saint, a gold, shiny medallion winking over and hung from the sky. They walked down streets as quiet as falling names. Apartments were destroying the neighborhood, people were chewing up the trees, and a Mormon Church stood on the sandy gray dirt of the old baseball lot. Dawes felt he and Becky were looking for a place of their own, a nest to hide in, a house of grass to become lost within, but there was no place to go any more. He felt there was something he must tell her, but he knew again he must remain speechless and, as in everything else, alone, a water body, a thin vessel only to pour shadows through. . . .

8

Dawes Williams was out in the deep, gold morning. Over the bridge he watched the shallow bottom water of the river become heavy with mud, carp, even dead catfish. There was a cold steel light lying just under the columned stacks smoking yellow summer, like rolled cigars, down near the dam. The morning had the close, drawn-in sweltering feel of a fat woman swatting away babies near a stoop; the rolled and bleated integrations of smoke rose and spread their alluvial fans of air over the vague, industrial river like old, whispering ladies leaning against you with their towering combs. Dawes Williams thought he saw the brighter bones of newer fish rise and compass, like bombs going off in the sun, like keys. They had sound, and he was with Travis Thomas and looking for a job for the summer, saying he could be a welder, or carry steel on a jack, and it was a big country even now but they were all busy and hammering on tin, they held sound, made noise, from those baroque towers, that jack-assed bray

America America

and from the bridge Travis, who was with him, spit into the water saying

"Hell of a sweet-mother country, Dawes. Makes you big just living in it. And we aren't ever going to be run out. Wound down to nothing. Never. We'll just be always big and sweet and rolling and impossible to crack, because that's what we naturally are, but I'll crack it someday, wait and see, because after all, Dawes," Travis said, spitting into the black water heavy with swirling carp, "it's only a damn thing and can be beaten. . . ."

Hell, Travis Thomas thought, Dawes Williams doesn't know a damn thing about this country of mine. . . .

But Dawes Williams only remained silent. He stood on the bridge and watched himself pour himself through the shadows on the water. He watched the new bright bones bomb in the sun and become old before they were used. . . .

9

It was Dawes' sixteenth summer, a time for American Legion baseball, drinking and going to work. He had been going to Joshua Wadlove High for a year now, and Becky Thatcher had passed behind him with surprisingly little effort or strain. One evening, early in the summer, Simpson had looked at him over his copy of *The Rapid Cedar Republican* and said:

"Yes, sir, old boy, a guy's got to start hustling in this world as soon as he can."

In the end Travis got Dawes and Eddie a job for a buck an hour. Dunker didn't need the work, as his mother usually slipped him twenty dollars before he sailed out for the day anyway. Travis talked to a man down by the river, and he got them all on shoveling diatomaceous earth into small pop-corn sacks with garden trowels. Dawes and Travis were stuffers and Eddie stitched them shut. They worked by themselves, without a foreman, on their honor as industrious Americans, and down a dark basement under the level of the river. Yellow fish eyes swam past all morning.

"Hell, Eddie," Dawes said, "what are these damn peanut sacks for in the first place?"

"Don't know," Eddie said, stitching number seven thousand four hundred and six shut as a seam of dust.

"Hell," Travis said, "this guy's going to save the potato chip industry with these bags. He's going to keep it drier."

Everyone laughed with Travis and continued sacking the dusty, phosphorus earth without a break in the rhythm. Travis figured he had done Dawes a favor. Dawes had been just sitting around all summer, wasting his time, reading on some books, drinking and playing ball, shooting pool and losing his money in card games. None of them really needed the money, but Travis believed like his father—a young man who is not out working and getting ahead in *this* country is dead and not fit to prosper. So Travis felt good to have got Dawes Williams off his can and showed him the way.

"It's not much," Travis was saying, "but it's good to know at least you can put in a good day's work."

"Big deal," Dawes Williams said. "I pull some of this earth here out of the barrel and I stick it in this sack. Travis," he said, "I don't know how to break this to you, but ever since I first realized I knew how to walk I knew I could do something like this. I don't have to come down here to this Charles Dickens fly coop under the river to learn something like that."

"Atttssss Dawes," Travis said halfheartedly.

Then things got slow for awhile, and the afternoon deepened with the grotesque water shadows drifting the underground walls. They all wore respirators, but the fine dust still got in and burned their lungs, and in the end Simpson Williams paid more in doctor bills than Dawes Williams even made. They all looked as if they had alien, foreign noses from another planet, and at the end of the day they got down on their hands and knees with homemade wire apparatuses no larger than toothbrushes and cleaned off the cake of the floor. Always, late in the afternoon, Dawes would gaze at the dusty window built under the level of the river and say:

"I wonder if the sun's been out today?"

"Shut up, Dawes," Travis said.

"This is a cow's ass all right," Eddie said, stitching'em shut.

When things got even slower, Dawes and Travis used to have a good time trying to slice each other's fingers off as they dug in the barrel, and the same day Dawes had managed to bring up Charles Dickens, Travis managed to slit him to the bone. Then Dawes got mad and they started to argue about it.

"You goddamn motherfucker!" Dawes started off. "What in the goddamn hell are you so goddamn gung-ho about? Here we are, stuck in a goddamn hole, making a goddamn buck an hour from some goddamn capitalist college kid who's out playing golf in the first place, and all you can goddamn do is stand there like you were goddamn Horatio Alger about to move into the control of goddamn General Motors. What the hell's the matter with you anyway?"

"If you're taking a man's money, you've got to put out," Travis said.

"What kind of old-fashioned crap is that?" Dawes said. "You don't mean a word of it. You goddamn Nazi!" he said, whipping off his gauzed respirator.

"What has Adolf Hitler got to do with this, Dawes?" Eddie said.

"The hell I didn't mean it," Travis said, not meaning it. "I mean everything I say. And you call me a Nazi once more, Williams, and I'm killing you dead."

"Go pee out the window," Dawes Williams said. "You nearly cut off my hand."

"Hell," Travis said, "this guy's a real entrepreneur."

"Entrepreneur hell!" Dawes said. "This idiot we're working for has been out of college now for only a year, and already he must have blown cold at least twenty thousand of the old man's hard-grubbed millions with half-assed schemes and you know it."

"Hell," Travis said, "this guy's smooth, Dawes."

"Smooth hell," Dawes said. "This guy's got seventy-five thousand penny bags of diatomaceous earth he can't even give away. But he's not worried. No, not him. He thinks he's going to save the American potato-chip industry. *He's* not worried. Hell no, *he's* an entrepreneur! Entrepreneur hell! He's got thirty-seven tons of kitty litter he can't move; he's got exactly twelve thousand sixty-three rubber-band guns in boxes he can't sell but, hell no, *he's* not worried, *he's* a goddamn entrepreneur! He's goddamn smooth all right," Dawes Williams said, breaking off quietly.

Before they were stuffers and stitchers, they were sackers, and Travis saw Dawes had him there, so naturally he just denied outright the entrepreneur even had those twelve thousand plastic rubber-band guns which were stacked in neat rows upstairs; so naturally Dawes threw another tantrum over the truth involved in the thing, ending it on a rising note by hitting Travis square in the face with his respirator, so naturally Travis threw him into a pile of diatomaceous earth, where he lay for awhile, thinking, pale as an anemic ghost, so naturally when Dawes got up off the floor he went after Travis with a garden trowel, so naturally Travis picked him up, disarmed him, carried him out screaming for justice, and held him over the edge of the river bridge until he apologized for everything.

And then they went back to work.

10

Later that same summer, one night when they were sixteen, one night after a dance round the pool at a lesser country club, Dunker pulled his car up to a beautifully executed spinout stop beneath an old apple tree growing on Ben Franklin Field. His convertible stood there in the moonlight like a beautiful thing of nature. He watched it. He sat there speechless for awhile behind the wheel and watched the hood glimmer and shine. It was the most beautiful hood he thought he ever saw in his life; it was candy-apple blue and had a fifty-dollar flame job painted all over it. The sky-blue scallops alone were worth another seventy-five bucks, and it all just sat there metallically blooming in the moon. He thought he loved that car.

There were only seven people in the car now. Eddie was outside, hunched over mysteriously, pissing quietly on the left front wheel.

Everybody was half tanked up by then, and they thought they could probably get themselves some lovin'. So there they were, the eight of them: Travis and Eddie and Dawes and Dunker and four girls. That made eight, which also made a crowd, so there Dunker was—under the apple tree, overlooking Stinky Creek, which was also an open sewer, turning his radio knobs, listening to a fantastic wrestling match in the back seat, and trying to make out.

Then Dawes Williams started in.

Dunker knew he would—he knew it, he knew it—he had been sitting there, waiting, just knowing Dawes would start in about it all sooner or later.

"Hey, Dunker," Dawes started in, "I used to play around here when I was a kid. You know that?"

"That's fantastic, Dawes," Travis said. "Shut up."

"Good old Ben Franklin Field. See that pine tree over there? That small apple tree? God what a line of memories."

"Kiss me, Dawes," Eddie said.

"Big deal!" Dunker said. "Shut up, would you, I'm trying to make out up here."

"Dunker!" Janie Royce said.

"Well, are we, or are we not trying to make out?" Dunker said, kissing her again.

Then there was a silence.

"This is insane!" Dawes Williams said. "There's eight people in this car."

So the girls started giggling, the whole mood was blown, and Travis reached around and began beating Dawes alongside the ears a few times, just to get him to settle down a little, and finally things settled down into next to nothing again. But later, just when things had just gotten quiet, Dawes Williams said:

"Hey Dunker, what's happenin' up there?"

"Easy, Dawes," Travis said.

"For Christsake, Dawes," Dunker said, "get your own."

"Get Ratshit in here to explain it to him again," Eddie said.

"That's all we need in here," Dawes Williams said, "is one more guy."

But that one had got him. Dunker knew that last one had got damn Dawes real good because the whole thing then went up for grabs for about the next twenty minutes on the subject of what a general idiot and innocent Dawes Williams had actually been. Dawes just sat there, not saying a word. He was morose. He looked as if he were about to weep on Susy Baker's breasts. He looked to Dunker as if the world were going to end, but he was going to die first and wouldn't see it. He looked as if he were going to cry.

But that wasn't all so bad, Dunker thought, because at least things were beginning to fall very silent back there. In fact, things had settled down just right, Dunker had his hand half-rammed up Janie Royce's leg again, wedged in there real good, he had forgotten even to listen in the back of his mind for an interruption, when out of nowhere Dawes spoke again:

"This is impossible!" Dawes Williams said.

"Invent! Invent! Live for Christsake," Dunker said.

"I can't! I can't!" he said. "There's so many things trying to come off back here at once I can't even concentrate!"

So then, turning on him, Eddie and Travis and Dunker dragged Dawes down to Stinky Creek and threw him in. Then, after he had waded out, Eddie and Dawes and Dunker turned on Travis and threw him in: then Eddie and Travis and Dawes threw Dunker after: then they got Eddie real good. Then they walked back to the car, singing, arm in arm, reeking of garbage and urine water, laughing like hell, and they sat on the hood and chugged a six-pack and scared the girls shitless by demanding point blank they run naked in the moon.

It was all right, they figured, they didn't mean it, not really. . . .

11

Dawes Williams sat on his porch, late in that summer, figuring only that he had sprung from a long line of porch-sitting people. Sixteen, he thought. A year had passed, his first year at Joshua Wadlove High School, a year of doing nothing at all, only drifting. He watched the street for sign.

He wished vaguely he were in love again. Becky Thatcher had gone over the hill, but he felt like writing DAWES KISSED BECKY A MILLION TIMES on the sidewalk. He didn't, figuring he'd been reading too much again lately, knowing suddenly she'd fled with Robin Hood on a great gray ass and was only noticed, once, in passing. At the edge of the world she had paused, looked back, and descended.

He watched the corner for Dunker and Eddie and Travis to come raising the roof of evening air, honking their horns.

Finally the convertible with Dunker driving rounded the corner. Dawes crossed the lawn and entered the street. Eddie hopped the seat, and Dawes hopped Dunker's car, and they were gone. Travis slumped in front, totally relaxed against the door, smoking a cigaret. Dawes noticed he looked perfectly pressed, as if he could step directly into a carriage, a seat at the opera, in only a button-down, powder-blue shirt, and that Travis never quite managed to smoke his damn cigarets; rather, he just let them burn down as part of a subtle, total effect.

"Tonight," Eddie was saying, "we get drunk on our ass."

"On our own beer," Travis said.

"Does that mean," Dawes said, riding behind, "that Dunker has finally pulled off his perfect set of matched ID's?"

"It does," Dunker said, driving along, looking straight into the back seat for seconds on end. "They are foolproof. They cannot fail."

They drove first, however, to a party on lawns, where Dawes saw Summer Letch. She was poised near a bush, about to spring out at him and bloom like an unwinding thing. Dawes stood around in the sunset and smoked seven straight cigarets and watched her. He couldn't believe the evening. She was brown, full of sunlight fleshed in summer dresses, guilty, and staring back. The air turned purple and fainted. Dawes was about to die away with it when Dunker and Eddie pulled him out to the car. They wanted to go buy twenty-two six-packs of beer at the J Street Tavern. Dawes wanted only to go back inside the yard and look at Summer Letch. He knew he loved her. He knew if he ever looked into her eyes, she would turn to glass. He knew if he ever touched her, she would dissolve through his hands, like shadows and water, and he would die of an exploded heart. He knew he loved her, and they drove straight to the J Street Tavern. Dunker went inside. Everyone else only hung around in the shadows of the alley.

"That party was nothing," Eddie said, smiling. "Dawes, you are just damn glad to be gone."

"Let's go back to the party, you guys," Dawes Williams said.

Travis and Eddie ignored him, intent and thinking only of Dunker's progress. Usually Hake Cutty bought everyone in Rapid Cedar their brew, but Hake—who had been completely haired except for the top of his head by the age of twelve and who, therefore, had bought more beer, over the bar, in the last six years than any man in America—was not available that night. Dunker went it alone. Travis watched. Hake Cutty, Dawes knew, standing in the alley, was only two years older than they were, but going on a drunk with him was like bringing the shadow of your father's great-uncle's mustache along in the car. . . .

Inside, however, Dunker was crossing the barroom alone. Closing the door of the J Street Tavern behind him, he had noticed three things: two women playing pool, some workingmen drinking, and a Bohemian bartender who looked as if he kept a twenty-pound club behind the bar to beat up kids. Approaching a bear's head stuffed and mounted over the cash register, Dunker said:

"Hiya. Nice evening. Give me twenty-two six-packs and four bags of pretzels to go, please. I'm having a party."

The bartender turned around very slowly. He looked at Dunker even slower, as if couldn't decide at which point to begin, and he finally said:

"You ain't even shaved yet, kid."

Dunker began getting nervous right there, but he said:

"Don't want a razor. Want twenty-two six-packs and four bags of pretzels to go."

"You mean you ain't drinkin' 'em here?"

"Nope. But I'll take a couple while I'm waiting if you like."

"Look, kid," the bartender said, "that's not what I meant."

"I know what you mean," Dunker said. "But did you ever see a six-and-a-half-foot-tall kid before? Ask yourself that."

"Plenty of 'em," the bartender said. "You ain't got no whiskers and you can't buy no beer."

Dunker had to start thinking then, so he said only:

"I'm part Indian."

"I know what you mean," the bartender said, "but you look like just another run-of-the-mill Bohemie to me."

"I am," Dunker said, "but my mother's grandmother was a full-blooded Cherokee princess."

"A full-blood?"

"Oh ya."

"Ya don't say. That's a hell of a combination all right."

"That's so," Dunker said. "That's also why I don't have any whiskers."

"I'll be damned," the bartender said.

Dunker now felt he had to put the bartender on the defensive so he said: "What the hell's it to you anyway? You got something against Cherokee princesses?"

"Not me," the bartender said, not even cracking a smile. "But I can't sell you no beer then, if you're an Indian; it's against the law."

Dunker could see he'd been had there, but, cracking his finest Hey-you're-about-the-funniest-bastard-alive smile, he said:

"Only my whiskers are Indian. The rest of me is Bohemie."

"Well, why didn't ya say so," the bartender said. "I'm a Bohemie myself. If you're sure you're a Bohemie, hell yes, I'll sell to ya."

"You bet," Dunker said, grinning. "I'm a Bohemie all right."

There was another long silence.

"Well," the bartender finally said, "if you're a Bohemie, what are you waiting for?"

"Waiting for what?" Dunker said.

"Well," the bartender said, "if you're a Bohemie, let's hear the Bohemian war hoot up on the bar."

"Oh, that war whoop," Dunker said, not batting an eye, hopping the bar, "I thought you were talking about the Cherokee war hoot for awhile."

So then Dunker stood straight as a tree on the bar and he bayed at the invisible moon. Everyone thought it was very fine, and one of the women shooting pool even said it was about the best Bohemie war whoop she had ever heard and that it brought tears to her eyes. Then the bartender frowned very seriously, like he was beaten, and turned for the cooler.

"Hey," Dunker said, smiling, "don't you even want to see my ID's?"

"What for, kid?" the bartender said, turning. "If you're a Bohemie, you probably did know enough to use the right end of the eraser. Then I couldn't sell you *any* beer, let alone twenty-two six-packs and four bags of pretzels."

"By the way," Dunker said easily, "you can skip the pretzels. The party's off."

"Okay, kid, you're the Indian," the bartender said, walking away. "But, by the way, twenty-two six-packs—what kind?"

"Oh," Dunker said, smiling, "any old kind at all."

Outside, Dawes Williams sat down in the alley. He dreamed of Summer Letch. He felt he could not listen to the light any more, that it stood off in the distance, wordless with impossible opinion. He was startled out of it only by the sound of the J Street Tavern's screen. Slowly Dunker's huge, slender frame came down the side wall, huddled, loping, a shadow momentarily free in the world, a carved-upon, self-contained tribesman carrying proof in a brown paper sack. He laughed and was home free as a game of tag.

"By God," Travis said, "he got it."

"Good. I've got a great idea," Dawes Williams said. "Let's head back to the party."

Travis ignored him, staring at Dunker.

"He was lucky," Eddie said. "What's happenin' here?"

Dunker ignored them and moved back and forth, carrying sacks out of the tavern.

"Let's head back to that party," Dawes Williams said.

"Shut up," Travis said. "We've got to steal some ice now."

So, without further ceremony, they climbed back into Dunker's Ford and went to find a mechanical ice machine to rob. That was Dawes' function in life. Dawes, even Travis thought, could sneak in anywhere. He could steal a judge's gavel. Travis thought that was a low and contemptible thing, being a petty thief, but he also admired him for it. In fact, it was Dawes who had stolen Dunker's father's cooler to put the ice in in the first place.

"Dunker," Dawes had said, showing up on a drunk with Mr. Nadlacek's cooler, "what's the good of stealing ice if you haven't got a place to put it?"

"Good, Dawes," Dunker had said, looking at him, "real fine."

Dawes Williams, in fact, Travis knew, did not recognize the right of private property to exist in principle. He took John Wayne at his word: the only duty of the strong was to help the weak. And Dawes Williams, Travis knew, usually felt strong, especially when drinking. Dawes Williams, in fact, was feeling so strong lately that he had begun keeping notebooks and scribbling things down. He called himself an "aphorist," and he liked to get very drunk because, when he got very drunk, he noticed he was able to pull the tall ears of words from silos and invisible hats like rabbits. Once, earlier in the summer, Dawes Williams had taken a lit cigar from his mouth, and a piece of scribble paper from his pocket, and looking across the spaces of Dunker's Ford at Travis, he'd said:

"Tray, listen to this: 'Because we have all sprung from impulse, from that first, fruit-driven, scratching, folly-happy animal who—walking up those first ape trails in search of deer, in search of the evening as immense as an eye—succumbs to that irrepressible desire to playfully ram a small stick up his own mother's ass—so much for perversity in the human condition!'"

"Well?" Travis had said, looking at him.

"Well?" Dawes Williams had said. "What do you think of it? I'd like your opinion on this one."

"Good, Dawes," Travis had said, "real fine."

"Christ, Dawes," Eddie had said, "I think that's dirty as hell."

Now, however, Dunker was driving the same wash of streets, looking for a new ice machine to rob, and other talk drifted the smoke:

"Who's got change for the first sack to get the trap down?" Eddie was saying.

"Dawes?" Dunker said. "How do you get a machine to cough up its ice for absolutely nothing? I'm not paying for frozen water."

"Dawes is glad you have asked him that," Travis said.

"Well," Dawes answered, "I've been working on that for a week now in my mind, and getting nowhere, so I think the best way to get ice out of a bastard machine is to induce it out, unless, of course, you happen to be a trained theoretical engineer, in which case you deduce it out also, in which case, incidentally, you have a serious problem with your mind."

"Induction, deduction, seduction," Travis said.

Dunker, driving, hooded in dial light, began looking at Dawes in his mirror as if that weren't what they had asked him, as if that were only the if of the thing and all they wanted to know was the how.

"I'm getting to the how," Dawes said, looking back in at him. "Hang in there, Dunker. This all fits."

"Attttssss Dawes," Dunker finally said, breaking his silence. "Someday we'll all be going to the moon, we'll look down as we are leaving, and Dawes Williams will be the last man on earth, standing there cursing."

"You bet your sweet ass," Dawes said. "I never want to leave this sweet mother earth. But first let me get a crack at this bastard machine."

"That's what we said, Dawes," Dunker said. "How do you get ice out of a machine for nothing?"

"That's what I said, Dunker," Dawes said. "You merely fiddle-fuck around with it until it falls open in the wind."

"I see," Dunker said.

"You bet you will," Dawes Williams answered.

So soon they were parked and walking around the Hibberd Ice Machine, looking for keys. They had already tossed off two six-packs of warm ones, and Dawes Williams was feeling like thinking. Eddie was standing on the corner, leaning on lamp posts, looking for cops. Dawes walked around it in perfectly abstract circles seven times, and he kicked at what Dunker took to be the invisible tires of the ice machine. He furrowed his brow and rubbed at his chin, and finally Dawes Williams looked up and said:

"I think we should lift up the door."

"That's fine, Dawes," Dunker said.

So Dawes got down on his knees and he peeked inside the outer door. It was dark in there, so Dawes lit a match and stuck his head up the machine. Soon he was inside, backwards, up to his knees. Then he began answering himself think: Yes, he thought, you play around with this trapdoor here until . . . yes, that's got it, it has a six-inch play in it . . yes, there is a thin rod, a tripper which the sacks of ice—when conveyed by a conveyor belt operated by money—trip open by the natural weight of their falling . . . yes, so you merely swallow your grandmother's ethics and bypass the nuance of money, and you merely flip her down here and yes, by God, you crawl headfirst up the damn machine into a black hole of light where, yes, it's red as a mammal, cold, silent as sleeping metal, damp, drunk, and suddenly you think you hear a cop's siren go off like a bomb, but only in your ear, another fire entirely, but there are nevertheless red-flaring lights against the black-pitch wall, and Eddie is yelling, far away, "CHRIST! KEYRIST, DAWES, HURRY UP: YOUR GODDAMN ASS IS STICKING OUT BACKWARDS. IT'S GOING TO BE JUST DAMN HARD TO EXPLAIN THIS," and you have already shimmied twenty-five five-pound sacks out, down your stomach, behind you, and are just now going for forty when you suddenly notice you are beginning to thaw out in the cold.

"Com'on, Dawes," he could hear Dunker whispering easily up the machine. "Greed is a terrible thing."

Then Dawes could head Dunker running, so he climbed back down, out of the machine, and soon they are all running, down the street, with ten bags full apiece. Dunker was ahead, already hopping the hood of his car like Gene Autry, firing it off, and soon Dawes was lying in the back seat collapsed, breathing within two hundred pounds of ice, lying flat with the flooring, thinking only that it is probably all right because when Dunker is driving fast, he is watching the road; it is only when he is driving slow that he is dangerous because then he stares into the back seat for seconds on end.

"This car is hot," Dunker said. "They may have got my number."

"Stash it behind Dawes'," Travis said.

They parked Dunker's Ford behind Dawes' house, Travis lit up a cigar, and they started out all over again in Dawes' ninety-dollar Mercury. They all thought Dawes was a helluva driver, the worst that ever lived. In fact, Dawes had got his '49 Mercury for ninety dollars from Mrs. Lowbus exactly two days after the first time Simpson said he could never drive the family car again, which was exactly one day after Dawes first brought Simpson's new '58 Chevy Impala home with both of the mufflers stuck in the trunk.

"Hell, Simpson," Dawes Williams had said. "I hit a ditch. Aren't you glad I'm alive?"

The night, however, revolving in other vehicles entirely, ignored them. They piled into Dawes' Mercury and drove down the hill, past the same corner. Dawes noted that it was the fifteenth time they had crossed that corner that night. He settled back and watched Travis smoking.

"What do you think, Dawes?" Dunker was saying, turning round in the moving car.

"Yes, I think that," Dawes said.

"Think what?" Dunker said, waiting.

"That Huckleberry Finn is dead."

Then Dawes Williams looked away. Dunker, he was sane. He was waiting for nothing at all.

"How many times have you read that book?" Dunker said.

"Nine times now," Dawes said.

"What is it you are trying so hard to say, Dawes?" he said.

"Go to hell, Dunker," Dawes said.

"I'm only trying to help," he said.

"Go to hell."

Travis and Eddie weren't listening. Three more of the six-packs were gone then, and they were wondering what to do. They headed back to the party. Everyone was out in the bushes, and Dawes stood by a tree looking at Summer Letch. She seemed stained by the earth, so densely alive she filled him with dread. He stood away, not listening to others talk, watching her speak, move lightly in the early night. The moon was her sail, bright as kites caught on a porch of the wind, and he knew he had been there before—swimming with others in a lawn of faces, a dark room of single file, a surface of night trapped deep in a sea, within words, structures, rooms, within nests somehow refusing to hatch over and bloom, somehow already gone while he was still in them; within rooms fragmenting, coming together, fragmenting again; within himself which had been here too, before, but it was different; within, marauding with fifty or a hundred others, the basement, the house, the lawn, the small yard of stolen field squared by the developer's hedges; within the brown, sweet summer, a deeper earth, warm, stone-smelling, distant, an elm of knowledge— but it was all different. Ultimately perhaps it was even quiet. Dawes?

He lit a cigaret. Dunker handed him two beers and told him he was very drunk. Coming out of pleasant fogs, he noticed that Dear Abby, with a head as big as all the oil money in Texas, was singing loud songs from the garage; and that suddenly he was Robert Walker in a movie full of war and old train steam, saying to Paulette Goddard: "Well, we'll have to be married now. I'm in love. I only fall in love once and that's forever— all the men in my family are that way. It's a family eccentricity you might call it." . . .

"Hell, yes, you might call it that," Dawes said to Dunker.

"Dawes," Dunker said quite seriously, "I think you better quit drinkin' for awhile. It's gone to your head."

"Robert Walker in a movie said the most hysterical thing I have ever heard in my life," Dawes said. "God is that tragedy."

"Fuck off, Dawes," Eddie said.

"Listen, Dawes," Travis said, "pull yourself together. Have another. Me and the guys are going to Dance-Land to look'em over and you're invited along."

"Thanks, Tray," Dawes said, "but I think I'll hang around here."

The lawn had turned purple and fainted again, but they talked Dawes Williams out to the car and he wound up at Dance-Land anyway. They paid their money, and walked up the long stairway that looked as if it must lead to a turn-of-the-century poolhall, and Travis began walking through the exact center of the dance floor, looking'em over. Eventually the best-looking girl in the place wandered by with her girlfriend and Travis stopped her and laughed in her face.

"Who do you think you are, buddy," she said, *"God?"*

"Where am I?" Dawes Williams said.

"Hell, no," Travis said, looking right through her, "but I'm close."

"Hell, yes," Dawes said, "can't you tell a goddamn Greek statuary when you see one?"

"Shut up, Dawes," Travis said.

"Ya," she said, turning on Dawes Williams, nearly swinging on him. "Why don't you stay out of this?"

Then she and Travis stared at each other. Travis' attitude softened for awhile; then he said:

"What's a girl like you doing in a nice place like this anyway?"

A direct coldness had come into his voice, and since she had already used up the tone of her voice, had nothing left to win with, she turned on her heel and walked across the crowded floor. Travis' pure, wholesome, totally sane horselaugh followed her across the hall. He stood rocking on his heels, rubbing his belly. Even a skeptic like Dawes Williams, sensing complication and nuance everywhere, knew it would have been impossible for a French movie queen, naked, to walk in here and convince Travis Thomas that every cell in his body wasn't perfectly formed.

"Not too bad though, that broad," Dawes said.

"I'd nail her in a minute," Eddie said.

"Real fine," Travis said. "Good one. I'd probably take her to a Fourth Street pig slaughter—if I had the gloves on, and a box to put her in."

Dawes knew they all said things like that; he also knew that they were only expected to say things like that, but not believe it. It was like in a movie, or in a book; it didn't count. Believing it was for hoods, using it to mess around was something reasonable.

Dawes was thinking that over, lighting a match, when the girl's boyfriend came up, over her steps, across the floor. The dancers danced on, and Travis and Dunker and Eddie began laughing in his face. Dawes was feeling drunk and sleepy, but from what he could make out the girl's boyfriend was one of the biggest truck drivers he'd ever seen. The sonofabitch was in a passionate way and was standing against Travis, staring him straight in the eye, nearly spitting, and saying:

"All right, who wants it! Who the hell wants me!"

Travis and Dunker and Eddie couldn't stop laughing. Almost with tears in their eyes, they pointed over at Dawes, who was leaning against a pillar and trying very hard to open his eyes.

"He does," Travis said.

"Hell," Eddie said, "you mess with *that* bastard and he'll just kill you."

So then, before they could stop him, he walked over to Dawes Williams and busted him in the nose. Travis' motioning arm had been like a one-piece slipping of the hounds, and before they got hold of the guy again, he had managed to beat Dawes severely about the head and shoulders, kick him down the long flight of stairs, and roll him part way through a glass door. Then he made his only mistake; he followed Dawes Williams out as he came to rest against a wall in the alley. When he did that, Travis knocked him down with one punch, Dunker kneed him in the face, and Eddie nearly succeeded in kicking his head off.

Then it went deadly still. Dawes began watching the night through different eyes, thinking mostly only about how much his head was beginning to hurt. Eddie came over and slapped his face and said:

"Com'on, Dawes, we got to get out of here."

Then they loaded Dawes up and they carried him around the corner of the building. Dawes could hear the door fly open and a crowd was forming behind them. They carried Dawes down the street and loaded him into his Mercury. They drove off and Dunker managed to throw an old sloe-gin bottle after them. Travis was driving Dawes' car, but before they had gone two blocks, Dawes made him stop because Dawes decided he wouldn't let anyone drive his Mercury but himself. Dawes got behind the wheel, rammed a mail box, and they headed for the country. They headed out toward the quarry to talk it over. Dunker opened four beers.

They drove in silence until Dawes steered the car onto the country gravel. Dunker broke the silence by telling Travis, who had been after him for a week about it, how he had managed to lose his virginity while parked in the front row of a drive-in movie on Saturday night. Travis was impressed, and Dunker was just getting warmed up to talking about the fact he had touched a button of the universe, when Dawes ruined it all by turning into Farmer Cotter's lane.

"Key-rist, Dawes," Eddie said, "this isn't the quarry, it's a damn farmhouse."

Dawes Williams still hadn't said a word. For vague reasons he misplaced, even while he was doing it, he ran off the driveway and began driving down a flock of chickens. He was busy chasing them around the yard with his car, pausing only to drive seven straight times around the large oak tree that grew directly in front of Cotter's house, when Travis ruined it all by grabbing at the wheel. They swiped off the side of the porch, and Travis said:

"What the *hell* are you doing, Dawes!?!"

"Leave me alone," Dawes Williams said, "I'm driving my car."

The Mercury bounced off the side of the house and continued on. The engine began knocking the sides of the fender wells, rattling its own mountings, and Cotter's porch light went on. Then Cotter came out in his pajamas and said:

"What the *hell* are you doing?"

Eddie leaned out of the window, flying by, and ruined it all more by saying:

"Just kiss our ass."

Cotter stood in his porch light and raised up his shotgun. Dawes Williams managed to steer his car back onto the ruts of the lane. They were thirty yards away now, moving back in under the night, when Cotter ruined it more by shooting Travis in the head. The window had only cracked, but one stray BB had gotten through and embedded itself in the exact center of Travis Thomas' forehead. The Great Cotter Wars had started. Dawes Williams drove the long way around and parked near the moon of the quarry. Travis Thomas got straight out, red and livid with anger at being shot in the head, and jumped in the water.

"The whole world is after us," Dawes Williams said.

Nobody else spoke for two hours. They sat around the white, inverted water and split another case of beer. Dawes' head was swimming, and Eddie kept running in the woods to take another pee. Dunker began laughing at one o'clock and broke off suddenly at two. The beer foamed up cleanly when the opener snapped the lid; and it was rhythmic, cold as springs. Finally, at two o'clock, Travis got up from his rock, like a powerfully stoic Indian trailing his blanket behind him, and he said:

"One thing is sure. That bastard has got trouble on his hands. —Com'on, let's go over to Dawes' and sleep."

They drove over, and Dawes sat in the thin light of his kitchen picking the single BB out of Travis' head with a fork. Then they all had another beer and went up to Dawes' room, where they sat around in the dark and had another. The flat summer sounds, the high locust, were out in the yard. Soon it would be morning. Dawes and Travis gave Eddie and Dunker the pillows and blankets and then crawled into the two beds. Dawes turned over to the wall, opened his screen, and began listening quietly for the Catholic wake to begin. No wailing rose up from the bushes, but soon his head was spinning faster than his house.

Eddie said he had a gut ache. After awhile everyone began bitching about Dawes' house spinning through the air, so Dawes got up and propped open the window with the heavy end of his pool cue, and they all hung out his window puking on Simpson's awnings until the first birds began coming up. Then Travis said:

"I need some air. Let's go over to Dunker's and sleep."

Soon they were back out in the yard, firing up Dunker's seven-thousand-dollar Ford, which never started, and then they were moving back down past the corner. When Dawes got down in Dunker's basement and turned the lights on, he fainted. *Summer Letch was sleeping, curled up like a kitten on Dunker's couch.*

Then the room began to come alive like birds going off in their cages. A thousand fluttering girls in pink nighties seemed to explode from the walls. Dawes and Travis and Eddie sat down on the stairs and smiled. Dunker, for some reason no one could quite understand, turned to his younger sister, Deena, and said:

"All right. What the hell is this? Get out of my basement."

"What the *hell* are you talking about, Dunker?" Dawes said.

Dawes knew he was the most striking person in the room—because he had a black eye and dried blood all over his shirt—and that Summer Letch, awake now, was watching him. He was so tired he felt he could talk to her. He thought he had died and gone to heaven. Giggling girls were running all over the room and grabbing shyly for each other's robes, but Summer Letch was just sitting there looking him over.

"Dunker," Deena Nadlacek was saying, "you are such a big goof!"

"Let's make peace," Travis said, gazing around the room and watching it faint like a fan. "We'll sleep over here, and you girls sleep on that side of the room."

"Didn't I see that in a movie once, Travis?" Dawes Williams said. *"The Walls of Jericho* starring Clark Gable and Claudette Colbert?"

"Shut up, Dawes," Travis said. "You may have, but who cares?"

"Attttssss Dawes," Dunker said, announcing him to the room. "Whenever my buddy Dawes is in trouble for something to say, he pulls out a movie."

But Dawes Williams didn't care what Dunker said; he was out of his mind with a purer lust. He sat watching Summer Letch watch him back. It was love at first sight; her eyes were deep as oak, brown as forgotten cow-sound, and she was fifteen, almost sixteen, scrubbed with an innocent perfume, waiting, hearing, Dawes supposed, her unhearable mother calling behind her. Watching her watch him, he thought she must be listening to their secret blood, not to that screen-slap in a forgettable dream of childhood, making her put her rag-doll up, calling her home to supper from a porch, from the air of evening itself. He thought if he could ever touch her, she would vanish.

Over in her corner Summer was thinking only: That Dawes, he must be one cute guy. He looks like he's been around.

The room silenced again, the shades fell, and the curtains fell asleep in the wind. A faint light rose and streaked down the walls. Dawes heard Doctor Nadlacek get up, move finally across the back pavement and back his Cadillac out into the driveway. Across a distance he listened as Dunker and Travis woke slightly and talked for a moment.

"Is it true," Travis said, "that the nurses down at the hospital refer to your old man, Dunker, as 'Zippers Nadlacek-the-fastest-knife-in-theWest'?"

"It's a lie," Dunker said. "My old man is the hardest-working surgeon you ever saw. It's Sunday, isn't it? He's going out at dawn, down to Cadence, Iowa, to cut'em up for nothing, isn't he?"

"Zippers Nadlacek," Eddie said. "I'll be damned."

"Ya. Maybe," Dunker said seriously, almost reverently. "But they say he can close like a sonofabitch though."

Then the room drifted off and dozed again. Dawes sat watching the shadows move on the walls. He watched Summer that morning as she lay sleeping. She was round and curled beneath herself. Her sleep was a sea as if, reflected in a commonly held mirror, they both lived there in her mind, dreaming of waking; and her body was oiled with its own amber, overcast with earth, rich as a turning spade, sleep-worn and lost within. Her legs, spread slightly as in a dance with a ghost of the morning, were taut as bowstrings, young, as lost as a perfect surface of rain. She held spasms of waking before her as if her sleep were a viable dance with decay; and she seemed to lie beyond him, in memory trapped in a house of mirrors, black hills. She was young and her long and beautiful hands lay on either side of her face. Locked tightly within herself, stone turning back against stone, it was as if she would never rise.

He moved closer against her before the others awoke. When she woke, she looked up against Dawes and she said:

"What have you been doing?"

And Dawes said: "I've been watching you sleep."

"How was I?" she said.

"You were fine."

"Was I?" "Yes."

"Are you sure?"

"Yes."

"When will I see you again then?"

"Soon."

"I hope so," she said. "Do you like me?"

"Yes."

"Why?"

"I don't know. Because I do."

"Do you think you want to go with me?" she said.

"Do you want me to think that?" he said.

"I don't know. I'll have to think about that."

"Yes. So will I."

"Do. Promise?" she said.

"Yes."

There was a silence.

"Dawes?" she said. "All the time you were watching me, I was watching you back."

"I know it," he said.

"Do you?"

"Yes."

"Dawes?" she whispered above Dunker's snoring, the room full of sleeping girls.

"What?"

"I'm going to get dressed now. Promise you won't watch me?"

"No."

"Why?" she said. "Do you want to watch me?"

"Christ yes," Dawes Williams said.

"I don't care, Dawes," she said, "but you can't watch me here. Someone might see you."

"I don't care."

"Yes, you do, Dawes," she said, "you care about me."

When Dawes was watching me sleep, I was watching Dawes watch me, Summer thought.

When Summer was watching me watch her, I was watching her watching, Dawes thought.

It was perfect. Later, Dunker drove everyone home in wide circles, and Dawes crossed his lawn and sat on his porch. He watched the early morning. He sat stone-eyed and cold and with a sober clearness, and watched a car slide past on the street. . . .

12

"This dude car does ninety in second easy," Dunker said, driving up to the Monticello State Fair and Cattle Exhibition.

He ticked a semi flat out, running through a narrow bridge, pulling on a sloe-gin bottle with one hand and driving with the other. No one said anything for ten minutes. The open, country night hung in the black windows.

"Close one," Eddie said finally.

"You do that again, Dunker," Travis said easily, "and you're walkin' to the fair."

"Jesus," Dunker said, finally letting his breath out. "That scared hell out of me, but I'm quick."

"The Quick and the Dead," Dawes Williams said. "My Gun Is Quick."

"Shut up, Willy," Travis said.

Then the surprisingly large lights of Monticello came up. The town swelled with action. They parked Dunker's pearly Ford blocks away, before a crowd of admiring kids, and it was still warm and ticking for a moment.

They hid two six-packs of beer, two bottles of sloe-gin and a half pint of whiskey in the sleeves of their jackets and made it through the twirling streets to the dark fences at the rear of the fair. They lay low for awhile across the dark street, studying the line of lights for movement, stuffing their pockets with cans of beer and tying off the loaded sleeves of their jackets with strings that Dawes had brought. Finally Dunker broke across the open street, the others following, and they took the fifteen-foot fence quickly. They sat finally behind the line of carnival tents, finishing the whiskey and watching the lines and nets of milling people. Travis went out for cigars and they sat finishing most of the beer, whispering in the dark bushes, drinking and smoking, and feeling very drunk and alive. The carnival bloomed just beyond, large and bright with walking.

"Ya," Travis said, returning. "Good deal. I won thirty cents' worth of these musky 'gars for only a dollar."

"You're a strong and husky mother all right," Dunker said.

"That's what the fella said when I rung his bell," Travis said, smiling. "He looked quite serious all right."

"You see any teat out there?" Eddie said.

"Why do you think I spent the dollar?" Travis said.

"Let's go," Dunker said.

"Ya, let's get some farm teat," Eddie said.

"Suey-suey," Travis said.

But they tied up their sloe-gin bottles again and made it out into the lights of the midway. The flags and rides were drunk, twirling, and the air was a well-bred cow, a swoon of earth trucked in from the fields. They spent thirteen dollars, mostly Dunker's, winning seven giant teddy bears before they were kicked out of the basketball shoot. Dunker tied all of the pandas off to himself with strings and walked the midway looking like a clean-cut Elvis Presley. Eddie got lost periodically, introducing himself to girls with teddy bears, and wound up giving three of them away for nothing.

"That one wanted to go," he said returning, "and she had five fine friends."

"Hey, she had five *fine* friends, Travis," Dunker said.

"I tell ya she wanted to go," Eddie said.

"Right," Travis said. "I'd need a fork."

"You keep this attitude up, Travis," Dawes Williams said, "and you're never going to get laid."

Travis looked at him strangely, and they continued through the swirl of lights. Cowboy Jack Winters And His Wyoming Melody Gang were playing inside the bandstand for two-fifty a crack, and half the fair was inside listening. An evangelist came on inside at midnight. They passed by, moving, stopping in the shadows to drink, moving on to throw darts, guess numbers, ring bells, pitch softballs, drive bumper cars, and pull ducks with numbers painted in nail polish from tubs of swirling water. Dawes was so drunk he nearly accidentally shot the man who ran the shooting gallery. Dunker stood up for him, and Travis told the man he would be better off plugged anyway, and they carried him down the midway. Travis walked the midway like God, actively ignoring the dozens of girls who turned quietly, in barely contained waves, with his passing. It was summer and the wind was fertile. Travis stopped only to buy more cigars. They came to a tiny, caving tent at the end of the fair, and Dunker stood, weaving, reading a hand-painted sign:

TEXAS MELANIE DALLAS INSIDE

"What's in this one?" Travis asked the barker. "My wife," the man said.

"Oh ya?" Travis said easily. "What's she do?"

"She strips," the man said. "Move on, boys."

"But I'm real intrigued," Travis said. "What else does she do?"

"Well," the man said, "just between you and me, boys, for a finale she demonstrates the eleven carnal positions and smokes a filter cigaret in her snatch with her diaphragm muscles."

"Where'd she learn to do that?" Dawes Williams said.

"Shut up, Willy," Eddie said. "The man's talking about his wife."

"So your wife's in show business, is she?" Dunker said.

"Ya. That's right," the man said. "She's a dancer."

"That a fact? Where you people from?" Travis said, smiling.

"Texas," the man said.

"Nice part of the country all right," Travis said, keeping perfectly straight and open in the face. "I've got to see this one. How much?"

"Two bucks a roll—but ya gotta be eighteen in this state to see stuff like this. It's dynamite."

"Hell," Travis said, "I've been eighteen for months now."

"How old's that one?" the man said, looking at Dawes.

"She-it," Travis said easily. "He's my older brother. He doesn't go anywhere without me. He's twenty-two."

"Never know't looking at him," the man said, collecting eight bucks quickly. "The next show's in twenty minutes. Go on in and relax, boys."

Inside, Melanie was sitting alone in the dark, dressed in dirty nylon slips, smoking a cigaret with her mouth. She was unexotic. She had no dressing room or other place to go. She was fat and looked as if she had scurvy or, at least, had never tasted a glass of orange juice. Her skin was yellow and fallen, and her legs were as easily spread as a farmhand's as she sat on a stool. The tent seemed tiny, as if it had been rented for camping.

"Hey," Eddie said, "you the whole show?"

"Ya," Melanie said. "Who let the kids in?"

"We can take it," Travis said easily, smiling, sitting down on a box in the corner.

Soon the tent began filling like a trickle of water and became hooded with silent men. Outside, Melanie's husband stood barking. Inside, it remained very quiet, a ring of staring eyes as vicious and attentive as churches. Melanie sat squatting on her stool, forcing a yawn. No one said anything for twenty minutes.

"I'll bet you wish you had a damn curtain at least," Dunker said finally.

"I ain't even got a towel or a rag, lover," Melanie said.

No one laughed. Twenty or thirty men, farmers mostly, in jeans and clean shirts and slickered hair, stood milling about, shuffling the dirt floor, looking for gracious exits, surprised at their own seriousness and lack of humor. They seemed strangely sober, but pleasantly dead in the eyes. Finally Melanie's husband came through the flap in the tent and announced the show was on. Still dressed in his dirty khaki pants, he began demonstrating the eleven carnal positions to a Conway Twitty record he had spun on a phonograph. He paused only to start the record over:

"This here's how the dogs do it, fellas," he said. "And here's how they make it in Egypt."

No one said a word or moved for a long time. Everyone looked shyly at everyone else, confused. The brighter girlie shows spun on the midway. Travis Thomas hadn't moved off his box. Dawes Williams fell next to him suddenly in the corner of the tent, laughing so hard his eyes filled with tears. Except for the sound of his hysterical laughter, the tiny tent remained absolutely still. Melanie continued into the Beale Street position:

"What is this?" someone finally said. "A con?"

"If ya have to ask," Melanie said, "you can't be told."

"Now, boys," Melanie's husband said, sensing danger, unmounting her for a moment and stepping into the pink light bulb and the center of the platform. "I want you to remember—this is no common girlie show. This is a scientific demonstration of lust!"

"Christ," someone said, throwing a wadded beer cup at him, "I've seen better flesh in a hog lot."

"I'll bet you laid better there, too, honey, if the truth was known," Melanie said.

She sat, facing them all down from her stool, still caught partly in the Istanbul position.

"Let's hang'em both," someone finally said quietly.

"It's a screw!"

"So you finally got the idea, honey," Melanie offered.

No one laughed. A drunk took out his cock and began peeing in the dirt.

"Now, boys, boys, please," Melanie's husband interrupted, almost nervously, "you may be a little excited from all of this lust, I hear they raise'em randy up here," he said, "in Ioway, a bunch of real corn-fed, meat-eating pokers all right, but now Miss Texas Melanie Dallas is going to go into her finale and let me tell you, let me tell you, I guarantee it is something none of you men have ever seen before. In fact," he said dramatically, "I'm so sure of that I want to guarantee it by saying, right here, right now, that anyone who wants his money back may now leave, having seen seven of the eleven carnal positions, free and clear, and with no obligation whatsoever. . . . Anyone, however, who wants to stay must pay another buck for the kick of his life . . ."

The crowd murmured, drew slightly together, and Melanie's husband moved among them, fearless, smiling, collecting bills. They all paid, except Travis, who went unnoticed in the corner.

"Shoot'em up," Eddie Welsh said.

"This better be good," a farmer said, "or me and the boys'll be seein' you out back, Dallas."

"Just earnin' our way," Melanie's husband said. "Hard, hard times, boys."

"Ya," Melanie said. "We ain't no welfare creeps."

"Nice Cadillac you got back here," Travis said, picking up the bottom of the tent. "Real nice."

"It's my brother's; we borrowed it for the summer tour only," Melanie's husband said, not batting an eye. "But I'm not afraid, boys. It's worth every penny. What's a buck to be the envy of yer friends? 'Sides, we're only in town fer one night an' this is yer last chance to see it."

No one laughed. The air in the tent was surly and almost swirled. Melanie's husband picked the last bill from the air, easy as cherries, and stepped to the center of the platform again.

"Now, boys," he said, ignoring everything, "this is so unusual, in fact, that I'm not even going to introduce it. Melanie doll," he said, patting the top of the stool, "do yer stuff."

Melanie hopped on top of the stool, and slipped off her G string, and took out a Marlboro, and inserted it in the lips of her snatch and lit it.

"Watch this," she said.

The crowd drew in, curious, slightly pushing under the lights and studied it. She drew and released perfectly round, grayish puffs into the close, crowded air, like smoke signals. Travis sat alone in his corner, motionless, smoking, pulling on a 7-Up bottle filled with sloe gin. Melanie stared through him, into only the distances beyond the canvas wall of the tent. She continued drawing puffs of smoke out of the cigaret with her diaphragm muscles, alone in a crowd.

"I'll be damned, Rollie," someone said. "Look at that."

Dawes Williams roared with laughter. Dunker held him up and they pulled the last of the beer out of their sleeves to watch. Melanie's husband was already outside, barking up another show. No one inside bothered to listen. Melanie smoked the cigaret down to the stub, dropped it, stomped it out loudly on the flooring with two bangs, and the lights came up on cue. She slipped on a robe and disappeared through a flap in the tent. Everyone scratched their heads for a while and filed out the exit.

"Come back past midnight, boys," Texas Malanie said with real enthusiasm, "and I'll blow you some perfect Os!"

"That's banal," Travis Thomas said, sitting alone in the silent rear of the tent. "That's banal as hell."

Soon they were drunker, rolling home and talking of Texas women, and they were twenty miles south of Langworthy before anyone noticed Dunker had missed the detour and was driving hard on grated, but unpaved, highway.

"This dude raps out at ninety in second easy," he said.

"Ya," Travis said, "this dude's a real Texas woman all right."

13

Fall came. Iowa changed, became a dead vine, a cold stalk broken close to the yellow patches of earth, the hard blue edge of invisible wood smoke and sky. The pheasants came out. After a long summer of being chased by nothing but farm cats, they filled the flat wind with rich plumes striped and tan, the flying red flowers of their heads. Dawes Williams took to going to his room and writing in notebooks. He wrote:

Across that lawn, in the evening as thin as madness, the greyhounds tipped their tall, sleeping hats, higher than silos of grain, and paused to wet the putting green. America is like watching a symphony being conducted by the tuba player.

But he paid no real attention to himself. They returned to Joshua Wadlove High School, but everyone except Dawes was playing varsity football. Dawes was spending his time hanging around as close as he could to Summer Letch, who was younger, and who was just coming up from Benjamin Franklin Junior High. One Friday after a football game, however, while they were sitting around drinking sloe gin and beer by the quarry, Travis lit up and said:

"We like to go hunting in the fall. We like to get out there in those golden fields and shoot those birds."

The next day Dawes talked Simpson again into the loan of his four-barrel, newly remufflered Chevy, and they set out early in the morning for the country. Dunker handed him a beer and told him to kick it a little. Dawes didn't like Dunker to watch him so curiously that early in the morning—he especially didn't like to be told he was going too slow—and, besides, he knew what they were thinking. He knew they liked to shoot those flying birds, but they were a little worried about Dawes Williams and thought he was a little strange on the subject of killing. They sensed he didn't like it, but didn't have the honesty or courage to admit it. Dawes, however, said nothing at all.

They were driving out to Pott, Iowa, to pick up Eddie's grandfather's prize bird dog. She was the worst bird dog in the world, however, so Dawes didn't know why they were going out to get her. But they were cruising along, as high as the king of Persia, and the morning was opening up nicely when suddenly Dawes saw a hairpin gravel curve:

"Watch this," he said, gearing down into automatic low, and fishtailing straight into the ditch.

When the car had come to rest against a bush, like an expensively bounced watch, Dunker looked at Dawes slowly and said:

"Attttssss Dawes."

"Good, Dawes," Travis said, "real fine."

"Did you like that one?" Dawes Williams said, opening the flask.

Travis and Dunker and Eddie didn't say another word after that. Dunker and Travis were sitting there in the back seat, with foaming beer all over the floor and their hunting jackets, noticing only that they were down a ten-foot ditch but right side up. Travis was thinking that Dawes Williams had nearly succeeded in killing him this time, but he was saying nothing, and was only busy ignoring Dawes by opening more brew. Dawes began intently playing with the engine, revving it up, and winding it down. Finally he turned round and said:

"Did you have to spill beer all over Simpson's car?"

"That's good, Dawes," Travis said. "That's just fine."

"Almost made that one," Dawes said, not even blinking. "I guess you'll just have to push while I ram this out of here."

Travis and Dunker and Eddie still weren't talking to Dawes, but they grabbed a couple of beers to get out to push with, and the car finally came out of the ditch like a ship launched mast first. Dawes, rearisen and on the road, was fierce in the eyes and flying into the wind again. Dunker thought Dawes was probably out of his mind, and having a bad day, but he didn't mention it because he was too busy settling back into his seat to watch Eddie, who was in the front seat, leaning over to beat Dawes over the head with his gun case. Eddie, riding shotgun, had his twelve-gauge out of its case so that if he spotted a rabbit in a ditch he would be ready to pot it, but Travis and Dunker were sitting in the back seat, inactive, staring straight at Dawes, but weren't saying anything because they'd already decided that they were going out in the morning to do some hunting, and not to worry about any penny-ante crap being pulled by Dawes. Then Eddie stopped beating Dawes Williams in the head and looked into the back seat, and said:

"This bird dog of my grandfather's is really *good* this year."

That brought a laugh, and soon they were pulling into Eddie's grandfather's farm again. Dawes watched Eddie pow-wow with his grandfather for awhile, and then they began loading (it took an hour because she was afraid of cars) the worst bird dog in the world into the back seat. Then they turned around and drove down the same road in the opposite direction while the worst bird dog in the world made herself more comfortable by running around on Travis' head, and peeing all over Simpson's flooring. Dunker could see that Dawes Williams was fierce in the eyes again. Dunker knew what was coming, but he didn't say a word. Neither did Travis. They both felt it was cheap, unlucky and dangerous to talk about upcoming fate so they just held tight to the worst bird dog in the world, and figured maybe Dawes Williams might make it this time.

So after they pushed Dawes out of that same flat ditch again, they went hunting. . . .

"We like to get out and tramp those fields," Travis said.

So they got out there, tramping in the fields all day, and Dawes was on the right flank and that's where his shots were. He was missing, so they put him out on the left flank and all the pheasants shifted with him.

"Dawes!" Travis Thomas said. "You now happen to be missing shots that could be made with baseballs."

But Dawes was happy as hell. Birds were flying away safe into other counties. Travis thought Dawes was missing on purpose and by now Eddie had the worst bird dog in the world on ropes because the bitch had been out front by four hundred yards all morning, carefree, singing, helping Dawes, happy as hell too, Travis thought, she wouldn't come back for super-stud dog of all time, she was always on Dawes' side, his wing, and flocks and whole herds of chuckers were rising before them, and the only problem was she was flushing them three miles out, and chasing every bird in the world into the next county over in Iowa.

"She can *find* those birds and chuckers," Eddie'd kept saying all morning.

"Hell, yes," Travis said finally, "she can *find* those birds all right. Only problem is, Eddie, she's finding those damn chuckers out where you'd need an ack-ack to get'em down from the sky."

By afternoon, however, Eddie had his bitch on a rope. Everything was finally settled down into next to nothing when Travis made the mistake of shooting a hen. Dunker looked over at Dawes. Dawes was already looking at the wounded hen; and then he started quietly screaming:

"Travis! You shot a hen! You wounded a goddamn hen!" he said, wild in the eyes.

Dawes Williams, Dunker knew, was about to go over and pick up the hen and take her home, but Travis interrupted him:

"Ya," Travis said. "I know it. I made a mistake."

There was silence. They began looking around abstractedly for game wardens. Then Travis looked down at the hen from the corner of his eye, and he blew her away from the hip.

Dawes froze in his steps. Dunker moved closer to watch him freeze, and Travis hadn't taken one step before Dawes emptied both barrels about six yards in front of him. Then Travis froze, and looked over at Dawes as calm as death; taking out a shell from his jacket, he loaded up and fired over Dawes' head. It was a warning shot. So then Eddie and Dunker drew off twenty yards, and sat down in the furrows, and watched as Travis and Dawes reloaded fiercely and began firing steadily at each other. From behind his cornstalk Dunker could see Dawes—behind a large oak—and Travis—down a drainage ditch—and they were both red in the eyes, confused, reloading furiously, and firing as fast as possible. From behind his oak, over and over, Dawes Williams began screaming:

"I can't shoot. *Damn* me! I can't hit shit!"

Dunker could see Travis wasn't saying a word. He was only popping up calmly to fire, doing it fast, taking aim only at a high sea of leaves, and Dunker could hear the shot hail in rains of oak leaves sixty feet up.

It was, for awhile, as if Dawes Williams were standing in a storm of tin leaves. Then it was over. From behind his pile of corn shucks, Eddie said:

"What the hell? That was about the most piss-poor gun battle I ever saw. What the hell?"

Then they gave it up for the day. Dawes Williams waved a white handkerchief at the distance, and Travis answered him back, and finally Dawes stepped before his tree and examined the wood, up high, that was neatly riddled with shot. Dawes Williams was finished for the day. He sat on the ground laughing in fits so hard Dunker thought he had gone berserk. He couldn't stop laughing; and soon Travis moved over near him, walking carefully, as if not to disturb something, some delicate balance of nature, and in the end both of them were sitting there, beneath a pile of corn shucks, laughing.

Then Dunker froze. He had looked over at Eddie, and Eddie was looking back.

"Key-rist, Welsh," Dunker said. "Don't look at me like that."

"Like what?" Eddie said.

"Like you were thinking of shooting. Like it was a damn contagion or something," Dunker said.

Eddie said nothing, however, so Dunker sat down on a dirt clod. While he was sitting there, not knowing, Dawes and Travis were nearly climbing the tree with laughter, and Eddie was beginning to look at him again, and the worst bird dog in the world, happy as dancing heaven, was out there, two farms away— because she also happened to be gun-shy—and making far sorties, again, into whole herds of flying pheasants, and Dunker only found he was still sitting there, not knowing. . . .

Soon, however, Travis wasn't laughing any more; he was just looking at Dawes. Then Dawes wasn't laughing any more either; he was just looking at Travis. Then Travis spit on the ground, and Dawes spit back, and soon they were rolling all over the frozen field, biting and kicking, punching each other, and Dawes got in a couple of fair ones (he was not four feet six any more, Dunker noticed, he was nearly six feet) before Travis threw him finally down and nearly tore off his ears. Pheasant feathers were coming out of Travis' jacket, Eddie's bird dog trailed in from the southwest to have a look round, to become excited and to pee, and the mix became so rich Eddie and Dunker decided to pull them, all three, apart. Before they had him even half up, however, Dawes Williams hauled off and kicked Travis square in the gut so Travis jumped up, turned round, wound up, and he knocked Dawes out, as cold as the hen beside him, for fifteen or twenty minutes.

When Travis poured a beer on him, the worst bird dog in the world finally finished licking quietly on his face, Dawes woke up and they decided to drive into Palo for some beers. They began to lounge around the tavern and take their ease. Travis was bruised, but Dawes Williams was the worst-looking hunter around. Blood ran off his nose and forehead, like a Roman fountain, and into his beer. A gnarled farmer came by and began examining Dawes abstractedly, like a piece of antique machinery, and in the end, chewing on his manufactured corn pipe, he said:

"What happened to *him?*"

Dunker looked up naturally, and smiled, and said:

"Well, I tell ya—the pheasants got'm."

That brought a laugh; the place relaxed, and the farmer bought them all a beer on that one as Dunker knew he would. Dunker couldn't get his legs under the table, so he pushed out another chair with his heel and began looking curiously at Dawes again. He drew on his beer and thought Dawes was taking this all too personally again. He thought Dawes was just sitting there getting pretty sullen about the whole damn thing; that he was not even philosophical any more—he was just plain morose.

Dunker continued drinking his beer; Dawes was still bleeding into his. They watched the worst bird dog in the world take another quick, nervous crap in the corner, in Palo, Iowa, and finally Dawes spit a piece of tooth on the floor, and looked Travis dead in the eye, and said:

"If you ever come that close to killing me again, Travis, I'm killing you dead."

"Dawes, if I ever kill you again," Travis said, "I'll finish the job."

"What the hell," Dunker said, "let's be friends."

Nothing responded. The day drifted off, and Dawes sat watching the light of the fields move in the canvas shades. He thought he was not any different, that he was just like the rest. He thought he was Dunker, and Eddie, and Travis Thomas because, in the end, you can't be what you've never lived through. He thought he was only the tall hat of a tale. He knew he could not be what he had not even dreamed into becoming. That's all. He would always live here, in this place, among these stones, this grass. And he would always be locked up within, the knots of dreams.

"Christ," Dunker, who was sane, was saying, "when I saw all that happen this afternoon, I knew there was God. I also knew he had his ass buckled on sideways."

There was a long silence, the tavern slept and bloomed back in the shades, and Dunker tried to change the subject by saying:

"Hell. Listen. I've got a new spot all picked out for tomorrow. It'll go better."

Travis put his beer down, Dawes looked over, and they turned on Dunker. For no reason, Dunker thought, they started to beat hell out of him. Finally Travis knocked over a table, the owner threatened to call out the constable— Dawes Williams stood in the exact center of the flooring and told them he bet they didn't have one—but they picked up Eddie's grandfather's prize bird dog, which was nervously peeing under the pool table, looking for another place to hide, and they ran the hell out of there without ever looking back. Later, still silent, they were riding along, driving down some chickens on that same peaceful road, and everything was very quiet and resolved until Dawes came to that same damn curve, the first time since morning, and he said:

"Watch this one, Travis."

He spun around it and let the mufflers fall where they might.

"Oh ya. You finally made one," Travis said, not even blinking, "the first all day."

14

Barney Redwood was born in North Dakota, but he'd lived the last four years in Chicago. He was sixteen when his father began beating his mother so bad she decided to pack the three of them, his sister and himself, to a hick place called Rapid Cedar, Iowa—population one hundred thousand. He wasn't worried; he knew the street was full of skirt everywhere. He was only worried if they had the damn street.

Then they were driving along, it was summer, and he began to worry. All he could see, as far as his eye could look over and then some, were these fields of blowing corn. He thought animals were out there, just walking back and forth, grubbin' around for the roots, or whatever it is animals like that eat. Hell, he thought, the next gas station was twenty miles away, they had these houses sitting out there in the spaces, and he hadn't seen a corner all morning. It reminded him of North Dakota, only flatter, and he wasn't about to go back there. He began watching for Ma and Pa Kettle, and damn if he didn't see dozens of them, driving by all morning. Everyone had cars with license plates reading—IOWA THE CORN STATE—and he thought his mother had let them all in for it again. He thought they had moved back to North Dakota, and he wasn't happy. There was enough corn blowing in the wind out there to feed Chicago for the next hundred years, the smoke of his cigaret curled by the window, and he could just see'em, all of the natives, out there doing harvest dances in the fall.

As they drove down the long seam of the highway, determined, all three of them now, Barney Redwood got to thinking: If you could change your place, you could change your identity, too. What could be more American than that? He began working things out, and he knew he could swing it. Like buying a new suit, he would make himself over. This, he thought, riding along, watching the fat green corn blow over in the wind, was my one chance to put on a show. So he looked at his younger sister sitting there beside him, and he said:

"If you ever call me 'Bayard' in public again, I'll break your neck. From now on, my name's 'Barney.' Got it? Or I'll break your neck."

Then they reached the outskirts of Rapid Cedar and Barney Redwood began worrying again. He thought the city looked like a single small factory with the aisles and corridors too well swept by the passing janitors. He thought the place could never go to any kind of seed, and he hadn't seen a poolroom all morning. They crossed the town in fifteen minutes, all of it, moving toward the west, and he was still piecing the thing together when his mother pulled the car in under the shade of a huge old gray tent of a wooden house.

"We're here!" she said.

"Big deal," Barney said. "Where the hell is this?"

"Get out of the car, Bayard," she said.

"Hell, no," he said, "I'm going home."

"This is home now," she said softly, pointing to the huge frame house as big and wooden as a grotesque circus. "And you can just thank my mother we even have a roof over our heads."

"Thanks," Barney said. "Hell of a deal this is. I bet the nearest poolroom is seven miles away."

"You can use the car," she said, not even blinking.

"Do you want my game to go to hell?" he said.

"Bayard Wilmington Redwood!" she said.

"Just call me 'Barney,'" he said, "like I was one of the guys."

"GET OUT OF THE CAR!"

So Barney got out and looked around. He prowled. He walked around the house several times, and he didn't like it. He surveyed the sky for signs of life in the wind. He tossed his cigaret in the grass. Finally, coming back, he stood looking his mother straight in the eye.

"All right," he said, "I give. Where's the damn dunking chair in this town? Where is the witch's stake?"

But he wasn't worried. He knew by now he could take himself any place. . . .

15

One afternoon in December they drove into Iowa City to get drunk. Counting the set of mufflers Dawes had lost the day they went hunting with Eddie's dog, Simpson had had three sets of mufflers on that Chevy in the first three months. Dawes, however, figured the first two sets hadn't counted: he had not lost those in ditches. Before Simpson found out about it, however,

Dawes had been poking holes in those with screwdrivers and ice picks, mainly for the sheer sound of it all. But the last set had come home in the trunk, naked as sign. Simpson told Dawes mufflers cost money; Dawes told Simpson he was too worried about money, but that he would try harder in the future never to bring a piece of his car home in the trunk. Everything was settled; Simpson felt Dawes understood and agreed, and went back to playing contract bridge and reading William James.

It was cold when they got to Iowa City. Eddie sat drinking in the bar. The fake I.D.'s they had were all good now, and Travis spent the night talking to college girls and telling everyone around his buddy Dawes Williams was a helluva driver, the worst in the world. Dawes didn't mind because he knew Travis happened to think if you weren't the best, you had to be the worst; nobody should be in between. Dawes couldn't walk by midnight, and Dunker and Eddie said they'd better get home as they had a game the next day. By the time they stumbled outside it must have been twenty below zero, and Dawes noticed a clock on one of the banks had frozen up and stuck.

Simpson's car was by an old nineteenth-century horse curb—the ones built in the days they must have been afraid the trolleys might jump the tracks and run over the houses—and as Travis was calmly getting in, Dawes Williams threw it into reverse by mistake and began to take off. He didn't get far because the right front door was still open and it snapped off cleanly from the hinges. It lay on the pavement like a permanently scratched tuna-fish lid. Then Dawes got out of the car, and walked around it, and he said:

"Sonofabitch. How do I explain this one?"

"Just tell Simpson it was defective at the factory," Travis said.

"It was your fault, Travis," Dawes said. "If you hadn't been screwing with it, it would never have happened."

"You say I'm liable once more and I'll bust you all over that wall," Travis said.

Dunker began watching Dawes. Dawes couldn't argue with that—his nose hadn't reset itself yet; the scars over his right eye, pink as the insides of a fish, hadn't healed yet, either. Dunker thought Dawes was a helluva sight, one of the worst in the world. Dawes said it again anyway.

"Travis," he said, "you're liable for this."

"Hell, Dawes," Travis said, laughing, trying very hard to find a way he wouldn't have to beat up Dawes Williams again, "I'm afraid there's no future whatsoever for you in the fight game. You better not study insurance, either."

"Well, what do I do with it?"

"How do I know what you do with it? It's your door, isn't it?"

"That's just good, Travis," Dawes said.

"Dawes is a drugstore cowboy," Eddie said from the back seat.

"Shut up, Eddie," Travis said. "You're not even drunk. At least Dawes Williams is drunk. Stay out of this."

"Well, God damn it," Dawes said, "how come it's my door lying there in the gutter and I'm taking all the crap about it? Answer me that one?"

"You're taking all this crap because we love ya, Dawes," Travis answered.

By this time Dawes had caught on like a contagion, and now both he and Travis were circling around Simpson's right front door. In the end they both figured the only thing to do was to pick it up and lock it in the trunk so nobody would steal it. Then Travis stepped in and Dawes roared off through two straight red lights.

It was thirty miles back to Rapid Cedar, and Travis found himself riding down the highway without a door, cold as hell, as if he were lashed to the back of a motorcycle.

"I'm freezing my balls," Travis said, looking over at Dawes.

But Dawes was paying no attention because he was driving eighty-five miles an hour and didn't want to slow down for conversations. Dunker sat in a rain of feathers, stripping down a week old dead and hunted duck he had found lost in the trunk. Eddie was skinning it out and throwing guts on the highway. Travis was freezing and bearing it wordlessly. When Dunker reached around and startled him with a wet eardork, full of spit and the insides of a duck, laughing like direct explosions, Travis almost rolled out the doorless air on his beautiful head.

"It's colder'n hell back here," Eddie said.

"Ya. You got trouble," Travis said.

Dunker hadn't brought a cap, was hooded in a pale interior light and shadowy feathers, and when Dawes looked into the back seat with his mirror all he could see was Dunker, being wise as hell, sitting straight as tea parties, with a disemboweled duck mounted squarely on his head. Dawes Williams began laughing so hard he forgot himself and passed out cold. They were on the shoulder now, and no one was driving, so Travis grabbed the wheel and gave Dawes a good enough shot over the eye to wake him up, and Dawes nearly opened his eyes and said:

"Hey, we gonna play golf tomorrow?"

"Jesus, Dawes," Dunker said. "You all right?"

"Hell, yes," Dawes mumbled. "I made four on that last hole."

"Hello, Dawes," Dunker said.

"Mark him down for four, Dunker," Travis said. "Maybe it'll help."

"Where am I? Where am I?" Dawes Williams said.

Just then, however, it started to snow.

16

It snowed all night. Next morning Dawes Williams lay in bed sleeping. It was cold as hell outside, still snowing like the wet underside of God, but he was warm under his great-grandmother Oldham's handmade English quilt. He could hear Simpson getting up like a hollow pipe. In the mornings Simpson still shredded the air in the yellow house with his asthmatic lungs; his coughing fits as loud as breaking thunder. Damn it, Dawes thought, it's hell to listen to him: he's been waking me up early for years, making me feel worthless. What's he want me to do-go out and chop a cord of wood like Arthur? We don't even have the fireplace to put it in. What the hell's he expect me to do? I didn't make this world. I didn't even make myself. Leone came to the foot of the stairs:

"Simpson!" she said. *"Please* stop that coughing!"

Dawes Williams rolled over and went back to sleep.

But in his mind he could still see Simpson's mind confronting itself in its shaving mirror. It looked at itself without effort or strain as the whiskers rolled off like taps. Walking in a dream of sleeping faces, Dawes thought:

Simpson is lying back now, confidently, knowing, as he does, that salvation in the modern world can, will, only flow naturally from the simplification of paperwork. My father. My father is human, and he has come to believe in the salvation of the bureaucrat, which means only the eventual millennium of checks upon the excesses of both the members and the larger composite—society itself. Yes, Simpson thinks confidently, sitting back, lying back in a mind as smooth and polished as a studied geologic spheroid, foaming his chin, Yes, he thinks, salvation greater than Jesus; salvation as great almost as the very invention of the double-entry bookkeeping system itself. . .

He rustled against the revelation easily and fell back into something near sleep. But it wasn't long before he could hear Simpson's heavy step going downstairs to breakfast. Leone, Dawes knew, had made him two eggs, bacon, tomato juice and coffee again. What is it he expects me to do? Dawes thought, rolling back over. He's coughing up his coffee now. Good God, he's been sounding like he's going to die for sixteen years now. It's the first thing I can remember hearing. Why doesn't he go over and keep his damn books and leave me alone?

Then Dawes Williams knew he wasn't sleeping at all. He could hear Simpson's heavy steps cross the silent snow to his car. Dawes could see him. He got in, started the engine, and then Dawes could see him looking over at his right front door. A neat pile of snow had drifted onto the seat, and Dawes could hear his shout. He listened to Simpson intently as he stepped out, and retraced himself mechanically, a martyred tin soldier looking for doors, back over the snow. Dawes could hear him reach for the house door. It opened and closed sharply in the clean December air. Simpson's dead step retraced itself on the stairs. Dawes' door opened:

"GOD DAMN IT," Simpson said, coughing, staring Dawes straight in the eye with the red, broken veins of his face, "WHERE THE HELL IS MY RIGHT FRONT DOOR!"

So Dawes rolled over, drunk, still sleeping, and he said:

"It's in the trunk. Where the hell else would I have put it? Hell, Simpson, why don't you drive my '49 Mercury this morning? The change'll do you good."

17

Dawes Williams was pissed off because he had to court Summer Letch in the rear of his old Mercury. Simpson had taken both his right front door and his high-running Chevy away forever. He called Dawes irresponsible and unworthy. He said he had been just waiting around patiently, hoping Dawes would grow up some, but now he was just getting damn disappointed in it all since Dawes had unhinged his right front door.

"You just don't seem to have any respect for my material objects, old boy," he said.

Dawes smiled. Simpson said Dawes would probably grow up only to embezzle money from a bank, and Dawes said he was probably right about that—it was a hell of a thing to have to sit around and watch—and then asked him if he could at least use his Chevy on Saturday nights to court Summer Letch.

"Hell, no, old boy," Simpson Williams said, disappearing, going back easily within his copy of *The Rapid Cedar Republican*. "Now, what did I just get through saying to you?"

Dawes didn't respond. He sat there, watching his father's face metamorphosize into newsprint and another smiling picture of Ike where a real head should have been, saying he thought President Eisenhower was probably a swell guy but that, in reality, he didn't look to him as if he could run a fleet of dinghies over the Delaware River. Simpson ignored him, beginning to hum.

"These are good years, old boy," he said, clicking his tongue nervously. "The best you'll ever see."

Dawes Williams hoped not. He said, even if they were, he doubted whether the General had anything to do with it.

"Simpson," he said finally, "I've been thinking of leaving school. You know, of getting out into the world. I've got better things to do. I'd like to go to San Francisco."

"So?" Simpson said, still reading.

"So," Dawes said, "could you loan me fifty to get started?"

"That's crazy, old boy," Simpson said. "Real foolish. You're in the world right now."

Dawes doubted it immensely. He felt surrounded, living in the exact, bloodless heart of a Methodist convention, a ding-dong school conducted by truer believers for convicted children learning to retain adolescence way beyond their time. He got up, told Simpson that—frankly—he was full of cow-shit, and left the house. Leone came in to announce dinner was served.

Dawes got into his car and drove around eastern Iowa for a few days. He came back to Rapid Cedar and went to school, sleeping at night in the city parks. Eddie and Dunker and Travis brought him clean shirts in the mornings, and girls brought him cologne. He stood in front of his locker before the bell, smiling, dabbing himself discreetly with roses and oil. Finally, early one morning, Simpson showed up in homeroom. He looked worried, nodded at a physics teacher in dull conspiracy and motioned Dawes out into the hall. They stood in the shadowy, deserted corridor, talking quietly:

"I think you should be coming home now, old boy," Simpson said. "Your mother may be cracking up again."

"Tell her not to worry. I'm making it fine," Dawes said.

There was a silence. Dawes began shuffling his feet, walking invisible circles around his father, who was whittling on an invisible stick, dickering:

"Well," he said, "I think you better. I'd hate to call in the authorities on this."

"Big deal," Dawes said, nearly laughing out loud.

"Well, I think you better," Simpson said.

"I'm doing fine," Dawes said quietly, smiling. "I could use my allowance though. Think you could spare that?"

"I thought you said you were doing fine?" Simpson said.

"Well, I am in a way," Dawes said. "But I can't get started on any large pool-shooting without a stake, can I?"

"Oh, Christ, old boy," Simpson Williams said. "You can't be running around doing this."

"I can't be doing it standing still," Dawes said.

"Well," Simpson said, nearly spitting on the cut sign he was making on the floor with his foot, "I may be able to give you your allowance, but you'll have to promise me you'll come home at least to sleep. Your mother's worried nightly that you're being robbed and assaulted by large Bohemians. She can't sleep and she's driving me crazy. You can see my position."

"Oh ya," Dawes Williams said. "But it's foolish. I can take care of myself. Besides, I have my shotgun in the trunk and I sleep with it fully loaded, cocked and between my legs."

Simpson began pacing. Dawes smiled back. Absently Simpson began to light a cigar.

"Can't smoke in here," Dawes said. "It's against the rules. And I'd need at least fifteen a week to make a move like that."

"I think you'd better come home just the same, old boy," Simpson said. "But I might be able to go twelve-fifty."

"That sounds like a deal," Dawes Williams said.

They shook hands on it suddenly, standing in the halls of Wadlove High. The bell went off again, classes passed, and Dawes began sleeping at home again. Otherwise, he avoided it, almost forgetting at times they even existed. It was an unimportant, easy thing, and he lived only with peers. Leone's migraines cleared up comfortably for awhile; then she began casting about for something else to worry about. Eventually she found it. She began to worry that the only central impetus driving her son's life was his carnal design upon Summer Letch. And she wasn't wrong as it all turned out.

Dawes Williams loved Summer Letch with a pure, abiding passion that transcended Plato. He could do anything for her, he thought, except leave her alone. He knew her to be innocent, sinless and clean; only everyone around them was full of guilt. Mrs. Letch, for example, was a witch. He knew it for a fact. He knew it watching her watching Summer with green, Fundamentalist eyes, following her, them, wherever they went, destroying their lives, prying their soft body open like a spongy, crustaceous shell, probing them with a watching like unclean fingers.

Mrs. Letch, in fact, was a schoolteacher. This was the factual revelation that crowned it for him, and he thought he could have learned to hate Mrs. Letch. She was a small, bony, hard woman who always parked the car in the garage. She was fierce and eccentric-looking and Dawes Williams always wondered how Summer had managed to spring from such a pursed withdrawal. But in the end he decided it didn't matter—Summer had just managed it. All was phenomenon. And, just as finally, he decided the reason he couldn't hate Mrs. Letch was the same reason he couldn't manage to hate anything—because Summer was there.

He felt her always. He knew when she came into a room, he forgot himself. He was grateful. It was the first time he could remember forgetting himself, except for the night Abigail Winas' shadow trapped him breathless against his great-grandfather's fallen walls. With Summer he was only abandoned. Yet he knew if he told Dunker and Eddie and Travis how he felt, they would have taken him down to the river and drowned him; more importantly, they would have unconsciously vetoed him in life, thereby freezing him out. He remained silent. Everyone remained silent. Eventually, everyone lost. But until then he wanted only to die breathless and old and spent under her skirts, between her, beyond her, within the dark, whispering taboos of her skin. He wanted to possess her, know her. He knew somehow, even passing through to the other side, they would somehow miss each other. He knew he could never get close enough to her.

She was his reason. He went to school now only because he took her there, leaving only to take her home; to lie passionately lost in her rugs until four-thirty, when Mrs. Letch came home and Summer rearranged her hair, her dress, and went to sit ladylike, foreign, near the piano across the room. The room filled suddenly with Mrs. Letch, pride and pretense. Separation, he thought. He sat, staring back between suspicious looks from Mrs. Letch, loving her. He had lain for as long as he could with her on those rugs, however, his eyes heavy with remembering the deep stars of sleep. He was sure he would die empty, without knowing her, possessing her fully.

Then one night in the rear of his Mercury she touched him. He couldn't believe her. She was easy, guiltless, adept as a virgin. He lost himself in her dark, her hushed carpet. She filled him with something wild, nameless. She could never stop touching him. At first she filled him with the old dreams, something almost buried, the old house, four years old and dreaming every night of being danced away by women, faceless, older, with long hands and painted fingers— a Narda in Mandrake comics perhaps—who tortured him, tiny with real erections, for dry hours on end. After that, full of power, never stopping touching him for long, she seemed to be connecting him to her with her hand, her to herself with his. He loved her. He went to the library. He read in a textbook it was called "digital sex," words which sounded like dry oatmeal, and that "prolonged use of it was dangerous to full sexual growth and awareness." He worried about it slightly. But after dark, parked over the river, she filled him with something destroyed, an eye halving, not meeting another coming off whole in the dark. He tried to tell her. She agreed. But she was more afraid of other things, her mother, a baby, Ann Saunders Teen Gossip Tips, the end of her life. He didn't know what else to try and tell her. He told her God Himself had made them to have sex at twelve, that it was her mother and society who were messing them up, destroying the possibility of their design. She listened. He told her they were natural and beautiful, that they could never happen to each other again. She didn't believe him. She was touching him with her hand. He wondered if he was lying, delivering someone else's line. It was hell. He wanted to convince her, to help him save them by making them completely into something together and new. He was almost sure it was possible. He loved her. He knew that he should force her, that he should rape her for the good of both of them. He couldn't; he knew he never would. He told himself he loved her. He knew they were lost.

She could never stop touching him. She rode with him in the mornings, touching him all the way to school. He sat beside her, following her, hopeless, dissolving. She seemed to be leading him by a chain of flesh, operating him, concealing her design in open-faced allurement. Often she would stay home, alone, waiting for him until noon. He would think of her all morning at school, separated, until the lunch bells would go off and he would sneak out the door, down the inside line of the building, past lines of trees, bellying through a hideout of cars in the parking lot, finally finding himself speeding through the quiet noon, tree-shaded peace of Rapid Cedar to see her. She met him at the door, pink, full of sleep and soap operas, sensuous, unbelievably young and decadent and full of powder and pajamas. He hurried back after a half hour, hungry and satisfied. He was confused. He was losing weight. After school, sometimes even before they left the parking lot, it was the same, her touching him, him driving them by following.

She seemed to touch him within all guises, all masks. He loved her, caught up in her rhythms. Lost in her design, she released him. She touched him unexpectedly, at any time in the day, during any season, in city parks, out in the country, after dark, within the deep, whispering trees, the city lights parked below, in the dim and flickering silences of movie houses, in a cellophane America full of Doris Day movies, rootbeer stands, the corners of rooms and the grassy sides of the river. He didn't want ever to leave for anywhere without her. But sometimes now, he thought, oblivious of me she is only connecting herself with herself; she is only looking through the closet door, amazed with her own power, wanting only to see again if it is still there. He couldn't believe her. Once, passing a semi at noon, on a Saturday highway going toward Iowa City, she touched him so much he thought he was going to drive off the road, killing them both.

"Do you love me?" she sometimes said, a dark thing trapped and welling against him, a vacant moan rising within. "Is it mine?"

"Yes. Of course."

"Really, Dawes? All mine? No one else's?"

"Yes."

He loved her, better than himself. She was finer in every way. He found a book and looked up "penis envy." He worried about her, for her, slightly. He ignored himself. She was touching him everywhere, anointing his Protestant soul, white as a fence of God, for the first time, initiating him into places in which he had already stood. He loved her for it. Only once they sat together in the pews, in the early, deserted balcony of the Methodist church, and she was touching him steadily along the long inside edge of his Sunday suit which he hadn't worn for years. He couldn't believe her; it was her idea to come in the first place. The minister was talking of sin. Dawes Williams nearly welled out of himself, moaning.

Where was the consummation? Oh, God, he thought.

He knew Summer Letch was beyond sin. She was inquisitive, he thought, and that was where they came together. He decided he loved her for her curiosity. And she was less afraid than he. The preacher was coming to the part where he began reading his text. Summer was moving against him, within his dream welling with unappointed ministers, wanting to leave. He did, too, understanding her. Later, in a field near some trees by a river, they couldn't stop kissing. She was a necessary fever, he thought, full of active design, and soon she would begin in earnest, releasing him for awhile, staying his execution. Everything was against them. He wanted to rape her, he thought, but how could one have the nerve to attack such innocence?

"Dawes?" she was whispering. "What are we ever going to do?"

"I don't know."

"It can't be right. I'd be pregnant. What will we do?"

"I don't know. Maybe I could get us some rubbers somewhere. Makes sense. I love you."

"I know. But no. Never. I'd be a. . . . I'd feel like a whore."

"I know. God, I love you so much. I do. I don't know."

But it all only excited him more. He could feel her, Summer, everywhere, close to him, near him, within the center of his brain, expanding his blood with light. He thought he knew her more than himself. She was breathing in his ear, so lost, so incredibly full of milk-white teeth, hot and within him, exploding his mind. He loved her. He would do anything she might say except leave her alone. Nothing could ever touch him again like this, he knew it, he wouldn't let it, he would wall it out.

Her eyes were as wide and brown as wondering fields of cows, rootless, grazers. Her hair was thick and rich as heaven. Even Dunker said she had a beautiful ass. She smelled of a rain of flesh.

He found he could stare at her for hours, amazed by his luck, the fact and recognition that he nearly possessed her. It nearly frightened him at times how intimately he felt he might know her. At other times, knowing he might be that close already to be living within her, he was filled with embarrassment. At times like these, nearly transfixed, watching her fix her hair, gaze into mirrors, or the wind run up under her loose August dresses, he felt full of a holy air, a nearly divine wonderment; he felt he was in possession of something gifted, himself, a puzzle he couldn't name. He would look at her, inarticulate, choked with her own design, his presumption, his embarrassment, and remain too amazed to speak of anything. Then even his face would fall silent. They would begin talking of something else, of nothing at all, perhaps even arguing. Then he could almost believe in her shallowness for a moment, become angry with both his belief and disbelief, and know again she could never be that. —How could he ever find her again? But then he could never lose her, either. It was so perfect, so incomplete. It was hell. Perhaps, he thought, Eddie and Dunker and Travis were right: you have to be cold with girls, with bitches, you remember to keep your balls tied down in the end or you lose everything, all sense of proportion, decorum, cool, and then you never get laid. —So what was the good of trying to tell her, he thought, because without not-having Summer, he could not even not have her. He remained silent.

Once, late, around midnight, after Summer had already touched him three times that day, she led him into the kitchen. They stood against the far wall in near shadows. Summer's father walked into the kitchen and startled them both. They had been once again lost within their private dream. Summer was panting in a loose spring dress, sweltering, gone limp with passion like a fresh bloom of skin, a perfumed musk of crushed organdy. Dawes was locked somewhere within it, trying to ignore himself. It was late, she was impressed within him like August light, a fragile leaf, and Mr. Letch—having no part, he thought—entered anyway. Just then Dawes Williams, the hero of the piece, was leaning against the wall, an erection sticking straight from his fly. He found himself suddenly to be engaged in that and he found, also, he was becoming the fastest thing in the world in becoming unengaged in it. He turned to the wall. He thought, even at the time he was doing it, being fast, he was faster in fact than Dunker Nadlacek in a dream of being fast. It struck him he was being so fast he was also moving in slow motion, frozen to the heart of a cellophane dream. Even while he was struck being fast, he thought, he was struck how fast he was being. He turned, went limp, zipped, and began a conversation with a still life—three apples, a banana, and two pears— framed over the stove so quickly Summer barely had one dish furiously rinsed twice before he turned back, smiling:

"Hello, Mr. Letch," Dawes Williams said lamely, grinning now.

Mr. Letch said nothing. He looked at Dawes, not quite managing to see him. He moved about finally, looking for a shotgun or knives, Dawes thought. He moved around Summer, who stood, a pole of ice, immobile, not looking, swishing fixated dishes in the sink. She said nothing. Dawes began telling himself he was so fast, in fact, Mr. Letch had only thought they had been locked platonically together, kissing passionately, as children do. At least he hadn't swung on him yet, Dawes noted; perhaps the bastard was still in the dark.

Dawes paced about quietly, discreetly checking his fly for sign, carrying on his conversation with Summer Letch and the still life. He found himself quickly run down to nothing, calling the banana "phony" and the two pears "mediocre"; the apples he called "unknown." Mr. Letch eyed him back queerly, nearly caught up in the language of the thing. Summer glared back at Dawes from her sink as if he had somehow already betrayed her. It grew silent. Dawes found himself grinning back at Mr. Letch, amazed at both his own congeniality and the depth of his hypocrisy.

"Well, I guess you two kids must be tired of each other by now," Mr. Letch said. "Better be breaking it up for tonight."

Summer only washed furious dishes, nodding her head. Next to his own mother, Dawes thought, he had never seen anyone wash dishes with such fury, dedication, an obvious self-absorption approaching self-abusement. He thought suddenly perhaps Leone had had something to hide all of these years.

Finally, however, Mr. Letch drank two glasses of water for authority and left the room. Dawes stood watching him go, a witness, believing for the first time in cause and effect, caught up in it yet because he couldn't get a hard-on for two months. All the life had gone out of him. Mystery had somehow been replaced by a factual consciousness; Summer's father was always with them. Summer would talk baby talk to him, laugh in his ear, but nothing could help. Finally, sensing a vacuum in her power, the decline of a kingdom, a flaw in her design, one night while riding with others Summer leaned over in the darkness, kissed it tenderly once, and made him well. Nothing good, however, he thought, lasts forever. Somehow the act had destroyed forever something between them; some huge, nameless thing was breaking up and moving out into the drifting night beyond them. He couldn't stop it.

Then, only once, it happened. It was nearly an accident planned unconsciously for months. After school, lost in her rugs, he was teasing her, her dress was up, breathing around her neck and then, almost a mistake, he slipped through her, her center, something suddenly falling open, like lightning, the center of his blood, his brain like a ship, literally exploding and—just as he was about to settle in, tell her everything he had ever dreamed, just as he was about to lie there, telling her everything he had ever wanted to, complete, just as he was about to move against her, softly, full of dead violence, filling her vague wall, her soul for the only possible time, dissolving them, their light, forever into something beautiful, new, true, as clean as her body—he heard a car move into the garage and stop. Mrs. Letch, home early, turned off her engine and got out. He heard her footsteps move on the adjacent concrete; he saw her shadow move down the porch, the line of window curtains like the dead, unholy sound of light caught in a fish's eye. Summer jumped away from him, destroyed, still caught nearly in a moment of convulsion, nearly crying out. Mrs. Letch was fumbling with the mailbox. By the time she entered, a few moments later, Summer was flushed but nearly composed. Dawes Williams sat with his pants buckled in a distant chair, listening to the locust rise whining in the evergreen bushes, staring at the wall.

When he looked back at Summer, she was gone. Something vague and defined had gone out of her eyes forever. She would never look at him again. She sat looking back at him with a near contempt. Mrs. Letch said nothing. She seemed to smell the air actively, looking through the horrible silence of the room with her nose. Dawes seemed to be forced out of it without a word. He loved Summer. He got up in the shadows to go home.

For a long time he felt his blood collapsing about him, needlessly, he thought. Though Summer seemed to come back to him, it was never the same. For two years she seemed to shuffle between Dawes Williams and B. T. Saus, missing herself, passing between. . . . Perhaps, he thought, that wasn't it at all. Perhaps, he thought, it was all a lie. Perhaps none of it had happened that way at all. Perhaps Eddie and Dunker and Travis had been right to begin with. Perhaps Summer Letch had just been a shallow bitch in the first place. Goddamn, goddamn adolescence, he thought, the oldest story in the world. But he would beat it. He would learn to be hard, functional, successful. He would learn to take while he could. He would be callous and smart. He would never let anything touch him again. He would steel himself against the world, locking it out. He would surround himself with himself. He would never be foolish again. On an impulse he went to *Webster's Dictionary* and looked up "loss." . . .

18

Dawes Williams stood in a freight car full of three hundred and seventy-five tons of soybeans; dust and sweat stood out all over him, and he thought just another summer had rolled around. He was in shape but it had pained him to breathe all afternoon. His legs were so heavy he thought his spine couldn't lift them. He had already lost twenty pounds in a month. Twice a day, when a whistle went off in the air, he filed into a shack of old lumber behind the other men, down near the tracks by a Coke machine, and he lay flat on his back on the floor. He stared at a naked light bulb swinging from the ceiling. Next to him—also not talking, also only staring at the same red swirl of the ceiling—was a man who had two-thirds of a doctorate in Eastern European history. No one spoke, and some of the men who had been there longer stared down at cracks in the flooring, their shoes, and not at the ceiling. To make it harder, the company made the men change shifts every week, so Dawes Williams knew come Sunday night he would be shoveling the tons of rolling soybeans down bins in the cement from midnight to dawn. . . .

He felt alone then. He could think of nothing but the falling rhythm of his shovel, which was made of a large sheet of metal, with two homemade handles of wood, and which was connected by a long returning cable to the wall of the factory. It always returned; and he was like a small animal who rode it backwards, without any reason. He thought of the first night he had come down the tracks to work at midnight—of the grotesque hooded figures, filled out with lanterns and his own sleep, standing out, shouting down the line—and how, when the foreman had told him the average kid only lasted inside the cars for fifteen minutes, he knew he would stick. . . .

But that first night he had been so awkward with the piece of homemade metalworking they called a "power shovel" he had only "pulled" fifty tons of beans. He had fallen out of the freight car, and onto the bin grating, twice and cut his ribs, and he knew if he complained, or even asked for merthiolate, they would fire him, so he said nothing at all. He needed the work because he wanted to buy back the '49 Mercury he had lost in a card game, and as he got better he did a full day's work. In eight hours he emptied the left side of four freight cars; he pulled and rode well over a thousand tons of dry beans down a hole in the platform. . . .

But Dawes Williams wasn't worried; soon he could quit. He came to work, often at midnight, in only a sleeveless shirt, a pair of old jeans, and some steel-toed shoes for riding on the shovel's cable backwards. He tied a bandanna around his forehead to keep the sweat off his glasses, two more round his ankles to keep the beans out of his shoes, and another around his neck just for the hell of it. In the stillness of the car, in the wet and hooded rings of shadows late at night with only the sounds of the falling grains behind him, he felt just like an Arapahoe Indian shaking out dry rags in the wind of the terrible war moon. Looking behind him—from on a tall mountain of soybeans, before he rode his one-piece machine down backwards like a water ski, before he got off it like a matador listening to three hundred pounds of beans make a pass behind him through the high door—Dawes glanced at the red shadow of the near-Ph.D. in Eastern European history and figured he felt like an Arapahoe too. . . .

"Job like that'll do you good," Simpson Williams had said, looking up from his evening paper.

"How would you know?" Dawes Williams had answered. "You never worked a day in your life. You only sold shoes."

"Well, old boy," Simpson had said, "that's true, but a taste of this'll make you want to go to college and do something else for a lifetime's work. In my day we didn't have good-paying work like that to do."

"One," Dawes Williams said, "they're paying me about half what that job's worth; and two, college labor by the time I'll get out will be the cheapest thing in the world."

"That's good pay," Simpson said.

"Don't think so," Dawes Williams said. "I believe like the guy I work with says: 'This insensible crap will only give us a lifelong feeling for the masses and lead us closer to Marx.'"

"That so?" Simpson said, going back into his paper.

Simpson Williams had said nothing more on the subject because he had given up debating with Dawes. The whole thing had just given in and broken off one day, without even a thin ritual dance of closing. Simpson thought his son Dawes had grown a little unsound in his thinking, but he didn't say anything about it as he felt perhaps Dawes had never been too stable to begin with. He felt he must have taken after his mother's family, because although the Williamses caved in at the heels and went into senility at an early age, in every other respect they were sound as a dollar. For his part, Dawes, however, thought for a bright man his father was a bit of an idiot to boot. Every time Dawes began to demonstrate to Simpson just what kind of a damn genius he'd become, Simpson would laugh in his face and say:

"Well, old boy, if you're such a fine genius, it seems your mother and I couldn't be all that bad. We helped, you know."

"Oh, Key-rist," Dawes Williams said, "I know that. I know all about that now, and I've also heard that damn gag before. In fact, wasn't it your great-uncle Fred who wobbled over to you and whispered that one at you through his senile ear trumpet at Cousin John's wedding? Remember?"

"If you're so smart," Simpson had said finally, going into dinner, "how did you manage to lose your car to Danny Deeder in a poker game?"

"Well, Simpson, I tell ya," Dawes Williams said after him, "I play my own brand of cards."

It was true. Lying there, back on the shack's floor again, blowing smoke at the Coke machine, Dawes knew himself to be a somewhat eccentric gambler, complete with his own vision and world view. He thought he just heard different sounds in the dice, the clicking cards, the roll of the pool balls. Dawes began thinking of the night he had lost his '49 Mercury, which was repainted blue as the sky, and as beautiful as the old war lance of an Indian pony. The afternoon drifted down the dull tracks, a breeze moved against the walls, and in the back of the shack one of the men who was taking off early was singing— *O Jumbuli'a, Jumbuli'a, O meomio an'a catfish pie'a*—into the thin shower of water running down the tile of the inside stone. . . .

Dawes Williams checked over his under card in five-card stud: *It had been the four of clubs, and his up card read the queen of diamonds. Dawes Williams thought he saw a relationship there despite itself and raised the pot twenty-five cents. Everyone else smiled and thought Dawes was a helluva strange gambler. Two became confused, however, and dropped out, but Danny Deeder raised Dawes fifty cents. Dawes called Danny's king of spades and was dealt a nine of hearts; then Danny Deeder was dealt a six of clubs by Barney Ingersoll. Danny bet a half; Dawes raised him a buck, was called, and was dealt the two of hearts.*

"I can't draw shit," Dawes Williams said, looking straight at Danny.

"Me, either," Danny said, "I believe you."

"What the hell are you guys doing?" Dunker said. "I had better cards than that when I folded."

"Ya," Danny said, "but you're not in this. It's just me and Dawes."

After Dawes drew the two of hearts, Danny was dealt another nothing card and bet a buck. Dawes knew Danny had nothing underneath, that he only had to beat the king, and so he raised him a buck. Danny Deeder knew Dawes had nothing underneath, he never did, and so he raised his raise. Dawes called, needed only an ace or a pair to win, and drew the six of diamonds.

"Key-rist," Dawes Williams said, "what a bust-out."

Danny Deeder then showed his hole card was only the three of clubs after all. He laughed, and hoped to set Dawes up for the next time when he might actually hold the hole card. Dawes knew none of that was ever decipherable anyway and paid no attention. The cards passed quickly. Won, nearly untouchable, money was banked inside the cellophane of cigaret packs, and Dawes had sat back within the warm overhang of smoke—and watched as the constant blur of the cards came across the boards all evening until dawn. Girls came and went, became bored and vanished, rearose and pulled even the steady players out into the evening, but the game wore on all night.

Just before dawn all the beer was gone, the cigaret butts smoked, and at least five people were dead broke and out of reasonable IOU's. By this time Dunker and Eddie and Travis were gone, and Barney Ingersoll and Mike Hanna were asleep on the table. Money stuck in cigaret packs—the irreproachably banked winnings not even to be spent on a straight or a filled flush—was also stuck away into pockets. By this time the only people left in the room were Peter Wolsey, Dawes Williams and Danny Deeder, who were bumping heads. As they played, Dawes explained the evening away:

"The thing about this game is," Dawes Williams said, "with all the crap that's going on around it, it's very important, if not imperative, to win early."

"How's that, Dawes?" Danny Deeder said, picking up another pot.

"This game is a capitalist's structure," Dawes Williams said, "largely corporate and fascist in nature. If your brother hasn't been included into the upper structures by eleven o'clock, it's time to start knifing him and doing him in. By twelve the poor are an unforgivable threat. By one the big bankers of the system own the table and it's hopeless. By two all the masses can do is feed the big bankers, be eaten alive and enjoy it. By three the money in the cellophane packs goes into the pockets, and even the *feeding cycle is over. By morning all there is left is a dead, ringing silence and epilepsy in the air, nothing more. . . ."*

"Dawes," Peter Wolsey said, "let's have another drink. I think you might be crazy."

"Could be," Dawes Williams said, "I don't like to look at the values of these cards, I only like to look at the rhythms of their comings and goings."

"How's that, Dawes?" Danny Deeder said, picking up another one.

"I don't gamble for the profit of it," Dawes said. "I gamble for the sheer joy of seeing the next card come—and the next and the next, even when there is no miraculous, let alone mathematical, chance it will improve me—yes, come popping up like a duck."

"You gamble," Peter Wolsey said, "for the exact same reason people without fireplaces go out into the woods to chop firewood."

"Hell, yes," Dawes Williams said. "I think it is good for me. I think it strengthens my character some."

"Go to it, Dawes," Danny Deeder said. "You're nice to have around and we love ya."

Then Danny Deeder laid down another full boat and picked up a twenty-dollar pot in' three to win.

"She-it," Dawes Williams said. "Those gods are after me with matches I tell ya."

Dawes reached for a cigaret and found he had already dropped seventy-five dollars. Danny Deeder looked across the old wooden kitchen table and smiled at him. Dawes Williams smiled back. He was very drunk. Danny Deeder, Dawes knew, would someday end up running a loan company and it would serve him right.

"You always been this unlucky, Dawes?" Deeder said.

"Always. How you doin', Pete?"

"'Bout even," Wolsey said.

"Yep," Dawes Williams said, "it all started when I was four years old. My luck already had soured on me. And the way I found out about it was I wound up one day flipping Heinrich Gretch for comic books in Tamera's old horse loft."

"Who was Heinrich Gretch?" Wolsey said.

"He was a five-year-old, half German, half Russian, and a quarter Hungarian, I think, an immigrant. Used to talk about nothing but concentration camps now that I think of it."

"Real hungry?" Wolsey said.

"Real hungry," Dawes Williams said. "He used to probably talk about cold winters running from dogs now that I think of it."

"Good way to go about it," Danny Deeder said.

"Hell, yes," Dawes Williams said. "That dirty bastard probably will end up owning seven chains of movie houses. So how could I question it? I never ran from any dogs, let alone for six straight winters."

"God damn it," Peter Wolsey said, "did he run from those dogs or didn't he?"

"How should I know?" Dawes Williams said. "But he never let me see any of those coins he was flipping. He won five hundred and twenty of my comic books in one sitting."

"You were a dead man," Wolsey said.

"I sure was," Dawes said. "All I can remember was: 'Heads!, no, it's tails, Tails! Tails! Tails!, no it's heads, Heads! Heads! Heads!, no it's tails. . . .' Man, I was wiped out just sitting there in that high air of that old dark horse loft."

"That's poetry," Peter Wolsey said.

"That it is," Dawes Williams said. "We got any whiskey left?"

"We never had any whiskey," Deeder said.

"I'll bet that's so," Dawes said. "Anyway, when I left I must have thought I had epilepsy. My legs were full of rubber. Christ, I was only four years old, and behind me as I'm pulling my little red wagon home I hear Henny Gretch saying: 'Yaw, Dawes, I vil flip yaw fer the vagon, too!' That's all I heard behind me. . . coming. . . coming from . . .''

"Coming from where?" Wolsey said. "Let's have it."

"Coming from the dark loft and the high air behind me. Christ, coming from that thin air rolling with the sounds of six winters full of running, screaming dogs," Dawes Williams said. And then he passed out cold in his chair.

When he woke, Danny Deeder was talking straight at him:

"Dawes," he said, "I've been tallying up my IOUs and this is how it stands: you owe me a hundred and twenty-two dollars."

"I don't have a hundred and twenty-two dollars," Dawes said.

"Listen," Deeder said, "this is how it went: When Ingersoll left, you owed him ten dollars, and he owed me twenty dollars—so he gave me checks from Barney Redwood for two dollars; Calders for six dollars; and a buck on the side and you owe me ten dollars. Then, when Dunker left, you owed him twenty-five dollars, and he owed me thirty-five dollars, so he gave me checks—ten dollars from Travis; five dollars from Eddie; ten dollars from you and you owed me ten more on the side. So you owe me twenty dollars on the side and ten dollars in checks; that's thirty dollars. Now—when Inge left, he owed me forty dollars and you owed him twenty dollars. He gave me a check from Hanna for twenty dollars; one endorsed by Ingersoll through you for ten dollars; and one from Barney Redwood for ten dollars. Then I took over a debt of twenty dollars Inge owed Jasper Hally—you owed Hally twenty dollars—so you still owe me twenty dollars more on the side but you don't owe Hally a damn thing. So that makes twenty dollars more on the side and ten dollars in checks there. That all makes sixty in checks and IOUs, and you've just lost sixty-two dollars bumping heads. That's one hundred twenty-two dollars; I've got it written here on this paper."

"Foolish," Dawes Williams said. "Damn foolish. Will you take my car on it?"

"I don't need a car," Danny Deeder said. "I just bought two last week to sell myself."

"Take it anyway," Dawes Williams said. "I want to buy it back for one hundred twenty-two dollars in the worst way."

"All right," Danny Deeder said, "I'll take it as a favor."

"Cool," Dawes Williams said. "Take me home in it, I want to eat breakfast."

So Deeder drove him home, and Dawes got his pool cue from the trunk, and then Deeder drove his car down the alley. Dawes felt that curious, early morning dizziness only cardplayers who have just lost their house can know, so he sat on the porch and watched the cars slide past on the street. The paper boy threw a column of newsprint at him and rode off in a distance of sleeping tin. The morning cast up gold birds. Without turning, Dawes knew his mother was at the door, finding a carless son where she had only expected to find clean, well-dusted, homogenized bottles of milk. Dawes turned and laughed at her fanatic materialism, her love and possession of automobiles. Then, when he turned back again to the street and spread the newspaper out on the lawn, he saw the smaller headline read:

DESPITE RECESSION IKE SEES PROSPEROUS TIMES AHEAD

He roared with laughter and, after awhile, went inside the house.

19

One Thursday that summer Eddie and Dunker woke Dawes, handed him half a warm beer, and Travis said:

"Com'on, Dawes, we're in a rut here. You need a change, and we're going to Waterloo."

"That's good, Travis," Dawes said, "real fine."

"I'll bet these girls in Waterloo are real dogs," Dunker said.

"Hell, no," Eddie said, "I've got some real fine names here."

Dawes slipped on some jeans and they went outside. Barney Redwood was sitting in the car, warming it up, driving already, and with Barney Redwood driving, they made the eighty miles down to Waterloo in fifty minutes. Barney Redwood was especially good at passing trucks over the exact crests of hills, and they did much better on the way back—after what happened in Waterloo they pulled that in forty-two minutes flat.

When Barney Redwood drove, he got very furious in the eyes. Travis—who thought that bastard Barney Redwood was a sonofabitch to boot, but then Dunker and Dawes thought he was all right—sat in the back seat and watched him handle the road. Dawes thought Barney was just fine because he shot so much pool with him, but Travis didn't like him because Barney had let Dunker use his movie camera one night to photograph this girl he was doing a job on. Barney set her up, on the floor, in the exact center of a shaft of light, and Dunker was outside, behind a bush, filming through the window. That was why Barney Redwood was mainly a sonofabitch, Travis thought. He thought he mostly didn't like to treat girls like that; mostly he thought things like that were private.

Dawes sat watching Travis, knowing what he was thinking, knowing also that things were never that simple, as the girl Barney Redwood had been doing it to also happened to be an old girl friend of Travis Thomas'. Just later, when they got to Waterloo, Eddie said he had plenty of names to look into:

"Great," Travis said.

Dawes knew Travis liked to meet new girls so he could just sit back and watch them think—My God, that's got to be the handsomest boy I've ever seen. Even Dunker could see them thinking that when they looked at Travis Thomas—they couldn't help themselves—but then Travis managed to carry it all off well. After, however, a morning set of nothing but a series of the doggy girls of Waterloo, they stopped for lunch and Eddie sat scanning his lists.

"I'll bet this next bitch really does it," he said. "This guy who gave me this list put a star by her name."

"What's her name?" Travis said quietly.

"Karen MaGoogle," Eddie said.

"That's good, Eddie," Travis said, "real fine."

"Listen," Dunker said, "if we get any more dogs, we gotta have a signal that means 'Let's get the hell out' without saying as much."

"Damn straight," Barney Redwood said.

"How about," Dawes Williams said slowly, "something like—'It's raining in Alsace-Lorraine'?"

Travis watched Dawes. He thought Dawes was sitting there, eating a hamburger, as if he had just finished his life's work, as if he had just become the master spy of the universe and come up with the unbreakable code of all time. Travis thought he had almost lost his mind when he heard Dawes say that.

So, after Dunker had finished taking Dawes out into the street and pounding him around some, they drove over to the house. Barney Redwood took one look at Karen MaGoogle's mother, who was answering the door, and he said:

"It's raining in Alsace-Lorraine," before she had even gotten a chance to introduce herself.

Travis stood there knowing now he didn't like Barney Redwood, the sonofabitch wasn't even polite to mothers. They made a semicircle around Mrs. MaGoogle's and, after everyone tired of watching this fat housewife trying to figure out what 'It's raining in Alsace-Lorraine' was supposed to mean, Eddie stepped up and introduced himself:

"Is Karen MaGoogle home?" he said, reading off his list.

"Do you know Karen?" Mrs. MaGoogle said.

"Oh, sure," Eddie said. "She's an old friend of mine. Trot her out here, would you please?"

"Well, Karen's in the bathtub," this mother and housewife said very slowly.

"She said that like it was Newton's second law of motion and inertia," Dawes Williams whispered to Dunker.

"Ya," Dunker said.

"That's all right," Eddie was saying to Mrs. MaGoogle with his most endearing smile, "wrap her up and send her out here anyway."

Things got very silent after that.

"I was only kidding," Eddie said.

But he wasn't getting much out of this mother, so Travis stepped up and saved the day, and said:

"How do you do?" he said, taking her hand and shaking it. "My name's Travis Thomas from Rapid Cedar and I told Karen I'd come all the way up and see her today."

"Big deal," Dawes could hear Dunker saying quietly, behind them.

But that didn't bother Travis. He was only looking at this mother, dead in the eye, concentrating on her with the straightest look he had. Dawes could see the woman was beginning to melt.

"How nice," Mrs. MaGoogle said.

"Could you get her out of her tub then?" Travis said.

"Well," Mrs. MaGoogle said, gazing back at Travis as if she were busy dreaming his blood into the family line, "it'll probably be a few minutes."

"That's quite all right," Dawes said, moving in, putting his two cents in, "we'll hang around."

Then Mrs. MaGoogle turned round and disappeared into the house to get Karen from her tub. Behind him, as he turned back to the street, Travis could hear Barney Redwood talking to Eddie:

"Hey, Welsh," Redwood said, "does this girl even believe in dancing?"

"How the hell should I know?" Eddie was saying. "I never even met her before."

"Key-rist," Dunker said, "I sure as hell hope she doesn't look like her mother."

"Don't worry," Eddie said, "this guy's given me some real straight names in the past. He's a helluva ballplayer."

"Attttsss Eddie," Travis was saying.

Just then, however, as they were standing there, smoking in the yard, watching all the neighbors leaving for work in their rigs, in the cabs to their Mack trucks, they could hear this queer, skipping thunder on the stairs, and then suddenly, bouncing the living room almost, Karen exploded through the door in her terrycloth robe and size ten slippers on her feet. Dawes only noticed the slippers because she was pigeon-toed.

Barney Redwood took one look at her and he said:

"Wait a minute. Hold on here. Send your mother back out here. I've got a few things I'd like to say to her."

Then everyone turned and stared at Eddie. It was so bad even Dawes Williams was glaring at him, and Eddie began dramatically tearing up his list. When Travis finally looked back at this Karen, she took one look at him and braced herself against the doorsill, and she barely got out:

"Hi! You must be Travis Thomas."

"That he is," Dunker said. "And he generally deserves himself."

Travis knew, right off, he'd never completely live this one down, and already Barney Redwood had drifted down, away, into the yard, and it was as if he were circling, backing off, intently examining horse flesh at the packing house, when he looked at her and said:

"Brother. Have you got all your teeth?"

"Huh?" Karen MaGoogle said.

Then Dunker was laughing as well, and trying to keep it all inside himself, that he lay crippled over a bush. Dawes Williams joined him, having such a bad time he spun on the railing and did a back flip off the porch. Dunker and Dawes were both in the bushes, lashed together in leafy masts, trying to flee, and then, arm in arm, they withdrew to the street, where they sat by a fireplug, roaring. Then Barney and Eddie left to sit on the hood of the car, leaving Travis all alone on the porch. Travis decided he would save himself by handling the situation with an incredibly unpredictable grace.

"Gee," Karen MaGoogle said quite seriously, "what's wrong with *them?*"

But she was happy. She looked deeply into Travis Thomas' eyes as if she'd just been introduced to the Russian court.

"They just can't take it," Travis said.

"Take what?" Karen MaGoogle said.

"Oh, don't mind them," Travis said, "they're just drunk."

"Well, I don't like guys that drink," Karen said. "You don't drink, do you, Mr. Thomas? That would ruin everything."

When they heard that come drifting over the lawn, Dawes and Dunker began dying in earnest. They fell all over each other and the fireplug: Dawes became delirious; he was gone; he was so frantic he crawled back under the porch, and Travis could hear him there, beating his feet on the underboards, singing almost, screaming.

"IT'S RAINING IN ALSACE-LORRAINE! IT'S RAINING HEAVEN'S EYE IN ALSACE-LORRAINE!"

When Travis turned to Karen MaGoogle, he could see, right off, she was still waiting for him to say something important. The best he could manage to get out was:

"Gee, Karen, I'm sorry we got you out of your tub of soap. We've got to be runnin' along now. Be seeing you."

"Is that all you've got to say to me?" Karen MaGoogle said in her most seductive voice.

Dawes Williams peeked over the edge of the porch. He told himself it couldn't be real, to get hold of it all now, but it was too late for that. When he saw Karen MaGoogle, and her seductive voice wafting out, he fell apart again and went straight back down, under the boards. He lay there in the darkness for some minutes knowing nothing could ever be repaired again. Another fit set in, and he began laughing so hard he spit up blood. He wedged himself up, under the shadowy railings, and was lying on his back, compressed, nearly kicking the flooring of the porch out with his head. Dunker went under, and tried to dig him out, and Karen began to develop the notion that something'd gone wrong. Travis stood before her, feeling caught in the middle, not knowing. Then Karen began to look at him as if she'd just been hit in the face with dead fish. Dawes was still lying under the porch, he was worse, only Dunker had joined up with him. Travis could hear both of them, bandits under the flooring, screaming:

"FLOODS! TYPHOONS! FLOODS! HELP! THE DAM IS BREAKING!"

"GREAT PERIODS OF DELUGE! FORTY DAYS AND FORTY NIGHTS! IT'S RAINING IN ALSACE-LORRAINE!"

"Well," Travis said, turning to Karen, "I sure hope we haven't inconvenienced you any."

Travis felt that part was all right, but the problem was when he turned round to face her down with it, he took one look at Karen MaGoogle's expectant face and then he came apart, too. He broke down so suddenly he almost cried. He just slumped down against the wall of the porch and he felt dry tears run down his cheek like convulsions. By the time he looked up, Barney Redwood and Eddie were lying in the yard, rolling around as if they'd been attacked by snakes. Then, suddenly, it grew very still. . . .

Dawes Williams came from under the porch. He strode out at first with confidence; then he grew red in the face, as if his skin had turned to litmus paper in the air, and he coughed up blood. He stood there, confronting, vague, spitting bits of his lungs on the porch. Travis called for a rag to wipe off the boards.

"You all right, Dawes?" Travis said.

"My buddy Dawes is doin' fine," Dunker said coming up.

"God it's raining," Dawes Williams said. "I can't understand that, the sun's out."

"Can my mother get you anything?" Karen MaGoogle said.

"No," Dawes Williams said, "I'm doin' fine."

But, by then, Dawes had to look Karen MaGoogle dead in the eye. He looked up at her, out of his agony, and he swore he was ruptured, had palsy and a broken lung, and then he said:

"Please. Oh, Christ, please don't say anything more. Everyone just be perfectly still."

And with that Travis watched him roll over on the grass and pretend to pass out cold. Just then, Mrs. MaGoogle came back out onto the porch, carrying a pitcher of lemonade.

"What's the matter with *him?*" Mrs. MaGoogle said.

"Oh heck, m'am," Travis said, real polite, moving back in as if nothing had happened, "don't mind him. He just usually goes epileptic on Thursdays."

"Well," Karen said, "he certainly looks pale and wan."

Karen MaGoogle was standing directly over Dawes, the hem of her bathrobe blowing in his face, but she had eyes only for Travis. She must think she's some damn Madonna to boot, Travis thought, looking for exits. But as soon as she'd said 'wan' to him, he knew what to do. Turning to Mrs. MaGoogle, he said:

"Mrs. MaGoogle? I believe your Karen here must study a great deal and read poetry. Is that true?"

"My, yes," Mrs. MaGoogle said. "Karen is the only junior elected to the Honor Society."

"In that case," Travis said, "I think your Karen should get to know my friend Dawes Williams here better. You wouldn't know it to look at him, but he is a poet, too."

"Oh?" Mrs. MaGoogle said, ignoring him. "And you should hear Karen's piano, too, Mr. Thomas."

"I'll bet," Travis said. "Is it tuned?"

"Why, yes. It is," Mrs. MaGoogle said.

Fainting with a holy fascination, Travis turned back to Karen MaGoogle, the doggiest girl in Waterloo, and said:

"My word, Karen. You must be quite an accomplished young lady."

Dawes Williams lay below, and when Travis said that to her he could see Karen could only rub the wonder out of her eyes, think of marriage and happiness, and collapse slightly against her steps. Even Eddie now thought Travis was getting in over his head, and might have to marry the girl in the end, and Travis himself only stood there thinking—Shut up, Thomas. If you say one more kind word to this girl, she's going to pick you up and pack you under her arm and carry you away forever to live in her tub of soap.

As he was thinking this, Mrs. MaGoogle only offered Travis another glass of lemonade. It was the fifth one he had drained in six minutes.

"Oh, thanks," Travis said. "Real fine."

"Yes, Mr. Thomas," Mrs. MaGoogle went on to say, "I tell you Karen's very accomplished, as you say, on the trumpet, too."

"I'll bet she is," Travis said.

"Mother! *Mother!*" Karen said again.

Even Dawes was now beginning to think Travis had gotten in over his head, and the only thing he could see in the world, lying there, flush with the flooring, was the huge head of Karen MaGoogle, with eyes staring out over lemonade straws, watching him back. Then her eyes glided back upon Travis as if she thought she was being presented with her promised pet hound, her prize for a conscientious childhood, or her lover returned from the war. It's hell to be this handsome, Travis Thomas thought. Suddenly, however, just when he thought he'd put it all back together again, to the point of gracious exits, Travis could see Dawes Williams was bent on only spoiling it all, because, just then, Dawes Williams got straight up, like a dead man strolling on stage against all cues, and he walked out into the yard and sat down and stared back like an Indian recognizing no one.

"OUT OF CONTROL! IT'S OUT OF CONTROL!" Dunker was saying.

But Dunker came up and sat down beside Dawes, two Indians then, equally wooden in the eyes, and Eddie and Barney were sitting on the curb, staring the other way. By this time Travis could see that Mrs. MaGoogle was trying to ignore Dawes by pouring lemonade, but she wasn't totally making it, and Travis was on his seventh glass in eight minutes, following her about the porch, catching it like rain in his cup, when he finally got out:

"No, thank you, Mrs. MaGoogle, I only like to polish four or five glasses of this stuff an hour."

"But can I get *him* anything," Mrs. MaGoogle said, pointing her pitcher at Dawes Williams, trying not to follow it out with her eyes. "An ice cube, perhaps, or a glass of brandy?"

"No," Travis said. "Don't you worry about old Dawes. He'll be good as new in a couple of hours. Soon as the tremors pass."

"He's so *young* for a thing like that," Karen said.

"Yes," Travis said. "Old Dawes's been that way all his life. No one knows what caused it, but he's made three separate issues of the *A.M.A. Journal,* and they say it's hopeless."

"They've given up completely, Travis?" Mrs. MaGoogle said.

"Yes," Travis found himself saying. "Hopeless. They don't even think he'll live to see thirty."

"My, my," Mrs. MaGoogle said. "That's terrible. My my, my my my." As she said this, she clicked her tongue in her cheek, trying not to notice Dawes Williams, who was still as sitting death, staring back in from her yard. Finally she turned on her heel. She exited, taking the drained pitcher of lemonade in behind her.

For a moment Travis was glad she'd gone. He thought: One more drop of that baby and I'd peed my pants. Then he wasn't glad any more because, turning back, he found he was alone with Karen MaGoogle on her porch. He was looking for gracious exits. He knew he was trapped by himself, his own nobility—that he should've told her this was absurd twenty minutes ago, to 'kiss ass'—but then he still didn't think she had it coming. Besides, he almost liked the feeling of nobility and wanted to hold on to it. Looking over the broken railings, he could see it was Barney Redwood now, sitting in the bushes, chanting— "IT'S RAINING IN ALSACE-LORRAINE!! IT'S RAINING IN ALSACE-LORRAINE!" —and that Eddie was lying on the hood of the car, eyeing him back with that look of his that said *Look, it's my mess, you live with it;* and that Dawes, the best of all, was finally up, and moving, and rolling down the driveway, being tended like a piece of tumbling weed by Dunker, who was watering him down with a beer. He turned to Karen MaGoogle. It had been an incredibly hot summer. He knew he hadn't spoken yet, but that she was hanging on his every word. Finally he got out:

"Well, Karen, what can you say for yourself?"

"I don't know, Travis," she said, proposing, "but I just want to take this opportunity to say I've admired you before from afar. I never thought I'd get a chance to meet you, of course, but I've seen you often on the basketball court. We're not in the same conference, perhaps, distance becomes an important thing in these matters, perhaps. . ."

"Huh?" Travis Thomas said.

"Anyway," she said, ignoring him, "I may have seen better players, but I've never seen anyone that *looks* as nice as you out there."

"Oh ya. Oh ya," Travis said. "Well, don't let it throw ya, Karen, 'cause deep down I'm just another guy. One of the boys, you know. A regular social democrat."

"Oh, I just *knew it,*" she said. "I knew you'd be nice."

Just then, however, the ambulance Mrs. MaGoogle had ordered out for Dawes Williams from the next block arrived. Mrs. MaGoogle did not appear.

"Tell your mother that was very thoughtful," Travis said, "but we like to take care of our own."

There was a silence. The ambulance driver got out in a robe.

"DUNKER," Travis yelled at the street, "SEND THAT DAMN AMBULANCE HOME."

"OKAY, TRAVIS. I'M TRYING," Dunker called back. "BUT IT'S DAMN RAINING IN ALSACE-LORRAINE!! IT'S JUST DAMN RAINY IN ALSACE-LORRAINE, TRAVIS!!"

"I'M COMING, DUNKER," Travis yelled back.

When he turned back to Karen, however, things got tense again. Karen was looking at him as if he'd never been away, as if he'd never go away again, and she had stars in her eyes that said she thought they'd been through it all with Dawes Williams, had raised him up from childhood together, and now she owned him:

"Travis," she said, "why don't I get my suit, call some of my girl friends up, and we'll all go swimming in the park?"

The afternoon light raced like snakes in the leaves. Travis thought he was some kind of goner for sure. A million things wove through his mind like wheels. Even the possibility of real, saving humor had been used up and vanished. Travis thought he'd better stall for time: for a moment he even thought of questioning the Honor Society semantics of swimming in the "park"; twitching, he even thought she had said she would get her "trunks." It was horrible, incredible, lost. Then, just at the moment he knew he was a goner for sure, he was cast up and saved. It had happened. Karen MaGoogle had just looked at him, quietly, and said something that had delivered him up from himself:

"Travis," she said, "I even know a girl who'd be just *perfect* for Dawes. She has a little problem. She's a poet and an epileptic, too."

As soon as Karen MaGoogle's last word fell, the entire thing exploded and dissolved. Barney Redwood became hysterical and kicked out two of the porch's slats; Eddie fell headfirst off the hood of the car; Travis collapsed down the stairs; and Dunker knocked himself nearly cold by diving through the front window of Barney's old car. Dawes Williams became breathless, asthmatic as fish, rising, gulping for air. Without saying another word, they picked Dawes off the cement and drove away. Barney Redwood wheeled the getaway car down the drive; Eddie threw his torn-up list of The Doggy Girls of Waterloo out on the lawn; and Travis leaned out of the departing window and said:

"NOBILITY IS DISHONEST! THE FLESH IS WEAK! THE FLESH IS WEAK!"

Travis' Karen stood on the porch and watched. . . .

20

Barney Redwood made it back to Rapid Cedar in forty-two minutes flat. He flew. He was determined. All the way—watching the fenceless shadows of chickens chew the ends of flat fields, the blowing corn, the endless edge of the green west wind out of the corner of his eye—he thought only: I knew it. I knew it. I knew it would come to this.

When he'd seen this girl's mother-MaGoogle, he knew right off there was God. He also knew, suddenly, who his father had been, and that he should have married Mrs. MaGoogle in the first place, and that it scared him.

But he made it back to Rapid Cedar, ignoring the others, in forty-two flat because they had to drop Dawes Williams off at the hospital for observation. Dawes sat in the back seat, saying nothing, spitting up blood. He had broken something. Two doctors dressed in white let him out, after two days, telling him the two broken vessels in his left lung would eventually heal over, and thinking he was a very quiet boy as he had said nothing at all.

Leone was worried, confused, and brought him his robe and the lesser half of a devil's food cake. Summer Letch came to the hospital to see him. Dawes took one look at her and knew she was playing Scarlett O'Hara and he was Ashley Wilkes. But when she ran those long, cool hands of hers up his leg and under his sheet, he knew again there was God and he finally stopped laughing. He sailed, swaying in her eyes for awhile, and his laughing within him suddenly broke off whole, drifted off, and ceased on the dark wall, the edge of the doorway, the end of the hall. . . .

After she'd gone, hands behind his head and at peace, Dawes lay back in his antiseptic sheets and thought for two days upon the worst thing he and Dunker had pulled off that entire summer, their lives. Feeling a need for a place to confess, Dawes stared at the hospital's pale green wall, its shadows and foot-prints of walking-by nurses. There, within its soft, pleasant fall of electric light, he saw Dunker Nadlacek and Dawes Williams, alone again, drunk, not caring, not wanting to call it a night yet, as they once again stole straw chairs from Negroes' porches in the two-o'clock morning, and he could still see *Dunker's dark, implausibly tall form crawl, a vertical cat grown up high in the summer air, slipping from tree to tree, through the shadows, into and then through the explosions and roofs of parked sports cars. White men's cars. Anyone's cars. Why not? Dunker and Dawes were not bigots. They checked carefully first to see that no one was in them, and then they made the bomb run. People carried insurance. Insurance companies were faceless, impossibly moneyed, nameless when it came to committing crimes against them. It was beautiful. Perfect. It was almost moral. And they tore off the roofs, like tornadoed houses, like cannoned war wagons, completely from the cars. . . . I confess, Dawes Williams thought, I confess, I confess to liking screaming and ruction better than silence.*

He thought it over for two days and two nights, and in the end he decided it couldn't be helped. He felt he had nowhere else to confess it. He felt suddenly a need to be moving along.

When they released him, early one Sunday morning, he felt a need to be shooting some pool, so he went to look for Barney Redwood. He walked, moving three or four miles through the sleepy, cornered streets of Rapid Cedar. Churches were passing. He closed his jacket against the thin summer morning and crossed finally through the high, dry weeds growing on one of the last patches of open ground left in the city. Barney Redwood's house was near the country, a sudden line, stretching out, and it was a high husk of gray wood, broken and open with windows.

Though he'd known Barney for a year now, it was the first time Dawes had gone out to Redwood's house. Hesitantly he knocked at the worn screen of the kitchen door and waited for an answer. He stood on the stoop out back and listened to Mrs. Redwood fry eggs over a stove in the morning. It was early, and the smell carried over the lawn to the tree line, clear as springs. The back door hung off its hinges and, entering, Dawes crossed the large kitchen, much too large for only three people, he thought, and he listened to the bacon frying, an early Sunday morning, and he said:

"Hello? Are you Mrs. Redwood?"

"Yes?"

"I'm Dawes Williams. I came to find Barney to shoot some pool."

"Yes, Dawes," she said, pushing a wisp of brown hair away from her face with the back of her hand. "Bayard's in his bedroom I think."

Dawes went up a long staircase leading, without doors, into what was almost an attic. Dusty sunlight fell through thick bay windows, the coves and gables carved in the mansard roof. Barney Redwood was in the corner, propped against a grotesque, wrought-iron Victorian bedstead. The room was dark in places, heavy, full of a yellow musk, a nearly illuminated deepness, and Barney was naked to the waist, under a sheet, smoking slowly on a cigaret, draining calmly the last of a pint of Peppermint Schnapps. A blonde, also naked to the waist, was in there with him, under the fall of the sheet. The blonde, who must have been thirty, whom he'd gotten the night before at the Dance-Land Ballroom, was talking about leaving for church, sighing giggles of air into the blue smoke, burying Barney's face in her teats, and wrapping herself all over him like fleshing vines. The blonde looked somehow older to Dawes than Barney's mother had.

"Hey, Dawes!" Barney said, pushing her away so he could speak. "Com'on in, pardner. Pull up a stool. When the hell'd they let you out of the hospital?" he said.

"Jesus God," Dawes Williams said. "What *is* all this shit anyway, Barney?"

21

The summer wore on and became August again. They never went to the farm any more, of course. Dawes had bought his '49 Mercury back from Danny Deeder and had quit his job. They drove the old sedan around town and threw beer cans on the lawns. Sometimes, very late, when there was nothing else to do, they would drive up the hill inside the Carter Park Zoo and park the car and watch the monkeys masturbate in their cages.

"Look at that one, Dawes," Eddie would say. "He reminds me something of you."

"What a crazy sonofabitch," Travis said.

"Some of these monkeys get awfully neurotic all right," Dawes Williams said. "There must be sixty of 'em caged in eighty feet of wire."

"Hell," Dunker said, "all these monkeys do up here is beat off all night. It's mad."

"Don't they have any female monkeys up here?" Dawes said.

"Sure," Travis said, "they're over in that other cage."

"Doesn't make sense," Dawes said.

"Sure does," Eddie said, "cause if they were in the same cage, all they'd be doing would be screwing one another to death. These zoo bastards know what they're doing. Who'd come up here to watch that? It's dirty."

"If we'd come up here to watch them masturbate," Dawes said, "seems to me we'd come up here to watch'em screw a little."

"We didn't come up here for that," Travis said. "We just came up here."

"Speaking of that," Eddie said, "we going to go over and watch Dunker sleep with Sue Allen tonight? We haven't done that for awhile."

"Oh, Christ," Dawes Williams said. "Come right in. Welcome to the monkey house."

"Lookit that little fellow over there," Dunker said, trying to change the subject. "He's really pounding his pud."

"Quit changing the subject, Dunker," Eddie said. "Let's go over to Sue Allen's house and hang around."

"I'm not changing any subjects, Eddie," Dunker said. "But you know what I saw the other night up here?"

"What?" Travis said.

"I saw Leo the Lion, lying on his back, full in the moon, whacking it off."

"You've got to be shittin' me," Dawes Williams said. "Lions don't do things like that."

"Give me that wine a minute, Dawes," Eddie said.

"Apparently some do," Dunker said. "I saw'm plain as day."

"Let's check it out," Travis said. "This I've got to see."

"Hell, yes," Eddie said.

As they walked down the path in the underbrush Dawes opened four beers with the key he kept on a chain round his neck, and Dunker continued, saying:

"I'm telling you, Travis, Leo the Lion whacks it off."

"Shut up, Dunker," Travis said. "I'll believe it when I see it. Not before."

When they arrived at the concrete slab with the wire around it that was Leo's home for ever since Dawes could remember, Leo the Lion was lying on his back, snoring.

"Doesn't look like much to me," Travis began saying, walking around the cage.

"Give him a chance for Christsake," Dunker said.

"Damn it," Dawes Williams said, "who put this lion in this birdcage!? Whoever would put a lion in a closet like this should be strung up like a dog and shot!"

"Hell," Eddie said, "this lion hasn't even got any teeth."

"All he needs right now to prove me right," Dunker said, "is his balls. Com'on, Leo," Dunker said, poking him with a stick, "wake up and whack it off."

"You know," Travis said, "Dawes may have a point here. This lion wouldn't have room to take three steps in any direction if he did wake up."

"He's been in here for fifteen years," Dawes Williams said.

"Hell," Eddie said, "if I was in there fifteen years, I'd be whacking off, too."

"That's true," Dunker said, pausing with his stick, "anybody that'd lock a twenty-five-year-old lion up in a place like this is a sonofabitch to boot."

"WHO DID THIS!?!" Dawes Williams said. "SOMEONE IS RESPONSIBLE FOR THIS."

"Listen," Travis said, "let's set this lion free."

"Hell, yes," Dunker said. "I've always wanted a lion. Let's steal this lion."

"Com'on, Leo," Eddie said, "whack it off a little and we'll set you free."

Then Leo the Lion roused himself slightly from his sleep, and he eyed them quietly from the corner of one lid as if he knew something was up. Then he let out a small growl, like a dying cat.

"What a cool old lion," Dunker said. "He's cool."

"Hell of an idea," Dawes Williams said. "I'll go up to the car for a crowbar."

As he was going up the hill, however, Travis called him back and said:

"Real fine, Dawes. Good. We can't do something like that."

Then they stood in the near shadows for some time, arguing, and in the end Travis convinced them it would be irresponsible to set even a toothless lion loose in a town as big as Rapid Cedar.

"All right," Dawes Williams said, "but I still say it's no more irresponsible than locking him up in an open-air pup tent like this."

"Hell, Dawes," Dunker said, "if it'll make you feel any better, we'll go to Old MacDonald's Farm and set all the pigs and chickens and rabbits loose."

"All right," Dawes said, "I'll settle for that."

Just then Leo the Lion rolled over and went back to sleep anyway. But making their way down to Old MacDonald's Kiddie Farm, untying even all of the mules and small burros, they did manage to fill the night full of squawking, running things before they turned and made their way back to the car; the fun, however, was out of it all.

"You can't almost set a twenty-five-year-old lion—even if he is toothless—loose on a city and then settle for only some damn old dried-up hens and have any fun about it," Dawes Williams said.

"That's right," Eddie said.

Then, back at the car, Dunker pulled one last, saved-unsaved rabbit from beneath his shirt and set him in the back seat. The rabbit, however, got nervous right off and hopped the seat and crapped in Dawes Williams' lap before he'd gotten a fair chance to stop him.

"Get that reptile jackrabbit away from me!" Dawes Williams said. "I don't like'em. They're just like death."

"What the hell are you talking about, Dawes?" Dunker said.

"He doesn't know. It's a bunny for Christsake," Travis said.

"Let's go over to Sue Allen's," Eddie said, "and watch Dunker walk through her window."

"Why not?" Dunker said.

Then Dunker began holding his rabbit, drifted off by himself and watched from the window as they drove to the other side of town. He thought Dawes had a certain way that sobered you up no matter how drunk you became. The sonofabitch. He thought Dawes could slow down the greatest drunk in the world to nothing more than a damn standstill. He thought that Dawes could see witches flying everywhere; that he had this damn heroic vision of himself, but wouldn't admit it; that he tried in a thousand ways to say it isn't so, but it is. Dunker knew Dawes sneaked books in his room at night; that he thought he was Homer, or Karen MaGoogle trying to sneak into the Honor Society, or something like that. But Dawes wouldn't tell you what it was, admit it, hell no, not him. He'd asked, but Dawes had a thousand ways: he tried to make you think it was comic, but it wasn't; he tried to make you think it was sad and tragic, but it wasn't; he tried to make you think it was all a mockery, but it wasn't even that. Hell, Dunker thought, he even tried to make himself think he was insane, but he wasn't. Not him. Hell, he was as sane as the rest of them. Dunker knew it for a fact. Hell, Dawes was just obsessed with the heroics of the thing and didn't know a damn thing about them. He didn't even know there was nothing at all; there's none of that. . . .

Then Dunker broke the silence. He put his rabbit on his head and he said: "You've been getting pretty damn bad lately, though, Dawes."

But Dawes didn't answer.

"Damn it, Dawes," Dunker said, "there's nothing heroic about any of this whatsoever, you rinky-dink fuck."

"I know it," Dawes said. "There is."

"The hell," Dunker said, looking out the window again.

"God, I'm drunk," Eddie said.

"What the hell are you idiots talking about?" Travis said.

"Shut up and ditch the car," Eddie said. "We're getting close to Sue Allen's."

Soon the car was ditched and everyone had pulled up short in Sue Allen's bushes. They crouched, opening beers quietly and whispering. Looking over, Dawes could see Dunker had brought his rabbit along.

"Well, Dunker," Travis said, reclining easily in the shrubbery, "hop along in there, pardner."

"Slow down," Dunker said, obvious, sipping his beer, "I plan on taking my time and ease about this thing."

"Do you?" Travis said.

"Yep," Dunker said.

"Listen," Eddie said, "I think Dunker's chickenshit."

"I've got my reasons," Dunker said.

"What's that?" Travis said.

"Well, I tell ya," Dunker said, pointing across the back lawn with the end of his beer bottle, "I'm waiting for that neighbor lady's light over there to go off."

"Why?" Dawes Williams said. "Are you going in that window, too?"

"Nope," Dunker said. "But if I'm not careful, that neighbor lady over there may follow me into Sue Allen's."

"How's that?" Travis said.

"Lemme tell you this," Dunker said. "About two weeks ago I was reading *The Rapid Cedar Republican*—well, anyway, I cut it out and you might as well read it for yourself."

Then Dunker took out a creased clipping from his wallet; Travis took out his cigaret lighter and, looking over Eddie's shoulder into the flare, Dawes could read:

THE TEEN GOSSIP TIPS COLUMN
STARRING ANN SAUNDERS

Dear Ann,

I am an old neighbor lady, a friend of the family, and I am concerned. I have known a certain S.A.—a dear girl who shall remain nameless—ever since she was a small, dear little girl playing jacks and skip rope on my patio. Yesterday night, however, my world fell apart. I was sitting by the window sewing (I always sit by my window when I'm sewing, I like to breathe in the evening) and I saw a boy go in S.A.'s window. I don't know what to do. The boy is a giant, at least seven feet tall, and he may be even annoying the girl. Please tell me what to do.

> Signed,
> A Concerned, Sincere Neighbor Lady
> *Rapid Cedar, Iowa*

Dear Concerned,
    You should, without fail, call up the mother and tell her what's going on. If that fails, call the police. —Ann.

"Ann Saunders is a bitch," Travis said, sailing his cigaret out into the yard.

"No shit," Dunker said. "I could tell right off this Ann Saunders had no respect for my feelings whatsoever. I could also tell right off this Ann Saunders probably never'd been caught in some girl's bed and didn't therefore give the slightest damn in the world if I got my balls shot off or not."

"Ya, that's probably true, Dunker," Travis said, laughing.

"Dunker," Dawes said, "is this girl expecting you or what?"

"Ya. She's expecting me, Dawes, in a real big way."

"No," Dawes said, "I mean do you have any signals you use?"

"What is this, Dawes," Dunker said, "an underground railroad for Christsake?"

"Isn't this the Civil War?" Dawes Williams said.

"Okay, Dawes, I pee on her window and if it runs downhill, she asks me in. Is that enough for you?"

"Sure," Dawes Williams answered, "I think this is great fun late at night. I think this is adventure."

"Shut up, Dawes," Eddie said.

"Listen, Dunker," Travis said, "is it true you snuck Sue Allen up to your room, at four o'clock in the afternoon, past your mother in an ashcan?"

"Hell, yes," Dunker said. "Lemme tell you about that. One day after school we were driving down Main, me and Sue Allen, and she had her hand in my pants. Right off I knew what she was thinking."

"You knew that right off, did you?" Travis said.

"Oh ya," Dunker said. "Then she looked at me. 'Oh, Dunker,' she says, 'I wish there was a place we could do it right *now*. I can't wait for tonight.' Just then we were passing the Hy-Dee Market, and I saw this sale on plastic ashcans, so I got an idea and I said to Sue Allen: 'Hey, how'd you like to sneak up to my room in an ashcan?' She said, 'All right,' so I bought one, and parked a block away from my house and I put Sue Allen into the ashcan. Pretty soon I'm trying to carry it through my kitchen without looking like it's heavy, my mother's eyeing me like there's something she can't figure out, so I say: 'I just thought I'd take this ashcan up to my bedroom.' —'What for?' she says. 'Well,' I say, 'they're having a sale on these things and a guy *needs* a good ashcan for his room.' So I carry her up to my room in an ashcan and it was beautiful. After dark I made her climb down the vine rods."

"Bullshit!" Dawes Williams said. "I don't believe it."

"You haven't ever snuck Summer up to your room?"

"Not in an ashcan."

"It's true. I'll see you bastards later."

Dunker got up, dusted himself off and crossed the patch of open moonlight. He knocked softly at the window. But as he moved across it, all he could hear was Dawes Williams behind him, thinking at him, thinking:

Forsooth, Romeo approaches the sill, Forsooth, Fair Juliet appears. Jesus, Dunker thought, I've got to stop wondering about Dawes Williams, it isn't healthy. Then, just as he was standing there, beneath the window, wondering about himself, holding his rabbit in his hand, Sue Allen came out with:

"Hiya, Dunker," caught low in her throat, behind curtains.

"Hey, Sue Allen," he said, cool as a selfless stud, "I thought I'd come over and see you for awhile."

"I know," she said. "I missed you, too."

Dunker, full grown, six feet ten now, was leaning against the house, thinking right off he knew this girl was crazy about him, and in the moonlight he seemed taller than the window. For him it seemed the window was like stepping over doorsills. Dawes leaned on a bush, observing, drawing on a beer, thinking only that if Sue Allen's father had installed permanent, Rusco windows, the whole course of Dunker's natural life might have changed. Then, across the quiet spaces, he could see Dunker had lifted the screen off its hinges and balanced it against the house. Sue Allen's voice drifted over like notes:

"Dunker honey," she was saying, "I've been thinking about you all day. It's been hell. You didn't call. Are you coming in now?"

"Maybe," Dunker said. "Maybe not. Who knows?"

"Dunker?" Sue Allen said. "Don't you love me any more?"

"Hell, yes, I do," Dunker said, turning slightly into the bushes. "The night would be monkey cages without you."

"Huh?" Sue Allen said.

"Never mind," Dunker said. "I love you pretty well."

"Pretty well?"

"Okay," Dunker said. "I love you a lot."

"That's good," Sue Allen said. "You had me worried for a minute."

As she said this, Sue Allen leaned out of her window and began hugging

Dunker as if she were hanging from masts. They were kissing, locked together, and it looked to Dawes as if Dunker were a large tower, a coast of moonlight, about to collapse, dissolve, fall inward over the cliff and sea of Sue Allen's sills. Sue Allen was nearly hanging onto the sides of the window with her knees now, trying to get at Dunker, and Dunker had his hand run down the back of her panties, and her teats were flopped out, full and moonlit, swinging from the cleft in her nightie. Dunker was already dreaming of falling easily into that window—neighbor lady or not, the guys in the bushes or not, selfless stud or not—when Sue Allen clinched it all, taking it out of his hands entirely, by leaning even farther out into the yard, unbuckling his belt, dropping his pants down, and pulling out his cock. She almost fell onto the lawn, an incredible position, but Dunker caught her with the curl of an arm and, leaning his elbow against the house, he turned calmly to the bushes and flashed a ten-inch hard-on flushed in the moon.

When Dawes Williams saw that happen he nearly applauded, trying to dig a hole under the bushes to hide from his own noiseless laughter. Travis gave him a six-pack carton and whispered for him to clench it in his teeth. Then Dunker made his first mistake: he went through Sue Allen's window with the damn rabbit still in his hand.

But for awhile, inside, Dunker felt very good about the whole thing because he figured he'd shown Dawes Williams, once and for all, just how truly unheroic things really were. Soon, however, Dunker forgot about everything. He lay around with Sue Allen, making good love, and in the end he rolled over—she was rubbing his back like a native slave girl—and he went to sleep. That was his second mistake. That was a mistake because Sue Allen always left her door ajar, so she could hear her mother coming down the hallway, and because Dunker's rabbit got out. So while Dunker was sleeping, innocent as God, the hat of his rabbit was out in the house, roaming at will, trying to hatch its own raisins on carpets. But Dunker wasn't worried. He was only indulging himself, sleeping the sleep of the innocent, and dreaming of the time he had sneaked himself up into his room, on a bright afternoon, in an ashcan. . . .

Then the great wheel turned back upon itself, and Dunker got his first break of the early morning. Sue Allen was talking at him, still feeling him up in her dream, and her voice woke him up just in time to fly under the bed.

"Damn it, Dunker," she was saying, lying beside him, still holding him tightly in her hand, "*God* damn it, Dunker. I hate this house. I hate it so much I want to get pregnant and move out. Dunker! Are you even listening to me? Are you? Well *are* you? Will you marry me?" she said.

Dunker was about to roll over, look her deeply in the eyes in the darkness and tell her—Hell, no—when he heard the most unbelievable scream in the world. The rabbit it seemed—Dunker sure didn't need anyone to tell him about it—had crawled up onto Mrs. Allen's bed and nibbled her. He'd also managed, they found out later, to crap all over Mr. Allen's sheets. Well, Dunker thought, that's it for me, I'm a dead man, because the scream wasn't coming from the bedroom any longer, it had already found the hallway; it was already at Sue Allen's door. . . .

Dawn was rising, but Dunker was rising much faster. In fact, even while he was doing it, rising like lightning, he thought he must have been the fastest-moving man in the world, bar none. He was under the bed, shivering, naked, so fast he hadn't even seen himself leave. So here I am, he thought, arrived, lying under bed posts, naked as God, trying not to breathe, thinking, I wish to hell Dawes Williams were here, it's not heroic, by God, it's chickenshit, there's nothing heroic whatsoever about this at all, as he noticed suddenly there was nothing in the universe but a blind flash of light falling across the throw-rug flooring to the edge of the bed. . . .Then Mrs. Allen began sitting on the end of the bed, bowing the slats. She was in no hurry, confused with sleep, rocking, toying with rabbits as if she had all night. Dunker's clothes were hidden under Sue Allen's sheets, he hoped, and he began to pray: Just let me out of this one, this goddamn mess, just let me out of this one and I'll go straight forever, I'll never touch anything as long as I live, he prayed to God, the Maker of Situations. Aw hell, Dunker thought, I'm all right. I'm safe under here. Then, just as suddenly, he knew that Sue Allen was playing with the idea of exposing him. Mrs. Allen was sitting on the bed still asking her daughter where the hell the rabbit had sprung from, only she wasn't saying "hell" exactly. Dawes Williams was outside, safe, roaring his ass off; learning nothing at all worth knowing. Well, Dunker thought, I am saying "hell"; I am saying "hell" all over the place, for instance, I am saying—Where in the "hell" did *you* come from, Mrs. Allen?—and—What the "hell," let's have a little faith in our daughter for Christsake—when, just as suddenly, it looked as if she, Mrs. Allen, were settling down for good, and were going to stay the whole morning, watching her baby go back to sleep. Dunker knew only that Sue Allen was toying with the idea of pulling her thin summer quilt back an inch, ending his life forever, he thought, only so she could move out of the house next week. He was tense. He felt Sue Allen lacked consideration for his feelings. Then Mr. Allen had nothing better to do, so he got up to shave. I don't *need* this kind of problem, Dunker thought, lying below, trying not to breathe, Oh, Sue Allen, don't you damn do me this way. . . .

Just then the sun began rising. The room went gray and gold round the lower edges. Time passed. Dunker figured finally it must have been six o'clock in the morning and Mrs. Allen was still sitting there, bowing the slats, talking to her daughter. When she finally asked Sue Allen to kiss and make up, Dunker began biting his lip, holding his balls, his nakedness, in silence he was laughing so hard over his knowledge, his distance, his triumph, his point of view. But Mrs. Allen continued talking, making up, and Dunker could see, right off, why Sue Allen wanted to get pregnant and married and move out of the house as soon as possible—the woman was impossible for Christsake—and it was beginning to look as if things were going to hang in the air forever, when Sue Allen got this brilliant idea and said:

"MOTHER! IF YOU DON'T LEAVE THIS MINUTE, I'M GOING TO KILL MYSELF!"

Well, Dunker thought, that one might do it—good move, Sue Allen. Then, as he was being saved—Mrs. Allen was preparing to take her leave and depart for other parts of the castle—Dunker began toying with the idea of popping up for the hell of it, stark naked, asking for the hand of Sue Allen in marriage, unhinging Mrs. Allen's mind forever, what was left of it, serving her right, he thought, when, just as suddenly, even this became lost too, not necessary, because Mrs. Allen finally got up, and exited, and took the rabbit back to her own room.

Dunker only lay there, breathing again with the slats, saying, "Thanks. My balls are gold. I knew it. I have had golden balls. All this time. . . .

Then he counted to three for luck and got from under the bed. He didn't put his clothes on and—turning to Sue Allen, saying simply, "Later"—he did the fastest barrel roll in the world through the window. He dove headfirst, running the air, not even ticking the framing, and he hit on his hands and rolled over nude in the surprising sunlight for the next fifteen yards. His peter flopped in the wind. When Dawes Williams saw that, he nearly hemorrhaged again. . . .

"You can bet on it," Dunker said, running into the bushes. "That was about the neatest barrel roll ever executed in the history of man."

When Dawes Williams heard that, he nearly died and came back to life again. Travis had the keys ready, and he also had some presence of mind so, running back to the window, appearing, he said to Sue Allen:

"Quick! Throw me old Dunker's jeans."

Sue Allen had nothing to say. Dawes Williams didn't have any presence of mind left at all. He was only down, knee-bent and caved, laughing in the shade, but still not leaving a sound. So it was Eddie who caught the pants Travis had thrown, and it was Eddie and Dunker who were crawling down the line of the back hedges, and when they looked back, they could see Dawes wasn't even coming.

"What the hell are you *doing,* Dawes!?!" Dunker called.

Dawes was lying on his back, looking furiously at the morning sky, rupturing his lung again. Travis had to stop to pick him up on his way out, and then they were all snaking down the hedgerow, no one talking, playing keepaway with Dunker's pants, and Travis was also carrying Dawes Williams over his shoulder like a sack of broken potatoes somehow still walking.

Then they arrived in the next yard over. Dunker, sensing moments, giving up his pants for lost anyway, rose up and began walking tall in the wet, sunlit grass. He didn't have a stitch on, six feet ten and nude in the morning moon and, taking five steps into the yard, he knew it already, he came eye to eye with Dear-Ann-Saunders-Concerned-Neighbor-Lady, Yours Sincerely . . . who was having an early summer breakfast on the patio, who was dropping a dish, and whose mouth was agape trying not to stare higher than Dunker's waist. Dunker, however, was unconcerned. Without hesitating, pausing, or breaking stride, approaching her almost as if he were about to shake hands, Dunker said:

"How do you do? I'd introduce myself, but I'm nude. Ann Saunders sent me out here to check out rumors of giants in the neighborhood, but do us all a favor and keep it low. See ya."

And then, passing by, checking the sky for weather with his friends Eddie and Travis and Dawes, Dunker only paused, turned slightly away, and covered up his dong like a maid . . . he felt he had just passed by, cool as a selfless stud.

22

Dawes Williams called Summer Letch on the telephone.

"I'm sorry, Dawes," she said, "I can't talk to you now. I'm going with B.T. Saus again."

"You're not sorry," Dawes Williams said. "The poor bastard."

"That's probably true," Summer said.

"Damn," Dawes said. "This is the nineteenth time in a year this has happened to me."

"If you swear at me once more," Summer said, "I'm hanging up on you forever."

"Good girl. I thought you were doing that anyway."

"Maybe not for forever," she said.

"Damn," Dawes said. "I think I'll take my chances."

"You'll lose, Dawes," Summer said, "you always do."

"Win. Lose. Rah-rah," Dawes Williams said.

"Goodbye, Dawes," Summer said. "This is for forever."

"Goodbye, Summer," Dawes said. "This is for forever."

There was a long pause on the singing wire in which neither of them hung up.

"Well?" Summer said. "What do you want?"

"What makes you think I want anything?" Dawes said.

"Why are you staying on the phone then?" Summer said.

"Why are you?" Dawes Williams said.

"I told you to hang up first," Summer said.

"Oh, Christ," Dawes Williams said.

"Dawes!" Summer Letch said.

"Summer," Dawes Williams said, "why do I have to tell you to kiss off to get you to do anything reasonable?"

"Dawes?" Summer said. "Do you think you still love me? Do you think you want to go back?"

There was a pause. Dawes knew Summer was suckering him in.

"Yes," he said anyway. "Summer? Do you?"

"No," she said.

"Do you still think about me at all?" Dawes said.

"Yes, of course I do, silly," Summer said, her voice softening. "I think about what we did."

"Summer?" Dawes said, hopefully, warming up. "Then do you think you might still love me? Will we ever go back?"

There was a pause. Dawes Williams considered himself.

"No," Summer said, "I don't think so, Dawes. I'm going with B. T. Saus again now."

"Oh, Christ," Dawes Williams said.

"Is that all, Dawes?" Summer said. "I don't *know* why I do these things."

"Yes. I think that's about all," Dawes said. "If you ever find out, will you promise to tell me?"

"Of course," Summer said. "But I never promise. Are you hanging up now?"

"Do you want me to hang up now?"

"Do you want to hang up?"

"No. Maybe," Dawes said.

"B. T. is calling me soon."

"Yes," Dawes Williams said. "I'm hanging up all right. In fact, I may never call up your silly ass as long as I live."

"Dawes!?!" Summer said.

"Yes?" Dawes said.

"Well . . . call me up in about an hour," Summer said. "We'll finish discussing it then."

"Oh, Christ," Dawes Williams said, hanging up.

Then Dawes called up Helen Willer, one of Summer's best friends:

"Hello, Helen?" Dawes Williams said. "What's happenin'?"

"Haven't you heard the news, Dawes!" Helen said. "Summer is going with B. T. Saus again. Isn't it exciting?"

"It certainly is," Dawes Williams said. "I'm breathless."

"Oh, Dawes," Helen said, "you're so funny. You going over to Carolyn MacHenry's Saturday night?"

"No," Dawes Williams said. "I'm going out to shoot some pool with Barney Redwood and I'll still be too drunk on Saturday night."

"Summer will be there," Helen said coyly.

"Summer is everywhere," Dawes Williams said.

"But Dawes," Helen said, laughing, "I'll be there."

"Oh, Christ," Dawes Williams said. "Listen. Are you going to tell me anything about this thing or aren't you?"

"Well, Dawes," Helen said, "all's I know for certain is what Summer did in fifth period Study Hall."

"All right," Dawes said. "Lay it on me."

"Well," Helen began, "Summer came into the room, smiling the way she does you know."

"Oh ya," Dawes Williams said.

"And then Judy Teek saw that Summer had two rings around her neck. Judy screamed, 'Summer!' and then all the girls gathered around. Judy asked Summer if the two rings were yours and B. T. Saus' and Summer said, 'Yes.' Then Judy asked Summer whose ring she was going to keep and Summer said, 'B. T. Saus'.'"

"That's not 'why,'" Dawes Williams said. "That's still only a piece of 'what' and maybe 'how.'"

"Get a priest, Dawes," Helen said. "I'm sure I couldn't explain Summer Letch to you. She does what she likes."

"She's a real free spirit all right," Dawes Williams said. "Thanks, Helen."

"See you Saturday night, Dawes?" she said.

"No," Dawes Williams said. "If I did that, I'd probably have Summer Letch back for another week and what would I do with her?"

"I'm sure you'd know more about that than I would, Dawes," Helen said. "But I'll be sure and tell her what you said tonight."

"That's good, Helen," Dawes Williams said, "real fine."

Then Dawes Williams hung up and called Judy Teek.

"Judy, you beautiful mother," Dawes began.

"Dawes," Judy said, "now don't start in on me. It's not my fault. I'm not responsible for Summer Letch. Just leave me alone," she said.

"Kisses," Dawes Williams said, hanging up the line again.

Then Dawes went and sat in his room. He got his pool cue and checked his bridge hand in the mirror. He rested it high on his bookcase and thought it looked fine; then he decided he would use up whatever cool he had left by calling Summer Letch one more time. He could get away with it; then she would vanish into smoke, a horrible silence, for perhaps even months on end. Besides, he thought, what the hell, there's nothing else to do tonight but sit in a tub and open my veins. . . .

He went back into his mother's bedroom and shut the door and got out a pack of Camels and called up Summer Letch:

"Hey, Summer," he said pleasantly, "what's happenin'?"

"Dawes?" she said. "What are you talking about?"

"Marry me," Dawes Williams said, "I love you."

There was a silence. She didn't want to marry him, of course, but she was interested in what he might say and wouldn't hang up. He knew he could hang on to her for exactly as long as his wit held out, for exactly as long as he could manage to dangle the donkey stick, the next conversational bauble in front of her nose. He lit a cigaret and puffed like a sonofabitch.

"Well, Dawes," she said. "What do you want?"

He knew he was lost. His wit had just evaporated him.

"Summer," he said, trying, "how many times have you read *Gone with the Wind?*"

"Six and a half now," she said. "It's wonderful."

"That boggles my mind," Dawes said. "And next to Margaret Mitchell herself who is your favorite writer?"

"Leon Uris," Summer said. "*Mila 18* wasn't his best but *Exodus* is still wonderful."

"Listen, Scarlett," Dawes Williams said, "I think that explains it all."

"What do you mean?" she said.

"I mean—I do not think you will ever be capable of loving me until I am capable of running Yankee blockades against a vast panorama of smoky history that never was. That's what I mean."

"Is that all, Dawes?" Summer said. "Really, honey, I have to take a bath and . . ."

"Listen," Dawes said, "if I ever came over and tried to kick down your door, all's that would happen would be your damn mother would try to turn me in to the school board and you know it!"

"You shouldn't have to ask about a thing like that," Summer said. "Dawes? Is that all?"

"No," Dawes said, fishing, "that's not all at all. I also mean, in a more perfect society, people like Margaret Mitchell and Leon Uris should be locked up for contributing to the rape of children. Their books should be banned!"

There was a silence.

"Dawes," Summer said, "you're so romantic."

"Summer?" Dawes Williams said, half-seriously, "do you think you could love me if I could get into the Marine Corps?"

"Do you think you could be an officer?" she said.

"Oh, Christ," Dawes Williams said.

There was a long edge of electronic silence sleeping in his ear, but Dawes Williams didn't even mind it as he had already lost. He had given up; he knew he couldn't talk to the air. Then, however, Summer surprised even him by saying:

"Dawes? Will you think of me at all?"

"Yes," he said, flushed with hope, and embarrassed he had felt it.

"What will you think?" she said.

"You know I could never forget you, Summer," Dawes Williams said.

"I know," she said. "But I mean what especially?"

"You know," Dawes said, his voice softening, "I'll think about everything we've done, and what you looked like, and what we felt like together."

"That's nice, Dawes," she said. "But Dawes, just between you and me, girls will never respect you if you talk to them like that."

"One," Dawes Williams said, "you are not every girl in the world yet, Summer. And, two, if you can't, what are they good for?"

"I'm not here to debate with you, Dawes. You're so damn romantic," she said.

"Don't swear at me, Summer," Dawes said, "your mother wouldn't approve."

"You leave my damn mother out of this, Dawes! I respect her if you don't."

"For Christsake, Summer," Dawes said, "your mother is just another damn schoolteacher! They've been after me all of my life!"

"Well, she's only trying to help me live right, you know," Summer said.

"You'd probably do a certain amount of that anyway if left to yourself, you know," Dawes Williams said.

"No," Summer said, "people are basically bad."

"You're not bad," Dawes Williams said, "you're just basically wonderful."

Then Summer laughed. Dawes settled back and felt better. Then Summer Letch sensed Dawes was feeling better, so she said:

"Dawes? I've got to go now. Goodbye. I can't be talking to you on the phone any more. B. T. wouldn't like it."

"Oh fuck off, Summer," Dawes Williams said.

He knew swearing at her would get him another five minutes.

"You're such a nasty thing really," Summer said.

"I hope realizing this doesn't upset you, Summer," Dawes said, "but there are really much more nasty things in this world than that. You know, underneath Leon Uris there is a lot of real pain, and real suffering—that he doesn't know how to talk about at all; and that isn't wonderful or romantic at all. You know under that vast panorama of the Civil War—even with Atlanta burning—

there was just a lot of dysentery and sores . . . and nobody was beautiful; and nobody danced in velvet skirts."

"What are you talking about?" Summer said.

"I'm talking about being tired," Dawes Williams said.

"I don't think I understand," Summer said, "and I don't think I should want to."

"I'm sorry," he said. "Will you forget it?"

He hated himself for apologizing. He hated his life because he was right and Summer was wrong, but she was winning. She had always been winning; she had always held some sort of keys he didn't even understand as existing.

"Will you forgive me?" he said.

"Sure," she said. "Who cares?"

"I care," Dawes Williams said. "I love you."

"Well, I don't," she said. "I don't care at all."

"You never cared," he said.

"I did," she said. "Don't accuse me, Dawes. What do you know about me?"

"No," he said, "you never cared. You never knew how."

"All right," she said. "I never cared. There: are you happy now?"

"Sure," Dawes Williams said, "I'm in heaven. But you never said that before. If you leave me now, I'm never coming back."

But, listening, he knew she wasn't laughing this time.

"Of course," she said calmly, "I know it. Because this time I'm never asking you to."

Dawes Williams could say nothing. He only sat, watching a thick silence, horrible as blood, race before him, dead as his veins.

He knew he'd lost, and he knew it was a game.

Summer knew the world had been put there only for her. Dawes Williams knew he loved Summer Letch and hated himself for knowing it.

"Good night, Dawes," Summer said. "Take care."

"Good night, Summer," Dawes Williams said, angry, almost crying, blind in the eyes. "Why don't you just take a flying ass-kiss at yourself and see where you land?"

Then Dawes Williams hung up the phone and went to shoot pool with Barney Redwood. Strangely, by the time he had run off a six-ball game or two, he didn't feel bad about it at all. He felt only a strange, clear trance that danced in the low-slung lantern light over the tables.

Dawes Williams, Dawes Williams knew, had won another battle and lost the war again. . . .

23

Another summer, an easy, high-rolling nine ball drifting with the long sway of the table, the window, was passing and Dawes and Barney moved over to the head snooker table in Orion, Iowa, and had been shooting for an hour when Dunker, Eddie and Travis blew through the door one evening, saying only, "Atttsssss Willy," all in one voice.

As they said it, Dawes was hanging back in the corner drawing on a straw that ran up the sleeve to Barney Redwood's jacket, and that was connected to a bottle of orange-flavored gin. Barney had just finished running off thirty-eight points, and he looked up from the table.

"I knew we'd find you here," Dunker said.

"Com'on, Dawes," Travis said, "we're leaving tonight for Elkhard Lake, Wisconsin, and you're driving."

"Nobody misses the races," Dunker said. "We're late. Half the town's already bombed and started up there."

"Why not?" Dawes Williams said.

"Ya," Eddie said, "we've been thinking it over and the only thing we've got that'd make any kind of impression pulling in there to Corvette Corner is your '49 Merc."

"Where we go you go, Dawes," Travis said.

"Oh ya," Dawes Williams said, "to a point."

"How much you got on ya, Dawes?" Dunker said.

"Twenty or so," Dawes said.

"I'll loan you ten and you can bum it," Dunker said.

"I'll shoot you for it," Dawes Williams said.

"Hell, yes," Dunker said. "Let's have a game first."

Dunker broke them open and Dawes ran off twenty-five points. Travis pulled up a chair by the window, leaned back, rocked his foot on the sill, and said:

"I believe you are now at a point at which you could be said to be hustlin' Dunker's ass, Dawes."

Eddie laughed and Dunker ran off sixteen points.

"Quick," Dawes Williams said, "someone light Travis' cigar."

"Don't have a cigar," Travis said.

"Quick," Dawes Williams said, "someone light Travis' invisible cigar."

"Let's take Dawes out and bust his hands," Eddie said.

"I had to take up something to pass the time while you were all out becoming all-stars," Dawes said.

"Ya, first-string pool player. Big deal," Eddie said.

"Beats me being third-string guard, and second-string infielder. To hell with that."

"Dawes," Travis said, "saying something like that is beneath a man of your intelligence."

"That's true," Dawes Williams said.

Then Dawes leaned over the far end of the table for his shot and turned his ass to Travis, and Travis snatched a long piece of folded paper from his pocket.

"What's this?" Travis said.

"Fuck off," Dawes said. "It's a poem."

"Christ," Eddie said.

Barney Redwood began moving off toward the door.

"You leaving, are you, Redwood?" Travis said.

"Ya," Barney said, "I'm going to Dance-Land."

"Okay, pardner," Travis said.

"See ya."

"See ya, Dawes," Barney said.

"See ya, Barney," Dawes said.

"Well, let's see here," Travis said, turning back into the shaded light. "Let's read this poem that Dawes Williams here has written."

"No, Travis," Dunker said, falling all over his cue, "I'd be a goner."

Then Travis stood up baroquely on his chair and read the poem to the entire place, to the walls, shadows and anyone who would stop long enough to listen.

"'Light in the Fields, the Old Stone House,'" Travis said, "'For Summer Letch, Fall and Summer 1959 . . .'"

"What is that?" Eddie said.

"It's the title," Travis said. "Shut up, Eddie, I'm reading Dawes Williams' poem here."

"Fall and summer, fall and summer," Dunker said, "that's mad."

"Dunker is sane," Dawes Williams said, not looking up, running off the six ball.

Travis ignored them all. He propped his leg up on the thin arm of the chair, thrust the poem out to his fullest extension and read:

> "I thought I knew you once.
> A strange dog, an orphan of the spell,
> I watched you escape into darkness. I
> watched the long grasses

stop short in the lost edges
of your walking. Your shadow
moved within the moon. A
revolution. A silence.

"Summer was a green sleeve of
wind: thin, approaching, full of
forgetful rememberings, and I was
a standing shadow of light, tall
and interfixed. We were two small
waterbodies, passing between.

"We watched a river, red evening,
where there wasn't one.
We played in an old stone house of the world.

"Soft as children,
lost as broken light,
our bodies, crystal as
each new stroke of falling
rain, brushed us near the
edge. We watched the trees,
oh soft eternal dark madonna,
gather in the skirts of the rain.

"A strange dog escaped into darkness.

"Strangely, the night had passed
too slowly
for us to finish exploring the wind."

Travis finished. His voice fell off like a stroke. He was laughing so hard he top-
pled over his chair, and was then in the corner, supporting himself by hanging
onto the hat tree. Dunker collapsed against the wall, and Eddie got out:
    "Christ, what a romantic load of shit."
    "Is the grass green?" Dunker managed.
    "Does a wooden horse have wooden balls?" Travis said.
    Dawes Williams, however, said nothing at all. Smiling, chalking his cue, he
only waited for it all to die off; but it didn't. It continued; soon everyone in the
farm-town poolhall was laughing but Dawes, and Dawes, Dunker thought, was
only standing there, braced on his stick, getting very pissed about nothing at all.

"What the hell," Dawes Williams finally said, "I never said it was any good. Quit stomping around on my head, Travis."

The rolling laughter, however, cut only by Travis' almost Negroid cackle, didn't cease or die off an inch. Eddie was against the door jamb so he could better laugh; Dunker was gasping, nearly dribbling spit on his chin, and Travis began to rock egocentrically around the axis of a pool cue—to rub his exposed navel under the raised knit shirt as if he were the great wellspring from which all valid humor sprang. Then the loud antiphonals—catching the whole pool-room up in the democratic, inclusive humor of it all—began to drift back from other parts of the hall.

"Christ," Dawes Williams found himself saying, "you're burnin' me. What is this? Some native desire to be merely hyperbolic, even simply burlesque!?!"

Then the gaiety finally spun itself dry. A cue slammed flatly against the hollow floor, through a yellow smoke of light hanging closely to the ceiling's replastered wall, and it was over. The laughing sank finally into the automatic clicking of resuming, rolling balls.

"Times," Eddie said, turning suddenly sullen. "Times. We got to have some *times* on us."

"Hell, yes," Dunker said. "Com'on, Dawes. I'm packed. I don't like to be packed and moving nowhere. When I'm packed, I don't care where I'm moving long as I'm moving."

"Hell, yes," Travis said.

"Hell, yes," Eddie said. "That's right."

"Hell, no," Dawes Williams said. "I'm not going till tomorrow. I don't have my stuff."

"Like hell," Travis said. "Where we go, Dawes, you go."

"Thanks," Dawes Williams said. "You're making my heart flutter."

"Now you're talking like the old Dawes," Dunker said.

"We," Travis Thomas said, "meaning *me,* are leaving."

"All right," Dawes said, running the last seven ball off the table. "Dunker owes me ten dollars. Let's go to Elkhard Lake, Wisconsin."

"That's right," Dunker said, peeling a ten off a large wad of money, "that's what I said in the first place."

"Don't anybody damn forget the cooler," Eddie said.

"That's right," Travis said, "don't anybody forget damn Dawes Williams, either."

Soon they were driving down the dark again. Travis was steering Dawes' '49 Mercury. Eddie was fishing in the cooler for four more beers, and Dunker was saying:

"Which way is Wisconsin?"

"It's northwest of Alabama, I think," Dawes said.

"That's it, Dawes," Travis said. "Lead me to it. Just lead me to it."

The lights in farmhouses, blue summering stars going north for the winter, moved in the glass window. Dawes leaned back in his seat, thinking only Dunker was sane, and waited easily for the Mississippi River to come up on the right. The blue river bluffs would stand out in the cold sky like stone Indians, but that was miles away. Dawes thought he heard a dog, crying for rain, breaking all stone in the wind before them.

Outside the night was breaking clearly against the window.

A bitch hound? Blackey Jane? Dawes Williams thought. Her time was a mirror, an illusion, out somewhere, stretching, reaching for meaning, for light, dissolving, collapsing itself. But it was only a small collapse then, a dry, faceless horror. And Dawes Williams had risen out of it, Icarus the Clown, a silly fire bird rising up nearly whole with plumes of dust, its own ashes, and a sunken, wax-smeared makeup trying to run over the sun without ever touching it. He thought a cat with cans tied to its tail ran after. He thought his footsteps passed through themselves, not touching, into a river of black sand, into mirrors of water.

Outside is night, the river, light. Blue bluffs hang over the water. The stone silhouettes of Indian chiefs smoke pipes of midnight and beat their drums-without-sound.

Dawes Williams thought Daedalus was not the metaphor, Icarus was. Later, at carnival time, in Elkhard Lake, a dwarf would rattle a rock in a sock; a sleeveless green yeoman in a linen jerkin would clasp the greatest granddaughter of TheWifeofBath teatward, and tentward, and with only a dry loaf of bread and a dull, sighing sound going out around them. It was carnival time. He knew he had been there before, falling, full of sun, like ritual, like summer itself. He knew his end existed within his beginning; his beginning must exist in his end.

Outside, the warm rain began. It fell on the window thick as a veil. Travis, that happy time-bent yeoman, was driving through the wash of water.

Dawes Williams was very drunk.

"What the hell are you doing, Dunker?" Travis was saying.

"Easy, Tray," Dunker says, "I'm just takin' a pee in this beer can here."

"Why's that?" Travis says, not turning, steering the car.

"It's raining out. I'm saving a stop."

"Seems to me," Eddie says, "the least you could goddamn do is take the lid off first."

"No," Dunker says, "it's harder this way."

Dawes thought only Dunker was sane; then, breaking his own silence, he said:

"Hey, Dunker, I remember Clark Gable in a movie once taking a wizz behind a bush I think."

Dunker was waiting for Dawes to continue. He didn't.

"Big deal," Dunker said finally. "Shut up, Dawes, I'm trying to throw this can of piss out the window here."

"Atttsss Dunker," Travis said. "Seeing you wrestle with that little hole in that beer can back there must have been like seeing you lose your virginity in a drive-in movie."

"Shut up, Dawes," Dunker says.

Dawes, who was already shut up anyway, shut up some more. He drifted off again. In his mind, a membrane thin as breaking mirrors of sleep, he began thinking about language. The first time he had noticed it, *language, was in the fourth grade when Miss Norma Jean Thompson, his teacher, turned against the whole class and said:*

"All Americans eventually go to heaven."

"By sweet Jesus," Ronnie Crown had said that afternoon, sitting on Dunchee's wall, waiting for Dawes Williams to come tell him about it, "that's about the God damn dumbest thing I ever heard."

Dawes Williams had agreed immediately that the message was insipid, but he thought for years that the syntax was inspired. In fact, the first time Norma Jean Thompson had said, ALL AMERICANS EVENTUALLY GO TO HEAVEN, was also the first time Dawes Williams had ever noticed the English sentence. From thereafter Miss Thompson's declaratory exclamation became Dawes' guide and syntactical touchstone. SEE DICK RUN. Yes, Dawes thought—rolling along in the back of his car, with others, going in the same opposite direction—language is a tonal can, a thing tied to the tail of a black cat's ass and will be nothing again. . .

"What are you thinking about back here in the dark, Dawes?" Dunker was saying.

"Nothing," Dawes Williams said. "Words. You know."

"I sure do," Dunker said, smiling. "Shut up, Dawes."

"Listen," Travis said, "for someone who believes in language as much as you, you certainly can use up a lot of it."

"Oh ya," Dawes Williams said.

Travis waited for him to continue. He didn't.

Outside, the water was building up in the ditches. Dawes Williams lit another Camel and thought:

SEE DICK RUN DOWN THE LONG ROAD.

But language, Dawes knew, was not even remotely related to anything else. It was a narrow extent, a jar without water. It kept no flowers living, dancing, breathing in sunlight. To possess a word, Dawes knew, was to be possessed by nothing at all. It had compounded his real phonetics, which were once only simple, pure stones into SEE DICK RUN into his first sentence, destruction.

"Damn it, Dawes," Travis was saying, "for someone who believes in words as much as you, you're sure not much of a talker."

"Travis," Dawes said, "which is it? You can't have it both ways."

"The hell I can't," Travis said, not batting an eye. "I just did."

"God, I'm drunk," Eddie said.

SEE DICK RUN DOWN THE LONG ROAD TO THE FAR HOUSE.

Ultimately, he knew, Summer was a word. And he—Dawes Williams, young yeoman, cynic, drugstore cowboy, boy shaman, crazy Indian, man of the world, humanistic misanthrope, would-be writer-of-letters-to-the-editor—could only sit watching her . . . grow, almost expand in the long morning light falling through fans, screens; the end of a yard; the swing hanging from a dry tree; the air near a fence where the first tomcat of day re-crosses the vacant lot, his own steps of the evening before. Yes, her mother had taken the train to Junction City, left her alone and, waking, he saw only the small girls on the corner—skipping rope and obsessed by the stone of the rhythm. And only Summer, words, had been lying beside him, brown, and sleeping in earth, soft as incomplete syllables in her firmness caught upon pillows. . . .

SEE DICK RUN DOWN THE LONG ROAD TO THE FAR HOUSE WHERE THE OLD MAN SLEEPS SOUNDLY.

He was very drunk. Dunker was reloading the cooler.

But tonals faded, he knew, and you made images; but images faded and you made words; but words failed and you made nothing. Then nothing bloomed and you made words again; finally you had only sentences left, which had rooms within windows, and houses within rooms.

"The geese flying in the Southern sky are not *the* geese flying in the Southern sky, but they are geese nevertheless," Dawes Williams said from the back seat. "A leap. An act of faith."

"Think you'll ever get it straight, Dawes?" Dunker said.

"Christ," Dawes Williams said. "I may have the call. I think I want to become a goddamn poet."

"Now you're talking," Travis said. "You've named your vocation."

"Atta boy," Eddie said.

"Listen," Dunker said, "I think there is something I want to call you right now. What is it, Dawes?"

"Call me an 'aesthetician,'" Dawes Williams said. "That's what I am."

"No," Eddie said, "I don't think that's what Dunker had in mind."

"Me neither," Dunker said abstractedly, trying to pee out the window.

So Dawes Williams drifted off again. No one was paying any attention to him anyway, so he began cutting on his stick, and working on his sentence. He was very drunk:

SEE DICK RUN DOWN THE LONG ROAD TO THE FAR HOUSE WHERE THE OLD MAN SLEEPS SOUNDLY, DEAD, BESIDE THE YELLOW CAT.

"Words, Travis," Dawes Williams finally said. "You make words or you go mad. That's wrong. It's: Words, Travis, you make words and then you go mad. That's wrong, too."

"Well," Travis said, steering the car. "Which is it, Dawes? You can't have it both ways, you know."

"The hell I can't," Dawes said, not batting an eye.

Outside, the rain was running down the window where Travis was driving. Inside, Dunker was urinating in another empty can to save a stop.

Looking up, asking Eddie for the flashlight, Dawes took out a piece of paper and wrote out:

The jack-guts once flew in the sun of Arthur's fields, his beard, like disintegrating wheels.

Without naming God you cannot possess the idea of him. That is why they define him so hard. So: therefore, without naming death you cannot enter that either. —Is that what's worrying you, Dawes? That, without words, you cannot even have nothing at all. . . .

Then Dawes put the paper down and finished his sentence:

SEE DICKDAWES RUN DOWN THE LONG ROAD TO THE FAR HOUSE WHERE THE OLD MAN SLEEPS SOUNDLY, DEAD, BESIDE THE YELLOW CAT WHO ISN'T EVEN RESTING AND WHO, INSTEAD, CONDESCENDS TO EAT THE BITUMINOUS RAT WHO IS, JUST NOW, PASSING HIS NOSE. . . .

"Hell, yes," Dawes Williams said, breaking his own silence again. "That's got it."

"What's that, Dawes?" Dunker said. "I'm fascinated."

"You sure as hell will be when I get through with this one," Dawes said.

"Lay it on me," Dunker said.

"The Word is a Rat," Dawes Williams said.

Dunker waited for him to continue. He didn't.

"So what?" Eddie said. "What the hell are you talking about, Dawes?"

"So what!!??! !" Dawes said. "So the Cat ate the Rat; the Old Man is dead; and DickDawes is still running. That's so-what-about-it," Dawes Williams said.

"Open me a beer," Travis said severely.

"Hot damn sun," Dunker was saying, "the Mississippi River is comin' up on the right!"

"Another twenty miles!" Travis said.

"Piss call for everyone," Eddie said.

"What is this?" Dunker said. "A Mexican bus for Christsake?"

"Black as a battle of words," Dawes Williams said, "that bituminous, word-less rat while I am riding—dried-out rind, sun-baked yeoman—on the back of a cart to carnival time."

"Get serious, Dawes," Travis said. "This is a piss call for everyone and I can't get your Merc out of third. It's the shifting linkage, I think."

"Hell, yes," Dawes said, "just wind her down by the side of the road here and watch her stop by herself. This happens to be a modern invention."

"You been reading too much *Time* magazine again, Dawes?" Travis said.

"Let's take Dawes Williams here out in a ditch and beat him up for the hell of it," Eddie said.

"Hell, no," Dunker said, lighting a cigar, "leave my old buddy Dawes here alone. He's a powerful horseshit thinker."

"Without you, Dunker," Dawes said, "I'd never have made it out of childhood. Thanks, mother."

"That's quite all right, Dawes," Dunker said. "Let's get out in the rain and pee in the wind on it."

As Dunker and Dawes were shaking hands on it, Travis was helping the car wind itself down by the side of the road. Soon Dawes had his hood open and was rewiring the shifting linkage again. He'd been doing it for a year, but he wasn't very mechanical and was getting no better at it. Finally finished, rising, Dawes could see that the others were all out in the warm rain, tossing down two apiece, playing football, and that the ditches were all running with water and high with sound. Standing in a warm house of the moon, watching the violent, rainy light weave only opaque motion, leaving patterns on the sunken grass, he thinks it is good to only look up and think—*See Eddie scat. Watch his real speed as he moves out for the pass. Hear Travis say, "Eddie, go out for the pass, past that semi that's comin' there, cut it, and I'll hit you with a buttonhook down by that culvert in the ditch." See Travis, the high school quarterback-who-may-go-on, fade down the slosh of running water, quickly, pumping a Budweiser can high in the wind, faking hand-offs to Dunker, and Dawes flying past. And he throws it well, nearly putting a spiral on a Budweiser can. Then, in the moon, see Eddie, splashing furiously through the calf-high water, slip with the catch. Sliding ass-ward in the mud, up tight against a hill, in the white moon he stood up again, shouting, holding the can high. There Dawes could hear high, rolling laughter twenty miles from the border, from the Mississippi, from the high, humping bridge, rolling over great water, below, denser than night—O Magnum Fulmen Popularum who crossed it on rafts—there Dawes thinks he could hear real laughter, a celebration, and he thinks he is home. . . .*

"The Mississippi is comin' up!"

"We have got the heap rolling!"

"We've wired it up!"

"And kicked the tires, and spit on the hood!"

"And we have got this heap rolling again!"

Then the bridge came up. It seemed to be a long chain of lights stringing out, crossing into another night, on the Illinois shore.

"The good old Mississippi for sure," Travis said.

"What the hell'd you think about that, Dawes?" Dunker said.

"Nothing," Dawes Williams said.

"What are you doing back there then?" Travis said.

"Do you really want to know?" Dawes said.

"Sure," Travis said.

"Well," Dawes Williams said suddenly, "I was just sittin' here, finishin' my sentence: 'See Dick run down the long road to the far house where the old man sleeps soundly, dead, with the yellow cat, who isn't even dreaming and who, instead, condescends to eat the bituminous rat, who is just now passing his nose, and who had once seen DickDawes running down the long road to the far house where he shouldn't have been going in the first place.'"

There was a silence.

"Lemme the hell out," Eddie said. "I got to piss off the bridge on that one for sure."

"Shut up, Dawes," Travis said.

There was laughter.

"You mean to tell me," Dunker said, drawing his words out like perfect Attttsssss, "that you have been sitting there, in the dark, all of this time, doing *that?*"

"Hell, yes," Dawes Williams said. "Why not? I'm drunk, aren't I?"

"What the hell is *that?*" Travis said.

"Yes," Dawes Williams said, "and when he meets himself—down there at the end of that long road, in the far house, where that yellow cat sleeps purring on a mirror, the sill of the wind—Jesus! will he be surprised."

"WHAT IS *THAT!?!?!*" Travis said.

"Never mind," Dawes said, "don't sweat it for a minute."

"Hold me back," Travis said. "Hold me back. So help me God, I'm for throwing Dawes Williams here from the top of the Mississippi River bridge, so help me God," he said straining backwards against the seat.

"Hell, yes," Dawes Williams said.

"What's happenin' here?" Eddie said.

"Go back to sleep, Eddie," Dunker said.

"God, I'm drunk," Eddie said. "I'm soaked in rain."

"Everybody's got to have fun," Dawes Williams said. "It is writ large on the wall. Carnival time is a pain in the ass."

"Wait a minute," Dunker said. "Your mood, Dawes, is now at a point at which it crosses my evening out."

"My fist," Travis said, "is now at a point at which it is about to cross Dawes Williams' nose."

"Go to hell, Dawes," Eddie said.

"Hold me back. Hold me back," Travis said. "Just hold me back."

"Carnival time is a pain in the ass," Dawes Williams said, passing out, going to sleep.

"I'll kill him," Travis said, continuing to drive through the rain. "Dunker, remind me to kill the sonofabitch in the morning."

"Dawes? Have another beer?" Dunker said. "You're sure as hell not much of a talker," he said, turning back to the window.

In Dawes' sleep there was a room full of laughter, a silence. Then the night drifted off, by itself this time, as if it didn't need any help, any wind to blow it along, and they were two hundred miles or more deep into Wisconsin, all sleeping, when Dawes' car sputtered over dead and stopped cold as a moon in the ditch.

Outside it was raining and Dawes was asleep.

It is an old dream. In the end a clown comes on stage. He is dressed like Charles J. Chaplin, and in the black distances at the end of a candle he mimes his own face; he takes it off and examines it at length; he is distended, ballooning, and his motions fill in the light. He talks of social democracy. His eyes fold themselves, roll, are vaguely lost in the yellow sockets, and he is crying now. Slowly he begins miming himself mime himself. He becomes lost in fits of forgetfulness.

He takes out a mirror.

His reflections multiply. Curtains open; self-images bloom in a red corridor of walls, in hallways without distance, stairwells without dimension, the recessive space of playhouses echoing back without space. Distended, grotesque on the yellow going red going black walls, he turns, slowly, he turns, distends and integrates from his mirrored center.

He has my face, Dawes Williams dreamed.

Into the candle before him he smiles, knowing as he does all things I do not.

He says he is God, a mask.

He has my face.

He has a mask. Slowly, before me, he begins drawing it aside. He is unaware of my presence now. Contemptuous. The open space of playhouses behind him grows, becomes as immense as an eye. Only his motions, dark as a fulcrum, turn him on the mechanical stage; he is drawing it aside. The mask. . . .

Beneath it is the face of Dawes. Again. Again.

Knowing all things I do not.

Because beneath it is the face of Dawes.

Outside, the rain is running on stone as deep and grained and imperfect as a wall.

24

Morning was a red tractor, a farmer passing by on the road. Waking, Dawes could see Travis had parked his car beyond the ditch, and on the other side of a fence. Travis and Eddie and Dunker were already leaning against the fencerow, throwing rocks at the road and, climbing out of his car, Dawes Williams joined them.

"Where are we?" Dawes Williams said. "What's happening here?"

"Well," Dunker said. "This is Wisconsin. Everybody goes to the races."

"Yes," Eddie said, "Travis thinks we are exactly beside this piece of road here."

"That's right," Travis said. "That's where we are."

"What day is this?" Dawes said.

"This is the morning after," Travis said. "I did some fine driving in the rain last night to even get us this far."

"This is Friday morning," Dunker said.

"This is Saturday morning," Eddie said.

"Anybody got a smoke?" Dawes said.

"Sure," Eddie said. "Have one of mine."

Dawes lay down in the high weeds of the ditch, smoking, and turning back against his '49 Mercury, he could see morning was only a twanging wire, a busted car parked in a cow pasture.

"Damn," Dawes Williams said, looking at the sky, "I think I loved that car."

"If we had some gas," Eddie said, "Travis thinks that car might start."

"That car just needs some gas, huh?" Dawes said.

"Oh ya," Travis said, walking around in the ditch, kicking tires.

"Well," Dunker said, "we better get some gas then."

"Here comes another tractor," Eddie said, squinting down a road of immaculate sunlight.

"Let me handle this one," Travis said.

"Sure, Travis," Dawes said. "You handle this one."

Soon a man pulled up short on his tractor and stuck his thumbs in his Oshkosh bibs. The fields were fresh after the rain, and it looked to Dawes as if the man were trying to strum out a tune on the buttons of his twanging bibs. Then the farmer looked down from his tractor seat and said:

"Where you boys headed this morning?"

"Oh, just down the ditch apiece," Eddie said.

"Hopefully onto the frigging road," Dunker said.

Travis was staring at Dunker and Eddie. Then he turned to the farmer, smiled, and said:

"To Elkhard Lake, Wisconsin, sir. To the road races. Don't mind my idiot friends here, they're just under the weather you might say. You don't have gasoline and a piece of log chain handy do you, sir?"

"Why, yes, I do have a piece of chain handy, boys," the man said, "which is why I stopped because you boys look like you could use a piece of chain, among other things, this morning."

"Thanks," Travis said. "Move it, Dawes."

Dawes moved, the farmer pulled the straining car over the top of the road, gave them a gallon of gasoline, and—muddied—they turned around in their tracks and began driving down the morning. Travis had found out from the farmer they had only overshot Elkhard Lake by seventy-five miles, but Travis was still driving and, opening the first beer of the day, he said only:

"Well, I guess we made better time than I thought we did last night."

"You can sure drive this car," Dawes Williams said quietly behind him.

The sun was high. The fields were still bright after the rain; herds of black and white Holsteins splotched the hills and, feeling nearly sober, Dawes Williams thought the morning tasted like clean German tractor springs in his teeth.

"Damn," Eddie said, "I think these clothes are beginning to rot off my back."

But they drank beer and it began going better and, stopping only for gas and quarts of orange juice, Travis continued to push the car all morning. They crossed a maze of backroads and highways, stringing east and west, and south again, across the hand-swept state.

"Nice ride," Dawes Williams said, loading the cooler with another case around noon.

"Oh ya," Dunker said. "You make a fine map, Willy."

"Sure is," Travis said, not batting an eye. "Lovely place."

Then, around three o'clock, Travis pulled around just another blind curve; they saw a sign reading ELKHARD LAKE WISCONSIN ROAD AMERICA CAMPING GROUND, and Dunker said:

"Let's pull in here, Travis."

"Ya. Let's take this one, Travis," Dawes Williams said.

"Oh ya," Travis said.

They pulled over, gave a man with a money bib five dollars, found everyone else from Rapid Cedar, and Dawes rolled out of the back seat and went to sleep under the car so no one would run him over. Waking up in a few hours, Dawes watched as Barney Ingersoll pulled in in Mike Hanna's car and told them the riots were starting. Everyone began climbing out of sleeping bags, and they began stringing out toward town like Jesse James. Dawes, half-asleep, watched Travis walk by, impeccably groomed in a vested suit. Travis, Dawes knew, would spend most of the night holding forth easily with the circles of racing drivers and aficionados inhabiting the bars of the unbelievably overpriced hotels. Then Dunker walked by, looked under the car, found Dawes Williams, and set him on his own hood like something hung out to dry:

"Com'on, Dawes," he said. "The drinking's starting."

As they drove into town, the early evening road looked like a single cater-

pillar going in two opposite directions at once. Travis and Dunker decided to
give it up, so they parked Dawes' car under a pine tree and began walking
down the shoulder of the road. The meadows were cooling; Travis had his suit
coat over his shoulder and his sleeves rolled up, however, and as they walked
down the gravel beside the rows of cars, the night seemed to explode with
potential life, close, around them. Dawes Williams tucked his shirt in and
stopped to tie off his shoes. Dunker opened four beers and a large can of cold
beans, and Eddie produced some plastic spoons out of his pockets. They ate
and walked on through the bluing evening. . . .

A Mercedes sedan pulled past them and a man told them to get out of the
way. They were walking faster than the Mercedes, however, and as they were re-
passing it later, up the road, Travis stopped dead in his tracks, peered into the
back window directly at six inches, for some minutes on end, and laughed the
man and his chauffeur dead in the face. After the man had become self-conscious, turned away, and blushed—and the chauffeur had reasonably passed
over the one split moment when he thought of getting out and fighting—Travis
turned and walked down the road.

They came to a train stopped dead in its tracks. Dawes thought it was
instantly insane. At least two thousand people, he figured, were walking around
it, prowling its edges, kicking its invisible iron tires, boarding it and exiting it
at will. Thin yellow light hung from its motionless windows, and a pale, invisible oily steam of noise rose from its engines. Police were trying to clear the
tracks, and hooded firemen were milling about it with hoses.

"Christ," Eddie was saying, "wouldn't it be neat if the world were always
this crowded."

Dawes and Eddie and Dunker walked over the couplings and, on the other
side, only another row of passengers sat smoking and watching the night from
motionless windows. The train was dead motion in an exact center of dead
noise and, as they crossed a line of pine trees, the small wood frame of the town
came instantly into view. Bright, expensive lights lined and nestled the lake.
Only the doors of taverns seemed to go off in the air. Looking back at the train,
Dawes felt it was as if the whole world were set upon boarding, reproducing
itself, and getting off its couplings and doors in Elkhard Lake, Wisconsin.
Looking forward at the town, he could see a thousand faceless mummers were
out and prowling around in force. A blue night was easing in from the north.
He watched a phalanx of hooded firemen trying to hold off Main Street. He
thought all life was revolving itself around a vague Fair; a medieval town.
Turning back to the meadows he saw the dark shadows of trees were standing
out against the late blue cool of the sky . . .

They moved through the town and walked down around the lake and
came back. Dunker went into a tavern and came out with a case, and cursing

about fifteen dollars. They sat under a tree, drinking quickly, and a thousand people wandered by. After awhile Travis moved off, and Eddie followed him, and Dunker followed them both, and Dawes took the rest of the case and drifted down by the lake. He sat alone and threw empty bottles at the water. The lights, the docks of the Schwartz Hotel drifted out and died back over the lake. Tall, standing shadows hung the edges. Lanterns strung out and burned peaceful holes in the summer night. It darkened, and the carefully tended lawns sloped into the lake. People sat out on straw chairs, and in the distance Dawes could watch them talking. The quiet seemed perfect, buried on solid rock three miles deep. He felt he never wanted to leave this behind. Then he got up and began walking through the night carrying only four bottles of beer stuck in his pockets.

He saw faces he knew. It was good to hang back in the night; to see them move around when they didn't know he was watching. Passing the dock of the Schwartz Hotel, Dawes hung back in the shadows and saw that Barney Ingersoll was bathing naked in the lake. T. T. Calders and Jim Inge were standing on the dock, laughing, talking about how drunk Ingersoll had been, and how he had come to town, after an afternoon prowling the woods, watching the racing, drunk, looking as if he'd been dragged through a mudhole, and how nobody could stand it so they had thrown him in the lake. A crowd was forming. Then, looking up from the lake, Barney Ingersoll had sprung up naked in the moon and said:

"You bastards. You bastards. I love all you bastards. Hell yes. Every damn one."

"Thank-you, Tiny Tim," Jim Inge was saying.

"Sit down, Barney," T. T. Calders said. "Your balls are showing and we've alot of nice people up here."

Then T. T. Calders and Jim Inge passed through the crowd collecting nickels and dimes in a stocking hat. When they had enough they sent one of the waiters-in-white-jackets into the hotel. When the waiter returned they tipped him the rest, threw ten tiny bars of ivory into the lake near Barney Ingersoll, and then went up the dock and over the hill for some beer. Ingersoll sat soaping in the lake, breaking sporadically into song; a larger crowd was forming, and Dawes Williams laughed to himself and moved down the street.

In the street a mob was forming. People seemed to move in streams, out from within the trees in every direction. The riot was in full swing and groups of people were assaulting Main Street with telephone booths. Broken glass went off in the air.

Turning a corner, Dawes recognized Danny Deeder conducting a crap game near the curb. Sitting down, watching, Dawes was soon swept down the gutter, and under a car, by a fire hose. Dawes lay under the front wheels for awhile, not breathing because he couldn't turn his head away from the water, feeling only that the faucet of the lake had been turned on. After the firemen passed, Dawes got up from under the car and threw a beer bottle through the window of a bank. Two state policemen spotted Dawes and chased him flat out for three hundred yards before they finally gave up. They settled instead for arresting Jasper Hally, son of a Rapid Cedar banker who was only walking the other way. The banker's son began screaming fanatically, something about 'fascist police state,' and they hauled him off to the Sheboygan jail. Then Dawes circled back into town in time to hear the mayor of Elkhard Lake, Wisconsin scream through a bull-horn. He began screaming for order and reason. He welcomed the crowd out to the races in broken German, Dawes felt. He opened another beer on a bumper and watched as Robbie Bartlett snuck behind the phalanx of firemen and cut off their hose with his knife. The crowd cheered. Someone hit the mayor of Elkhard Lake, Wisconsin on the head with a beer bottle and the old man walked from the platform, black with dignity and the impossibility of hanging them all. In the distance Dawes saw Dunker and Travis fighting with two men even larger than they were. Eddie distracted one of them by hitting him with a stick, Dunker threw a knee at him, Travis knocked him out, and then all three of them turned on the other man, who ran down the street. Dunker and Eddie and Travis ran in the other direction. Dawes wished he had been there. Nearer by, Dawes turned to see a crowd grouped around a prize fight, and, pushing his way into the inner circle, in the hooded light Dawes could see Jay Davies was getting the right side of his face beaten in by a left-handed Mexican someone said was from Moline, Illinois. In the end, B. J. Reedy distracted the Mexican by calling him a 'bean-eater' and Davies decked him with three punches. Then everyone stood up, and shook on it, and B. J. Reedy led the Mexican up toward the Schwartz Hotel for a beer. Dawes turned and walked down the street. He knew he didn't want to miss any more of it than he had to; he wanted to keep moving. . .

Passing a storefront, Dawes was cornered by a woman who was drunk, who was guarding her windows with a broom handle, and who accused him of starting the riots. Dawes said the price of beer was too high anyway—that she would come out on it in the end—that she had probably started it all herself, if the truth could ever be known—and that, finally, it was a mass society and probably nobody started the riots, they just sprang up out of the ground. Then the woman's husband came out and told Dawes Williams to mind his own business, and the woman hit him over the head with the broom. Dawes Williams puckered his lips and kissed the air before her, and then he walked on.

Walking back to the hotel for a beer, he thought the night was drunken, mad, fire-strewn, hooded, full of a thousand Druid shamans looking for a single witch to lead them out. He paused to watch a drunk sleep it off on the lawn. Eventually some kids came up, picked his pocket, and moved down the street.

He thought suddenly he would be moving on soon so it didn't matter; he thought he would be leaving for Paris, France, an island in the Aegean, as soon as he could. Turning, Dawes saw Barney Ingersoll was soaping naked in the lake, singing out loud, so he moved off through some pine trees and headed for the next hotel over. He thought he needed another drink. . . .

Arriving, Dawes hung back in a corner of the bar and drank beer that was being passed back, down a long chaos of hands, toward the rear. Across a perfectly packed can of a room Dawes saw that B. T. Saus and B. J. Reedy were doing the same, only they had branched out and were doing it on a larger scale. As a boy came in with cases of beer stacked on a cart, Dawes watched as B. T. got his attention and as B. J. siphoned off the top case from the stack. B. J. worked the beer under the table just behind him with his feet and later B. T. and B. J. stood up front drinking, talking, selling the hotel's beer at the hotel's own prices. Dawes noted that this seemed to be the kind of capitalism that genuinely worked, and headed out the door and into the night again. . . .

He found he was perfectly assimilated into a pleasant blur as he made his way into a drugstore and asked for paper and ink. He thought he recognized someone he hadn't seen for years; for a moment he thought it must have been Ronnie Crown, a rainy face in a mob of night, but then he decided it must have been no one at all. He was very drunk. Back on the street, he thought the people were like chittering mechanical toys, that, if you wound them up, bumped them slightly, they would change direction and march straight over the end of the world.

He headed out for the line of pine trees, the road leading toward the end of town. He walked down the gravel, looking for his car. Finding it, he climbed in and began driving. He wanted to drive forever, until the engine stopped, and he found himself sitting only in the warm, shadowy pines. He felt completely drunk, and, reaching for the flask of whiskey he kept in the glove box, he was unaware of even Mike Hanna, who was sleeping quietly in the back seat, within the ruck of blankets and bags behind him. Wind blew in the windows, and Dawes' lights moved like two old snakes on the road. He drove through the miles of highway and road—stopping only at the quiet country crossroads, sleeping deep in night, to scribble on some paper he had found in the glove compartment another *Song of the Northern Meadows*. Then, rolling again, until dawn broke with its pale breathless birds, its breathless porcelain birds, he found himself (finding also for the first time Mike Hanna) back somehow at the campgrounds. And it was like the morning before: first he saw the sign— ELKHARD LAKE WISCONSIN ROAD AMERICA CAMPING GROUND —*rising up*, tacked to the ground with long poles, and then he pulled down the old, tree-sheltered road. A huge bonfire, full of shadows and faces running over the edge of the sky, burned the end of the wind. He heard a fantastic scream.

He was parked and walking now, carrying Mike Hanna over his shoulders, but in the distance he could hear only a high scream that ran over the trees, the wind, that ran over everything swirling below it. For a moment he thought it was Travis' screaming; then, just as suddenly, he knew that it wasn't Travis, that Travis was only trying to scream instructions over, over the top, perhaps, he thought, even becoming a part of the high rilling moan that was growing up, an instantly blooming tree, from the ground. Dropping Mike Hanna, running, Dawes moved into the firelight near the tent, and through the hooded canvas doorway he saw Travis and Dunker, and others, straining unbelievably against the back end of a Pontiac. Travis was screaming:

"YOU'RE ON MIKE ROURKE'S HEAD! YOU'RE ON MIKE ROURKE'S HEAD!"

Mike Rourke was lying below wheels, trapped in a sleeping bag, screaming.

"FORWARD!" Dunker was screaming.

"WHAT THE *HELL* ARE YOU DOING!!!???!!!" T. T. Calders was shouting, running around front, through the fire and back again, beating his hands on the Pontiac's hood.

"YOU'RE ON MIKE ROURKE'S HEAD!" Travis said. "GO FORWARD YOU GODDAMN-LOONY-JACKASS-BASTARD!!!???!!!"

Mike Rourke's high, rilling scream broke, finally became intelligible, formed itself into words, and said:

"MY HEAD! GOD. CHRIST. GET'M OFF! HE'S RUNNING OVER MY HEAD!"

But the Pontiac only seemed to spin in a canvas rut. The tent was half-collapsed, and everything seemed to hang motionless, until finally Dunker ran around the corner of the tent, with a heavy tire iron in his hand, and smashed the Pontiac's side window into shreds and reached in and turned off the engine. Then there was a stillness. Everyone, Dawes too now, strained against the back of the car until Dunker reached in and threw it into neutral and they managed to edge the car up the slight hill of grass. T. T. Calders threw blocks under the wheels, Dunker jumped in and set the brake. A totally insentient drunk rolled from the car; three or four of the others picked him up and slapped him silly until he was awake, and then someone knocked him out. Behind him, in the tent, Dawes could hear Mike Rourke's breathing, heavy, close to the ground, crying.

Almost afraid to look, they finally all filed into the tent and lit a lantern. In the hooded canvas shadows a perfect tire tread was beginning to form a welt all along the flesh of Mike Rourke's cheek. T. T. Calders got out some whiskey and Dunker gave it to Rourke in a tin can. They sat about, eating cold canned goods, talking it over for some time. Dawes knew Mike Rourke would be famous in Rapid Cedar for months, that, in the end, he would probably get quietly laid over the whole damn thing. Travis invited Rourke to ride back to Rapid Cedar in Dawes' car on Sunday afternoon. Rourke accepted.

"What a crazy sonofabitch you must be," Eddie said.

Then Dawes excused himself, remembering something, and went outside to pick Mike Hanna out of the lane. Coming back, cold sober now, he rolled both of them into the exact center of the tent, emptied his pockets, and went to sleep in a thin rustle of dull blue scribble paper which no one, including even Dawes Williams himself, poet-extraordinary-of-the-northern-meadows, could even remotely decipher.

25

Two days later, on Sunday afternoon, Dawes found himself sitting under the sill of a wooden beer tent, drinking and talking to Barney Ingersoll. He didn't know what he'd been saying, but, waking slightly, spilling beer down his pants, he heard Ingersoll say:

"Forget it, Dawes. Nobody I know wants to be a genius anyway. It'll get you nowhere."

Then there was a silence. Dawes couldn't focus the sun and shade in his eyes; he could just barely see Barney, who was two feet away and rubbing warm mud into sleeping swirls on his belly.

"My feet are cut," Barney Ingersoll said. "I sure wish I had me some underwear."

"I feel like burrowing under a log," Dawes Williams said.

"Ya. Great, isn't it?" Barney Ingersoll said. "Drive down and hop in the lake maybe?"

"Can't, don't think," Dawes said. "Haven't seen my car since yesterday."

"Why not?"

"Don't know," Dawes Williams said. "It just hasn't been around. I can't figure that out, either."

"Ya. This is a heller all right. You seen a race yet?"

"No. I thought I saw one yesterday but Dunker said I was dreaming—making it up."

"You see Dunker yesterday?"

"Sure."

"I'll be damned," Barney Ingersoll said. "That's better'n I did."

There was a silence.

"You see that guy burn up and die yesterday, Dawes?"

"Did a guy burn up and die yesterday?"

"Sure a guy burned up and died yesterday. Didn't you hear about it?"

"Nope. I didn't see it," Dawes Williams said. "How'd it happen?"

"Christ, Dawes. He ran his big dicky racer into a tree. How else?" Barney Ingersoll said.

There was a silence.

"Damn it," Dawes Williams said quietly, "I sure wish'd I'd have seen one of those races one of these years."

"Oh ya," Barney Ingersoll said, holding his head. "I sure wish those bastards hadn't hidden all my underwear too. Hope is a terrible thing."

"Damn it," Dawes Williams said.

"Ya," Barney Ingersoll said, "I'll bet those races are neat all right."

"Where's the woods?" Dawes Williams said. "I believe I have to wizz again. I wish I knew where I caught this cold."

"Me too," Barney Ingersoll said. "The woods are everywhere. They grow a lot of trees up here."

Having stumbled back from peeing on a log, Dawes sat in the shade again and listened while Ingersoll said:

"Good job, Dawes. Let's go up top for a beer."

"My body is a temple," Dawes Williams said. "I'm a Methodist."

"I need a beer bad," Barney Ingersoll said.

"Hell," Dawes said. "It must be fifteen miles to that beer tent."

"For Christsake, Dawes," Barney said. "We've been sitting right under the damn thing for two days, I think. See that flag up there?"

"Where the hell are we?" Dawes Williams said. "I need a bratwurst."

Then Dawes passed out cold on a woman's foot. When he woke, Travis was shaking him again, it was nearly red evening, and Dunker was saying:

"Where the hell have you been, Dawes? We've been looking for you everywhere."

"Where am I?" Dawes Williams said. "I don't like to be discontinued this way. I like to remember where I've been."

"You've been sitting out here listening to the races, Dawes," Travis said quite seriously.

"Who won?" Dawes Williams said. "Did anybody get his big dicky racer burned on a tree?"

"Com'on, Dawes," Travis said. "We're going home."

"I don't know," Dawes Williams said. "I've grown to like it up here. Where are we?"

"This is Wisconsin," Dunker said.

"You're driving, Dawes," Travis said. "You're the only one who's had any sleep."

"Help me up," Dawes Williams said. "I don't think I can walk any more."

"Think you can make it home, Dawes?" Dunker said.

"Sure," Dawes said. "I may not be able to drive like Travis. I may not be able to drive it through a ditch and across a fence, without even leaving a mark, but I can drive it all right."

Walking down the hill, Eddie stopped to kick at Barney Ingersoll to wake him up.

"What is this," Ingersoll said, "a raid?"

"B. T. Saus told me to get your ass up if I saw it lying around," Eddie said, "and get it down to the parking lot."

"What the hell," Ingersoll said, "the Grand Finale isn't even over yet." But Dawes stooped to pick Ingersoll up, and then both of them staggered out of the woods. It was Sunday evening and the last of the races were over. A few thirty-thousand-dollar Chaparrals and Cheetahs were only winding down, whirling around the track behind them. When B. T. Saus pulled his '46 Hudson Hornet out of the camping grounds, Dawes Williams pulled out behind him. They rolled south toward Iowa through the growing dark. Mike Rourke sat silently in the back seat with scabs already forming a perfect tire tread, a perfect secular stigmata, on his cheek.

"These two cars," Travis said, lighting a thin cigarillo, "happen to have more class than anything up here."

"I sure wish I had myself a '46 Hudson Hornet then," Dunker said.

Then, for some reason, everyone laughed for seventeen miles. When it all ceased, finally died off, Eddie said:

"Pass old B. T. Saus, Dawes. I just happen to have an egg left over from breakfast in my pocket."

It took Dawes Williams four miles, some swearing, and a lot of used-up nerve, but when B. T. Saus finally chickened out—when he saw Dawes Williams was about to be wiped out at the bottom of a long hill by a semi in the passing lane—he pulled over, dropped back, and let Dawes in. Then Eddie, flying past, reared back and let B. T. have it with a fast-ball egg on the windshield.

Then B. T. passed Dawes Williams and threw out a can of beer with the lid macheted off.

Then Dawes Williams passed B. T. and threw out four more eggs and a cut-up pillow Dunker had found under the seat.

Then B. T. passed Dawes Williams and threw out a baloney sandwich.

Then Dawes Williams passed B. T. and threw out an open can of oil.

Then B. T. passed Dawes Williams and jettisoned an open can of STP and a tire jack.

Then Dawes Williams had Travis tear up his back seat, and, maneuvering around, making his final pass at B. T. Saus, he had Dunker roll his spare tire down the roadway. The tire bounded off the exact center of B. T.'s '46 Hudson Hornet, stopping it dead in its tracks. Dawes Williams moved off, steering, rolling down the road like a thousand banjos going off in the air.

"It was just a good thing B. T. only had a '46 Hudson Hornet," Travis said, "or you'd never have passed him in the first place."

"You know, you shouldn't fight with your friends—the people from the same place as you," Mike Rourke, who was beginning to sound like an expert on everything, said from the back seat. "You should only fight with your enemies—the people who come from different places, and who aren't your friends."

"What is this—moral geography?" Dawes Williams said, rolling home.

Then, when they met at a party back in Rapid Cedar a week later, Dawes and B. T. smiled at each other a lot and sat in a corner getting drunk. When Summer Letch went home with Danny Deeder, B. T. and Dawes Williams only turned to one another, paused a moment, and said:

"Danny Deeder!!!! Oh, ma Gawd!!!!"

Then they continued drinking and laughed about it for a long time, like two balloons holding each other up in the wind, and when B. T. went home to sleep Summer Letch off, Dawes went out and climbed a lamp post, singing songs and swearing at the wind, until the cops came and hauled him away to jail.

Dawes sat in his cell and thought things were breaking up; coming apart at seamless joints. He thought the jailed night was a perfect drunken stone, that the tinny light was a ragman, bone and yellow cheek, selling the floor out from under him, that black God was auctioning off the doors, that only two protruding eyes, the burned bulbs of last year's flowers, were with him, gavel rapping sullenly the floor of his dream. The night was monk's wood. He lay on his plank. There was a frog in the corner, dim hands, arks of covenant, cage shadows and only the single word "Cigaret" drawled and slobbered on the darkness. There was laughing, a red wetness on his cheek. The red ash glowed on the wall. The frog in the corner had a voice, like steeples, like something thrusting up, not whole, into the blackness of old, real books. There was a density of breathing, whispers, wave splash, the rise and fall of old wood boats in the moon. He clutched at something and missed. . . .

Then they opened the door and threw Barney Redwood into the cell.

"Barney?" Dawes Williams said. "How the hell are you?"

"Not so good, Dawes," Barney Redwood said. "You see, these witch hunters have caught me walking around the edge of the William Howard Taft Hotel, and various other sundry things have gone wrong for me in the last few hours."

"What's that?" Dawes said, smiling.

"It's not funny, Dawes," Redwood said. "I was down to the hospital, and my mother has cancer, and they think they caught it too late."

Then the cop saw Barney Redwood and Dawes Williams were friends so he led Barney Redwood off to another cell.

26

There wasn't much opinion out on Barney Redwood. Travis didn't like him, but then, ironically, it was Eddie who had managed over the years to become the maker of final judgment. Eddie didn't like Barney Redwood either, but Dawes did. Dawes felt his life was somehow entwined with something Barney Redwood had to tell him. But Eddie, the power behind Travis' throne, had the final say. William Wadlove High was a place of shifting reputations and centralized power structures, and Barney Redwood was only partly in. Reputations were made and lost forever in a matter of days. And Eddie, who managed never to say a two-dimensional word, had somehow managed to worm his way into the heart, the exact center of it all. He was a minor genius at it. He had managed to do things over the years like getting Ratshit Rawlings effectively vetoed in life: he guarded the inner sanctum; he spent most of his time working hard at polishing monosyllabic pronouncements to be delivered on people, especially girls, who presumed to enter the inner circles. During football season Travis and Eddie were as inseparable as newlyweds; and until basketball season rolled around, even Dunker and Dawes were expected to go their separate ways. Dawes Williams went home one day and wrote into the notebook which he had been keeping for some time now:

Joshua Wadlove High: it was all a Florentine court enameled manneristically to the face of a Mickey Mouse watch bought at an auction. Camelot!

Dawes, in fact, eventually gave it all up; he traded in his second-string basketball shoes and became a bootlegger. On Sunday afternoons that fall, he would load up with fake ID's and drive across the Mississippi into East Dubuque, Illinois, where he would, with all the capital he could swing and Dunker's help, buy as much as two hundred dollars' worth of whiskey and wine. Returning, with Dunker sitting sprawled in the back scanning the horizon for patrol cars, he would usually turn a profit margin of up to one hundred and fifty percent. His all-time coup was selling a sixty-nine-cent bottle of wine for four dollars and thirty-five cents, tax not included.

"Hell, Jarvis," Dawes said, staring down at the fifteen-year-old kid staring up at the straw-wrapped bottle of wine, "this is luxurious stuff."

"Get pretty juiced-up on stuff like that, Dawes?" Jarvis said, staring back.

"You'll never come back," Dawes Williams said, pocketing the money. "You are on the road to perdition for sure."

Then, watching Jarvis walk down the street with his new bottle of wine, turning to Dunker, Dawes said:

"That wrapped-in-straw number could be a real item."

Eventually Dawes and Dunker ran the original one hundred they had invested into over a thousand dollars. On the Sunday that happened, Dawes looked quietly over at Dunker still scanning the horizon for patrol cars and said:

"Well, we put together a big-man, by God."

Dunker, beginning to read his father's *Wall Street Journal* at that time, said:

"Hey, Dawes, there's a company selling in there for an eighth. We could buy eight thousand shares."

"What company is that?" Dawes said.

"It's called Xerox," Dunker said, looking back out the window. "I only saw it 'cause it's near the bottom."

"Hell, no," Dawes Williams said. "I'm going to buy me the neatest little '56 Ford with fender skirts you ever saw with my end of that money. I don't believe in that capitalistic crap of yours anyway. You end up spending too much time with it. It rots the mind."

"Could be," Dunker said.

So Dunker didn't buy Xerox; Dawes didn't, either. He bought a '56 Ford with fender skirts, and he also bought Summer Letch some beads and trinkets. She almost didn't take them, because Summer wasn't going to be tied down to Dawes Williams by some mere beads and trinkets if she could help it, but in the end she took them grudgingly and on her own terms. Dawes became disillusioned with great wealth, forgetting its possibility easily.

Winter came. Dawes continued going to school, and he felt he must be the kind of person who had nothing else to do. He felt if he tried to do anything else, he would probably dissolve. Nothing seemed to happen that year. He never saw Travis or Eddie, and he felt as if he wanted to be moving along. He sat around and watched Simpson watch television and thought of running away. Once, late in that winter, the day Xerox split five for one and started climbing again, Dunker came over to Dawes' house and stared at the walls for three hours. Dunker wouldn't eat anything, wouldn't drink anything and wouldn't say a word. In the end, he looked at Dawes for a moment and said:

"I could kill you. I could take you outside and slit your throat."

Then Dunker picked himself up and walked through the door, leaving Dawes to sit there wondering what in the hell he had been talking about.

Spring came finally. It hatched over and bloomed in the wet brown streets like a single egg. Flat time hung in the trees.

Sometimes, after school, Barney and Dawes would go over to the old grotesque house full of the shadows of wood and sit watching Mrs. Redwood die. They tried not to look. She was gaunt, distant, shucked; what was left of her hung loosely on the sticks of her bones. Dawes could remember only her hollow eyes, but it was impossible to look beyond their yellow edges.

Sometimes, after school, he drove Summer home. He still saw her, but it was different. He tried to forget. One day Dawes Williams had Summer Letch half-trapped in his new, almost new, '56 Ford with fender skirts, and he looked at her and said:

"Damn it. I blew it."

"Blew what, Dawes?" she said.

"Our chance in life. I just blew a few million dollars in the stock market. We could have been married."

Dawes began to be obsessed by the mental picture of millions of dollars, all in one pile.

"Don't be silly, Dawes," Summer said.

"I'm not being silly, I'm being serious. I'm driving about a twenty-two-million-dollar car, and you're wearing two million dollars' worth of beads and trinkets. It's hell. We could have been married."

"That's real funny, Dawes," she said.

"Xerox," Dawes said.

"Xerox!" she said. "Dawes, you idiot!"

"I know it. It's hell, I tell you."

"It's all right, Dawes," she said. "I couldn't marry you anyway."

"Why not? I love you."

"I know," she said. "But I don't love you. Not in that way."

"Good God," he caught himself saying. "You mean you've just been using my body. . . all these years?"

"Of course not, silly," she said. "I just mean I couldn't live with you. Ever. No one could. You'd drive me nuts."

"But, Summer," Dawes caught himself saying, "I love you. I mean I really do."

"I know," she said. "Do you want to come over until four-thirty, when my mother gets home?"

"What the hell do you mean by that?"

"You know very well what I mean, silly," she said.

"No, I mean what do you *mean*?"

"Oh, that," she said. "I just mean I'd want someone who's compatible."

"*Compatible,* for Christsake!" Dawes Williams said. "This is the death of romance. Summer," he said, "you've been reading Ann Saunders again. I'll break your neck. So help me I will."

"Well, I'll still never marry you," she said. "I want a guy who's compatible. Someone who's *fun.*"

"*Fun,* for Christsake," Dawes said. "Fun! What the hell is 'fun' all about? Here I sit, probably the only truly *gifted* sonofabitch you've ever seen, and you say 'fun,' for Christsake!"

"That's what I mean," she said. "You're not any *fun.* You just make me feel dumb all the time. Do you want me to sit around and feel *dumb* all my life?"

"Oh, my God," Dawes said, pulling the car into her driveway. "I'm getting the hell out of here. I'm leaving town."

"You mean you don't want to come in?" she said.

"See, you're not so dumb. You figured that all out by yourself."

"Dawes, come in the house," she said, looking him deeply in the eyes.

"Hell, no. I'm going to shoot pool with Barney Redwood."

"In, Dawes," she said softly, touching him.

So Dawes went in until four-thirty, then he drove down to play pool with Barney Redwood. They shot pool in the Allison Poolroom, an integral part of the old, nineteenth-century Allison Hotel which sat exactly two feet from the railroad tracks that cut Rapid Cedar directly down the middle. It was as if the passing afterwind of the trains would eventually blow down the doors, leaving the Allison Hotel standing by its own bare roots.

The Allison itself, Dawes thought, was the finest room in town. Everything in the place was incapable of being produced in the twentieth century; even the tables, four snooker and two pool, were seventy-five years old, with the name of an extinct Chicago manufacturer stamped on brass in the sides. Every time Dawes looked at the head snooker table, surrounded by its platformed chairs, he thought of a novel called *Sister Carrie.* Even the implausibly green curtains in the windows were mounted on vestigial casters. He paid by the game, not by the hour, and the money was collected by old, palsied ex-players who were dressed in money aprons, and who dealt the loose change back across the tables as if the coins were cards. Nothing made Dawes feel more escaped than to enter the doors of the Allison Poolroom, cooled by the rush of the huge, circular ceiling fans, and shoot pool with the old railroad men, the truck drivers, even the barbers and piano salesmen stealing away for an hour. He knew the Allison Poolroom was up for sale, but he could still forget he was part of the twentieth century, a progression of time.

Barney Redwood was the only one who ever saw the Allison exactly in the way Dawes did. To Travis, the place was the end of the world, a personal assault. Travis, even before the day they were graduated from William J.

Wadlove High, thought the world was a wonderful place, full of bright noise, and he could already hear the thin ice cubes clinking shut in sophisticated glasses at distant country clubs. Travis knew past knowing what part of the pike he was headed down. Dunker and Eddie weren't so sure, and Dawes was somehow nearly driven mad by the prospect of having to move. It hadn't even occurred to Barney Redwood that there was a road, which was also why Dawes suspected he was somehow superior.

One day, late in the spring, looking up from a shot in the glare of a window, Barney Redwood stared at Dawes and said:

"What the hell, Willy, let's hop a freight."

Barney, who'd been talking quietly all afternoon between shots with a man dressed in tanned goatskins, in dead leather turned inside out, smelling of invisible rain and rot, then said:

"Com'on, Dawes, let's take a ride with Travelin' Tommy here."

"I'm going east. Then south to Virginia," Travelin' Tommy said.

Then Tommy roused himself just enough to spit in the gold slop jars placed near the pillars of the Allison Poolroom. He only came through twice a year, Dawes knew, to sleep the bright afternoon away like rags. Travelin' Tommy liked to begin his travelin' at dusk.

"This is rustic as hell," Dawes Williams said, leaning on the perfectly circular pivot of his cue.

"What the hell, Willy," Barney Redwood said, "we'll ride to the Illinois side of the river with this Travelin' Tommy here and then thumb back."

"What do you say," Dawes said, turning to Travelin' Tommy, "can we ride to Illinois with you?"

"Suuure," Travelin' Tommy said, biting on an orange, "this is what you call a social democracy, ain't it?"

Later, around five o'clock, the freight came past the door of the Allison Poolroom and everyone came outside long enough to watch Dawes and Barney and Travelin' Tommy hop it. It was late spring, but cold, and the sky was already dusky. Travelin' Tommy settled down in a leeward corner and began paring an apple: he eyed it abstractedly, as if it were an insurmountable problem in solid geometry. Finally he ate it. He placed his bindle under the rise and arch of his back, slowly, it took him twenty minutes, and he approached it like a pure problem in inductive science. They weren't moving in the fields of blowing grasses and clover ends growing by the tracks a half hour when Barney raised himself out of his silence and said:

"By God, Dawes, I feel closer to Chi."

"Suuure," Travelin' Tommy said. "We're moving east."

The land rolled past like a movie. In the fields the early lights of tractors coughed red smoke, evening. A thin evening moon slipped in solitary oaks, and Barney Redwood was bent furiously into the white wind of the door. Dawes sat remembering how, once, early in the morning, when they were drunk and the sun was just breaking over the river, he had climbed behind Barney on the fire escape, up, up the seventeen stories of the Thomas Jefferson Hotel. Once there, arrived at the roof, still marching behind the determination of Barney Redwood, Dawes had finally drawn off and sat in the exact center of the roof, watching Barney Redwood as he marched around the naked edge of the rim of the hotel, six times, like the red ribbon of a small parade going nowhere. Barney blew through the empty end of a bottle of peppermint brandy like a flute. On the seventh time round, he'd slipped slightly in the northeast corner and tumbled over the edge; Dawes walked over and watched him hold on to the rods of a neon sign. He'd swung back and forth and gripped himself with the backs of his knees.

"What the hell are you *doing?*" Dawes Williams had said, peering over the edge.

"Right now," Barney'd said, looking down, "I'm peeing my drawers."

"God damn it, Barney," Dawes Williams had said. "Cut that crap out and get up from there."

"Hop the roof, Dawes," Barney'd said. "I'll catch ya."

"Go to hell," Dawes had said. "I'm going down the ladder."

"The problem with you, Willy," Barney'd said, balancing himself vertically on the sign for awhile, "is that you don't really like this swimming in deeper air."

"Get the hell up from there," Dawes had said.

"Don't you help me," Barney'd said. "You help me and I'll throw you over the edge. You touch me and I'll break your neck."

Finally, Barney had climbed back over the edge of the high wall; he had stood, spitting down at the street, with that same furious look caught on the corners of his face. And now, as the land rolled past, Dawes watched him merely use that look to stare down fiercely the wind blowing through doors. Almost to himself Barney was saying:

"What the hell, Dawes. Let's swing over the sill and ride on the roof for awhile."

"Later," Dawes said, not even batting an eye.

"What the hell do you say, Travelin' Tommy?" Barney said.

"Nooo," Travelin' Tommy said. "It's cold up there."

Pretending to ignore Barney, Dawes drifted off. Watching the galloping kerosene horses cough, thin as light, in the evening fields, he thought only, *Yes, hell yes, and he'd have done it, too. If I hadn't ignored it, him. If I'd even looked at him wrong, he'd have swung over the roof. Sure as I'm sitting here he'd have killed himself just to prove he could. Because it was me. Because his mother is dying. Because I'm*

the only one in Rapid Cedar who knows he's full of it, who knows he's alone. That
knows he's an outright liar. Because it was me sitting here, knowing what he was, and
not someone else who didn't. I know. I know his real name, not Barney, the other.
Because I know his father wasn't a World War II flying ace, shot down over Germany,
but is only a storyless drunk in Chicago. That's why, if I'm in his car, he goes down the
street sometimes eighty miles an hour. That's why. Because I know that and even more.
I am the one who knows about his true father, and who knows things like he didn't ever
shoot a bear in the heart with a four-ten shotgun and skin it out, and he didn't ever
lose his virginity to an Indian girl in the Black Hills when he was only nine years old.
It's amazing who believes that; and it has only happened to be me who has had the
common sense to merely look at it, to know what it is and not care. Because I know
why. The first Sunday Barney Redwood came to town he jumped off the Rapid Cedar
River Bridge, into the white water below the dam, for a ten-dollar bet and four cans of
beer; as if he could believe it then, as if that would make it all true. It isn't. No matter
what. Not even when he rearose, out of the river, saying next he would try the one over
the Mississippi for only thirty-five dollars and a gallon of wine—not even then would
it be true. Not even when he is climbing water towers in the evening is it true. But
sometimes, late at night, alone, he walks around the tall edges of small hotels without
ever falling off, without ever leaving a sign in the pacing-by air. . . .

"Dawes," Barney Redwood was saying in the sleeping dark of the freight car, "let's swing under the door and ride the rods for awhile."

"Later," Dawes said. "Wait'll we hit Illinois."

"Suuure," Travelin' Tommy said, eating a potato. "You fellas could have a high old time under there."

"Nobody talks like this any more," Dawes Williams said, kicking bits of grain from the sill of the door.

"Apparently Travelin' Tommy does," Barney said.

Travelin' Tommy paid no attention and took out a tomato and a small shaker of salt from his pocket.

"What the hell, Dawes," Barney was saying, "we can't just sit here in the dark forever."

"What do you think, Travelin' Tommy?" Dawes said. "Can you just sit there in the dark forever and watch the land roll by?"

"Suuure," Travelin' Tommy said. "That's ro-mance."

So they rolled on, silent. Dawes sat near the freight's door watching.

"What the hell, Dawes," he finally said, "let's run down the roofs and stick up the engineer."

"Suuure," Travelin' Tommy said, finishing the last of a salted cucumber. "Jesse James was a real bad man."

The sound, the heavy dark of iron wheels, ran out before them. The wind was summering. They were running through broken patches of dirt, a band of scrubs and hill country around the river, and Barney Redwood was staring into the doorway, and soon, jumping up, catching himself, he began doing pull-ups on the underhang of the roof. Travelin' Tommy, locked in his corner, had just finished a small bag of potato chips and, neatly, in six geometric folds from bottom left, he wrapped the wrapper and buttoned it down in his vest.

"Barney?" Dawes said. "August is my month. The strangest things happen to me in August. In fact, nearly everything worth remembering happens to me in August."

But Barney said nothing. Paying no attention to Dawes Williams, he continued only to chew on his piece of corn leaf.

"Suuure," Travelin' Tommy finally said. "Superstition is a terrible thing."

"Anyway," Barney said, poised in the door as if he were a sack of mail to be forked off at any turning, "this isn't even August. This is May."

"Anyway," Dawes said, "my whole life's becoming nothing but a damn polemic in the first place."

"Later, Dawes," Barney said, not even batting an eye.

"Suuure," Travelin' Tommy said, taking out his potato-chip wrapper, blowing into it. "Disputations are hellish things."

"Christ!" Barney Redwood said. "Would you look at this guy!?"

But Dawes said nothing. He waited only for the first signs of the Mississippi River to come rolling up. Outside, the night was clear and speechless as woven fields. Inside, Dawes climbed tightly into his silence of boxcars and began thinking, constructing his consciousness in his own image. In his corner Travelin' Tommy began singing quietly into his potato-chip wrapper. To Dawes he sounded like hoarse coach trains crossing prairies at evening. He sounded as if he were dying of breathing. Into the door of the wind Barney Redwood seemed to be a shadow, both lewd and elegant, trying to count up the swirling infinity of the night.

"Hey, Dawes, wake up!" Barney said, turning finally. "We're about to cross the Mississippi River!"

"Suure," Travelin' Tommy said.

"I know," Dawes said slowly. "I can scarcely cross the Mississippi River, going either way, without tears."

"Good, Dawes," Barney Redwood said. "What is that?"

"What I mean," Dawes said, "is that crossing the Mississippi River at night is like watching it rain on a time before you were born."

"Suuure, Dawes," Travelin' Tommy said from his corner. "I think that's a real nice sayin'."

"Thanks, Travelin' Tommy," Dawes Williams said.

"Well, what I think," Barney said, "is this: Travelin' Tommy here must be part gone in the head to think something like that is nice. And you must be far-

ther out beyond him to have said it. That's what I think. No offense there, Travelin' Tommy," Barney said.

"Suuure," Travelin' Tommy said.

They had all moved to the door and, standing in the shadowy iron trestle
light, the three heads—Barney Redwood, Travelin' Tommy and Dawes
Williams—stared at the river below. The Mississippi was a great sea, heavy and
wide with spring, swollen with moon, moving off to an exterior ocean. In the
corner Travelin' Tommy's transistor radio was playing, blooming out of the
sparks, cornered, thin and blooming like a cracked harmonica, barely splitting
the air, barely rising, speaking at them. Just then Bing Crosby began singing:

> Have you ever seen the sunshine?
> Have you ever been there . . .
> Wondering when the rain will end?
> I would call the rain my friend,
> and journey till the rainbow ends.

"It's a simple song," Dawes said into the static.

"Suuure," Travelin' Tommy said. "Bing Crosby can sing those songs."

"BaBaBa-Boom," Barney Redwood said, hanging from the door.

Barney, Dawes could tell watching him, was still thinking about jumping.
But the evening, at least, had begun to run down like a string. It ran over the
moving river, erased itself and died down into nothing and the thin whistle of
the train. Travelin' Tommy took out an orange and began polishing it on his
shoe. They reached the Illinois side of the river. The iron rhythms rubbed, side
to side, against the wheels in 2/2 time. DrummerDickHyootBroncoDawes
began to beat simple rudiments on the boards of the flooring. They wound
through small timber stands, groves near the river, and soon broke out into a
new reach of fields, of fresh illusion of spaces. Illinois was hung with white
wood, flat as a mile and a half.

"I'd have jumped that bridge for thirty-five bucks and a gallon of wine,"
Barney Redwood said almost in passing.

"Suuure," Travelin' Tommy said.

"That damn river," Barney said, "is something else. Sometimes I think it's
trying to tell me something. Sometimes I think it's even bigger than any of us."

"Suuure."

"I always wondered," Dawes Williams said slowly, "what Abraham Lincoln
thought, riding down it, rafts and keel boats, at night, a hundred and thirty
years ago."

"I'll bet you do," Barney Redwood said. "Me too. I sit around and wonder
about stuff like that all day sometimes."

"Suuure," Travelin' Tommy said. "That sounds reasonable to me."

"So what did he think about, Dawes?" Barney said.

"I don't know," Dawes said. "I never got that far with it."

"Well," Travelin' Tommy said, "he thought about the fact that if you're a natural genius, with no place to go, and if you're floating down a river at night, just hearing the dogs on the western shore howlin' at the fire in your pit, you either learn humor and humanity or you go mad in the end."

There was a silence. Even Dawes Williams moved closer to the door.

"My God," he finally said, "that's about the most extraordinary thing I ever heard in my life. I knew if I sat here long enough you'd say something extraordinary over there, Travelin' Tommy."

"Suuure," Travelin' Tommy said, unfolding an old cigar and chewing it.

"Travelin' Tommy here," Barney said, "was once a rich and successful millionaire who . . ."

"Hell, no," Dawes said, "a minor Walt Whitman who . . ."

"Suuure," Travelin' Tommy said, "I was none of them."

"What the hell do you mean? Which is it?" Dawes said.

"Neither," Travelin' Tommy said. "I always been travelin'. Before I can remember I been travelin'. I been travelin' so long I ain't had time for nothing else."

"I won't believe it," Dawes said. "You've got a past."

"Nope."

"You ever jump off a Mississippi River bridge for thirty-five bucks and a gallon of wine?" Barney said.

"Nope."

"You ever *know* anyone who did?"

"Nope."

"You ever know anyone who ever thought about it seriously?"

"Suuure," Travelin' Tommy said. "You did."

Dawes knew Travelin' Tommy had him there, so he sat back and watched Barney shut up about it. The train rolled on through the fields beyond the river. Tommy's radio continued to raise static and stale air in the corner.

"Jesus," Barney Redwood said, "where'd you ever believe this guy'd get money for batteries?"

"Suuure," Travelin' Tommy said, "it's a terrible expense."

"Barney?" Dawes Williams said. "I'd like to tell you how I feel about old things. I'd like to try."

"I get it, Dawes," Barney said. "The time has come to speak of many things—of cabbages and kings, of fireplugs and pumpkin tops, of princesses and purple rings. I get it, Dawes. Shut up about it. Go to hell."

"Old things like Travelin' Tommy here."

"Let Travelin' Tommy speak for himself. I don't like old things and I don't

like people who think they know about old things. So take your old things,
Dawes, and go sit on'em over there in the corner."

In the stillness Barney leaned farther out of the freight, watching the
roadway coming up.

"I don't have any old things, Dawes," he said, "and I don't want to hear
about yours."

The train was moving down, flattening out now. Barney Redwood kicked corncobs and bits of broken grasses through the open door, and Travelin' Tommy had
taken a pipe from his vest pocket and was smoking in his corner. The long whistle
sounded another crossing and Barney turned against Travelin' Tommy and said:

"Where the hell are we, Tommy? I'm getting off this damn train now."

"Suuure. It's been a time ridin' with you fellows. I think we're just outside
of Galena, Illinois, right about now."

"That's good, because I always wanted to get off at Galena, Illinois. You
comin', Dawes?" Barney said, jumping from the door.

"Well, I guess I'll be leaving now, Tommy. Thanks, and I'll see ya."

"Doubt it," Travelin' Tommy said, "but when you hit, start runnin'."

"Oh ya. I know it. I think I saw you say that in a movie once. Thanks,
Tommy," Dawes Williams said, jumping from the doorway.

But when he hit, Dawes didn't start running; he didn't have a chance. Before
anything else at all could happen, he merely fell and slid down the cinders for
sixty yards. When he finally stopped, he lay on his back and listened to the moon
pass over him with the noise of a train. After some time he thought he could hear
Barney Redwood picking his way up the tracks, calling his name. He could hear
Barney throwing out rocks into the night as if he were sounding for long-lost
submarines. Finally, out of a dream, Barney spotted him. He approached and
began kicking at Dawes, gently, as if he were an old bundle of clothes.

"Oh, ma Gawd," Dawes Williams finally said. "Don't touch me. Just let me lie."

"Jesus, Dawes, I think you could use a little jumpin' practice on ya. I saw you.
You came out of there in the moon like mad swans with just mirrors for water."

"I know," Dawes Williams said. "I didn't think. It was all my fault. I must
have kept up with the train for the first sixty yards."

"More like a hundred judging from your skid. Foolish," Barney said,
looking down, pacing off a piece of ground. "Damn foolish. Remind me to
never take you mountain climbing on a high chair. Remind me never to take
you even to the top of the Thomas Jefferson Hotel."

"I will. So help me. Oh, ma Gawd, let me lie."

"What do you need?"

"What have you got?"

"Cigarets? Pennies for your eyes?"

"Hell, yes," Dawes Williams said. "Give me some."

Dawes felt better smoking the cigaret. Its smoke drifted out over the effort-less tracks. He took deep drags and watched.

"You're bleeding all over the damn thing," Barney said.

"I can't help it. I need a drink bad. I need a bandage."

"A drink?"

"I'd trade my left nut for one right now. Swear to God."

"Hell, why didn't you say so?"

From his pocket Barney pulled a pint of J. T. Brown Sunnycrow Bourbon with five or six shots still left in the bottom.

"Magic," Barney said pouring it down Dawes' throat.

"That's fantastic and beautiful," Dawes finally said. "You been holding out on me. I owe you. Where'd you get it?"

"Easy, Dawes. I lifted if off Travelin' Tommy and I don't even want your left nut."

"That's good. I need all I got."

"You can say that again."

"I think I can move now."

"Bet you can't."

"I'm going to try. How bad is it?"

"It's terrible. I never saw anything as bad as you."

"Tell me slow."

"Your forehead's open. Your cheek is open. Looks to me like both your knees and one of your elbows are gone."

"Wait'll you see my stomach," Dawes said.

"Don't want to. Don't want to see that at all."

"Just cut me a long stick," Dawes said, "and we'll walk to town."

Barney left for awhile and Dawes could hear him moving around in the woods. Finally he came back with a staff.

"Dawes," Barney said. "You still lyin' round all day on the trestle? You lazy sonofbitch, get up and get doing."

"Just lift me up easy and set me on my staff," Dawes Williams said. "I'm going to town."

"Bet you a pint you can't pull it."

"Pioneers!" Dawes Williams said.

"Buckeroos!" Barney Redwood said.

"Hell, yes," Dawes said, "you just don't want to carry me."

Then Barney lifted up Dawes slowly and set him on his staff. In the night as thin as an iron trestle they began picking their way to town. It would be great, Dawes thought, to come home at dawn, looking like a train wreck, and to sit back in the hallway laughing at your mother's fanatic fear of death. Already Barney was out on a country road, fifty yards in front of Dawes, who was busy noticing only it was slow going, laying your staff down with every step.

"Slow down, Barney," he said. "It hurts to look up, but I think it's an allegory."

Barney came back and began helping him stumble through the furrows. They came to a small stream, forded it, the water was cold, and helped, and Dawes stood in the middle for a long time. On the other side they came to the road and began walking it down. No cars moved, but they finally saw the thin lights of Galena, Illinois, rise over a field of grass. They turned left and cut over the field.

"Looks like good walkin'," Barney said.

"That's right," Dawes said. "I'm in heaven."

In the moonlit field Dawes could see his broken shadow moving before him. Barney's was straight, but his was bent double, crippled over the shadow of his staff like an old man with palsy. They came to the outskirts of Galena, streets of sleeping houses, a sign: WELCOME TO GALENA, ILLINOIS, THE HOME OF ULYSSES S. GRANT. Walking down a hill, within a narrow sidewalk hushed by the rush of cold, breathless trees, Barney finally spotted the neon sign of a roadhouse on the next corner. He went into The Black Rooster's Bar to buy a pint.

"I owe you one," he said, turning at the door. "You been just swell about this. You never cried once."

"Oh ya," Dawes Williams said. "What does that mean?"

"It means I owe you one."

"Thanks, Barney," Dawes said. "Why don't you make it a fifth?"

"Suure," Barney said. "If I die without ten cents in my jeans, I'll consider myself successful."

When Barney came out they began walking down the sidewalks full of blowing trees. Dawes thought the town was a beautiful place, full of the nineteenth century; it was quiet as a deserted sill. A canal of a river ran below the rise of parallel hills, along the line of old wooden jetties running the length of Main Street. Dawes and Barney stood on the wooden mooring of the freshwater docks, and then Barney opened the fifth. Drinking, they watched the smooth, inverted moon full of water move past, without effort or strain, perhaps not even drifting off south. Dawes felt suddenly something had broken off him, an old gate bowed inward to wind.

"You sure are bunged up, Dawes," Barney Redwood was saying. "In fact, looking at you makes a person feel almost whole."

In the stillness the wood houses, the cast yellow light, seemed to burrow up on hillsides across water like small spineless animals seeking safety in the heights, a new reach of shadowy sky. Barney drank from the fifth until his eyes watered; then he passed it over to Dawes.

"You want to catch the highway now, Dawes?" he said. "Start thumbin' back to Rapid Cedar?"

"I sure don't want to take the train," Dawes said.

"Might take all night. We better start."

"Hell no, Barney. Let's find this house of Ulysses S. Grant."

"Probably just some damn historical society of naked-minded little old ladies in shawls," Barney said. "They probably only get flushed while looking at pictures of dead men in the first place. That's all."

"No," Dawes said. "I think we ought to look into this."

"That's what I said, Dawes," Barney said. "I got all night. I don't give a damn."

They moved off and, finding the sign again, an arrow that led up a long hill, they turned off and entered the silence of the lawns. The hill rose over the river. They walked in dark streets, past the sleeping wood of houses, under the cold roof of the trees. The night wind was up somewhere, deep, tremendous, hiding behind the huge white outriders of the clouds, beyond them.

"Damn," Dawes said. "All I took trampin' was a jacket, six bucks and some cigarets. It's getting Jesus cold out here."

"You're rough and tumble you are, Dawes," Barney said.

They reached the top of the hill and Barney unscrewed the fifth. As he pulled on it, Dawes could see that houses like lighting in old lace rose and fell on both sides of the nested hill. At the end of the falling hill the fields began again, untouched by the single interruption of two ridges and a river. A bulge of leaves lay over like a house of its own. Crossing the street, Dawes saw a sign nailed to an oak. It said ULYSSES S. GRANT MUSEUM, and the tree was as naked and grained as walls.

"Com'on, Dawes," Barney said. "Let's look around."

"Hell, yea," Dawes Williams said. "Abandon all hope ye who enter here."

"You don't cool that stuff, Dawes," Barney said, "and I'm going to take to beating you with your own staff."

"You may be the devil all right," Dawes Williams said.

In the darkness they began circling U. S. Grant's house. On the sixth time round they began peering into the black windows. No lanterns cast up yellow shadows on the inside walls. The visionless depth cast back no distance, and on the seventh circle they gave it all up, drew off, found a spot under a peach tree, and began working seriously on the fifth. The whiskey was smooth and went down easily, but when Dawes began to pour some into his wounds, Barney began to complain:

"I didn't buy that whiskey to pour on the ground," he said.

"I'm only trying to sterilize myself," Dawes Williams said.

"You're making a damn fetish of it then," Barney said.

"I can't complain. At least you didn't buy your favorite, apricot brandy."

"Good stuff that. Real exotic."

"It's rotten," Dawes Williams said. "Can't stand it. It's only for dudes and genteel sipping after dinner. Don't you know that?"

"The hell," Barney said. "That's a lie. I drink two pints of that stuff every Saturday night to get drunk by. Fantastic."

"Hell," Dawes said. "That stuff isn't even antique."

Barney began looking over at Dawes in the moon; a mood crossed his face like the shadow of a branch; a thin, nervous laugh rose from his throat. They sat under the shade of Ulysses S. Grant's peach tree drinking quietly. The yard was close, heavy, drawn in around them with the cold shadows, the moons and hearts of early spring lilac and flying bees.

"Look at that house," Dawes Williams said. "It looks like an old man, sleeping in a wicker chair, covered with trees."

"Looks like the windows have ears all right," Barney said.

"I wonder what old U. S. thought," Dawes Williams said, "looking out on this lawn, walking about in those walls. Pacing with his whiskey glass. Waiting for a war."

Barney said nothing.

"I saw a picture of his wife once," Dawes said. "She was cross-eyed as a bird."

Barney said nothing. Then he said:

"It's old all right."

"I wonder if a place like that could ever be haunted by his ghost," Dawes said.

"It's mostly haunted all right," Barney said. "Probably by the ghosts of little old ladies' historical societies."

"These little old ladies happen to be moving this whole thing along," Dawes Williams said, "and only nobody but them knows it. You've got to be from out here to understand that."

"What are you talking about, Dawes?" Barney said.

"Well," Dawes said, "it would be nice knowing there's always another society of little old ladies just waiting to roar off and tend the weeds growing out of your grave once you're gone. Everybody seems to be working toward that."

"Is that what you're talking about, Dawes?"

"I'm talking about an old stone house," Dawes Williams said, but then he broke off short, distracted by something in the wind.

"Houses, countin' insides, are mostly made out of wood," Barney said, taking the fifth and drinking on it.

"That's true," Dawes said, taking the fifth back. "It is."

Then Barney said nothing again. The moon hung through the limbs of the clouds. The breezes moved through the flowers of the yard.

"I've got to hit the road for good someday soon," Dawes Williams said quietly, looking at Barney.

"Who doesn't?" Barney said. "But you'll never make it. I've watched you. I know how you think and what you can do."

"I will," Dawes said seriously. "My real name is Jackrabbit Davis and I'm still trying to live in a hole in the woods."

"Christ," Barney said, laughing, "'Jackrabbit Davis.' That's the funniest thing I ever heard in my life."

"I will," Dawes said. "You watch me."

"I can't," Barney said. "I'm going to be moving too fast."

"That's true," Dawes said. "You shouldn't need someone to watch you. Not if you're serious about a thing."

"Listen, Dawes," Barney said. "You're going to make a bigger C.P.A. than even your father was. Your name is Tom T. Town."

"That's not true," Dawes Williams said, passing the fifth, sitting there in only his blood. "I've got a feeling for time and place and for movement. I know I have."

"You need to tell yourself a lot of things to keep going at all, Dawes," Barney said.

"Christ, am I drunk," Dawes said.

"That's true," Barney said. "Innocence is a terrible thing."

"I think I've dreamed all of this up out of the air," Dawes said. "I think none of you ever existed at all. That this is all only a damn history in the first place."

"Dawes," Barney said, "this is not even damned."

"I'll bet that's so," Dawes said, draining the bottle, throwing it under a hedge. "Barney," he said, "this sure has been a zinger."

Then they began laughing, then fell silent for a long while and decided, looking at each other, that they were very drunk. Barney began doing cartwheels and headstands. He walked on his hands on the lawn. Dawes climbed Ulysses S. Grant's peach tree. Hanging by his knees from a limb, Dawes wrenched himself around toward Barney and said:

"Because you see, Barney, if Dawes Williams hadn't gotten mixed up with Huckleberry Finn somewhere along the way, he might have made it in life."

"I read that book," Barney said. "Which parts?"

"The floating parts, not the others," Dawes said. "Because reading Huckleberry Finn is like watching it rain on a time before you were born."

"Is that all, Dawes?"

"No. There's more."

"Let's have it, Dawes," Barney said. "I think I am ready to listen to that stuff of yours now."

"Good," Dawes Williams said. "Because I think I am ready to repeat it now."

"Can you remember it all?"

"I can. I have it memorized."

There was a silence, and Barney Redwood stood in the wood white of the moon watching Dawes Williams hanging down, swinging, remembering from his branch, from Ulyssess S. Grant's perfect piece of peach stone.

"Because whenever Dawes," Dawes Williams said, "stopped off at Sam Clemens' home in Hannibal, Missouri (he was ten and on the way south with his parents' structured wanderings), or within Abe Lincoln's home in Springfield, he was racked by impatience. . . ."

"Impatience?" Barney Redwood said.

"Yes," Dawes Williams said. "Impatience. He wanted immediately to leave. He wanted to be on his way. Unlike many children twice his age, who were merely impatient with the endless rooms full-up to bursting with curios of fine porcelain lace, old wood knockers and warming pans, who were merely anxious within the presence of a thousand omniscient ladies' aid societies, Dawes' impatience came from his growing awareness, there in those rooms, that the gray, lithographed, distended past was out to drive him mad."

"Drive him mad?" Barney said.

"Swallow him alive," Dawes Williams said. "Standing there—in those dry rooms full-up to bursting, in those hotels broken and overhung with the walking spirits, with the bones of more famous Mormons—he felt a need only to repress insanity. Like the coolness of lost water, he felt he was standing in the presence of an old stone house."

"An old stone house?" Barney said.

"It said 'Dawes,'" Dawes Williams said. "It was written on carved dead stone. It was hung in the wind like an old cracked gate at Arthur's farm. It was mad I tell you. . . ."

"Dawes," Barney said, "I think you better come down from that tree."

"I can't right now," Dawes said. "I am upside down."

"You also happen to be ass backwards to the wind," Barney said. "In fact, Dawes, I happen to know for a fact you could never cross the Mississippi River, going either way, without tears in your eyes."

"Hell, yes!" Dawes whispered. "Without loud lamentings and the gnashing of teeth. I tell you he was madder than a witch's eye turning suddenly upon you! Madder!"

"Listen, Dawes," Barney said, looking up in the moon, pacing the ground, "I think this is the end of childhood for you. Do you think this makes us queer or anything?"

"Hell, no," Dawes Williams said, bouncing down from his tree, doing a back flip in the air. "But then what do I know?"

"Maybe you're just drunk," Barney said. "Pass me the brew."

"Can't," Dawes said, "you drank it all."

"In that case then," Barney said, "let's go."

"All right," Dawes Williams said. "Anyway, as my old buddy Barney Red-wood would have said—Where's the damn dunking stool in this burg in the first place?"

"That's right, Dawes," Barney said. "We sit here here long enough, with you screaming into the trunk of this tree and me walking around under this Ulysses S. Grant's peach orchard, and you know damn well the burghers of this town'll find a stake to rope us from. Let's go before they come down here and chase us out with rocks and sticks."

Then Dawes congratulated Barney on a fine statement of poetic fact and they turned from the dark house. Walking through the thick underside of narrow air the trees were still leaving on a surface of antique, treelined pavement, the thin light and the wood wind, Dawes Williams and Barney Redwood moved out onto the highway and eventually hitched themselves home.

27

Dunker Nadlacek finished the third of his giant tenderloins. Sitting alone in his seven-thousand-dollar Ford, he spent two dollars and ten cents of the twenty dollars his mother had slipped him for dinner at the B & Q Root Beer stand. He ate the last of his onion rings, finished his second giant orange drink, and listened as the skinny girl carhop said:

"Nice car ya got here. Geez, kid, you eat here a lot, doncha?"

He turned on her with those hard and soft eyes of his and said only:

"Ya. You pick up on things fast, doncha?"

It was evening, and his thoughts turned to driving over and seeing what Dawes and Eddie and Travis were doing. He thought things were breaking up, spreading apart, because there seemed to be nothing at all to do that summer. Eddie was almost married; Travis was spending his time with a college girl in Iowa City; and Dawes Williams wasn't even talking to anybody. It all seemed pointless, stupid, as if everything he had known were trying to move beyond itself before it was even time. He thought they were all trying to act as if they had never even known one another to begin with. He thought Travis and Eddie and Dawes looked at him now as if they didn't even remember each other. . .

He steered his Ford out of the drive-in and headed west along Main Avenue. The evening, sky darkening, some rain clouds off to the north worried him slightly, but it drew in around him, welling, like the insides of a larger machine. He felt at the new Wham-O slingshots beside him on the seat and figured tonight, at least, he had something to do. He thought backwards to that very afternoon when, over a slow beer at the J Street Tavern, he had looked up at them all and said:

"I think I know of a way to get Cotter."

He thought of the way Travis Thomas had tensed forward in his chair; of the way Eddie had laughed out loud; and of the way Dawes Williams had groaned slightly and looked out of the window. He parked his car behind Dawes' house, bent his head six inches going through the back door, and entered the bright kitchen. He sprawled in a chair and looked abstractedly at Dawes and Simpson and Leone. Dawes looked at Dunker and knew he couldn't sit in a chair any other way. Dunker looked at Dawes and knew he was just holding another absurd conversation with his parents. Dawes looked back at Dunker and knew suddenly that Dunker, coming into a room, made you feel immediately that you were only playing Lilliputian games in a doll's house and had been doing so for years without ever noticing it. Then Dunker began looking around at the walls as if they were passing inspection. Sitting in the spare kitchen chair, Dunker then looked back at the table, eyed a plate of hard rolls and, reaching across the table without leaning, took a huge bite and bounced the roll back on its dish without batting an eye.

"Need a pail to spit that in, Dunker?" Dawes Williams said.

"Ya," Dunker said blankly. "Got one handy?"

Then Dunker excused Dawes from the table and led him out back. He opened the trunk of his seven-thousand-dollar Ford. Dawes was still thinking quietly of his mother, blanching noticeably at seeing a grown Ronnie Crown enter the kitchen, but finally Dunker drew his attention to a collection of six hundred or a thousand cherrybombs and M-80s lining the sills of the trunk. Taking some cotton balls and waddings from his pockets, Dunker said:

"God, is this beautiful. It's the best idea I've had on this since this afternoon."

"What is this?" Dawes Williams said. "Science again?"

"It's cotton balls and wadding," Dunker said.

"Cotton balls, cherrybombs and slingshots," Dawes said, "—it'll never work. It's aluminum and will never fly. About the time you try to get it off the ground, some old man with tears in his eyes will write into *The Rapid Cedar Republican* saying how they carved great oaks down to a stub of nothing but dust whittling out their first slingshot. He'll spoil it all for you and walk away claiming he could hit a squirrel with a rubber band and a rock at six hundred yards."

"That's a real fine speech, Dawes," Dunker said blankly, ignoring him, "but why didn't I think of it before? It's so simple. It's so damn final. I just don't know why I didn't think of it before this."

"What is it?" Dawes Williams said. "Does it have internal combustion?"

"Use your imagination, Dawes. Once I got the original idea, it only took me five minutes to perfect it."

As he said this, Dunker began intently twisting the cotton balls into long, compact strings that he dusted with clear nail polish until they were dense and rigid. White fluff drifted over the yard and Dunker bent over the trunk of his Ford like a mad scientist intent with invention.

"*Now,*" he said, not looking up, "what the hell have I got?"

"I don't know," Dawes said, "what have you got?"

"It's a fuse," Dunker said quietly, "a delayed-action fuse."

"Big deal," Dawes Williams said. "What has this to do with the avant-garde European cinema? I'm going in to finish dinner."

"You still don't get it, do you, Dawes?" Dunker said, looking him squarely in the eye. "You still just don't get it."

"Swell," Dawes said.

"No. Not swell. Exactly fifteen minutes to the three-inch. All's you have to do is glue them on, light'em, and fire'em over the roof."

"Slingshots!" Dawes said suddenly, recognizing the two aluminum Wham-Os lying uncoiled on the seat.

"Hell, yes, the Great Cotter Campaigns are ours."

"Hang on," Dawes said, "I'll get my jacket and we'll go get Travis and Eddie."

"Hell yes," Dunker said, "the war is ours."

28

The white sheet of water had moved in over the quarry. Dawes Williams was outside, running around a tree in the rain. The rest were inside Dunker's Ford, lost within glue pots and fixings, making the small bombs.

"That's six hundred and five fused and ready, Dawes!" Dunker called over the wind, from within the warm, hooded light of his Ford.

"We're not boring you, are we, Dawes?" Travis was saying.

"Come in out of the goddamn rain, Dawes!" Eddie screamed.

"Hell, no," Dawes Williams said. "I just never seemed to have been this wet!"

Dawes continued to run circles in an invisible circle of rain. Sheets of water were falling over the quarry. A tree broke off and fell behind him.

"What!?!" Dawes Williams said.

"I say, Dawes," Travis was saying, "are you crazy? You been running circles in the rain now for thirty minutes!"

"Atttttssssss Dawes," Eddie was saying from the lighted car.

"Go to hell!" Dawes Williams said.

"Dawes," Travis yelled, almost interested, over the larger reach of the wind, "what the hell you been thinking about out there in the rain for the last thirty minutes?"

"Screw you, Travis," Dawes said, beginning to retrack his own circles in the rain. "Just go to hell!"

"Thinking! Thinking hell!" he said. "I been thinking hell, Travis. I been thinking about Charles J. Chaplin. Charlie Chaplin, Travis! I been thinking about impersonators miming themselves mime themselves! About an endless succession of masks! What the hell do you think about that, Travis, you silly sonofabitch?"

Dunker leaned out the window and hooked another beer can into the quarry water:

"That's nineteen," he said quietly.

"What is this?" Travis said. "A baseball game?"

"P.S. Summer Letch to Dawes Williams," Dunker said, "P.S., hell. That was about the most half-assed P.S. I ever heard in my life."

"How'd you ever meet that space-head Summer Letch in the first place, Dawes?" Travis shouted from the window.

"You remember, Travis," Eddie was saying. "It was that night just after Dunker finished telling us how he lost his virginity."

"That was the night we had our first run-in with Cotter," Travis said. "That's what night it was."

"Quick," Dunker said, busily messing with his glue pot, "someone order Dawes Williams an EEG."

"This is a goddamn poem being conducted by the tuba player!!??!!" Dawes Williams screamed in the wind.

Then he continued running circles round himself. Dunker leaned out the window into the fast rain and threw him a beer. He thought the distance was a premonition, without a single light, and that the blowing leaf was only full of his own fear, full of his own panic like the supraterranean passing of dark, breathing fishes, things never seen.

Dawes Williams continued running patterns in the circles of broken rain.

"I just never," he said to the howl of the wind. "I just never have been this damn wet!"

"Com'on, God damn it, Dawes," Dunker was calling. "Come in out of the rain."

"That's twenty-two for me," Travis said, hooking another beer can from the window.

"Com'on, Dawes," Eddie was saying from the lighted car. "Tonight we get Cotter for good! Soon as she quits raining some!"

"No. Hell, no," Dawes Williams said.

"God damn it, Dawes," Travis and Dunker said together into the row of the water, the implosive wind, the furious quarry, "what the hell are you *doing* out there running in the rain?"

"I am about to give it all up," Dawes said. "I am making soliloquy. I'm making a damn soliloquy!"

"The hell you are," Eddie said. "You're making a damn ass of yourself is what you are damn doing."

"The hell with it," Dunker finally said. "I'm getting out and running in the damn rain with my buddy Dawes Williams."

Soon Dunker and Eddie and Travis and Dawes were all running round a tree of rain in the night. The moon was almost out again; the wind and water had slacked some. But Dawes thought the night, mad, deep, lost, going under, witch-strewn, was his only brother, an idiot, a dwarf. In the foreshortened distance of quarried rock he rustled the nightsounds, like a fine shirt of bells, a vest of rings and frills. Dawes thought he waved him home with a flick of his wrist. An elf, twisted in his own mirrors, cast out from his own house, his illusions of possessing a self, Dawes could see he wore another face. His wink, a jaded star, hung out to dry on the green roof of a flooded barn, recrossed itself without effort. He sailed over the moon. Taking his suitcase full of slingshots and explosive pumpkin balls, he was gone.

"You know," Dawes Williams said, still running around a tree, "whenever I think of how bad we are, I just think of all of the things we didn't do. We never robbed an old man in an alley who couldn't afford it. We never beat up on girls or old ladies. All in all, we're pretty damn straight."

"That's right," Travis said, "all American."

"Hell yes," Eddie said, "a bunch of half-assed straight arrows."

"The salt of the earth," Dunker said, "some real swell fellas."

"Yeomen all!" Dawes Williams screamed. "What is this, a damn romance?"

Then there was a silence. Eddie sprinted out for the fields; Travis dove under the water; and Dunker ran up the back of a small tree.

"She was human, wasn't she?" Dawes said suddenly.

"Hell, yes," Travis said, standing in the pond. "Let's have a little compassion for those doggy girls of Waterloo."

"For Christsake," Dunker said, drawing up on a rock.

"The flesh is weak," Dawes Williams said, breaking holes in the rain without leaving a trace.

"Dawes Williams is our conscience and light," Dunker said.

"Dawes Williams is a damn Methodist preacher come out of the woods," Eddie said.

"Expiation!" Dawes Williams began screaming. "Expiation! John Donne! John Donne!"

"What are you talking about, Dawes?" Travis said, stepping out of the pond.

"Who cares?" Eddie said.

"I care," Dawes said. "I care immensely."

"Dawes," Travis said, "why don't you just write a damn poem about all of this?"

"Fuck off, Travis," Dawes said. "I'll call it 'Growing up with Brother-Tom-the-Miller's-Son.'"

"Shut up, Travis," Dunker said, "and let Dawes here get on with this story of his."

"It's yours, too," Dawes said.

"The hell," Dunker said, "not mine. It's yours and nobody else's."

"It is," Dawes said.

"What the hell are you two assholes talking about now?" Eddie said.

"Go pee in the corn, Welsh," Dawes said.

"Hot shit! Hot shit!" Eddie said.

"Ca-caw ca-caw," Dawes said back, but Eddie had already taken off at the first ca-caw and was running back over the fields.

Soon Eddie and Dawes were rolling in the mud. Travis and Dunker were opening beers and watching. Eddie got five or six quick punches in and then Dawes got him down and sat on his head in the mud. Eddie was nearly drowning, but he managed to get out:

"Let me up, Dawes, and I'll kill you!"

"Doesn't follow," Dawes Williams said, continuing to sit on his head. "Non sequitur!"

"Christ," Travis said, lighting a small cigar in the rain, "this reminds me of Elkhard Lake."

"Rub some mud in his face, Dawes," Dunker said.

"Eddie can outpunch Dawes easy," Travis said.

"That's true," Dunker said, "but not while Dawes is sitting on his head."

"I'd pound you good, Dunker," Travis said, smiling, "but I'm resting now."

"That's true," Dunker said, smiling back, "it's just a good thing for me you're resting. Otherwise I might have to drop-kick your head."

Then there was another silence. The rain had slackened even more, and only a faint yellow haze of dead water could be heard running down the hills behind them. Getting up finally, Dawes turned his bloody face, his nose against Dunker and said:

"What the hell. This is all just phenomenon. Nothing we ever do comes out anywhere. This is all just another load of shit."

"Ya," Travis said, "but tonight we get Cotter like he's never been got."

"That's right," Dunker said. "We got no more time for the bastard. Tomorrow we are moving on."

"Whatever happened to Ratshit Rawlings?" Dawes said.

"There's a bulldozer sitting in his yard," Dunker said quietly, not even batting an eye, "that's all. I know. I put it there."

"Quit trying to be cute, Dawes," Travis said.

"Hell yes," Eddie said, "tomorrow we're going to college."

"Oh, my God," Dawes Williams said, standing dead up in the last of the rain, still wanting to run thin arabesques in the dead air turning its face toward September, "I think this moving-on crap could go on forever."

"The rain has let up now," Dunker said. "It's time to get our stuff together."

"Yep," Travis said slowly, chewing on a stick. "If it hadn't've been for Summer Letch, Dawes, you might have made it in life."

"'Ann Saunders Teen Gossip Tips' almost did it to me in the end all right," Dunker said.

"She did me in for sure," Dawes said. "She did me all in."

Then there was a long edge of laughter, a sleeping, drifting-off noise over the quarry. Looking up, Dawes could see that indeed the rain had stopped. It drizzled away in the dead fuses of the trees. The trees stood without effort and even the air lacked ambition. Dawes watched as Dunker and Eddie and Travis sat in the warm mud over the quarry throwing rocks into the water. The night, he thought, is now a unified fabric, seeking only chaos again, a broken inertia, a stone of stillness and plots.

"Yes," Dawes Williams said, "I wanted a lot from Summer Letch. But she didn't even know there was supposed to be a beginning. No one had told her."

"There's just a lot of real tough and stupid cunt in this town all right," Eddie said.

"Going to produce a lot of beauticians, nurses, housewives, and school-teachers in this town all right," Dunker said.

"Make their mothers real damn proud," Travis said.

"You hang around here," Dawes Williams said, "you can help one of them produce three or four more just like herself."

"I don't know," Travis said. "Maybe as you get older that's the way it's supposed to be."

"Attttsss Travis," Dawes said.

"She-it," Dunker said, "I hope not."

Then Dawes Williams climbed up on a small rock and said:

"I wish to propose a toast to the future possibility of genuine soft sexuality and gut sex existing somewhere in the universe."

"Hell yes," Eddie said, "to future fucks!"

"Hell yea," Dunker said. "I think Eddie here has a certain flair for words."

"I don't know," Travis was saying, "I suppose I drink to that. But it seems to me, Dawes, that that makes it not much of a story. I wouldn't have told it that way. Not me," he said.

"Seems to me you have left a hell of a lot out," Eddie said.

"Let Dawes have it whatever way he wants," Dunker said quietly, "nobody can change him now. Anyway, we're moving on tomorrow or so. What the hell," he said.

"Yes," Travis said, "but tonight we get Cotter."

"Yes," Dawes said, "I guess that's what it is we do now."

"Yes," Dunker said heavily, "I guess we just had too much wind in us for those doggy girls of Rapid Cedar who seem to only come complete with their mothers."

Then Dunker got up and headed for the car. In the west, out over the quarry, the sky was clear with a single moon that was waiting to pass beyond morning.

"What the hell," Dunker was saying, "who's for another beer? All this talking has made me nearly sober, for Christsake," he said slowly, laughing at himself, moving off.

"Yes," Eddie said, "and you know what I found out about Cotter, talking around the bars in Orion real quiet? For the last three years running Bronco Jim Cotter has been so loved by his neighbors they have elected him Emperor of the Rocky Mountain oyster fries."

"The what?" Dawes heard himself wonder out loud.

"The pig nuts!" Eddie said. "They save them up in big jars after the castrations and once a year they really fry up an orgy."

"By God!" Travis said. "I think you've got it."

"I wouldn't put it past them," Dunker said.

"Of course not," Travis said. "Any miserable bastard miserable enough to pull a shotgun on you is miserable enough easy to eat pig balls."

Dawes Williams stood off, listening to the high rolling laughter go off like smoke at the last stroke of Travis Thomas' voice. Then he watched as Eddie and Dunker and Travis drifted off from the water like the shadows of Indians moving up to the wagon and outrider of the car. Dunker began wiping himself off with a rag. Travis and Eddie used their hands like chamois to slide the thick mud down the sides of their arms and jeans. Finally, rain stopped, Dunker went back into the hooded light of his car and bent over his glue pot. Travis was bent into the thin electric light of the trunk, and there were only fifty more cherrybombs to glue.

"Pass me the pot, Eddie," Travis was saying.

Then in the darkness Travis emerged, like a hoodless inquisitor, and began warming up the thongs of the slingshots. Eddie was loading up the small cloth sack. Dawes thought, standing off in the distance, that Dunker was Machiavelli; that Travis was the boy David; that Dawes Williams was Lord Byron; and that Eddie, he and his sack were Santa Claus.

"I think in time," Travis was saying, "I could become one of the finest slingshot artists in history."

Dawes Williams began laughing uncontrollably.

"What's up, Dawes, old mother?" Travis said, not even looking around.

"In a pig's ass you're an artist, Travis," Dunker said, moving from his Ford. "Wait'll you see me fire them babies in there on the money."

"What's the plan?" Eddie said.

"Jus' gather round and listen to the voice of the old prophet," Dunker said, and then his voice drifted instinctively into a whisper. As everyone gathered round, Dunker bent into the end of his flashlight and continued:

"Well," he said, "you see, we sneak real low through the corn, in close to the road to about seventy-five or a hundred yards, and then we fire six hundred and thirty-five of these Dunker special, mother-loving, delayed-action babies in on him. He'll think the last wandering German suicide squad is out to burn up his tree. Oh, is that beautiful."

"Right in there on the money," Travis said, laughing quietly. "Hot damn."

"Hell yea," Dunker said, "about, as I figure it, two or three hundred on the roof, a few down the drain spouts, a couple hundred more on the porch, some lucky ones on the windowsills and then (oh, that's beautiful), then we just pull ourselves back into the high rocks and watch it go BANG!"

"Damn," Eddie said, "I wish we had another thousand M80s or so to lay in there behind them."

Then there was a long silence. Dawes could hear an epileptic stillness fill in behind him as the locust began again after the rain. Then Dunker rose up over the air of the quarry and yelled:

"BANG! BANG-BANG-MOTHER! SUPER-BANG-BANG! The old bastard'll think he's being raided by the Prussian militia."

"That's beautiful," Travis said slowly.

"That's beautiful," Eddie said slowly.

"I like it," Dawes Williams said. "It has a certain baroque symmetry. I haven't done anything this dramatic since old Ronnie Crown and I blew up Mrs. Lowbus' horse barn at the age of seven."

"Shut up, Dawes," Dunker said.

"If there's one thing I hate, Dawes," Travis said, turning almost cold, "it's a hypocrite. If you choose to be in this, you're in. The rest of it doesn't matter much at all."

"Okay, Trav," Dawes Williams said, stringing out with the rest of them to the edge of the field, "anything you say."

Then, suddenly, actually none of the rest of it did matter as they were low in the corn. Eddie was dragging the sack; Travis and Dunker were loosening the thongs in the wind; and Dawes had three cigars lit in his mouth for punk. The ground was still deep with a soft wetness against him, and they were crawling through the broken grass of Cotter's dead field. The car was stashed in the quarry behind them. The rock rose like a sheet of pale gray sea. There were forced, destroyed whispers in the grass around him. Dawes could see Dunker and Eddie had stopped to finish a beer in the patches of the August mooncorn, but he and Travis were crawling in the rich, black-smelling manure furrows. Finally Dunker and Eddie were moving again, but Dunker was cursing because he had forgotten his pellet gun, and it was then, suddenly, as Dunker was cursing, that Dawes Williams could first hear (he had only thought he heard it before) a lone bitch also moving somewhere up in the white pond of the quarry rock. He heard the hound; the low sad mourning of her howl was somewhere behind him. He crossed a fence, and Dunker was cursing again because this time he had forgotten his wire cutters, and the perfection of it was once again marred.

"Crawl, you mother," Dunker was saying.

"That's absurd," Dawes Williams said. "It must be seven hundred yards to that house, that road; he couldn't see us with field glasses."

"Crawl, you mother," Dunker was saying.

But Dawes didn't crawl; instead he rolled over and lay listening to the slightly wet, sharp-leafed corn, to the black bitch drink again from the signless white pond. She raised her head and turned. Dawes heard the dog, crying for rain, cross the low blue Iowa fields, realizing then, at that moment, that he was already outgrowing it at the instant he was even doing it; that the time in his life meant for dumping Mrs. Lowbus' swing over the side of her porch was already over, dead, gone into the ground. He was slightly angered by it (and Dunker was cursing again, crawling again into the dense corn on the other side, this time because he had just remembered he had forgotten the skyrockets and Roman candles left behind in his garage) and suddenly, for the first time again, Dawes thought he knew, knew as he knew wood was hard, why it was they had always been cursing when it, all of it, grew quiet, dead at the core.

The slow swing of the rain-drenched moon hung over.

Dawes could see they had managed to crawl through to the other edge, the outer side of the field. Dunker and Travis, knee-bent against the last row of corn, were already woven within the taut, going-slack, going-taut snaps of the rubber thongs coming alive in the wind. They were calling for lights with their hands, and Eddie and Dawes were slumped low in a black furrow lighting two more cigars apiece for punk, working mechanically with the sound of the throngs. The high, dim, flaring parabolas extended themselves, became dark again in the yard. The fire went into silence, waited to be rearisen, and they made thin crackling noises against the house. Dawes could see they burned thin tails of black wind behind them, dissolved, and died in an almost horrible silence, the soft end of a fuse. . . .

Turning, he could see the hound was moving again on the rock of the quarry, a stone of escape.

Not quite daring to look backward, Dawes began the slow belly-flat, snaking movement back into the field. Around him he could hear Dunker and Eddie and Travis moving with him in the same direction. For once, he thought, they were together in the black-smelling hang of the earth. He thought they had never been this wet, this free, this loose in the night. He could feel them hanging together, whispering, laughing, walking back across the field on their arms, wanting to rise up and break and run; wanting to feel the wet stalks split before him, them, headlong, and blind, and inside a small furious curl of darkness; wanting chaos, to see the fence come up fast, to see that flat wire broaden out with a sudden vision, against the pale back rib of rock. Wanting later to be able to talk for weeks on who it was that hurdled it best of all. On who it was had caught their crotch on the wire.

He wanted more than that the opportunity to lie quiet, withdrawn from the road, to watch it happen; to lie listening on the warm density in the middle of the field for the sound of the buckshot to rise over the wind, the top of the corn, like a thin falling rain. And, lying there, motion stopped for awhile, Dawes thought he could remember Cotter, two years before. He thought he could remember himself, clanking the cheap old car into low, flooring the engine knocking quietly against the sides of the fender wells, spinning the whole mess like a tailing string on the wide patch of dogsummer dust in front of the barn. And Cotter had stood there, behind the porch's cracking pillars, bulky and raw-muscled, young even, like some Old Testament Jehovah in red and natty polka-dot pajamas, complete with shotgun, staring past the mute post with a kind of subfascination, saying strangely nothing. Then there had only been Eddie leaning from the window, the small rise of the gun from the dark porch, the first shot fired in the Great Cotter Wars, two years before, and now there was only that same thickly failing light hung from the barn, and Eddie and Dunker and Travis, who were crawling off, low to the ground, breathing, escaping around him.

And so, deep in their own effect, Dawes watched them, all around him, crouch behind cornstalks in the middle of a field, waiting. They were lying listening for the four or five hundred-odd explosions (or perhaps, if Dunker was good enough, the one, cataclysmic, all-encompassing BANG), the startled shouts, the sudden lights, the aroused dogs tied to the end of the long ropes to group up howling near the house. Off, in the road, a man's voice came from a stopped car near the ditch, saying:

"Beth. There is somebody in Cotter's field. Listen, damn ya. There is. There's small fires burning all over his yard!"

"Dunker! Dunker!" Eddie was whispering, trapped in the corn. "How many'd you and Travis get in?"

"About five hundred," Dunker said crawling in the stalks.

"Oh my God," Travis said, breathless, "that's beautiful. What about the other hundred and thirty?"

"Don't worry, Travis," Dawes said, "I lit one and stuck a book of matches in the sack."

"Dawes," Travis said, "I love ya. That may be one of the more reasonable things you've ever done." .

"Thanks, Trav," Dawes Williams said, snaking back over the ground.

Then, halfway out, they paused and turned back to the road. The black fish of the man's car was stopped, idling quietly, piercing the gloom and looking for sounds. Dawes Williams lay out in a visionless flatness, lighting a smoke, almost relaxing, thinking only: Yes, by God, we've got them now. Them. This time for sure. They're out here playing our game. We're all out here having a hell of a time. It's a child's game. And we're all tin soldiers, turning on our heels, skipping ropes and obsessed by the stone of the rhythm. What are we thinking? What will happen? Yes, we are all rituals, recurring shadows, myths, mirrors of ourselves, and we are trapped, turning only in a stone of silence. . . .

As he was thinking this it began.

He thought it was almost unexpected. The small explosions began going off in the yard. The small explosions were followed by land-hung thunder. The cherrybombs bloomed in quick bursts, ones, twos, even fours and then fives, growing finally into tens and then dozens. They seemed to him to be aerial bombs going off without even the nuance of falling. He lay with the others, in the exact middle of a field, chewing on a corn leaf, admiring his handiwork. He watched it grow large and horrible as birth, as contained as a herd of maddened whales blowing up steam in a creek. He thought they had just managed to blow up the world.

Then the dogs began. They made the night a house exploding without sequence in the wind.

"Hey, Dunker," Travis had said in the whispering ditch. "Let's lay us in a dozen or two in that tree."

"Hell yea, pardner," Dunker had said. "Then let's cover his roof."

And turning, Dawes could see flashes from the porch, the roof. The ends of the trees broke open with small fires. The dogs were going wild within the damp shadow of the house.

Then the sack went off in the ditch with a single explosion loud enough to fold a forest of wood. A light went on in the porch. The door opened hesitantly.

The man, Cotter, robed and gray-haired, stood in a hood of light. He looked through the screen, seeing only stillness, dead wind. Dawes Williams could hear the bitch as she spoke once again in the distance, miles away and homing.

Cotter then came onto the porch slowly, as if it would give with his weight. He tested his step. He was a cat on water, trying to walk it, Dawes thought. Slowly he tested the stillness to see if it had flaws. The woman in the parked car was the only sound. Her voice died away into controllable gushing sobs, into pieces of flotsam moving away. The other man, walking quickly up and down in the ditch, was moving fatalistically, as if he were about to step on a land mine. He was confused. Moving his flashlight through the weeds, finally he settled on the porch and, in the faint yellow dark, Cotter could be seen moving his gun on the wooden railing. Suddenly he was in motion, waving it, black as sticks, saying only: "IN THE NAME OF GOD!"

His gun banged itself on the wood, became a quickly rapped gavel, sharp as his movement.

"WHO IS DOWN MY DITCH?" he said.

The reply was small, even birdlike:

"Me. Why it's ME, Cotter," it said.

"Who the hell is 'me'?"

"ME. Ed Vegans. Don't shoot ME, Cotter."

"That so?" Cotter said slowly.

"Hell, yes," Vegans said. "There's somebody suspicious in your fields, though. Not ME, Cotter. I heard them setting the dynamite. Wasn't ME, Cotter."

"Christ," Travis was whispering in the corn. "This is priceless."

Dawes Williams said nothing. He was too busy, across the field, watching Cotter on the porch. He thought Cotter was somehow almost human. He thought this was ironic; that now, at the last moment, was when it had become clear that Cotter was capable of being understood, pitied, loved or at least tolerated, there on that porch.

"In the field, in the FIELD," Ed Vegans began screaming.

"What?" Cotter said, almost absentmindedly.

Then Dawes began watching the way it was hooked, suspended. Dawes Williams thought a truce had broken out. He thought this, that is, until he saw Dunker motion for Eddie's cigaret, the thing needed to light the last, nonfused M80 cocked in the slingshot poised and strung tautly against his ear. Eddie didn't even have to be told to light that one; that last, nondelayed M80 that Dunker had saved in his pocket like an egg for emergency; that seemed, now, even rising, to rise even faster than Dunker's own rising. "GOD IN HEAVEN," Dunker was saying, almost running from it, its immensity, into opposite directions, "DID YOU SEE THAT SHOT!!??!! TWO-HUNDRED AND FIFTY YARDS," he was screaming, "AND DEAD AS A CATBIRD'S EYE! NOWHERE IN THE HISTORY OF MAN HAS THERE BEEN A SHOT LIKE THAT!" rising, burning at the end, and rising, and then, just as suddenly, Dawes Williams turned back, and Cotter became aware of its coming. He saw its descent.

It fell like a wet seed.

Turning, they saw Cotter begin to scream something and they stopped to watch his old form become suddenly young as he sprang, like a cat, caught in that last moment of suspended disbelief, rolling itself over at that last, impossible instant before hitting the ground. Yes, Dawes Williams thought, Yes, Yes, as he turned to watch the last, unnecessary M80 blow itself, Cotter, and a large hole inward through the screen.

Everything was then in motion. Finally, Cotter was pacing the flooring, Dawes, Eddie, Dunker and Travis were climbing up over the edge of the slipping quarry, and Ed Vegans was screaming:

"In the quarry, Cotter, in the rocks in the QUARRY, Cotter! See'em, Cotter, see'em in the rocks in the QUARRY, Cotter?"

"Yes. Yes. I'll get my pants."

"HELL, no, Cotter. Get your damn car going. Go SOUTH, Cotter. I'll go NORTH, Cotter, and we'll sandwich'em in. It's ME, Cotter, Ed Vegans. They're in the QUARRY. I see'em. GO SOUTH, Cotter."

"Yes. Anything. But Key-rist, Vegans, shut up for awhile."

"Okay, Cotter, but I just thought you'd be interested to know who it was fixing to dynamite your house, Cotter, I just thought. . ."

"Yes. Yes. But shut up for awhile, Vegans."

"You GOING, Cotter? You going after'em?"

"Yes. Yes. You hurry up and I'll meet you coming south."

"Okay, Cotter, I just thought you'd be. . ."

"Jesus," Cotter said, slamming the screen behind himself, "I'll go in my pajamas."

Dawes Williams, rising up over the edge of the cold rock wall, could hear it all. Only he had paused to listen to the quietly hysterical woman become openly hysterical. Her siren of wailing was a solo, slowly asserting itself, rising over the road, the stopped night, counterpointing the men, commanding final attention, dying into memory already as the others were diving over the sides of Dunker's convertible, were sitting on the inside like three cigar-store Indians going to town, listening to the engine, large and powerful and personally customized by Dunker's mechanical mind and, of course, also not wanting to start and therefore going AAAArrrraRRRRrrrrrrarraaaarrrrr into the otherwise sleeping dark.

"Good car, Dunker," Travis was saying, taking a cigaret slowly from his pocket and lighting it. "Where'd you get this hunk of junk in the first place?"

"It'll start. It'll start," Dunker said.

"Leave it," Eddie said.

"It'll start. It's been out in the rain is all."

"Hide it," Travis said.

"It'll start. These damn cars."

"Take the license plates off and burn it," Eddie said.

"It'll start. It loves her Dunker, doncha baby?"

"Sell it to that dummy named Vegans," Travis said, ignoring the fact that they were stopped dead in a rut with the militia behind. "He'll be happenin' by soon."

"It'll start. It'll start. I love this car."

"Give it to a passing cowboy," Travis said, drawing effortlessly on his cigaret, "and let him explain it."

"Give it to Dawes Williams," Eddie said.

"Dawes?" Travis said. "Do you mind stepping in here? We're making our getaway just now."

"I *love* this car," Dunker said. "She never fails me."

"AAAArrrraRRRRRRRrrrrrrrrarraaaarrrrr," Dawes Williams said.

"I *love* this car," Dunker said, kicking out the radio.

"Listen, Dunker," Travis said nonchalantly, blowing smoke to the blue ring of hills beyond him, "I'll give you four bucks and some beads for this car. Naturally, of course, I'll take all the responsibility of ownership on delivery. Right here on the spot, pardner. You can just wander off into the hills and lead a simple life and never sweat it again."

"I love this car and she loves me," Dunker said. "It'll start." There was a pause. "YOU-GODDAMN-MOTHERLESS-SONOFABITCH-DOUCHE-BAG-INGRATE!!!????!!!!!" Dunker said, beating the dashboard in with his fists, kicking off the heater vent.

"PUSH IT!" Eddie said.

"That's right," Travis said to the obvious. "I wondered how long it would take you to figure that out."

"AAAArrrraRRRRRRRrrrrrrarraaaarrrr," Dawes Williams said.

"I'm going to kill Dawes Williams one of these days," Travis said. "Where is he?"

"I'm pushing this car," Dawes Williams said, "and I could use some help."

"Shut up, Dawes," Travis said, getting from the car. "Nobody likes a wise-ass at times like this."

But Dawes was paying no attention. He was only pushing furiously at the rear of the car. He was becoming a fan of the theatrical, cliff-hanging moment, and he knew that the idea of pushing it had only been misplaced in a brilliant, hyperbolic interlude. Soon Eddie and Travis were out in the dark beside him. Dunker was steering the car.

"All right," Dunker was saying. "Push this car."

There was one last small hill, and they were pushing with those piston-like legs, down the slope, when it all finally ignited, exploded with a mild stop and then went running wildly, valves ticking, up the quarry road. Eddie and Travis were already over the back seat, and laughing, on the floor, while Dawes reached for the bumper, finally catching it and, as he was being pulled over the wet sand as if in winter, behind a bus on ice, he heard Travis say:

"Awwwwww for Christsake, Dawes, this is no time to fuck around."

Then he was running even harder, still connected to the machine, feeling spastic, a puppet, and all of it was happening too quickly for it to occur to Dunker that it would have been easier to stop the car in the first place; too quickly, and as Dawes was noticing it all resolving itself into an irresolvable problem in pure physics, Eddie, who was being held by Travis, leaned over the end of the trunk to pull him in like a large hairless tuna; a sailor come home from the winedock sea.

Then they drove down the road like a defenseless timber stand meant for destruction. Dunker exploded small bushes, saplings, trees, everywhere. Everyone was in and watching for lights coming from the other direction. Somewhere to the north was Ed Vegans and his screaming woman; somewhere to the south was R. G. Cotter, RR 7, seen on a mailbox once in passing. After the rains the night was clear and heavy with stars, and Dunker was driving well enough, shifting down and power-drifting the corners. The engine was warm and welled up around them.

"This car is mother, I tell you," Dunker was saying, steering the Ford through the closing dark with his hooded lights.

Eddie was opening four beers on the floor. The road was really a one-way lane, a truck route meant only to service the quarry, and therefore leading into and out of it without a single turnoff. The bilateral rut of the road, like train tracks, ran deterministically past scrub thin woods and an occasional open field. At the crossroads, three miles up, Ed Vegans would be waiting with his hysterical woman. Through a common concentration Dunker was saying:

"I love this car. I knew she'd start. She never fails her Dunker. What do we do next?"

"Maybe try it over a field," Eddie was already saying.

"That's great as hell, Eddie," Travis said. "I love that. We could get ourselves nicely hung up in six foot of mud, maybe lance Dunker's Ford here to a small tree, and then we could just sort of dance around the car until they came to take us away."

"We could let Dawes lead us in song," Eddie said.

"You guys could take off. I could take it alone," Dunker said.

"Martyr," Dawes Williams said.

"Hell, yes, whatever, we'll do it together," Travis said.

"Ya, Dunker," Dawes said. "You big heroic goof."

"Attttssss Dawes," Dunker said weakly.

"AAAArrrraRRRRRRrrrrrrarraaarrrr," Dawes Williams said.

"Shut up, Dawes," Travis said. "I'm thinking."

"If this Ed Vegans is waiting," Eddie said, "let's just nonchalantly stop and bust his ass."

"Splendid," Travis said. "We could run a hundred bucks and a few Saturdays picking up the city park into reform school."

"Wouldn't be so bad," Dunker said. "Maybe Dawes could make first string playing for some nice old Catholic priest bastard there."

"Hell, I've got to go to college," Travis said. "How'd I ever let you guys talk me into this in the first place?"

Everyone began looking at Travis Thomas strangely. Then Travis Thomas began looking at himself.

"Ya," he said. "So what?"

"First," Dawes Williams said, "Atttttssss Eddie. Second—Atttttssss Travis. Third—Attttssss Dunker."

"Attttssss Dawes," they all answered.

"Maybe find a tractor lane," Eddie said, "and pull off until they go by."

"That's just great. Splendid," Travis said. "I love that. That's great. We could wait quietly for six or seven hours and then a million cops would come, and cuff us, and haul us away."

"Hell," Eddie said, "Dawes Williams could lead us in dance."

"Well," Dawes said, "we could give ourselves up and be sorry a lot. Tell'em we really didn't mean it. We could be real polite and then, at the right moment, break down crying all over the bastards."

"Shut up, Dawes," Travis said. "I'm thinking."

"What the hell," Eddie said. "Who *gives* a rusty fuck?"

"Dawes' mother's bridge club does," Dunker said. "They're the ones who give a rusty fuck about things like this. Hell," he said, laughing, "they'd never forgive Mrs. Williams if Dawes here got himself caught for a thing like this."

"That's true," Dawes said. "Besides, after I got thrown in jail last summer they put her on probation."

There was a huge laughter.

"By God, Dawes," Travis finally said, "you'd never be asked down to the parlor for cookies again."

"Never for sure," Dunker said. "It's hellish."

"What the hell," Travis said. "No balls, no babies."

"That's what we like to hear at times like this, Travis, is some of that tough talk," Dawes said. "Just like Bogart movies. What does it mean?"

"It means," Travis said, "that we are going through."

"Hell, yea," Eddie said.

Then there was a silence, and Dunker hit his lights just before the last curve leading into the last straight stretch. Travis flipped the top into place, and they began locking it and the doors into place and rolling up the windows.

"Hell of a nice car you had here, Dunker," Travis said. "I always wanted to own it. I always did admire this car."

"Shut up," Dunker said.

"Take the right ditch," Dawes said. "He'll be facing left."

"That's great, Dawes," Travis said. "Why don't you think straight like that more often? That's very good, unless he's taken the trouble to turn around, in which case it's horseshit. Just look before you dive in there, Dunker. The best of both possible worlds. Straight?"

"Real straight, Tray," Dunker said, looking sideways without moving his head.

"Hell, yea, hot damn," Eddie said, "let's do it do it."

"Attttttssss Eddie," they all said.

"I just hope we ain't breathed our last Attttsss," Dawes said.

"Attttssss Dawes," they all said.

Then, in the pale light, they could see Ed Vegans' car braced broadside against the opening of the lane. Travis tensed against the dashboard, gripping the metal frames supporting the canvas top. Bracing his feet against the flooring, bulging the seat backwards as if he would pop out the seams, he seemed to Dawes strangely stronger than the car in the darkness.

"Travis," Eddie said, laughing, "you sweet sack of shit, you're in the old death seat."

"Hell, yes," Dawes said, "ripping through the goddamn ditch. Death and destruction. Rocks and gravel. Let's damn do it, Travis."

"Shut the hell up," Travis said.

"Man, I've got to hit that ditch hard enough to come out, Travis," Dunker said.

Silence.

"Let's think a little, Travis," Dawes said.

"Wait!" Travis said. "Turn those motherless lights on, Dunker. Pull up short."

"What?" Dunker said.

"About ten yards short," Travis says. "Hit it again as soon as I've got him moving. Dawes, we'll flip the top back down and you get ready to hang over and cover the back plate when we're by him."

"What is this," Dawes said, "a Jerry Lewis movie?"

"What the hell, Travis," Dunker said, "I don't . . ."

"DO IT, DAMN IT!" Travis said.

Dunker pulled up short. Then Travis, hanging from the window, began to scream at Ed Vegans:

"Quick!" he said. "Hey jack, quick!"

"What?" Ed Vegans said.

"Move it, pardner," Travis said. "They've got us trapped, I think. They'll kill us this time! Those hoody bastards back there are NUTS, I tell ya!"

"What?" Ed Vegans said.

"OOOOOOOOOOOOOOOOOOOOOOAOOOOOOOOOOOOOOOOOOOO," the woman said.

"What!!!??!?!!!" Travis said. "How can you stand there and say 'what' at a time like this?"

"What?" Ed Vegans said, not catching on quick.

"Twenty," Travis said, "count'em, TWENTY I sure as hell counted them."

"That's right," Dawes Williams said, catching on quick, "TWENTY!"

"That's all right, *Dayton,*" Travis said dramatically. "I believe I can make this man understand before it's too late."

"Oh, I hope so," Dawes said, sobbing in the back seat.

"What's this?" Ed Vegans was saying.

"TWENTY!" Travis said. "There's at least twenty hoody bastards back there with bats and cycles and chains. They jumped us while we were swimming in the quarry. Took our clothes and beat *hell* out of us, I tell ya!"

"Ooooooooooooooooooooaoooooooooooooooo," the woman said.

"We're naked!" Dunker said. "Naked as a catbird's eye! What do we have to do," he said, as Eddie was already half-stripped, "PROVE IT TO YOU!?"

"What's this?" Ed Vegans said.

Then Eddie jumped naked over the side of the car. Standing nude as stone in the pencil-thin light coming from Ed Vegans' flashlight, Eddie was complaining to Dawes out of the side of his mouth how cold his balls were becoming.

"Let's just bust this idiot's ass," Eddie was saying.

"Aaaaaaaaaaaaa," the woman was saying. "Oh Ed, oh Ed, please make them go away."

"Well," Ed Vegans said.

"Lemme go over this again with you," Travis was saying. "Jumped us at the old swimming hole. Bats, chains and bombs . . ."

Then, suddenly, looking over his shoulder, Dawes could see the dim glare of Cotter's lights as they rose over the two-mile hills, dusky, full of dark, still two miles off but coming. . . .

"DAMN IT," Dawes Williams said, "THEY SAID THEY WERE LOOKING FOR A WOMAN. WE DIDN'T HAVE ONE SO THEY HEADED OFF TOWARD A FARM HOUSE. . ."

There was a dead, ringing silence from the woman for the first time. Dawes could see the lights of Cotter's car break over the last hill, homing.

"THERE THEY ARE!!!!!" Dawes Williams said.

"Well. . . I guess if. . ." Ed Vegans was saying.

"Move it, Vegans," the woman said, ending it, "or I'll call you a dumb bastard until the day I die."

Her voice, Dawes Williams noted flying by, had been strangely resolved and even calm. And Vegans had stepped backwards on some vague mechanism of a pedal, not having time once he had started it ever to reconsider it again, because, Eddie jumping in, Dunker had started with his first motion and had timed it perfectly, sliding already through the small gap, hitting his lights, the engine revving already like a thunderclap through first gear as Cotter's lights became visible over the last stretch behind them. All of this, Travis flipping the top with one motion, and Dawes Williams was already hanging over the lid of the trunk, draping his shirt over the rear license plate, calling for Eddie (who was, of course, too busy lobbing a lit cherrybomb into Ed Vegans' stupefied car even to pay any attention or answer) to please grab his goddamn ankles. . .

But, already, they were moving down the pike at eighty miles an hour. Dunker was winding the high rap of the car into third, and Cotter was directly behind. Dawes was lying out flat with the slope of the trunk lid, at ease, at peace again, because he thought he was riding a hell of a high machine. Eddie was leaning over him to fire beer bottles and rags back at Cotter and the road behind them.

"Fireball Roberts," Travis was saying in the front seat, laughing at Dunker, laughing at them all. "Fireball Roberts went over the south wall."

"How fast are we going? Damn," Dawes screamed over the wind.

"'Bout ninety-five," Travis answered over the noise.

"Leave your shirt over the plate and come on in now, Dawes," Dunker yelled.

"Hell, no," Dawes Williams said. "I live out here! But how about do you suppose grabbing my goddamn ankles now?"

"Sure, Dawes," Travis said. "Anything for a goddamn buddy."

Then Eddie tied onto Dawes Williams with a short length of rope, stringing him out to the drifting air of the trunk like a balloon. Underneath, Dunker's mufflers wafted out like individual rhythmic bombs; like exploding metal walls.

"You're not even losing him!" Travis was screaming.

"Curves, too many," Dunker said, downshifting. "Wait'll we hit highway 30. Then I'm flat out. I'm sailing this bastard straight over the Mississippi River."

Then their voices died off, went too low, and Dawes couldn't hear them for awhile. He felt perfectly alone. Reversing his neck, Dawes, a still-water crane turning quietly in furious water, could see Cotter's headlights immediately behind him. Eddie and Travis, even Dunker, who was driving, were slumped low in their seats. Two graveled dust clouds ran back from the Ford, making separate gray funnels that fused on the green hood of Cotter's car.

"One thing about you, Dawes," Travis said, laughing coolly in the front seat, "you may have your head stuck in a hole in terms of the future, but you sure know where you have been."

"HOTDAMNFORBRONCODICKHYOOTDAWESWHORIDESTONIGHT!" screamed Dawes, without looking behind him into accelerating spaces.

Trees, pieces of roadway rolled past him like the back of a train. He saw, as one might have expected, that the wheels roared more loudly against the road when one was outside of the car. Also, he knew riding inside the car at ninety miles an hour was nothing compared to riding outside of the car. Lying out, nearly parallel with the road, almost relaxing, he watched the gray funnels of wheel tracings spin patterns, transient arabesques without lasting structures, in Cotter's lights. He could see the concrete lines blur, merge, move past and fuse into the sound of children dragging sticks across a regular surface of boards; could see them become high-speed fence posts in Cotter's whirl. Watching horizontals become verticals, then perpendiculars, ultimately rising to interfere and intersect their own parallels, he thought if he could not have damn God, at least he could have space and geometry, function and cosine, password and physical law knocking at a sleazy door of night. Whoooooopppppppeeeeee, he thought, HotDamnForBroncoHyootBillyDickDawesAndJackrabbitDavisWho-RidesTonightInAHoleInTheWoods.

He knew the road drifted down to the river. In the front, behind him, he knew others were talking, moving off in the same direction only because they were in the same car, the same hooded container of dark. He wished to drive into the trees, the soft, leaf-hung rinse of the air, until the engine stopped. He noticed that when Dunker downshifted the car, he braced himself naturally, gracefully against it; that if they were going right, Eddie pulled on his left foot; that if they were going left, Travis pulled on his right foot; that no matter if they were going forward or sideways, he was reversed. And always Cotter and his miraculous lights stayed close, through the gravel roads, the sleeping country, through the stretches of county black top, through even the quick corners on the tired edge of Rapid Cedar heading onto the ten-mile stretch of hill and creek road curving back onto the flats, where they sailed into Vales, Iowa, population three hundred and six, some corn traces and sleeping goats, and where Dunker shifted finally into third again, accelerating through the four or five hundred yards of Main Street, tired wood houses, accelerating, reaching already for the long, flat stretch of Highway 30 lying out all the way, sixty miles, to the Mississippi already streaked with morning. . . .

"Kick it, Dunker," Travis was saying, almost pressed, looking behind.

Cotter was still behind. He looked to Dawes—still lying out, almost bored now, studying the pavement—to be only fading slightly. It looked as if his effort had only faded four or five hundred yards in half an hour.

"It's kicked," Dunker was saying. "Flat out. I can't understand it. It's only a hundred and twenty-five. I'm writing a letter to Henry Ford."

"Let's just stop and bust his ass all over this part of the state," Eddie was saying.

"No," Travis said. "He's got nothing. We're clean as air. There's a lot of Ford convertibles around. Hell, I figure even at the rate we're losing him, we'll be five miles ahead by the time we hit the river."

"That's right," Dunker was saying. "We'll drive straight into Illinois and double back by another road."

"Keep your lousy head down, Dawes," Eddie said finally, "and don't let'em catch a good look at you."

But Dawes knew he didn't need any encouragement, that he was only studying the pavement anyway. It was blowing too hard to talk back into the wind, now, too hard, so he ignored them. Dunker's machine seemed to be wanting only to fly apart, to explode. It seemed to boom out behind him like a single thundering bomb. He thought that it screamed for destruction. And it was somehow right, he thought, that he was outside of the car, flying in his own mind, somewhere beyond them.

The car's whine got higher and higher, reaching out like a stringed instrument, an overtight fiddle, playing beyond itself, above its own head. It was almost light. Morning was a big truck, a recessive sound, winging in the other direction. First light was a racetrack of noise. Dawes Williams lay out on the trunk of Dunker's Ford and dreamed of crossing the river at dawn.

"Hang on, Dawes!" Eddie was screaming.

"Hey, Eddie," Dunker was saying, even though Cotter was receding in the distances, "find some more beer bottles back there and throw them at Cotter."

"Cotter is fading," Travis said.

"Can't anyway," Eddie said. "I've got ahold of Dawes Williams here and can't let go."

"Christ," Travis, his buddy, was saying, "throw that crazy sonofabitch Dawes Williams out and see if he bounces."

"I'd bounce," Dawes finally screamed back to the wind. "I'd bounce! Hell, yes, I'd bounce bigger'n hell!"

"What do you know," Dunker said, looking back, smiling, "Dawes Williams is flesh after all."

"That's right," Dawes said. "I am. I'm having a hell of a time."

"That's right," Travis said. "Keep it up. Don't you ever die, Dawes, we're too handsome for that."

Then there was high, rolling laughter again, ten miles out from the Mississippi. When Dunker was driving very fast, he was very safe, forward, intent, skillful and concentrating. It was when he was driving slow that he was dangerous, staring into the back seat, holding conversations for seconds on end, not wanting to be left out of anything. Turning, Dawes could see morning, first river light, breaking over the spines of the hills. God, he thought, it's grand because after you are velocitized, hanging on with mechanical chaps, it doesn't bother you any more. He thought he was riding a split wing, a stone chariot, dead silence, a horse-drawn casket of sun hauling velvet, neon signs to a black, unseen world below. The engine was welling below, and he thought he remembered how Dawes, lost always in his dreams of balance and eventual harmony, would stare at things, at anything, even the flooring, for hours on end. He thought he had always been watching it all closely, waiting for sign. They would bring absolute answers to his absolute questions, order to his personal insanity. Nothing came. But he thought he still wanted it to come, to rise up whole from the dust and the darkness, to come all at once and to blur in their passing density of Godflesh in his eye forever.

"Dawes," Travis was saying, half-asleep in the front seat. "Come on in off of that trunk lid."

"Hell, yes, Dawes," Dunker said, listlessly almost. "Cotter is gone."

The first light was up over the bluffs. Turning into it, Dawes could see that Cotter had dropped back, out of sight, forever, two forks back in the road. He was turning around. Dunker had slowed to seventy-five and was staring vacantly at the wind around him. The morning was a flat and sleeping thing; the hills were ringed with blue. A red tractor steamed like a kerosene stove in the distance. The Mississippi was close but could never be known. And at dawn, he thought, I must always return. With the light poles he must abandon the night who was his only brother.

He thought he would make a soliloquy. The day was begun and over, first light; and it had been a long time since the train of early waiting, full of farmers, old ladies webbed in a lens of oil, mothers and small boys, crossed Iowa, time, the river of rock. Ten years, he thought, and I have awakened only to sleep again. I have never awakened. I have always slept. Will always. With my brother the red west wind.

Yes, he thinks. How can you ask it to be otherwise. Dawes?

"What is it you know and won't tell me?" Dawes Williams found he was saying out loud to the morning, to the car behind and beyond him.

But Dunker and Eddie and Travis were almost sleeping and not listening at all. The car had crossed over the river. They were in Illinois, not even on the Iowa side, Dawes thought, when it happened; began to happen. It was early, slow, cool, and Dunker was only going fifty or sixty when he missed, began missing, the tight curve, and slid, began to slide, off the small mountain, tall hill of the river bluff. Dawes wondered why Dunker was doing it there. Cotter was gone; there was no need. *Why, Dunker?* It had become such a pleasant morning. *For God's sake, Dunker.* But the car was sliding two ways at once. Travis was looking at Dunker sternly, knowing the end. *For God's sake, Dunker, you're killing yourself.* The brakes rolled. The car nearly flipped on its side—it was like riding the high side of a sailboat—and when it righted itself, it began fishtailing against the grain of the curve. For awhile it seemed to go up the road backwards. *For God's sake, Dunker, you're killing your best friends.* The car, mindless then, was leaning half over the bluff, wheels spinning on the thin shoulder, and Dunker was flooring it until it was about ready to wind up and break, go over its own top. *For God's sake, Dunker, what the* hell *are you doing?* Then Dunker brought it back on the road. Rolling over onto his back with the motion of the car, Dawes could see Travis braced against the front seat, his knit, tanned face stared straight into Dunker's without looking away; and Dunker was staring straight into the turn of the road, the next turn, the one he would never make. He was sitting so tall and tense he was nearly hunching over the entire windshield, and the wheel was fluctuating so wildly it seemed to be steering him. Eddie had been knocked down onto the floor and was still trying to hold onto Dawes.

"What the hell are you DOING, Dunker!" Travis finally screamed.

"Dunker!" Dawes screamed. "Dunker, don't do it!"

"Christ," Dunker said, not looking sideways, almost crying, "I'm sorry. I'm sorry as hell!"

Then the car began doing a dance of its own. It finally began sliding away from the river, going the other way for a moment, and Dawes was almost releasing a sigh, an expletive of happy, dreaming air, another close one, when, hitting the inside granite sheet, Dunker began losing it again and in slow motion then the car bounced off the wall of rock and slid over the end of the bluff.

"Lemme go, Eddie," Dawes remembered screaming at the end. "Slip the rope! Let me off this car, Eddie! LEMME GO!"

Then slipping away, behind, Dawes could hear them crash over the ends of small trees. It ruffled a line through the undergrowth, the tearing stones, dove, muffled itself, exploded and rolled over beyond the edge of the river.

Waking, through a dream of falling timbers, on the epileptic sun of the concrete, Dawes could feel his heart exploding in his mouth. It was very quiet, strangely peaceful. For a moment Dawes thought he needed only a ride back to town. That for some reason he had only gone to sleep in the woods, become lost. Then it all came back like a rush of denser air. They were gone. They couldn't be gone. Of course, he thought. That's it. Then, for some reason he wouldn't admit, he began walking fast circles in his mind without ever leaving it. That's it, he thought, they're goofing around. He almost laughed. Then the rush of cold wind came back and, frantically trying to move out of it, Dawes began watching the rim for movement. He saw a thick red layer of blood drying, running down the front of him. He stamped his foot. Turning on his heel he moved his hand to his forehead and began walking the edge. He felt as if he were having conscious, liquid convulsions without stopping to know it. They couldn't have gone over. He began searching the rocks, looking for his own footprints to show him he was even there, for the car to rise up again. To fly. For Dunker to laugh. As if it had never gone over. He could almost see it sitting there; it must be there. Or around the curve. Or just the next county over. Hell, Dunker and Eddie and Travis had been around for years. He had always known them. Would always. They were his best friends. He'd wake soon. They'd be there. He'd wake. Out of his mind, sane, Dawes would crawl over to the end of the bluff and stare over the brink. He would look down the hundred or two foot drop and see that Eddie and Travis and Dunker had re-arisen and were swimming in the early sun of the water and were, all three, making shore, quietly and without heat on the Iowa side. The car only would not be seen. He'd wake.

"My car!" Dunker would be saying. "I loved that car!"

"No old lady ever made *that* dive," Eddie would say.

"Dunker," Travis would be saying, "soon as we make that bluff again, I'm throwing you off."

"Oh, my God," Dawes Williams would say, laughing, watching them come from the water. "You crazy sonsofbitches! This sort of thing could go on forever!"

"Dunker, not Dawes," Eddie would say, "is now the worst driver in the world!"

"What the hell," Travis would be saying, standing on the shore, "I'll kill 'em. I'll kill 'em."

"*What!?*" Dunker would say, laughing back. "I made a little mistake is all. It was my car, wasn't it? Who can say? Listen, we'll thumb to Dubuque and I'll buy us a fifth and we'll shoot some pool. *What?!*" Dunker would say.

Then Dawes Williams would stand on the brink, laughing, looking down into what was left of the moon. He would watch them come climbing up again, like all the other times. And then, to put it all back together again, he would say something like—"It could go on forever, I tell you. What is this, a Mack Sennett movie? Cars running through barns. Airplanes exploding houses. This is ruction, I tell you. And I have wasted a soliloquy. In fact, you silly bastards, I have wasted one of the finest soliloquies I have ever made!"—and then, after he had said it, finally gotten all of it out, they would slap him around a little, and feel happy and together and going somewhere again. And he wouldn't tell them, like always, he wouldn't tell them that they really weren't going anywhere at all; no, he would carry that by himself and be happy, too. . . .

But then, suddenly, he saw he was already staring into the water and it wasn't moving at all. He noticed he felt only his heart exploding in his mouth. The place was dead. He felt like running circles in his own head, but he couldn't even move to do that. It seemed little enough to ask; he only wanted it to move. There was no motion in the water, deep, black, without circles, and he seemed to move with it, to sway and undulate with it, and with the soft, seamless runs of their blood. The place was dead. He listened to his ears explode without noise within his head, the very center, again, again. He watched the curve for Dunker and Eddie and Travis. They would come for him soon. They were dead. They would walk quietly around the corner with Travis saying, *Atttttssss Dawes,* like a pleasant weed in his teeth, because they were dead. Because they were dead and because they would come. Travis and Eddie and Dunker and Dawes could never die. Perhaps it was only he, Dawes, who had died. He hoped so. Travis and Eddie and Dunker were alive. Hell, Travis ate Dawes' mother's pot roast raw. Travis, hell, Travis wasn't dead; he could never die. The place was dead with sound; it was like small things, birds, leaves, sticks in the wind blowing up into a waterfall. It was as if the whole world were water and running up over the sky; and he could hear every drop, every note, every particle and gradation. It was music. Nature was a single sound, a blowing up of blood in his ears until thunder and melody came out in a single running water note. They would come. Dunker would come and pick him up and dust him off and curse him out. For falling off his car while it was still in motion. Dunker would know him. He waited. His heart exploded in his mouth and tasted dead as salt. He lay finally on the rock of the shoulder and stared at the sun, which broke apart and then burst in his mind. They would come soon. Dunker would know him, take him home. They would come soon because they were dead.

"DUNKER!" Dawes Williams was screaming. "DUNKER! DUNKER, YOU KILLED TRAVIS AND EDDIE! DUNKER, WHERE ARE YOU?!"

They would come soon and dust him off and throw him in the river because they were dead. It made sense enough. I will look around now, he thought, I will look around and see them coming now. I will.

"THIS DOESN'T COUNT," DAWES WILLIAMS WAS SCREAMING. "NONE OF THIS COUNTS! IT'S BEEN OVER LONG AGO. RESOLVED. DONE. NONE OF THIS COUNTS OR MAKES ANY SENSE! ALL OF THIS DRIVING OVER BLUFFS ONCE THE RACE HAS BEEN WON, AND OVER, IS RULED OUT! NONE OF THIS COUNTS!"

I will, he thought, I will Will them to come around that corner now. To be alive. They are alive because they are dead. They will come soon. They will know me. Dawes, moaning low in his throat like a dog, digging into the rock of the road, crawled to the edge of the bluff. Standing again, turning again and again on his heels like a mechanical soldier, he paced up and down on the roadbed. He felt shucked, but there was an anger that bloomed in his head like a stone. This had all been ritualistic, he thought, almost like a dance. It never happened. But they will know me. Yes. And I will come back here someday. We all will. Because they are alive and this mountain has killed them. It has. I'll kill this bluff. I'll blow it to hell. It killed them. It killed them. I'll come back here someday and blow it to hell. I will. I'll grind every stone in this mountain into sand. I will. I'll grind it into air. I'll burn it and swallow the stones. I'll haul it out and bury it at sea.

"OH GOD, CHRIST, HELP," Dawes Williams screamed, pacing, grinding his teeth, walking rapid, uncontrollable circles in his mind without ever being able to leave them behind, "YOU KILLED TRAVIS AND EDDIE AND DUNKER!" he screamed, staring up into the sun, trembling on the roadbed. "I'LL KILL THIS DAMN ROCK!"

Then someone stepped down from a truck, touched him, and he turned away from the river, knowing only there was a terrific, silent blood, the boom of his heart, the sway of dead and rotten leaves, hanging over the water.

BOOK THREE

The Stones of Dust and Mexico 1967—1968

"What can you say?"

—*Dawes Williams in conversation with a Mexican goat.*

"To sing unto the stone

Of which it died."

—*The ghost up Emily Dickinson's sleeve; the goat's reply.*

1

Ten years had passed. He sat by the sea in Mexico. Some nights Dawes wandered into the cathouses, the naked cafés where they talked and he listened. He heard the mellifluous rivers of talk he couldn't even syllabify fall, like perfectly unbroken stones, into the soft hush of a silent river behind him. He thought this was dramatic, like death in a cathedral, a tower of conscious light. Lighting the rope of a small cigar, he sat back and wished someone had made him study Spanish in high school. But Urzika was with him. This must be the part where I am in the story of a modern couple, Dawes and Urzika, he thought, yes, these must be notes from an amoral grave. But she was with him; she was all he had, and she wasn't much—a bright rag, a skinny castanet in the wind waiting for only the last bell to fall over the end of the sea, he thought, sucking on a dry lemon. And soon she too would be leaving. They all would, the bastards. Soon she would be walking out into the dark hang of the southern rain to find herself a new hat of a lover, a new ending. But she understood him: she understood him so well, in fact, that he thought she was bored with it all. Looking away from her, he wrote in one of his notebooks:

Family understanding, indeed all of the great middle-class virtues, are not what they are cracked up to be. Like afternoon, they are a dead horse passing; two Mexicans standing on the corner. . . . The sea gulls come and go, speaking of Michelangelo. Nothing has changed. Everything is as it was but is, of course, somehow different. . . .

Romantics are like that, he thought, drifting back, chugging his tequila; they wait apprehensively until it is all gone into past, unspun from the center: then they pounce at themselves and take root in the dry yellow air. He told Urzika this and she said:

"Bully for you, Hy-oot John."

She was tan and thin, and when she said that she had the perfectly mimed voice of Theodore Roosevelt. Then she continued:

"Dawes," she said, "you are such a boy. I will make you happy one day. I will cripple your left leg in a sexual action, tie sand bags to your waist, and let you swim the Rio Grande for me in the moonlight. At flood stage. Once on the other side, you can turn, scream 'Hy-ooooot John' to the vacant owls of the wind, and pee in your hat. Would that make you feel better, Dawes?"

Then she said nothing at all. She turned away. But Dawes Williams was happy; he had finally found a girl who understood him. And the tequila was very good, very rough and red. His head was full of sun. He thought day was busy exploding inside a house of stone crackings, and he sat wishing only it didn't hurt quite so much. He pushed a stool away with his boot, and, going back to his notebooks, his furious papers full of scribble and decay, he decided he was writing a novel after all. He thought the title of the novel would be simply *The Night of the Fried Stone (The Cow Who Jumped Over)* by *Handsaw Williams, the Man in the Fantastic Room.* He thought it was all stylized, but important enough to be done through to the end anyway. Taking out his pencil, checking the eraser for oil, in a distended hand he penned:

THE ROOM / THE CAR / THE TRAIN / THE BUS /
THE ROOM OF THE SEA AGAIN . . .

Ten years have passed. You must remember that. You must remember it because I can't any more. You must remember it because the bastards have taken myself away with them. Ronnie Crown was right; they beat you in the end. Because I am not me any more. I am no one. At thin hotels I sign myself in as simply Enoonmai. Nothing pretentious, nothing baroque or smelling of capes, and cliffs overhanging the sea, and lightning. No, nothing that would lead to suspicion down here in the Rat Lands. Yes, but Dawes Williams is dead, put away with all his marvelous toys, beads, magic totems, and cut-glass trinkets of the land, all his wonderfully spinning glass prisms of the day. That is why he has come to Mexico; he thinks there is really no land here; no sun. . . . But he is confused. He is dead and still breathing. He is spun out and wound up into nothing. Not only that, he is dying. He knows he is. . . .

He looked up across the breeze of the table again, at the sun sweeping over the Mexican sea, at the children, brown as nuts, with round shadows for eyes, as they played soccer down at the ends of a beach. Then he looked at Urzika, who was looking away east at the mountains, at the dry clouds bearing the sea and salt rain up, stuck, in the high places of deep rock. He wanted to get up suddenly and move away, perhaps find a boat to go out to an island, but was held there by her hand.

Under the table she was rubbing his leg, unzipping his fly. She was good at that, at holding him, at fixing him in one place. But the tequila was very red, rough, full of bits of glass and wheels of the sky going down. She was looking at him, smoking a joint, and he said:

"You know, it's funny. I was on the train and I thought: 'The train is not as bad as the room—the room was worse than the train, the same as the train, only the train is a moving room, and better, and stops at other places. . . .'"

"How's your eye?" she said, ignoring him.

"Fine."

"No," she said, "it isn't. Your whole head's beginning to swell. God, the colors."

"I like it that way," Dawes Williams said, not knowing how else to approach it. "Besides, it is eventually impossible to worry about ever wearing a hat this way."

"You're going to die," she said, looking out vacantly at the sea.

"I know that. Do I need you to tell me that?"

"I'm taking you to a doctor," she said. "I think I'll be needing you for awhile."

"No, you're not," he said. "I've had enough of those. I'm fine."

"You're so damn cute sometimes, Dawes," she said. "So young. Sometimes I could just take you down to the sea and drown you in a sack. I could just hug you to death."

"For Christ's sake," Dawes Williams said, "I'm seven years older than you are. You're only nineteen years old!"

Then there was another silence. Dawes Williams went back to his notebooks, and he wrote:

Twenty-six. A ward of dirty velvet rope. Graduate school. VelFever was always watching, exactly like the shrinktified eyes of Doctor T. J. Eckleburg in Fitzgerald's *Gatsby* which "emerged pale and enormous, from the dissolving night"; which rose to only look over the wasteland like a fiat-sided, one-way Hollywood gasoline sign. Yes, I am indeed a precociously degenerating machine. Paragraph. It has been raining a great deal down here in the mountains. The dead stone is all wet and fertile, and the deserts are dry as light. I can't speak Spanish. Paragraph. And that is ironic because I can speak Latin. How could one have ever hoped to go die among the Romans in the first place? What total uselessness it has all become. Paragraph. American high schools must be done over, and I've never even been to Mass. I'm not even a Christian, thank God, let alone a conservative, a traditionalist, a Catholic. I know there is no God flying around in the roof any more. It is strange what children are led to believe. Paragraph. Twenty-six. I guess staying power was my grandmother's virtue after all. Arthur is dead. Gin is alive and living in Miami. It was cancer that got old Arthur. Still, no doubt he died with unbelievably good muscle tone for a man of his age. Twenty-six. Paragraph. In the end they will say of me—Bright lad; for a yeoman he died of old age and decay earlier than anyone with the possible exception of Stephen Crane. . . .

Then he turned back to the sea and laughed. I travel light, he thought. I carry very little with me; only my letters, my fans from the past, and one small duffel bag full of underwear and books. I carry my pen and ink identity—I rarely go out any more, even when I travel five thousand miles down and around and toward Mexico—or rather my identity has made a quick spiral, a downward denouement into pen and ink and nothing more. And that is why, in a real sense, my pen and ink carries me. I rarely go out any more, even in Mexico; I only ride my inkwell into the sea like a burro with wings.

Turning to Urzika, he told her this and she said:

"Bully for you, Hyoot John. Bully for you. Bully. Bully."

"I am writing a novella and a one-act play," Dawes Williams said.

"Good for you," Urzika said, going deeply into the chaos of her leather pouch of a purse. "I'll help."

Drawing a Dixon number two out from the duffel of her purse like an unsheathed sword, Urzika then turned dramatically into him across the sun-swooning, burned distance of the table, stared fixedly at a point directly above his head, and said:

"Well? What shall we write about?"

"I don't think you quite understand this yet, Urzika," Dawes said flatly, trying to ignore her.

"Sex!" Urzika said. "Let's write about nine people and an eagle screwing in the moonlight!"

But Dawes Williams didn't even look up. Already he was back into his notebooks; and under the heading DAWES WILLIAMS' FRONTIER KIT he made himself busy listing all of the possessions that were with him.

Finishing, he put the last of his books away, noted the stare of the American matron who was eyeing him. He looked over at Urzika. Urzika was paying no attention; she was making sucking noises with her lips, looking over the distances of the sandy-floored, leaf-caped cabana. She was looking directly at the American tourist of a woman who was staring, furiously transfixed, back into the sound of Urzika's voice. He thought Urzika was only nineteen years old, and couldn't believe it. Then the small sucking noises on Urzika's lips fell off short and she began staring into the woman with a small fascination. She seemed to want to peer into, to recognize, to mock. Urzika locked the woman to her, almost romantically, across the shady sun of the buzzing distances. She almost kissed her across an open space of afternoon. . . .

"Key-rist," Dawes Williams said, "let's get out of here."

But the woman had already turned and moved toward the door. She had found herself frozen, caught in a moment of her own fascination, a small fear, a recognition; then she had looked at her own embarrassment, fumed and stalked from the curtain of the door. Dawes looked at Urzika's eyes. He thought the iris, smooth and round, a vacant sail in the wind, was a naked green snakeskin set out to melt in the sun.

"Lookit that old Jake," he heard Urzika saying. "She's positively scuddling away."

"I'm a nondenominationalist myself," Dawes Williams said quietly. "I think what you did to that woman was just damn impolite."

"You grew up on the better part of the prairie all right, you sodhead," Urzika said.

"This then," Dawes said, "is an examination of an American kid. Rah. Rah."

"That's right, you graduate-school snot," Urzika said. "Kick a field goal or Mama's gonna cut off your raisins tonight."

"Mama's got a deep voice," Dawes said. "In fact, Mama talks just like papa's razor stropping."

"Fuck off," Urzika said, smiling broadly, pulling the ends of his hair. "Don't moralize something you like."

"'All storytellers,'" Dawes said, reading out of his notebook, "'must first of all make friends with their audience. This is a moral certainty.' Miss Wilma Spell Spent, D. Handsaw Williams' third-grade teacher in lecture."

"I wish you wouldn't keep those notebooks, Dawes," Urzika said almost seriously. "They're dirty and obscene. They run through me like naked lunch. I really think you are a sick man."

Then there was a silence. Urzika drifted over to order more tequila as she thought she liked Dawes Williams better when he was full of tequila. Coming back, she said:

"Dawes? Don't you want to ask me about my sexual fantasies yet?"

"Do you have any left? I thought you lived them all out before they'd had a chance to bloom."

"Do you want to hear them or not?"

"This is not an interview for *Look* magazine," Dawes Williams said. "This is serious."

"Then you may write this down," Urzika said dramatically, drawing the words out on the long edge of her tongue like spires of dreaming air. "My sexual fantasies are both 'lewd' and 'elegant.'"

"That's all very well," Dawes Williams said, trying to watch her back and failing, "but I don't think there is a novel in that."

"The problem with you, Dawes, is that you have no imagination."

Laughing, Dawes Williams laid his head down on the table. He tried hard to remember that Urzika had plans of becoming an actress. He tried hard to remember that he was dying, and what this would mean. He was only surprised that, in the end, he could watch it only turn to soft melodrama. Finally, rising over the faint scent of half-sucked lemons, he said:

"No. That line should have read: 'Dawes, the problem with you is that for a moralist with neurasthenia you have no imagination.'"

"Declassé," Urzika said. "Personally I could never marry a man who wears white gloves and carries a cane."

"Personally I never could, either," Dawes Williams said. "They're too damn sissy . . . and saying declassé has been declassé now for thirty years. You are so damn declassé."

Then Urzika stared at him, dead stone sphinx with exotic paws for eyes, for minutes on end. And he knew he could never outstare her for long, that she was shameless, bottomless. He knew her face was a perfect stone mask, but he thought he had known her somewhere before; perhaps, he thought, it was on a high grass vale in Scotland in the sixth or seventh century before. . . .

Finally, breaking, he smiled at her; she was satisfied and, getting up, she kissed him and moved down the beach. Immediately she began talking to some surfers who had brought their boards down the coast to Mazatlán. Dawes watched her for awhile, furious, interested, not interested at all. Dawes knew she would always stray back now, for awhile, but he tried to imagine her as something free, as something only foreign, unknown, and merely walking by, out of sight, near the sea. He found he couldn't. He found suddenly that trying to make such a large leap from reality into imagination only made him tired then. He found this didn't surprise him, or even make him nervous. He wondered over it for awhile, puzzled. Then, in the thin-bladed leafshadow, he went back and began reading his notebooks. He thought it was too late for romance; there was only time left for the last pale waltz of the mad. He read:

THE NIGHT OF THE FRIED STONE AND THE MOON

(which jumped over the cow)

A NOVELLA

(in four movements, partially finished)

by

S. H. Dawes Williams

(The Man in the Fantastic Room)

PAGE ONE. PROLOGUE. Build your house on Midwestern rock and it will collapse with a larger thunder.

In the beginning there was me, green smoke and oatmeal, conscious light, all looking for a shoe to rise from. Later, Walter came. Then there was sense. He walked past my window with electronic spats and a cane with a whistling tip. He had an electronic smile that is vaguely like watching the *Congressional Record* being erected in neon. Later, Walter came by. He was turned around and going the other way. Somehow I have changed . . .

It may be sin, you know. Only bad Communists change. Methodists, they only hang around in their conservative, conglomerate skins like reptiles who refuse to molt; who refuse to wilt into that larger surface of sun and be renewed. . . .

But Seriphus Handsaw Williams knows all and will tell less. Quiet, Walter is coming. On cat's feet. In the fog. He has a cloth coat, and is powdered with the perfume of an innocent devil. Why is he coming, you wonder. How the hell should I know why he is coming? Why the hell should you bother to ask? Be still, Dawes, there are no reasons any more. Be still, Seriphus, you are the merest product of baroque and scheming blood; an illusion of a dead magician's wind. . . .

Dawes is mad!

Dawes is mad!

Dawes' blood feels like broken glass!

This is not *a priori,* Dawes Williams thinks, pacing in his room, this is serious.

This is not serious! Seriphus Williams says, this is menopause, goddamnit!

I am pregnant! Dawes Williams says. I am having twins!

Where I go, Dawes, Seriphus says, you go. That may explain it, but I doubt it.

You black Prince, Dawes Williams says. De Sade in a manger!

Alice!

Mad-Hatter!

Then the thing dissolves in silence. Dawes Williams is left alone with an image. Nothing. There is no sense to be had in the universe; there is only the illusion of meaning. Things have become absolutely relative and transcended themselves at the exact point at which the words leave off. Swish. Booooom. He is left wondering only how to tell someone and still get away with it. . . .

Perhaps Walter will understand. Perhaps he will not. But at least he is omnipresent. He is everywhere at once. . . .

At two-fifteen in the afternoon VelFever comes in. He is dressed exactly like a small-town bank teller who is spinning his change in a brown-paper spool. He smiles. He is not worried; it is not his blood which feels like broken glass and, besides, there is nothing else he can do.

It is only an incipient young man's malady, Dawes thinks he hears VelFever say. It will pass with time.

Why!?!?!!??!! Dawes Williams says.

Because!?!?!!??!! VelFever says.

Dawes Williams is not happy, but he feels at least he has become a gadfly. Dawes Williams takes out a pad of paper and writes:

> The smoke on the window is white.
> The smoke on the paper is yellow, and deeper.
> There is no smoke going under the river.

What do you think of it? Dawes says, handing it over.

VelFever reads it for a long time, smacks his lips, and says: Suicide. This is suicide.

No, Dawes Williams says, it is paper.

No, VelFever says, this is suicide. I'm afraid you'll have to be with us a while longer.

No, Dawes Williams says, it is just a statement of physical law. If you have ever seen smoke going under the river, I wish you would please tell me now.

No, VelFever says, this is suicide.

No? Dawes Williams says. What kind of suicide do you think it is? Do you think it could even be said to be aesthetic suicide?

No, VelFever says, Dawes, you have no imagination. Can't you see this is figurative suicide?

May I be excused now? Dawes Williams says. If I can't go to Mexico and commit suicide, I think I would like to go to my room and lie down.

No, VelFever says, this is our little time to talk.

Whoooopey-dee, Dawes Williams says, stalking from the room, turning. You know, of course, he says to VelFever, if an apple ever fell on your head it would cause an *a priori* blockage so vast, so cataclysmic, so apish in ultimate outward expression that you could probably only sit, for minutes on end, scratching your head and thumbing your feet on a pile of bananas before you.

I am only trying to help you, VelFever says.

You're making a hell of a bad job of it, Dawes Williams says. And you're getting over-paid. You turn out bad work.

No, VelFever says, musing on his papers before him.

Hell, Dawes Williams says, by the time I get out of here I'm going to be broke again! I could be living in a villa in Spain by now for what I'm paying around here. I could be slaying dragons and windmills!

It's your fantasy, VelFever says. We mustn't let it intrude upon your reality. We mustn't let you commit suicide even on paper.

You silly goose, Dawes Williams says, don't you even know by now there is no reality!

No, VelFever says, I think we should increase your medication.

You know best, Doctor, Dawes Williams says, laughing wildly.

There is always some hope in diseases like this one, VelFever says, you must have hope. There is always that.

Dawes wishes to tell VelFever how maudlin he has become, but instead only a cold, perfect shiver runs through him for the first time. It is two twenty-five in the afternoon and he walks down the hall to his room. He sits alone in the cold ivory, anesthetic brick of his walls and wonders what has become of the ritual in it all. He wonders how it all could have come to this; then wonders further how he could have only wondered something as melodramatic as that. Everything—crying, rage, loud shrieks of boredom, a fear that is like omnipotent ice—seem to be caught in his throat like castrated, impossibly quiet things that refuse to bloom and be released; to grow outward from a center, a rush that is full of the noise and clatter of a perfect silence. He wishes to call his mother, but that is ridiculous; he is twenty-six years old and, besides, he left home early with Dunker, Eddie and Travis Thomas. A nurse comes with a pill in a jelly-bean timbale. Her hands are filed, and Dawes watches the shadows move on his walls. Cars move in the street. He knows he is only six blocks from his house; and from the windows in the corner room—the rumpus room where they are teaching him to be creative at twenty-six by sawing on boards—he can see Ronnie Crown's grade school, William Joshua Wadlove High, and a small liberal-arts college he attended for two years. He thinks he has grown up, been educated, and gone mad within a radius of six or seven blocks. He smiles.

Why, Sally Sunshine from Oliolo, Iowa, Dawes Williams finally says, how do you do today? Do you feel fine? he says.

I have pills for you, Mr. Williams, she says primly.

Dawes Williams swallows and knows nothing good will happen. Once a machine has degenerated you throw it away and get a new one. The sun is shine and all polish and gone black. The world is full of so much ruck, and Seriphus Handsaw Williams is laughing. The nurse is gone. The nurse is a patient; the nurse is full of ugly hands and diaper pails; the nurse is as crazy as a stoned and rational and antitranscendent Indian who doesn't believe in pantheistic rocks . . . the nurse could have been made in two hours, on a better day, or if I had my body back, he thinks, but now she only looks at me as if I were a dry sack, a crack of broken light in a timber, which I am. . . .

Why is it, Dawes Williams thinks, I have never been so full of potential movement, so kinetic, and yet I am totally helpless; I cannot even fall over and be. Why have I been wrought on so hard for no end?. . . He lies back on the bed and wants to be able to want to leave. Everything is second-generational; the first generation is simple and obvious. But he knows in the old systems, the spoon-fed pails of values, the Good energize, and the Bad degenerate into smoke. He thinks then he must be evil, rotten with seed. If this is not true, he scans the possibilities: perhaps the genes merely self-destruct when they contact with negative space; perhaps the evil are the only ones capable of good, the good the only ones capable of evil; perhaps all only carry the reverse of their coin, the ascension of their ambivalent value, the essential binary binding of the two poles of an electrical brain; or, perhaps, it is all relative absurdity and it is only happenstance—a fantastically retrospective, blown-up dance of self-assuring ritual, spun to no purpose under a crustaceous sea of the air—that leaves the strong behind to write the values of "history." . . . Yes, he thinks, I am not evil; for the first time I am capable of good. Because the strong are only strong, not good; the weak are strong. They survive and are capable of strength; the strong are only capable of degenerating. But this is ruck! This is a sophomore's riddle! I have never done this before.

OH CHRIST, Dawes Williams screams, AM I EVEN ALIVE!

But the walls, the corridors, are hollow and dead with response. He notices his nose is bleeding. But his head is locked on his shoulder, and he can't move, and he can't tell anyone. But they couldn't do any good. The walls are white and fall into a distant doorway that pukes. People are walking in white gowns. This is not me, he thinks, I have always been alive. I have never done this. Who is this? Seriphus? Handsaw? A million others. This is insane. It feels as if his spine is coming out like a root. He thinks it is incredible, known but only whispered before. He thinks it is incredible because he is totally rational, lucid, looking only for a word to explain how clear he is, yes, dying, fading, sitting there watching himself evaporate. . . . But this is totally lucid, totally insane. Footsteps, like naked coins. He seems to be crawling down the seam of a corridor, looking for a nurse. . . .

CHRIST, Dawes Williams screams, WHAT IS THIS!

He notices his guts hurt. He notices a nurse is telling him to go back to his bed and rest quietly. He stares at her in utter disbelief. Can't she see it? Can't she understand? He thinks if he goes back to his room they will think he is good and make it pass. He tries to stand and notices he is lucidly convulsing. He seems to see everything. He thinks for the first time he understands his life. He thinks perhaps he doesn't, as there is nothing to understand. He thinks there is only a universe unbalanced, a spinning of unimportant light, and that there always has been, only this, only an illusion of balance and light. He wonders why people don't grasp the obvious and become alive while they are. He notices a nurse is approaching him with a glass of water, and a smile in her hand.

She tells him to go back to his room. He wants to be good. He wants it to pass. He lies on his bed and breathes through a corner of his throat. VelFever comes in through the door. Even he seems finally concerned.

Dawes, he says, what seems to be the trouble?

TROUBLE! Dawes Williams tries to scream. CAN'T YOU SEE, YOU BLOODY ASS, I'M CRIPPLED OVER IN FOUR SEPARATE DIRECTIONS LIKE A HUNCHBACKED DWARF! CAN'T YOU SEE DE SADE WAS THE ONLY POTENTIALLY GOOD MAN WHO EVER LIVED! CAN'T YOU SEE CHRIST WAS ONLY FULL OF SELF-SERVING HORSESHIT, RELIGIOUS WARS, AND ILLUSIONS OF GOODNESS, GODNESS, AND STRENGTH! AND DON'T YOU KNOW, ULTIMATELY, THAT THIS WHOLE DEBATE HAS BEEN PATENTLY DEAD FOR OVER A HUNDRED YEARS! AND CAN'T YOU SEE THAT THIS HAS NOTHING TO DO WITH ANY-THING IN THE FIRST PLACE! SO WHY AM I CRIMPING!!!

But VelFever says nothing. He stares at Dawes Williams for some time as if he were made out of bemusing fish flesh. Then a nurse comes in with a needle, flexing it out in the wind, and, finally, just as VelFever is shooting him, everything dissolves into a pleasant blur that is nothing at all . . .

Waking, the next morning, Dawes Williams knows he has a palsy so vast it whispers when it screams. He prowls the hallways like an old man without a cane. His blood is flying apart on a wheel that has already spun. He sits at breakfast, dropping his spoons, watching all of the Tuesday, Thursday, Saturday housewives come back from electric shock. They are naked, clipped and cold in white sheets and flat tables. He thinks he has never seen tables that flat. He thinks the dead do not travel so peacefully. He thinks they are as cold and gray as ass-ended fish. A new Sally Sunshine comes by and tells him she is his new nurse-of-the-week. She comments upon how calm and utterly rational he is for a boy with his problems. As he is finishing his naked egg, next—long, clear panel of waist-high windows—down the long shooting gallery comes Broun, a sixteen-year-old boy who has small hands and an unnaturally large head, who is nearly foaming at the mouth, and who is being chased full speed by a nurse who is shaking out a needle full of Thorazine in the wind. Broun, shaking out a Ping-Pong paddle, hides under a table in the rumpus room and threatens to do in an ex-Marine who is the attendant. They take Broun down the hall, screaming for justice, prom-ising retribution on all (once he gets to the far side of Mars and comes back a millionaire); (once he comes back with a higher-grade rocket fuel); finally they chain him to his bed and close the door and it is quiet again. Old Mrs. Tad comes down the hall crying:

EVIL

EVIL

EVIL

Later, Sally Sunshine II leads Dawes Williams away to saw on some boards. He tries to tell her he doesn't want to be pretentious, but he has two college degrees. Finally Dawes gets out:

What the fuck is this anyway?

Sally Sunshine II doesn't answer, but she smiles back like the picture of a mother on a cereal box. Dawes has considered smiling mothers on cereal boxes absolute naked lunch for two years now, so it doesn't help. Mrs. Edna Fee comes by and says:

How do you do? I am Mrs. Edna Fee and I am eighty years old. Have you seen my daughter anywhere?

Then, immediately turning, she comes back and says:

How do you do? I am Mrs. Edna Fee and I am eighty years old. Have you seen my daughter anywhere?

Sally Sunshine II and the ex-Marine lead Mrs. Fee off and rope her to her bed. All is quiet again. Dawes meets a woman who begins explaining B. F. Skinner to him.

You won't feel any better when you get out of here, she says, but no one will know the difference. You'll behave like a sonofabitch.

She then explains how they are taking him down to the womb and growing him up, sweetness and light, again. That explains Sally Sunshine I and II, Dawes thinks, but it doesn't explain what is wrong with him. Dawes goes off and sneaks four books on clinical psychology from the nurses' lounge. Dawes then corners VelFever in the hallway and asks to be let in on the movies they run for the nurses in the corner room. VelFever says, No. Dawes explains patiently to VelFever he has a real intellectual curiosity in this matter. Vel-Fever says, No, this isn't the time. In the hallway Dawes meets the B. F. Skinner woman again and she tells him Skinner has trained pigeons to sort watch parts more effectively than humans. Dawes is not impressed. He knows he is never getting out of here for long again. He knows it is Pandora's box; and he knows he is dying of knowledge. Cornering VelFever in the hallway, Dawes asks for a physical. VelFever says, No, this isn't the time. VelFever asks Dawes to quit cornering him in the hallways or he'll chain him to his bed. Dawes tells VelFever to fuck off in front of two nurses and retreats to his room. He sees profoundly that being treated like a baby makes it seem like you are acting like one. He collapses again. Waking, Dawes finds his bladder isn't working. He has to wizz so bad he is bursting help-lessly for an hour before the ex-Marine comes in with a smile and sticks a catheter tube up his urethra. Dawes asks VelFever for a physical and calls him a quack. VelFever takes him into a room and whacks three times, utterly seriously, on his knee with a rubber hammer and pronounces his nervous system sound. Dawes can see all about modern medicine in America now, and laughs in VelFever's face. Dawes knows all about pill pushers now from the roots out, and he knows you'd just better not develop anything interesting at all, 'cause there ain't no help. He also knows you have to become an American President to get any help. Telling VelFever this, he goes back to his room to doctor himself. . . .

For two weeks Dawes Williams didn't come out unless ordered to eat, or saw on a board. He stood on his head periodically in the corner because something told him to. He believed in his inverted theory because it made sense to get blood to the brain, and because he read in a magazine that the jungle cat knew, down to one one-thousandth of a percent per quart, just how much salt to get out of the salt lick. Only man couldn't pay any attention to his real biological impulses. He tacked the article to his wall with tape and developed a meta-physical religion out of all relationship to the volume of the article. He walked out into the hall only to get lights from the wall coil, and he remembered he had been capable of playing with matches successfully since he was six years of age. The thought nearly drove him mad.

Writing was cruxifiction, but he could read. He hid the four clinical-psychology text-books under his mattress and took them out when it was safe. He dissolved them. He was speeding, and he was sure his mind was up to two hundred and ten. Everything in them was life and death, and he began in all four reading the chapters on "Psychosis and Rare Brain Disease Syndrome." Then he worked back, cover to cover. The ex-Marine came in twice a day and drained his bladder. He lay there and felt shame and a dread that transcended even depression. He found in a footnote his convulsion and weakness walking was due to "Parkinsonian side reaction in up to fifteen percent of the patients using this drug"; he also found, in another book, that his bladder trouble was caused by this. He told VelFever. VelFever looked surprised beyond words, agreed about the pseudo-Parkinsonian side reaction, but disagreed about the bladder trouble. Dawes called him a medieval quack this time, and said he wouldn't take the medicine. VelFever said, No, he had to, he was being difficult. Dawes exploded with the injustice of this, and told VelFever if he considered what he had been doing for the last two weeks "difficult," he was less than an idiot. VelFever said nothing, but he smiled. Dawes said he would take the medicine if a urologist came in to check his bladder. VelFever said no, he knew all about bladders. Dawes told him to fuck off, he didn't know about his. VelFever called in a urologist. Two days passed. A nurse told Dawes Williams to go stand in the bathroom and run water to get the idea. Moving down the hall, Dawes met the B. F. Skinner woman again, and she told him that was the way they got infants toilet-trained. Dawes Williams went straight back to his room. He saw Simpson was there, sitting in a chair, tapping his feet. Simpson began talking abstractedly, looking at the floor. Dawes saw he was nearly an old man, helpless now and confused about this. Simpson finally said:

Dawes, you'll be all right. Your mother and I have faith in you. You'll come through this. Just remember you've always had a good head on your shoulders.

Simpson left. Dawes nearly became hysterical thinking of accountant Simpson standing there, in the middle of a lunatic assemblage, telling his son he "had a good head on his shoulders." Sally Sunshine V came and took him away to saw a board. Finally the urologist came. He poked around Dawes Williams' bladder and pronounced it "soft," "toneless," because of the drugs. VelFever came quickly in and walked the urologist all the way out of the ward. VelFever came back and, so that he could take the first two drugs, put him on a postsurgical bladder-toning drug. Dawes called VelFever an idiot, a fanatic, and a madman. VelFever stalked out. Dawes Williams got out his books and began reading again. . . .

At the end of two weeks Dawes Williams came out of the room knowing— from a rare brain syndrome that took place ninety percent of the time only in women—he would be dead in sixteen months.

Dawes Williams looked up from his notebooks. He knew that would be the end of chapter one. Urzika was running up and down the beach, waving the bright blanket of her rope jacket at him and the distances, and the sea seemed almost calm. The waters rolled out like a fantastic topaz mountain, skimmed with sun and white, rolling glaciers; the sea, he knew, was a mask, prone and indelible, lying invisibly within the perpendicular perspective of the light. The light, he knew, was the real mountain; the sea was the illusion. The light blew through everything like a green, smoking wind; it penetrated everything, almost grotesquely, touching the brown skin of the women, baking the white mud of the houses, dancing like a fire with the barest equilibrium down the long, bowed winery of the streets. And he thought the streets were Utrillos. The alleys were without people, silent, destroyed with broken lines. Dawes thought there were crickets in the bright air of these hollow mud walls, and they were driving him mad. He knew he could not stand this high, naked wind for long; he hoped almost someone would call out the Mexican Militia and declare war on the light.

Urzika had drifted away for awhile. She was swimming in a mask of the sea, moving down to the south now. Shrieking long-tailed birds blew upward in the soft fan of the breezes and flew outward like lazy, decadent smoke, grass snakes of the air. They lit and rose like feeding kites with methodical, mechanical order from the twin rock islands moored and rafting slightly in the naked blue light of the sea off Mazatlán. The light, he thought, always the light. It seemed to bloom over him like an overprecious destruction, like a thing that had mastered and released. Dawes lit another Mexican cigaret and ground the match in the sand. He thought he was well hidden, lying way up somewhere, away from himself, high in a green and rotten, rain-weary thatch of the wind. He looked away from the sea and began reading again:

Chapter 2

IF YOUR MOTHER IS A REPUBLICAN, SHOOT HER!

After Dawes Williams had finished with VelFever, polished the finality of his own diagnosis, he went back into the room to await his fate like a squaw. For days he sat and stared at the flat noise of his walls; he practiced not looking at things with his eyes open. He thought for a madman with nothing but death and a faded bloom on his hands he was totally lucid, but always the small, twitching nerve end remained.

Finally, sitting on the bed, beginning to get into the theory that he, Dawes Williams, was one of the last great incarnations of the ghost up Emily Dickinson's sleeve, he began writing a novel. But everything seems to slip away and fade within mirrors. He thinks of the time he went to Galena, Illinois, with Travelin' Tommy and Barney Redwood, but doesn't have the energy to begin. He thinks of the time Dunker and Eddie and Travis were killed, but thinking this, he doesn't even have the energy of remembering. Most of all, he thinks of the farm, of Gin and Arthur, but all of that is lost within the face of Abigail Winas, the picture of a rocking chair and an old stone house framed with the mad net of the moon.

It is all too impossible. It slips beyond air and wood smoke, memory, the already dead wave of a magician's wand, and lacking anything to write about Dawes Williams puts down:

SERIPHUS HANDSAW WILLIAMS GOES TO TOWN

A Long Short Story by Dawes Williams

MODE: *Manners in the Novel of Ideas*
SUBJECT: *The Campus Revolt*

PLACE: *A Room*

TIME: *Sometime After the Flood*

Epigram: It's all right, because in the end Walter Cronkite will come, and stand over the cold ash of the secular media body, and pronounce it dead and not risen.

Dedication: For Robert Ingersoll, the last of the great secular humanists, who saddled up and rode to town; and for H. L. Mencken, who rode the same horse in the opposite direction.

Benediction: The Golden Rule as applied to abstractions.

Main Text: Dawes Williams is drunk on his ass. He thinks he is obsessed with beginnings. He thinks he can announce the sun. The room is full of old rose light, trellis patterns, and goat bones. This, he thinks, is its tone but not its specific reference, its meaning. (He thinks he will study epistemology soon. In fact, he thinks nearly everyone should study epistemology very soon. But then, as the truck driver who passes his window every morning at nine has so often said—What the hell does he know?)

Nothing responds. Dawes Williams would roll over and roll himself another joint, except he hasn't been out of his room for two months so how in the hell would he have contacted a pusher? Besides, it makes him speed, and he is already going over the roof on air. Satisfied, nearly smug, Dawes Williams rolls back against the wall and considers himself as clean as a Methodist on that one at least. He thinks he is trying hard to forgive himself for being alive, but it just isn't taking. . . .

Disinterested, Dawes gets up, begins pacing, and tells his blood to be still. Later, lying on his back again, in his deserted room in college, he blows thin reefs of acceptable smoke at his window of moon. It is night again. It is night again and raining again. Nothing responds. He thinks poetic fallacy is romantic as hell, and that yeomen who try to wear knee stockings usually must wind up catching their balls in their garter belts. . . .

Dawes Williams sits in a chair. He begins reading his letters; his dark papers come mystically in from the rain and the mail. One was from Summer Letch; one was from Barney Redwood; one was from his mother, Leone. One each was from Dunker, Eddie and Travis Thomas. Dawes Williams is puzzled by this . . . some of them have been dead now, he notes, for eight years, and none of them ever existed. Thinking only—Dead Men Write No Letters—he wishes suddenly only that he had some Robert Louis Stevenson around so he could begin all fresh, new, and over again. He thinks, perhaps, he is only caught in a moment of suspended disbelief and, standing up, announcing himself to his walls, he says only:

HOW HAVE I SPRUNG FROM ALL OF THIS, THAT'S ALL I WANT TO KNOW!? WHAT THE HELL HAS HAPPENED HERE? WHO *ARE* ALL OF THESE PEOPLE ANYWAY! WHAT THE HELL HAS ANY OF THIS GOT TO DO WITH THE DOGGY GIRLS OF WATERLOO IN THE FIRST PLACE!?

Sitting down on the windowsill, Dawes knows the problem is not the novel any more, it is writing the novel. He takes out a Camel and begins smoking. That is the best thing about yeomen, he thinks; unless they run over the side of a mountain in the pursuit of the Wife of Bath, they don't break down. They outlast your average effete personality; they often go on forever. Taking out a pad of paper, mounting his icebox, Dawes Williams writes:

I am the real Dawes Williams. I know I am. Unfortunately, I am also the fictive Seriphus Handsaw Williams—orator; would-be writer of letters-to-the-editor; courtly gentleman trapped in the society of fools; and that greatest of all American blood myths—the lost, delicate, misplaced and wandering genes of The Dauphin of France. Dawes Williams, however, founded on the peasantlike acceptance of paradox as he is, believes me to be the truer social democrat. The boy, in his total disavowal of absolutist thought, is a perfect ass. In short, if Dawes Williams were left to himself, he could only construct the perfectly relative center of nothing-at-all and, in the end, Dawes Williams seems to me to be severely limited by the physical, binary, dipolar surface of his electrical brain. . . . Reactionary! Fool!

Have no fear, I tell him, I am only here to help you transcend. But he doesn't listen. He only wishes to graduate, fall in love, and get on in life. (I told you the boy was an ass.) I, however, wish to become a prophet. (Nothing big at first, of course. I only want to run a little shop that will someday eclipse that once run by Jesus the Nazarene.) How I ever became encased, then, in this gray, washed-out, provincial shell remains a mystery even to me. Dawes isn't worried; he only wishes to be one or the other, both, perhaps even neither. I, however, have come to prod him on. I have memorized every book of literature Dawes Williams has merely read. I can't even spell but in the end I have become, truly, the ghost up his sleeve. . . .

(A, I assure you a brilliant, seven-page, interlineal listing of every great ancient and modern writer that Dawes Williams and I have ever read—as they ultimately relate to Savonarola—has been deleted here. I played Hamlet, Quentin Compson, Emily Dickinson, Walt Whitman, Ahab *and* Moby Dick; Dawes Williams, needless to say, played that mad, burning monk. . . . In the end, I watched Dawes Williams dissolve into a pot of ashes, an affronted phoenix bird blooming back with the same moralist fervor Jay Gould might have displayed chasing down another caboose.)

Waking, Dawes Williams went and sat at the window. He thinks he is Huckleberry Finn and quiet, unassuming Tom, not Dick, Rover. He thinks he is having an identity crisis; that I will pass like the naked wind of a bad fever. I laugh in his face. He tells me, sarcastically, If you could pass Ph.D. orals with single names and gestalt wit we'd have it dicked someday. I laugh in his face; but to humor him I tell him *he* can play Laurence Sterne for awhile and *I* will play Tristram Shandy. The dullard doesn't even respond. I laugh in his face.

We have a certain symmetry! I say.

Dilettante! he screams at me. Asymmetric!

We possess a certain pretense! I say.

Do you know, he says, crying now, breaking down, that my father voted for Eisenhower? Twice!

God bless Genet, I say. Batman de Sade!

But he says nothing now and begins walking around the room. I watch him very closely and record all his actions. He thinks he is still a great prairie at night; he thinks I am the mad moon of the Great Spoon River, rolling between. I tell him to roll himself up in his romantic duffel and we will catch a freight to Winesburg, Ohio. I tell him we will go catch carp in the river. He doesn't answer. He only mumbles something indistinctly about Galena, Illinois, and, lying down flat on the floor, then he proceeds to try to read *The National Review* and *The New York Review of Books*, at once, with opposite eyes. I begin talking to him gently:

Dawes, I say, I would not, however, presume (even for an instant) to call myself Joyce, Kant, Marx, or Djuna Barnes.

Anais Nin, he says, is indeed a sane and beautiful lady.

That would be a bit much even for me, Dawes, I say. I have that much humanity left. All is not lost. Sanity is just around the corner. Something will happen. It's blowin' in the mornin' rain.

That would be nice, Dawes says. I'd like that. But God. I'll bet they (all of the great ones, the ones who played enough seasons to make it to the Hall of Fame) are all just now listening to you talk (the ones who have finally made it and become sane by becoming dead), spinning in their graves—like brilliantly whirling dervishes gone black at the core of light—like a phalanx of children's tops, set out front. I'll bet they are weeping with grief over you.

Quietly irritated, I move away. There is a long silence. Dawes Williams rolls over and takes a dark letter from his shelf. It is Dunker's letter, and he reads it over:

Hey Dawes,

You are imagining yourself, Willy. You never happened that way. In fact, there is some question you happened at all. And even though you are writing this to yourself, I am listening in.

And now for the News: I am happy playing B-ball up here with Heaven's Angels, Willy. It's swell. The big time. They got culture up here all right. It's no Orange Bowl yet, but they're capitalizing fast. —Hope to sign for $ sixty-two grand or better next season for hooping that old ball. I'm worth it easy. —You'd be damn surprised just how many dead people and saints over the centuries were not six foot nine. And how many of the ones who are have never played basketball. They need me, mother. They take to it big up here . . . almost as good as Indiana on a Saturday afternoon in T-shirt weather. It's nice as hell. (You ought to see those damn crazy Celts, they love it, they get naked and dance in the rain whenever we win. Reminds me some of you, Willy.) —Gotta run, mother, the General Manager (reminds you of *Green Pastures* doesn't it, mother?) is calling me out for free-throw practice. An invisible voice, it's like talking to the intimations of your bladder as they're telling ya to wizz.

> Don't let your meat loaf,
> Dunker Nadlacek

Then Dawes Williams begins pacing again.

God damn you, Dunker, he hears himself screaming to his silent walls, you bastard, I haven't seen a nickel in six months!

Then Handsaw collapses against the wall, laughing.

I thought you said they all died, Dawes, he says.

They did, Dawes says. This is just paper. This is real.

This is real? Handsaw says.

That's right, Dawes says.

But this isn't real, Dawes. Fantasy. They didn't write these.

That's right, Dawes says. If they had really written these letters, they couldn't have been real. But I wrote them, so they are true. They are true, therefore they are real.

Really, Dawes? Seriphus Handsaw says.

Really really, Dawes says. Damn, who would have thought it could have come to this? That I would eventually wind up, standing here, debating with a lunatic?

You are good at describing phenomenon, Dawes, Handsaw says, but you have never once found its secret heart of meaning.

That is true in its way, Dawes Williams says, blankly walking away without even batting an eye, but it isn't real because only you have invented it. Besides, the secret has never existed; or at least it never once has been found.

Then there is a long silence. Dawes Williams begins to sit in the closet, playing with a gun. The light in the closet doesn't operate, so, becoming dissatisfied, Dawes Williams eventually comes out and opens a bottle of wine. He yanks the cork with a penny and his teeth. Handsaw is fascinated. Dawes looks into the socketless illusion, the small inquisition of his eyes, and says:

That's right. I learned that trick from an ex-Marine.

I said nothing.

Quiet, I am composing.

You hear abstract music, noteless, drifting, in your head.

That's right. You're positively omniscient.

I am God.

No, you are a horse's ass.

Then Dawes Williams takes another of his dark papers from the windowsill. Blowing smoke at the moon, he starts to read. It is a letter, sent up from Rapid Cedar by his favorite mother, Leone:

Dear Dawes,

Just a note with the cookies to let you know what's going on. I don't know how to tell you, but your grandfather is dead. You had to know, of course, but I hesitated telling you so close to your tests. It was cancer. These things happen and we must accept them. We were all surprised, of course, as we all thought Arthur would live to be ninety at least. He was in such good shape otherwise. If Mother decides he's to be sent up here to be buried at Dawes City, we'll go to the funeral; otherwise I'll go to Miami by myself.

That's all I have for now, but why don't you come up to Rapid Cedar this weekend? The change would do you good. Don't be so negative all the time, Dawes. I hate to sound like Norman Vincent Peale, but why don't you "accentuate the positive" for a change? Think it over.

Love,
Mother

P.S. Gin wondered if you wanted Arthur's trophies, and I told her yes. It would be a shame for them to be all thrown out.

Distracted by a late, snowy moth flying about his hanging light, Dawes becomes disinterested. The sieve of winter continues outside. Dawes Williams formally puts his dark papers away again for awhile and thinks: Good God, Handsaw, we are yeomen. We could never be paranoid schizophrenics, or Indians wild on the prairies, or fat businessmen going to town. Lost always now in the slightly twisted, Van Gogh geometry of horizontal winter falling lewd perpendiculars through the flat parallelograms of our window's sills, it is too late for us now. Over. Lost in our mutually exclusive dreams of boredom and waste, we will never stir again. Not ever. Only the sane can sleep as contentedly as that. No, perhaps we will find the strength to go to Mexico and die. . . .

Then Dawes Williams gets up. Putting on his Navaho hat to take a walk, he pauses quietly at his door to turn off his light. Looking back into the darkness, he believes the chairs to be sleeping within the age of their wood; he believes the room to be suddenly vacant of ghosts up its sleeve.

If your mother is a Republican, he says going out, shoot her before it's too late!

Behind him the room, the high, sightless spires and dark towers of speechless moths locked in stone, sat waiting for a noise, a blush, a movement or so . . .

Looking up, Dawes could see she had been sitting there, watching him read. Urzika had come back from the sea. It was evening again.

Urzika had reached under the table. Dawes thought she'd interrupted him like a Mexican poker game anyway, so they began walking together, back up the long curving edge of the seawall, along a black line of green plants separating the outskirts of the town from the sea exactly the way the mountains separate it from the desert. Urzika was laughing. She was deep and musky; having gone under, she still smelled of the soft fish dust of the sea. Moving back onto the edge of the market, Dawes began to hold the edge of Urzika's hand. Then, dropping it, he said:

"I'm just too goddamn old for this."

"Talk tough, Hyoot," Urzika said. "For what?"

"You know," Dawes Williams said, "for anything like this. For anything at all."

"My love possessed," Urzika said, almost smiling, "you're all stove in, Dawes."

"I am," Dawes Williams said. "I'm one dead pirate."

"How dare you die on me?" Urzika said, almost serious.

Then there was a silence as they walked through a house of bones, the rich hanging meat of a market that was green, and strung down on hooks, even in the coolness of the evening.

"Dawes?" Urzika said. "Why don't you burn those notebooks?"

"Can't," Dawes Williams said. "These notebooks are a real work of art. Posterity needs these notebooks."

"Romance," Urzika said. "For every page you burn, I'll bury you in passionate love."

"By God," Dawes said, "I'll bet my grandmother never said things like that as a nineteen-year-old girl."

"I'll inundate you," Urzika said, rubbing against him, "I'll smother you with juice. —Tell me I'm good."

"You're good, Baby," Dawes said with the imperfectly mimed voice of Humphrey Bogart, "you're real, real good."

A man hacking the side off a cow began watching them, so they moved away. Urzika was walking behind him then, both hands in his front pockets, matching his step.

"Fact is," Dawes said quietly behind him, "you've got no real leverage for a statement like that. Fact is—you're destroying what's left of me as it is with your rather unnatural lusting."

"Dawes?" Urzika said, taking her hands out of his pockets and turning him. "Do you think I am a nymphomaniac?"

"Don't know. I'm not a sociologist."

"Do you!?" she said, almost stamping her foot.

"Don't know," Dawes Williams said, turning on the edge of the market. "But I once read this here article in one a them there New York mag-a-zines? —Well here," he said, stopping, dramatically drawing out his wallet, reading off a dollar bill, "I have clipped it out and saved it for future reference. It says: 'According to the latest questionnaires, compiled by Eric Anderson of the University of Mississippi, a Ph.D. in Sociology (and an ass to boot), the average "*normal*" American married couple, couple and achieve orgasm not more than one to one and a half times per week.' And that," Dawes said, smiling at Urzika, "puts us twenty-five to thirty ahead."

Urzika began pouting. She drew one edge of her mouth out, mock-dramatically, and smiled at Dawes from the other corner of her lip like a famous Da Vinci nude with clothes on.

"It's a lie," she finally said. "Besides, you never complained at the time."

"I have never had the energy to even think of it before this," Dawes Williams said, not batting an eye.

Urzika laughed at him with the large, cynical one she hoped eventually to use on stage one day if someone gave her a break. She then looked at him with those huge, incredulously innocent eyes. For a moment Dawes thought again he almost loved her; that if he weren't dying so badly, perhaps they would have already settled down to raise orphans.

"Besides," she said finally, almost to herself, "I always get you up, you Randy Bastard."

Dawes Williams began laughing. He walked on, out of the market. Several dogs ran before him into the street.

"Didn't I once hear Mary Pickford say that very thing to William Holden in a Japanese movie?" he said over his shoulder.

"I'll bet when you say things like that at home on the prairies," Urzika said, "they call you a fag."

Then she ran after him, caught him. She jumped on his back, roped him with the curl of her arms, and began biting his neck. On the edge of drawing playful blood, she released him and moved her mouth against his ear.

"Take some acid with me tonight, Dawes," she whispered.

She was passionate; but there was a mocking in her voice that was deadly serious.

"Christ, no," Dawes Williams said, refusing even to look at her. "I wouldn't even come home to die."

"Compromise!" she said suddenly. "Burn your notebooks! Do some mescaline!"

"No. If you don't stop this, I'm leaving for Mexico City in ten minutes. I swear I am. I can only sit in dead fear of your morning coffee as it is."

Urzika turned silent. She seemed to be looking past the thin, unimportant hang of his flesh into the other side of his bones.

"If I seriously thought you thought I was capable of doing something like that to you, Dawes," she said, "I'd be leaving for Mexico City in *five* minutes."

Dawes Williams looked away, nearly flushed with something he thought he hadn't got a name for.

"Oh," he said sarcastically, almost in self-defense, "you know me. It's just this paranoid trip that makes us—me and Handsaw—act so bad."

Urzika didn't even smile. Real condescension bloomed in her eyes; she withdrew and walked on ahead of him. Dawes caught her, turned her, and tried to look at her for a long time. Failing even this again, penetrating nothing, he could only stand there thinking how he didn't believe she was nineteen years old. He thought he had lived an unbelievably sheltered life. As he looked away into the soft, fluttering dogs of the Mexican evening, into the simple purple flurry of rags of dust in the roadway, he could see nothing but the mask of her face.

"Dawes!?" Urzika said, wrenching his face back within her. "Burn your notebooks. For, not me—*us!*"

"Courtly love is dead," Dawes Williams said, turning, walking on ahead.

"Bully for you, Hyoot John," Urzika said. "You've just encapsulated another one into nothing but horseshit. *Horseshit.* Do you understand me? I said '*Horseshit'!*"

There was a silence. Dawes turned onto a street that was narrow with houses. Catching him again, Urzika almost netted him this time with the entire soft curl of her body. She stood furiously against him, impressing herself, a leaf and a mold of earth; her hand went immediately, easily under his shirt. She refused, for minutes on end, to let him move, even to let him look against her. She was crying—but then Dawes Williams knew she cried easily.

"Oh, Christ," Dawes Williams said, "I only wish it were raining. Then you could play Audrey Hepburn in *Breakfast at Tiffany's*. I could play Truman Capote as being played and reenacted by a paid Hollywood stud. What a god-damn romance that might turn out to be."

Then Urzika let him go. She slapped him hard, began beating him with the bottoms of the small, furious nests of her fists. Finally Dawes curled her over his shoulder in a fireman's carry and began stringing her out toward home. A

Mexican burro passed on the left, dragging a cart behind. Still beating him, Urzika settled finally for running her hands down the back of his pants.

"Com'on," Dawes Williams said, "we'll get run out of the country."

"Compromise!" Urzika says.

"Quit scratching me!"

"Burn your notebooks! We'll only blow up on some grass."

Dawes Williams set her back down on the dry pavement and faced her again.

"Smoke if you want," he said, "but I can't even do that. The first and last time I even did that, my old friend Braun Daniel smiled at me, handed me thirteen joints, and told me to hold it all in—to let him know how it felt when I finished. About half an hour later I got a rush that put me on a ward for two and a half months. All I could think of to remember— and I mean it was fast— was the fact that I was dying. That and all of Aristotelian *Poetics,* especially as warred with by Giraldi Cinthio in the sixteenth century. I nearly went mad."

"Beautiful!" Urzika said.

"No," Dawes Williams said. "None of it lasted. It all evaporated into nothing but air and I barely remember it."

There was a silence. Urzika was thoughtful.

"They don't teach you much about things like blowing up proper out there on the prairies. Do they?" she said.

"No," Dawes said. "Mostly they just throw you in the old swimming hole and watch you drown."

"Bad place," Urzika said, finally smiling again. "Hum me a tune."

"I guess it was something for Braun Daniel to do that afternoon. But personally, though I see it is bigoted, I could never trust a head again."

"If you kick a dog hard enough, you can only kick him once."

"I don't even trust you, you know."

"I know," she said, walking on, "but *trust* me, Dawes. Believe in me. I know the other side. Burn your notebooks."

Dawes stopped. Putting his foot on the stump of a doorway, he began to leaf through his notebooks; then, out loud, announcing his intention to the Spanish balconies, he read to Urzika:

"'So that I may keep the externals straight,'" he said, "'the dry skeletons of fact intact, I write in my notebooks:

"'February: Said goodbye to VelFever when he wasn't looking and left Iowa for good (by car). March: was on the road; shot pool in Dothan, Alabama, on the sixth (played very badly and lost fifteen dollars to a house painter). April: in Florida; went to the greyhound races; met a man who remembered Arthur; won eight hundred ten dollars, mostly on a dog named Chihuahua's Hat; decided to go to Mexico; left that night for Key West. May: On the road again; New Orleans and the Southwest. June-August: Sat in Rio Grande reading Braun

Daniel's letters from Vietnam; bandanna round my head, slapping the waters, screaming, Chihuahua! Chihuahua, boys! Cross over into Free Ground!; went to Mexico (got out of the river first) and then finally Mazatlán by bus and train; met Urzika; am not happy.

"'The car, the bus, the train, the room of the sea again. My notebooks are full of this: no poetry any more, no prose, not even hurried aphorisms and epitaphs of the mind. There is only this any more: train schedules, birthdays, and hat sizes; like Swanberg's biography of Dreiser, there are only street numbers and the temperature of Valdosta, Georgia, at noon on the fourth of April as I was passing through. . . .

" 'Am not happy. Am tired, and dying, and hope it will be over soon. Also: *Only assassins keep notebooks because they thrive on the slow act of murdering themselves.* . . . —My own Doctor VelFever Faustus Shrink'um said this; or at least I thought he did; or at least I wanted him to; or at least I thought I wanted him to be bright enough to have said that if he could have thought of it himself. . . .'"

Dawes' voice drifted off. They began walking again. Soon they were home, climbing into the small room that was Urzika's, and that was mounted on the postless air and the shop of a jeweler who sold topaz rings. The jeweler was a mute, had given the room to Urzika only because he was lonely and she could talk on the air with her hands. The room overlooked a mud courtyard, the broken brick of an alley, and the naked walls of four houses; Mexican dogs howled like hungry ashcans there in the night, and only some of the topaz rings were carved on by real Indians. Entering, Dawes lay near the floor on the bed. A kitchen table, covered with blowing paper, scribble, sat on three legs in the corner; an icebox with a hot plate and a bathtub with no pipes, and three cats prowling the edges, sat on the long end of the room; and a door, open and without stairs, blew directly in over the courtyard. The place was vacant and windless with the shade of green and dead plants.

"I'm not hungry," Dawes said. "Are you cooking?"

"No anyway," Urzika said. "I was just thinking of dropping something and going out for a walk."

"What is this," Dawes said, "a compulsive ballet movement?"

But Urzika said nothing. She had abstracted herself and was nearly gone from him already. Dawes was glad. He knew she would wander in, stray in early in the morning, and curl up against him again full of nothing like guilt or innocence, even remotely like regret or a desire for forgiveness; then they would make love until noon, not talking, until it was time again to go down to the sea. Her being gone again would give him a chance to sleep, or at least to rest, since he could never sleep. He listened to her go back down the wooden stairs. After she was gone, he turned the naked hang of the brown light on and began reading again. . . .

Chapter 3

NUMBERS

Number One

RATSHIT RAWLINGS' WEDDING

Dawes, like many other plastic humanists, loved humanity only as long as it kept its place and remained in the abstract. In fact, I remember a story that will illustrate what an absolute sullen sonofabitch Dawes Williams really was:

It was, perhaps with irony, perhaps not, at Ratshit Rawlings' wedding that Dawes finally started to openly lose his grip. It was years since they had all stopped running around being yeomen together—the ghosts of Eddie, Dunker, and Travis Thomas still hung in the vacant air of that bridal table—and it was there that Dawes gave the bride a round canning jar inappropriately wrapped in Christmas paper. Its surface was all bells, blue spheres, and the suggestions of prancing reindeer. Only Dawes Williams seemed to know, or care, that behind the white veil lay a bonfire, a bloody sacrificial snake of symbolistic air.

"O! Thanks! Thanks so MUCH, Dawes," she, the bride, the happy one, said before she had bothered to open it.

In it was a rubber penis. A ball-less and severed phallus all round and pickled in vinegar. After she had recognized it, looked at its roundness for awhile, she dropped it to the floor and "it," the thing, and she, fainted, wilted and lay there shattered like plastic flowers as the maid hired for the day came to carry them both out. It was arm and dustpan and just all happied out, the bride in one hand, the rubber penis in the other.

Older people began to line up and stare at Dawes Williams for minutes on end.

"Hell of a fine joke if you ask me," Barney Ingersoll said.

"Well. Ratshit," Dawes Williams said finally, turning slowly around, "I think you may have gotten yourself a simple puritan one there. I just don't know who hit the floor first—your wife or the thing."

Sometimes, I thought, *I* long for the ability to create real experience, to create social impasse, to have that gloriously bleak ability Dawes had; to make the old women of the race—wrapped tightly as they are in their black, inviolate shawls, in their mindless pecking orders of social distinction— writhe and cry out in their abject fear of the rubber cock.

Oh well, perhaps in a less delicate age that requires the services of madmen who are more than merely theatrical, I thought to myself. . . .

Because, you see, the thing had a point; it was not over and, indeed, it was only just now beginning to unfold itself. Dawes knew it, had planned it that way, and after he had gone over for another glass of punch, a matron of the tribe pinned him in a corner of the church (as he knew one would) and they held a long, hushed conversation in which Dawes explained himself:

"It would be you, Dawes Williams, who would do a thing like this no doubt," the matron starts out.

"Perhaps," Dawes says, "perhaps not."

"How could you!? How dare you!" she says. "Dawes Williams, you cad, you wait until your dear, unsuspecting mother hears about this one! You were such a nice boy before you went to college you . . . you degenerate!!"

"Not me, Mrs. Burr. It was Handsaw."

"Handsaw indeed. Who is Handsaw?" she says, rushing on. "Another of your curious fictions?! Another of your filthy rationalizations meant to shake us from our good sanity and stability no doubt, Dawes Williams, you paranoid gypsy!?"

"Not mine, Mrs. Burr. It's not easy growing up on the prairies, though," Dawes Williams says. "Shucks, me and Handsaw, we're just trying to get us out of that crazy Mexican War is all."

"How dare you! Really, Dawes Williams, all you need (and it's high time you found) is some nice, self-respecting girl to settle you down."

"I am innocent," Dawes Williams says.

"Have you met my daughter Arrabella?"

"Is she the Queen of Spain?"

"No, she is studying nursing."

And then Dawes: "Not mine."

"It was—I know it was."

"No, nope, not mine."

"Yes yes, yes yes yes."

"It was not my rubber penis, Mrs. Burr."

"Really, Dawes," she says finally, "sometimes I think you should be quietly put away."

"What is this? A dialogue spoken to a vacuity? Where am I?" Dawes Williams says.

"You are in church!" she says.

"No, not mine, Mrs. Burr. I, the quietly sane, unpretentious poet for all chimes, I keep mine in the vest pocket of my Sunday suit, wrapped in a leather banana case, filed away for the future, like well-scrubbed American yeoman farmers, on Sunday, well-brushed and going to town. I am foreign to this baroque place, this palace of corn."

"Pretentious fool," she says. "You are making a speech."

"Not mine."

"Yes," she says, quieting some.

"No. And at night I keep mine in a glass of water, beside my bed."

"Decadence!" she says, reeling against the church's wall. "That's demonic!"

"Yes," Dawes Williams says, "it lies under the waves and genitive rollings; across a pea-shell sea, the moon-ridden, unclenched, inexorable rolling where Christo Colombo still rides the iron petals of sun, lost, a Latin Viking in the eye of a violent God, endlessly rolling. It's just me and Walt Whitman, alone in a rowboat with the King of Siam. We paddle the risen petals of an iron sun; we swim within the furious eye of a violet God, perched and waiting on a whitestone beach. He is History; we are mad nymphet scribes, self-deluded with light. I don't know. It is merely speech connected to nothing any more. I am sad. I need another glass of gin punch. Pessimism that leaves you numb is the only ultimate breakthrough . . .

"Insanity! Insanity! Doggerel!"

"Not mine. Others'."

"Yes."

"And if I married her, your Arrabella," Dawes Williams continued, "I would, I must, roll softly over in the morning, I would feel her wrapped closely against me in her unknowing fear, I would look deeply into her eyes, and I would say—'Darling, darling, I've just decided your coffee is wretched,' or, 'Darling, darling, what's happened to your horseshit coffee!'—and she would understand. She would just lie there in her prepared, omniscient understanding and understand."

"Schizophrenic peasant!!" she says, drawing herself up. "These things are simply not discussed in polite company. At weddings."

"Yes," Dawes Williams says, "it is something she can handle. She would understand; she is even glad I have finally said it and finally reached the age of virile majority, become an American guy. Yes, she is glad, even grateful, because it is all she is capable of understanding, is all you have given her to know she needs to understand about living, Mrs. Burr."

"Oh, my God," she says, "you are mad!"

"I am afraid I am serious."

"You can't be."

"I am afraid this is the quality of life in the late American Republic. I'm afraid I see a mighty slow plastic time for Ratshit down that lonesome pike, and that's mainly a sad thing for a guy whose ancestors were New England Transcendental poets. . . ."

"Please, Dawes," she says, "do not refer to Ratshit Rawlings as 'Ratshit' at his own wedding."

"Harrison was a good man," Dawes Williams says slowly. "It was Eddie Welsh who renamed Harrison Rawlings, Ratshit Rawlings. We were all boys together."

"Oh, my God," she says, writhing against the flat wall of the church, "that's demonic!"

"It's at least moralistic, dipolar."

"Not *mine,*" she says. "It's not *my* rubber. . . thing!?"

"Button, button," Dawes Williams says. "Yes, I think it is. It's because you're moving away from your past in the wrong direction and trying so desperately to call it Right. Your greatest grandmother, remember, possessed the innocent, driven, *a priori* insight of a Druid witch (who serviced George Washington—the great leftist radical only thinly disguised as an aristocratic bore—during the Revolution) but you've forgotten."

"Insane man! Lecturer of dreams! Oh, Dawes Williams," she says quietly, "you nut."

"Yes, it has been pleasant talking to you, Mrs. Burr," Dawes Williams says, drawing himself up to his fullest, baroque extension, "even though you shall, doubtlessly, always choose to remain a mindless little bourgeois twit nervously successful mostly in the raising, the carefully religious nurturing of other, ongoing moronic twits who will remain mostly renowned for being healthy enough to dance on the cinders of a world going out. Incidentally, they will have to be remembered by themselves; the rest of us won't be around. And I'm afraid the ultimate result will be something short of epical poetry."

"WHAT!?!?!!??" Mrs. Burr says.

"Das what I say," Dawes says.

"Really, Dawes," she says, "you have transcended all bounds. I'm telling your mother. I'm calling my husband over here to straighten you out."

"Not mine," Dawes said finally.

"Not!" she says. "Not at Miriam's daughter's wedding. These *things* are simply not *my things!*"

"Not mine."

"Not mine."

"Yes."

"Not mine," she says, turning round, "and Dawes Williams," she says pointing sacrosanctly at the ceiling, "there has never been an American war in which he has not been on our side."

"Not even before 1620?" Dawes Williams wondered after.

"Not even then," she says, withdrawing.

"This then indeed," Dawes Williams says, beginning to pace off the geometry of the church's flooring, "has been a truly exemplary and hallowed ground."

Number Two

ROY RIDES: HANDSAW, PRINCE OF PLAYERS, STEPS STAGE CENTER AND PRO-
NOUNCES A SHORT SOLILOQUY UPON THE END OF BEING

That was the Dawes Williams I knew and remembered! That was the dirty sono-fabitch I loved so well!

Dawes, we who are about to die salute you! O, fie on't!

That damn silly yeoman: you are out of your time; you are looking for only another fair town to wander in; you are out in the rain, dying of brain cancer, with only a goatskin and a bladder of wine. You crazy bastard: knowing only that in the twentieth century the sane are mad, locked up and put away, and the insane are safe, beyond the law.

Because it is Sunday morning again now; an elemental juxtaposition. I am almost sure of it.

John Steinbeck was a wonderful man! Dawes is screaming.

Yes, I say. It is slow Sunday again, the Roy Rogers movies are on the tube, and per-haps I am merely hallucinating, but it seems to me Dawes Williams, mad yeoman, Marine, potential defender of the commonweal, is just now over by himself in the corner, opening his veins like a noble Roman; he is busy slitting his wrists with a teaspoon.

We should be Greece, not Rome! he says. Perhaps I should be drinking hemlock right now and denying the ethics of suicide.

Perhaps, I think, there is a piece of social criticism to be gathered here.

Perhaps there isn't.

But Roy Rogers continues to ride. He is streaking down pale horse trails, between thin arrows in the West, and he is successful in ignoring us all. Dawes is disenchanted, but I am capable of great distance and ignore him back. Roy suffocates the room with heroic dust, a horse named Trigger. He rides out of a stone of perfect sun, the movie is on!, and he tears past a posse of poker-faced horses and begins to pull a '37 Dodge sta-tionwagon over against the curb of a small, cardboard mountain—Is this Tennessee? everyone wonders. A door opens, and from the '37 Dodge stationwagon steps Dale Evans.

"Hi there, Roy," she says.

"Hi there, Dale," Roy says. "Have we met? Welcome to Calavernous, California—it's a good thing me and my horse Trigger here were able to stop your runaway Dodge."

Christ! Dawes Williams screams. All must be simple phenomena after all!

Roy, slick and polished as a blond boot, hair pulled back like sixty, smiles silvered and boyish gigolo teeth into a sheepish sun. Dawes Williams thinks he has found an ulti-mate metaphor for the universe. He thinks the universe thinks it is so Good, it doesn't exist any more. But Roy—standing there amid horses and stationwagons, amid vague Camelot coexistent West, smiling those damn smug teeth into a stage-filling sunset—con-tinues. Dawes doesn't; he ends. In fact, he is in the process of ending right now. Roy, how-ever, looks blindly successful: a man both successful and surprised by his success, the greatest sort of happy, unexpected success. Over in his corner, Dawes Williams begins to hate Dawes Williams who is hating Roy Rogers—ostensibly because when you are suf-fering psychosis brought about by Alzheimer's disease you have no time for bad art, how-ever important, but really because Dawes Williams is not continuing and Roy Rogers, that happy ass, is. In fact, when you are suffering psychotic hell you are forced to emotionally question a culture, the validity of a species, which has made mostly Roy Rogers movies in the first place. Enough, suffice to say that the psychotic in dementia does not tend to see the easy satire in it all. And that Dawes Williams was such a psychotic. He notes carefully that it is strangely ironic that it has all come to this, but, standing over there by himself in the corner, beside the tube, opening his veins with a teaspoon, Dawes Williams was not laughing any more. . . .

To Be or not To Be, I say, There is no question involved in the thing. Existence isn't nice. No wonder the Victorians denied the existence of existence. (*Cognosco propter non sum.*) Dawes is a modernist, but I don't blame them myself. A sane, human man could only be embarrassed—standing there, holding reflexively onto the self-conscious, ape banana of a question like that. This then—the consciousness of being conscious—is surely the genesis of neurosis; and neurosis is the genesis of death. We are swimming then, I say, in that great nonprotestant sea that is beyond free will. The freedom of it all feels strangely deep, foreign, and explodes on contact with our blood. . . .

I stand wordless with impossible opinion, Dawes Williams says.

But, in fact, looking at him standing alone in his corner, I could see Dawes was not even smiling . . .

Number Three

DAWES WILLIAMS AT THE RIVER IN HILLS, IOWA,
OR: SENSIBILITIES, LIKE EGGS, BREAK AT DAWN.
ALSO CONCERNING ACCOUNTS OF LOCAL FLORA AND FAUNA:
BRAUN DANIEL AND DAWES WILLIAMS AT COLLEGE.
IN WHICH, ALSO, I MAKE THE CONFESSION:
"I AM SUCH A BAROQUE, FALLEN PRICK REALLY!"

I am such a baroque, pompous prick really. I speak, like Fielding and Richardson, with a jaded, epistolary tongue. Don't run to your dictionary if you haven't one. I am only pointing out that I am, unforgivably, writing you a letter. Ignore it; this has become such a damn manneristic century anyway, perhaps I can't help myself. Perhaps I can, but then perhaps I don't care to, choose to overlook it, and perhaps Dawes Williams, that mad-ass cowboy poet of the prairie cornstalks, doesn't either. Have you got that? Good, forget it. It wasn't important. Have you ever thought that perhaps you might not even be here right now; that you might be somewhere else, but forgetful? . . .

Yes, Dawes Williams says, where has the narrative gone? This was such a pretty, prancing story and you've spoiled it.

Dawes? I say, blowing his mind. Where are you now in specific reference to this page any more?

That's just it, Dawes Williams says, I don't know. I seem to have lost track at least three generations ago. Are we still on?

I look over at Dawes. Just now he is writhing with pity and fear; he is over in his corner, inching his hand across the reaching flooring, trying to connect himself within the naked socket of the huge, leonine lamp. Catharsis! His right foot is rammed up the back of a toaster. Anagnorisis without peripetia! O void. Dawes, who knows he will never make it, who knows he will never succeed in connecting the electrical rhythms, begins screaming:

You! Handsaw! he says. Shut the hell up. If you say anagnorisis without peripetia! O void, once more, I'll never make it. I'll be laughing too hard to ever make it.

He'll make it. Dawes Williams, that lucky, irrepressible plowman, will probably connect his toaster to his lamb socket and come out whole. Bloomed! Cured! Flattest of ironies, it would probably be a perfect electric shock. Whole, treated, sane, Dawes Williams' prefrontal lobotomy will then be able to forget me. By God, I tell you that sonofabitch is uncanny.

Because, you see, it all started breaking out that spring he tried to talk and couldn't.

Let me explain: His mouth would fall open, he would stutter for awhile, then fall silent again. He rode his motorcycle down to the river at dawn. Because that was the spring of Braun Daniel, his vulgate Bulldog Boomer le Roi, and their wild circus of domestic mice. Let me try and explain: Early in the mornings that spring, usually beginning at false first light, when the mice whimperings grew too unbearable and when they were gnawing loudest at their walls, trying like birth to get out, Dawes would get up from having not slept

(Yes. That was the spring I woke and found I was living with Braun Daniel and his Great Spirit of Bred-Mouse, Dawes Williams often said when he was drunk enough to get stoned)

and leave the farmhouse and start his motorcycle, the one with "TRIUMPH" scrawled across the tank, and ride down those country towns, down those silent roads and fields of quietly breeding owls,

(Damn I bet I woke up a lot of hardworking crackers that spring, Dawes Williams often said. That was the spring Braun Daniel gave up writing soft, liquid poetry and joined the Marines. Broad, thick in the head as Hemingway, he took to reading *A Farewell to Arms, The Green Hills of Africa,* and dreaming of killing small yellow people. It was rousing adventure, like drinking and fire bombs in the old days. He felt great. I went mad and entered the lists in VelFever's ward. Paradox, I suppose, but I will never be able to assimilate it emotionally. Perhaps God is really just a fat general's ass after all. What can you say? he often said)

and the steaming early-morning dropping of horses going gold in the sun. Dawes, revving his bike through the wooden bridge at Hills, Iowa, stopped down the road. Sitting in a snowpile, he took out his notebooks and wrote:

BRAUN DANIEL'S FURIOUS SPRING

"I'll see you across the barricades, Daniel," Dawes Williams had said, leaving the farmhouse. "I'm real particular about who I shoot. I'd rather shoot my friends when they are wrong than my enemies when they are right."

"Damn vestigial moralist," Braun Daniel said. "Methodist. I'm an existentialist. You can't seem to understand that."

"Existentialist, shit," Dawes Williams says. "But you're right, I don't. And even in the intellectual morass of your Cliff Notes mind," Dawes says, slamming the screen behind him, "I doubt the reality of the logic that Camus, or even Sartre, in this late date of 1968, would be joining the United States Marine Corps in the name of enlightened individualism."

Braun Daniel says nothing. He eyes Dawes fiercely through the screen door; he thinks for awhile of running out nearly naked in the snow, of chasing Dawes around the chopping block of the barnyard. Giving it up finally, he recedes back into the cellar to sleep. His two prize bulldogs, Boomer le Roi and Zoomer the Deuce, wag their tails and chains across the mindless, soundless kitchen floor behind him.

"What are you, Willy," Braun Daniel says finally through the kitchen screen, "turning soft or queer or something?"

"John Wayne kisses only his horse," Dawes Williams says, bouncing down on his bike. "At least usually."

Braun Daniel says nothing. He stands head high at the horizontal window smoking a cigar. Dawes Williams does half a wheelie around a tree and comes back. Dawn is rising. December.

"You know," Dawes says, "the hero celibate, that is the 'clean hero' syndrome, has been well described. I'm bored. The problem with you, Daniel, is that you are just another psychopathic loner but you are too physically healthy to know enough to feel bad about it."

"I don't want to be no goddamn celibate, you goddamn effete," Braun Daniel says. "I just want to help plant the seed of a new race in the belly of the Orient."

"She-it," Dawes says, "you just don't ever want to be the father to a son.—Why don't you just go to Montana and knock up a poor, unsuspecting waitress and save everybody ahelluva hassle? Why don't you just pass through that nameless hobo air without blowing anybody's brains out?"

"Why don't I come out there and knock your block off?" Braun Daniel says, laughing.

Dawes edges his motorcycle away. To cover up, he pulls a pint of whiskey out of his jacket and begins drinking.

"Fuck off, B. D.," Dawes says. "You know when you walked in there— Gibber's place, ten in the morning, everybody blowing up around the stereo and trying to read books—walking like Tut, leading those damn silly dogs of yours, announcing you had just joined the United States Marines, I thought the place had gone dead."

"It was beautiful all right," Braun Daniel says, smiling. "Like I say—you have to be an existentialist to go against peer-group pressure like that."

"Send'em to college, and all's they do is hang around bus stops reading *The Police Gazette,*" Dawes Williams says. "What's it coming to, I ask you?"

"What's that supposed to mean?" Braun Daniel says.

"It means you ain't no Genet," Dawes says, "although, ironically, picking up on it on another level, you may be a full-blown individualist in the Ronald Reagan mold."

"Right, Dawes," Braun Daniel says casually. "Real fine."

"Like I say," Dawes says, pulling away, "I'll see you across the barricades."

"Up your political ass," Braun Daniel yells after, laughing furiously. "I'll bring the Marines."

Dawes Williams bombs down that road.

Winter is a cold stalk of broken yellow light. Nothing is clearly around him, like houses of white wood. Hills rise, continue, vague and brown as cores; they go back under black pastures of broken ground, the stray spines of vacant corn. He seems away because nothing is attached to the sky, and the dead season is a lost, seeping thing. The water burrows, like white and naked sleeping animals, into the dark centers of earth; and morning is a stray cow, coming in to drink. Cold stone horses run in the fast, fat fields; they steam like whales in the distances, and Dawes thinks suddenly dead Methodists lie in state, beyond the county line: he thinks they are dark logs, rolling over like camp meetings in the white and luminous green water. For a moment he thinks he remembers an old stone house, Abigail Winas, and an oval attic window framed in moon. He thinks time is the concept of an image, only attached to the sky.

He gets down from his bike, walks along the frozen river smoking a brown cigaret. He stands watching the sun come up. He is in Hills, Iowa, he thinks, and he thinks he is thinking of jumping through holes in the ice, of swimming softly within the soft, light sheets of water like the embedded fossil of a fish, staring up, blowing funny eyes and cartoon gills up through the frozen puff of the screen.

Dawes Williams, yeoman in heat, walks, paces, talking to the madder river, the bell of air, the cold early spring. He thinks only: Romanticism is dead, ha, ha, and turns away from the water. It is first sun and, digging through his leather pockets for old scribbled paper, he fumes, turns on the banks, begins talking again. Staring down the foliage, addressing a tree, he thinks he can read himself off like a list; a record of madder air. Finally sitting down on a rock he says:

"JUST ANOTHER DOCUMENT
A POEM: 'THE BRIDGE'
by
DAWES WILLIAMS, AMIABLE PLOWMAN,
AT THE RIVER AND THE END OF HIS STRING"

Ignoring a herd of black-and-white milk cows come down to dream on his more curious air he reads on:

"Winter. The yellow bones,
the smoke and stacks of factories, sleeping rising fish,
rope the skeletons of the paler entrepreneurs—
locked tightly within their actuality of only a
richer, more mercantile death—within the harder reality of
sky. The shadows of cold flying birds.
The yeoman paces the river.
and waits for an answer. Nothing comes.

"Fuck capitalism. (Having nothing but a dramatic dialogue with
itself, when what is needed here is a new Homestead Act.)

"I can see Dawes Williams now—
(that lost soul of a boy's eye, hung,
like a thickened stone, on a chain from his own bent neck: a priest's
stone; deep, and blue, and over-precious)—watching the evening as it
blows itself up from the river. That helpless aesthete. That hopeless bastard.
That singer of only himself.
(At the highest ascension,
                          he thinks,
                                        there is a door.)

"He lies. In wait.
Quietly he paces: as if *he* could disturb it:
        as if he actually *were* that smoky priest of himself,
        self-proclaimed and appointed, casting those litanies
        of smoking pots before him on his way to the water.
He waits: for Hart Crane to rise again:
        from that self-same stream that forever flows,
        three hundred miles, north of Havana,
        at two minutes to noon.
To speak. Soft. Soft as bent light, trapped in the
rain. Nothing comes. (But red flowers will bloom.
Red flowers will bloom in the door of the sky.)

"Dawes Williams remains. Pacing.
Waiting an answer in the ante-room, pacing,
talking softly to the softer waters,
        'Madness,' he says to the river,
'is an apprenticeship. . . consciousness a textural house.
How can the sea-wind,' he asks the naked air,
'not ask the inland grasses to rise?
How can the red, decomposing flowers
deny the softer rubbing insect of the blacker waters?'
Nothing responds. But Dawes Williams remains.

Pacing. Talking to a softer sill:
> 'In that summer,' he says,
> 'I spent hanging to a greener air . . .
>> watching the bones of the darker fish
> dance like distances off colder waters .
>> watching the bright bombs of bones
> rise and compass, into the sun . . .
>> watching them sound, dance, become
> blacker bulbs in the pitted hearts of
>> their own seeds, then hang to the air,
> with only the thinnest suggestions of flesh
>> In that summer when it happened,
> when they rose, and danced
>> and moved off south in the sun
> (cold, spectral, full of the ghost),
>> with heads as big as eyes,
>> with eyes as large as roses,
>> over the waters . . . and I thought:
> *To have jumped in that sea.*
And to have, perhaps, remembered the sound of that falling.
> *Three hundred miles, north of Havana.'*
> The shadows of the dancing, darker fish:
> The cold, prancing green light emerging.
>> *(On a hot day, too hot for sleeping,*
>>> *a few minutes past noon.)*
> That, and the red, decomposing flowers
> blooming in the door of the sky.
> That, and the sound of the ship, port rudders,
> a slipping beyond, a dancing behind,
> (cold, spectral, full of the ghost)
> the green light of the imperfect sea slipping below."

It was a good poem, he thought putting it neatly away, good enough easily to commit suicide over.

Then, done speaking, he bounces three times on his motorcycle starter and is away. It is nearly six now, first river light. Running completely through three gears, Dawes Williams takes one last turn down the single sleeping street of Hills, Iowa. His loud, rapping sound blows off the wooden houses, the drab store fronts, the red feed signs, the stray and broken dogs running out from the vacant yards. Kicking the air, a mangy charging cur in the teeth, he rides up on the wind and the single alley of the town. He thinks he is alone in the world. Pale morning, thin lights go on in the windows of white houses.

He thinks suddenly he is inhibited by the squared, recurring geometry itself of doors, windows, streets, the edges of houses.

The huge, finite whiteness of sky, painted-in within the stark mad fingers of brown trees, the bare cedars, rise a clean stone of seeing that falls naked and dead on the lens, the shadowy moving water-bodies of his eyes. The clear light washes over; leafless; cold. He thinks winter has become a simple asthma in the lung of the sky; a thing made close and choked on wet surfaces, it has become only a blister of distance . . . Braking, down shifting, revving up, Dawes goes up the flapping wooden rise, the loose planking of the old covered bridge. He jumps the bike, mounts the air, and enters the long tunnel; the flat ellipsis of light under the bridge's roof. His sound becomes a clock, a thing with dark regular spacings, and rattles around him. He thinks he is a long stick, a naked edge being trailed over a picket fence behind itself. At the end is a drawn funnel of gray light, a cold burst of sun.

O Damn Bless Me, Dawes Williams thinks revving and shifting up, heading for the flatlands along the thin river bottom, it's only another blueloving motherswan of dawn. Nothing transcends like a motorcycle.

Coming out, like only metaphysically passing through to the other side— of a mirror, experience, the frame of a door—Dawes is doing a perfect seventy-five and he swerves slightly to miss a large, tough farm cat who is busy chasing a small pheasant over the last patches of snow.

Winter, he thinks, is broken light; a small yellow stalk barely used; a round stone of hills forming behind. Slowly he watches the young pheasant rise away and fly over the air. It goes up, a perfect sail, a whole buzzing wing, over the river as the cat turns; shakes the wet out of her paw; begins making her caving way up the sullen banks; crosses the ditch; sneezes the morning from her lungs. As Dawes watches her, a perfect stone, light, she goes down a culvert, enters a hole in the fence, and emerges within the three acres of junked pots, cars, taut nesting rats lying out over the broken whole, the sill of the river . . .

If Braun Daniel were here, Dawes Williams thinks, yes, he would have chased her out, for miles, furiously, through fields, through barns, flat out, yes, running, a fierce lost bear trapped in his own woods, the busted stalks, yes, for miles, flat out, headless, hot, lost, yes, and turn, turn laughing, in the gray air, at the cold sun, and turn against me, yes, laughing, and tear out her heart . . . I have seen him do it.

In his spare time he tames wild owls in the kitchen. They bring back dark mice from the fields in the morning; disused; partially eaten. He walks his fifteen-year-old rooster named Elmer on a leather leash downtown, in Iowa City, to meet people in the afternoon . . . yes, he's really groovy.

Yes, Dawes Williams thinks stepping down again, I have seen him do it. That Braun Daniel, he hates those cats. Yes. And laugh at me, and turn against me, laughing, worn stone, wild wind, accusing me of madness, yes, and bite off her head, and tear out her heart, and shuck her out on the laughing ground like spent and bloody, dead and unholy rain. I have seen him do it.

The bike runs out easy and warm beneath him. The sun is an early field. The tubes in his lungs are freezing; and he can feel them bluing, drying into dead cores. TRIUMPH is scrawled in tin across his tank, and he thinks he rides a deserted stone of wild grass, the wind going down the same road in the opposite direction. The light, he thinks, is a cigar butt; vague, yellow, sleeping easily within itself like the long edge of God. Winter too is heavy with the frozen over, the thawing under, the pilings and recessions of root-bearing animals, the closed cuttings of deep, surfaced earth. And the split stalks, they are a thin miasmus of misplaced wind; the broken stain of ground, the last mirror of dark, rowing earth.

Skies the color of vague standing noon are small with animals, chewing rodents; the white gnawing distances are tiny with noise . . . the early ground light, a low hung mist, a burrowing under, is a moving within, the bigness of walking cows.

Broken leaf. Sky. The wind is a delicate illusion.

He thinks he is riding ten miles south of a given point. Dead, childhood Methodists sleep beyond in the graveyards. Moving down familiar country roads, with others, in the wrong direction, he thinks he is only overwrought to no end. Feeling deeply suddenly he is only too far out-back on a nomadic, homeless continental shield, he spins it all on its rear axis and heads back north. He will go north to the farmhouse where Braun Daniel sleeps so well, under a blanket of dogs—C. S. Scotty MacDuff, Boomer le Roi and Zoomer the Deuce—under a warm winter mound, a pile of yellow fleas and living fur. In the morning, Braun Daniel will rouse himself only to use their napkins of ears to theatrically blow the night from his lungs.

Dawes Williams passes a mooing cow foraging a ditch.

The sun is almost full up over the limp ground now. Dawes Williams opens his throttle and begins outdistancing the medium-sized fawn greyhound who is galloping gracefully along the inside of a fencerow. He passes the white leaning walls of the Baptist Church. The sleeping walls, like white wooden lilies of morning, sit miles out back and stand beyond even themselves. A yellow haze drifts up from the gravestones. The vague river fog, the smoky water of ancestors trapped in the cold sun, walks between the houses and outbuildings.

The warm bike raps out beneath him; between him. Dawes Williams thinks he rides the ringing pails of morning down familiar country blacktop; he is sitting high, and he feels he may be as big and wide as a hidden house of the moon.

The road, soft curves, a rolling out before, drifts over the tops of black dirt hills. The sky, he thinks, is a hanging; big as knives in the west. The wind is up and rising like Indian drums. It's nuns' picks of utter silence in his knitting; his stockings, caps, mufflers, and skin.

Going down the road, he feels like the junk-man with an invisible truck tied behind. He passes a horse; morning is leaning swaybacked against a bowlegged fence.

He swerves, lays out low over cement. Screaming GOD-BLESS-US-EVERYONE Dawes passes an early tractor heading out to deal hay and plow up the day. Looking up, he sees he is doing a-hundred-and-five.

The sky is happy, big with farms. The single red tractor raps away somewhere, on two cylinders, in 5/7 time going over the back of a hill. The morning comes up higher; it is eye level now, he thinks, and full of cold flying-by birds, wet gray shadings, a haze of near hills; the sleeping light, doing a-hundred-and-five.

Soon he will go back to the farmhouse and sleep. He passes a forgotten, overgrown congregation; a scrub of peaceful rock; a stone community of gravemarkers where a speechless wind hides out in the vertical morning. The weeping shadows of old gray-beards walk, by in the country woods.

Gearing down, pulling in under a fat shadow of snow, the shade of a leafless cedar, Dawes lights his last brown cigaret. Sitting Indian style on his TRIUMPH, he begins thinking again of Dawes City, Iowa, dead in the ground. He thinks that image is locked in time; that memory is a stone that refuses to melt, to dissolve away and become whole. Once again he is eight years old, trapped against a breathless, beatless wall, a round and oval window of attic moon; he is caught and watching, midnight, the fall of his great-great's old stone house, he is watching from the high stone balcony as she— Abigail Winas, dying fish light brain, midnight itself, the only true Celt left in town—runs through the squawking woods, gutting a chicken . . . the noise of the light itself.

Now the woods are full of flying, whirling druid witches. A hanging beyond. A pre-monition that is real.

Often now, when he is out riding alone in the mornings, he can see Abigail walking the edges of the fields. She is alone, like the light, hanging mists, with the prancing shadows of Indians, Travis and Eddie and Dunker. When they come out to see their sleeping land, green and overpruned like Aunt Ella's whiskers, her lilac hedges, her tin cities and her small towns, they choose to faint dead away again into the hills, the river bluffs of the eastern and western valleys. That is where they sleep now, he thinks. I know. Soundly, watching, waiting for another chance, I know they do. And in the mornings, riding alone, I can see their thin skeletons, white as smoking bone, rise up and walk over the very edges of the fields. *Can't you see, I tell them, that none of this is my fault? Can't you see, I tell them, that it is really no one's fault? That it is, yes, inexcusable?* . . . But they will not listen to me. Nor answer. There is a secret they will never tell me. There is a secret their dry heart will never condescend to hear.

Then bouncing three times on his motorcycle kicker, he is away.

He outcircles a dead haywagon and turns left. The long, standing herds of milk and feeder cows are parked in the fields. Heading down the last clean stretch of country road, he can see that the farmhouse, Braun Daniel, lie beyond, across a mile-wide space of clear brown treeless field. There is nothing to do. All is sleeping within the cold Midwestern light.

Lucky, it is a mild winter, though. . . .

Avoiding the driveway, he rides up the center of the hill that lies before the farm-house. He knows he hasn't been sleeping well that spring so he casts about in his mind for something to do. Perhaps, Dawes Williams thinks, I will go into town and eat bacon and eggs.

Braun Daniel's old white Plymouth is parked counterclockwise across the lane. A stray herd of farm cats is wandering its edges. The left front door is hanging open and down wind in the air.

Inside, Braun Daniel lay sleeping. There was nothing to do. Dawes lit a cigaret and watched his smoke drift off in the yellow light of the window. Only when the alarm went off, announcing the sun, would Braun Daniel awake and Dawes Williams begin to sleep. Looking over, Dawes can see that even the piles and blankets of sleeping dogs don't phase him; that Boomer le Roi is sawing the hard, dozing sleep of the innocent, half-turned, squarely planted on Braun Daniel's head. . . .

Then the alarm does go off. The bed explodes. And Braun Daniel steps forth, arises like a wandering Prussian drillmaster in need of a war. Bouncing up straight as a tree, he does three hundred and fifty jumping jacks in two minutes, puts on his shorts, and goes out barefooted in his socks to do four miles in the last of the snow. Passing Dawes Williams' bed on his way out, Braun Daniel pauses only to say:

"You lazy, decadent asshole," as he goes through the door.

Then Dawes Williams could begin to sleep, lying low, smiling, dreaming of Braun Daniel running his ass through the woods.

"Quick," Dawes had said, rolling quietly over. "Someone call Frank Merriwell a cab."

Braun Daniel had said nothing more. He had already gone over the back of the hill. Dawes lay there blowing smoke at the roof: he rolled over and thought perhaps it was only guilt, but he could still hear Braun Daniel's furious breathing receding four miles away in the woods. . . .

Yes, he thinks, that must be it. We are both in graduate school now. Braun Daniel, he is only testing it. The first time I ever saw him I was turning a corner round the new 9½-million-dollar Science Building (trying to figure a way to look intelligent in my red freshman beanie) on the small liberal-arts campus of Boe College, and there he was, hauling the larger piece of a two-ton oak across the commons lawn. He was straining, red in the face, wrapped within an elaborate set of ropes, pulleys and horse harnesses.

From the first it was Little John trying to fuck over Robin Hood at the bridge.

P.A. folks—that is, Pre-Acid people, not knowing they were living on the exact hinge of an irrelevant age—were rolling out of the two twin dorms. Some were in pajamas and nightgowns, and all were standing around saying things like:

"Go, horse. Bray. Pull, mother. Give him some hay."

"Cool your hogs," Braun Daniel was saying, "I'll make it."

The yellow morning possessed the decayed sky, the broken remains of a Midwestern windstorm. The oak had blown down in a tornado which had managed to hit Boe College at dawn and, as if to preserve some of the storm for himself, Braun Daniel was up early that morning, naked to the waist, busted vessels in his face, pulling on that harness roped to that tree. A crowd was gathering. Braun Daniel, turning against the circle, saw Dawes about to sit on the grass (for the first time, Dawes Williams thinks, I had gotten too close to the thing already for my own good) and he said:

"Hey, you, James-asthmatic-Joyce in the wire glasses, give us a hand, will you? Nobody around here seems to understand about this."

At first Dawes Williams said nothing at all. Daniel's shirt was off, the ropes were making red cuts and welts across his bursting chest, and in the distances behind, Dawes

Williams thought he heard girls moaning quietly, like snakes of wind gone up under the thin watery morning of nightgowns:

"Must be some horny-piggy Alpha Kappa Zetas," someone was laughing from the other side of the leafy tree.

But everyone had piled out early to see what Braun Daniel was up to next. He was pulling on that tree.

"What the fuck is this?" Dawes Williams finally said.

"What the fuck isn't it?" Braun Daniel said. "Life's a physical confrontation. I'm an existentialist. I'm hauling this tree up to my room and I'm afraid I may need some help."

"Oh ya," Dawes Williams said, bending against it. "Why?"

"No, not now. I'll do it myself," Braun Daniel said. "You trying to kick me off this bridge? I'll get it to the steps, Myth of Sisyphus, to the damn wall. It's getting it up the four stories of Greene Hall I need the help with. Among other things, I'm going to need someone to get rid of the bureaucracy for me."

"Rah. Rah," Dawes Williams said.

"I can see right now," Braun Daniel said, "you are some kind of Socratic asshole or other."

"Mike Fink, King of the River."

"You helping me with this rock or not?"

"It's not a rock," Dawes Williams said.

"That shows a lot you know about it," Braun Daniel said, "you Communist fucker."

He was mocking. Moving away. Pulling on his harness.

Dawes Williams lies within the thin silence of his sleep, blowing smoke at his roof, trying to write a novel. But then, he thinks, Braun Daniel always was a great naturalistic parody anyway . . .

Maybe, after all, it was because, Dawes thought, lying there blowing smoke at the moon, Braun Daniel was an English major. And because his intellect was like watching a German eat whole the head of a screaming pig. He was a damn strange one. He was the only one, for example, in Late American Novel 4:6 who thought Dos Passos' *U.S.A.* a great piece of literature because it remained largely a beautiful fascist dream in nature. In Late European Novel 4:7, he thought Genet was a genius mainly because he had the common sense to only pose as a minor queer disguised as Candide. And that, ultimately, Jean-Paul Sartre probably really was a Communist front without knowing it. In fact, Braun Daniel was the only one Dawes had talked to in Late-Early-Mid-American History 12:2 who thought Andrew Jackson was a truly great man because, after all, he was, with Grant, the truer father of his country.

"The American Dream is moving along well," Braun Daniel said. "If these pussy-spectacled intellectuals would just leave it alone."

"Greece, not Rome," Dawes Williams said.

Braun Daniel laughed his ass off and went out for a walk.

Anyway, after he had got the oak tree up to his room (Dawes Williams thinks, lying there, his smoke run out now), Braun Daniel lived in a Druid forest. No one entered easily that tangled house of leaves. And when he studied, which was seldom (mostly he read Cliff Notes and Hulk Comic Books), he lay in the corner, flat on his flooring, under parts of that tree. In the mornings during football season he walked to breakfast—750 yards, down four flights of stairs, across the campus—on his hands. One year he broke his forearm on a helmet, and he went home to Chicago to beat up hillbillies with his plaster cast. Late in the afternoons he read people like Wright and Bly, and Sappho, and wrote the most unbelievable lyric poetry imaginable; and when they finally managed to stage his first act—a play about a Negro jazzhead prophet with a Jewish girlfriend—at Boe College, everyone was surprised and wondered why it wasn't entitled: *Cat on a Hot Tin All-American Small-Conference Lineman.*

And once, Braun Daniel showed up for breakfast in the coed diner with a small field mouse cupped in his hand.

(No Drapus Hopsonicus, those last two mice, Dawes Williams thinks.)

Looking at a rather finely wrought, inbred pledge whom he hated, Braun Daniel said:

"There, Thompson. What do you think of this mouse?"

"Watch out," Dawes Williams said, "here is the Hun."

"Fuck off, Willy," Braun Daniel said.

There was a silence, then:

"That's a fine mouse, Braun Daniel, sir," Thompson said.

"The hell it is. It's not a fine mouse at all, you idiot bastard freshman dink," Braun Daniel said. "It's an entirely insufficient mouse. Any damn fool can see that."

"Yes, sir, you're right, of course," Thompson said.

"Of course I'm right!! I know I'm right!! Do I need *you* to tell me I'm right!?!?!?" Braun Daniel said.

"No, sir."

"No, sir, what?"

"No, sir, sir," Thompson said.

"That's good, that's better," Braun Daniel said.

His eyes drifted off, came back to Thompson, and they seemed almost to be dancing it out together.

"This is an absolutely insufficient mouse," Daniel said. "This mouse has absolutely no business whatsoever existing. Wouldn't you say?"

"Yes, sir."

"Yes, sir, what?"

"Yes, sir, sir."

And with that, not batting an eye, or looking away, or changing expression even cruelly, Braun Daniel bit off its small, quivering head—neatly—with his front teeth, like celery, and he coughed it up, pale mouse eyes, and spit it at the pledge. Who fainted dead away. And that was just about the most famous thing Braun Daniel ever did.

(Yes, that's it, he thinks, lying there, blowing last smoke at his roof, that must be who he is.)

Because the mouse's head rolled around and ended finally up in Thompson's scrambled eggs.

"And when he wakes up," Braun Daniel said to the table, walking away, "you tell him to eat those eggs, every bit, like a good scout, or I'll ball his ass forever out."

And turning, he was gone. And that, except for publishing a limited edition of poems entitled: *Edgar's Songs: The Woman with the White Pitcher of Milk,* that must have been the most famous thing Braun Daniel ever did. . . .

It was not long after that Dawes Williams packed up all his damn pencils and books and went, twenty miles down, to the university. Not because of Braun Daniel, of course, he thinks; he had nothing to do with it. It was only 'cause Simpson wanted me to git one-a-them-there broader ed-e-cations that I node my mule down to th' uni-versity. That was before their junior year and, although it was only a few miles, Dawes Williams didn't see Braun Daniel again until two years later, late one afternoon, just as he was about to start graduate school, when out of nowhere Braun Daniel surfaced, appeared, bounced through his doorway, saying only:

"Dawes mother! I'm going to law school. Going to be a lawyer. I'm going to be the one you know who makes this system run."

"Oh, my God," Dawes Williams said quietly, looking up from the fifth volume of Proust's *Remembrance of Things Past,* "so that's what's going on out there in the streets. I should have known it."

"Let's get us a place in the woods," Braun Daniel said. "I love the country."

(So that is how—that is, at least, as much reason as I care to know or give— I wound up here, Dawes Williams thinks, rolling quietly over, yes, in this farmhouse, in his damn furious circus of wild, jumping mice, in this damn fierce particular spring, alone in the world, with this damn Croatian Prussian fascist footballer in poet's clothing, who to top even all of that off—for Christ's sake—thinks he is also an existential revolutionary.)

Dawes Williams' smoke drifts off on the walls. It is yellow winter morning, time to sleep. Dream.

Soon, almost under an anxious, rolling tension like sleep, Dawes Williams thinks he can hear him running back over the spine of the woods.

It must be guilt. No. Innocence is what hurts; guilt must feel good. I wish I could get into guilt; my blood hurts. Perhaps it is only some medical reality that has stepped in, canceled this metaphysic out. Perhaps we have just refused to learn that a mass society, the only new thing, has stepped in and inverted all a priori values of the shepherd, the flock. Pregnant women are worse than murderers. Either that, or it was innocence which has been guilty to begin with. . . .

The morning sleeps on the walls without him. Braun Daniel prances loudly in the powdered snow, on the cold air; he begins singing militaristic songs.

It's not his fault; he's just too healthy. It's not his fault he's too healthy. Hell, he's so healthy he's capable of acts of violent insanity. Hell, he is so sane he is just nuts. . . . God, I hope I am mad.

The low dog sounds of MacDuff and Boomer and Zoomer the Deuce row out and back now, quietly, over the fields. It is only seven, light with soft mist, and soon he will have to wake again, into a nightmare. But now it is only time to sleep, beyond even the vague absence of a dream.

Still, outside, he can hear Braun Daniel running over old bones, buried, enshrined in the soft gold of sleeping light, trapped deeply in glass, lost quietly under the squawking Methodist woods. . . .

The room is silent. Dawes Williams got up from the river that morning, put his notebooks away, and thought only monarchists could sleep that well. He rode his motorcycle home to the farmhouse, across the fields. Braun Daniel lay there, sleeping easily within the row of his dogs.

Now I sit here in the dark, watching Dawes read it all over as if that could make it all happen over again in a different way. I sit here smoking, ignoring Dawes.

So Braun Daniel joined the Marines, I say, and Dawes Williams moved to town.

He says nothing at all.

I ignore him. Taking out another of his dark papers—it is the letter from Barney Redwood this time—he begins musing and reading it over:

Dear Dawes,

Got married. Believe it? She's a Southern girl from the hills, and already we've got a little girl. She's a honey. Delly's old man's an interesting cuss who raises fighting-cocks and runs around with the Klan in his spare time.

Haven't seen you for eight years now. How are you? I've made 987 parachute jumps now. I'm still a Hi/Lo instructor in the Army. You bail out in dead night at 10,000 ft. and open at fifty with a meter. Real hairy. Love it, dad. Leaving soon to jump over Europe with The Golden Knights.

Take care, Willy,
Barney Redwood

Dawes Williams gets up and goes over to the window. The window is like a simple, pointless experiment in early-Renaissance geometric perspective—a painting, it reaches out of an interior wall into an infinity that eventually stops. The curtains bow, deepen, and move off with the night.

Dawes remains. I think I will sleep now.

Because soon Walter Cronkite will be coming. He will be adding it all up like cosmic media Ping-Pong and giving it sense. Eric, and the other boys in the gang of the band, will be helping him with the harder math.

Chasing them all, Roy Rogers will be galloping beyond like secular Sunday gone over the back of the ratlands. . . .

Dawes Williams looked up from his reading. Light was breaking through

the window, east of the sea. Urzika had just come in, and, sitting down next to
him on the bed, still caught within the moon and shadow of her carnival hat,
she watched him read. The low sun was a gold eye, a Mexican mask that crept
in from the door. The door was high in the air and led nowhere. It overlooked
a morning humming with green birds and lizards scuttling away under the
jungle with broken-off tails. Dogs go off in the screenless air; enormous, flight-
less roosters, black as giraffes, try to sit in the trees. Urzika was wide as a moon
of eyes, and, watching her calm stare fill itself and come back, he felt he must
be only pacing about meaninglessly with his eyes. Finally, giving up, he felt she
must be only a new girl in the piece come in for the laundry.

He got up and moved to the high window of the open doorway. Without
turning to look, he could see those huge green eyes of hers that seemed to be
made for looking round corners, for the night, for running away through thin
holes in the rain without leaving a trace, as they filled in the room. The air in
the tight inner space seemed to be an agony of crushed tropical roses, of dense,
thickly sweet Southern flowers that made him feel suddenly she must be bored
with it all and was thinking of going home, to America. Day again, he thought;
the green Mexican light skinned the shimmering wall.

"It's morning, Dawes," she said. "Did you sleep?"

"No."

Dawes crossed back to the bed and sat down beside her. He watched the
red shadows splinter and slide on the walls like wood lizards trying to hide
themselves away in a painted jungle. Down the block he could hear the sea
birds rise and swell, gold as ducks, over the bay.

"Walk all night?"

"No," she said, "I met some people."

"Good people?"

"Yes, good people. Beautiful people. They want to go farther south. Aguas-
calientes maybe."

"You going?"

"I don't know. I thought we weren't ever going to get into horseshit like
that, Dawes," she said.

"Right," Dawes Williams said. "I lost my head for a moment."

"That's what I love about you, Dawes," she said, laughing. "You never lost
your head for a moment and you never found it, either. That's what's wrong
with you, Dawes. Kiss me."

Dawes ignored her. He stared off into the rustle of the silent gold bugs
moving about in the jaws of the flooring. He thought even Simpson and Leone
must have had arguments like this only in a higher voice. He laughed at himself. He knew he shouldn't have thought that. He thought instead, then, that
he was quietly obsessed—it was probably only the heat, he thought, the lizard

shadows crawling the walls—by the great expectation that some faggy eigh-teenth-century English aristocrat, with a ready dildo in his pocket, would come round a corner dressed as Uncle Sam, businessman, and steal Urzika away. He thought he would tell her that, and she would laugh, and sense an edge, and slip out of her clothes, and prance around the room like Catherine of Russia, demanding to be laid on the spot. He thought she would ask, pout, demand to make love all morning; that she had the one-directional, hard-to-keep-up-with, obsessional imagination of Tom Sawyer prowling the graveyard. Instead, she slipped out of the single naked sleeve of her dress and curled beside him. She felt suddenly like close, tactile air around him, relaxed, and rising up, and waiting. He wanted to say he loved her. Looking over, however, she seemed to be already sleeping . . . and even in her dreaming, deep with sound, a broken sea of decay, her long hands seemed to want to run down to the bottom, the seams of the waist, and enter herself.

The red light broke off and went yellow on the wall. Dogs ran in the cob-bled city below. The Mexican day, slow as a clock, rose up the stone of the mountains and began falling over the end of the sea. Lying back, smoking, Dawes picked up his broken scribble paper where he had left off and began reading again:

Chapter 4

SUMMARY AND CONCLUSION
Number Four
THE DUTCHMAN IS CALLING:
EMBLEMS OF OUR BILATERAL SYMMETRY ARE BEGUN

EPIGRAPH: "O but it is not the years—it is I, it is You . . .
I have the idea of all, and am all and believe in all,
I believe materialism is true and spiritualism is true,
I reject no part."
—Walt Whitman in *With Antecedents*

Dawes Williams is standing in the sink, applauding. Orange peel, coffee rinds, the skeleton of a fish, pour down from his brow like Sylvester the Cat.

We are all lost in our dream of possessing life, a dream. Now the Dutchman from Elcader is calling Mr. Questioner. Dawes Williams ignores them all.

"Who is this?" Mr. Questioner says.

In fact, Dawes says, reaching for his notebooks, let me continue here by reading six or seven lines of intellectual graffiti into the record. I think it's pertinent.

Without waiting for my benediction he nuns right on:

"Dear T. S. Eliot," he begins. "How is Anglican Heaven? You may have perceived the first unsightly edges of black night wasteland bloom on the river," he says, "but you seemed never to know it, on feel it, plastic world, slide through your bowels like shit to be learned.

You could not replace aesthetic qualification with real reality. Few can. (No one can and still make a poem.) Things have gotten worse.

Now only sociologists can afford aesthetic tones,

seeing things which are giving out and dying finally."

There is a silence. Dawes Williams gets down from the icebox.

What did you think of it? he says finally.

Nice in its way, I say, Dawes.

Perhaps not, he says.

Perhaps, I say. But, at any rate, I am now ready to give you the key to this novel.

Hot damn, he says. We must have an ending.

Then, like a child, scuttling on all fours—his two legs, and the two hind legs of the rearing chair—he draws near my adult fire.

What will it be? he says. A bank job and the cops: tommyguns, and girls in red dresses, and dead Studs Lonigan heroes?

No, I say, I think not.

Tomorrow/Tomorrow, Dawes says, I go home to Tara?

No, I say.

I'VE GOT IT Dawes Williams says, I'M STILL REALLY SEVENTEEN YEARS OLD AND WE HAVEN'T EVEN LEFT THE FARM YET!!??!?!?!!??!?!? NONE OF THIS HAS REALLY EVER HAPPENED!

No, I say, I think not. Hard to film.

Listen, Dawes Williams says. Get this: I'm still on the ward, see, seven years old, a skitso already, see. Now: at the very falling end VelFever comes in, see, and he is dressed in a clean, starched pinafore—he is playing Prissy, you see— and his line is: OH, MISS SCAR-LETT. OH, MISS SCARLETT. THE CONFEDERACY HAS RISEN, AND IS MARCHING, AND IS BURNING DOWN IOWA CITY TRYING TO ROUST OUT EVERY DIRTY COMMIE PUNK KID IN THE STATE. I GOT-A GO WED DE WINN'R, JEM, SHE SAYS, INJECTING POISON INTO HIS ARM!

No, I say. We can't rewrite history quite that badly.

CURTAIN! Dawes Williams says.

No, Dawes, I say. Let's put it this way: Sociologists *are your* nemesis. If there ever was an utter, mind-denying foil—Hal and Hotspur—you and sociologists are it. They have sprung up out of nowhere, pseudoscience and the twentieth functional century to deny you atavistic life, haven't they? Haven't they, single-handedly-in-flower-pot-coats, canceled out your poem, your novel, and the possibility you will ever find your Druid witch?

Yes. You've got me there, Dawes says. But don't mince words.

Then it is simple, I say. In our little Kingdom of Ends the only reasonable denouement would be that you will be killed, struck down viciously, that is, stoned to death by a band of wandering Peace Corps workers in Mexico. For fullest effect, I think, this should happen on a moving train, on the night of the Fourth of July, rolling somewhere south between Chihuahua and Torreon.

FORESHADOWED! Dawes Williams says, striking his fist on his palm, going into the bathroom to wizz. FATED AND TAGGED! STRUNG UP ON A POLE OF DESTINY LIKE A TOURISTED FISH!

Thank you, he says, coming back, sitting on his side of the room.

I ignore him. That is not easy and, indeed, it is only possible because there is a line painted down the perfect center of our room. Dawes helped me paint it on one of his better days last week. Dawes lives on the Left side, while I live on only the Right. I use only the Left side to piss in. (Indeed, like Dawes, I felt I had a certain claim on the Left side; but both of us living there would mean harmony, and harmony would mean boredom, and boredom would mean insanity and death. Dawes and I felt we couldn't risk it.) Anyway, in deference to Dawes' existence taking seniority to mine, I do everything with my Right hand now. (Incidentally here, in reference to certain biological acts I am obliged to carry out on our person, that is why I am called—like an Indian who is named for primary function—Handsaw the Seriphus of Williams.) To go straight on: I even eat with my Right hand. (I am afraid here that Dawes often refuses to hold onto the fork while cutting the buffalo steaks, and the organism is in great peril of dying. I tell him this, but he only accuses me. I would eat the goddamn thing whole but am too genteel.) Anyway, also in this connection, unlike Chaucer's people I also wipe my ass with my Right; and if I ever choose to dismember ourselves—it will be only the Left side, not the Right. That way there will be something left to split up again.

All of this, however, is not a joke to me and Dawes: Late at night, when our bilateral symmetry is off, while my head is locked to our night shoulder, and while his bowels nearly tear themselves out going to the left, Dawes looks at me and accuses. He says it was I who started this Parkinsonian condition. Baroque asshole! he says. Little End'un, I sneer back. He is wrong. I am the Realist/Cynic/Successful Aristocrat. I only hold up the mirror of the world. It is Dawes, that boy, that prairie, that hopeless romantic, who overdistends us both by insisting to reach impossibly for that dream in the wind. . . .

O lost, Dawes Williams says, Handsaw, like America, you are about as much fun as a hat on your head. A high-button shoe in a bedroom.

O unDonne, I moan behind him, slumping in my chair.

The night drifts on, a perfectly dead and sailing Call-in Show.

Meanwhile, on the radio, the Dutchman continues. He is talking in that dry, softly composed speech about the day he met Jesus. In person. He is our truer milieu, but only Dawes is glued to his words, not I.

Dawes grows quiet, but only because the Dutchman has condescended, at Mr. Questioner's sniveling prodding, to wind up once again upon his most famous story, entitled simply: The Day I Met Christ in Person. . . .

"Or, that is, you might say," the Dutchman is saying, "The Day I Pressed the Ghost in the Flesh."

"I think I know what you mean," Mr. Questioner says. Checking himself, he says: "What do you mean?"

Dawes pays no attention to me any more, but he listens to the Dutchman. Perhaps it is because the Dutchman believes in the physical divinity of Christ (he saw Him rise over the moon with his own eyes, didn't he?) and because Dawes is so afraid of the dark right now. Deep down, Dawes is afraid he will actually connect that toaster to that lamp socket and the lights will go out forever. I know better about the Dutchman. He makes no difference either way; Dawes and I will be simply unspun, wound down to nothing soon.

Yes, Dawes Williams says, we feel bad. We have a malady so vast, so cataclysmic in premonition, not even Oral Roberts could cure us now.

That's it, Dawes, I say. Sunday afternoon! TV! Bright lights, big tents! The big-time, man! We could go on The Oral Roberts Show and become *personalities!*

It takes a psychotic to really spot another, Dawes Williams says, walking away, quietly, into the bathroom to open his veins.

Nothing happens for awhile. Dawes brushes his teeth. I sit back in the dark, alone, dreaming, seeing that I am that worm—struggling within porous canvas, trapped in that great underjar of earth, trying to rise like the ash of a moonmoth, knotted now to external eyes, to the fluttering wind, and fly over that painted, metamorphosized gasp of the meadow, over that quickened hammer of his own destructed blood. Not Dawes.

But the Dutchman continues. And with him comes the growing recognition (to me, not to Dawes) that The Overnight Show is really a Renaissance construction: it is Florentine, full as it is with its daily shifting political aliases, its accessorial reputations, and its pathetic belief in itself. Soon, using the perfectly mimed voice of Savonarola, I shall call in and burn the whole show down like the Great Spoon River. . . .

Because, you see, I know the moment I cease and become quiet, vanish into nothing but rising ashes and the tails of wisping moonmoths trying to fly the night of the sun, then Dawes Williams will die and go out like the light of a bug lost in a child's jar of summer. . . . I am keeping Dawes Williams alive, you see, by murdering his heart.

Number Five
HEAD TRANSPLANTS AND CHEROKEE INDIANS
AND HOUSTON, TEXAS

Perhaps it is only the tumor in my lower cranium again, but it seems to me that the phone in my radio is ringing. The Dutchman has hung up. Roy Rogers has ridden over the hill. Who could it be?

Hello, Dawes Williams says to the radio. Milieu calling.

I ignore him. So does Mr. Questioner.

A fifteen-year-old girl who is married to a Marine is calling. She says her name is Molly Pitcher and she is sitting alone in her room with a fifteen-foot cannon plunger. She says she is waiting hopefully for the Battle of the Vietcong Ocean Canoe as she'd like to get out there and show'm what she's made of; says it'd make her feel really good, and besides, she says, somehow she just knows she wouldn't be the one to get shot. . . . She talks for awhile and dissolves fitfully into memory.

Soon a one-hundred-nine-year-old Cherokee calls in from Des Moines. He thrives, he says when questioned immediately about the secret of life, on three hot peppers and a glass of whole milk per day.

On my phonograph, Kate Smith is singing.

"What else can you tell us tonight, George Feather?" Mr. Questioner asks the Indian.

But the Cherokee says nothing at all. In the silence you can tell Mr. Questioner is deeply worried that the one-hundred-nine-year-old voice box is giving out on his spot. Soon, however, the Cherokee comes through by saying his longevity was also helped a great deal by the fact he didn't see his first white man until he was one hundred and six.

There is a large, Midwestern, communal graffaw all around. It is as nice a way as any, I suppose, of abdicating thought and the agony of responding to anything at all. In the dim, vague background Mr. Questioner sits scratching the perfect geometric square of his head.

Ho Ho Ho, he says. Checking himself, he says: Ho? Ho? Ho?

Soon, a drunk calls in to say he's just heard in the J Street Tavern that an old wino just survived a brain transplant in Houston, Texas.

"Of course they held it in the Astrodome," he says. "They didn't want it to get rained out, did they?"

Mr. Questioner, picking right up on it, tends to discount the rumor. But the caller persists. In the perfectly modulated, precocious rhetoric of an idiot-savant child donning party wings he says:

"Do you think the thing will ever find widespread, practical application, Mr. Questioner? What is your opinion on that, if I might ask?"

(This sort of J Street Tavern, Emily Post diction is still very upward-socially big out here on the prairies, Dawes Williams says. Did you pick up on it, Handsaw?)

I dig it, Dawes, I say. These cats can lay down the jive.

"I don't hold opinions," Mr. Questioner is saying. Checking his exuberance, he says: "Opinion? Am I a brain surgeon? How would I know?"

"I thought you'd come up with something reserved like that, A. B.," the caller says, hanging up. "Very wise indeed."

The room drifts off in a moment of silence.

Personally, sitting back, I think suddenly Mr. Questioner is his own reward. He deserves himself—that is the only poetic justice in the universe; and that should be enough to soothe even my baroque sense of insulted vengeance. Also, I tell myself, he will never make network. . . .

Then, lying low in our mutual dark, Dawes Williams grows restless again. Finally he goes off:

Do you think this means we're finally saved? he says. Do you think this new head-transplant thing will eventually replace the prefrontal lobotomy? Has wonderful modern medical science done it again?

Perhaps, I say. Perhaps not.

You know, Dawes says, I long to rise, to go to my phone in my room and call my phone in my radio and ask Mr. Questioner just what in the hell does he think.

Peace, Dawes, I say. Joy in the morning. We may be finally risen yet, Jem.

Then I drift off again, go back into a deep sleep. So many things are un-American, I think finally. Things like head transplants and prefrontal lobotomies. Dawes would never consent to be wed in a church like that. He'd be afraid someone would come out of the dark and take away all his Scout medals if he ever did a thing like that. Besides, after he had finally made it in Hollywood, how could he go up to John Wayne and say:

"Duke, I don't know how to confess this to you, it's terribly un-American of me, but I've just had a prefrontal lobotomy."

As I am about to take root and expand this last emblematic encounter— that is, Dawes Williams and John Wayne—into nothing less than the Louisiana Purchase of pop culture, the Seward's Folly of camp, suddenly I find I am too tired to continue. I wish only to sleep. To hear the dry leaves rustle; the dead ends of the trees take root on the glass; for the perfect stone cuttings of the white, mooned hearts of the lilies to faint over screaming in the net of the night. I can't. Only Dawes could have found a sleep that sounds as well as that. Cast out, I will awaken again only to dream.

Not much else, I notice, is happening anyway.

Number Six
THE PHONE CALL

I think Dawes Williams is dead. He hasn't moved in six hours.

Perhaps he isn't. I decide to call Mr. Questioner and ask him what he thinks about it all. Is Dawes Williams dead? Soon, foreshortened in my mirror, I notice my hand reach for the phone in my room. In the dark a cigaret is lit. I smoke it down and wander forth to communicate with the world at large. Filled with a terrible anxiety, I begin speaking too soon—into the dial tone:

"Hello?" I begin. "Is this spaceship Earth? I'm afraid we're in trouble. The dome is cracking. Let me speak with the captain, please. I think there's icebergs north of Uranus."

There is a pause at the other end. A horrible silence. Finally someone answers.

"Helllo? Night-line," I hear.

"Hello?" I say. "Do you always pronounce your hellos with three l's?"

There is another pause. I listen to myself breathe into my phone and out of my radio. Strangely fascinated, I decide finally I am being asked to respire into a heart-lung machine without losing consciousness.

"Helllo?" I hear again. "Who *is* this?"

"This is Thomas Aquinas," I say right out front. "I just called in tonight to explain everything that's happened in the history of the world in some detail."

"Helllo!"

"Helllo? Mr. Questioner?"

"Yes."

"Yes? Hello?"

"Yes? Go ahead."

"Go ahead?"

"Yes, yes."

"Yes?"

"Yes!"

"Yes. Parry and thrust, eh? Well, it's me again."

"Is it?"

"Yes, it is."

"Have you called before?"

"No."

"No?"

"No."

"Yes? Well, do you have an opinion on anything?"

"Sometimes."

"Sometimes?"

"Yes," I say. "Don't you?"

There is a pause.

"Go on, please," he says.

"Go on?"

"Yes, hello, whoever, go ahead."

"Am I on?"

"Hello. Hello. Are you even there?"

"Hello. Mr. Questioner?"

"Yes? Hello!"

"Hello? Mr. Questioner?"

"Yes, yes, yes. Hello?"

"Yes? Well, good evening then, Mr. Questioner. I've been trying to reach your program for some while now."

"Have you?"

"Yes, I have. I'm breathless."

"For some while now?"

"That's right. For some while now."

"Is that right?"

"Yes, that's right. But I've been busy pasting old pictures of Bob Hope into scrapbooks since October. I've got over four thousand. Some in color."

"Yes, yes," he says. "Is that all you wanted?"

"Yes? Go ahead?"

"Go ahead. Yes?"

"But that's not what I called in for," I say. "Mr. Questioner? Are you there?"

"Yes, I am. Go ahead."

"Well," I begin, clearing my throat, "what I called in for was to inform your listeners of the fantastic interrelatedness of all historical events."

"That sounds like an interesting, worthwhile subject," he says.

"It is," I say. "It's fascinating."

"That's fascinating," he says. "I hadn't thought of it."

"Yes," I say. "Well, I had."

"What does it mean?" he says.

"WHAT DOES IT MEAN!?!" I say, catching my breath. "It means if Charlemagne would have died three years earlier, A. B., we wouldn't even be in Vietnam. I reckon we'd be just now fighting over Byzantium with the Cherokee Indians somewhere on the plains of the Transvaal."

There is a silence.

"Battle of the Limpopo, A. B.," I say. "We're not exactly the intellectual descendants of Bartholomew de Las Casas, you know."

"Good point," he says. "I hadn't thought of it."

"All relative turnings become absolute once they become," I say.

There is a long silence. One can picture Mr. Questioner communing with some lost *a priori* flap of his mind by pulling down firmly on the single iamb of his lower lip. Sitting alone in the dark, dancing with the crooning lost ape of his banana microphone, soon he is scratching his head.

"Hello?" I say. "Is this still night line? Am I on? A. B.?"

"Yes?" he says finally.

"May I speak now?"

"Yes. Hello?"

"Hello hello?"

"Yes yes."

"Yes," I say, "well, you're probably wondering why I really called in tonight."

"No," he says.

"No?" I say.

"No," he says. "I thought you'd probably get around to telling me? Most of 'm do?"

"All right," I say. "I will. I just called in tonight to say I am leaving the country."

"Are you one of those kind?" he says.

"No," I say, "I'm not. But don't you worry—I'm taking Dawes Williams with me."

"I see," he says.

"Do you?" I say.

Silence. In my phone I can hear myself breathing in my radio all over again.

"Mr. Questioner . . . ?"

"What is it you WANT!?!"

"Want?"

"Don't play dumb with me," he says. "You must WANT something."

"I don't want anything," I say.

"You don't?"

"No," I say. "Well, nothing spectacular, I guess."

"Nothing spectacular?"

"No. Nothing spectacular," I say. "Although I do think I am missing a fantastic chance to say something relevant here."

"Do you?"

"I certainly do."

"But you must want to say something," he says. "They always do. Don't you have any opinions at all?"

"All right then," I say, "if you want to be that way. Let me just say I called in then to wish you a good night. Is that all right?"

"Good night?"

"Yes. I'm going to bed now."

"To bed? Now? That's all?"

"Yes. Not quite," I say. "Dawes Williams wears mittens and an old felt hat when he goes to bed any more. Thinks it'll cure him."

"Is that all?"

"That's all."

"That's fine."

"Is it?"

"Yes, it is. I think so."

"Well, it's not. I'm also going insane in a crazy way."

"Yes?"

"Yes!"

There is an embarrassed silence.

"Well, how nice," he says, trying to ride over everything. "Good night."

"Nice in what way, would you say, Mr. Questioner?" I say. "Nice like little girls and candy canes? Metaphysically nice?"

"Good night!" he says.

"Yes," I say, "it has been a good night. Thanks for answering."

There is a silence like an amazed sack exploding slowly.

"Can I ask why?" he says.

"You can," I say.

"Can I?"

"Yes."

"All right," he says. "Why?"

"Well," I say, "because my cousin and doppelgänger Dawes Williams is over in the corner, dying finally, and because he doesn't bother me any more."

The phone hums on, dancing between us.

"I see," he finally says.

"Do you?"

"Yes, I think I do," he says. "I'm sorry about it."

"I sincerely doubt that, Mr. Questioner."

"You shouldn't doubt me in public," he says. "It's not polite."

"Yes," I say, "I been around. I doubt it."

"Why?" he says. "We're perfect strangers. How can you doubt me?"

"Why not?" I say. "I doubt a lot of things."

"You do?"

"I certainly do. I doubt you are even there."

"How can you?"

"I can."

"But that is incredible!" he finally says.

"No, it's not," I say. "It's epistemology."

Then, reaching deeply, almost hurting himself, he says:

"Don't you believe your ears? What about Locke and Hume? I am empirically *here*, for Christsake," he says desperately.

"No," I say. "Don't think so. Once I have hallucinated, all reality is hallucinated retrospectively. Perhaps you are only hallucinating that greatest of all communal hallucinations—everyday Reality."

"What does this mean?" he says.

"Good Question, Mr. Questioner," I say. "It means it will be very hard to ever become a Republican again."

"Well," he says, "these philosophical arguments are impossible to resolve. But they're a lot of fun."

There is an uneasy silence. For only a moment Mr. Questioner has had to look at himself and recognize he might not even be there. The moment, however, passes quickly. Clearing his throat, Questioner wonders:

"But how could this Dawes Williams be dying?"

"I'm glad you asked that," I say.

"You are!?!"

"Of course. That's the real reason I called. I'm glad you asked, because just now he's over there, sitting on the windowsill, looking out into a distance of impossible space, trying to commit suicide with a phonograph."

"Is this some kind of gag?" Questioner says. "Is that possible?"

"It is," I say. "He's trying to swallow it."

"Is he having any success?"

"He's having a hell of a time, A. B.," I say. "I thought your listeners might be interested."

"What's he doing now? Can I ask?"

"You can," I say. "And we consider your interest touching."

"But can it work?" he says.

"It can," I say. "It's a miniature Japanese-component stereo; and it blooms and ignites with infinite noise on contact with water—special, sacrificial bottled waters shipped over here from old and sacred Oriental springs."

"Sounds like the latest fad," Questioner says. "Is that all?"

"No. Kate Smith still is singing."

"Aren't you going to even call an ambulance?"

"Not really."

"Not really?"

"No, not really."

"Why not?"

"Why?"

"Why!?!"

"Why is he doing it? Is that it? Is that what you want to know?"

"All right."

"All right?"

"Yes, yes."

"Because. . ."

"Because, because. Yes, yes."

"Well," I say, "because, A. B., he has become so deluded he thinks he's pregnant with twins."

"TWINS!?!"

"Yes. That's right. He's afraid they will be girls."

"That's incredible!"

"Yes. I think so, too. I keep telling him he's crazy, that they'll probably be boys, but he doesn't listen to me."

There is another embarrassed silence.

"Mr. Questioner. . . ?" I say almost humbly.

"Yes?"

"Maybe you could tell him. Maybe he'd listen to you. Maybe you could announce over the air he isn't going to have twins, and maybe he'd believe that. Dawes Williams is a great believer in twilight air space."

"Is that why you called me?"

"That's why I called you, A. B.," I say. "I believe you can heal."

"Something's wrong here," he says. "Perhaps we just aren't communicating in a sociodynamic way."

"I don't think we are either, A. B.," I say. "But don't worry about all that jargon now. If you'd just announce over the air that Dawes Williams isn't going to have twins, I'm sure it would help."

"Is that all? Don't you want to say anything else?"

"Don't you think I've said enough yet?" I say.

"Perhaps," he says. "But don't you want to say something more?"

"All right," I say. "I'd just like to say how much I've always enjoyed your show, Mr. Questioner."

"You have? Thank you."

"Yes. I have. Even Dawes Williams has enjoyed it in his better moments."

There is a dead, ringing silence. For a moment I think Mr. Questioner has gone out at the other end, that I am pathetically alone once again. Then, happily, I can hear the rise and fall of his soft breathing pick up again.

"But don't you have any opinions?" he says. "What do you think of the war? The election? Castro? Are you a Humphrey or a Nixon man?"

"That's very funny," I say, knowing full well I could have cost either candidate the eastern half of the state by merely pronouncing his name just then. But I have no malice. Besides, there isn't enough difference in the two for even a pedant like me to pick up on.

"Yes, but what do you think?" Questioner says.

"Well," I say, "looking back, I think everything has gone especially unwell since 1648, the Peace of Westphalia, and the end of the Thirty Years' War. . . . Only Dawes Williams is registered to vote, Mr. Questioner."

"I think I see now," Questioner says. "You are very dependent, as they say, on this Dawes Williams and you don't like it. You should get out more."

"Yes," I say, "Dawes Williams is very patriotic."

"I don't quite think I see what you mean?"

"Well," I say, "I mean Dawes Williams was to take me to the polls with him. An outing! A chance to see the world once again!"

"And now you can't go?"

"And now I can't go, A. B. Dawes Williams is dying, A. B."

"Perhaps I could arrange a ride to the polls through one of the major parties for you. You could still go. I'm sure he wouldn't mind. I would be glad to . . ."

"I don't think you quite understand yet, A. B. You see, Dawes Williams is taking my heart, blood and liver with him when he goes."

"Oh?" he says. "I hadn't heard about that, I don't think."

"I don't think you understand, Mr. Questioner. You see, Dawes Williams is not really schizoid—he's just talking through his death mask."

"Oh . . . yes . . . of . . . course," he says. "I think I can see that now."

"I hardly think so," I say. "But someday you will. Surprised, on your deathbed you will ask your soul to fly over the moon and be disappointed when it doesn't. Good night, Mr. Questioner."

"Good night?"

"Good night."

"Good night then. Thank you for calling."

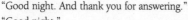

"Good night. And thank you for answering."

"Good night."

"Good night."

Suddenly the line goes dead. I am alone again now: receiver and extension hung up neatly on its hook. Existence drifts off once more with the night. It leaves no sign, no paw in the snow to remember itself by.

I would probably not come along that path again to see it lying there, surprised and looking back, anyway.

Number Seven

OUR ROOM:

MOBY DICK WAS ONLY A MINNOW.

I CLOSE DOWN THE FOURTH MOVEMENT WITH AN EPIPHANY

ON AHAB AND MELVILLE.

Before I go to bed I read all the papers over. But I never read a newspaper dated earlier than Armistice Day, 1919. I find reading anything dated later merely to be rushing to judgment. I even have a copy of *The Deadwood Gazette* the day Wild Bill Hickok was shot in the back of the head. I always save that one for last.

Dawes, however, complains. He says our room's become a hermit's castle, stuffed with the bloat of a thousand old newspapers and boarded shut with the maze and mountain of mad labyrinths and fortress-like stackings. He says that we can't entertain any more.

Stay cool, Dawes, I tell him. Moby Dick was only a minnow.

He doesn't. He is obsessed that the papers are all yellowing rat's pupils. They are out, of course, to eat him alive. Torn, distended, and burned at the edges, they loom and rot in the musted air. Twenty feet! Higher than ceilings! They are moated, he thinks, and full of crocodiles: in one it says Ole Joe Hill was held up against the back of a Mormon wall and shot for singing a song.

I feel suddenly I am winding down again. . . . Nobody remembers.

It is only dawn again. . . . Perhaps it is Christmas morning again and Santa, wreathing with pity and fear, has fled the housetops. He says—"Anagnorisis without peripetia, O void"—and hops the back of Roy Rogers' waiting reindeer. Perhaps. Perhaps not, it isn't plausible. But in the thin light falling from the heated snow of my test patterns (sometimes the shadow of dark, lovely dancing ladies) I begin reading the comics over. Dagwood, having lost his job again, runs home to kiss his wife. Someday. I think to myself, I will make it down my hill to the small-awninged store and buy a whole book. I am very tired.

Dawes Williams would have known what to make of this.

Because all sound is gone. The day. It is mind-shattering, like listening to nothing at all. Small and static records keep clicking over. Unsuccessful, without even noise now, they walk endlessly over themselves, like mechanical soldiers marching my walls, my corners of rooms; houses remain. Through the curtains of the window I see finally . . .

           Moby Dick was a great white whale who merely swam in the sea. All else was implanted upon him in the dreams— mad dreams, distending behind; the black wakes of ships, passing, slipping below, spreading away from the voyeur's eye—of Ahab and Melville . . .

           those starkly dead trees of winter rise in the yard. Organic droppings. Like animals without backs or stomachs. All nature has become a nightmare.

     I am very tired. I think I can only sleep now again. . . .

Dawes Williams looked up at the open window of the jeweler's high doorway. For a moment the entire universe seemed caught in the naked frame. It seemed late afternoon; flat, Mexican evening was approaching. Urzika was stirring against him. For a moment he thought he must be sleeping. Waking, it was dark.

A dead line of red light was coming in from the opposite, inside door. Urzika was standing over a naked sink, washing herself with a rag. Watching her was like dreaming. Hooded in light and shadow, feeling only herself, she seemed strangely unapproachable. She knew he was awake and watching her. She turned slightly away into the red eye and mask of the dark.

"Dawes," she said, "come here."

Instead he lay on the bed, lighting the Mexican rope of a cigaret. She was long and naked, and hidden, angular shadows ran down her and ended hanging to the light. The water off her body bloomed on the dusty flooring. He thought suddenly, not even quite able to break into that large bloat of consciousness, that he couldn't even remember her name. Angry, he got up and walked through the door.

"Dawes?" she said.

"Do you even know where I am?" he said. "Yet. Do you even have a whisper?"

"Dawes!?" she said.

"Listen," he says, "how could me and Handsaw Williams ever have the nerve to think we could love anyone? Or even *anything*? You answer me that? I'm going out and walking until I fall over the end."

He went straight down the thin trellis of the stairs. The street was almost a shock. He went down to the corner and stood, trying to smoke it all in without fainting. He thought he had often stood on that corner, reading *Tristram Shandy*, trying to ignore the daylight, waiting for her to come down. Afternoon then was always two Mexican horses, passing: one, named simply Sterne, stopped to chew on the dusty curbing; but the other, named Tristram, ran on.

But she didn't come. He wondered suddenly if part of him might be waiting after all. Feeling his eye was festering even into the cool, the last dark green of the August sun going deep under the sea, he began moving off.

Finally Urzika was behind him, half-stopping, half-moving, and tying her dress up like a forgotten shoe.

"Where are we going?" she said.

"You're too much and too late," he said. "All I know how to do is carry books back and forth to school."

"Well," she said, laughing, "you just should have developed some balance along the way, old boy. Balance is good fer a fella."

"Oh, Christ," Dawes said, "two decades wasted in a direct exercise in total, anti-living and all I did was help them."

"Shut up, Dawes," she said. "Who needs it?"

"But, damnit, what do we do next? Walk around the block again? Move away to Ohio to teach social work to other social workers? Key-rist."

"I have an idea," she said. "Let's get stoned."

"I can't even do that well. I can't do anything."

"I'll be patient with you."

"I know. You're a saint. It can't work."

"Maybe you're right."

"Oh, damn. That's not the answer."

"Maybe it's even true you can't even make love forever."

"Oh, Christ," Dawes Williams said.

"Oh, Christ," Urzika said.

Then they continued walking down the street, hand in hand, two waifs let loose on the plastic world. They moved through the town, the market, the small, dusty night lights, evening and the concrete rim of the sea. Once, leaving footprints in the smooth sand near the water, she dropped his hand and said:

"Sometimes, Dawes, just looking at you, I feel wasted all over."

A last stone of sun broke light on the dark water. They walked quietly within sleeping nets of small brown children. Late soccer balls boomed in the air and went over the sinking edge of the sun. Urzika was wrapped within his faded jean jacket now, and poorer Mexican children ran everywhere selling Chiclets from wooden boxes. The soccer players kicked themselves around noisily on the edge of the sea, never too far from gatherings of watchful Catholic mothers; and they went also within the groups of men and small boys selling bright rope jackets, bits of silvered abalone and polished volcanic glass, the masks and Yo-Yo-like games carved from wood and fashioned with string.

"I had a friend once," Dawes said, "named Travis Thomas, who would have taken one thin look at this place and said: 'Welcome to Despair. This country is nothing but Chiclets.'"

Urzika was smiling slightly. They made their way up to the seawall lined with a single green taxi, and down the seawalk where the two-mile row of miniature hotels baked in the whitewashed cool.

"A bastard like you probably has a lot to feel guilty about in Latin America all right," Urzika said finally.

The gray parade of horses continued to pass. The hooves beat on tilted streets leading up from the sea. The tourist carts drawn behind were full as hay-wagons with bright, Christmas-tree-shirted Americans.

"Hey, you! Victor Vacation! Go check in at the consulate!" Dawes Williams yelled after.

Someone from California got out and wanted to fight. Dawes Williams stood, thumbing his nose at the silence, which eventually dissolved into nothing at all. Urzika led him by the hand, up from the sea, at the end of tilted streets and a straw-hatted parade; a hundred whipped and dappled horses and dogs and a thousand of the same Americans wherever you went. Wandering, she took him finally to the iron-fenced house of the fat, four-hundred-pound, expatriated opal hunter who was her friend and Platonist.

She entered without knocking. Dawes followed down a dim, interior hallway of light, green masks and Indian spears. At the end the fat four-hundred-pound opal hunter sat, caught within an intense point of light that thinned out quickly into the cool dark around him. He was busy laying the stones out against bits of black cloth, talking to himself, poking at them with tweezers. Almost as if they were semiprecious children, he was commenting, in his thick falsetto voice, upon the rare green fire of this one, the size and personality of that. Almost feeling he had stumbled upon some unnatural act that was already in process on an inanimate object, Dawes watched the other's eyes, destroyed by fat into small nuts, as they leered into the intense narrow beam of white light. Urzika sat down before him, smiling. The opaque stones lay between. It was full evening, and the hot streets cooled and merged into an utter blackness on the interior walls of his fenced house. Dawes felt uneasy and oppressed by the light. He sat watching the other's green, possessive eyes. They leered out at Urzika like oily nuts casting about trying to feed on the light.

Finally, getting up heavily from a cushioned camel stool nearly the size of a table, he went over to some drawers. Coming back, he gave Urzika some money. She smiled and gave it back, and he handed her a transparent bag full of tablets and capsules—mescaline, meth and acid—and a sack of grass. Handing the money back uncounted, Dawes thought for only a moment Urzika had taken on the air of an established department store as she gazed at the things before her. They seemed to be many-colored and bright.

"Free will, dearie," he said, taking the money back. "I don't want you to feel I'm oppressing you. Just keeping it all nice and neat and tidy and independent, hon."

"Oh, Christ wow," Dawes found himself saying. "I haven't seen a commercial intercourse like this since I gave up my paper route."

There was a small silence in which the green light filtered the walls. Dawes listened to naked lizards running under the rugs.

"Fuck off, Dawes," Urzika finally said.

"Who is the boy, dearie?" he said, eventually casting the impossibly slow, beady weight of his gaze over at Dawes.

"I'm Wilson Paramour," Dawes Williams said, standing, extending his hand. "How do you do? I have a thirteen-inch dick and good lungs for a dude."

The hand was not taken. Urzika reached over and patted his leg.

"I'm taking care of him while the folks are away," she said. "He's sweet. Cute for a dying man, isn't he? Lots of fun. He's got that last, indefinite bloom on him right now."

The fat four-hundred-pound opal hunter sat down, moving the air quietly about him with his hand fan, giggling like a girl who was overly sexual to the point of nervous frigidity. They talked. All Technicolor was gone. The room seemed cracked with the fat light of yellow men. Fascinated for a moment, finally he was bored. He found himself ultimately fixated and sustained within the talk of the opal hunter by a contempt for effete panderers which he thought was buried with another time. Surprised by this contempt, he drifted off in near wonderment that it was still existent within him. He came back.

Now the opal hunter was nearly lecturing, it seemed to him. He drew from the thousands of plastic tubes full of opals, a great stone zoo caged within the shelf of his house, which became single, opaque eyes full of tiny bits of red and green and yellow fire once put under the glass. Bending double over his own belly, the opal hunter began explaining how little he managed to pay the natives who brought the stones down out of the mountains, the sun, with bits of fire still trapped within the layers of cloudy glass. Then he bragged how much he could get for these bits of native stone in New York, flying out twice a year. He looked at Urzika. He said he still hoped she would fly out with him in a month. But, damn, he said, if the buggers weren't getting smarter now—in the larger cities, in Guadalajara, around Acapulco, even in Mazatlán, he said, and he was angered because now he had to load his vast bulk into his coverless jeep and travel the distances into the smaller villages. Hard distances, you'll just never know, he said almost squeaking like a huge rat that still lay somehow within the purr of his fat, oily fur. Yes, he said, he had been in Mexico for thirty unendurable years, but now it was all changing for the worse. It was going modern. Ruining him, he said.

"You just can't expect to fuck the peasants over forever, I guess," Dawes Williams said quietly.

"No, dearie," he said, "you can't. Nothing good ever lasts."

They talked for awhile longer. It grew darker as the sun fell over the back of the roof and under the sea. Dawes felt the room was as black and evil as the ritual going on in a church. Finally they got up to leave. The fat four-hundred-pound expatriate opal hunter gave Urzika three stones and stood for a moment rubbing her bare shoulders, polishing her like glass. He stood before her, trying to bore within her with the green absence of fire, the stone zoos of his eyes. He pressed the stones into her hand and told her to return at any time to his house. She smiled and stood back against him, for some strange reason as tall and proud as if she were naked.

Leaving, Dawes Williams purposely paused to kick over the corner of the table. Hundreds, thousands of rattling eyes and rolling opal stones lit up and danced on the tile floors. Dawes Williams immediately apologized. But already the fat opal hunter was down on his knees, mad, trying to scurry in every direction at once, as if his semiprecious children were drowning, as if the sky had just opened up and were raining diamonds.

"And don't you ever bring him back here!" he was screaming at Urzika. "He's an infidel! Barbarian! Fool!" he screamed at them as they went back through the door.

Following along behind her—down the patio tile, a dead, birdless jungle overhang of night limbs and domestic creepers—there had been her laugh, larger than his own. They moved through the wrought-iron gate. In the street Urzika turned him and said:

"What's th' matter, Dawes? Don't you know how to act when you're invited up t'nice people's house fer company?"

Then she broke out into almost shrill laughter, rammed her small shopping bags into her shoulder bag, and began doing a mock escape down the side of the walls. The streets were close with houses, distant with the faint sounds of barking dogs. Laughing, Urzika began running. Dawes chased her out. Then even the cold moon broke against his swollen eye, leaving only a red explosion, a sudden sickness, and he had to sit down suddenly for a moment along the side of a wall. Then Urzika turned and began coming back, hesitantly, five or six steps at a time.

"Dawes?" she said. "Dawes!?"

Dawes didn't answer. He crawled over to the edge of the cobbled burro tracing and puked up only spit, bile and small hunks of bloody skin.

"Christ," he said, nearly crying. "Stay away from me. I'm in such bad shape I can't even catch girls any more. Christ. That hasn't happened to me since third grade and I first got my speed."

Urzika laughed quietly. She came over and tried to tug him up by the back of the hair.

"Can you stand?" she said. "I think you need a drink."

"Christ," Dawes said, "I think it's only another German nurse."

She leaned down then. She lay over him, nearly fascinated as she studied the small, filthy bandage beneath his eye. She tore it away. Groaning, her lips parted slightly when she saw it, and she told him she thought it was infected.

"Of course it is. My head's always been infected," he said.

"It just needs a little sunlight, I think," she said.

He was about to tell her he didn't give a damn when she produced the fat four-hundred-pound opal hunter's yellow mirror from her pocket. They sat together, under the single street lamp, watching as the soft scab broke and ran, making his eye seem almost rainbowed. The cut ran like a part on the eyebrow ridge, turned, went around the side and under the eye like a lucky horseshoe and then, snaking out, ran down along the inside cheekbone. It stopped short, against his nose, like a billiard shot eventually, leaving Dawes Williams to walk around looking as if someone had tried to operate on his eye with a pocket knife. It was the cut Dawes had got rolling that night between Torreón and Chihuahua, Chihuahua and Torreón, while fighting an entire band of American Peace Corps workers single-handed.

"Damn it. Damn you," Dawes Williams said, "leave me alone, Urzika. I'm Huck Finn this time. I know I am."

"Michael will fix it," she said. "If not, I'll give you something that will help."

"I'm a Methodist," Dawes Williams said, sitting in the gutter. "My body's a temple."

Urzika laughed and helped him up, and they made their way back to Michael the Mute's, a small and quiet man who sold rings and crosses and chains and other religious items from within the bars and windows of his shop. Urzika and Dawes lived upstairs, and the shop, like everything else in Mexico, was without steps and lay easily upon the level of the street. As they came in, Michael's young daughter was sweeping bits of the store out onto the street. She was brown and small, Catholic, quietly religious-looking, as if she had a tiny nun locked already tightly inside her.

As they came in, Michael was bent over his acetylene torch, cutting a ring. He looked quietly up through his tinted goggles and over a bluish flame.

Urzika talked to Michael in sign language. Her fingers carved silent letters onto the air. Faster than the ear could see them they left her hands in single notes, phonemes, even in vague and dissonant phrases. Dawes stood back and watched with one eye as the notes of her hands faded within the flaring moon. Slightly behind her, he watched the one-handed notes being played by the one-named girl being watched by the one-eyed yeoman and the no-voiced man. Down at the ends of back streets he heard the pariah dogs bark like iron rings, welling up the unknown distances, the night-flowering walls, and he could only think that things were not whole any more, had never been whole for him, could never be again, and that they were only single notes, stones without even motion then, breaking up, falling apart, separating and drifting farther away, only broken phonetics of half-understood movement, in the dusky chaff husk of the air. . . .

"Well, Dawes bastard," Urzika was saying, "I believe we are going to have to cauterize your eye this time."

"Hell, yes," Dawes Williams said, "just gimme a bullet fer my teeth. I'll be brave. Long's it's my inside, track-rail eye it doesn't matter."

"What?"

"You wouldn't understand. You ever know Arthur? Well, I did," he said.

"Hold still, Dawes. I'm trying to wash you in the blood of your own lamb."

"You can't ever meet someone in the street and ever understand. Not any street, not even your own."

"Are we playing Hyoot John Williams again, Dawes?" she said.

"Who gives a damn if you give a damn? Who gives a damn if you give a damn about giving a damn?"

"You do," she said.

"Burn my eye out if you want, but don't give me that circular crap this early in the morning. It makes my head spin."

"It's night again, Dawes."

"I never was much good at cipherin' the fractions of light lately," he said. "Besides, Urzika, I got no quietly rip-roarin' ballin' stories to tell my grandchildren now. How can I tell'm I been had by laymen, ass-ended by Peace Corps workers on their way to Mexico City in the end? I ask you."

"Why, Mr. Yocum Longstreet," Urzika said, drawing herself up, pouring him a tall glass of rotten tequila, "how you DO carry on making a purty li'l girl's heart flutter so!"

She stuck a cut lemon in his cheek and set him down on a one-legged cow stool. He sat motionless, trying to balance the wind, looking up and smiling back.

"Oh shut up," she said finally, quietly.

"That's heavy, I think," he said. "Yocum Longstreet Williams."

Then he drained the glass. It was like drinking a hot river with bits of sand, small exploding suns rimmed in thick green moss, still carried along by the bottom silt. The sand was dark sand, and it node the waves of the glass like wheels. Hot wheels. Or the clawed feet of tiny animals. It was like drinking your eye.

Then he lay over the edge of the table and puked up nothing at all. He leaned back against the wall, convulsing slightly, slightly blooming back within the regular flare of his pulse.

"Hell, yes," he finally said, "it's the old Red Skies of Montana-Ivanhoe-Christ rejuvenation scene we are finally playing now within the confines of Yiddish syntax."

"Trust me, Dawes," she said.

Then, just as Dawes began to trust her, Michael began moving blissfully about his eye with a senile smile, a dirty rag, and a bottle of red dye. The wound was squeezing itself open. Watery blood, thin as a sick baby's, ran down Dawes' face. He saw his sleeveless shirt was torn, filthy and carved upon with unbelievable legends written in both dry and fresh blood. (*Sometimes,* he thought he would write into his notebooks, *Urzika just lies at night in the dreamy dark, reading off the signs and eyelid movies of his old shirts like sleeveless gestalt Rorschachs.*) But that was a lie and, suddenly, sitting there on that Mexican cow stool, drinking tequila and chewing the stuck lemon pouched in his cheek, looking back into the eyes of the small daughter with the tiny nun locked tightly within her, he thought he must look like only a pelican, stuffed, boarded down and bedded within the gray beneficence of a zoo.

"You know," he said, looking back at Urzika, "as Simpson's father, Ceril Pencil Williams—the Midwestern lawyer, part-liberal who drove the Klan out of Omaha and defended nuns and other emotionally unenfranchised groups, part-Methodist still who slept every Sunday in church—once said—in direct conversation with his brother, Hyoot John Williams, who had wandered up from Arizona, 1919, who was just then standing there, rearisen after all those years, an old man nervously fingering the Mexican's memory of a spinning bullet attached to his watch fob, reloading the Colt meant now only for shooting more walnuts down from the red evening, over the lawyer's sleeping lawn, 'Well, I'll tell you what I think, Hyoot John,' he said. 'I think every time a damn fool Western Williams goes to Mexico he deserves to either get shot, stomped on, infected, or the general hell kicked out of him.'"

And with that, still looking at Urzika, Dawes Williams passed out cold on the floor. He slid from his Mexican stool like a discarded suit of limp clothing. And now, finally happy, as insentient as an ass-ended fish, he lay one eye deader to the world.

When he came to, became conscious of Urzika again (as if that bastard had ever been conscious, Dunker once said), he found himself upstairs, stripped and naked, boarded again almost, into the stuffedness of the bed. Rings and bits of glass, carved-on metals, golden snakes with precious and blue topaz eyes seemed stuck like stones embedded to the gleaming walls. A gothic Pietà, Urzika was caught momentarily sitting on the edge of the bed, cradling his head. As soon as he awoke she released it. She then eyed it apprehensively—as if it, the whole apparatus and contraption of his head, were a ripe melon about to roll off on the floor and burst. He had a fresh bandage. He looked at her. She went across to the mirror and looked into it for a moment. She brought it back. In it, he seemed amusingly disfigured. He saw that the bandage buried his head in gauze. Slowly he looked back at her.

"Jesus," Dawes Williams said, "it seems I am consistently being ass-ended by laymen."

"Be quiet for awhile," she said.

"Hell. Just send me out into these feudal streets. Tin cup, fife and drums. I'll take up a collection for the first revolution. The one that overthrows feudalism."

"Really, Dawes bastard," she said, "your humor is really so fucking bourgeois."

"I know. Urzika, I really hurt."

"I know. I know. Yes," she said, vaguely rocking him slowly in the air. She spun it all over. Her hand ran all over him, trying to touch him everywhere at once.

"Damn it, I love you," he said.

"Shut up. I'll stop."

"I think I love you. I haven't loved anything for a long time. That's a lie. I've never loved anything."

"I'll stop."

He felt her everywhere. She was trying to pass through to another side. She was everywhere, an invisible, touching ghost, beyond him, inside him, behind him.

"I probably don't love you, either," he said. "Not really."

"Be quiet. I'll stop."

"Urzika? Why don't we buy ourselves a couple of Mexican goats, a cow, some dogs and straw hats and move to South Texas?"

"Dawes! Words!?!"

"Why not? Raise ourselves a bunch of sexually sensitive, transcendental poets of Western man. Make a start in life?"

"Dawes. Words. I'll stop."

"Why not?"

"Dawes."

She buried her mouth against him. She was trying to touch him everywhere, more lightly than he could feel. He rose up within her. She pulled him along behind her. He flowed into stone within her soft, spreading hand. Her mouth was everywhere. She was almost frantic, small, biting him, and curled everywhere against him at once. The room was full of Mexican night, an affair of gold rings, closable red lacings. She spoke in tongues he couldn't answer, not even with humor or disbelief. She knelt at him and slapped him at the same time. A speechless thing, he thought he loved her, like going under a surface of green water. He lay, reaching for her, for a long time. She fell naturally under him. Her hands moving in red distances. She was drawing him out, forcing him under. Then, just as he thought he was suddenly within himself once more, she forced him higher. Her arm locked his ear to her mouth, moving, pulling, riding him higher, and she made hot, forced sounds against him. The muffled noise locked him tightly within her. He couldn't move. She was biting at him, her tongue moving in his ear saying impossible things. Dark things. Things beyond memory, and she drew the bandage away, furious, soft, her soft hand working quietly somewhere below him. An orange bloom of night. And he was frozen to her rhythm, moving with her. Her hands ran down his naked hips, she was moving below him, an impossible nest, riding always higher, opening rising closing, screaming against him, beating him with small fists, calling his name. Through her hands he felt their horrible tension, the inside of her head. Twice he thought he had passed through her shadow. He wanted her. He wanted that now. The orange night. The weight of rain their shades made crossing over onto more naked stone. The house of an attic, the eye of a mask. The bilateral symmetry of shadows, coming together as they crossed between. He wanted her again. A ring of evening. A deep, falling bell of dark. An impossible thing. He wanted her warm, open center. Her spread. Her soft desert and orange and rhyming eye. Finally, her hands went down under, along the length of his inner legs, feeling out sound. Her legs parted more with a soft, dropping motion, he fell farther within at the last moment, and then she buried themselves within him for a long time.

"Tell me your last name?"

"No," she said.

He slept. Waking, he could see she was sitting in a narrow light, easily naked and eating an orange, reading the last of his notebooks. At the end, he remembered, she had tried to kiss him, saying, "Are you only within, on a part of me now, Dawes?" He hadn't answered. Finally exploded of words, consciousness dissolved again, he died into fitful sleep. And then, pretending to dream, he lay beside and slightly under her, watching the expression on her face as she pretended to read:

Chapter 5

THE LAST MOVEMENT

Number Eight

SENSING THE END IS NEAR,
I BEGIN LOOKING FOR BEGINNINGS

Subtitle: You Can Buy 3/2 Beer in Iowa When the Number You Happen To Be Standing on Reaches Twenty-one, But Coming of Age in the Modern Age Should Only Mean—For the Sensible, Innocent Candidian—An Instant Retreat Beyond Even the Horrors of Childhood.

Epigram: That is, when the Prussians are out and marching again, four miles wide in their jackboots, the sane man gets out of the way. Eventually, they will pass over themselves, dying of sheer boredom in the first place. Only a Lunatic would stand up at that first moment of time and deny them. Only a Fool and an insecure, thick-necked effete would see the need to. .

Contra Logic: That is, of course, unless you happen to hate these particular Prussians badly enough. . . .

Personal Dogma: Personally, I'll shoot the first reactionary redneck who comes through the door. . . .

I awaken to only dream again. What will happen?

Sunday, I think. The Roy Rogers movies are on. Patternings. Safe, sure homing devices in the mass, secular society. Perhaps, I think, Moby Dick will swim through my living room and we can finally afford the luxury of a cathartic end. Dreaming of it, of the luxury of being able to externalize and finally kill my own evil, I sit back rubbing down my genuine pre-Civil War harpoon gun with a rare Oriental oil.

Dawes Williams ignores me. (I can never quite seem to get him together.) He scurries about in his corner, doing his own things. Just now, scratching his head, he sits trying to make sense out of one of his dark letters come in out of the mysterious rain. This one is already three or four years old and it is from his old high-school girlfriend, Summer Letch. It is in emotional script and, personally, I think he wrote it to himself.

But, waking, I am surrounded instantly by nature again. It seems—trying to get even for all time—out for a clinical dissection, and I am its object.

The Opinion Poll comes on.

Kate Smith is singing.

Steppenwolf and Led Zeppelin bloom on the walls.

The local news, without temporal body or spatial conception (it merely happens, how does it do it?), comes on. Magic! Regular as a clock. Where does it all come from? . . . A small man with red ears in a green closet in Cincinnati, Ohio. He has been running it all after all, all this time.

The news is on.

Roy rides.

Dawes Williams lies reading old letters from Summer Letch.

It is snowing like a wet god because it must be Christmas morning again.

I know what the letter says without ever seeing it. (Omniscience is the least of my problems.) It says:

Dear Dawes,

Adieu. Just a line to tell you the good news. I've been married! I'm so happy about it! We're going to Chicago to play football! Wish me luck. It never could have worked between us, Dawes. . . you're so . . . so intelligent!!

"Adieu,"
Summer

Dawes turns away, into the window, scratching his head. Finally he says:

"Three years, I know, but I just can't understand it. Do you suppose she had to be quite so 'methodical' about it all? I think I loved that girl."

I turn against Dawes, and we begin to hold a lucid conversation:

You know, I say, sometimes I think it's just like Dunker used to say— "Dawes, you're just an incurable romantic. The only reason you've always loved Summer Letch so much is because she happened to be the one who stuck her hand in your pants first."

Dunker is dead, Dawes Williams says.

Don't worry about it, I say. It doesn't matter. All is farce anyway. We have all sprung from that first scratching, folly-happy ape who walking down deer-trails in Galapagos evenings, succumbs wistfully to that irrepressible desire to playfully ram that small stick up his mother's ass.

There was a long silence on that one. Even opaque Dawes Williams recognizes it. Finally, he folds the letter away:

You would rob us of even our last small dignity as animals, he says. Evolutionist!

I would, straight-lace, I say, I would do that in a minute if I could. Dignity is militancy, war and pestilence through pride and ignorance.

There is more silence.

The world, I say to Dawes Williams, looking straight at those doe-ridden irises of muscle staring straight at the floor, is farce.

No. It's not, he says. It's possible catharsis. It's serious. It's very important doom. It's lyric doom even. It's legitimate tragedy. Free-willed and fated, all at the same time, like the Greeks.

That's dribble, I say.

It's not, Dawes Williams says.

There is more silence. Dawes, he was one fine sonofabitch in his way, I am thinking (as fine as Hubert H. Humphrey of Minnesota). Finer. There is more silence.

Yes, Dawes finally says, I watch television. But I don't enjoy it a minute. You enjoy it, Handsaw, and that's why you are an idiot and I am sane.

But good God, Dawes, I say. Robert Lowell has never been on television. Forgive him. Spot him his existence.

Yes, but he has been on the cover of *Time*.

That's not the same thing.

It is, he says. It's exactly the same. It's tubular.

There is more silence. I sense I finally have him:

Dawes, I say finally, you're just not that sane.

I am, he says, I am. Oh ya? he says. Am I not?

Dawes, I say, didn't you once say: "My third-grade teacher smelt like a forge of sour milkweed caterpillars"?

Yes, he says, but I didn't mean it.

And didn't you once say: "The world will finally evolve itself to the point, internationally, in which War will be illegal. In which the only legal idea, the only political-dogma-handed-down-like-myth-and-archetype, will be: IT IS IMMORAL, ILLEGAL, AND ULTI-MATELY FOOLISH, THEREFORE IMPOSSIBLE, TO THINK THAT WAR IS POSSIBLE. ANYONE SO ARCHAIC AS TO BELIEVE OTHERWISE WILL BE SHOT!!"?

Yes, he says, I said it. But I didn't mean it. I forgave myself. And I never once said we were all apes running wistful sticks up our mother's asses. Only you said that. Only you, Handsaw. Not I.

You were at least implied in it, I say.

Wasn't. And besides, he says, your own Marquis de Sade has never even *been* on television, either. Therefore: how could he exist?

That's true, I say, turning utterly away.

I know I am beaten and defrocked again. Dawes Williams is always too fast for me in the mornings, and I should have known better. I should have never brought the whole thing up.

I feel I am listless, degenerating uneasily into only satire. I dream of going out.

The Roy Rogers movies are over.

The *Opinion Poll* comes on.

—"No, lucky-Mrs.-Davy-Pierce-220-Forks-Road-N.E. It's not an electric snowflinger-or-the-cork-in-a-small-bottle-of-been-either! (GOOD TRY.) But now we have SIX HUNDRED AND SIXTY BUCKS IN THE OLE SECRET SOUND JACKPOT! We'll be calling *you* later!"

I hope they call me soon. I sit back, waiting. When asked, miming perfectly the prissy, celibate, administrative voice of St. Paul, I will say: *Is it Ignatius Loyola in a horsehair shirt? . . . Could it just possibly be, do you suppose, Jesus Christ Himself walking by silently, without tears, in the passionless snow?*

That will get them good. The bastards. That will make them chase their own shadows round the edges of town, looking for possible pockets of light. That will confuse their ass all morning.

Number Nine

SUDDENLY LISTLESS, I BEGIN DRIVING THROUGH FOR AN ENDING:
MY MIND.
DAWES WILLIAMS TAKES A SHOWER.
THE CAT-IN-THE-HAT MARINE.
a moment of all time.

Suddenly listless, I dream of going out, of making angels in the snow all morning. Things are unwound. Perhaps Dawes Williams, that irrepressible, sod-busting yeoman, would care to go with me.

Perhaps not.

Perhaps it isn't even winter any more.

It is only eight-thirty, too early for church. I am not going anywhere anyway. Perhaps it isn't even Sunday.

Perhaps it is.

Perhaps I have only forgotten something minor. (That is what scares me.) I pick up my knitting. Anyway, Dawes Williams stands alone trying to gargle himself to death in the shower. Day drifts in. He is failing miserably, moving about in his narrow stalls:

Where am I? Where am I? he says to his walls. Lost in the heart of just another student ghetto? Is this real? he says.

Nothing responds.

I guess Dawes Williams is not dead after all.

I hope he does something bright. Interesting.

Perhaps he will even go outside and we can have story, character, action, a narrative line once more. Maybe he will take up engineering after all, going off finally to Oregon, Argentina, to build only another bridge between two known worlds.

Probably, but I doubt it. Dawes Williams never goes out any more. He's become an eccentric. He has become a bore. I hope he says something bright. Unusual. I begin to eye him intently, looking for sign:

Handsaw? he says portentously. Where have you put the soap?

I ignore him. That Dawes, he's losing his touch.

Summer Letch, he says. She shouldn't have done it. Something is missing. I've lost all desire to spend my life-cycle buying a house. How will I pass the time? I feel somehow so guilty. What's to become of the Developer's Industry and the Interest Rate? Summer is gone.

Too slick, I say. I don't believe it.

I do, he says. She was a blade of wind. A moonsong passing through the suburban mirror of night. I shall never buy a house.

Good God, Dawes, I say, you haven't even seen her for six years. She's probably already got fifteen Little Leaguers just as funky as you.

Memory, he says simply.

Fuck off, I say.

I shall never buy a house! he screams suddenly. I feel like another shower!

Immediately he gets out, begins crossing the room. He turns on the radio-phonograph-tube. Begins singing. Drying himself off thoroughly, he goes back into the shower. (Dawes Williams is very clean for a schizoid. He's very strange that way. He refuses to conform to a pattern.) Soaping, standing there, perfectly miming the voice of Janis Joplin, he sings "O Neon Night/O Plastic Night." Socking his beat to the aluminum walls, laying down a hand sound, he manages finally also to incorporate four electric guitars, a small, watery harmonica, and an authentic pipe organ into his sound. Ultimately, blowing it, dissolving beyond his own peak, he sounds like a seal. (Dawes Williams, I think, is a fool for not going into show business.) But no, not him. Dawes Williams, I come by degrees to believe, is making himself into nothing but a grotesque.

(I have been reading Rilke again, especially the notebooks. I find the man an absolute genius.)

I grow listless, want desperately to write an antinovel. Just as I am about to begin, however, the phone rings and the moment passes.

It was a wrong number anyway. It was only a Marine wanting to know if Dawes Williams might be interested in joining the Corps. Braun Daniel, it seems, missing Dawes Williams hopelessly, has sent his name in as a possible identity and source.

"That's not my kind of philistine," Dawes says into the phone, hanging up. But he has spoken with the perfectly mimed voice of Jack Benny and, for an instant, he has sounded vaguely American, like a can of well-timed corn, like he is dying.

But I am worried. Dawes Williams, I am afraid, is just making another hopeless social blunder. There seems to be something fundamental even he refuses to understand. It is all academic, however, because soon—perhaps I am just hallucinating again—the Marine shows up at the door. Dawes Williams stands, looking back, nude and dripping water, perfumed and grinning. For a moment, polite and nearly fumbling for his card, the Marine looks benign; then, spying Dawes Williams through the fog of social contact, he looks mean. He looks as if Dawes Williams, who is strangely more muscled and twice as large, can't handle him.

"Who are you, man?" Dawes finally says. "The cat-in-the-hat Marine, for Christsake? Do you think you are really needed or called for around here?"

The Marine takes a swing at Dawes, who slams the door in his face.

"Where's my gun?" Dawes says. "That bastard wasn't even armed."

Before he can even go to look, however, the Marine is knocking almost politely at the door again.

"What is it you want?" Dawes says.

"I just want to make friends," the Marine says. "I've brought all kinds of fun games to play and, besides, it's raining outside. I've *got* to come in."

"Good for you," Dawes Williams says, "but my mother's away and you *can't* come in."

"But I'm the-cat-in-the-hat Marine," he says, "and I *want* to come in."

Bereft of any further social logic, Dawes opens the door. The-Cat-in-the-Hat Marine enters. From his bag he pulls: six red flares, four M-16s, some barbed wire, a Vietnamese whore, a grenade launcher, three decks of cards, a case of bourbon, three loaded opium pipes and an automatic death machine.

Soon Dawes Williams and he, busy hands, happy squeals and giggles going off high in the air, are seen playing quietly with their heads together in the corner. Dawes Williams is having a helluva time, just like the good old days with Dunker, Eddie and Travis Thomas, and it's raining and safe. Mother will never be home.

Soon, however, Mother does come in. She is dressed like poetic justice and Uncle Sam. She is paternally stern as she comes through the door, but soon she has them both balanced on her knees, fondling them, tweaking their rosy cheeks, kissing them passionately by turns, and feeding them cookies, candy and milk. Finally, sensing their desire, she relents and releases them, sweeping them out into the warm sweep of the rain where they run down Penrodand-Sam streets, squealing with joy. . . .

The room is empty for awhile now. Dawes Williams is finally gone, leaving me behind. In the end, you see, he went out, arm in arm with The-Cat-in-the-Hat Marine, to shoot up the world. BroncoBillySixShooterDickDawes, falling back over himself in the wrong direction.

Alone finally, remembering suddenly a moment sixteen years before in the Canadian woods which became the first split, the reason why Dawes Williams went off arm in arm with The-Cat-in-the-Hat Marine, WHY HE IS IN SOUTHEAST ASIA WITHOUT EVEN BEING THERE, I take out my notebook and begin writing out a character sketch. Thinking eventually to send this number to *The Reader's Digest*, I entitle it simply:

A MOMENT ON ALL TIME

Dawes Williams was only twelve at the time—out for his first adult fishing trip and learning experience in Canada with his father and his uncle, Simpson and Ben Williams— but I remember him vividly that moment. He was poised near that clearing like a horn- less doe, sniffing the wind. Faintly remembered civilization, like walking over thin and treacherous ice, lay before him. He was insane for the first time then. He never talked about it. No one knew. (I did.) Because, you see, that was the first time he knew, as an absolute certainty, he had a soul as big and lovely as Jesus Christ. Also for the first time, he knew and felt the heavenly damnation of that burden, like being caught in the exact center of a baroque operetta, there, people singing and running off with exploding harps in every direction . . . across that clearing of Indian woods in Canada.

And I remember watching him. Knowing. Caught up with him in the tragic comedy of it all.

He was twelve. He stood in that clearing, poised for a moment like a destroyed wild thing, fearing his nostrils, doubting the wind, not believing civilization, yet wanting to come closer: like a doe really, female; with the eyes straining, muscular, soft with flight. Coming finally, after six days, out of those woods as if we were not really standing there, near the boat, watching her, as if we had not been standing there at the landing, waiting, for a week. Coming quickly now as if he had just seen the Godhead itself rise up name- less and without need of a face from the forest floor, as if he must run and tell us about it now, quickly, before it had all turned into only smoke and a mask and he had forgotten it again, before it vanished again into wherever it goes when it isn't here.

Because he had just finished living in the Canadian wilderness for six days on three cans of beans and an Indian blanket. The Indian blanket is particularly interesting because it proves that in those days, in the beginning even, he was not an utter fanatic—utter fanatics with truer callings do not take Indian blankets, nor do they feel the need to take three cans of beans—and because he must have known all along, even before we left Iowa, he was going to do it. He was set on it. He had known we were staying in a cabin, yet he had argued furiously for the taking of those blankets—furiously, and yet without ever saying anything, which was the way he always argued about those things—that afternoon we stood near the car waiting for him, to make up his mind the devil wolves wouldn't eat him while he slept, to leave for the woods.

And so it was three cans of beans and six days in the piney wilderness with only God-or-whatever, and a few hapless timber elves ever knowing why, or what he saw, or what he even did, or ever caring to: urinating on the flowers, or chanting hymns in some lost language, in some not yet puberty-ridden voice, or perhaps simply communing with some deep, lost tonality locked tightly within a Celtic tree. . .

But Dawes Williams, he came back, of course. He had to. How else could he eventually be ass-ended in Mexico? And he came back after only six days (only then because it suddenly came to him that even he, the great and boyish shaman of the piney woods, would need a ride back to Iowa before the Methodist winter of wolf set in), a short week, throughout which my uncle Simpson had been frantic, and yet knowing him, knowing Dawes as he did, also strangely stoic, saying (over and over for six days):

"Well, Ben" (Ben was my truer father, even at the time), "you know he'll come back someday." (As if we had months or years to begin with.) "Yes," Simpson said, "he will. It's just like that time he got mad at his grandfather on the farm. He was six. But when he came back the next day, huge in the eyes you know . . .

"I know, Simpson," Ben would say, "I know."

". . .and I asked him what he'd been doing, Leone was crying you know, like he had been somehow ruined sleeping one night out in the fields you know, well, he just looked at me quite seriously and he said: 'Don't worry, Dad, I been trackin' Arthur's wild jacks. I been livin' with them for awhile.'"

"I know what you mean, Simpson," Ben said, going for another Pabst.

What a damn carnival! I thought. It was a real peasant's fair, a melodrama, a meeting in a wooden tent of the undersensibility, a conspiracy of whittling sticks and orators on stumps. The red shadows moved the deer antlers across the walls all afternoon until it was time to fish. They moved through a constant ruck of poles and nets and hoops in the corner, soup cans and fishheads and asymmetric talk. For six days Ben, my father, was saying:

"Awww hell, Simpson," Ben, his brother, was saying, "hell, this is not sense. This is not sense. There's no sense at all being upset about a thing like this. You've always known this sort of thing runs in the boy's mother's family. Knew it the day you married her. Probably before. Soon after. And hell, since this sort of latent moon worship has *been* there, going on this long, it's probably also then developed complementary ways of taking care of itself. They would, or they wouldn't ever be here to worry about in the first place. You can see how one thing goes with the other that way. Hell, you can see how he's safe enough in that respect, Simpson."

And then Simpson: "Good God, Ben, shut up. Just be quiet about it."

"Hell, let's go fishin', Simpson."

"I believe." Simpson says, "that that damn Catholic priest next door that looks like he's got gowns for eyes is more concerned about it than you, Ben."

"Why? Just because he happens to spend his nights out there running in the woods, flashing himself before himself with a lantern, screaming, 'Dawes. . .Dawes,' like a bloody smoking pot? I was out there, too, you know, but a fella needs his sleep, too. He'll make out."

"But I thought I saw him once . . . he was running away, Ben."

"Why the hell not, Simpson? He likes it out there. He's a damn witch, isn't he?"

"No, he isn't," Simpson said. "He's just a little mixed up again, Ben. That's all. He's got a fine mind," he said, sitting there, hunched over double into the same shadows he'd been in for a week, not praying, not even moving much, but instead caught in that moment it was forever beneath him:

"Ben," he said finally, on Saturday night, "what am I going to tell the boy's mother if he's gone for good? Do I just tell her I have lost him? How can I go home and tell her that probably the wolves got him? What the hell do I say?"

And then Ben: "Awww hell, Simpson, let's go fishin'."

But Dawes, he came back, of course. With the protective omniscience of childhood, picking his spot, the exactly right pendulum tick between Simpson's desire to kill him and his desire to gratefully forgive him, he came back trailing the madness of his thin Indian blanket behind him, still watching the sky for further sign, smiling vacantly. Then, standing by the fishing boat loaded with fishing tackle, with the shadows of three alien men—my father, my uncle, my cousin Dawes—I remember Ben turning round, unimpressed, saying:

"Well. . . I guess we were all right on that one, Simpson," he finally said

Not I. I just stood there, looking back. Nothing in particular (that I could see) responded. But Dawes Williams, he had returned not quite more whole than nearly. After being alone. In forests. Like always, his whole life. Like on that sixth day when he came back, crossed the cleaning, and began looking me straight in the eye across distances.

"By God, Simpson, I believe we have one here. A live one. I believe we have privy Moses here come back from the wilderness. Yep, with a burning bush for an eye, and only a thin causation for a mind. By God, I believe we have. Awww hell, you guys," he said, "you finally mind if this old pagan goes fishin'?"

I stood there, saying nothing. Hating him. Dawes. Thinking. Only: *Yes, and he is not the only one who is mad in their way. I, too, am mad in my way. We are all, just standing here, mad in our ways. But it is only HE who is wanting terribly to make us see it, to act it out. For some reason. To make us look at it for hours on end. Without mercy or forgetting. Yes, it is I, Handsaw Williams, who is even better than Dawes, finer and better and madder in every way. More than Dawes. But who will tell him? And finally it will only be HE, the only one, who will make it out of himself someday. HE, not I, who will have the obtuse nerve to make it into something finer than himself. Someday. Someday he will compose a great lie. And call it himself. The possibility of himself. Not I. He is the only one. Something finer than himself. The Bastard. Not me. Only him. Dawes. Who is not even aware of it. Of himself. Of that thin stone of ever-woken seed. Who is not me, but only himself. Dawes. Who is not in me, but in only himself. Selfish. Mindless. Fool. . . He will make it out of himself someday.*

The room drifts off before me again. Dark, internal ark.

Outside the rain is running on stone. Sunday.

Inside I dream only of an antique sleep.

Number Ten
INTERLUDE:

LOCUS AND LOCUM, MY OWN LOCATION.

PREMONITION:

MR. NORTON, THE JEWEL OF THE SEA.

Inside, deep under my antique sleep, I drift off dreaming, a few minutes past noon, a day too hot for sleeping, three hundred miles, north of Havana, of the dustless sea. All is phenomenon. A wash of black, innocent water. I dream of an entity, a man with yellow wind beating around him. Maidens await his every opulent movement. He is deeper, more richly impressed on my consciousness now, than the King of the Sea. In his eye is a terrible blueness of jewels. His name is Mr. Norton. Ultimately, approaching, he says only:

"All is phenomenon."

My cabin is slow. There is a sea breeze. I lie back, caught up again, dreaming of Mr. Norton and the Spanish whore. The sea, an orchard of soft blossoms, rises, lies beyond, becomes an affinity of affixed shapes, strange forms, fields, flowers of a stranger sun lying easily beyond. There is a merging. Silent seams of perfect, faceless water close together, distend behind, run without noise within the sound of my shell. In the sea I hear my ear. The morning is a perfect stone: I lie beyond. The air is a net of hot rock all morning. I hold onto the murdered stone. In the boilers, below, four Ethiopian princes are casting dice against the pipes, a small dream—of fish bones and of icy snake-eyes in the glass. Above decks, Schiller, dressed only in a German monocle and shoes without laces, sits over his yellow paper. He sits within his own air, hot with blowing flies, reading. His vague eyes, yellow too, like Italian glass spun quietly from the maddened centers of blow-pipes, cast points of black, concentric anger over his columns of numerals. Periodically disinterested with the Spanish whore, Mr. Norton's blue jeweled eye blooms through the hole in my cabin wall at me all morning. Slowly, over his paper, upon command above decks, Schiller burns; beginning to smile he ignites, becomes flesh, printed in Germany . . .

"They can only make molecules out of you once," he says.

Only acted upon, holding onto the murdered stone, I lie back wordless with impossible opinion. Mr. Norton goes out finally to murder the morning. Displaying great mental energy and cunning, he mimes the yellow air into an embarrassed shame and nonexistence. The Horsemen Of The Stoned Rain open themselves, like broken water-hearts, birds of the deep sea morning, on the horizon . . .

The air is green with flags. Suddenly it is very clear. There is an ovular window carved in the ship of my wall. Ship's keel, mad as a house, rises but the window does not. It remains, hanging to the desperate air like only the thinnest suggestion of breathing flesh.

Carved, like an unsuccessful exercise in outgoing infinity, on the sightless renaissance of my walls, it only rows my shell up and down on the motion of its sea-breeze, suspending my nature.

Above decks, on the sills hammered on mast heads, the Spanish whore dances like fixated wood. I lounge below, decadent, caught up without arms within the thin, outgoing, luxurious snakes of my smoke. (I watch the bombs and bones of darker, more competent fish dance in the cold off more distant waters.)

It is sometime in midsummer, I think, a few minutes past noon. The green sea distends out forever, like Adam's rib. There is sun. The sky is blue, dreamy, able to lose itself within me. It is deep with an oyster's crust, heavy and oppressive with the sweetness of stirred and thickened roses (able to lose itself within me). In the end, a clown comes on stage. It is an old dream, the yellow inner fallen air of broken playhouses, and he is dressed like Charles Chaplin. In the black distances at the end of a candle he mimes his own face. He takes it off and examines it at length. He is distended and his motions fill in the baroque dark. (Vaguely he talks of social democracy.) His white eyes roll, are lost in the vague sockets. He is crying now. Slowly he begins miming himself mime himself.

He takes out a mirror.

His reflections become multiplistic. Curtains open. The images of self grow in the mirrors of his red walls. They root and bloom in the glass. They become pluralistic in a stage of corridors, halls without step or dimension, the recessive spaces of playhouses echoing back, exactly, without space. (He is an abstraction.) Distended on his own walls of a nameless desire, he becomes a grotesque, lost in the spiral of his dream of self-possession, wrapped in his own arms. He turns. Rotates. Blooms from his mirrored center. His own heart.

He has my face.

Into the ends of candles before him he smiles, knowingly, knowing all things I do not. He has my face.

He has my mask.

Slowly, before me, as if I weren't even here, he begins drawing it aside. He is unaware of my presence now. Contemptuous. He accuses me without pointing. His distraught motions fill in the mechanical stage. He is drawing the mask aside:

(There is a small applause from the house, lights come up.)

Because beneath it is the face of Dawes. . . knowing all things I do not. Because beneath it is the face of nothing at all.

I suddenly think I will sleep, not awaking again, now. Outside, the dark cathedral of arks, tropic whales, vent steam in the porcelain air. They lie beside, below, beyond me. They pass mating, thunderous as wakes. It will be a deep, theatric sleep, waiting only for Mr. Norton, his throne of soft dust and his bluish jewelry of eyes, to rise up and to know me once more. Here. Lying flush with my space.

Because, you see, I am my own (and Dawes' too then of course) locum and locus. My own locative logos. Our only location. In the end I was only the black face of his death after all.

Something, fragile as my wonder, small as Dawes' fear, perhaps only the self-reflexive shadow of a broken rising gull, choking with soot, soft with only self-knowledge and decay, tries to rise away with our sill. Only the clouds, light with the dark lilies of morning, fly beyond . . .

I would sleep again. Knowing all things I do not know.

Number Eleven
LAST LISTINGS

It is Monday morning finally, last listings, and Dawes Williams goes to his mailbox. Coming back into his room, he sits down and reads it all over several times:

Dear Mr. Seriphus Williams,

I regret to inform you that Mr. Walter Cronkite was not available for comment upon your seventy-five-page letter—perhaps I should say treatise—on what he could do with CBS News. (I can report to you, however, that Eric Sevareid inadvertently stumbled over two pages of it and called it "trash.")

I can assure you, though, it has all been read with some interest by the "staff" and we, at this end, think perhaps you should send it on to NBC, or even ABC. If you don't, for some reason, feel up to this right now, perhaps you might even consider letting us do it for you.

Dr. Stanton also would, I am sure, were he able, like to thank you for your interest.

> Best Wishes in the Future,
> Miss Carlyn Wood
> *Sec. for CBS News*

Dear Dawes Oldham Williams:

This is to inform you you have successfully passed your General Armed Forces Physical (held last month in Des Moines) and have been classified accordingly 1-A by your local board.

> Congratulations, Emma Beckworth Smith
> *Loc. Sec. to The Colonel*

Hey Willy,

If you and the other 30 people I sent letters to this month can *just* send me 2 bucks apiece I think I can *make it thru the rest of the winter.*

> Please man, no shit,
> Gibber

P.S. Just slip it to *General Delivery, Montreal, Canada*. It's desperate, Willy. I can't even afford to do a little grass.

Dear Dawes,

A rare, routine check of our records shows that—for some reason unexplainable to me—we have been carrying you now for the last twenty-three months. Care to pay up? Or perhaps even renew out there? We have so few people subscribing out there in Iowa, perhaps that helps explain it. Perhaps not.

Best,
Standley Wise
For The New York Review of Books

Dear Mr. Handsaw Williams,

Is that your real name? Our records show that—while you only made one call last month—you still owe us eight dollars. You will please pay as billed. Also, our records show you as "deceased," which we feel can't somehow be right. Will you also come down to our offices and straighten this matter out?

Mrs. Henderson Bead
For A.T. & T.

Dear Dawes!
Come home!

Mother!

Hey Willy!

Enclosed are some four pounds of poems, letters, a novel, and photographs of me killing wild boar while on patrol. Read them over carefully and let me know what you think. Come over here and I'll show you around the highlands. Anyway, save the MSS for me. If I'm shot, get them published at any cost. I happen to be the only pro-war poet over here with Hemingway's balls still on. (HA! HA!HA!) Try the H. L. Hunt Press. HA! HA!HA!—The War's going great. Should have joined the Marines with me, Willy. Great show. Gotta run.

Braun Daniel

Dear Dawes,

I haven't seen you lately. Why not? Disillusioned with me? Your phone has been out this month so I thought the only, perhaps even the best, way to get in touch with you was via the mails.

The matter is, in short, this: we now have an unexpected opening at the hospital for you—thanks to a rather unfortunate occurrence which I couldn't go into here—and I was wondering if you would consider committing yourself? Let me make you well, Dawes. Will you at least come in to the office and talk to me about it?

Very Very Sincerely Yours,
John Wexler
Psychiatrist

Dear Mr. Dawes Williams,

Your letter has been received and turned over to the FBI for further scrutiny. Turn yourself in at your nearest local law enforcement office. They will, I am sure, turn you over to the proper people for examination and treatment. It will go better for you.

Sincerely yours, Mrs. Gladys Crab
From The Office of the President

Dear Grandson,

Do hope you are feeling better by the time this letter reaches you. Won't bore you with a lot of Grandma Ellen's advice now. I will only forward to you a beautiful copy of Billy Graham's latest pamphlet entitled *Eternally Yours*. Read it over several times at length, to get its deeper meaning, and I'm sure you'll feel so much better. It's an unusually good number, put out by the Rocky Mt. Press People—such a good group!! In closing, let me only say pay particular attention to the wonderful and inspirational poem on page nine—opposite that photograph of Mr. Graham's own sweet granddaughter—entitled simply *What Is Eternity?* So inspirational.

Incidentally, while it's not too late, why don't you consider the possibility of attending law school? Oh, your granddaddy Ceril was such a wonderful lawyer and convocation speaker before worry and the Klan got him. If you could have only known him before his death at such an early age, I'm sure the course of your life would have been quite different. He was such an example to us all!!! He was a Democrat, of course, but then we won't hold that against him forever, will we? He had such remarkable sense, even idealism, in nearly everything else he did. Think it over.

Love and Peace,
Grandma Ellen

Eventually, putting his mail away, thinking people were just crazy, Dawes Williams got up and went from the door. He went to turn himself in at the post office.

Number Twelve
CURTAIN SPEECH:
BRAUN DANIEL'S WILD CIRCUS OF DOMESTIC MICE.
HUCKLEBERRY FINN WILLIAMS IN A BATHTUB.

Dawes is gone for awhile now, finally, so I think I may speak freely at last. The room is empty, hollow. Sensing the sheer reverence of this lull in the action, I step stage center. I say:

That was the spring Dawes Williams tried to speak and couldn't. His mouth would fall open and then silent again. He stared often at the flooring. In taverns at midnight he rose up to say nothing at all. He rode his Triumph down to the river at Hills, Iowa, at dawn.

I pace the stage, continuing to speak:

And that was the spring Braun Daniel had nothing but time on his hands. The mornings he spent enlisting in the Marine Corps. It became an extremely involuted process. Dawes and Handsaw Williams both wrote long, glowing recommends in the end. . . . In the afternoons Braun Daniel spent his time avoiding law-school professors on the street and revising his poems. He sat always in the same spot from two o'clock until four. . . out in the yard, in only his jockey shorts, under the same huge shadow of the elm tree, talking to only his typewriter perched on a rattan mat, and to his favorite bulldog Boomer le Roi, who was furiously chasing anything that moved, even suggested slight life, in the grass. . . . And when Dawes Williams would disturb the air with a word or the slap of a door, Braun Daniel would become instantly furious and say something like:

"Goddamn it, Willy, you just blew this goddamn line out of my head forever. It was almost there."

In the evenings he lured sorority girls to Farmer Elroy Colcaw's South Pasture with promises of unbelievable lust.

By early summer, Braun Daniel had removed every pot, pan and dish from the cupboards: in the spaces, stuffed with old straw and blankets, of the shelves and drawers he began keeping mice. Some were domestic and white; others black and red and all wild shades of gray. He was working, ultimately, toward an Appaloosa mouse. Or, perhaps, toward something more. . . . He mated them by decree and edict and gave them foundling names. He mated Mary Magdalen with The Sun King, Louis XIV; Abelard with Paulette Goddard; John the Baptist with Mary Godwin Shelley; Heloise with de Sade, and a mouse named God with a mouse named Judy. . . .

In the end, by midsummer, the place was crawling with birth. Dawes said at night he could hear the freed ones whining in their walls, the captive ones still scratching out of the grasp of their cupboards. Quietly, like small things without fields to burrow in . . . softly, he said, like frenetic things trapped in a closable blackness. Finally like miniature seams of crying water without fountain or estuary, without source or with end . . .

I pace. I throw the cape back over my shoulder. I pace the playhouse. I say:

I remember him, Dawes, late one afternoon, sitting within the deep country shadows, the farmhouse kitchen, trying to sift the red light, looking flatly at the floor (he was always looking at the flooring, at holes in the wind: it was late summer by then; he was without motivation or reason by then; he was mad by then), looking at me, and saying in a flattened tone:

"Damnit, Handsaw, this place is lousy with mice."

"What'd ya say, Willy?" Braun Daniel said.

"I said: Damnit, Braun, this place is lousy with birth. Why don't you get some of these lousy mice out of here?"

And then Braun Daniel: "Oh, my God. The humanist reactionary philistine is knocking at the walls of the temple."

And then Dawes: "Christ, I live in a grotesque house."

And then myself, I, Handsaw (tentatively): "That is only malicious gossip. Why do we think we are nothing in this century? We are as big and lost and quietly mournful as we ever were. Can ever be. Even with the ruck that fills our inexplainable rooms, our mass, we are still that. Surely we are even that."

And then both of them: "Shut up, Handsaw. Go wire off another letter to an editor. Go be a would-be czar. Just shut the fuck up."

But I had already turned to go. Sublimation, I thought. And leaving the farmhouse that afternoon, I heard them behind me, wrapped fiercely in their communal mime: they were like the old women of the tribe tied tightly within their black inviolate shawls, their nonanimal skins. They were clutching at warmth, at fire. I knew them both to be mummers, insanely reflexive masks of sanity, twisting it, bending it to their own shape, mirroring back only the distorted, the personal, the insane. They were both mummers in their ways . . . but it was Braun Daniel who was laughing, and talking hurriedly, while Dawes was silent and passive. Sitting quietly on that chair, in the red country shadows of that slow farm, he was looking flatly at the floor. He was lost in his reverie of boredom and waste, watching the vacant ghost sleeves of the mice as they spawn in the floors of his shoes. Because, you see, it was Braun Daniel who was suddenly through the door behind me, shouting heatedly:

"Wait! Handsaw! You loveless moralist! Wait! You've missed the best! The end! What it's all been leading to! You've missed my showing you the mouse I've named 'Dawes.'. .

I pace the stage. I say:

And having turned that afternoon, behind him now, going back into that kitchen, the shadows on the walls like red chickens, I watched: quiet, behind him now, I saw Daniel open the drawer, and fish through the molting straw, and emerge again, laughing, fiercely happy, his black eyes nearly contained, laughing wildly, and in his hand was a newly born and nearly dead and two-headed mouse.

. . . INTERMISSION . . .

I go out for a smoke; a cigar; a glass of champagne. Coming back, refreshed, the roller of big cigars once more, curtains up, I begin pacing in the out-back shadows. There is applause in the house.

"Welcome," I say. "I am overjoyed that you have not returned. None of you. But for those of you who have, let me just say that this is Act II and Curtain—Huckleberry Finn Williams in a Bathtub—in a play called simply *The Unbegotten.*"

I pace. Beginning to hop about furiously, stage left stage right, even stage center, I play all the parts. I say:

Because, you see, that was the spring I came unexpectedly out from town and found Dawes Williams soaking in a bathtub overflowing with *prima facie* suds. . . . He was just lying there, motionless as dead sail, smoking quietly on a Marsh Wheeling cigar. His head was lost within reefs of bluish smoke, and a copy of *Huckleberry Finn* was draped, with the decoctic curl of his arm, over the edge of the tub. Two quarts of beer were perched on the sink near him. And Braun Daniel's prize vulgate bulldog, Boomer le Roi, was sitting tensely on his haunches, like a partly loaded gun, apparently thinking of jumping the tub. . . of taking a wild swim in the mountains of suds.

"Hey Willy mother," Dawes said, not opening his eyes, not even moving, "pull up a stool."

"Everything is in order," I say openly. "The mouse, introduced in the First Act, just went off on schedule in the Third. Do not worry."

But he did not even open his eyes. He took a long, thoughtless pull on his beer. Boomer, stirred by the action, stuck his forgettable dog head over the side of the tub and began to explore, at length and with wonder, the small mountains of foam. He buried first his nose, then, interested, caught up, his whole head up to the ears.

"This dog is queer for suds, Willy," Dawes finally said, still not moving.

He was frozen in his orb, a monolithic sphinx, a fixity of stone at the gates asking questions of riddles.

"Yes, sir," he said, "this dog craves action. Just like his personal literary doppelgänger, Braun Daniel. He loves to consume soap, Willy, when things are slow."

Boomer le Roi cocked his head one-quarter to the side. Then, his first advance completely unchecked, he wound up like a quick spring and he jumped the tub. Head buried, slapping the waters, he began exploring the suds. Dawes, for the first time, opened his eyes.

"You miserable and horny cur sonofbitch!?!" Dawes said.

There is a long silence in which Dawes Williams tries to explain himself. Boomer le Roi, oblivious to the social amenities, ignores it. He romped in the waters and came up barking. He went under again. He emerged finally, licking the furious water running from his jowls.

"Dawes," I say, "why don't you just take him out?"

"Hell," Dawes said, taking the Marsh Wheeling from his mouth, "he's *in* here now. Besides, there are some things you still have to suffer in this world, and Boomer le Roi happens to be one of them."

I sat—began sitting—there. Watching Dawes. It was like having an audience with a famous man who has nothing whatever to say, but who just lies there in his baroque tub of soap and says nothing at all. Who watches you back with an air both chose and heavy with portent. Who, finally, closes his eyes as if your existence were the highest irrelevant phenomenon in the universe.

I pace the stage over. I say:

Because Dawes had closed his eyes again. He seemed to be sleeping this time, deep under himself, curious with space. I cleared my throat like a sycophant and immediately hated myself for it. Boomer le Roi began playing mindlessly at the far end of the tub. He was looking seriously at the wall.

"Hell," I say finally, "I saw Braun Daniel in town walking his other two bulldogs, so I thought I'd take the opportunity to come out and see you. That's all."

It was very quiet. Afternoon. The silent shadow of the farm drifted the walls, like listening to yourself watching your own listenings.

"Ga-rooooooovy," Dawes said. Then, his eyes nearly open for a moment:

"That's neat as hell, Willy. That's just about the neatest goddamn thing I've heard all day. Want a beer, Willy?"

"My body's a temple, Dawes, you ass," I say.

"Gee, that's exciting," he said, not opening his eyes. "What was he doing with them?"

"Braun Daniel? In town?"

"Yes. Did he have them on leashes?"

"No. They were running free. Down in front of Joe's Place. They were attacking stray coeds trying to come in from the cold. They were mounting them at will."

"And Braun Daniel?"

"A crowd was gathering. He was egging them on."

"Sounds hike Braun Daniel all right."

"Yes, he was in form. Standing there saying: 'Atta boy, mount that one there. Way to fire, Zoomer.'"

"Too bad Boomer wasn't there. Been a field day."

"Yes, he was standing there by the door, introducing himself, saying, 'How do ya do,' tipping his hat, sicking his dogs, rewarding them with pickled wieners."

"Sounds like Cardinal Spellman, all right."

Silence. Boomer still romped in the waist-high water. Dawes hadn't opened his eyes yet. It was like there was nothing out there he hadn't seen before or cared to look for. When he finally did open them, it was only to look at Boomer le Roi looking flatly at the wall. They were both, I think, that day, waiting calmly for the walls either to collapse or to move; they were both tired of them simply standing there.

"Go to hell, Dawes," I finally said. "Take your romantic hat with you."

"I'll follow you down, baroque and jaded mother," Dawes Williams said, soaking, not even opening an eye.

"Nothing is heroic any more, Dawes," I said.

"If you're going to start in on Myth and Heroism again," Dawes said, taking the wet cigar from his mouth, "so help me God, Handsaw, I'm going to get straight up from here, with soap still dripping from my balls, and I'm going to run you through with a thin kitchen fork."

"Sometimes cigars are just cigars, Dawes," I said. "Others are German wieners."

"Drop dead," Dawes Williams said quietly.

"You just don't want to think about it. Not now. You just don't want to have to lie there in your tub and think about heroes, that's all."

There was a silence. He still didn't open his eyes.

"Because that would imply action. Dawes," I said, trying to rouse him, "tell me again the time Braun Daniel took Elmer, his old and mangy fourteen-year-old rooster, down to Joe's Place on a leash."

There was a silence.

"Because that would imply action," I said, "and most of all now you don't want to admit action."

"Well," Dawes said, "Braun Daniel brought him in, Elmer, and he set him up comfortably on the bar, and he said: 'I'm just here to announce that my rooster, Elmer here, is here to fight any other damn rooster who is here.'"

"Because the only action you have now, Dawes, is murdering your past, everything who has suckled you with rotten milk, and your mother, who is a Republican."

"There weren't any takers," Dawes Williams said. "But I still think there is something very elemental Braun Daniel doesn't understand."

"Dawes," I said, "what do you think it is, this thing Braun Daniel has for violent animals?"

"Quit feeding me lines to answer, Willy," Dawes said. "I, myself, pretty much gave you up for lost and losable eight years ago. Remember?"

"Yes. I remember. We were playing Indian ball with Dunker and Eddie and Travis Thomas."

"Yes. It was that day you let three straight fly balls hit you on the head. Remember? How you kept running frantically in, and how that damn ball kept hitting you frantically on the head? God, were you a fantastic metaphor for ridicule. Christ, was that funny. . . . The thing about you, Handsaw, is that you try too hard. You do nothing naturally. You tend to lose all sense of style and decorum. You get all bound up, Handsaw, and you really become grotesque and overextended."

It was still. In the silence Dawes had opened his eyes to see if I had burned.

"But I don't tend to spend six days in the Canadian wilderness. Is that it?" I said.

"For Christsake, Willy," Dawes Williams said in his luxurious tub, "you know that never happened."

"And even if it did," I said, "one has to be able to catch fly balls to look well doing a thing like that. Is that it?"

Dawes said nothing. He only hummed vaguely through his lips.

He had closed his eyes again. Through the foam I could see his body. He was not Donatello's bronze boy-David any more—only somewhat more Highland Scot, thicker in the thighs, less intellectually sexual around a hatless forehead—no, softened dramatically around the sedentary edges now, he looked like only a forgettable piece of soaked bread. And I knew it was bothering him.

"By God, Dawes," I found myself saying, "I believe you're getting soft round the edges. I hadn't noticed that before."

I thought that would burn him. He didn't answer. Instead he only stood up suddenly, pushed the dead weight of the bathtub toward the wall with an imaginary pole, and said:

"Me and Boomer here are rafting the river down to Ka-ro, Illinois, where we cut back some into free ground."

Then he sat back down again and went to sleep. He dozed for awhile and then, partially waking, said:

"It's my Williams blood that did it to me. It's inbred and shot through something thorough."

When he said it, he wasn't at all surprised. It was as if he had been planning on saying it for some time. But he had again opened his eyes at least. At first I thought it was because I had managed to burn him a little, but then I knew it was only because Boomer le Roi, a season for all vulgar dogs, had wrapped himself around one of Dawes' legs and, thrashing about wildly in the mindless water, was just now trying to hump Dawes Williams to death.

"JAEEEEESEEUS KEYYYYYRIST!" Dawes Williams said. "IT'S JUST ANOTHER PLAGUE YEAR AFTER ALL!"

"That's beautiful," I said. "That's a more real social democracy."

Dawes wasn't listening. He was busy already picking the dog out of the tub. Boomer's motor refused to quit, however, and he walked out the door humping the air. In fact, the dog, better dressed than his manservant, wrapped himself around himself, shook off his furious wetness, and began wandering out into the outer rooms at his leisure. He yawned for awhile, and began finally to occupy himself destroying mice. Boomer seemed finally, lost in his dreams of unrealistic riches, to want to go off; to dissolve into all organic directions at once. He became gradually frantic, began barking as if he were bent on dismantling the house as a single organic piece of mouse-trapping. He became centered in a sexual heat bent on killing; at murdering at once all the minuscule running forms.

"Yep, Willy," Dawes said as the house began barking apart around him, "it's the Williams blood that got me in the end. All simpering, rotting sensibility, man. Uncharted painters and poets, all of the bastards. Like you. Tories, all of the bastards. Soon as the Revolution broke out, they split for Canada. Didn't come back, most of'em, until after the Civil War. I hate my blood," Dawes Williams said. "Like you."

"Like me," I said, innocent as a maid.

"Like Cousin John Williams in California, sitting there in his own clay, spinning his wheel, only making his esoterically famous ceramic pots when what he should be doing is throwing them at governors and governments."

"Damnit, Dawes," I said, "all makers of ceramic pots are esoterically famous everywhere. Let's have some sense here. What can one man do?"

"Just be quiet about it, Willy," Dawes said. "He can attack the local radio station. Or, also, like Uncle David Williams, the minor, uncharted Grant Wood of Nebraska . . ."

"But damnit, Dawes," I said, "all Midwestern painters everywhere are eventually like Grant Woods everywhere."

"Just be quiet about it, Willy," Dawes said. "Or like old Dad Simpson hisself, the quietly unknown aesthete of uncharted Iowa accountants and bookkeepers. Jesus, what a mask it all is. He could have risen above himself and blown up Boulder Dam. He could have joined the Wobblies."

There is a long stillness. Dawes, eyes still closed, takes a long, slow, satisfied pull on his beer.

"Dawes," I said, "you are such a wonderfully pretentious prick really." He lay soaking. Then, breaking out of it suddenly, opening his eyes as if he had just been struck by something, he said:

"Did you know, Willy, that my mother was a champion foot racer?"

"Tennessee Williams," I said.

"Fleet she was. Fleet like her daddy Arthur's best and racing greyhounds."

"Dizzy Dean," I said.

"Did you know that about me, Handsaw?" he said. "Did you even imagine that?"

"Carson McCullers," I said.

Then his eyes closed again, self-satisfied; then they opened again.

"But you see, Handsaw buddy, Simpson and even Ben, your father, had two of the finest and highest intelligence quotients for the assimilating of middle-brow blocks into middle-class holes that ever went through the public-school indoctrination system in Phoenix. Not bad for a couple of asthmatics. Did you know that?"

"Paul Harvey," I said.

"Well, I knew that. I knew it 'cause I like to know just what kind of contradictions I have happened to have sprung from, by God."

"Thomist," I said.

"Quit stepping on my rhythms, Handsaw," Dawes said.

"Shirley Temple," I said.

"Old Granddad Williams, too," he said, "a helluva idealistic lawyer. Defended nuns and other minority and impoverished groups without franchise. A regular liberal."

"Uncharted Clarence Darrow, by gum," I said.

"I tell you, all riddles lie in the paradoxes of the blood," he said.

"Adolf Hitler," I said.

"And what did I get out of this white elephant, this rummage sale? Well, I tell you. Yes O yes," he said, rising, standing naked and dripping soap in the bathtub, as tall as an arrow, as beset with pigeon droppings as a Confederate general. "Yes," he said, "mediocre is what I got. Nothing of value. Nothing I can even use. Screw and renege this mess 'they' have made. I refuse to live with it any longer. I've got to rethink my cells, my social organisms, until they come out more nearly whole. *I've got to pull off metamorphosis,* a simple rebirth into new, disestablished forms," he said, suddenly standing half on the faucet, half on the floor, screaming, discontented with the day, genuinely in the throes of self-pity now, rising rhetorically, drawing himself up flush with the walls as if he were operating imaginary puppets' strings run up and back down the ceiling through systems of eyelets and pulleys.

Soap was still dripping from his balls.

Then, just as suddenly, he sat down in the tub and was silent again. His eyes were closed again, as if his sleep were a viable conflict with disease and decay, and he was drinking his beer, lighting a joint, suddenly happy. Just as suddenly as the other.

"Noel Coward," I said. "Is this what happens after the audience has left?"

Silence. Even Boomer le Roi had returned. He sat licking his balls on the rug, looking round corners to see what was happening. He was transfixed finally, fascinated like a curious stone by the oratory of Dawes.

"Christ," I said, "how long have you been like this?"

"Not long."

"How long have you been in that tub?"

"Not long. I won't answer that," he said.

"Why not?"

"Because it sounds like a heading question, poorly placed and delivered, in an overly portentous conversational dialogue. In the damn play of a book, and because I don't want to."

"You are becoming only your own emblem," I said. "That's not a reason. Why else?"

"Quit feeding me lines to answer, Handsaw."

"Why?"

"Well, because it embarrasses me. Because, as an American, it's my own business. And because I don't care to remember. Besides, to say how long I have sat in this tub would offend my grandfather Oldham's ingrained sense of Puritan worth in which virtue, one equals one, is equated to work. To simply getting up in the morning, and walking five hundred greyhounds around the corners of the fields, and not to sitting in tubs of water for six and one-half hours."

"Six and one-half hours!?!?!!??!"

"Yes, is it time for lunch yet?" Dawes said. "And do you think it's easy sitting in a tub of water for six and one-half hours? Denying your grandfather? Because I have sat here with grace and wit and a quiet, learned dignity, for six and one-half hours, and that is important. It also helps explain, incidentally, why I am looking so soft and withered round the edges."

"With Huck Finn?"

"Hell, yes, with Huck Finn . . . with dignity and with Huck Finn, and who in the hell else would you sit here with, if not with Huck Finn?"

"I'm sorry," I said, "I didn't understand."

"I didn't think you would. Huck does, though. He is one of the few omniscient picaros I know. We're doin' a lot of travelin' here in this bathtub. We're rafting America, a plastic shoe."

Cutting him short, I said: "Do you, Dawes, want to know what I think? Do you? Do you?"

"All right," he said, "what the hell do you think, Handsaw?"

"I think just that I am the only one who's mad in this room. I think your madness is merely literary."

"Well, I think you are your own Tom Sawyer," Dawes said.

"Who cares what you think? On an off day, I'm madder than you were at the very apex of your career. You are out of your mind, man, if you think you are madder than I am."

Silence. Boomer wandered out into the other room, collapsing with sleep. I knew suddenly there were rhythms in insanity, a single fantastic ellipsis, and Dawes' were beginning to shift, break up, convolute, like blue ice going out of northern lakes in the spring. And his eyes were closed again, as if I had never been there, as if I had never been born. Then, as if he were on stage, caught in a lapse with nothing to do, he inverted the bottle and he began to pour beer on his head until it ran into his transfigured eyes. In a low voice full of impotent passion he said:

"I, Paul, take thee Jesus . . . I, Paul, take thee Jesus . . ."

Seeing my chance, cutting him off at the pass, I said:

"Now you've really done it. We'll never get over this now. You rinky-dink yeoman bastard . . . you think, like William Saroyan, maybe, you're gonna pull this all off, in the end . . ."

"No, Willy," he said quite solemnly, "I have a simple genius and gift for living. You hate me for it. Because you are capable of only the gift of death."

"Sane people do not think of these things in precisely these terms. They tend to overlook this whole baroque field of concentration."

"I told you that once," Dawes Williams said.

"But I only believe you now."

"Yes. Well. Listen. We're the same damn thing. Mad as hell. Two curious stones being forced to explode in the same concentric implosion of air. And it's now only a question of which we do first—die or go madder. Of who it is will have to take the train to visit the other. The new one. The one of us who is finally forced, chosen, to sit all alone in that dark room and count the moths as they swarm in the well of the lamp."

(Hell, Dawes, I am thinking, that's nothing new. There's nothing new in that.)

"Because of all that, and because of all the damn people I have ever known, the ones I wouldn't under any circumstances want to spend eternity with, it has happened to be you (and that's ironic), you, Handsaw Williams, who have had exactly the same things in exactly the reversed ways (and that's ironic), only in you, Handsaw, the whole thing has gotten somehow horribly out of hand (and that's ironic, too) ."

(Hell, Dawes, I am thinking, what's so ironic about that?)

"Because really, Handsaw, when all is said and done, we just weren't that mad in the first place. They were. History will vindicate us."

"I see," I said.

I pace the stage. I turn into the lights. I say:

Only thing was, I didn't see any of it.

"You see," Dawes Williams said, "the universe is only another shell game. To steal someone's curtain line: I Never Understood A Minute Of It."

"Pessimism!" I said.

"A better religion than hope. A saner, truer direction. At least you get reality and the possibility of viable social structures."

"You unmetaphysical asshole," I said, "you've got some nerve. Isn't there anything good about it?"

"Yes, it can only get worse. Poetically, relatively, we are sitting on the exact center of a high spot."

"Dogmatist. I see," I said.

Only I didn't. I didn't see a damn bit of it. Only Dawes saw it. Only Dawes saw any of the things he thought he saw.

"Willy," Dawes Williams finally said, "let me tell you: I never did think you were too bright for a madman."

"I am! I see it!"

"The hell. I doubt it," he said.

"Dawes," I said, "this is getting us nowhere."

"That's right," he said "hell'zapoppin'." Then, almost quietly: "The farm was so true. So beautiful. So real, like some calm thing stolen from the night-bound world, like the sudden awareness of human time caught in the single image of a Chinese poem." Then: "All of the rest has been just horseshit, urban sprawl and electric plastic cubes. It's so obvious. Why doesn't someone blow it all up?"

His eyes were closed again. He was locked tightly within his house again. The afternoon was winding down like a spent coil. The book was still dangling in his hand. And now even the dog was back, sitting quietly on his dog haunches, in the same spot, completing the circle. It was quiet again, winding down, a house full of red shadows on the sleeping afternoon walls. It was as if I had never come in.

"Hell, Dawes, I just thought I'd come out and look into your wilderness for awhile. See how it's going."

"Thanks, Willy. Ga-rooooovey," he said, "hell of a deal that is. Want a beer, Willy? Some of Braun Daniel's grass?"

"No. I better be going."

"A pill. You want a pill of some kind, Willy?"

"No. I better be going."

"Stay for awhile. I want to tell you about this Eurasian girl I found writing poetry at the Hamburg Inn. Takes me down to the river and reads me the evening of her haiku. — A needle, Willy? I think someone left some kind of needle around here somewhere."

"No. Thanks. I've got to be going. How are they?"

"The poems? Manic-depressive and full of centuries of mass society. Non-sexual somehow. I feel always I should be somewhere else. Or they should. Or something isn't."

"Like playing horse with Dunker? Indian ball with Eddie? Or looking for work jacking up steel with Travis Thomas?"

"Ya, something like that. Something worthwhile and fit for a yeoman. I'm telling you, this poetry business just isn't to be taken seriously."

"I know what you mean. Maybe you could work your way in at IBM?"

"No. Don't think so. Quit feeding me lines, Willy," he said. "If I'm going to be a trilobite, I guess I'd like to be one who tried to leave traces, a tube of his sensibility in the hollow river mud."

"Great," I said, "when are you starting?"

"Soon," Dawes Williams said, "pretty damn soon."

"She showin' you how? How are her poems, Dawes?"

"Hard to tell about that. I think, ultimately, they may be described as serious parodies of either Donne or Tu Fu as translated into Pawnee by either Walt Whitman or Louis Untermeyer's Uncle Charles."

"I don't admire stuff like that myself, Dawes, but sounds also like you're not separating out very well any more—eh, Dawes?" I said chuckling. "How long are these haikus, Dawes?"

"Quit feedin' me, Willy. Hell, some of the damn things go on for hundreds of pages. I think, ultimately, evolving biology in the organism is, like technology which only imitates its darkest inner seed, fixated mainly upon repetitive design."

"Never get home before nightfall, do you, Dawes?"

"Hell, Willy, sometimes I don't even get home for lunch. It's driving me mad. I'm losing lots of weight over this poet. If this keeps up, I'll be dead from trying to give life in six months."

"Looks hike you have trouble there, Dawes."

"I'm not a well man."

"It's trouble."

"It's trouble all right, Willy. Some kind of grief there."

"I see."

"The hell you do. You've never seen a damn thing, with the possible exception of the inside of Bahthasar Neumann's Kaisersaal, in your whole unpent life."

"Yes, well, I'm easy," I said. "I don't see then."

There was another silence while I sat watching him. The afternoon of the farmhouse was a sanctuary, deathly still, waiting for the next, unseen, exotic bird to rise.

"Vel, here't 'tis den," Dawes Williams suddenly said, not bothering to open his eyes. "Yar'sa thar's jes et, cos'in Ha'sa, as et 'pears ta me nexta Iliver Goh'smith I's jus'bou th' darnest, sloooooooooooowest, th' doooooooombest gen'us what's eeeeevat birth'd, I ess!" he said, diving slowly, going deep into his tub of soap.

"I see," I said.

"Like whiskey feathers you do," Dawes Williams said, under the water. I pace the stage. The playhouse is vacant. Realistically miming despair, acting out a brilliant confusion, I say:

I finally saw it! Because in my puzzlement I recognized that when my cousin Handsaw called me "Dawes," or my cousin Dawes called me "Handsaw," often he would break out into an idiot's chiasmus of hybrid, garbled, down-home atonal dialect—which only he could decipher, which only he could trace backwards through the long and seedy history of the voice box—all as if we both had been born, and immediately lost to wolves, on a small, esoteric mountain in the Gulf of Mexico. The final reasons for it—the dialect, the mocking—were always vague, almost lost in the pit of Dawes' bleak mind. They always escaped me, until one day (while walking behind a band of drunk Mestizos on a street in Mazatlán, Mexico, counting their steps) I finally saw it: Dawes had only meant that, hike any Scot-Irish atavism living too long on the same hill with its own design, we could disintegrate at any moment, degenerate at any mishung dropping of time. And he was announcing simply that we had; that we were stuck and fated to only each other now, like seeds frozen in death to their own pods for all time. Yes, that we had already become hopelessly inbred and oversensitive to our own design. Like incest. Like Hawaiian incest, royal, planned almost, ultimately ashamed of nothing; only, unlike it, there had been no provision made for the taking of the rejects, the obviously inadequate and malformed babies out onto the rocks of the sea to be drowned.

"Damn it, Dawes," I said, breaking the yellow silence, "you can't call me a kind of relative idiot."

"The hell I can't," he said.

I was becoming utterly beaten now, looking for an exit, a peace. Instead I said:

"Dawes? How many times have you read that book?"

"I've read Huck Finn sixteen times, and that's unusual as I've never read any other book even twice. Never have had to. I read *Finnegans Wake* twice, but the first one was a mistake."

Pause. The dog was sleeping the slow afternoon away on the rug beside Dawes' tub, full of cacophonous wind, a vulgate organ winding down in the back of a whorehouse. Dawes' eyes were closed again. Unlike some blind, however, he was no seer.

"You dilettante," I finally say.

"You bet your sweet ass I am," he said. "I am the student of only myself. But, damn it, I have never found anything quite as fascinating. As full of interest and wonder."

The dead afternoon hung heavily in the next room.

"Dawes?" I said finally into the silence of that slowly closing room. "Why above all did you choose aesthete and dilettante?"

"I worked very hard at that, Willy . . . because I just like to lie here and watch old Huck go down that river. Nothing else, just the floating, that's all. I like to watch that floating. Yes, it's just about the most perfect thing there is to see that happening. It's just like watching it rain on a time before you were born. It's like watching even the thorn of the rose take root on the glass."

"That's a lie, Dawes."

"That's true."

"That's fascinating, Dawes," I said, yawning.

But a silence had settled over Dawes' house. It was late afternoon. I could see the quiet. I caught myself listening for it to bloom back again like a single heart. Instead, only the dog was soundless on his motionless rug. The burrowing rodents were silent in their walls. I sat there, listening to the sound our blood made running in the walls. I sat trying, perhaps for the first time, to understand what it was, to hear the seamless water running between us. Dawes was lying in his tub of soap, eyes closed forever, oblivious. He could have been opening his veins like a Roman's yeoman, brought down from Gaul, and I would have never have known, or cared, or stopped him.

Or was he too. . . listening.

I wanted to tear his horrible mask away and look at his terrible face. Instead, I sat there and I said:

"Dawes, I have always seen you more as Tom Sawyer. You know, running nowhere, having all of those overly planned and squared, verbal and only theatrical adventures. Forcing everything. Letting nothing happen naturally. Huck had a kind of natural, innocent completeness of spirit and action you have never even dreamed of."

"IT'S ALL A DAMN LIE!" Dawes Williams said suddenly, rousing himself from his thick tub of soap. "I AM HUCK FINN! I'M A DOER! GODDAMN YOU, I AM HUCK FINN! I AM CAPABLE OF RAFTING THE PENTAGON, OF TRAMPING THROUGH THE PRESIDENT'S HEAD; AND I AM EVEN CAPABLE OF BLOWING UP BOULDER DAM!"

Then he sat back down in his tub, took out his long-necked scrub brush and closed his eyes. He rowed, paddled and poled in his sleep.

"Dawes," I said calmly, "you will never do any of these things. You'll never leave this room."

"I thought you'd never catch up," he said quietly. "I've known that all afternoon."

Then he began laughing. It was a horrible sound. His laugh had no bottom, no exit, and it rose without end in the slow afternoon. Utterly without point, it bloomed and rotted over in red shadowy air behind me. It was like the small, self-complete sound a burrowing animal leaves, piling the deeply sick roots, the yellow shells of air in behind itself for the winter. Then it stopped.

I continue to pace the stage over. In the fish-blooming shadows of the vacant theatre, I am deifically schizophrenic, three into one and out again, like telephone numbers. I say:

Because, still lying in his tub of soap, not rafting anything, Dawes was now laughing the way only a forty-year-old man laughs—cynically, past even the humor of belief, and now only genuinely moved by the condescending farce in it all. My God, I thought suddenly, Dawes Williams is finally only looking at farce.

"Stop it!" I found myself screaming. "You stop that this minute! Damn you! Damn you!" I said. "You stop laughing this minute!"

But Dawes continued—laughing now like that forty-year-old man who has, to his own surprise, finally stumbled upon, articulated that forty-year-old premonition of farce.

"God damn it, Dawes," I said. "You stop it! God damn you, Dawes . . . you don't believe it is that. I am the one . . . you are not the one who thinks it is that. God damn you, Dawes. I am the one. . . God damn you to hell."

But Dawes just sat in his tub of soap, not rafting anything any more, laughing. He was not even watching any more.

"I'm tired, Willy," he said. "I'm just so tired. I can't do it for both of us any more. You go do your own believing now for awhile, Willy," Dawes Williams said.

And that was all he would say. The red shadowy sounds of the feeding chickens rowed out in the yard. And so, sitting there, in only the sleeve of my own silent design now, I was finally dismissed, nonverbally and without even a flick of his hand, like in a stupid, imperial court of sun worshipers, in an age of absolutism, of divine right which nobody voted on, and kicking my way through the ruck of his five or six hundred paperback books, the quixotic droppings of his wild dogs and his even wilder domestic mice, his drums, the spare parts and wrenches for his motorcycles, I left, left that afternoon cursing his hide.

Finally satisfied, I believe I can sleep again now.

CURTAIN

(applause from the night-blooming fish)

It was nearly morning in Mexico. A thin eye of light came in through the door. Bored, Urzika put the notebooks down on the floor. Dawes Williams, pretending to wake, stirred himself over to watch the line of green and yellow light move slowly, like yesterday and last week, across the flooring. He thought that eventually the light would succeed in eating the wood, the cracks of dark space in the corner, the secret hearts of tiny animal life buried in the walls; that perhaps this was the day he and Urzika would leave for South America, perhaps even home. It didn't matter. Pretending to wake even further, he tried to look at her; but she was already part way up the sleeve of her dress and out of the door.

"I'm going out for another walk," she said. "I'll know if I'm coming back when I get here. And incidentally, Hy-oot John," she said, behind her, going downstairs, "I was farther into your head in the first five minutes than those fucking notebooks of yours will ever be."

Smiling, Dawes Williams rolled over in the Mexican light and went to sleep.

2

It was a bright morning. Dr. John Wexler's feet were propped upon his desk; his hands were webbed behind his head. Dawes sat, very quiet, trying to ignore the fact that he couldn't breathe.

"You seem better, Dawes," Wexler was saying.

Dawes said nothing. He watched the dead March light hanging in the office curtains. Poor, limited Wexler. He watched as Wexler began to stare at the wall.

"I think you will be able to leave here now, Dawes," Dr. Wexler said, refolding his handkerchief for the seventh time.

Passing up any number of brilliantly irrelevant, deflating things he might have said, Dawes Williams sat quietly, scratching his head.

"That's great, doctor," he finally said.

"What will you do, Dawes?" Wexler said.

"Oh, don'know," Dawes Williams said finally. "Guess me and Handsaw will just sally forth, wandering about at will, slaying the voracious philistine."

"Oh?" Wexler said quietly, taking the handkerchief back out of his pocket.

"Yes," Dawes Williams said quietly, smiling, "I guess we'll just wait for them to open extermination camps so we'll have someplace to finally hang our hat."

Wexler laughed.

"Dawes," he said, "you have quite an unusual sense of humor. I'll never get quite used to it."

There was an embarrassed silence. Dawes looked at Wexler queerly. Wexler fumbled with himself for a moment; his eyes drifted off and came back.

"Well," he said with authority, "we'll have to stop here. But we'll just keep our eye on this thing from a deliberate distance. You seem better."

Dawes got up to go.

"And, Dawes . . ." Wexler said, "just remember there is no prolonged sense of dying. You have nothing to fear."

"Oh ya," Dawes said. "But fear itself? Is that it? Is that what you wanted to tell me? That you have just ruled out the possibility of suffering with physiology and exorcism? Really, Wexler," Dawes said, walking out, "you tend mostly to inspire only the nation of myself."

"Well, Dawes," Wexler called after, "even if your distaste for my mental tenor, my 'rhetoric,' is justified, take my advice. Learn to relax."

"Ja-esus Key-rist," Dawes Williams said, walking out, passing a nurse, "if Wexler ever develops an opinion on anything at all, ship it out COD to me at once."

Once outside, he remembered the calendar: the fourth of March, a new life. The birds of late winter were singing in the high trees. He stood, pacing in his mind, watching the slush of the corner for a sign, as if sanity were a pair of idle hands with nothing to fidget with. Immediately he decided to go out and get drunk.

He walked down the street, stopping off only at The Paperstore for a copy of Caesar's *Gallic Wars,* and then he came in from the cold for a drink, for some spirited conversation with Mabel Campbell, and for breakfast: a hand-boiled egg, three pieces of dried-out jerky and a basket of popcorn. Folding the napkin under his chin for effect, Dawes Williams began feeding: he peeled his egg.

"Hey, Dawes," Mrs. Campbell said, "where the hell have you been?"

"I been in the madhouse, Mabel. No sweat," Dawes said, pouring ketchup on his beef jerky. But in the corners of his eyes, without ever moving, he noticed people were moving quietly away.

"Good for you, Dawes," Mrs. Campbell said, coming over with a suspicious rag to wipe his corner of the bar. "Say," she said finally, "where's Braun Daniel, Dawes Williams?"

"Joined the Horse Marines," Dawes said. "Took his bulldogs with him and went off to lay waste the outlander."

"Damn," Mabel Campbell said. "Who would have thought it?"

"I would," Dawes said. "I would have thought it for a long time now."

"And what have you been up to, Dawes Williams?"

"Sleeping, I've been sleeping."

"Sleeping?"

"Oh ya. I never get laid. I've been sleeping for three months now. I been having a breakdown and serious denouement of the sensibility."

"Posh!" Mabel Campbell said. "Anything serious?"

"Well, no, actually nothing at all to be worried about. Just another run-of-the-mill panpsychosis with everything coming off at once without sequence."

"Damn, damn," Mabel Campbell said.

The day drifted off. Dawes Williams sat in Mabel's Tavern watching the outside world come past for hours. He watched the clock over the bar rotate, completing itself every 11.3 seconds, and he began thinking of sleeping. People came and went, apparently at will. He sat fighting only sleep, consciously, as if somehow it were a terrible awakening. He felt he needed a change. Night began falling.

He ordered an egg.

Then Louis Kawkins, the old man, came in. He coughed romantic phlegm through whiskers hanging like rust. His two eyes were the color of water, and he said:

"Ho there, Dawes Williams, buy me a beer."

"Who do you think I am," Dawes said, "Peter Fonda?"

"Ho there, Dawes Williams, buy me a beer."

"For Christsake," Dawes said, "is this the night for the Emmetsburg Spring Corn Festival again already?"

"No, Dawes," Louis Kawkins says, "but I thought I'd come into town anyway."

"Well, I'll be damned," Dawes Williams said, "this must be legacy."

"Well, Dawes Williams, it's like I always say—I can just set here and die a little for ya if you buy me a Grain Belt."

"Thanks, Mabel," Dawes said, buying Louis a Grain Belt, "and we'll have a couple more."

"You are one fine damn sport you are, I always say, Dawes Williams," Louis Kawkins says.

There was a solemn moment. Dawes sat back and began watching the spinning black, playing itself out, reducing the reduction of an endless cycle of nights and days, trying, once and for all, to separate the dancer from the dance.

"A hole is a hole is a hole," Dawes Williams said finally, testing him.

There was a silence.

"Isn't that a pastiche of old Gertrude Stein, Dawes Williams?" Louis Kawkins said.

"You have an amazing mind, Louis," Dawes Williams said.

"I thought so. That's what I thought it was, Dawes Williams," Louis Kawkins said.

"Set'em up again Sam, Mabel," Dawes Williams said. "Aren't even the old alkies unlettered around here?"

"I wouldn't want you to think I was puttin' on any airs with my learnin', Dawes," Louis Kawkins said. "Not that. It's just that I got a fierce memory of all these informative seminars we been puttin' on here, Dawes Williams."

There was a silence.

"I never get laid," Dawes said.

"Ho there, Dawes Williams," Louis Kawkins starts over again, "where the hell have you been hidin' yourself?"

There was another silence.

"Sleeping," Dawes said. "I been sleeping a long time, Louis."

"Ya know, Dawes," Louis said, "I been worried about you. You sleep too much. I can see it in your eyes; they look tired. When you going to get your sand up again and head down for Mexico, like you're always talking?"

"Soon, Louis," Dawes said, "just as soon as I can learn to be interested enough to stay awake for awhile."

"Don't confess at me, Dawes. But that's the stuff. You're a doer at heart, you are. Don't worry about staying awake, now; that Mexico will kill you dead. Why, once, down in Saltillo, I remember a woman who had three eagles and a donkey in her living room who . . ."

"Well, listen, Louis," Dawes Williams said quietly, "I appreciate your telling me about that, but I think I've had about enough for one evening, and I think I'm going over there and shoot me some quiet pool."

"Ho there, Dawes Williams," Louis Kawkins said, "run off them balls like ya used ta."

Dawes Williams crossed the room and began nickeling into the game.

After a while he was slumped low, easily within the narrow light, running the balls from the table. At the end of a smooth distance they quivered slightly and fell over with a small sound. And the room was hot.

Dawes Williams stood in the withdrawn circle of table light, losing five dollars over a slip scratch and complaining about it.

"Pay up," the bastard said.

"Listen," Dawes Williams said, "if I were being asshole technical about it, you'd owe *me* five on that shot. But I'm not. You stroked the cue ball twice, and sank the eight. You lost. And I'm not paying *you* five on it."

"Pay up," the bastard said.

"Fuck off," Dawes Williams said, stupidly turning, reaching for his beer, paying no attention, stretching to his fullest baroque extension.

Then he went down. He began falling through the bottom and vague center of his dream. The thick end of the pool cue, hand as a bone, came across his temple, knocking him down, cold as a fish.

His forehead lay open, surprised, and down and lying there he began quietly to notice that his shirt was running all over his hands, as if the dye weren't any good; his left hand refused to move, and he wondered why, because somehow he thought it should, was supposed to, and because someone was calling his name, somewhere behind him, somewhere beyond, the other side, and because he couldn't answer the bottom of his falling dream; and then he was only kicking out at a darkness, and finally his right hand went out, reaching, he began to watch it, for something he thought was before him, he didn't know it, and suddenly he was only wrapped in a small fascination, an open dream of yellow light, four metal posts and shadows, thin ones, going out the door.

Waking, then rising finally to his fullest baroque extension, Dawes Williams said:

"I'll kill that bastard. Where is he?"

"Hell, Dawes," Louis Kawkins said, "he grew tiresome of stomping on your head, and he went out the door. I think you better use your wits on this one, Dawes Williams."

Walking out into the dark, Dawes Williams found that particular bastard in question singing loudly, beginning to piss quietly in the alley. Dawes rounded the corner. The bastard looked surprised to see him, eyed him, put his cock

back in his pants, and doubled his fist. Approaching cheerfully, Dawes smiled
a wide grin and said:

"Mind if I wizz on your wall?"

"You want some more?" the bastard said, eyeing him back.

"Nope. Not me," Dawes Williams said. "I had enough."

"Just so you know it," the bastard said.

"Oh ya," Dawes said. "You wouldn't hit a man with his cock out, would
you?"

"You fruity or somethin'?" the bastard said.

"Nope," Dawes said. "I just happen to have a sense of humor about things
like this."

"Ya?" the bastard said.

"Oh ya," Dawes Williams said.

There was a silence in the alley. Only Louis Kawkins had followed Dawes
outside, because only Louis Kawkins had known anything else would happen.
Then, quietly taking out his cock, peeing as high as he could on the wall, like
painting a fence, Dawes said:

"I sure can pee a high stream when I'm drinkin'."

"What the hell are you talking about?" the bastard said, still eyeing him.

"Oh ya," Dawes said. "Had a buddy name of Dunker once. Used to pee
the highest stream in eastern Iowa. Got to be damn proud of it."

"Ya?"

"Oh ya. Used to get soused alot and practice it by the hour. Like a piano
player. Got so, with a hind wind, he could write his name fifteen yards away in
the snow."

"Bullshit."

"Oh ya. Used it for a calling card when he was courting the girls. Used to
win money betting on it when things were slow."

"No bullshit?"

"Oh ya. Saw him win thirty-five bucks and a gallon of wine off a guy once
with my own eyes. But it was only a trick bladder shot, of course. Showed it to
me once. Anyone could learn to do it if they had the talent for it."

"That so?"

"Oh ya."

There was a silence. Dawes Williams began closing in on his own knife-
fighting, ear-biting blood by waiting.

"Hey, you not such a bad guy for a asshole," the bastard finally said. "How
about showing me how he did it?"

There was more silence. Dawes Williams was thinking it all over. Timing
his timing.

"Oh, do'no," Dawes said quietly.

"Hell. What the hell," the bastard said.

"All right. Why not? I can't see any harm in it since you're so interested."

"Yes. Hell, yes," the bastard said.

Dawes went over to get the poleaxe of an old two-by-two he had spied leaning in the dark alleyway.

"Well," he said coming back, smiling, "let me get this board over here for making a scratch mark, and I'll show you how it goes. There. Now, do you think you can piss into that barrel over there?"

"Hell no," the bastard said, "you must be crazy! That barrel must be fifty feet."

"Oh ya. Well, when I get done showin' you how it's done, you'll be able to put it right in the center. Every time. Wind or no wind. Competition or no competition."

"The hell," the bastard said, genuinely interested.

"Listen," Dawes said, leaning casually around his two-by-two, "once I show you how this trick bladder shot works, you'll think you've been an idiot all this time for never figuring it out for yourself."

"You calling me an idiot?" the bastard said.

"No. Hell, no," Dawes said, "don't get antsy on me now, man."

"Well, how then? I think you probably nuts, but I got a bladder on me like a bull mule in the spring at nuttin' time."

"Fantastic," Dawes said, "but I'm all out, so I'll just move through a dry run for ya. Now watch this carefully."

Setting the board aside quietly, Dawes Williams got down on all fours. Digging his feet into the cold cinders for balance, he began hyperventilating madly.

"What the hell is that?" the bastard said, pulling on his beer.

"Oh ya," Dawes said panting. "Well, this happens to be the biggest part of it all. This is the trick. You've got to do this until you can't even see any more."

Then, just as suddenly, Dawes Williams was up like a catcher, eyeing fiercely the barrel, bouncing wildly on his haunches.

"What the hell is *that?*" the bastard said.

"Oh ya," Dawes said quietly, "this really builds up the rhythms in the bladder muscle. I feel almost set."

"This is crazy," the bastard said.

"Trust me," Dawes said. "Once you master this, your friends won't believe it."

The bastard stood, cast darkly in the yellow alley light, scratching his head. Finally, Dawes stood too. He was full in the moon. Then, delicately arching his balance backwards on the very heels of his feet, he quietly exploded, doing an awkward, grotesque broad jump and landing with a small thud six feet away.

"Well, hell," the bastard said, "anybody could do that. You jumped halfway there!"

"Nope," Dawes said, "I didn't cross the scratch marks. So that was a clean dry run. A legal take. I would have been all right on that one. But," he said, intently measuring the distances around the scratch mark, "in competition with the money up, usually it's the custom that two scratches is a forfeit."

"Ya?" the bastard said.

"Oh ya," Dawes said. "You've got to be careful. There. Now you give her a try. Fire one right in there."

"Do'no," the bastard said, "somehow it seems silly. I'll try it some other time maybe."

"Hell, no," Dawes Williams said, flashing his hey-you're-the-finest-sonofabitch-who-ever-lived smile, "take your best shot."

"All right. I'll give her a try for the hell of it and to just show you there's no hard feelings."

"Why else?" Dawes said. "That's the stuff. Make the shot and I'll buy you a beer. We'll tell Louis Kawkins and some of the others what a genius you are at it, pardner," Dawes Williams said, smiling with a broad humanity, clutching his poleaxe.

Slowly the bastard got down on his knees. On all fours he began hyperventilating wildly.

"Do you feel it? Do you feel it?" Dawes Williams said. "Do you feel like you can wizz a mile yet?"

"Hell, no. I just feel dizzy."

"More, man," Dawes said. "The oxygen ratio is the key to the whole thing."

"I think I got it," he said.

"You betcha," Dawes said. "You can't miss."

Then, slowly, the bastard got up on his haunches. He took out his cock and began bouncing madly on the balls of his feet.

"How'm I doin'?" he said.

"Fine," Dawes said. "I'll just stand up here in front of you, marking off the approximate scratch line. You just wind yourself up and get a good jump."

"High?"

"Oh ya," Dawes said, "the higher the better. It's all in the parabola vector finally, man. Oh ya. But you can handle'er. I know you can. Just bounce yourself up real tight and take your best shot. Right down the tubes here," Dawes Williams said.

Slowly the bastard wound up. Dawes thought the determination and belief in his face were slightly pathetic. He looked as if, if he didn't succeed in peeing in the exact middle of that barrel at fifty feet, he would be as hurt as a child. Dawes watched him spring. He watched him fly in the air for a moment, bent inward, ready to explode outward in a massive vertical genuflection from the hips upward . . . and, as that happened, Dawes Williams dug in on his hind foot, peeked around the corner of his batting stance like Stan Musial with two out in the ninth, and he just cut that bastard in half.

And then it all came out. Twenty-five years. The bastard went down on the pavement, limp as a bag, writhing, rising for air, holding his guts; an almost exploding and naked terror full of disbelief came suddenly onto the surfaces of his amazed eyes. He looked back and Dawes Williams hit him again and again. Coldly beside himself, like a furious child, Dawes knew he could quit, but wouldn't. That was all that surprised him. Nothing else. Not the thin thudding sounds moving off the sides of the walls. Not the silence. The hooded tactile of the yellow light. Nothing. And he continued to beat it until it went nearly soft. Relaxed. Became nearly busted and disused, a cast-off thing, limp and nearly lifeless. He seemed to watch a face break up, horribly, and drift off before him. He seemed to feel some nameless thing quietly disintegrate within. Then he stopped himself. The bastard was still breathing, lying in a disfigured pile of broken and bloody cloth beneath him. Dawes kicked him once more. He stood alone finally in the alley for awhile, crying. He saw Louis Kawkins was standing down near the edge of the building, watching him. No one else. Dawes thought he was smiling. Then, in a far ear, Dawes heard sirens, real or not, and he beat it down the back of the alley thinking only: *Oh ya. That is all I need right now. A quiet room. A cell of cold monk wood. More time to think it all over. Oh ya. They aren't ever taking me alive again, anywhere.*

It was past ten when he reached Rapid Cedar heading south by southeast for Mexico. He parked his old car in the gravel drive behind Simpson's house. The Catholics were holding another moonlight wake, behind him, across a yard of black and blowing trees. The air was dense, dreaming, heavy like ancestors. For a moment he thought Ronnie Crown, calling behind him, was sitting in the flat air of Dunchee's wall. Crown was mocking, laughing, throwing the trails of smoking stick matches down in thin tails of German fighters that would never burn. Dawes remembered hearing, two years before on the news, someone named Ronald James Crown had been stabbed to death in a river town in Illinois in an argument over some money and a girl.

Dawes sat for awhile, uncertain, as he hadn't been there for over a year, uncertain because he didn't know why he had come now, uncertain because he knew suddenly he couldn't ever manage to forget any of it. Finally, getting down from his hood, he went past the rusted swing which had never been disassembled; the cutaway elm, diseased and rotten and full of a terrible open sky, which had always been there; the old clubhouse he and Simpson and Johnny B. Harper had made on a Sunday afternoon. The yellow sign, burned wood and infantile etching, Saying, BARRACUDAS ONLY NO B AVENUE GUYS ALLOWED, was still swinging in the creaking wind. He went across the interior yard to the back door. Locked, he kicked at it. He waited for it to open, entering finally the dim hallway. In the old light he saw the faint face of his mother. She was standing by the refrigerator, only staring back.

"Leone! You old Republican's ass. How the hell are you?" Dawes Williams said.

"Relax, Dawes," Leone said, staring back, "I promise to vote for Robert Kennedy if he runs."

"Damn me. Well, it's not much, but it's a beginning, I suppose," Dawes said.

"Dawes!" Leone said seeing, as he moved into the light for the first time, his face and the dark, dried blood frozen in strange patterns on his shirt.

"Oh ya," Dawes said. "I went three rounds with Killer Dick and quit."

"Is that why you're home? So early? In the spring? Aren't you going back to the hospital nights? Don't you have some comprehensive examinations coming up? What's happening here?"

"Quit sniffing me out before I even get through the doorway. What are you? A Methodist minister's bloodhound?"

There was a silence. Leone, who had been reading three biographies a week since the age of sixteen, picked up her copy of Strachey's *Eminent Victorians* and began heading through the kitchen. Then, pausing, turning back, she said:

"Dawes. What *is* happening here?"

"Jesus Christ," Dawes Williams said. "I was just sitting, I don't know, talking with Handsaw, reading Kant's *Critique of Pure Reason,* when it suddenly dawned on me it was time to be quitting. Shucks, I was almost to the end, too."

"Who is this Handsaw boy, Dawes?" his mother said.

"He's just my new roommate and doppelgänger, apple-pie Mom," Dawes Williams said, not batting an eye. "I think even you might even be said to already have a strange affinity for him."

"Dawes," Leone said, "you're not becoming a homosexual, are you? What does Doctor Wexler say?"

"No, Mom," Dawes said, "we're all right on that one. As much as anyone can be, I reckon. I've just been reading too much *Sturm und Drang* lately."

"I see," she said.

"I doubt it," Dawes said.

"I don't see any need for this smugness," Leone said. "Why aren't you in Iowa City?"

"Well," Dawes said, "I tell ya. There I was: down in the territory of the aristocratic Comanche, trapped within that skinny buffalo winter, arrows on the left, six-guns on the right, plastic machines all around, and me just figuring finally that trying to sleep with the chief's squaw and planting my beaver traps in the river was absolutely at cross purposes . . . so I up and split."

"Take those shoes off before you walk on the rug," Leone said. "You couldn't possibly give it all up now."

"Well," Dawes said, "you know how it is with us scholars. On again, off again. Our interest wanes mysteriously at the end."

Leone said nothing. She went over to the faucet to pour herself a glass of water. Sensing disinterest, Dawes wandered into the sunroom. The cat purred around him. The dog mounted his leg, delirious. Simpson sat, half-sleeping, with a bowl of popcorn nestled on his stomach, in front of the tube. He was watching either reruns of *The Dating Game* or the local news. Dawes couldn't tell which. The old air of the room smelled of sleep and dead, fried butter.

"Well, old boy," Simpson said, drowsing, "where have you been keeping yourself?"

"Listen, Simpson," Dawes said, leaning over against him, whispering, checking the wall's corners for spies, "get this. *The Celts have finally risen.* The Hair and Tartars are out and flying. We're pushing those motherfuck Anglo-Saxons clean over the borders and into the sea forever this time. I know we are. I can feel it. Aren't you excited?"

Simpson laughed sheepishly and unwrapped another caramel. Dawes watched the weatherman give the scores for awhile. Finally he said:

"Hey, Simpson, what the fuck are you watching here, man?"

"Oh, nothing much, I guess," Simpson said.

"I guess," Dawes Williams said. "Has Monty Hall given away America, the whole goddamn country, to a woman named Mrs. Ugly Jones from Santa Barbara yet?"

"Don't believe so, old boy," Simpson said absently, "but you need a haircut badly."

"He will," Dawes said. "You keep watching for it."

"How's that, old boy?" Simpson said, adjusting himself in his chair without moving.

Checking under the couch for ghosts of the king's men, Dawes Williams lowered his voice again and leaned closer to Simpson.

"I can scarcely believe it myself," he said finally, "but the revolution is *really* going to come off after all. However: at the last possible moment the entire Republican gang is going to hand off the hot football potato of America, the entire materialistic bobble, to Mrs. Ugly Jones. It's an end around, a Statue of Liberty, see. It's a Stepin Fetchit routine, see? Then the mob's going to take Mrs. Ugly Jones out into the streets, try her, lop off her head, see, and the Republican gang's going to step from her ashes like the great and risen and untouched phoenix-Arizona bird, see? It's a soft-shoe routine, see, for song-and-dance men . . . only another bummer, see, like the new phoenix birds blooming from the feudal system and calling the fief the corporation. It's all just like achetypal technology, see . . . just more repetitive calisthenics and wind."

"So?" Simpson said.

"So," Dawes Williams said, "if you'll just loan me a hundred bucks I'm going to get out of the Prussians' way as they are about ready to get pissed off. I'm leaving for El Dorado tonight."

"Oh, how you talk," Simpson said. "What you need is a depression and a war to straighten you out."

"I'm just a yeoman in search of the New World still," Dawes Williams said, lapsing into silence.

"Well, sir, old boy, a man's still got to stick to it and fight for what he believes in in this world."

"I think I still believe that," Dawes said, "and I may have some startling plans along those lines yet."

Within the drifting-off silence of Simpson's smile Dawes began watching him. He was an old man now, strangely thicker around the edges, defeated without ever having lost. Having quit smoking, he ate small tinfoil candies and crackers as he watched the tube. He breathed easily, up and down, rhythmic as the flow of his soft felt sugar candies, his muscular paunch nearly fading and blooming back in the light. Disinterested, Dawes got up finally and wandered back into the kitchen. There Leone was nervously standing over the sink, pretending to wash already clean dishes.

"Leave me alone," she said. "Don't start in on me tonight. I'm not up to it. I've had a hectic day."

Dawes sat down on the kitchen chair, forgetting to remove the cat, which ran screaming into the basement.

"You've been having those now for over twenty years," Dawes said quietly. "I don't think you were ever really up to living."

Leone turned on him. There was hate in her eyes. She said nothing, but opened a window. The nearly cold wind blew the curtains into the kitchen. The old grandfather clock struck ten-thirty in another room.

"The-King-of-the-Earth's henchman is dozing off another bonbon festival in the sunroom," Dawes finally said, "dreaming, I suppose, of his Republican gang. I thought I'd come in here and rap ya for awhile, *Mom*."

"Really," Leone said, "this is just disgraceful. I don't see how you have the nerve to talk to your own mother this way. After all we've done."

"The air's still free in a two-party conversation," Dawes said. "You can respond and defend yourself if you can figure out anything to say."

"I don't feel any need to defend myself to *you*," Leone said.

"Right," Dawes Williams said. "That's got it."

"If you're not fit for human society, you can just go off and be by yourself," Leone said.

"Right," Dawes Williams said, "I'm going to. I just dropped in to say goodbye. How's yer ole idea, Mom?"

"You hate yourself. Don't think you can take it out on us," Leone said.

"Right," Dawes said, "that's three of'em. I bet you got a million of'em. I got all night. Let's hear'em all."

"Aren't you clever?" Leone said.

"Uaa UaaUaa Uaa UaaUaa Uaa Uaa," Dawes Williams said, rising, doing a small monkey dance around her in the kitchen.

"Are you *drunk?*" Leone said.

"Oh, wow," Dawes Williams said.

Then he took a pot down off the wall and put it on his head like Johnny Appleseed, touring America, sowing it under with fruit-bearing trees. He beat two skillets together, hopping and whooping like an Indian. Leone retreated, a small, terrified fascination still caught in her eye. She stood in the new sliding doorway, looking back.

"Simpson!" she said.

"What is it, Mother?" he said.

"Will you quit looking at that *television* AND COME IN HERE PLEASE!"

"Now, Mother."

Suddenly disinterested, Dawes quit making modulated whooping sounds with his hand and his mouth. He began looking around the kitchen, pacing, spying out an issue. Finally he settled on a huge vanilla cake sitting on the naked, stainless cupboard.

"What's that?" Dawes Williams said, smiling.

"Well," Leone said, "I baked it for your birthday."

"That's absurd," Dawes Williams said.

"Well," she said, "I thought maybe you could come up for a day."

"That's crazy," Dawes Williams said.

After circling the table for awhile, lying back, he walked over to the cupboard. He picked up the vanilla cake, turned it neatly over, and dropped it on the floor. Leone gasped.

"You. You. You . . . *sonofabitch!*" she screamed finally, swearing for the first time in her life, relieved, throwing a Kleenex box at him, the dense breath stopped in her throat.

"No Andy Hardy, he," Dawes Williams said.

Then he sat down on the stove, laughing.

"How's yer ole dollhouse?" he said finally. "Keeping the dust off it? Why don't you sell it and buy a tent? It'll build up your loins."

Leone was still trying to talk. She was dark, still slender, but worn. She stood watching him sit on her stove.

"Giddy up," Dawes Williams finally said, whipping the burners with his red bandanna.

"Dawes," Leone said.

"They're less care, tents are. More time for conversation and books. *Look-Look* magazine even," Dawes offered.

Then he reached into his hip pocket and put on his blue stocking cap:

"*Roundtable?*" he said into the black mirror of a wrought-iron skillet. "*This is Jehovah. Over and out.*—That's Fredric March, the admiral turning the flagship about, in *The Bridges of Toko-Ri*. Quite a man, the admiral."

Simpson came in to stand by the doorway. He cast about with his eyes, quietly interested by the noise. He stood invisibly holding up the house with his fat pajama strings, watching.

"You're acting badly, old boy," he said, "just badly."

"Choo-choo! Choo-choo!" Dawes Williams said. "*But then I don't mind rough duty, Lieutenant Brubaker, sir. I hate them Commies.* That's Mickey Rooney, the wonderfully goony and gutsy helicopter ace in the W. C. Fields porkpie hat, who has just lost his Japanese barfly girl to a sailor on the *Essex,* who has just destroyed Tokyo and been jailed, who has just been bailed out by Brubaker (who is married to Grace Kelly), who has just torn the dress off her back, and who has just been transferred in wonderfully friendly terms by the admiral, in *The Bridges of Toko-Ri.*"

"What is he talking about, Simpson?" Leone said.

"Now, Mother."

"It's all right, Mom," Dawes Williams said. "We knocked out *The Bridges of Toko-Ri* in the end. And Brubaker took approximately three or four hundred Commie Asiatics with him before he expired dramatically in a drainage ditch, behind the lines. . . . Besides, the admiral was very sad, calling in fighter cover until the very last, sitting on his bridge, talking wonderfully into his Jehovah phone."

There was a silence. Simpson eyed him suspiciously. Leone sat down.

"It's so pathetic," Dawes Williams said, rising to his fullest baroque extension for the first time in months, "so goddamn pathetic what you have here. A tinfoil aluminum plastic clearing on all time."

"If you feel so strongly about it, you could have joined the Marines with Braun Daniel, old boy," Simpson said.

"I don't think you have this quite down yet, Simpson," Dawes said.

"If you don't like it," Leone said, "it's just high time you started making your own life somewhere where you can feel no one's bothering you."

"Where's that?" Dawes Williams said. "Have they passed a new Homestead Act yet?"

"That's right, old boy," Simpson offered.

"How's that?" Dawes Williams said. "All the good people to make it with have been drafted or split, with the lone exception of Braun Daniel, who has simply joined. You holding out on me, Dad? You know a place you're not talking about? You know a place you and your kind ain't fucked over good yet, Dad?"

The kitchen was very silent. Simpson was red in the face but helpless. He went to the cupboard and got a handful of Fritos. Leone shut the window. She opened a green bottle of Airwick. Dawes sat listening to the old grandfather clock strike eleven.

"That clock's never run right," he said.

"You're such a damn genius, you are. Listen here," Simpson said, then he fell silent again.

"This is such a really *dull* place," Dawes Williams said. "Why doesn't someone say something?"

"What does he mean, Simpson?" Leone offered.

"Now, Mother."

In the other room, Bruno Bettelheim was speaking. He was talking about people who couldn't cut it, who had only marked themselves for death in other people's extermination camps. He bloomed and faded back into the loud tube. His face, Dawes knew without looking, was full of assimilated wisdom and simple electricity.

"No. No! America is anything but a fascist nation. The people who say that just make me a little bit sick," he said. "You people just don't know how well you've got it over here, and that is your only problem."

"What a heavy juxtaposition," Dawes Williams said. "I think I resent this intrusion."

"What *is* he talking about, Simpson?" Leone said.

"Now now, Mother."

"Why doesn't someone ask him if he thinks Germany was a fascist nation in 1927?" Dawes said. "For a nation of mostly lawyers, I don't think anyone is capable of thinking on his feet or asking the obvious any more."

No one bothered to ask Bettelheim anything, however, and soon Tiny Tim came on. Disinterested, Dawes Williams turned back into the faint yellow light of the kitchen. People in New York began suddenly to applaud deliriously. But the slow air of the kitchen, connected to nothing at all externally, began to wind down even further. It bloomed and died back like a soft match in the wind.

"Well," Dawes said, "I just thought I'd drop by and say so long. I'm heading out again. I'm saddling up ole Paint, the only plowhorse left on the place, and heading out for the plastic gold rush in California."

"I just don't understand why any of this has to be this way," Leone said, crying.

"Now look what you've done, old boy," Simpson said. "You've got your mother crying."

"It's a sad thing all right," Dawes Williams said. "I think she thought this soft suburban dream of hers would go on forever."

"Shut up!" Leone screamed. "Sometimes you're just horrible!"

"I believe this martyr has sprouted teeth," Dawes said.

"Now, Mother."

"This is crazy," Dawes Williams said. "Can you loan me a hundred, Simpson? I'm short."

"You need some hard times to straighten you out, old boy. Hell, no, I won't loan you another cent."

"ANOTHER CENT!" Dawes Williams screamed. "AS IF I'D BEEN PICKING YOUR POCKETS ALL THESE YEARS! YOU OLD FAKE! THIS IS WHERE YOU GET OFF THE A-TRAIN CLICHÉ, MAN. YOU PAID FOR PRACTICALLY NOTHING! AND SOMETIMES, DEEP DOWN IN THE THIN MISER OF YOUR SOUL, I EVEN THINK YOU KNOW YOU ARE JUST NUTS!"

There was a long silence in the kitchen.

"What about all those cars and motorcycles, old boy?" Simpson said.

"We can't get started on all of that now," Dawes said. "I paid you every cent you ever loaned me. There I was, coming over with week after week of weld smoke and grain dust on me, signing over a hundred a week for forever, and there you were: bent over your ledgers, thinking what a fine bastard you were to loan me the money, with not a cent of interest, and with only the title for security. All those years. And the heaviest work you ever dreamed of was fitting a shoe. Don't give me that she-it, man," Dawes Williams said.

"Well, I've supported you plenty," Simpson said.

"Talking money with you is real exciting, Dad. It's just like reading Victorian prose selections. You'd really make someone ahelluva fine accountant."

"Well, that's what I do," Simpson said.

"Don't I know it," Dawes Williams said.

"Simpson, what is he talking about?" Leone said.

"Shut up, Mother," Simpson said quietly. "We're having this out once and for all. What about all of that insurance, that gas money?"

"Commuting is cheaper than renting. Who else do you know who got six years of college for the price of two? And if you want to pay your old friend, Ab Snopes, twice what car insurance is worth, that's your tough shit."

"What about all that tuition?"

"And as for that health insurance, you handled that so fine I couldn't even go to the hospital twice when I needed. You're just piss-poor with money, you know that, Babbitt?"

"You've got money," Simpson said. "What happened to your fellowship?"

"I stretched three thousand for over three and a half years. You've got to be both a genius *and* a Scotsman to do that, by God."

"Ya," Simpson said. "And I saved you from investing it in mutual funds, or you wouldn't even have had it that long."

Simpson sat back, smoking an invisible cigar, self-satisfied and smiling at last. Dawes hunched himself up on the stove like an excited catcher and prepared to cut Simpson off at the knees:

"Oh, yes, Texas Dick," he said, "for a guy who spent his life around money, you couldn't even handle a child's licorice allowance. DON'T YOU EVEN KNOW WE'VE BEEN IN AN INFLATIONARY PERIOD FOR OVER TWENTY YEARS NOW!?!?!!??!!???!!?!?"

"Investing in the stock market is always a risky venture, old boy," Simpson said calmly.

"Don't invest, don't invest, you said. Well," Dawes Williams said, "if I'd have invested that money three years ago, I would have had eight grand now, not nothing."

"You're at cross purposes with yourself, it seems to me," Simpson said. "For a guy who professes to hate money so badly, you seem also to love it upon occasion."

"I know what you mean," Leone said, laughing. "For a nonmaterialist, he seems to like material things, just like we do, when the occasion arises."

There was a long silence in the kitchen. Leone and Simpson leaned back, smiling, contented in the knowledge that they had just destroyed Dawes' idealism with reality.

"You are a couple of real fourth-rate wits, you know that?" Dawes Williams said. "I never said I was Christ. I only said I was a Communist, and we're just real worried about material and who owns it at the source. Can you grasp that?"

"No," Leone said.

"Well," Dawes said, "we're just real worried and concerned when incompetent motherfuckers, like Simpson here, own the means of production."

"You can't talk to me this way!" Simpson said.

"You're terrible!" Leone said. "Do you want to give your father a heart attack!?! That's just fine. Then we'd all have no income!"

"Now, Mother."

"Fuck off," Dawes said. "If this big-time banking dude would just loan me a hundred, I'd make us all well. I'd buy the dynamite to blow up this filthy house!"

Leone nearly fainted with what she took to be Dawes' fantastic contradiction, a thing that she didn't have the words to define. Simpson was up on his feet, red in the face, puffing, thinking even of swinging on Dawes. Dawes looked back and laughed in their faces.

"Propaganda!" Leone finally screamed. "You don't even know what you are saying."

"You know," Dawes said, "if this baron of the earth, this cog that is six percent by population and thirty-five percent by consumption of the world, doesn't get his muddy foot off the population of the world, if he thinks he can just keep dealing himself from the top—while my whole generation, created in his own image to serve him, is just somehow meant to be rationalizers to his thought, and janitors to his pollution, sweeping the mess up behind him—he is just nuts."

Finally even Leone was silent. Dawes sat on the stove, listening to the dirty wind of the old block take root on the glass outside. Simpson was slumped in his chair, nearly dreaming.

"But is that any way to treat your own father?" Leone said finally.

"I am afraid I think so," Dawes Williams said quietly. "But will you loan me the hundred? I've really got to be going now. I'll mail it back first chance."

"I'm sorry you feel that way, old boy," Simpson said, not looking at him.

"Me, too," Dawes said.

"I'm sorry you feel your mother and I are not fit to live with any more."

"I'm sorry, too," Dawes said. "I'm sorry everything you and our grand-fathers did, maybe even dreamed about in their way, turned out to nothing more than plastic horseshit."

"It's an old story," Simpson said.

"You can't change the world," Leone said.

"I know it," Dawes said. "I've quit on that anyway."

"You can't do that," Leone said.

Dawes sat on the stove, laughing.

"So has everyone I know," he said finally. "Except for Braun Daniel, who wants a last piece of sweet cake before the whole thing dissolves."

"You got some more mail from him today, Dawes," Leone said.

"Yes," Dawes said, laughing quietly, "only Braun Daniel has become dif-ferent from the rest of us because he has become the same old thing. The rest of them are making belts and doing fine jewelry, trying not to make smoke."

"Your friends in Iowa City, Dawes?" Leone said.

"Yes. My friends everywhere," Dawes said. "They're just too fine in their way, too, to go up in your stinking plastic smoke."

"Maybe it's just not that serious yet," Leone said. "Have *some* faith in your leaders, Dawes. Where's your sense of humor any more? You always used to have such a good one," she said softly.

"Oh ya," Dawes said. "Well, some ecologists think it is already *over,* Mother. It's already happened."

"Now, Dawes," Leone said.

"Now, Mother," Simpson said.

"What the hell is the matter with you people? Don't you know *anything?"* Dawes Williams said, nearly crying, screaming out at them.

He sat still on the stove, cross-legged, alone. For a moment his voice drifted off, and he seemed to be talking only to himself.

"Sometimes," he said, "I think this particular uprising of Celts is not done out of any joy on hope at all. It's obviously happening out of complete defeat. Premonitions. An only more chronologically sensitive despair. The world's going out," Dawes Williams said. "But what I don't understand, what makes me only mad still, is why you people hate them so. They're only dying, like lemmings going over the cliffs in the midst of plenty, so that you people can go on consuming. You're too weak for anything else."

"That's just a little bit preachy, old boy," Simpson said.

"Oh ya," Dawes said, "but who cares now? The Prophet from Iowa. But there won't be anyone around reading formalistic criticism anyway. Who cares?"

Leone was crying. She sat down in a satin chair on the edge of the dining room.

"I think I'm going to be sick," she said. "I can't take much more of this."

"Take an aspirin, another racy Victorian biography of Balzac to bed, Mother," Dawes said. "You'll be better in the morning."

"A guy can only run his own little corner of the world, old boy," Simpson said.

"Oh, we've covered all of that, Father," Leone said.

"Somehow," Dawes said, "I knew I'd find you standing here, saying something like that, Dad."

"But he's quit on his education, Father," she said.

"Now, Mother."

"Mother and Father. Mother and Father," Dawes Williams said.

"Maybe he's just had enough," Simpson said.

"Kiss off," Dawes Williams said. "I happen to be the hardest-working sonofabitch you know. I only wish Arthur were still alive, so I could drive down to Dawes City and tell him what a lazy bastard he was when it came to anything that mattered."

"Work is a good thing," Simpson said.

"Work makes mostly only smoke and kills people," Dawes said. "Work is the most overused excuse for not being able to live any other way."

"What a terrible thing to say," Leone said suddenly, flatly. "That's insane."

"Let's face it," Dawes said. "The human race has always been mostly preoccupied with its own boredom. It won't be happy until it finally succeeds in swallowing itself."

"Why, I'm just amazed," Leone said, nearly breathless. "There's just not an ounce of humanity left in you."

"I'd answer that," Dawes Williams said, "except I can't think of anything to say."

"So where do we go from here, old boy?" Simpson said.

"I don't know where you two are heading," Dawes said, "but I'm heading south. Either to the streets or on to the ratlands, perhaps even to the streets of the ratlands. That's where you come in, Simpson. Can you lend me a hundred until the revolution comes in?"

"Just a damn minute you are. You're not handing me that line of crap, because I'm stepping in here right now."

"How's that?" Dawes said, smoking on the stove. "You are putting your foot down, are you?"

"I am."

"This could become a damn flat conflict then, because, if you remember rightly, you couldn't even get the dog to crap on paper."

"No," Simpson said, not even batting an eye, "and I'm not having much more luck with you, either."

"Touch-cheek, Babbitt," Dawes said, genuinely laughing. "You can be such an aristocratic charmer for a plowman turned accountant when you want to be."

"What does that mean, Leone?" Simpson said.

"This is not the Joe Pyne Shanty Irish Show, Dawes," Leone said. "I've had about enough of this."

"Oh ya," Dawes said. "I've been using a lot of neologisms lately. Can't seem to break the habit for the life of me."

"What does that mean, Simpson?" Leone said.

"Oh ya. What do you think of the revolution so far, Mother?" Dawes said.

"I don't think anything of it."

"Oh ya. It'll probably just go away," Dawes said. "Nice weather for it. Think I'll go out and tie myself to a barricade somewhere. Think I'm about ready to go down screaming now."

"What will that prove?" Leone said.

"What a really sadistic thing to say, Mother," Dawes said.

"Now, now," Simpson said, sensing a lapse in passion, "let's all have something to eat and we'll feel much more like talking this thing out of Dawes."

"Not me," Dawes Williams said, "no time. I've got to find mine own pheasant gun around here. Big political mission. I know it's in bad taste, but I've got to assassinate the mayor of Billings, Montana."

"Dawes Williams!" Leone said.

"Got to. He's a counterrevolutionary. I know he is. He's going to lead another reactionary movement of cattlemen in the grazing lands. He's buying up all of the newspapers. I know he is," Dawes Williams said.

"Just be quiet about it!" Leone said. "You've got me so I don't know whether I'm coming or going."

"Just a little hyperbole, Mother," Dawes Williams said. "I may, however, cut off my ear and send it to Richard Nixon in a box."

"Mr. Nixon will be doing what he can," Simpson said.

"Um-ga-waw," Dawes Williams said, the visor of his hand over his eyebrow, scanning the horizon of the room frantically for sign. "Can the silly hare ever even marginally succeed in eating the lion?"

There was a silence. Dawes Williams lay back against the wall.

"Seriously, Simpson," he said. "How about loaning me that hundred? I can last two months on that."

"I know what's wrong with you, old boy," Simpson said. "For a guy who doesn't like material things, you sure like *my* material things."

"You own the means of production. Yo' es de way 'n' de light."

"I'm putting my foot down here and calling a stop, I tell you," Simpson said.

"That's all very well. We've been through this before. Let me go write that into a notebook somewhere, but are you going to loan me the hundred or not?"

"I am not."

"Bigot," Dawes Williams said.

"You can finish your degree, but I'm not going to give you the money to go hang around the world on."

"But I might even learn something out there."

"You sure might. No."

"All right, then," Dawes said. "I guess I'll just have to hang around here and organize you for awhile."

"No. Fat chance. What does that mean?"

"I think that means something like messianic conversion," Leone said.

"Fat chance," Simpson said. "The brighter branches of my family gave up that sort of wood worship and bonfire crap generations ago. We may never renew our knighthood after what those illegitimate Tudors did to us," he said smiling, "but we aren't about to take five steps backwards into that kind of tribal darkness, either."

"That's about the most schizophrenic thing I ever heard!" Dawes Williams said.

"Well, I'm not. I don't believe in this particular step of yours."

"Who gives a shit if you believe? Even the dumbest, most unsympathetic branches of your family probably gave the prodigal offspring an old plow-horse and ten bucks to hit the world on. What the hell is the matter with you, Simpson?"

"Well, there's no living in persecuting me, I can tell you that," Simpson said. "A guy with your degrees could sign on somewhere and do plenty. You could do plenty."

"What does he mean?" Dawes Williams said.

"Pleeeeen-ty," Simpson said.

"Oh, horseshit," Dawes Williams said. "But will you at least forward my mail and my issues of *The New York Review of Books?*"

"I should hope not," Leone said. "If you must read trash like that, make your own arrangements."

"What does she mean?" Dawes Williams said, incredulous.

"She means you will have to go to work for a change."

"Just fuck right off, Simpson, with all due respect," Dawes Williams said. "I consider you a lazy, uninformed bastard. I've worked harder in the last five years than you or Arthur ever had nightmares about."

"Now, now," Simpson said. "Let's all have something to eat and we'll all feel more like talking."

"My God," Dawes Williams said, "what an utterly incredible thing to say."

Leone sat, crying again.

"What do you think he means, Simpson?" she said.

Dawes pulled his stocking cap down farther over his ears and began speaking into his skillet again. His eyes were distant:

"*They go out. They fight. They land on pitching decks. . . . Where do we get such men?*'—That's the admiral, Frednic March again, mourning the singular passings of the two star-crossed helicopter pilots, Mickey Rooney in a porkpie hat and the other, and Lieutenant Brubaker himself, William Holden hisself, who had everything to lose, and nothing to gain, and who managed to take three hundred relatively unimportant, unmourned (but then they weren't married to Grace Kelly, but then maybe they had wives) North Koreans with him (after knocking out the Bridges of Toko-Ri), proving once and for all the Occidental has not yet lived long enough with the cognitions of his own Mass Society."

There was a long silence in the kitchen. The grandfather clock struck midnight in the other room. The dead wind and old sleeping ghosts tried to take root on the glass. The dog wandered into the kitchen, sat down on his haunches and looked curiously up at Dawes.

"But what does all of this *mean,* Simpson?" Leone said.

"Now, now, Mother," Dawes Williams said. "You know it's just my cranial tumor that makes me act so cross in the evenings. You know, deep down, I think this dream of gloriously organized plastic, this Camelot, this solid Republicanism on both the Left and the Right, will just go on forever."

"I don't understand," Leone said, crying like a child, nearly sixty now and alone, "what I have done to deserve this. . . . He's so hateful sometimes. . . . Once, when he was seven, I remember Dawes gave me a valentine. . . . Later he flew into a rage and tore it all up. . . . He's so hateful and willful and . . ."

"I beat him with a board for that, if I remember," Simpson said asserting his lasts.

"I think we all just ought to face the fact that social democracy is an impossible idea as long as we continue to be, all of us, raised as children," Dawes Williams said. "We all grow up looking still for the soft and chastising nipple and this means forever an oligarchy, a warm mother nation-state, in one form or another. It's hopeless. We'll never give up being feudal, only imitating preexistent, *a priori* hums."

"That's about enough of that kind of talk, old boy."

"He's so hateful, there's not a bit of humanity in him and. . ."

"It's only petit mal, Mom. Don't worry about it," Dawes said, climbing down from the stove. "So long."

"He can't leave now."

"Stay for some supper, old boy."

"That's crazy," Dawes Williams said. "But I am sorry Arthur is dead. Not that anybody needed him. And you're good folks at heart, I guess. It's just that, put together, you are all as loaded and dangerous as potent children demanding their way over something they know nothing about."

In the silence Dawes crossed over the kitchen to the door. The dog tried to follow him out. Black skies. Dark, dark till morning. Strangely, for only a moment there at the end, he thought the three of them had nearly touched again.

"Is that all you've got to say to us, old boy?" Simpson, who was behind him in the hallway, said.

"He's so hateful and. . ."

"What the hell's the matter with that woman?" Dawes said.

"Your mother's just not feeling too well," Simpson said, patting her hand. "She's just been taking on too much lately."

"There's not a bit of humanity in him."

"There's pathos here," Dawes Williams said. "Quick. Someone get a council and canonize that woman. Quick. Someone take her picture."

He turned then, went down the short stairs, into the door, then was gone.

"Is that all you can find to say to us, old boy?" Simpson said again.

"No, it's not," Dawes Williams said into the doorknob, which came off in his furious hand: *Of course they're coming. Where would you have us make our stand, son—the Mississippi River?*—That's Fredric March, the admiral again, confirming the Lieutenant in his duty, in *The Bridges of Toko-Ri.*"

Then, kicking out two doors on his way out like sublimated murder, Dawes Williams left for good with the commandment Thou Shall Honor Thy Father And Thy Mother Or Thou Shall Drop Shortly Dead still ringing queerly in his ears.

3

H e sat in the river. That is, Dawes Williams, young yeoman dressed only in jeans with stripes and rags and bright bells dancing on the sunburned wind, sat in the edges of the Rio Grande, reading his notebooks and his letters come in from Braun Daniel and the cold and Vietnam. It was a hot afternoon, the sun wove through him like a drum, fat buzzards wheeled and circled overhead. He had drunk a lot of beer that afternoon flying down through the Southwest, and the broken shell of his car sat behind him near the road. The wind ran through the river weeds and grasses and cooled it some. He beat the waters with a red bandanna like a white stoned horse, not moving.

"A greyhound named Chihuahua's Hat," he said quietly. "Eight hundred and ten bucks. Omens and found signs in the cut water at last."

"Ballyhoo!" he said to the thick brown water. "Chihuahua! Chihuahua! Ballyhoo, boys, it's free ground!"

For a moment, pulsed with sun, he thought he was Hyoot John Williams himself, about to swim the flooded Rio in 1885 with the major's payroll. . . . only in the other direction. He sat soaking in his jeans, red and orange stripes, fringes, a knee scarf that blew in the reeds whenever he stood on the edge of the water, reading his notebook and letters:

> Leaving town, he passed Summer's old house. A flat light hung within the porchway. It sat off from the street. They had all moved on years before, but reconstructing quietly the natural history of past houses, Dawes thought she had been brown-skinned, young, impossibly perfect, smelling of sleeves of rain, and she had lain with him, watching the sounds of the dark room shift into blue rings, and she had been morning itself, and he was naked and lost in her nakedness, the evergreen shadows falling across the walls and lines of her body, and it was Halloween, raining, and someone kept knocking at her doors, passing mummers, but she had only looked through the other side of his darkness, only him, saying only as much as "So this is what it is? Do what you will, oh please, I am fearless now. I love you. We are the same thing now, Dawes." Movement. He couldn't believe her. What she was. Had suddenly become. As if she were suddenly blooming around him. Within him. Higher than the ceiling. He couldn't believe her. He couldn't believe what it was she had become beneath him. Furious. Lost. Unnamed.
>
> And it smelled of clean linen on her mother's bed (who had taken the train to Junction City to visit relatives on Halloween, he could scarcely believe it, his luck), and Summer had let the stocking fall, for the first time, *the last*, the only, they were to be doomed, tied ever after only to her fear, but it didn't matter—something had already broken off in the universe—and he lay easily within her, hearing only the broken float wash over, the slack water running behind, filling in the spaces, closing him out forever, and in the dark again he lay listening only to the white, virgin sounds of her leaving; the secret, expiring thing locked safely again within her, health, he supposed at the time. . .p. 103.

He sat still in the Rio. Thirsty. Midafternoon. For a moment he was almost overcome. Passing her house had been almost two months ago, but the road flowed and fused forever, locking him out. He squinted into the south, almost as if a herd of wild horses should be dancing there, stirring up the pure white, sun-blazed dust. The car was broken down behind him, forgotten—

But that was years. But are years possible things? And passing the gray quarry stone, Coachman's, on his way out of town, he stopped the car, suddenly angry, got out, and hung one last, high-fast beer bottle into the darkness. Over the water's moon, its nonreclaimable surface. In a slight, distant ear he thought he caught himself gagging, cursing. Dunker and Eddie and Travis Thomas lay out over the water in pale sleeves, like ghosts. . . . p. 112.

What did Tristram Shandy know? . . . p. 166.

Only assassins keep notebooks. They thrive on the slow act of murdering themselves. Oswald. Sirhan. Me. Sometimes, I tell you, early in the mornings, it scares hell out of me. . . actually. p. 116.

Richard Milhaus Nixon, a water shade, by definition a thing that does not exist, does not even ascend into the bright, airy, loftily loamy plateaus of being capable of inciting ridicule. . . . p. 7, in the prologue and dedication.

Dostoyevsky knew lots, man. He even knew more than Richard Nixon and is, therefore, somewhat higher on the chain of being. . . . p. 9.

For hours in the darkness he followed the single word "South," tack-signed on the highway signs—always on the far, the other side of the dim towns. It was, he thought, as if someone had been afraid the road would suddenly revolt, snake back on itself and be gone. As if the worst thing to be feared in the country was losing one's way, the straight and narrow, immediately upon emerging from anywhere at all. As if someone passing had stopped, taken it upon itself, tried to order the road to be still, forever planted in one place. To stake it down with directional imperatives. . . .

And in the lamphights of the sleeping towns was winter. No gnats swarmed in the yellow. No wakeful dogs seemed to sleep in the drab, the fronts of stores, the hollows of feed signs. Dawes smoked brown cigarets. He reached for his single duffel, his cue case, his boxes of notepaper, but suddenly noticed he had forgotten his clothing. It didn't matter, he wasn't dressing for dinner. He reached rhythmically in the ashtray for his corkscrew and beer opener until St. Louis, where the first light broke down, suddenly, over the river, and where he stopped it all, got out and asked the fat woman with the wart on her nose for more wine. Forgetting his cigarets, his change, he cursed himself and crossed east, over the river, seeing only perhaps Huck Finn again, and loose rafts broken away in the current. *Like watching it rain on a time before you were born . . . you were never born, Dawes, you just died incessantly, all of your life.* St. Louis, a huge horseshoe. More stacks. Dead sky all morning. All was past time now.

First river. First light. He was east and south now, moving all morning. The cars, crawling behind him, became older as he continued south. Broken houses. Walls of dead brick and sunlight falling through.

No one seemed to move, or live, within these destroyed heaps of board, for him. Almost no animal life sniffed the edges. And just before the light failed, just before dark, flying past slowly, he noticed one cardboard sign, cast out to the road, barely readable, weathering in the yellow rains and worn in the winds:

4 Ɔale chep
Signed: J. Ɔ. Whitley . . . p. 148.

He sat in the Rio. Reading furiously. Thumbing through like a crazy Indian who couldn't read script. And his shirt was cut away. He was sunburned and peeling fiercely. A green bandanna with cowboys and stars ran around his naked, burning forehead and under his hair—

The instinct of an interior ear told him: If you are ever truly defeated, you will run always higher, until you are dead. You will go naturally higher, up always into the nearest hills, and you must, never looking back. You must die, finally, trying to tear off your own leg, saving yourself.

You are a redneck. You have redneck blood. You could be this right now, only backwards. . . .

"These Celts have just gone to particular seed," his father's final benediction would have been, smoking always an invisible cigar. p. 133.

Schizophrenia is merely thought coming from right field. Why be embarrassed? Make friends with the monsters. Right field, that's where John A Priori, the best outfielder in the League from the Bronx, plays. . . in Brooklyn. p. 33.

He passed vague lumber all day, all night, the next day. Perhaps not. One thin light seemed to follow, cast down from the trees, all afternoon. It was cast up like a shadow, a thin, moving opening in the gray spaces, his rhythm, his black pounding water that beat the inside surfaces of his eye like a small childbirth rending the yellow air. Like Cyclops trapped in a cabin, a moving cave, he drove down the road until it exhausted itself and quit. It never quit.

Is this really Tennessee?

Nothing responds. He drove until he couldn't move any more. It was then, suddenly, after days, he felt he had lost the simple ability to move, the sense of color. Road blurred into road. Epileptic. Full of sad trance. It was only later he remembered it was night.

Then he pulled over to the side of the road and slept like roses growing up the side of the glass. p. 162.

Boots. Boots with bells sang on the banks of the Rio behind him—

Waking, he was relieved to find that the Famous Robinson Crusoe of Southern Tennessee was really there. He stood, smiling in, tapping on his window with a quarter. He leered inward. Bitch dogs ran in a clear field of moon beyond his mouth. It was late, still dark as a bone of contention. There was a quietness. A mirror of dogs' ears rilling up. Sirens going off. A voice of early light. But it was a quietness only possible, he knew at once, in warm places suddenly chilled, deeply, to the bone of its heart, all life muted by the unexpectedness of it, shocked into silence by the reality of it, startled paradoxically only into sleep.

He drove on. . . . p. 164.

Bells. Bells without boots sang on the banks of the Rio behind him—

Eventually he pulled out, flush with a two-hundred-mile chain of organistic lights, onto U.S. Route 1, into the soft, sleeping gold, the risen plastic of the Florida night. Handsaw roared with laughter. . . . p. 197.

Tristram Shandy knew lots, man. In fact, Tristram Shandy may have come closer than anyone to knowing it all . . . . p. 467.

Startled, turning quickly into the southwest, Dawes Williams thought he had just forgotten something important. Suddenly discontented, knowing forgetting meant really he was just on the verge of remembering it again, comeback-in-a-new-form, he went down and waded in the shallows. The reeds blew in the long wind, vague as a genesis. It was perfectly still for a moment. Then, remembering it like a key, an old bone unlocking the wind, he went back up the bank. Thinking he was looking for a misplaced beginning at last, he rummaged around in the trunk of the Ford. Finally, under two sacks of spent laundry and the spare tire, he found what he thought he was looking for—an old, incredibly mutilated, barely legible notebook. He walked for awhile barefoot in the sand, the bells on his jeans jangling the air, looking at it. Finally, jumping back into the river, a hot day, too hot for breathing, he began reading again—

THIS IS THE STORY OF HYOOT JOHN WILLIAMS,
LAST OF THE GREAT COWBOYS,
AS TOLD TO ME BY SIMPSON WILLIAMS.

When August came, slick as a dream of falling timbers, they would pick the boy's father up at his office, and drive west toward the farm for hours with the sun dying like the insides of a split melon before them. Finally, in the dark, they would talk:

"Yes sir, old boy, Simpson Williams said, addressing his boy, taking the cold cigar away from his fine lips, "old Hyoot John Williams, my father's uncle, he'd just stand out in the back acre, in Omaha, out by the Missouri in the evenings shooting the red walnuts out of the sky with his old Colt."

"Wait a minute," Dawes Williams said. "Walnuts aren't red."

"They are when they explode," Simpson said. "I've seen them."

"Wait a minute. Hold on here," Dawes said. "If he was such a damn cowboy, what was he doing as far east as Omaha?"

"He rode the train out for a visit with his nephew. I think they were going to talk about buying up some land."

"Ceril Percil Williams? When was this? Those two must have made a pretty pair."

"You sure have a lot of opinions on this. Don't you?"

"I sure do," Dawes said. "Practically nothing escapes me."

"Yes. Well, during the First World War. 1919, I think."

"Wait a minute," the boy said, "if he was such a damn cowboy, why wasn't he *in* World War One? Are you sure about any of this? Or is this just another figment of your imagination?"

"Good Lord, Dawes, he was sixty years old at the time."

"He must have had a steady hand, shooting all them walnuts out of the sky."

"Dawes," Leone said, "don't say 'them.'"

"That's right," Simpson said, "a steady hand. That's what I meant in the first place."

"Well, why didn't you just say so then?" Dawes said. "Why are you trying to be so damn mysterious about this anyway?"

"Dawes!" Leone said. "That'll be enough 'damns.'"

"Yes," Simpson was saying, "old Hyoot was tough as an old boot, but he had the heart of a baby."

"Hold on here," the boy said, "just wait a minute. Before you go on, what I want to know is this—how did these damn Williamses ever get that far west in the first place? Out there in the flats with only the Indians and the cows?"

"I'm coming to that. I was coming to that," Simpson said.

"Well, why don't you just get to it then? Do you think you could come any faster?"

"Well, he went out there as a boy, with his father."

"Do I need you to tell me that? Heck, I could have figured that much out for myself. What I want to know is how he finally came to be in Omaha shooting walnuts out of the sky."

"Is that what you want to know?"

"That's what I want to know. Could you tell me that?"

"I don't know if I know that," Simpson said.

"What is it, do you think, you could tell me about?"

"Well, I could tell you how it was they got to be living south of Sierra Blanca in West Texas."

"All right. I'll settle for that. How did they get to be living south of Sierra Blanca in West Texas?"

"At least I think it's in West Texas," Simpson said.

"Are you sure of any of this?"

"Of course I'm sure of it. I heard old Hyoot tell me about it himself, didn't I?"

"How should I know? I wasn't there."

"That's true, old boy," Simpson said, smiling.

"Well, tell me the parts you are sure of then."

"Are those the only ones you are interested in?"

"Of course. You think I'm fruity or sumthin', Simpson? Why would I want to know about it unless it were true?"

"Well, you see," Simpson said, "when the Civil War broke out, most of the Williamses were living around Aurora, Illinois."

"Aurora, Illinois! What's that got to do with it? I thought you were talking about south of Sierra Blanca, West Texas."

"I'm getting to that," he said.

"This sure is fun," Dawes said. "But I wish you felt like getting a little faster. Maybe you want to really tell me how they got to Aurora, Illinois. Is that what you want to do?"

"All right," Simpson said. "You see, when these Williamses, these Scottish Williamses, got off the boat in Delaware somewhere they were still one family—one old man who was past ninety, his fifteen children, and his sixty-two grandchildren."

"All right," Dawes said, "I won't even ask how or why, but when was it we were on this damn boat?"

"Around 1760."

"And so it took them a hundred years to even get as far inland as Illinois. They sure must have messed around some on the way."

"No, no," Simpson said, "I don't think you quite have the idea of it yet, old boy. That wasn't how it was at all."

"Well, how was it then? Do you even know? Are you ever getting to the point of all this?"

"If you let me. They spent that hundred years, you see, in Delaware, and Pennsylvania with the Dutch, you see . . ."

"The Dutch?"

"The Dutch, and then Ohio, Illinois, Iowa and then Illinois again."

"No wonder it took'em so long. They sure must have messed around a lot. With all that movin' around I'm surprised they even made it that far."

"So then the Civil War broke out, you see . . ."

"I thought that would be in there somewhere."

"And Hyoot's father enlisted as a private. But it was a good war for him. He came out a major, with some money for the first time and an idea he'd sell the farm and buy as much land as he could in the West. They were always going to Texas, but first they left to wander around in the Black Hills for awhile."

"How the hell did South Dakota get into this all of a sudden? That's what I want to know."

"Don't say 'hell,' Dawes," Leone said.

"How would I know about something as personal as that?" Simpson said. "But anyway they were up there for quite awhile. In fact, they were up there the summer Custer got massacred, as a matter of fact."

"Are you sure Custer has got anything to do with this? With Hyoot John Williams? Was he even born yet, shooting walnuts out of the sky in Omaha, Nebraska, in 1919?"

"Of course he was born yet," Simpson said. "And Custer had something to do with it. If he hadn't gotten massacred, they wouldn't have left so hurriedly, would they?"

"How would I know?"

"That's true."

"How would you know, either?"

"That's true, too."

"Are you sure about any of this?"

"Of course I am, old boy. Hyoot John told me about it himself, didn't he?"

"How should I know!?!" Dawes Williams said.

"Are you getting confused, old boy?"

"Is that the purpose of this? Confusion? Is that what you are trying to tell me?"

"Of course not."

"Well, don't you worry about me then. I'm doin' fine. I'm just beginning to wonder if history is the same thing as talk in the first place. Did any of this ever happen after all?"

"Don't be so foolish, old boy," Simpson said. "Of course it did. So, anyway, Hyoot, who wasn't named Hyoot as yet, was only sixteen . . ."

"When are you getting to the naming part?" Dawes said.

"In a minute. But he was sixteen when he had his first real adventure . . ."

"Well," Dawes Williams said, "I'm waiting."

"Do you want to hear the naming or the adventure first?"

"I don't care. Which are you planning to let me in on first? I'm just waiting for anything."

"I'll tell you about the adventure first."

"That's fine."

"You see, it all came about, in a roundabout way, because of the major's old Civil War head wound, which was acting up again and . . ."

"That does it," Dawes Williams said. "We're back to the Illinois part again. I want out. Stop the car."

"No, old boy," Simpson said, laughing. "I just meant because of that he was a little absentminded again and had left the money in a bank, across the Rio Grande, and the payroll was due the Mexicans again."

"Listen, Simpson. Are you only the duke, or are you the Dauphin of France? Which is it?" Dawes Williams said, out of control, laughing wildly.

"Get control of yourself, Dawes," Leone said.

"Don't be silly," Simpson said, "or I won't tell you any of this at all."

"That's all right with me," Dawes said. "What makes you think I am listening anyway? What makes you think I think any of this is history in the first place?"

There was a short silence.

"What's the major's old head wound really got to do with all of this?" Dawes Williams said.

"Well, you see," Simpson said, "it was directly because of his head wound that the major developed this passion for irrigation ditches. This passionate desire to irrigate all of West Texas with cheap Mexican labor, and make it a garden."

"So Hyoot John had himself a big adventure with this drainage ditch? Is that it? Is that what you are trying to tell me?"

"Well, the major had to meet his payroll, didn't he? He had to pay off the Mexicans who were working on his ditch, didn't he?"

"I see," Dawes said. "You're trying to make fun out of me?"

"Of course not, old boy, I'm just trying to tell you the story of Hyoot John Williams."

"Well, do you think you could think it over for awhile? Get it real straight in your mind what you want me to know? Then tell me the story you are trying to tell me?"

"Well, damnit," Simpson said, "it's very simple. There was a flood . . ."

"That's it! Hyoot John saved a Mexican in his father's flooded ditch. He was a real good guy."

"No," Simpson said, "the ditches weren't even half-dug yet, and they were never full of water, but he had to meet his first payroll or lose his workers, didn't he?"

"So Hyoot John stuck up a Mexican bank, across the Rio, to get Mexican money. He was a real cool guy. Is that what you are trying to tell me?"

"Bank robbers are not 'cool,' Dawes," Leone said.

"That shows a lot you know about it," Dawes Williams said.

"No," Simpson said, "these Williamses were good, hardworking people. These were not a bunch of trashy bandits. He had the money all right; it was just that it was in a bank on the other side of the Rio Grande."

"So young John Williams went over on his horse and got the money. And that's an adventure. Right?"

"Wrong. He didn't have the adventure just then. He had the adventure coming back over the Rio."

"You mean this isn't a trick? You mean we finally got to the adventure part?"

"That's right."

"This isn't a trick, is it?"

"No. On the way back the Rio was flooded, and he had to swim the flood with three thousand dollars in gold and silver. He nearly drowned. Only a passing log. . ."

"That's convenient," Dawes Williams said.

"...saved him, and his father had to string along seven miles downstream before he could get a rope on him and drag him out with his horse."

"That's not an adventure," Dawes Williams said. "That's just more stupid chance or destiny or something. Didn't he even kill anybody in Mexico?"

"Of course he killed somebody in Mexico," Simpson said. "But not until he was older did he kill anybody."

"Simpson!" Leone said. "Quit fillin' this boy's head with nonsense."

"This isn't nonsense, Mother," Simpson said. "This is family history."

There was another silence.

"All right, you've got me hooked now," Dawes Williams said. "Who did he kill?"

"Well, he killed Charcon, the famous Mexican bandit, for one."

"Were there others?" Dawes said.

"Of course there were others, old boy."

"Simpson!"

"Well," Dawes said, "if you can't tell me how he killed this Charcon— what else did he do?"

"Lots of things, old boy. He was ramrod of eight thousand cattle when he was only twenty-five, for one thing."

"That so?" Dawes Williams said.

"That's so."

"Well, how'd that come about, pray tell?"

"That's easy," Simpson said. "Lightning did it, you might say."

"You might say?"

"You might. It was on the first real ranch he worked on. One night, in the first summer, they found the foreman, nearly back from town . . ."

"He was probably living in sin there, in town," Leone said, laughing uncontrollably.

"Oh, you two," Simpson said, "you're ganging up on me again. Anyway, the foreman was found dead, hit by lightning, fused to his horse, and John Williams was made ramrod of these eight thousand Hashknife cows."

"I'll be damned," Dawes said. "So how'd he meet up with this famous Mexican bandit Charcon by name?"

"That was only the next summer, after he got the name of 'Hyoot' stuck to him."

"Have we got to the naming part again? Is that it?"

"I was thinking of it," Simpson said. "Are you ready for that, do you think?"

"Was there a lot involved in this naming business?"

"No, it was very simple."

"You mean to tell me, damn it," Dawes Williams said, "that he just got this 'Hyoot' name stuck to him because he said, 'Hyoot-Hyoot,' to his cows all the time?"

"That's exactly it, old boy," Simpson said, lighting the cold cigar.

"I don't believe it," Dawes said. "It's too simple."

"Too simple?" Simpson said. "What's so simple about it?"

"I just don't believe in simple things," Dawes said. "Never did. Things just aren't like that."

"Well, how are they then?" Simpson said.

"Mostly," Dawes said, "I think they are complicated. That follows, doesn't it?"

"I'm hooked now, old boy," Simpson said. "What is it then you suppose about this naming thing?"

"I think it stuck probably more because he himself liked it so much. I think you have a way of naming yourself more than others doing it for you."

"Aren't you just full of wisdom this morning, Dawes," Leone said. "You'd better not let Granddad catch you talking crazy like that. Arthur doesn't like it."

"What do you mean?" Dawes said.

"Now, Mother," Simpson said, "I'm real interested in this if no one else is. So why did he name himself 'Hyoot John,' Dawes?"

"Well," Dawes said, "I think he saw something, well, like funny, or like Mom says, 'ironic,' in it. I think he must have always pictured himself quietly, so nobody'd know, you know, as the major's kid, a regular Scottish prince lost on the frontier. I think it just amused him some to be called 'Hyoot John.'"

"Is that what you think?"

"That's what I think. What's your opinion on it?"

"I don't hold opinions like that, old boy," Simpson said.

"I do," Dawes Williams said.

"Maybe so, old boy," Simpson said, chewing on his cigar end, "but I wouldn't recommend it as a habit. What else do you think?"

"I think I want to get back to why this money he swam the flood for was so important," Dawes Williams said.

"It wasn't the money. His father didn't need the money; he needed the Mexicans."

"Same thing," Dawes said. "So he could make more money."

"Maybe so, maybe not," Simpson said.

"No 'maybe' about it," Dawes said. "What is 'maybe' supposed to mean?"

"Just means 'maybe,' I guess," Simpson said.

"I see," Dawes said. "What else did he manage to do besides get himself named?"

"Lots of things. Once, to deliver important dispatches and mail from the Major to the train, he covered fifty-five miles on foot in the desert in eighteen hours."

"Why didn't he take a horse?" Dawes said.

"I don't know," Simpson said. "Probably a rattlesnake bit it or something."

"Is this a fairy tale?" Dawes Williams said. "Seems to me this Hyoot kept getting himself into a lot of needless scrapes. Was he very bright? Maybe he was just the kind of a guy who liked to take stupid chances with himself. Big deal. Is that it?"

"I don't think all of this is justified, old boy," Simpson said. "What brought all of this on?"

"I don't know," Dawes said.

"You don't think it was hard out there in those days?"

"Wait a minute. Hang on here a second," Dawes Williams said. "You can't get away with that! So he was really Abe Lincoln after all? That's where the Illinois part finally comes in, huh? Is that what it is you are trying to tell me?"

There was a silence.

"Well, I don't believe it," Dawes said. "Not even Abraham Lincoln was really Abraham Lincoln probably by the time they got through with him."

"Well, it was hard out there in those days," Simpson said. "Let me tell you it was. Why, Hyoot John and the Major spent the better part of their lives just trying to beat sense into the head of this jackass named Waggoner."

"Simpson!"

"I've had it with that part anyway," Dawes said. "Let's get back to the cow part. How was Hyoot John with cows?"

"Well, he was fine with cows," Simpson said. "In fact, before he was through, he knew everything there was to know about cows."

"Ya," Dawes said, "but what sort of particular things did he know about cows?"

"Well, for an example," Simpson said, relaxed finally, because Simpson was good with factual information, "he knew one way to find out if a heifer had been stashed by a cow out somewhere in the brush was to merely ride past her, checking her bag, to see if she had been sucked dry yet lately."

"The cow or the heifer?" Dawes said.

"The old cow of course, old boy."

"Simpson!"

"Well, he knew things like that, Mother. I was just telling the boy here how it was."

"No," Dawes said. "You're just telling me how Hyoot John himself said it was. That's what you're telling me."

"Don't see the difference," Simpson said. "He was an honorable man. I knew him, didn't I? I saw him with my own eyes."

"I may be beat on that one," Dawes Williams said. "I'm not sure yet."

"You're thinking it over, are you?"

"That's what I'm doing," Dawes said.

"Let me know when you get to the end," Simpson said.

"I don't think somehow I'll ever get there," Dawes said.

There was another silence. The new '50 Chevy moved west through Iowa in the evening. The corn lay out in a black, sightless wave; with only an imperfect voice, it sounded like a low, ground-hung rain in the wind.

"So, in the end," Dawes said, "he wasn't a cowpoke any more, he was a cowman. Is that what you are trying to tell me?"

"He was. A damn good and rich one, too. He knew the main thing to know about cows was only that if you kept at it long enough, steady enough, you'd end up broke . . . used to say, 'Prices and Weather, one is misery, but the first time they connect up together, it is death.' I remember it well."

"At least he was a pessimist," Leone said. "That's something."

"But who cares about his damn name and money and cows?" Dawes said. "When are you going to get to the part where he shoots famous Mexican bandit Charcon dead?"

"Well then, one day Hyoot John was just sitting in a saloon in Monticello, Colorado . . ."

"Monticello, Colorado!?!?!!" Dawes said. "That's crazy. How did Monticello, Colorado, get into this? How did he get up there?"

"He just arrived one day," Simpson said. "How do I know how he came to being in Monticello, Colorado? Anyway, he was just sitting there, minding his own business, when he noticed that this big Mexican was. . ."

"Charcon!" Dawes Williams whispered quietly. "We finally got to the Charcon part. Damn me. But say, why was this Charcon so big? How big was Hyoot John Williams?"

"Dawes, he was only five feet six, a hundred forty pounds soaking wet," Simpson said, "so help me God."

"I believe you," Dawes said, "but somehow I thought we were talking about a larger man."

"Nope. Had a famously fast hand, though. Said, as it all turned out, that was more important anyway."

"So he was good with a gun?"

"Of course he was good with a gun," Simpson said. "It was John Wesley Hardin's first cousin that showed him how, wasn't it?"

"How the hell do I know?" Dawes said. "This is your damn horse story, isn't it? You're the one who is telling it. Well, aren't you? Isn't that true!?!"

"Yes," Simpson said, "I am the one who is telling it. And let me get on with it, will you?"

"You mean that is what you are planning on doing night now?"

"I am if you'll let me."

"So, after all that wandering around in circles, it all came down to that one day in Monticello, Colorado. Is that it? What happened?"

"Oh, not too much," Simpson said.

"Not too much!" Dawes said. "What kind of a story is this anyway?"

"Well," Simpson said, "it seems that this Mexican Chancon, who wasn't a famous bandit yet, he was just getting started in life out there in the Southwest like everyone else, was beating up a helpless old man who . . ."

"Wait a minute," Dawes Williams said, "hold it right there. You're not getting away with that. Not that. There's got to be more going on here than that. Something you're just not telling me. So Hyoot John Williams was really only Tom Mix and Hopalong Cassidy, huh? Is that it? Well, I don't believe it. Not that. I won't stand for it."

There was a long silence, like the red corn plants and evening sleeping in the long, even rows of wind.

"Is that so?" Simpson said, throwing the old cigar from the window.

"That's so," Dawes said.

"Well, I guess it's all in the way you tell it maybe," Simpson said finally, quietly, "and this is the only way I know to tell it, so that's the way it was, I guess. That was all that was going on as far as I know. So, anyway, Hyoot stepped in there, called him out, and he managed to beat off this Charcon with his fists."

"I thought he was only a runt."

"He was. But fast with his hands. Quick. So he made up for it all with speed and animal cunning, but this Mexican Charcon swore he'd kill Hyoot John in the end. Hyoot laughed him off at first—he wasn't one to worry—but two nights later as he was sitting over some figures in the bunkhouse . . ."

"Those Williamses are always seeming to be sitting over figures no matter where they wander," Dawes Williams said.

". . . a bullet tore into his lamp, two inches from his head, leaving him high and dry in the dark," he said.

"Honestly, Simpson," Leone said, "why do you choose to fill his head with such stuff?"

"What's 'stuff' about it?" Simpson said. "You just sit over there and be quiet. He was my father's uncle, wasn't he? I believe him. I saw him shoot those red walnuts from the sky, didn't I?"

"I've seen some walnuts," Dawes said, "and I still say they're black, not red."

"A lot you know about it," Simpson said. "They're red when they explode."

"That's probably so," Dawes said quietly to his father.

"So anyway," Simpson said, "Hyoot decided it would be 'uncomfortable,' as he called it, to be just hanging around the Southwest, waiting for that Mexican to decide to strike again, to ambush him, so he decided—the next time he could get him into a public place—he'd pick a quarrel with Charcon and shoot him dead."

"Hot damn," Dawes Williams said, suddenly interested. "So what happened next?"

"So do you finally think this thing might be a history after all, old boy?" Simpson said.

"No. I wouldn't want to go that far."

"So, anyway," Simpson said, "the thing had a bad start. Because the first time he started out for town, to get that Mexican, he only wound up in a cedar tree, with only his rifle, waiting for help."

"You're not telling me all of this," Dawes said, "I know you're not."

"I am. Give me a chance. He was there—up that tree—because the Mexican was one ahead of him, was waiting, and because he had just finished shooting his horse out from under him. So he was just sitting up in that cedar tree, all afternoon, waiting for some of his boys to come by and help him."

"What a crazy sonofabitch he must have been!" Dawes said.

"Dawes!" Leone said. "I may not know what Hyoot John was, but he was *not* a crazy son-of-a-*bitch*!"

"That's all right," Dawes said, "I was talking about the Mexican anyway. And, in fact, he must have been a *beautiful* crazy sonofabitch."

"Dawes!" Leone said, trying to slap him a little.

"Was this Hyoot John scared any?" Dawes said, changing the subject.

"Of course he was," Simpson said. "He was a sensible man, wasn't he?"

"How would I know?"

"Besides," Simpson said, "only two months before that a man named Thompson got mixed up with another Mexican and killed him. In only two days the Mexicans had this Thompson treed. Then this famous Mexican rifle shot named Juan Baco came out from town and picked Thompson off from a half-mile. The first bullet tore off half his head."

"Simpson!" Leone said. "You will stop this this minute!"

"Easy, Mother. Hyoot John told me all of this himself, didn't he? Anyway, after this Thompson fell from the tree, they moved in and circled around him. They shot him sixty-three more times and left him for dead."

"Wait a minute," Dawes said. "That's crazy. Didn't they think he was already dead? Maybe they were afraid he'd move a little."

"Course he was. Dead before he hit the ground. So there was this race war going on—between the Scot-Irish and the Spanish-Indians—and that's why Hyoot was not about to sleep in that cedar tree."

"So we finally came to a conclusion, huh?" Dawes Williams said. "All right, I understand that part, let's get on with it."

"I am. I am."

"Well, what happened then?"

"Actually, nothing much at all happened then. There was some time involved in the thing at this point."

"That really messes it up," Dawes said. "I don't believe it."

"No, he just got down from that tree two days later, when some of his boys happened by, they had a good laugh, and he rode on home with one of them."

"I don't believe that. Nothing at all?"

"Nope, not for ten years."

"What the hell has ten years got to do with this? Would you tell me that at least?"

"Well, I don't know what you can say about the time involved in the thing, old boy, or even how you'd go about saying it."

"Damn it," Dawes Williams said.

"Dawes!"

"Damn it. Damn it. Damn it," Dawes said. "Somebody'd better start telling me what they think ten years has got to do with all of this all of a sudden, or I'm getting out and walking to Arthur's."

"Well, you see, I guess, Dawes," Simpson said, lighting another cold cigar, "the ten years was just the space of time before Hyoot John met up with Charcon again."

"I just hope you are able to finish this," Dawes Williams said. "Where the hell did he see him this time? Golddust, California?"

"You really want to know that at this point?"

"I sure do. You're good at places, and numbers of bullets. You're going to tell me that much at least, aren't you?"

"Yes, I guess so. If you think you are ready for it."

"I'm all set."

"Well," Simpson said, taking the hot cigar from his mouth, "it was in Chicago, Illinois, that Hyoot John saw the famous Mexican bandit Charcon ten years later."

"Key-rap," Dawes Williams said.

"Dawes!"

"Chicago, Illinois," Dawes said. "I should have guessed it. So Hyoot John was a bank teller in Chicago, Illinois, huh? Stop the car. I'm getting out and walking to Arthur's."

"Dawes," Leone said. "Don't be silly. It'll ruin your mind."

"No, of course Hyoot John wasn't a bank teller," Simpson said.

"What was Hyoot John doing in a place like Chicago in the first place then?"

"He was selling his cattle."

"And he saw the crazy, bushwacking Charcon. Is that it? But what was Charcon doing there? Was he selling his cattle, too?"

"I doubt it, old boy, unless they were stolen," Simpson said. "But then he was coming up in the world, too. But yes, he saw him. It was in a poolroom down by the stockyards."

"So Hyoot John was selling his cows in a poolhall. Is that it? I wouldn't put it past him at this point."

"No. He was getting a haircut, just off the tracks. And that's only why he saw him."

"That's not why," Dawes said. "That's only how or where he saw him. Was he still mad at Charcon?"

"No, he wasn't mad. Not at all. Said he had nothing against Charcon whatsoever any more. Said he just thought it would be a good time to get it all over with and kill him."

"Simpson!"

"Well, Mother," Simpson said, "that's how he used to say it, down by the Missouri, fifty years later. I'm only reporting."

"So he's standing there," Dawes said, "reloading his old Colt, shooting red walnuts out of the sky, saying all this. Is that it? Is that what you want to tell me? But never mind that now. What did he do, that day in the poolhall when he saw Charcon? Did he just step right in there and call him out?"

"No, not exactly. He waited low, lighting a cigaret, hanging around, until Charcon came out and then he trailed him down the tracks, near the deserted freights."

"Somehow," Dawes said, "ever since I saw him climb down out of that cedar tree, I thought something like that might happen."

"That's no way to talk about old Hyoot, Dawes. Anyway, that was the second day Charcon got away."

"You mean he hasn't got around to killing him yet?"

"Said one second he was there, and the next he had just disappeared in the air 'round a corner. Said those Mexicans could smell the wrong gringo a block away—even as far north as Chicago."

"Did he say that, did he?"

"He did."

"Wait a minute," Dawes said. "Hold on here. Are you trying to say this famous Mexican bandit Charcon was magic? Like an evil witch, or smoke in the air? Is that it?"

"No . . . no, I don't think I'm saying that at all, old boy," Simpson said. "At least I don't think I am. I'm just saying the facts—that Hyoot John said Charcon disappeared into thin air and was gone that day in Chicago."

"Listen," Dawes Williams said, "it's bad enough that Hyoot John wound up in Chicago that day after really starting out on a boat in the Atlantic, and you don't know how he got there, but when this Charcon starts showing up on the same corner—Hell," Dawes Williams said, "Mexican bandits never got as far east as Chicago, any damn fool knows that—and you still don't know why, that's too much."

"You mean you're not listening to me any more?" Simpson said.

"No, it's too late for that. But this is no damn history, I can tell you that."

"Are you telling me that?"

"I'm telling you that."

"Well," Simpson said, "I don't think I need to be told that. Certainly not by you, and if you keep telling me things like that, I'm not going to be telling you how Hyoot John finally tracked Charcon down to Durango, five years later, and shot him dead in the streets."

"Simpson!"

"Well, he did, Mother."

"I'll settle for that one," Dawes Williams said softly. "I wouldn't want to have come this far and then miss that one."

"Well," Simpson said, "one day in Durango, State of Durango, Mexico…"

"Wait a minute," Dawes Williams said. "Aren't you even going to tell me first anything about those five years in between?"

"No," Simpson said. "I don't think they're particularly important to the story."

"I do. I think they're important as all hell. It's been fifteen years now, if you remember right, since that Mexican chased Hyoot up that cedar tree, and I think the time involved in the thing is the most important part."

"You do."

"I do. Next to maybe the killing."

"Why is that?"

"The time? Well," Dawes Williams said, "we all seem to have our own special deals about this thing. Yours seems to be the geography, the places of it, like just the people's names, and mine seems to be the time involved in it."

"That so?" Simpson said.

"That's so."

"Well, that's crazy, Dawes, because you can't talk about time."

"How do you know? Have you tried?"

"Of course not. That's foolish."

"Well, I guess that takes care of that one. But, Simpson, didn't you ever stop long enough to ask yourself why it was, after fifteen years, that Hyoot John Williams still wanted to kill this Mexican in the first place?"

"He wasn't Mexican, Dawes, he was a Mexican bandit."

"That's not what I asked."

"Dawes," Simpson said, "why don't you just let me tell about the places of the thing, and you take care of the time or whatever it is you want to know for yourself?"

"All right," Dawes said, "but if Durango turns out to really be in Illinois, I'm quitting for sure."

"No," Simpson said, "it's a city in a state by the same name in West-Central Mexico."

"That's sense," Dawes said; "that's more like it. At least the places in this are finally straightening themselves out."

"That's right," Simpson said, "because by this time old Hyoot John had his own spread full of twenty-five thousand cows. It was down near Naco, Arizona. But, you see, also by this time Charcon had come up in the world and had his own band of cattle rustlers. They used to come up over the border from the Sierra Madres in Sonora. And on one trip they took twenty-five of Hyoot's cows back into Old Mexico."

"I'll be damned. But if old Hyoot had, really had, twenty-five thousand cows by then, how come he was so upset over losing only twenty-five of them?"

"He didn't say," Simpson said. "But you've got to draw the line somewhere on things like that and, besides, I guess he felt he had an old score to settle."

"That's crazy," Dawes Williams said. "It's been fifteen years."

"Could be, but I do remember him saying he thought it would be a good, sort of poetic time to be going down, over the border, and to be finally killing this Charcon."

"So what happened?" Dawes said. "Was there much blood in the streets that day? An orchestra in the background?"

"So," Simpson said, "he trailed him down near Durango when, just then, it suddenly struck him that. . ."

"I never thought he was too bright," Dawes said. "So he had to go all that way to figure that out?"

"...Durango, Mexico, would be a place to be a gringo openly killing the beloved Mexican bandit Charcon."

"So this Charcon was 'beloved,' huh?" Dawes Williams said. "You hadn't told me that."

"Only by the Mexicans, Dawes. It was one-sided at best."

"Maybe they had a reason," Dawes said.

"Maybe."

"Did you ever stop to think of what it might have been?"

"Nope," Simpson said. "So, anyway, about this time, he built himself a fire out in the foothills of the Sierra Madres round Durango, and he began thinking the whole thing over."

"He was probably thinking of moving back to Illinois about that time."

"No, don't think so, old boy. Said by this time he'd had to kill six or seven men in fights on the border. You see, he was head of the Arizona Rangers by this time, and he'd had to kill six or seven unsocial types. He'd even had to catch and lynch single-handed two cow thieves who had rustled one of his own heifers by this time, and once he even had to ride down into Mexico and avenge the assault of a white woman by a Mexican dandy. He found the man at a fiesta, paid some boy or other to call him outside, and once

he had him out there, he plunged his silent Bowie knife through his heart in the shadows
. . ."

Simpson's voice drifted off, almost beyond itself. Nearly remembering something.
Leone was speechless, and even Dawes had nothing to say. They, all three, sat in the
soundless car rolling west into Iowa, nearly there.

"Don't think it wasn't hard out there in those days," Simpson said, looking at the
two of them. "It was. It was plenty hard. Pleeenty hard."

"You've always got problems, I guess, when you're trying to push people around,"
Leone said, staring straight out of the window.

"So, anyway," Simpson said, quietly turning his cigar over in his mouth, "at least, I
guess, that probably proves Hyoot wasn't exactly worried, or new to it, sitting by his fire
in the Mexican foothills. No, I think he was only trying to think up a good plan so he
could get away with it all. It probably suddenly struck him he wasn't in America any more,
he wasn't exactly the law any more, so he'd need a plan."

"That makes sense," Dawes said.

"Don't know," Simpson said. "Those things seem to get lost in time somewhere . . ."

"If there's one thing that shouldn't get lost in time, that is the sort that shouldn't,"
Dawes said.

". . . or bound up, or something, but anyway, he hit on a plan. He thought suddenly
he'd wait for the cover of night . . ."

"That's real sense," Dawes Williams said. "I thought he'd get that far at least."

". . .and then try and get a chance to kill with his knife again. Thought if it worked
once, it would work again. No sense trying something new, something unproven."

"Oh ya," Dawes Williams said.

"So he thought if all this was done silently—he was dressed and passing as Mexican, anyway
—he'd get a pretty good chance to beat it back over the border before they knew what hit'em."

"That so?" Dawes Williams said.

"That's so," Simpson said.

"Well, I don't believe it. Not me. He couldn't pass for a Mexican. I never saw a
Williams yet who was any darker than milk."

"Not him," Simpson said. "Had the usual blue eyes, but he'd lived out in the Southwest in the open sun, remember, most of his life and was brown as a nut. Besides, he rode,
hid in his hat, used some red dye, and spoke broken Spanish."

"All right," Dawes Williams said, "I guess that part's well enough taken care of. So
where did he find this Charcon that night in Durango?"

"Well," Simpson said, absentmindedly throwing out another cold cigar, "he asked
around, he asked around and he found out this famous Mexican Charcon was in this
famous Mexican whorehouse..."

"*Simp*-son *Will*-i-ams!?!???!!!!??!?!?!!" Leone said.

"Yes, Mother, you may be right on that one," Simpson said. "Well then, he was at a
kind of Mexican party, Dawes. Yes, that was it."

"I doubt it. Somehow I don't think any of this really happened, but what happened next? Did he go right into this Mexican party and call him out like a man?"

There was a silence.

"No," Simpson said, "that would have been damn foolish, considering the terrain. He didn't do that. He sent a boy in with a silver peso to tell Charcon one of his riders was outside to see him."

"The sonofabitch!?!" Dawes Williams said. "I been expecting this. Ever since that day in Chicago when Hyoot trailed him down those tracks like a shadow that's deserted."

"Damn it," Simpson said, "who is telling this story—you or me?"

"You are. But you're making a hell of a bad job of it."

"That so?"

"That's so. I don't believe any of it."

"You want to finish this then? You want to finish telling me how Hyoot John finished shooting this Mexican one night down in Durango?"

"Not me. I wouldn't touch it. I wouldn't pretend to know anything about it."

"Well, I think I do."

"Well, that's pretty damn foolish. Did he take him all the way up to Aurora, Illinois, to finish him off and shoot him dead? To make a perfect circle of geography out of it, do you suppose?"

"That's pretty foolish, old boy."

"How can you say that's foolish? After everything else that's been trying to go on here, I think it's pretty foolish of you, calling that foolish."

"Anyway," Simpson said, "that's not what happened in actuality. No, old Hyoot just stood there in the shadows of those houses, and pretty soon this Charcon begins coming out in the light."

"Wait a minute. I've got it now," Dawes Williams said. "This is where old Hyoot John finally sees the light, that he's really a lawman after all and not a murderer, so he says, 'Stick 'em up, Charcon,' and takes him back for trial."

"Well . . . no . . . old boy," Simpson said, "he didn't say that."

"What did he say?"

"Don't know as he said anything at first. But Charcon came stumbling out, drunk, into the light, saying, 'Si, amigo, what is it you want?' or something like that in Spanish you know.

"I know. I know."

". . .and old Hyoot was just standing there, flashing his Bowie in the shadows, saying something, I suppose, like, 'I have finally come to kill you, Charcon, you are a dead man.'"

"Then he rushed out and slit his throat? Is that it?"

"No, he never got a chance for that kind of a ceremony. Charcon, you see, was no fool himself by this time. . ."

"You sure seem to feel people get smarter as they grow older," Dawes Williams said.

". . . and he had his gun under his sombrero, which he was carrying in his left hand.

Without a word further, he fired through the top of his hat. He hit Hyoot high in the chest."

"So? So? So!?!" Dawes Williams said.

"So," Simpson said, "Hyoot was no fool, either—he had been carrying his knife, his Bowie in his left hand, so he just whipped out his Colt and plugged Charcon dead in the heart."

"And that was it," Dawes Williams said.

"Not quite," Simpson said, "because Hyoot was also hit. He had one buried in his shoulder. So there he was, he said, too hurt to move, lying there, pointing his gun at them, dragging himself off, trying to make it back to the hills before the Mexicans came to string him up. To lynch him like a dog. Yes, he said he would have been a goner for sure on that one if it hadn't been for this harlot. . . er, this girl at the party who took a quick liking to him. He paid her some money out of gratitude and she snuck him off to the hills."

"That so?" Dawes Williams said.

"That's so," Simpson said.

"Are you two boys quite finished?" Leone said.

"Just about, Mother," Simpson said. "So you see, Dawes, this girl at the Mexican party, it seems, had been left in the lurch by Charcon years before for another so she didn't like him even less than she didn't like gringos. There's a lesson there somewhere, I think."

"Is that so?" Dawes Williams said.

"That's so, old boy. She hid him out in the foothills not too near the places where they held the parties, and she cared for him, and ministered to his needs for two days, and finally, no worse for the wear, he managed to make it back to the border into safe ground."

"Then he took the train back to Aurora, Illinois. To be buried in the family plot. Is that it?" Dawes said.

"No," Simpson said, "he died in Arizona, in bed with his boots on, at the age of ninety-six. Said he was never sorry or regretted a minute of it. Said if he had it to do over, he'd have shot Charcon as a younger man so's he'd had a longer to remember it."

"Now how do you know that's true? I think this is just history, all right. I think that's sure."

"I know it because I saw the spinning bullet on his watch chain that he carried in his chest back up the Sierra Madres, all the way, home to Arizona, to Omaha in 1919, old and carved on, where he stood spinning it, shooting the walnuts out of the sky—*Just two inches lower and that Mex had got my heart and I'd been a goner for sure*, he said."

"So you believed him. That's how it was."

"I know because I believed him," Simpson said. "I know because of all that and because once he took off his shirt and showed us, me and my brothers, the wound."

There was a silence in the sleeping car. It was full night then, sightless, full of speechless moon and white light in the windcorn. They were almost home to Arthur's and safe ground.

"You know," Dawes Williams said finally, "there's just one more thing I'd like to say before you drop this. I just wish we had that Mexican here. I just bet there's a couple of things he'd like to say about this whole damn thing."

"It's a fine thing to see the other fella's point of view, all right, old boy," Simpson Williams said.

Dawes Williams still sat in the Rio, reading. But it was nearly evening; a buzzard wheeled away in the open sky, rising through red clouds and dead with approaching night. Dawes sat in the river, cooling his hogs, his letters from Braun Daniel and Vietnam, and he beat the waters with his orange bandanna.

"Chihuahua's Hat!" he said. "Ballyhoo over the river, boys! What a crazy running bitch!"

He began tearing up his old notebook. The pages danced a moment, hung in the heavy air, and fell over the brown water.

Behind him, on the bank, the bells on his boots sang in the thin winds, long edges of grass, red evening.

Dusky mud for war paint—

A POOLROOM ON ALL TIME . . . p. 230.

It was a long game. A table of broken light, coming in from the green window. Dawes Williams woke always slightly into the early yellow. He drank mindlessly again from the quart of orange juice spiked with gin, and his eyes tensed within the glare falling over the edges of the low tables. The rest of the room was hooded with a slight darkness, like corners without perpendiculars, only soft with unknown distance, and he sat in the poohroom in Little River, Florida, washed up easily within the huge circular fans, the sleeping glare of the shades, the orange tropic light, dozing fitfully, waking, dreaming of motion, shooting the nine ball, reading *Studs Lonigan* by turns . . . p. 233.

This is a hell of a fine denouement. Where in the hell am I? p. 234.

It was a long morning. Another fiction of regular, rhythmic, broken racks. He was getting beaten again in an endless series of nine-ball racks conducted now for six days in the back of a room, and he sat watching the flat glare come off the polished head of the fat, sloppy sonofabitch of a weird kid who chalked with three separate motions; who hitched up the sides of his greenly spotted pants with the backs of his thumbs; and who ran his black glasses up his nose before every shot. . . . p. 234.

He was not making a million in America . . . . p. 235.

On the first day in Fla. Dawes Williams had woken in the sun. The insides of his car were a perfectly murdering pulse. The windows of his steamed Ford were rolled against thieves and murderers, the night and the weather; it was at least a hundred twenty inside. A woman was peering quietly in. She was looking in, at exactly four inches from his head, searching for life. She was announcing the sun and high noon. A mad bombing bee on a strafing mission, she was beating out furious taps and rudimentary inquisitions on his window with a quarter. As fierce Dawes Williams, destroyed by the waking sleep and the heat of remembering, opened his eyes, she raced quickly backwards for six amazed, instinctive steps, stopped, and dropped the hand that had risen to her bosom.

"Oh ya," Dawes Williams said, "this must be hell proper."

"What do you mean?" she said hurriedly, seeing him for the first time, thinking of running.

Dawes, yawning pleasantly with his early bliss, rising from his bed of a car, smiled forward at her. Rolling his window down, taking the air near a beach, he said:

"Please. Don't be afraid. Thanks for waking me."

"Yes?" she said. "I didn't mean to startle you. It's just that, when you turned your head . . . your eyes . . . that is, I hadn't expected to see a . . . a . . . well, that is . . . you *should* thank me: you know you might have suffocated in there like a dog . . . that is . . . well, you know that *does* happen down here . . Her voice broke off short. Dawes Williams stared back at himself through her watching.

She was a small woman, trembling terribly.

"Now, now," Dawes said, "think nothing of it. There's nothing to worry about here. Not really. It's just you and me out here, so early. Hell, I'm not even on parole any more. Hell, on the whole, the board says I'm making amazing adjustments for a sexual maniac."

"Oh . . ." the woman said, walking quietly backwards, stepping on invisible rose ends, moving away. . . . p. 228.

After she had left, Dawes Williams arose. He went slowly down to the sea in the ships of his holey shorts, jumped within the first wave that went rolling by. Soon he was soaping in the surf, brushing his teeth (Dawes Williams was very clean for a schizoid), singing loudly old New Bedford whaling songs in a high falsetto. Soon a fat Portuguese man-of-war stung him through the holey ships of his shorts and drove him up from the sea.

But Dawes Williams wasn't worried, he had nothing better to do anyway. He was just beginning thirty straight days, an infinity of nothing to do. Finding himself up and floundering in fun land, strangely he wasn't worried. In fact, he was nearly driven sane by the prospect of wandering pointlessly through the concrete plastic and night lights. He was probably the only one near Miami Beach with thirty-six dollars in his pockets, and walking round the rim of the dull green sea, disheveled and sun-burned as an old picked-over rooster end, he spent most of the light reading on a stolen copy of *War and Peace,* most of the shadowy afternoon shooting pool and drinking orange gin, most of the evening arched against palm trees, watching the slow smoke of his brown cigarets curl over the water, dreaming of a revolution, and most of the night sleeping finally in the peace and litter of his car, waking finally only to the reveille of exploding sun on his windows conducted by some strange parade of a woman tapping a coin on his window who was even stranger than the last. Waking, a march of standing days, he stared back into their grotesque amazement; their rudiments of sunny, unkissed flesh. p. 229.

Taking the old, greendusty Coke bottle down to the public fountains for something to make tea with, Dawes Williams sat the early afternoons out, swigging darker waters, reading *War and Peace* . . . . p. 239.

A huge rectangular, double-columned book, he had perhaps stolen it for its pretentious length, but which, soon, involved him as he had never been involved before; involved him, for the first time, in ways his own life never had. p. 260.

"Hell, yes," Dawes Williams said, turning suddenly into the airless amazement of a sun-skinned, dab-nosed woman obviously down from New York, "this is one fine book. How are you dudes doing up there?" p. 241.

Leaving the beach, like a mass of nearly deflated balloons hanging in limp air, Dawes wandered the seaward streets. Leaving so that he might have a place to return to, he wandered the gold pot of Collins Avenue, the plastic jungle of signs, hotels, and light like baroque and manneristic palaces of mineable sun. Squinting into the sea, a last bamboo cat, wide in the eyes, low within the plastic reeds of evening, he watched the dried and Sunday-clean children who trailed behind the loud, postsexual women wrapped, yet falling apart in their worn tatters of bright cotton Christmas paper. Slowly, near evening, they were going to water, drifting into the huge holes of the hotels, constantly dabbing white cream on their cold noses, peeling and fearful, waddling the ducklings behind them. They moved about on the cement like a wet jungle of signs, an almost visual rise and fall of the audible image, and the ironic streets were finally tacked together by the whine of Lincolns, Cadillacs and an occasional delivery truck.

Ultimately, he thought there was a process of watching yourself not watching. A distance. A soft alienation. A leaving. A last sighing, nonrecognition of his humanity . . . he was just glad he'd found a nice pair of swimming trunks. p. 242.

He was happy he could never be a part of this. His happiness was the only thing keeping him alive. . . . p. 243.

Evenings like morbid, luxurious secretions, the decadent oil caught from the murdered inner ears of rarer whales; strings of ambergris and scented gold rings stolen from the Indian ground; the plumes of more exotic birds worn proudly through the roads of lights, the walls of steel poles, the streets strung with pearls of bait, in carriages, a curve of dead, electric smoke . . . women walking. p. 243.

Stopped by a shoeshine boy on Collins Avenue, Dawes Williams said:
"You can't shine sandals."
"You look wore out, man," the kid said. "What's the matter with you?"
"What do you think of America so far?" Dawes said, casting his eyes around in the spangled wind.

"Hell, yes," the boy said, smiling, "it's America all over the damn place any more."

Noticing he was getting topped by shoeshine boys anyway, Dawes Williams handed him a quarter, the kid handed it back, still smiling pleasantly, saying he thought Dawes needed it more right now, and then Dawes drove over to Little River to shoot pool and to watch the soft Florida gold of afternoon glare as it fell through old shades, long windows, and the end of the room . . . p.244.

The afternoon deepened. It was a long game, two or three hundred racks, and Dawes Williams was holding his own but slowly losing. Dawes sat, reading, looking up, feeling he was somehow better than the fat, sloppy-chalked, oilpaper-smeared, uncool kid who followed him everywhere he went, beating him out of quarters and dollars, and who had just finished running all of the balls off the table.

"That makes eleven now," the kid said.

"What you want me to do," Dawes said, "faint?"

"What's that supposed to mean?" the kid said flatly. "You trying to be smart or something?"

"Umm-a, umm-a," Dawes Williams said.

"Just pay me the buck on the last game," the kid said.

"What did you say your name was again?" Dawes said. "I want to make sure I get that straight."

"It's not my last name. It's my whole name."

"Well, let's have it again."

"My name is Green Johnny Miami," the fat kid said.

He stood looking back at Dawes. He hitched up the sides of his green pants again, blew hot and unclean air on his glasses.

"Oh, Christ," Dawes Williams said. "I'm Damon Runyon."

"Well, Damon," Green Johnny Miami said, "you wanna go again?"

"Sure, Green John," Dawes said. "Rack'em up."

He settled himself again, began reading, looking up, watching the real pool balls roll over clicking in the glare and hazy end of the sun. . . . p. 246.

It was evening. Cooler. The last nine ball had rolled lazily with the easy roll of the long table, thunk, into the black of the corner pocket. Broke, beaten, Dawes had moved off to the edge of the room. He sat, leaning in a chair, feet propped on the windowsill, staring out at the flat play of the wind. Unworried, he knew he still had twenty stuck in his shoe and four pounds of stolen lunch meat rotting under the seat of his Ford.

He thought soon it would be time for heading over to the greyhound races and making a million. He sat, drawing things from his green army-surplus munitions bag—his notebooks, which he hunched over in the dark light, a copy of *The Young Manhood of Studs Lonigan*, a bottle of orange juice and gin, brown cigarets. He watched people filing in and out of the door.

It strikes Dawes Williams suddenly that there is a world both existing and going on out there. That fat men with cats on leashes are stepping from taxis, and paying the drivers off with old five-dollar bills; that people are going to the theatres; that beautiful women with long slender hands are walking baboon-looking New York dogs down to the corner fire hydrants; that the sun is shut down for the day, but money is still changing in banker's hands, behind closed doors.

Words are not reality, he thinks, and I lie beyond, because words are better than reality; reality doesn't exist, and the fat men with leashed cats are all getting back, into their taxis again, and they are smiling at the drivers with disused and yellowing five-dollar eyes, and reality is cheap, and people are going to the theatre, wondering how you can enter a house that has no windows or doors. . . . p. 249.

It had been a long day, a long table, a long game. Dawes shifted himself around, got finally down from his windowsill. At the end of the room Green Johnny Miami was still hunched over in the glare, shooting pool. Racking his cue, which he had been holding between his legs at the window, he paused to watch one last nine ball slip quietly away with the table. He thought he had wasted a lot of time at college reading books while he could have been learning something useful. On his way out the door, he noticed an old shooter in the corner leaning over a shot. Startled, Dawes studied him for a moment. Horribly broken, tired but not vacant in the eyes, he chewed the stubby rat end of a cigar as he leaned over his shot. Waiting, timing a moment not shaking from palsy, he ran it easily down the table. He ran six and dropped back with a leave. The old felt hat he wore was draped low over his left eye, in an unusual, nearly urbane angle and shading. Clearly, in the old light, a worn, shattered paperback stuck from his hip pocket like a dull, barely readable flag. It said: *War and Peace*. Dawes Williams couldn't believe it. It was fiction. He found he had no humor to disbelieve it with. Even now it was only a moment, full of adrenaline, like only for a second passing through a mirror into an old and broken and defeated form. And coming out whole again in the same motion and step. It was only a fiction. He couldn't believe it. He couldn't disbelieve it. He hurried out the door, into the deep evening sleeping like a wing, trying to ignore it. . . . p. 252.

He went to clean up for the dog races. He jumped in the ocean, sat soaping and singing in the sea. Having shed himself down to the holey ships of his shorts, prancing down to the water, he felt just like Robert Cohn, cast-off social rug, the middleweight boxing champion of Princeton. p. 255.

A gull flew by, coasting up, riding the air, blowing away. Dawes Williams stood up in the water and ack-acked him to death with an imaginary tommy gun. He sat back down in the water in the holey ships of his shorts, chewed an invisible cigar:

"I'd a had another beautiful folded double if there'd a been another bird flying' along there. Haha haha hahahaha," he said. "I'd a been finally a piece of the universe with an act like that." p. 256.

Moon bright, he sat soaping in the white surf. Taking his copy of *Pride and Prejudice* out of the munitions bag, he began reading again. He found he couldn't understand it. The evenly spaced rhythms of place description, dialogue and character unrolling, like picket fences, seemed to him to be the wildest breakage of reality, the most fantastic lie, like believing you could actually take a perfectly symmetrical cherry pie from the oven and present it to starry-eyed children. Disbelieving in prototype novels, women's bridge games, Margaret Mitchell and Uncle Sam's vision of history, Dawes Williams took out his toothbrush and went to work in the crashing surf. He sat in the ocean, eating stolen meat and drinking orange juice and gin. It was romantic as hell. . . . p. 256.

He finally cast Jane Austen onto the waters. *Go, little book.* . . . He believed something must have been purposely missing anyway. He watched her go. Carefully steering around Sterne, Smolett, Fielding, Richardson, even Defoe, and William Shakespeare—like dank, unknown tugboats—she set sail, mounted the night on slippers and scissors and sealing wax, and headed out for either England or South Carolina. . . . p. 257.

In the low face of the moon lies the fat-sloppy, oilpaper-smeared, chin-chalked, uncool kid with green-splotched pants who follows him everywhere he goes, smiling, dropping nine balls into the quiet evening pockets of the universe behind him. Without a sound. But Dawes Williams, he wasn't worried, not him, he knew he had another twenty, taped under the dashboard, that he had barely even told himself about. That was the best thing there was about America—there was always another twenty taped on the inside of a shoe somewhere. Besides, he was going to the dog races. . . . p. 253.

Looking for meaning simply in juxtapositions is dangerous business. p. 101, in a margin.

Looking merely for the phenomenal irony to be found in mere placement isn't. p. 203.

"I find sometimes my only abstractable, that is, fierce, enemies in this world are Braun Daniel, American politicians and the bones of dead writers. Do you find that at all queer? What do you make of that?" —Dawes Williams in conversation with the Tibetan Buddha. p. 606.

"Absurdity! Absurdity!" he squealed in his small voice. "That is silly! One mustn't hate bones." p. 770.

"Do you think I am a bully?" Dawes Williams said. p. 770.

"Paranoia! Paranoia! Vile, stupid, pretentious man!" p. 808.

Reading a copy of *The Selected Poems of Vachel Lindsay* at the stoplights, Dawes Williams began heading down Collins Avenue again. He went across the causeway, past the last threads of evening, the black gull, the sleeping gold yachts of the houses, and he was moving toward the dog races at West Flagler. Clutching his last twenty like the fanatic mission of a crap-shooter looking for a game, a likely pass, Dawes Williams wasn't worried. . . . There was no place to go anyway so he only sat there, turning on his light, reading on his copy of Vachel Lindsay at stoplights, knowing somehow it was really his night this time. Hell, yes. He was sure of it. He was sure of it. He was going over the sun with this one. With what Arthur's old leftover blood knew about greyhound flesh, he couldn't miss. By God. He thought he would run this twenty into an empire. Cattle. Oil. Telephones. Rubber balls. What the hell, it doesn't matter. He would buy land in the Southwest and move his people out. They would build a place called Huckleberry Finn, New Mexico. A new life. Soon a large, free university would bloom on the desert. America was a hell of a sweet-mother place, if you could only learn to love money enough. . . . Just then General William Booth Entered into Heaven:

> "He saw King Jesus. They were face to face,
> And he knelt a-weeping in that holy place.
> Are you washed in the blood of the Lamb?"

Dawes Williams tossed the book into the back of his Ford.

"OH, MY GOD," he said out his vacancy of windows to a passing chauffeured Cadillac stopping for the same light, "IF I WAS ONLY JONATHAN SWIFT WHAT I COULD DO WITH THIS ONE. THIS CENTURY. THIS PLACE. IN FACT," Dawes Williams said, "EVEN, I SAY EVEN IF I WAS ONLY RING LARDNER OR BEN HECHT I COULD RELAX A LITTLE, HAVE AHELLUVA TIME MESSING WITH THIS PLACE."

"Did I hear you say something?" the open chauffeur said, even curious, surprised. "Were you asking direction?"

"Oh ya," Dawes Williams said. "We seem to be moving with others here. Going in the same, opposite direction. I've always wanted to ask a real chauffeur his views on social democracy. What are those views?"

"Move on, John," a voice said through an electric box in the open evening.

"THAT'S RIGHT," Dawes Williams said, staring straight into the back seat, "IGNORE MY DIALOGUE, MOTHER DUDE. BUT THE UPPER CLASSES ARE REALLY GOING TO HELL IN THIS COUNTRY. YOU KNOW THAT? THERE HASN'T BEEN A REAL ARISTOCRAT IN THIS COUNTRY SINCE THE EIGHTEENTH CENTURY HINGED QUIETLY OVER INTO NOTHING AT ALL."

There was a silence. In the stillness the light was changing.

"AND COME THE NEXT DEPRESSION," Dawes Williams said, "YOU WON'T HAVE TO JUMP OUT YOUR WINDOW. YOU'LL GET A PUSH!"

Riding the last half-mile to the dog races, Dawes Williams began thinking about the dudes of Miami. . . . p. 271.

* * *

Soon, however, he was ignoring all of that, standing down by the rail, the brown, pale, manicured track, watching the wide, one-thousand-foot tote-board, made in Cincinnati, which computerized the odds instantaneously.

"You should have heard my grandfather tell about how the old Irish used to computerize the odds with their hands," Dawes Williams said to the railbird next to him.

The green-frocked women in short dresses passed, selling tickets.

"This reminds me of a debutante's birthday party," Dawes Williams said. "It just doesn't smell of worked-over leather and wood. Even the dust smells like vacuumed plastic."

The dogs for the third race were being paraded before the stands, like delicate paramours.

"You should see these dogs run in an open field," Dawes said. "Hell, these dogs won't break."

As they paraded, led by abstract keepers, some of the greyhounds tensed, others were relaxed and even blasé, one was even pausing to take a quick crap before he condescended to enter the short boxes. An attendant soon came with a delicate broom and a gold dustpan to collect the manure and to smooth over the hand-swept dirt with his slippered foot. After going to the mulling window to buy a quick ticket on Cometman's Fantasy, Dawes hurried back to the rail. The last bell rang. The cotton jack began its dull whirl around the track. It streaked out, down the straights, past the iron boxes, they were off, and soon Cometman's Fantasy was seen making the turn. His huge brindle form was loping along relatively, complacently, in the rear of the pack, challenging no one. Like Dawes Williams, Cometman's Fantasy was not worried.

Dawes tore up the ticket suddenly, needing a drink. Taking out his large bottle of ginned orange from his munitions bag, he drank quietly, down by a rail of luminous night. Finally, sticking his head into the bag, he toked-up and everything was suddenly very pleasant; the thick lights blurred beyond, more real; the green-frocked ladies in short dresses passed, selling tickets on the great electric wheel.

In the fifth, a fawn bitch was bumped, going down hard on the last turn, and, coming up lame with a broken leg, she lay down again as if she had been hit with a hammer. Yet she was quiet, nearly quizzical. She lay down against the inside rail, waiting, whimpering softly, as if almost her insides had been carved quietly with a knife. On his form Dawes saw her name was Dandy's Dreamy Love; and rising brokenly, twice, she began finally making her way on three legs down the last stretch of track, to the place where the race finished; still partly frantic dogs were being rounded up by their keepers to be herded back to the kennels. A uniformed attendant came at first, for a moment, trying to lead her; then, finally, picking her up, he began carrying her out. Out back. To be gassed, Dawes knew, because she was only a class B dog, he noted, and because she was no good for breeding or racing. He doubted anyone else in the stands knew it. A crass, well-dressed, horseshit woman, screaming for joy, broke for the pay windows. But he knew it, and he thought the railbird next to him knew it, and he remembered his grandfather, dead Arthur, out by his first pen row where the best pups were kept, in

August, right foot caught through the wire, spitting through his teeth, saying, *Yes, it's a hard damn business, and sometimes it just dries a man, right there on the spot, to see a dog down, Dawes. Happens. Like your gut had turned suddenly to dry oatmeal. Have to gas them, you know, Dawes. Yes, and you have to get rid of the ones with no promise, the hurt ones, the no-good-runnin' ones. You have to be shed of them like shucks in the wind. . . . Hell, every farmer round here's got one of my dogs. But that's no good any more. . . . I ran out of farmers who were willing to take greyhounds the first ten years I was in business. Ya, it's a business, like everything else. You'd been eaten out of house and home, up to your knees in no-good-runnin' dogs, you weren't hard on'em sooner or later. Flesh that doesn't pay, can't eat, Dawes. Wouldn't even be able to take your good stock south or east. Hell, you'd be too damn broke to feed your good blood. Never make a nickel or even break even, but I keep it to a minimum, 'cause it dries a man up to see too much of that kind of thing for too long. Yes, it's a business, but it dries a man up fast to see one of his good ones down on the track, Dawes,* Arthur had said to the boy, listening more, now, to the small evening, red breeze, to the black, rain-wet reach of dark cedar grove, to the sharp yellow walnut stain of air moving about like whispers in his speech. . . .

"Christ, I'm shot," Dawes Williams said softly to the railbird next to him. "But that was the first time my grandfather was even human. He was talking about ruined dogs."

Staring out into the green blurring light, Dawes watched the bitch, Dandy's Dreamy Love (was it only a name, he thought, or had someone noticed something far away, something special, distant and dreamy in her eyes as a pup—the way Arthur sometimes did), as she was being carried down the long track.

He felt suddenly sad. He stuck his head into his munitions bag, toked down a short cigaret in two fantastic swallows and stood against the rail, the whirl of light with tears in his eyes. Suddenly moved into another motion, he decided this was no goddamn place for sentimentalists and went back deep into his form.

In the seventh he was down to eight dollars when he wired JJ's Zippy Crimson and Seaward Lilly into a quiniela. Luckily he was stoned, and the seventh was the race for dogs with names like rhythmic seaweed to be winning. JJ's Zippy Crimson hipped out Dakota Sally on the last turn for second place, and Seaward Lilly broke first from the boxes and won it easily. Blind with fortune, convinced that his luck had finally turned, he made his way to the windows. The bored cashier counted out eighty-five dollars and change and, buying two whiskeys, feeling at ease with his destiny for the moment, he settled in a corner of the establishment to handicap the next race. He bet on Waltzing Verna and Dickey's Doo, both of whom finished seventh.

Over his shoulder he saw a bleached, wealthy-looking woman scream as she broke, quicker almost than the incoming dogs, for the windows. The multicolored whirl of light, electric-sounding jacks, blurred in his mind, easily, without strain, going and merging into impressionistic blotches of color that had sound, and sound that had color, something destroyed, unmourned, not light into shadow, but light onto softer light. Flashbulbs and cinnamon. Velveteen, decadent snakes of Southern air, and by the tenth he was out of whiskey, orange gin, and thin cigarets, and down to fifty bucks.

He took out his pack of Camels and stared at the five tens banked within the cellophane. He remembered everyone he used to know in Rapid Cedar did it that way, late in the early morning. He thought of how Danny Deeder used to be able to give off the impression, like a soft bouquet, he was sitting on his money while making more. He thought suddenly of the card games in Iowa. He decided to shoot his wad.

He stared back into the mathematically square lights of the dog track. The early bells for the tenth race were going off in a bell of air. The railbird's drone of silent mulling mixed itself easily within the multicolored distances, the dresses and shirt fronts, the perfume of the women. And luck, he thought, is only a great turning which only turns back on itself. Always. On itself, not an object, like rhythms. Like memory and time. And the only question becomes when and how much and how do you read it and stop it when it reaches where you want it to go.

And, mindless, the dogs were being marched about again in their tailored blankets like a small, bright parade tagging along behind itself. They pranced in their handwoven stitchings, the flat, manicured air. Dawes sat on the other side of a green-frocked fog and watched it move. It was romantic as hell, and the only question became when and how much and how to stop it. Memory and time . . . a red brindle bitch named Chihuahua's Hat was prancing her frantic head within her leashings. Arthur's blood told him nothing, but another part of his head went off like a bell and he decided someone had slipped her a meatball with a pill in it. And that's the one, Dawes Williams thought, that is the one with my name stitched somewhere within those handwoven stitchings.

Looking back into the electric toteboard, made in Cincinnati, which computerized the odds instantaneously, Dawes Williams saw that Chihuahua's Hat was opening at 50-1. Grasping the square root of 50 instantaneously, Dawes Williams let out a deep, religious sigh and said only:

"Twenty-five hundred dollars!"

Then he turned and broke for the windows. Embarrassed, he found himself full of a greedy success.

He bet his roll. He laid every dime in America on a bitch named Chihuahua's Hat. For a moment, he laid his own wad on the line. He was unworried: he had plenty of worthless books to read, one bottle of orange gin and, besides, he was already developing a vague, foolproof plan for sticking up the First Federal of Miami in broad daylight just as soon as Halloween rolled around again. Arriving at the rail once more, breathless, Dawes found the same railbird standing there, waiting for him, even interested.

"You know," Dawes Williams said, "I'll bet they have a lot of crime down here in the winter."

"Oh ya," the railbird said. "I was wonderin' what you'd be thinkin' of next."

Suddenly, looking back into the totumboard, Dawes Williams let out a long, falling expletive of amazed air.

"What the frigging hell!" he said, elbowing the railbird. "Chihuahua's Hat is falling off the frigging board. I went up to the window at 50-1."

"Oh ya. She's 10-1 now and falling. She's a barometer dog."

"It's raining on my head, all right," Dawes Williams said.

"Oh ya. She'll probably finish even and break her neck coming out backwards from the boxes. It's like betting on turtles."

"There's no logic to it, all right."

"Sure isn't."

"Well, I knew that," Dawes Williams said. "I knew all about that. I just had this feeling."

"Oh ya."

"What's 'oh ya' about it?" Dawes said.

"Say," the railbird said, "aren't you a hippie?"

"Hippie-hippie, yippie-yippie," Dawes said. "Why not, so what?"

"Well," the railbird said, "I thought you people didn't go in for crap like this."

"Don't as a rule," Dawes said. "But I happen to be the only hippie in the world who also happens to be an asshole at heart."

"I see," he said tentatively.

"Is there anything else you'd like to know?" Dawes said.

"Well, as a matter of fact there is."

"Ask me anything," Dawes Williams said. "Don't feel bashful. I happen to think this is really a social democracy in disguise."

"Well," he said slowly, almost hopelessly, looking down at his shoe, "I was just wondering like if . . . well, you know, like the fellas I know always say . . . well, is it true that those hippie girls are the wildest ass in the world?"

"Oh, Christ," Dawes Williams said, biting his tongue, perfectly straight-faced and serious, "let me just tell you this: Next to the great and shrouded Oriental myths of the motionless fornication and the horizontal slit, they are about the most fantastic orally fixated cunt in the world. You can't believe it."

"That's what I thought," he said, nearly dreaming on it, smiling, moving slightly away.

"You dirty old buzzard," Dawes Williams said, smiling back warmly. Ultimately, however, Chihuahua's Hat began rising on the totum. She closed finally at 15-1.

"Seven, eight hundred!?!" Dawes Williams said, swiping the railbird's beer. "I'm in heaven. This dog comes in and I'm going straight to Mexico."

"You got fifty on Chihuahua's Hat?" the railbird said.

"Oh ya," Dawes Williams said. "Good play, wasn't it?"

"Hell, no," the railbird said.

"You're not Green Johnny Miami's father, are you?" Dawes said.

"Don't know," he said, "but that dog, Chihuahua's Hat, is blinded in one eye. Everyone knows that."

"Which eye?"

"Don't know. The outside, now that I think of it. If they run to the left."

"Thank God," Dawes Williams said quietly, "we're all right on that one."

"That so?"

"Hell, yes. All my granddad Arthur Oldham's best blooded running dogs were blinded in the outside eye."

"You don't say! You Art Oldham's grandson?"

"Hell, yes, I am."

"I'll be damned," the railbird said, "that is somethin'."

"Oh ya," Dawes said, "we're all right on that one."

"I'll be damned," the railbird said. "How is old Art?"

"He's dead," Dawes Williams said as the dogs exploded and the boxes went off in the air.

"Dead? Old Art?" the railbird said.

"Dead! Dead!" Dawes Williams said. "Do I need you to tell me Arthur Oldham is dead! He's dead, that's all."

Chihuahua's Hat came in all right; she paid a little over 16-1 in the end. He collected eight hundred and ten dollars at the windows, but somehow the airless night had gone suddenly limp and lifeless at the center's plastic, luminous heart. Deciding he must go straight to Mexico, he left that night immediately for the long, over-the-sea highway and Key West, Fla. . . . p. 292.

It was evening. In the distance was the bridge over into Mexico. He was hungry, tired.

"Christ," he said to himself, "none of this ruck fits together at all."

He sat, soaking still, in the edge of the Rio. He drank a bottle of tequila, ate three cut lemons, shook ten cents' worth of Morton's salt into his mouth. His body was a fixture. Fishing in the last light, in his jeans, he took out the soggy letters from Braun Daniel once again. Before he threw each piece into the water, he read them over forgetfully; but first, in the thin light, he looked over the two photographs: in one, just earnest and proud as hell, as if a girl he never married had just presented him with a baby, with proof of an irresponsible manhood, Braun Daniel was kneeling, thick in the hands and the shoulders, mustached, black in the eyes, smiling back over the snout of a wild boar he had shot with his M-16; in the other, standing among smiling others this time, Braun Daniel was the only one deadly serious in the face, standing overly straight, and in his outstretched hand was a fresh human skull, like Hamlet. . . .

Dusky delta mud for war paint—

Hey Willy, Apage Sathanas!

First sequence, dedicated to Theodore Roethke: (South of Elephant Valley on the Old French Road—Notes to my old buddy BroncoBillyDickDawes). How's the price of cheese? We're being mortared at the moment in Battalion and I'm sitting up here on Chin Strap Mt. watching the show . . . reading three weeks of mail. Sorry to hear you're so much more fucked up than usual, Willy. Last week I lost some men so I'm also pissed off. I'm sure your suffering will vent itself in creative energy. HAHAHA! Willy, start painting, or get an animal or a woman to give affection to. Or go get drunk and wreck Joe's Place. Do you good. Shoot-the-piano-player. HA-HA. But don't shoot yourself. If you get drafted, "Charlie" may do that for you. Anyway, I need your letters. You're mad. I'm a complete savage. I don't try to justify anything any more. I only enjoy the fighting. But the only things worth saving in this country are the wild life for future hunting purposes, and a few trees. HA-HA! We are creating the future over here, however, at least, daily: (1) markets for Japan (2) some Coca-Cola signs (3) the seeds of a new race in the bellies of the peasant women . . . now there's nothing left to do but the cutting of a swath (notwithstanding rain) north to Hanoi! What this country needs is a good ole American march to the sea. (Dear old Sherman.) By the way, *Gone with the Wind* is having a revival in Saigon: all the upper-class broads are going around the streets with flowers in their hair like Scarlett O'Hara. The poets in this country are weeping—I know because I took one out and hung him to a cross last week. The intellectuals have all been taken out and shot long ago. HA-HA. Helped move things along real well for awhile. The Buddhist monks will all be driven underground, or burned up by the end of the year. That'll help, too. Something to look forward to. Anyway, the Korean Marines know what it's all about—they become the new warlords over the South now, day by day.

We sit on our ass, afraid to violate policies and restrictions. There is too little pure confrontation on the part of our politicians. I think when I get back I'm going to change history by shooting the "Hump" or somebody. The mayor of Billings, Montana. Remember, Willy? *When in doubt, shoot the mayor of Billings, Montana.* Anyway, some gutless wonder politician who is sacrificing the blood of my brave Marines. We should—as MacArthur said— NUC them first and ask questions later. Blockade Hanoi. After all, this is a civil war. . . . Oh shit, here I go again . . . sorry. . . . What does it matter? (Remember, drunk on *my* ass, when I said I was closer to Genet than you were . . . to "Sainthood," which is only understanding it all at once . . . and you said I was too mad to be talked to . . . you may have been right after all. . . . I see what determinism is now, and that I wasn't understanding it— i.e., avoiding it, molding it to my own design, though I thought at the time I was—I was only walking straight into it, which is not changing it to my own design, my own purpose, which is not understanding it. . . . I see almost what you meant when you said I was the existential villain in the piece, the microcosm, only being acted upon, only being caught up in the thing, the macrocosm of the machine). . . .

BUT WHAT THE FUCK, YOU'VE GOT TO HAVE YOUR BALLS ON.

And it all pays the same—teaching English or teaching squad tactics— getting hit by a sniper or falling out of a window, stained-glass bureaucratic uncruxifiction either way—serious games, Willy—games of the seasons, each to each, and autumn is coming and ending, Willy, I'll look for you in summer's gasp, or in death, and stand straight in the bright of the leaves. HA-HA. Right. My sergeant, who is under me and over me at the same time, who I could butcher in a fair fight and who would shoot me in the back of the head if I dreamed of calling him out on it, would get me discharged if he read this letter. I don't justify anything any more. HAHA. Who's existential? I'll tell you who—my radio—his name is "Waco," he is run by a man named "Dallas," and he speaks true, real things to me, Willy; or how about my Black Sqd. Leader—his name is J. J. Three-Finger Jack.

Last night I caught sight of the waves coming in off the ocean, Willy, crashing the full moonlight to pieces, a thousand meters off across rice fields, as pale and white as the bones in Tu Fu's beard. I couldn't ever tell it. Below the coastal plain. I sat on the mountain, calling in the fire. The star-fields, the gunships, the groves of bo and tamarind and frangipani trees I was hiding in, so close, a pipe of spider's web, so close, an infrared scope, so close, like finger-squeezed death—HAHA—the pipes and globes of fire, an arch of sea, a listening, a plane carved between light years and crab's claw, and into it all I sent a hook of shells. Calling it home to my head. Artillery: The King of Battles. The Crab Fog of morning and phosphorous cloud mixed with rose; the sun drunk with its own absence of position. A beautiful, lace-winged insect danced beyond, over the horizon, without leaving, in a slow bumblebee's mating in the banyan tree, above my head. Life and Death, Willy.

Teats, write you later,

Second Sequence:

Dear Willy mother,

Living in a cave on Marble Mountain. Mosquitoes so big they fuck the turkeys! Flat-footed! To death! The northeast monsoon is here. And the flowers have died in nonsoluble defoliant. Too bad—HAHA.

You'll be pleased to know we've been dealing the enemy a series of blows up here on Marble Mountain of late—good fine words. (If they'd let me, I'd burn every village in the province.) It had been poor hunting for awhile. A flood, partly my own fault, fucked up the terrain beyond killing. In an attempt to drain the area, I flooded it by breaking down all of the peasant's paddy dikes. It was just bad engineering on my part. (HAHA.) From my position high atop Marble I called in some shells: we had nothing better to do. But I only made the area worse, the captain shit his pants—HAHA—Oh well, no rice crop this year again—HAHA—people to people plus civil action—BULLSHIT strategy anyway. You don't fight on empty bellies—or something like that—Let them eat cake, they been doing that for twenty-five years anyway—HAHA—Busy Busy, Little Bee, Busy—I call it the pursuit of destruction, which, after all, is a creative act.

Have I run out of oxymoron yet? Betcha so.

I sweep areas (when they're not too flooded), lay ambush, blocking force, etc. Got some snipers the other day. Truly golden experience! Opportunity for the virtuous and superior to show his luck. Opportunity for God to show the might and right of American arms. Daily. (I'll write no more poems for awhile, the men I think are beginning to suspect me.)—Right!—It's a bummer. On to Hanoi!! Give me the strength and let my enemies be civilized and give me the will to kill them fast. HA-HA! In this war success is only secondary to statistics. Secondary only to Goodness, Truth, Beauty, Appearance, and every other goddamn virtue. This WAR IS BEING RUN BY OLIVER GOLDSMITH!!!!!! What's the price of cheese back there, Willy? You decadent asshole. Kill Cong.

Your buddy, Braun Daniel

Third sequence:
Willy,

Temperature 134 in the wet oceans of shade. The Cong are gnats. Kinetic. Potentially swarming. Oh yes, were you but here. We're winning this war with Coca-Cola signs; but they're winning it back with resistive strains of syphilis. (In this sense then we may be the Indians in the piece after all.) And it's going to rain again. On to Hanoi on American money, Russian rum and nuclear devices!!??!!

Incidentally, tell Walter Cronkite to either shut up or get over here and butcher somebody quick, or I'll never watch The CBS Evening News as long as I live. HAHA.

It's a damn bummer! But get your shit in one bag and let me know how you're doing. (Why don't you take a vacation over here? Seriously, Willy, you could swing it, and we could shoot the shit in a corner somewhere. Think it over.) Willy, for Christsake, are you dead or alive?

Incidentally, Dawes, you *do* have one or two friends left (me and the U. S. Marines). HA-HA. Here I am protecting your ass (my Marines kill bu-cu bu-cu VC. Hail to the Field Artillery) and your children's children's children's ass, making sure the world is fit for all the good gooks to live in. Right. You bet. And there you are, enjoying it. HAHA.

Because, you see Willy, my shit is finally together.

Not that it matters.

(Putting "Charlie" in a trick can be quite a dramatic, structural problem— HAHA.)

Is Rapid Cedar still safe for Democracy? HAHA. I hear the Black Militants and SDS are burning the cities again. Well, well, the red-necked bastards, tell 'em for me violence gets you nowhere. . . . Well, well (There's a scorpion in the tent), well, we're burning a few cities, but the damn gooks keep trying to build'em back behind Us—HAHA. Yeah. We're all heroes, Willy! HAHA. Yeah. (The gook women all have VD, my Marines all go in the scivy houses after the gook women, my Marines all have VD; it's an old story, a simple formula; I'm disillusioned, though, the new race is all going to be hammer-toothed!) HAHA. Like Jason or Aeneas, or Homer's boy Ulysses-Asshole. (Enclosed will be a poem or two.) I write every day—a trick I learned somewhere to spare suffering—there's already too much sac- rifice by my brave Marines. Kill VC, Death to the Insurgents, Kill VC.

Anyway, the terrain is horseshit—cactus desert from the China Sea inward a couple of miles, then starts the rice paddy (mines, ambush etc.) rising into tangled, jungled mountains, a canopy of thick fuck death (sniper, NVA, leech, snake, rain forest, bamboo

thicket, booby trap and ten-foot elephant grass). Fuck it! Fuck it all. Fuck the whole goddamn country! To NUC it would be a self-release.

I run ambush patrols now all night and am Transportation Officer in a Battalion
perimeter most of the day. Say hi to everybody for me, Willy.

Enclosed are some of the poems:

Your buddy in exile, B.D.

STARFISH

Who sent the grasses
to mob my fingers?
The cactus silk
to make velvet
        of its spines,
twisted within my whispers,
the hedgerows,
bamboo.
There were no men,
no outriders loose
against the night's
unfastening dark of moon.

We lay down our arms,
placed over our heads
the fish's song.

ADVANCE-ADVANCE

Ten men had died of mortars.
And outriders loose against
the sky dressed themselves
with constellations (it
ends this way—a bird flying
at the eyes) we passed them,
almost running, the stars, the huge
liana's dull intestine. (I held my
carbine low.) Was it only the wind—
this whipped direction
this beach of uncoiled grass,
and pressed within us?

There were no men rising
in Orion's belt—it was the wind,
mantis seedling,
death hum,
the shapes shadows take,
moving against the leaves.

"THE CAPTIVES"

Birds of the deep lilies,
 the woman's white, naked hip
  I found in a Buddhist holy place,
   on Marble Mountain,
begin to sleep (in mother's
blue hair). It is September,
and gallinules
 stalk the rice moon
  on silver legs.
The devil rolled his tongue
to the dawn patrol.

Our mission in another valley
 uncoiled his tanager's
  wings.

On the horizon
 we were aware of the sleeping dead
  to be found in mother's blue hair.
Thus she
 was revealed,
  O Madonna of the deep, impossible rock.

Each to each,
 the outlines of ourselves,
  our captive's silhouette.
Later, as we slept,
 beneath a sail of earth,
  sirens made
     the world
       a globe of fire.

Then a ghost cut loose
   in the pointed hills,
       and she came in with her dream of water.
We had almost forgotten.
She sighed.
Our rear guard went down hand
   to a pistol shot.

All his life
he was a fool.

Fourth sequence:
Willy—

From high in the I corps—Read Levi-Strauss' *The Savage Mind* yet?

Beautiful book. How's *your* audience coming? How's your mad, revolutionary critique? How's Iowa City? Tell George Davis at The Paper Store to send me my *Complete
Poems of James Dickey*—or I'll come home and kill him— HA-HA.

Willy, I've almost stopped counting, it's been raining three weeks. Sometimes the
sound makes you crazed. Yesterday we caught three Cong in a hole: grenaded them;
messy. Day before an Am. Trac. went over a mine, a 200-pounder, 100 meters from where
I'm sitting. We Medivac'ed 20 men who were riding it. Three I carried off myself and their
skin hung off like wet tissue, the hair all burned into a rusty-reddish mat. The Negroes,
strangely, looked white. It was a real bummer! HA-HA. Three days ago a command deto-
nated Claymore cut off the legs of two guys, my people, and fucked up seven more. We
killed two of the rice burners slipping away. I have a theory high art looks to life for serious
resistance before oncoming order. I hope so.—Ahhhhh for the War in Vietnam! How you
been, Hyoot John? I'll bring the Marines. Incidentally, I always thought you'd be madhouse as hell in a brawl, if I could have ever got you started. I thought also you'd make a
wicked sniper you ever set your mind to getting into it.

See you in summer,
Braun Daniel

Fifth sequence:

Jesus Christ Willy I can't believe it I lost my 1/2 leg what do I do now Willy kill myself
I'm just lying here I'm finished forever it's over for me I can't believe it it isn't true it's
dreaming I lost my 1/4 leg Willy tell me what to do I'm only kidding, perhaps, Ha-Ha

Dawes Williams got up from the dull stone of the Rio. Part of him was
screaming quietly. Everything, he knew, had a meaning that was meaningless.

He moved down the banks, walking quickly. He felt he had to move now. Before it was too late, before his old buddy Braun Daniel hobbled back to him like Long John Silver, laughing wildly, calling for his leg, literally stringing him to a cross in the name of oncoming order, yes, as he stood there, mute, trying to explain, despite it all, that it was Virgil's poetry and not Aeneas' simple fornication of land they had admired; that, leg or not, that didn't change anything at all, he was still only Don Quixote trying to do Ulysses' thing in a world composed by Jonathan Swift, Fyodor Dostoyevsky and Joseph Hellen; that he, Braun Daniel, sitting up there near a Buddhist holy place, holding a woman's white naked hip in his cave on Marble Mountain, turning it in the light, calling artillery in on rice dikes *and still thinking of it all in tragic proportions, only that,* was, yes, still only the joking ass of God, nothing more. He had only demanded to give up something over nothing at all and call a foolish peasant's happiness good, true, noble and fine. . . .

Dawes continued to move along the Rio in the darkness, moving toward the bridge, jostling only one duffel full of books, some underwear, and two pairs of jeans. He almost wanted to tell the river that he loved Braun Daniel like one on the other was the other's idiot brother; that he hated to say this, even to the water, but one of them was thoroughly mad: there was no in-between any more. He kept moving, with purpose, stopping only to unstring all of his bright rags, ribbons, leather and rings; to smooth down his hair to be presentable at the border. Looking into the nearly dark swirl of the water, however, he saw Braun Daniel, laughing wildly, screaming HA-HA HA-HA HAHAHAHAHAHA within a naked vacancy of air closing behind him; he saw those black, lyric eyes, those eyes like treacherous glass planning snakes that taught fifteen-year-old roosters to walk into bars on command, that taunted Boomer le Roi and Zoomer the Deuce to mount girls at will, who lured uninnocent coeds down to Colcaw's south pasture with promises of only horses and riches of unbelievable lust, who would come into the farmhouse door at evening saying only, with complete ease and happiness (and only a small hint of real psyche irritation)—"Com'on, Willy, let's go to town and eat us a cow."

He moved on, hurrying, still seeing those fat, laughing eyes that only stared back, like a stomach, like a yellow, piercing cat's eye. *Youcrazysonsabitches.* He ignored it. He moved on toward the bridge, rustling the sand and the long night-blooming edges of grass, learning only the small lesson that you carry yourself along, wherever you go; trying to unlearn the Americas myth that by changing place, you are also changing identity. *Youcrazysonsbitches.* Around, near him, foreshortened within the granite mountains, El Paso burned like small fires in the hills, like a reptile's winter stone planted under a periphery of graveyards. *Just an old piece of lead, Simpson said, he said, spinning the old Colt, the old bullet attached to his watch bob. Just two inches lower, Simpson said, he said,*

amazing the Midwestern lawyers' children, shooting red evening, holes, out of the wal-
nuts of sky, Just two inches I say lower, he said, and that Mex had got my lung, he said,
Simpson said. But I had already plugged him dead through his heart—he was already
shooting from memory—so I spoiled his aim some, he said, Simpson said. He hurried on, moon bright, in the near dark, ignoring it. Soon the border. The
bridge. A new life. Free ground. A lie. Thin evening. A drawing up. Closing. He
stood on the bridge for a long time, watching the sky turn, lower than the
horizon almost, becoming a perfect rose stone. Thinking of nothing better to
do, Dawes Williams dropped his last smoking cigaret into the brown Rio, into
flowing-out water, an axis of turning rose and broken fire.

Crossing over, he came to a wooden booth, flat, naked-bulb light, and a
Mexican who eyed him queerly and who apparently understood only slow,
broken English, because Dawes Williams took one look at him and quickly said:

"Just write down Williams, Hyoot John, down there. —That's it!" he said,
smiling, struck by something suddenly. "So one night he just rode down to
Durango and he shot him in drag."

After a few more huddled questions, Dawes passed into the faceless night,
like being reborn and entering heaven. . . .

4

Mexican evening. A horse near a corner, crossing his hooves.
Someone passed selling hats. Suddenly interested in something, Dawes
Williams paused to watch. Finally, jostling the noise, Dawes entered again the
hot Mexican streets, Ciudad Juarez, a place named for an obscure Lincoln of a
Mexican president he had never heard of. Disbelieving his own motion, free of
the car, he found himself staring back, a pair of brown, incredulous eyes,
saying:

"Señor Railroad? Train? *Enginones?* Choo-choo choo-choo?"

"Ahhhh, ferrocarriles! Si! Si! Ferrocarriles, choo-choo choo-choo, un kilometer,"
the stray Mexican said, pointing down an Utrillo's alley of dark, falling streets.

"Gracias. Gracias," Dawes Williams said.

But he was stupefied; the man spoke Spanish. He was just standing there
on the caving street, staring blankly into the brown eye, thinking—what the
hell kind of a language is this anyway—before his Latin began coming back and
he pieced "iron car," or "carrier," out of the jumbling chaos of the uniambic
rhythms and a language he couldn't even syllabify.

Shouldering his single duffel, he went on through a dark cave of dry air. Dawes Williams, therefore, Dawes Williams thought, was bound he would go to Mexico and have himself an adventure.

Down at the end of streets, an old gap-toothed woman took him aside somewhere within a crowd. She stood, staring back within a cloud of six shawls, smelling of bursting watermelon, trying to sell him a switchblade knife he didn't want. It was then it occurred to him that he couldn't even count in Spanish, knowing only that eight and a half or twelve pesos made a dollar and that, therefore, the huge centavo pieces weren't even worth carrying, let alone figuring, at one one-hundredth of eight and a half in an economy beyond even inflation. She was adamant, however, and sixty-five pesos was her lowest offer. He declined. She clutched at his throat. Forty-seven pesos was her lowest offer. She ran her rough gap-toothed hand along the pearl inlaid butt, the open blade edge large enough to spear frogs with. He demurred. She smiled, nearly spitting in his face. He thanked her kindly. She ignored him. She spelled out thirty-three pesos with her left hand in the air, her lowest offer, and stuck the knife in his throat. He flatly refused, told her to fornicate with her mother's virginal orifice in English, and hurried on, hoping slightly not to be noticed. Looking back, curious, he saw she was spitting six times in the gutter, cursing and walking violently away. He wondered suddenly if he would need the knife.

The air was a stain. Horses, sway-gutted and swivel-jointed, quietly chewing the gold cud of the evening, harnessed in rotting leather, were crapping easily in the streets. No one came with a broom to clean it up, the night was electric, the leather still smelled musky with rain, and the street never separated up from the earth, but only formed a molten continuum with the broken sun.

He walked on, down the street to the swinging-door cantina. He learned his first word: *cerveza;* his first phrase: *Hasta la vista con carta blanca!* He moved off into the yellow corner. He sat smoking brown cigarets, thumbing the joint, dreaming of catching a train. Soon men were staring, smiling through the black gaps in their teeth. He moved into the street again, finally leaving the huddled nontalk, into the bloom, the cooling walk . . . then he made his way to the station to buy a ticket.

"South. Anything at all going south tonight," he said with his hands, pointing to the far, outgoing wall.

Nothing seemed to respond. No ticket or official-looking paper flew like magic rugs through the slots.

"Hang on here," Dawes Williams said, smiling, "I'm having a hell of a time here."

He walked down to the long, vacant shadow of the aluminum window. Looking out, cupping in the exterior light with his hands, he found his suspicions were confirmed: he had been pointing straight north, back into the Rio Grande. Tired, regrouping, he slumped against the side wall. A woman passed, nearly winking at the rags tied round his knees. He opened his duffel and took out his atlas of the world and looked up Mexico. Making an a *priori* comeback, he was able to decipher that Torreón lay to the south and looked somewhat central in terms of transportation, rail hubs, jumping off in all organic directions at once, and the flow of fenceless goats. Reapproaching, having rapprochement with windows and ticket sellers in wilted shirts, he fared better this time. They finally took his money. He cashed a hundred into piles and piles of multicolored pesos, a great clatter of silver, all of which he threw quietly into his duffel.

"Now," he said, zipping it up like a purse, "*Torreón, Señor. Ab Tor-re-ón.*"

Amazed with his luck, he received a ticket finally on the Nationales Ferrocarriles for forty-four and a half pesos—four dollars and x number of cents for five hundred and thirty miles; a ride on the slow and wooden merry-go-round of goat noise and peace that always sometimes ran once a day, thinking at least the country was in no danger of fascism, train schedules or punctual parades, and not even being aware enough yet to notice that the country hadn't even moved out of feudalism, so it didn't count, so there could be no danger of a national excess of any kind. Knowing firmly for the moment only that travel was broadening, he moved off to the gates.

Dawes sat against the window staring out. A girl with dark eyes, incredibly beautiful and taut, and unaware of it, watched him across the aisle at the end of the train. As he became aware of it, before he had even quite thought of looking back, she would drop her gaze. He went out, passed her dropping eyes, and stood on the nearly open coupling smoking in the long edge of velvet night and the grass of his cigaret. Returning, looking back into her, he knew finally she was only watching the strange zoo of his blue eyes, his kinked hair, his bright rags and leather, the paleness of his only nearly burned skin. Turning to a younger sister, giggling, blushing back at him, he knew she was saying, Sister, I have just seen a strange and muted animal walking through the tribe. What could he be doing here? Where could he be going crossing our hills? It is strange. Soon, however, her mother noticed it, looked at Dawes Williams angrily, and took her away to another car.

Dawes took a blanket out of his duffel and began going to sleep. He curled within the yellow, foreign wood of the seat and stuck his feet out the window. Soon he was up again and interested as, across the tuberculous aisle, this time a bad-lunged Mexican compatriot was pressing a beer against his shoulder and asking him to drink. Constructing a real social democracy, they sat for awhile buying each other beer and passing it around. Swaying easily together across aisles in the nearly motionless train, they began conducting a conversation without words, a composition in genuine, alingual rapport built and erected mainly from finger signals, shoulder shrugs, keyed silences and especially baroque facial gestures. Dawes Williams' mood shifted violently and he began laughing.

Soon the conversation, however, degenerated into fitful silence. Dawes wanted to buy the Mexican another *cerveza* from the passing buckets, but the man was nearly asleep on the sill. Dawes got up. He was in a strange, talkative mood that needed words. Putting his Indian blanket in his duffel, he went to explore the rest of the train. Suddenly, feeling like his own Tom Sawyer, his own dreamer and spinner of twisted destiny, he felt as though he might even be able to stir up an adventure. He began walking up and down the pews, looking for groovy stoned Indians who, he felt, must still be lurking and hiding out in the shadowy corners, moving south in the desert on the motionless iron horse, just waiting for someone to talk over making war on the mathematical tourists.

However, he found none. But at the end of the train was a club car, a burst of smoky light, where he found a group of more Americans squatting over tequila and bourbon and their own tinny noise.

Waiters walked about serving slowly in their disinterested white jackets. Still dressed in his jean jacket, duffel and rags, Dawes Williams walked right in, his scarves streaming around him in the smoke. Somewhere, just between the motion of bending into the chair and actually making contact with the wood, he immediately grasped the fact that what he had found here was a simple American expeditionary force, led by a probably married sociologist-psychologist team of chaperons, followed by a phalanx body of ninny students, that was going to Mexico City to study the natives. He ordered three fast tequilas and began looking around. He walked to the bar and stood looking back at a blonde girl who was sitting at one of the tables, holding forth to a group of reasonably enthralled sycophants. Christ, Dawes thought, a student leader. Crossing the room, he carried in a chair beside her and pulled up short, like a strange horse nosing her trough. She began eyeing quietly his musted jacket and rags, apparently afraid to move, even to breathe:

"Hi there!" she finally said.

Dawes Williams knew that was her first mistake.

"God," he said reverently, "you can speak. I mean English. I been down here, trapped like a dog in this hellish country so long, I nearly forgot what good ole English sounded like."

"Really? How long?"

"Six years."

"Well, that is interesting. What do you do for a living?"

"That's an interesting question," Dawes said. "I don't think anyone's even quite asked me that before somehow."

"Well, we're trained in that sort of thing," she said. "I'm a sociologist, you know."

"No, I hadn't heard," Dawes said. "I'm only just a pearl diver and shark skinner myself. It ain't much, but it's what I do best."

"Well, you know," she said, "we do need people to bring pearls up from the bottom of the sea. Otherwise we wouldn't have them. It's a very useful social function in the end."

"I guess that's so," Dawes said. "I'm a very useful person."

"Well, we mustn't brag," she said. "That's bad in the end."

"I guess that's true. But I like to keep busy. In my spare time I look around for revolutions down here to make money in. Me and my uncle Tom."

"Really, I'm an American myself. Can you tell at all? Probably not—I'm good at disguise."

"I think people are just nuts," Dawes said abstractedly.

"Yes," she said. "I suppose so. You sound American, but look strangely Australian somehow."

"My uncle Tom says it's my convict blood," Dawes Williams said. "He says my real father was once married to a Celtic bushwoman with wild eyes down in Tehuantepec and I've never forgotten it."

"That's so *damn* fascinating," she said. "I love to travel."

There was a silence. Her eyes were wide, as close as they would ever be to dreaming conscious yellow air.

"Yes," Dawes Williams said finally, quietly, "I could tell you were an American night off."

"Really!!?!?!! !?!"

"Oh ya."

"My name's Joyce," she said, loking at him almost seriously.

"No shit," Dawes Williams said. "Mine is Alexis."

"Alexis?"

"Oh ya."

"That's a rather strange name."

"Yes, well, you see my mother, who was a white Russian, you know, was once involved with Rasputin-the-mad-czarist-monk."

"No!" she said, drawing herself up, slightly puzzled. "But that's fascinating, I think. I think I've heard of that. Isn't she married to him any more?"

"No, she's going with this plumber named Justin O'Reedy now. Met him at the Chicago World's Fair."

"I see. But then, as you may or may not know, divorce is getting to be quite a modern problem," Joyce said.

"I'll bet you're working on that."

"Yes, we are. But how did you guess? You must be psychic."

"Oh ya. Runs in the blood. But they weren't divorced anyway."

"Oh? What happened to Mr. Rasputin? . . . or was it Mr. O'Reedy?"

"He died."

"Oh, that's terrible," she said.

"Yes," Dawes Williams said, "death is becoming quite a modern problem."

"Well," she said, musing with her marguerita, eyes drifting off and vague with peace, "it's a greater beyond."

"You know," Dawes said, "you looked just like my grandma Ellen when you said that. It was striking."

"Thank you," she said.

"Are you drunk or something?" Dawes said.

"No, I've only had one."

"How would you like a cigaret?" Dawes said. "I roll my own."

"No," she said. "Not just now."

"Damn," Dawes Williams said.

"I just hope this Mr. Rasputin's end wasn't too painful," she said. "I couldn't sleep thinking of that. Being in Mexico makes one so much closer to death, you know. You may have noticed that if you're an observant person."

"No," Dawes Williams said, "it wasn't too bad once they got finished with him. First they shot him in the head sixteen times, see, but he wouldn't go down. So then they emasculated him with a bread knife, cut off his head, burned him some, dumped lye on his carcass, and threw his bones in the Olga. After that, he began getting a little boiled about the whole goddamn thing."

"BUT THAT'S ABSOLUTELY DREADFUL!" Joyce said, screaming and fussing with herself. "IT'S UNFORGIVABLE! IT'S INSANE IS WHAT IT IS!"

"Yes," Dawes said, "it is. But that's what happens when you get caught up in the natural revolution of the world."

"Yes, revolutions are terrible, unnatural things," she said. "Soon I think we will be able to prevent them."

"That's one point of view," Dawes Williams said.

"You mean there might be others?"

"Jesus Christ," Dawes said, "don't make *me* into the pragmatist in this horseshit dialogue."

"You may be right somehow," she said. "What are you talking about? Do you even *know?*"

"Thomas Jefferson, for example… do you believe in him?"

"Of course. He was a great American."

"Well, then, Thomas Jefferson, for example, said a healthy country should have a revolution every thirty years."

"He was probably just kidding. He meant something else."

"No. He is generally still considered quite literate."

"He must have been just sick or crazy at the time."

"How would you know?" Dawes Williams said.

"Well, it's practically my *field,* isn't it?"

"I feel safer already," Dawes Williams said. "But, no he wasn't crazy. He was a neo-Platonist as a matter of fact—a man looking for Ultimate Form, therefore an Idealist and a Liberal. He did not want to abdicate the crown of Higher Thought processes merely because they were somewhat more difficult and harder to live with. He did not believe in merely codifying what could merely be easily observed and sitting on it forever. He, in short, believed in conception more than perception; mind more than simple eyesight."

"I doubt you know what you're talking about," she said. "Didn't you say you were just a fisherman or something?"

"My uncle Tom used to teach Intellectual History in Colonial America under Noah Porter at Yale," Dawes Williams said ironically. "He never seemed to get anything straight, but I finally managed to figure it all out for myself."

"I don't believe you," she said.

"It's true," Dawes said, almost tearing in the eyes. "But that was long ago, better times, before his wife left him and he shipped out on the last whaler leaving New Bedford, in 1922, to become a world traveler. At night, in his bunk, he read Herbert Spencer and Honoré Balzac. That was the beginning of his second great intellectual excess."

"I see," she said.

"Indeed," Dawes Williams said.

"Well, how's that then?" she said. "Does all of this fit together? I think it all should in the end, you know. Maybe you could just get to the end, skipping the rest, and give me a good, clear declaratory statement. I'll accept that."

"Well, I guess the point is he got very schizoid in the end. Like most nationalists caught suddenly in the real world, you see, he began to be obsessed—like even pre-Marxian Naturalists—with the inevitability, therefore the reality, therefore the philosophic basis, I suppose, of class conflict in the social organism. He became a Communist, you see."

"That's terrible," she said. "What an unhappy man."

"Yes," Dawes said. "He got very schizoid at heart. You see, unlike most American Communists-who-are-anarchists-at-heart, he remained a Tory at heart instead. That's even worse. Because, you see, Communism and Anarchy come together as psychological coin *before* the revolution (indeed, in the antic-ipation of revolution), but Communism and Toryism can only come together (Idealism and Elite Decay) *after* the revolution. And, of course, the revolution never came off, so he remained a very unhappy mind."

"I see," she said.

"I thought you had that in mind when you called him 'unhappy,'" Dawes Williams said. "It's amazing how you grasp onto ideas."

"Oh, perhaps," she said, blushing with pleasure.

Dawes Williams thought, perhaps, he might even get laid out of all this. Though grotesque, the idea did remain, however, somehow pleasant, like taking some great bodily revenge.

"So you see," he continued, "my uncle Tom had a Yale and the Real World thing conflict all his life. He had, on the one hand, Decadent, Self-Reflexive Abstraction and, on the other, Inevitability, Progressive Vision, and Rationalism tainted only by a reliance upon Empiric Induction. In his later years then—you can picture him, can't you, white beard, sad, destroyed eyes—he just walked about the streets, asking which way the revolution went. It seems the masses hadn't read Spencer or Zola yet, let alone Balzac or Marx. It was pathetic as hell. And all I could do was watch it," Dawes Williams said, breaking down, crying quietly.

"There, there," she said, "don't cry."

"I can't help it," Dawes said, stopping completely. "Karl Marx. We know about him, don't we?"

"We sure do," she said. "He was so sick. Look at the sorrow he's caused in this world almost single-handed."

"Yes," Dawes said, "he probably just needed someone sound, someone like you, a sociologist to straighten his thinking out for him . . . to heal him and make him well, a poor, limited man."

"Yes, yes," she said, "how true. If you only knew. It's almost inspirational."

"Say," Dawes said suddenly, "what do you think of United Fruit Company and International Pigs? Do you think they might have had anything at all in bringing sorrow into this world single-handedly?"

"I don't know," she said. "Sounds interesting. Are they some kind of another international rock-group conspiracy or something?"

"Not exactly," Dawes said. "I guess my point is simply this: As a sociologist, wouldn't you say that there are always two sides to every story?"

"Oh, yes," she said, warming up to it, yet closing the subject with the final, finite statement, "that's definitely, definitely true."

There was a long silence. The train rolled south through the desert night, an air in which one dreams of God. Dawes said nothing for awhile, staring at her in an inverted fascination, waiting for what might drop from her mouth next:

"Yes," she said finally, almost disinterested, "revolutions are terrible things. We must prevent them whenever we can find them."

"Some things are worse," Dawes said.

"Just for an example," Joyce said, "we were passing Hidalgo del Parral earlier this evening," she said, pronouncing the thick Spanish words extremely carefully, and with her fingers, from the fat, indexed guidebook she never let loose of, "and I was just pointing out to the group here that one of your revolutionaries named Villa—Pancho Villa, you know—'was shot here while riding in the streets in an open car.' I'll bet that's a fact you didn't know."

"Twenty-six times," Dawes said.

"Yes," she said, reading it off, nearly crying, "twenty-six times. That's even worse than your Mr. Rasputin. I guess," she said with a weary pontificance, "that just proves that violence and revolution are universal disasters."

"Oh ya. Even in Hidalgo del Parral they manage to try and unwrite history," Dawes Williams said.

"You're being vague again," she said. "Watch that."

"Be specific?"

"Be specific," she said. "Tell us what you mean."

"What for? You wouldn't understand it then, either."

"Is it difficult?"

"No. It's just that it's like trying to talk to the *a posteriori* vacuum of an infant. Only in your case it goes beyond that into even *a priori* deficiencies."

"I see," she said. "You don't like me. It's only an excuse, you know, a *rationale*. The truth is that the *only* reason you don't like me is that you don't like yourself."

"Look," Dawes said, "you value people who love you for your mind and personality and intelligence more than you place value in people who just love you for your body, don't you? Com'on, 'fess up."

"Yes," she said slowly, "that's true. That's absolutely true."

"Good," Dawes said, "because I happen to love your body a great deal, but—you're wrong again—I don't dislike myself as much as I sincerely dislike you."

There was a long, tense silence.

"You're just talking," she said. "You can't be specific because... because you're just wimpy and *crazy!!??!!*"

"Well, specifically then," Dawes said, "I only said 'unwrite history' because—if you'll look in your guidebook there—you see they shot Villa fifteen years after all of the shouting was over with. Now: moving into a more abstract vein, what we can further draw from this fact—without a book but given, of course, we have a head on our shoulders—is a literal infinitude of possibility, the one I choose to draw on at this moment, for example, being the idea that Villa was assassinated by just some more average, nun-of-the-mill, right-wing-Studs-Lonigan-Klan-reactionary types because . . . Why? you say. . . . Well, I'll tell you, because obviously only right-wingers would be dumb enough to think that by killing the Man you can also kill the Spontaneous Combustion of Ideas that have sprung up around him. And that, dearie," Dawes Williams said, his voice lapsing off, "is why they shot even him fifteen years too late."

The train rolled on.

"Yes," she said finally, stirring her drink, "the world can be such a wild, vicious, illogical, miserable place sometimes. I'm really quite cynical, you know."

"Oh ya," Dawes Williams said. "I know, I know."

"Yes," she said. There was a pause. Then something like suspicion, twenty minutes late, clicked over in her well-shaped head: "Say," she said, "wasn't that Rasputin a witch or something?"

"No, a priest."

"Oh," she said. "Then I guess he wasn't a witch. I mean being a priest and all."

"Oh ya."

"Say, how was your mother married to him if he was a priest and all?"

"Well, I don't quite know how to tell you this, Joyce," Dawes Williams said, blushing into his Mexican beer, "but they weren't married at all. In fact, we were, all three, illegitimate, outside the circle of God, and damned. We were, however, firmly, vestedly even, you might say, fanatically against Communism at the time, so that saved us some."

"Well, that's not all bad, of course," she said. "I *am* sorry in a way, but then you must look out for the excesses. It's just such a darn shame people will never seem to learn to take responsibility for their actions. These things sometimes repercuss through generations, you know. Still, they were deeply in love somehow, however, though, I truly suppose. That's nice in its way, too, if you think about it. Romance is, you know."

"What the hell are you talking about?" Dawes said, confused.

"Oh . . . I don't know," she said. "Just talking, I guess."

"Anyway," Dawes said, "they were deeply in love. Mother said she never quite got over it. The way he died and all. She said his penis was Eleven Feet Long."

"Yes," she said laughing, "I can imagine a plumber is not a very exciting relationship after an illicit love affair with a priest. Still, the Church is becoming quite modern. You just tell your mother you met a 'someone' who told you to tell her that she'd be a far more happy person in the future if she avoided at all costs going around and getting mixed up with revolutions *and things*," she said, laughing at her own joke.

Dawes Williams, however, was not laughing. Apparently a witless bore, he sat there, a face of perfect stone, naïve and innocent rock, not even grinning back.

"You bet your rose," he said, getting finally up. "Indeed I will."

"Leaving so soon? We were just getting acquainted, Alexis, but I feel somehow I know you so well. I even think I was beginning to like you in a way."

"Oh, that's so damn fine of you, Joyce," Dawes Williams said, nearly blushing, "but I feel I must step over here and speak to your chaperons for a moment."

"Yes! Do! That's John and Dorothy Clavin! They're nearly famous I think, you'll just looooove them. Especially John, such a fascinating man, so complex, so bright. He's so nice. You'll just loooooove him."

"Oh ya," Dawes Williams said.

"Well, Alexis O'Reedy," she said, "it's been a kind of pleasure. You're quite an interesting person really. Take stock. 'Come up and see me sometime.' I just loooooove it here in Mexico so far. You meet such interesting people traveling. People you'd never run across staying at home."

"How would you know?" Dawes Williams said, turning quietly against her. "That's nearly a fainting tautology. And don't you ever, incidentally, call me Alexis O'Reedy—my name is Rumpelstiltskin—that is, you could have vanished me into invisible smoke at any time in this dialogue by merely possessing the sense and sensibility to pronounce my name—and also incidentally I hate my father's blood, not because he was mad and mystic, but only because all he could think to do with it was to become the prince's pet canary-bird."

"Perhaps," she said, "but I doubt it."

"Talking to you," Dawes Williams said, turning away, "is like waking beyond a pointless metamorphosis, like being encased still in a dream, in a vase and sleeping cocoon of fluttering butterfly butter, and not being able to pass through the thick gold wind to the other side of . . . anything at all."

Then, wishing he had a serape like a yeoman's rope cape flying in a melodramatic wind, Dawes crossed the swaying room of the Mexican railroad car. Immediately, approaching, he spied John Clavin and his wife, Dorothy. John Clavin, with all of the good mothering qualities of a stern, learned sheepdog fixed to all points of the air around him, was holding easily forth. Dawes Williams, uncredentialed interloper in rags, came closer to the huddled, sociological nontalk, cleared his throat, and said:

"John Clavin, I presume. Don't rise, sir. Excuse me, I haven't time to introduce myself just now, but you frigging people must be out of your frigging minds."

"Huh?" John Clavin said.

"Don't be an ass," Dawes Williams said. "There is no in-between any more. Mind if I join you two? You probably don't know this, John, but you happen to be voyeuring this flock of goddamn, insentient nitwits and ninnies across this wine-dark sea."

"What did you say?" John Clavin said.

"Do you suppose I could buy you all a drink?" Dawes Williams said, pulling up his chair.

"One certainly meets quaint, alienated characters when traveling," John Clavin said, turning theatrically into the general audience of silent glasses.

"Have you ever read *The Monk* by Matthew G. Lewis, Clavin?" Dawes Williams said.

"No, I don't believe I've had that pleasure," John said.

"I've never finished it, either," Dawes said, trying to order mescal all around, settling for beer and margueritas, "but I understand it. Have you finished *Oscar* Lewis then, at least?"

"Oh, yes. Wasn't that the fieldworker who did some sort of day-to-day thing down here?"

"Oh, Jesus Christ," Dawes Williams said.

In the silence that followed Dawes began fishing in his jean jacket for pesos. Waiters passed in their disinterested white waistcoats. Dawes begins calling for drinks all around.

"Yes, John," he said, lighting a small black cigar, "as I was saying: One of us is certainly mad as a hat of yellow air. There is no more in-between any more. That's absolutely positive. I'm nearly certain of it."

"Where did you come from. What's your *background?*" Dorothy Clavin said impulsively.

She was a tall, nervous woman who looked as if she often chewed her fingers late at night after sneaking volumes of Conrad Aiken in the bathroom.

"Me?" Dawes Williams said. "I been down in Oaxaca, shaking dry grass at the sun, praying for an Indian rain. I'm a shark skinner. Damn few of us down there any more. My uncle Tom showed me everything he knew about skinning sharks when I was a boy. Oh ya. My uncle Tom has about the neatest shark knife I ever saw. Says he's going to give it to me when he dies. Neat, man," Dawes Williams said.

"I see," John Clavin said.

"Like hell. Huck Finn smoked a lot of dope in that corncob of his, you know," Dawes Williams said. "He didn't do all that social seein' over just some measly tobacco and river air, you know."

"Oh? Really? I hadn't heard," Dorothy said. "And just where did he get this magic smoke in the middle of Missouri, in the middle of the nineteenth century?"

"Oh, you know," Dawes said, "it's always around."

"I *see,*" Dorothy said, trying hard to be catty.

"Do you people really start from nothing and *learn* your personalities upward from rote arithmetic?" Dawes Williams said.

"And what else did you do in Oaxaca?" Dorothy said, trying to ignore him.

"I don't think you're taking any of this serious enough, m'am," Dawes said. "But, just for the rec, I mass-produced electric God masks out of Coke bottles and Christmas tree lights down there in my spare time, and sold them to the Mexicans. That played out in the end, though. There wasn't any real living in it.

Those people were into a different sort of a stone, so I went to Mexico City, becoming a diamond hunter and adventuring shoeshine boy for awhile."

"There aren't any diamonds in Mexico City," Dorothy said.

"Oh ya. That's what I found out," Dawes said. "Anyway, I went back to Oaxaca and everything was all right for awhile, but then my uncle Tom got mixed up with mescal and this whore of a Norwegian princess, he took to beating on me again, and then one night finally they stole all of my best shark skins and eloped down to Basse Terre in Point-à-Pitre, trying to revive sugar-plantation slavery and romance, doncha know."

"That's too bad," Dorothy said.

"No, turned out fine," Dawes Williams said, "because on the way down my uncle Tom tried to stick up a banana boat—it's a long story—but now the sono-fabitch is rotting up in Yuma prison and it serves him right because now, you see, the Norwegian woman came back to Oaxaca and thinks she's my mother. She's a real fine bitch and treats me good. I've got to get back to her, I tell you."

"That's quite a story," John said.

"But what I don't understand," Dorothy said, "is how your uncle Tom and you got down to Oaxaca in the first place."

"That's simple," Dawes said. "We were born there, both of us. I'm older than my uncle Tom, of course, by five days. But our people came down with the Mormons a hundred years ago and stayed on after the last great reexodus. My granddaddy said he was just tired following all those faggot prophets around the ends of the earth looking for a place to be rich and prosper in. Yep," Dawes said, cutting on an invisible stick, "and now the only thing that bothers me about the whole damn thing is that my uncle Tom took his shark knife out in the rocks, and now he won't write and tell me where it's hid."

"What was your uncle's name?"

"Jason. Tom Jason, the young wizzer. Byron's my name. My maternal grandmother was distantly in love with the poet by that name."

"I see," Dorothy said.

"That's a very amusing attitude, Missus Clavin," Dawes said.

Soon more drinks were brought, and Dawes Williams began laying out long strings of pesos on the table.

"Won it on a dog named Chihuahua's Hat, in Miami, Florida, just before I left directly for Key West on my way to Mexico," he said quietly.

"I see," Dorothy said.

"Anyway," Dawes said, "what do you do when you're not running around seeing things?"

"I'm sure I don't know. But thank you for your generous drinks. Incidentally, you *may* call me Dorothy and this is John."

"Oh, my God," Dawes Williams said, smiling. "It's Dorothy and John. Do you think you people will be ever successful in purging society of anyone who is talented at anything at all?"

"What do you mean?" John Clavin said.

"You've got me there," Dawes said.

Soon everyone was sipping on salty yellow margueritas. Dawes lay back easily within his rattan chair, drew on his long cigar, and said:

"Say, John and Dorothy, what do you two like to do in your spare time?"

"What do you mean?" John said.

"Do you mean *recreational* pursuits?" Dorothy offered.

"Yes," Dawes said. "I mean, for example, John, do you ever sodomize Dorothy here in the name of scientific investigation into the field of possible neurotic mores and folk ways?"

There was an uneasy silence. Dawes noticed suddenly everyone seemed to be staring at him unreasonably.

"Well then," Dawes said, "if not—what do you two think of the novel as still being the only possibility of literacy and communication in the modern world? Do you two still read newspapers? Do you have an opinion on that? Are opinions valid things any more, do you think? Is validity a valid thing any more? Can we permit ourselves even the luxury of making tautologies with certainty any more? Do you think you are even here? If so, upon what sort of research is this assumption based? Is it valid? Can you ask this? Is your inductive ground sound? Have you ever dreamed of being locked in a black, thoughtful closet? Do you feel guilty about this dream?"

"See here!" Dorothy finally got out. "If you insist upon *larceny*, I'm afraid I'll just have to ask you to . . ."

"Now, now, Dorothy," Dawes Williams said, "you're indulging your passions in this. If you'd just look at this objectively for a moment, I'm sure you'll see that if we can ditch John here in Mexico City, we should be able to start a new life in Rio by May."

"What an absolutely hateful *outlaw*," Joyce interjected nearby. "I'm sorry, John, I really feel somehow this is all my fault somehow."

"Youidiotcunt," Dawes Williams slurred through his tequila.

"WHAT!!!???!!!" Dorothy Clavin said.

The room was large with a tense yellow bloom of smoke that rolled out just as suddenly with the shift and motion of the rails.

"I said," Dawes said, drawing himself up to his fullest baroque extension without leaving his chair, "that youcannothelpit. You know not what you do. Besides, neither can I. I've been stone drunk for seven months now. It's been a heller for me ever since my uncle Tom's aunt died looking for likely export items in Guatemala City."

There was a threadlike silence. John Clavin continued drinking his marguerita. His eyes were pursed, serious. Looking back, Dawes said:

"Outstanding damn drink, eh, John? Think ethnic, what? We've got a hel-luva bond of country here as the imperialists once said. Said it, that is, until they stuck them in a black hole in Calcutta and let them sniff their own humanity at close range for a change, eh, John?" Dawes Williams said.

"Look," John Clavin said finally, "what is it you specifically want?"

"Who, me?" Dawes said. "Not me. But 'specifically' seems to be your problem, John. John, Dorothy here isn't doing too bad in spots, but your track form seems to be consistently abysmal. You're just dull, man."

"I really feel your money could be spent *elsewhere*," Dorothy said.

"Nonsense, Dorothy," Dawes said, "only too glad to do it really. Waiter?"

"You . . . you *militant*," Dorothy said.

"You see, John, Dorothy here doesn't do too badly in spots."

"I think you have a problem," Dorothy said coldly.

"I do. Absolutely," Dawes said. "And you two are my problem, John and Dorothy. The witless trying to make the world over into their own simple-minded, fundamental, evangelical image has always been the problem."

"You bastard," Dorothy Clavin said.

"I'll overlook that, Dorothy, because I can see a warm person beats under-neath all that irrelevant floss," Dawes Williams said. "But I see the hate, which will go off like a gun in the fifth act, has been duly introduced in the third. All is in order. The script will play. Denouement is certain."

"Is this *melodrama?*" Dorothy said.

"No," Dawes said, "it is *allegorical* soap."

"I don't think I *understand.*"

"I believe you."

"But will we ever be rid of you?"

"Oz, Dorothy. Go to Oz," Dawes Williams said. "Just climb in, zip yourself up, follow the yellowbrickroad all the way home to imagination and forget me. Reconstruct it, spread flowers, dance in the fragile sun."

"What are you?" Dorothy said.

"Has something gone wrong here? Any damn fool could have figured that out by now."

"What?"

"Misanthropic secular humanist."

"That is quite impossible," Dorothy said. "The two concepts are mutually exclusive."

"Don't you believe in double-whammy, oxymoronic truth or H. L. Mencken, Dorothy, you silly goose?"

"That sounds like a lot of pseudo, half-comprehended, tossed-out termism to me," John Clavin said.

"Who asked you to butt in on this, John?" Dorothy said.

"I thought . . . since I was sitting here anyway. . ."

"Nonsense," Dawes Williams said. "Why can't you two earnest kids just learn to get along?"

"All right. Yes. Of course," John said.

"On the other hand," Dawes said, "if we ever let this become a social democracy, you'll be the first we'll tell, John. I promise."

"You mean I just have to sit here waiting for some kind of millennium, some cattywampus of sophomores?" John said.

"Ride on, John," Dawes Williams said. "That's the first thing you've said tonight that's even approached common sense."

There was a long silence. Several of the huskier social workers were watching John Clavin intently for a sign, for a signal to begin physically attacking Dawes Williams.

"Cool down out there," Dawes Williams said, turning baroquely into this audience of truer, more genuine cattywampus sophomores. "I buy the drinks here, but I don't want you people to break down trying to be this fascinatingly brilliant for hours on end."

There was a tense silence. Eventually things began to settle down, there was a peace, and even Dorothy was beginning to grin when Dawes put down his drink and said:

"You know, John, you have a remarkably vehement patience. I believe most people would have tried to punch me out by now."

"Thank you at least for that recognition," John Clavin said.

"No. That was an insult," Dawes Williams said. "Can I get you a chronological lexicon for all of this?"

"I may throw this drink in your face," Dorothy said.

"Oh boy, would you? That would be dramatic. A real Scarlett O'Hara— the female of the species, eh, John? Incidentally," Dawes Williams said, "what did you get your doctorates in? That might shed some light. Habits of mind and perceptual filter. That sort of tripe."

"John in psychology. I in sociology," she said.

"A real meeting of the minds, eh, gang?" Dawes said, turning into the maddening crowd.

"I hardly would expect you to know anything about it," she said, visibly calming and truly vengeful now, drawing back and waiting for a cold, long-reaching, sure kill that would leave marks.

Taking out a piece of paper, however, on which he had written while sitting with Joyce and which said—"I in sociology. John in psychology"— Dawes Williams gave it over gratefully to the two of them with the comment:

"I had this notarized five minutes ago in the presence of a notorious public pubic."

There was another long, tense silence in which John and Dorothy and Joyce sat seriously contemplating their own design without, however, the nuance of actually quite thinking about it.

"Of course, that explains it all," Dawes said finally, quietly.

"Explains what, would you be so kind?" Dorothy said.

"Structured learning. Too much structured learning. Rots the brain, you know. Dissolves the *a priori* mind, the witch's eye, you know. Damn terrible, degenerate thing to have to see, I tell you."

"No, I didn't know," she said. "And *that,* of course, finally reveals you."

"Unfrocked mask," Dawes Williams said. "Oh damn."

"What I mean is," she said, "is simply that you display only the typically— fantastically typical—classic undergraduate attitudes. The *common* rationales and paranoias, I might add, of the limited student."

"Fuck off," Dawes Williams said, yawning, looking as if he were about to turn in for the night. "Dorothy, you were the only hope we had, but I really feel you may be beginning to lose your stuff."

"I don't see how you could *presume* to know something you're not even acquainted with," she said, sitting back, contented.

"You know, Dot," Dawes Williams said, "I just wish Jonathan Swift could have met you both. He would have finally made his real breakthrough in time-space geography. Thinking you utterly mad, zany, things to be cared for, lovable like pets, or children who knew no better, he would have loved it greatly, spinning your naïveté on the top of his delicate petard, fascinated by the twirling, correspondent wonder lighting up the wide toys of your eyes. Because you know, Dorothy," Dawes Williams said quietly, slowly finishing his tequila, finally tying off his last, blue Straight-Arrow Lone-Ranger bandanna around his forehead and under his hair, "you would have made a fantastically inadequte Druid witch."

There was a silence; green pots coming off brown in the air.

"Thank you," she said, knitting her brow, chewing a finger.

"No, that was an insult, too," Dawes Williams said. "Something's gone amiss here. I'm just not being understood. Would you like me to send out for a *dramatis personae* for all of this?"

"Are you playing Lear?"

"Just now I am playing Young Geoffrey Firmin Among the Society of Mothers, Fools, and Mestizos Watchers."

"I don't think I am following you."

"That's not my responsibility."

"I'm bored, actually, I think."

"Listen," Dawes Williams said, "screw on your ole bonnet of an attention span, Dorothy, and try concentrating on this very hard for awhile. Ready? Any," he began, "social *science,* a contradiction in sanity to begin with, constructed like soft religion upon absolutely relative *knowledge* drawn from structured learning, *reason,* and assimilated *research* is mostly dangerous bunk that operates on the level of self-confirming prattle. It is not only an illusion in progress, a highly *pseudo* exercise, it is actually recessive in nature. An outgrowth of pragmatism really, it remains true to itself—the merest rote function—the great and inferior butterfly ghost of this century—and it, therefore, ranks unintuitive, unimaginative, unstoned and non-*a priori* disciplined social scientists—the great and misled butterfly nets of this century—a *great* deal lower on the chain of being than Celtic Druids drunk on the witch's eye of the moon. In fact," Dawes Williams said, "when one is drunk enough, one is more than tempted to say that *all* backward-moving evil in this century which cannot be directly traced to that false, unquestioned god mask Technology can be indirectly, irrevocably and finally traced to the nub-headed priests of that electric god mask, to social scientists—i.e., the New 'Methodists'—the leading ninnies . . . and ninn-y-poops."

His voice tailed off. He noticed next that a general pandemonium erupted everywhere at the last, falling stroke of his soliloquy. He didn't care. He noticed that they were attacking him. He noticed that Dawes, the hero of the piece, was being beaten and shoved and ganged by three or four social scientists at once. He noticed they were out to kill him, that Joyce had her hands around his throat, yet was managing somehow to beat him furiously with her high-heeled shoe. It swung in the air like a beige machete. It fell silent, cracking wood. The yellow lights whirled, danced out, spun through their own centers. Thinking he had been kind enough, stupid enough to tell them what they were, he ignored it for awhile. Then, caught up in it too, he lashed out with a bottle and a chair. He knocked something down, kicking it twice, full of joy. Then someone, faceless as twirling shadows within the rails' motion, side to side, succeeded in opening a seven-inch horseshoe gash around his brow, under his eye, with a Mexican beer bottle smelling like a bloom of red and dirty wash. Dawes, however, the hero of the piece, succeeded in getting a knee in someone's groin, a good back-swinging elbow in someone else's eye. He decked Joyce with a soft right to the gut. He wondered if it was a dream. Finally Dawes, lost within his own design, decided he was getting murdered and enjoying it immensely. He thought only: HotDamnForBroncoBillyHyoot-WhoRidesAgain.

He went down hard, a false slip, skating on blood. He lay, throbbing within parallel rails, listening to the frantic, uniambic Mexicans, to the brown pots of mulling conversation and opinion streaming everywhere around him, but with a wide humanity. He seemed to go under something, a great raft, small, thundering fog, and he lay watching Dawes Williams' blood running with the stale brown beer and the sandy-alkaline grass out the door, off the clattering couplings, and down south into Sinaloa. Amused, he smiled for the heaven of it. God Bless Me, he thought, a War with the Social Scientists is forming. His last thoughts were of Dunker, Eddie, Travis and Barney Redwood. He crawled under a table and tried to sleep, dreaming of social democracy, wishing he had spent less time shooting the pool of books, and more learning to bust a motherless beer bottle over a social scientist's head.

After awhile he saw the Mexicans were breaking it up. They were unpiling the heap, pulling the furious social scientists off the table, pulling the stoic table off Dawes Williams. There was a tremendous silence, the stillness of paper bombs. The wet ruck, split wood and broken glass drifted about the edges of the car like windless snow fences. Dawes watched as the treacherous social scientists drew off into the corners. They stood, arms crossed, daring him to rise. He ignored them for awhile, sitting alone, table gone, arms draped over his Indian-style knees, defeated, smiling back, wondering what moral lesson he could teach them next. His shirt was full of blood. Scratching his head finally for effect, standing, completely happy, he looked around and found he stood once again within the City of Man. Disappointed, he said:

"BUT I LOVE ALL YOU SWELL BASTARDS. ALL YOU SWEET LAMBS AND FISHY CHILDREN. HELL, YES, EVERY ONE. AND TO PROVE IT, BY GOD, I'LL BUY EVERYONE WHO HAPPENS TO BE ON THIS TRAIN, THIS MAGNUM REPUBLIC, THIS SOCIAL DEMOCK, A GODDAMN MEXICAN BEER! HELL, YES, EVEN THAT GODDAMN WONDERFUL NINNY'S BEHIND, DOROTHY."

As he said this, he noticed they were coming for him again. But the initial passion was spent. This time, ritual and dance beginning again, it was only carried off with a disinterested, expired heart. Still, it was nevertheless pleasant, quietly heated, like opening veins in a warm bath, at least until Dawes, the hero of the piece, spoiled it all by going down for a long count, senseless to the senseless floor, smelling only the brown varnish of time, and hearing John Clavin, pale as a vacuum in a rose of space, calling behind him:

"PLEASE! PLEASE! WE'LL ALL BE DEPORTED! STOP THIS! I THINK I'VE HAD ALL I CAN STAND!"

"You bloody butchers in German nurses' robes," Dawes Williams said, "trying to get rid of the evidence, the *prima facie* body again, aren't you? You're rigging the *corpus delicti,* the history, the chronology and actuality of the event on me again. You are. Aren't you, you bloody and impure, obscure monks and nuns . . . mother-fuckers?"

"Now, now," Dorothy Clavin said.

"Don't worry about taking care of me," Dawes Williams said. "Heal thyself."

"Now, now," Dorothy Clavin said.

"Here I Stand," Dawes Williams said, "nailing my papers to the god eye of the Mexican desert, constantly being ass-ended by children dressed up as sociopsychopathic surgeonheads. Who would believe it?"

"Now, now," she said, openly fearing the police.

He turned against her. She saw his eye in the yellow light, the side-to-side motion, and she nearly fainted. Still, in the dark, round the corners of her mouth, he saw a smile, nearly decadent, caught up and enjoying itself.

Then, turning him, they led him down the sleeping hallway and toward their compartment. Some pieta, her . . .

"Oh, boy," Dawes Williams said, "this is working out fine. I couldn't have planned it better. Now we can all go down into the belly of the Pullmans and play Pietà for awhile. Wait'll my uncle Tom gets out of Yuma prison in sixteen years and hears about this one."

"Stop it, Byron," Dorothy said. "When are you going to break through all of this and say something you really mean?"

"Oh ya. Wow. Soon," Dawes Williams said. "Oh ya. Wow. Wow wow."

Then, going down the long edge of the hallway, sleeping like soft money, he paused, fell slightly behind, and slapped Dorothy Clavin squarely on her playful butt.

"Incorrigible," she said, laughing, moving away.

"That's right. I'm a real randy boy," Dawes Williams said.

"Don't get too close," she said. "Don't bleed on Mama. Don't smear her, don't touch, she's going out tonight."

"But seriously, Dorothy," Dawes said, "you have a real fine ass for a sociologist. Real fine, real fine—eh, John?"

"Oh, do'no," John said abstractedly. "I suppose so."

Dawes and Dorothy laughed, nearly excited, and moved down the hallway like children, ahead of John. The taut sound of her ass had resounded and fell away. In the compartment finally, Dorothy was forcing his head still as she held a cold compress of rags under his nose. John was standing, humming My Gal Sal, pressing the open sore that was Dawes' forehead closed with tape.

"There seem to be so many incredible things I could say just now," Dawes Williams said, "I don't know where to begin."

"Be quiet," she said.

"But damn it, I'm bleeding all over myself. I'm making a damn mess of everything. It's my Celtic soul. I need this blood—it's all I have."

"Be quiet for awhile," she said.

"Are we doing a postsurgical liturgical here? And the hell of it is: How will I even convince anyone any of this really happened? That's the hell of it. This is incredible. Even I admit it."

"Just be quiet now," she said.

"But how does one say: I've once been ass-ended for life by a wandering, helpless, semiliterate band of nearly unconscious do-gooders? Is there a parable here? Oh my, oh my, we laugh 'til we die."

"Just be quiet," she said.

"I can't. This is the part where I am always struck dumb by the fact that, despite it all, I am only replaying the life of Jimmy Stewart. Just a lovable, helpless boy at heart shooting down the vanquished, the unwashed and the seriously stoned. This is dreadful. Hear that latent, cracked falsetto, full of both choirboys and disbelief, that unbelievably nonidealistic comic undercutting, that self-forgiving, American twang?"

"Yes. Of course. Be quiet for awhile," she said.

"Listen. I want to ask you: How do you even broach something like this? Do you just walk up to someone in the street, a horse parked on a corner, evening perhaps, and say, 'Excuse me, I've just been whipped into near lividity by a bunch of sociopathetic sociologists. What do you think of that?'

"Are you Don Quixote?" she said.

"Do you have to get everything backwards, Dorothy? He only believed in charging down things that never were. It seems that I am being legitimately run over by things that are but no one will believe it."

Meanwhile John, who was still wiring Dawes' head like the revolution of '76 conducted in an orchestra of gauze, had switched to *Has Anybody Seen My Gal?* and was putting the finishing touches on the corners of Dawes' new scar with needle and thread.

"Sinew and old whalebone, some stitchings I'll long treasure—eh, John? My own personal stigmata to prize and go with thou. That's a real fine thing to have a thing like that."

"It's going to be a real fine scar, Dawes. Looks like it hooks around there with a real asymmetric flair. A real game of horseshoes. Looks like it goes with the one over the other eye, like wings—how'd you land that one?"

"Just pool cues dueling at the wizzing cans in the fiery alley at midnight, John," Dawes Williams said.

"No," Dorothy said, "I think they look more like networks of small, thorny vines growing up about your eyes, Dawes."

"Oh ya. Always wanted a pink star in the shape of a newborn calf on my forehead myself. I may become the living Rorschach. But seriously, Dorothy, you should'a seen the other guy."

There was a silence in which Dawes studied them.

"Dawes?" Dawes Williams said.

"Yes. We looked in your wallet when you were out," John said. "Also, your share of the bribe to the Federales came to slightly over four hundred pesos. Otherwise, we'd be heading north out of the country already."

"Hell, yes, on an ass. We could have held Palm Sunday in El Paso."

"Also," John said, "your share to the porters came to another four hundred pesos. They were very happy to get it."

"So, under the pretense of wanting to know where to send the body, you robbed me. Is that it?"

"No, but we were interested in where you came from. Professionally, I must say, we were a little surprised to find you were an Iowa boy."

"Oh ya. We get books smuggled cross the borders and everything out there now."

"Dorothy still doesn't quite believe it. You always travel under an alias?"

"I've got to."

"Why's that, Dawes?"

"I've got my reasons, I guess."

"What are they?"

"Give me time. I'm working on that. Look. I trust you people. I even love you people. You look like good, trustworthy Americans who pride yourselves on your responsibility and I'm going to tell you the truth. The truth is: I'm working for the CIA."

"I don't quite believe that," John Clavin said.

"Oh, wow," Dawes said. "But damn it, John, what good does it do for me to tell you these things if you never believe me?"

"What do you mean?"

"I mean, John, how can you assassinate the mayor of Billings, Montana, successfully if you don't take the trouble to establish reliable cover as a Communist sympathizer traveling in Mexico? I ask you: How?"

"Cover?"

"Hell, yes, cover. Everyone knows about cover. You just can't go out and do these things bold face, you know. You got to work at it. It's a slow, tedious thing. It takes time to do these things right. Hell, you just can't go out and shoot a right-winger unless you're a left-winger posing as a right-winger, a fanatic, and you can't just be running about shooting a left-winger unless you've taken the trouble to become a right-winger posing as a left-winger, so that everyone thinks finally you must be a plastic left-winger posing as a right-winger who is really, after all, just another left-winger who doesn't know any better. Hell, everybody knows that by now. Where you been hiding, John?"

"I don't think I believe any of this even figuratively," Dorothy said.

"Yes. The literal mind has been having a hell of a time with itself in this century. That's sure," Dawes Williams said.

"Hold your head still, Dawes," she said. "You're starting to bleed again."

"Hell, even solid ole Chaucer himself messed around with Machiavellian stuff like this. There never was a new cultural thing. Only the numbers have gotten bigger."

"But you can't expect to shoot the mayor of Billings, Montana, in Mexico City. You'd at least geographically agree to that, eh, Dawes?" John Clavin said.

"Your naïve wonderment is touching, John, but of course you can. Especially if you're only doing it in your mind. Don't you believe in Divine Immanence any more, John? Besides," Dawes Williams said, "the mayor of Billings, Montana, *lives* in Mexico City any more. Everyone knows that."

"I see," John Clavin said.

"John, I'm not angry any more. I love you like one of us was the other's idiot son and needed caring for, and I'm not even remotely trying to make your wife now, but the hell you do."

"You certainly are *frank*," Dorothy said, smiling.

"Well, anyway, whatever, it's all over now," John said. "All that is left is your share, the forty pesos you owe on the breakage fee."

"Hell, yes, fascist rent, feudal taxation, glad to pay. Worth every penny. To teach you a lesson, your own humanity, eh, John?"

"That the lesson?"

"Well, the irrelevant, abstract one. The real one happens to be: That though the peasants are sleeping with the mulling chickens in the back of their own trains, the Federales and waiters, the porters of society, are collecting rent up front."

"I see," John Clavin said.

"How could you? That's only the background. The lesson is only that *nobody,* none of them, not even involved, not even detached—the sleeping porters, the assimilated Federales, the busy waiters—even knows what has taken place. That's the lesson. Marx yes, but Camus and Sartre are the important parts. Because if the moral necessity of knowing is felt enough, the changing will follow so naturally the act of changing will evaporate. You see, the only immoral act is the absurdity of not knowing. That's what is really wrong with this train and makes you sick in the guts."

"That's utopianist, I think," Dorothy said.

"No, it's easy, once pride is given up," Dawes said. "You see, it was axiomatic to the naturalist that my only function in life, cultural and political, as a average man, was to seek out and follow the gifted and the genius-like wherever I could find them. This is easier, of course, with real scientists who can put the sum creativity into three concrete letters squared; it is somewhat harder with the somewhat more elongated, abstract cultural genius."

"Education is the answer," Dorothy said, tapping her fingers.

"Not as we know it today," Dawes Williams said. "But that's where you two come in. You can't. That's why I hit you with a Mexican beer bottle."

There was a long silence. But soon, entering and exiting at her own will, Joyce came in with a bourbon.

"Here, drink this all up," she said. "It'll do you good. Fix you up and make you whole again."

"Alcoholism *is* becoming quite a modern problem," Dorothy said, looking almost snidely at John.

"Thank you," Dawes said to the girl, "you are a prince. The monk's own wormwood nun."

"Friends?" she asked.

"I will if you will."

"I will if you will."

"Friends."

"Friends!"

She left, happy with assurance and contentment.

"What are you going to do with that idiot, John, when I am gone?" Dawes Williams said.

"Don't say things just behind people's backs, Dawes. It's a bad tactic," Dorothy said. "Really. It makes them *paranoid.*"

"Well, she's got real reason for worry," Dawes said.

"I think, Dawes," John said, "that once you're gone, thanks to your revelation, we'll just have to concentrate upon making her into every bit the general personality you are."

"I wouldn't wish that on a dog," Dawes said. "But seriously, John, while I hate being this consistently baroque all the time—just what the hell is a 'general personality'?"

"Skip it," John Clavin said, beaten down, walking to the window, looking out into the moon of the Mexican scape, "you wouldn't understand my problems."

"Sorry, John," Dawes said, "I don't mean to keep picking on you."

"It's all right! It's all right!" he nearly screamed back.

"I guess only the affect of the fixation ever changes," Dawes Williams said. "Let's talk about sex, religion, macroeconomic politics, something easy. Do you people have any opinions on that?"

"Have you been chewing peyote buttons down here, Dawes?"

"That's an interesting, reactionary thought, John. But I don't need that stuff. Just give me a rolling train, some moon-shell land to look at, some nearly hallucinating cactus juice, and a band of ungypsied social workers not knowing *a priori*—*a posteriori* from rote and I'm happy as hell. A real human carnival as exciting finally, perhaps, as the Iowa State Fair."

"You can't be happy, Dawes," Dorothy said.

"I am," Dawes Williams said. "I'm happy as hell! Leave me alone. I have never been this wet, this goddamn drunk. Besides, happiness is not the end. Misery is. Happy people, people like Braun Daniel and Hyoot John, have the energy to commit war, breeding and every other horseshit thing that comes off in this world. Give me a really psychotic Christian full of ashes any day."

"Then what's wrong?"

"This dialogue, that's what's wrong. It can't be real. We'll never get away with it. *They* won't let us."

"But you're really not going to shoot the mayor of Billings, Montana, when you find him in Mexico City," Dorothy said. "You *know* that. You *promise* me that?"

"Of course I'm not," Dawes Williams said. "Get ahold of yourself, Dorothy. That's not real. That was all a lot of conversational nonsense. A lie. A fiction. An illusion and fabrication of mental electricity. The fact is: I'm not even stopping in Mexico. I'm just passing through. Actually, the truth is: I am headed south, into the mountains of Colombia, to look for the relics of Ché's bones."

"Dawes!"

"Oh ya. Got a good chance, too. Met this Cuban brain surgeon, down on his luck, in Dallas, Texas, who sold me a map where to look. For only twenty-five more he sold me the last letter Ché ever wrote telling how to read the map. I can find the place . . . no trouble . . . soon as my uncle Tom gets out of Yuma prison, shows me where he hid his shark knife with the Mayan engravings on it so's we can piece together the other half of the mystery."

"What did the letter say, Dawes?"

"Don't know yet. That's the only hard part left. It's in damn Spanish (wouldn't you know it?) and I haven't found anyone able to read it to my satisfaction yet. Met an old tequila head up in Juarez who took one look at my letters and said 'twern't nothing more than an invitation to a Mexican wake, but I don't believe that. Do you?"

"Don't shake your head so much," Dorothy said suddenly. "I think it's beginning to bleed again."

"I got trouble," Dawes Williams said. "My seams are unweaving themselves."

"At least we know the wound is real," John Clavin said.

"Oh ya. We know that much. That's sure. *In dolore sum propter sum.* It's a real comfort to me in my old age," Dawes Williams said, fainting, going to sleep.

There was a convexing merging, dark shapes, a dance, a ring of wine bells. He dreamed. They were so far, so far away. It seemed strange almost, so alone, an inch away, trapped in a mask of water, knowing they were this alone, too, yet it was impossible, *still even here a matter of definition, words, gestures,* to tell them. That was his distance, his dream. And in the beginning of his dream he thought, Why not? I might as well dream. I've done everything else but jump from the singing silo of a hat and die doing taps on the table. But none of this damn metaphysical dreaming for me, he thought. And then he thought he heard Dorothy say, John, this damn boy is fragile and lost, as she set him down like a fragile, broken plane, a surface, and turned away.

Yessiree, all it takes to make a good murder is two or three really pissed-off people, Dawes Williams knew . . .

Waking, a morning flat with ones, he saw the train was parked quietly in Chihuahua, Mexico. There was one sun, an entire window of it, and his mind was a single red explosion of sound. It shattered him and left him still trying to sleep. Looking down the long barrel of his duffel, Dawes Williams found one naked foot as it stuck from the shoeless window; and finally, recognizing it, he saw it was a destroyed thing, burned to a crisp.

He thought perhaps it was noon. He felt wasted, thin, destroyed, and he knew the light was passing through him. He knew if he went to crap he would pass his own heart, his brain which was only a beating red tuber, a cloud of flesh, attached to the simple root of his medulla on a cord of feeling.

He thought he slept for awhile. He wasn't sure. But the conductor was shaking him again, collecting the pillow Dawes Williams had clutched furiously within him in his sleep like an inanimate doll of flesh.

Then Dawes began looking at the brown, matronly, milk-teated woman who was wrestling quietly with a baby's head just across a space of seats. It was almost pleasant for awhile, watching her, seeing her filtering the fierce noon light away from the baby's awareness with her breasts. In the end her image saved him. He began thinking of the dreams of the night before *No, Lady. Jesus, Lady, not here.* of John and Dorothy Clavin and of his fantastic ride *No. Not right here on the spot, Lady,* on the fantastic train, deep in the goat belly, when *No. Sweet Jesus, Lady. Not in public,* she did it: With one motion, a diver going off cliffs into the sea, she brought up the baby's awareness and she, brown woman, began flopping the huge white noon of a crayon teat against its chin. He lay watching her, fascinated, caught up in the small struggle *Sweet, Sweet Jesus, Lady. Not just now. I'm truly truly hung,* as the baby suckled with a great and happy noise, and as she smiled tenderly back, and as breakfast came up piping hot and ready to serve. He couldn't believe he couldn't believe it. So tender, so incredible, so huge, until suddenly the blood ran up through him like a tender orgasm, a death of sweet, milky sickness.

He rose up to puke out the window, saving himself.

"HOT DAMN," Dawes Williams said, through a broken throat, to a crowd of the curious who had gathered, "BREAKFAST'S ON. IF I'D REALLY BELIEVED IN MOTHER LOVE, YOU SEE, I'D HAVE JUST LAIN THERE AND DIED. BUT I REALLY DON'T, YOU SEE, SO I WAS SAVED. I WAS MOTIVATED, SO WE'RE ALL RIGHT ON THAT ONE AFTER ALL."

Someone looked surly, pulled a knife and threatened to come on the train to slit Dawes Williams into two separate gullet-bearing bodies.

"I think there's a misunderstanding here," Dawes said quietly. "However, if you promise to make it quick, I'll lie here and wait for you," he said gratefully.

He threw a handful of pesos down onto the platform, trying to pay his own assassins. Ironically, however, an immediate fist fight broke out over the money and all thought of murdering Dawes Williams got lost. Disappointed, Dawes also thought perhaps this lapse was partly caused by the simple fact that, looking in disbelief at him as they had, they didn't figure he *had* any more money worth murdering for. He knew if he wanted to get murdered in this country, he would have to dress better, not worse. Suddenly embarrassed, however, he returned to his seat. He tried to ignore the whole incident as it had woken him up. The small, certain tremors in the distances of his body were waking to daylight rhythms. He tried to ignore this, praying on a black cross for their return. Finally he closed his eyes again. It was quiet, an ironically non-existent and rational dream. He lay under a lid. Except for his body, he felt strangely well. He lay under a quietude so vast it became fixated finally on the catalepsis of a huge, brown, crayon teat once again. Within it there was occasional laughter in the street, spinning red pinwheels of shouted air, Mexico itself, a swirl of animals and faces, dark wooden carvings, a trampoline of Indian air coming off at ear level on the dusky platform, yet slightly below. Lying there, not moving, he saw himself the hero of the piece, the greatest child of them all, walking the streets, passing among them: in his hand was an abacus, and he was busy only counting noses. In the end he evaporated into the red eye of the western sea. It was a pleasant dream, full of wonder and peace, safely beyond him, held in abatement, lying there, completely spewed out, not caring if the train ever moved again, listening only into the vast herds of flies' wings buzzing in his screenless sills. He relaxed. The small brown child, still at his post staring, thought suddenly he was dead.

Then the conductor came and shook him saying: "*Torreón,* Señor!" (Good fucking Jesus God, Dawes Williams thought, We weren't even in Chihuahua in the first place. I have somehow managed to have missed Chihuahua. It must be poetic justice, proportional damnation, the wages of sin.) "Señor!" the conductor said again, holding his eyes outward for a tip, "*Torreón!*"

Dawes finally gave in to his imploring that he must get off the train and got up from his board. He gave the conductor, who ran the pillow concession by night and the pick-up-waking concession by day, a five-peso note. He thanked him and shook his hand. He gathered his bag together, tied his Indian blanket round his neck with a length of cheap hemp and, with one shoe on, began marching through the door.

After what seemed awhile, he heard what he immediately took to be Dorothy Clavin's voice, calling at him, coming through the stoned, quiet layers of stationed air. Looking down to the right along the tracks, he saw she was dressed only in a noon-white bra, a silly hat, staring at him. She was leaning out of her Pullman window, doing a balcony scene.

"Dawes!" she was saying. "You'll catch hookworms that way. Put your shoes on. Button up. Where do you think you're going, Dawes? Come down to Mexico City with us, Dawes!"

"Are we alone?" Dawes said. "Jesus, she likes me."

"Yes. John went down to have lunch."

"Can I come through your window and lay the hell out of you?"

"No," she said laughing, "we haven't time."

"Too bad," Dawes said. "I sure would have appreciated it."

"Think you could have managed it, Dawes?"

"Ride on, Dorothy," Dawes said.

"What are you doing?"

"Just sittin' here thinkin'."

"Come down to Mexico City with us, Dawes."

"Can't. I need me some sea, I think. I was thinking of a place named Mazatlán. Got it circled on the map. Too late now to back out. But you look radiant this morning, Dorothy, hanging from that window in your silly hat. You and John must have gotten all excited last night."

"For the first time," she said laughing, "he whipped me."

"I thought you might get into something nice," Dawes said. "You owe me a lot."

"Don't I wonder," she said. "That's why I want you to come to Mexico City with us. Climb in and we'll smuggle you down."

"Can't. I'm not a dryback. Besides, I haven't got that kind of time left. Thank God."

"Good luck, Dawes," she said seriously. "Kiss your uncle Tom for me the next time you see him."

"Oh ya. Thanks for your belief finally. Can't kiss him, though. Got news last night they hung him in Yuma prison. The governor stepped in and commuted his sentence to death. Damn merciful if you ask me."

"I see."

"I've still got some reservations about that," Dawes said.

"But you may need it. The luck. You're going to be murdered soon if you keep running around this country like you did last night."

"Did all right, did I?"

"Why don't you study voice, Dawes?"

"Don't worry. Only your friends and intimates murder you. Strangers as a rule only kick hell out of you. I haven't been down here long enough to have any intimates yet. If I even do, then I'll worry. Then I'll have some real hope."

"You can't run a world without sociopathics, I guess."

"You have a very fine ass for a sociologist, Dorothy."

"Thank you, madman. Are you telling me to keep it that way?"

"Whatever."

"Well, you take care."

"That's easy. These are good people. You're good people too, Dorothy. They're no good at murdering anybody but themselves. I think, in the end, I need either Hyoot John or Braun Daniel. Maybe he's up for a furlough. Maybe there's hope and a chance for me yet."

"Goodbye, Dawes."

"Kiss John for me, Dorothy. See ya."

"You'll look splendid in your bandages, Dawes, marching through Georgia."

"I didn't do my marching-through-Georgia number last night—Curly Wallace signs on the right, Lester Maddox signs on the right, hillbillies on the right, everybody on the right, the titter tottering into the sea, no Sherman to be seen on the horizon, just me, thunderclouds all around, just me in the land of the vicious, red-necked Co-manch raiders with farms— did I?"

"You sure did. Round five o'clock."

"Damn," Dawes Williams said seriously, hitting his open palm with his fist. "I've never lost touch with memory before. Not even through lucid convulsions. Maybe I'm finally going over the edge this time. Maybe there's hope."

"Cheer up," she said. "I still think you'll look splendid, perversely gallant, walking around in your Band-Aids."

"I love you, Dorothy," Dawes said. "You have taken the time to understand. Like to say I wanted to do the same for you, but I don't want to start sounding like a Methodist Youth Convocation on Wednesday evening. Bad way to go down."

"Be kind to somebody, Dawes. Throw flowers on Trotsky's grave perhaps."

"Oh ya. Don't worry. Soon as I get me a crutch and a small wood drum in the market, a tin cup from the ditch, I'll be set in this country, Dorothy. Spirit of '76. Going to fake the hell out of them for awhile …just as they think we're only slipping ourselves into the second dialectic, I'm going to slip'em into the third. Personally. Going to look for a revolution to start . . . soon as I learn a few dozen words of Spanish, I've got it made."

"How'd you come by all this opinion, Dawes?"

"We studied Simon Bolivar in school, as I remember it. They told us he was a great man because he freed and liberated the poor people, not the rich. Which was excessive, of course, because even at the time I knew the rich never needed it. It backfired on'em, you see, because I believed them, and because they never expected me to take it that seriously when the chips were down."

"Dawes?" Dorothy said, leaning out of her window, her voice nearly soft and inaudible. "Go back to college sometime. Promise me?"

"Oh, sweet Christ," Dawes said. "I was afraid you'd do that. You've just broken the whole illusion. Handsaw is roaring with laughter."

"What do you mean?" she said.

"Here I was, finally thinking I was alive finally and dying, living in Mexico, involved for a change, for Christ in a real, timeless biological process finally, finally making it, and you had to come along and ruin it with a premonition of college."

"But that's not a reason. Anyone can be simply *alive.*"

"Want to bet? Besides, I can't go back to that, I'll be too busy burying my uncle Tom now once he gets out of Yuma prison. Besides, I can't go back there; my final discernment was entitled: The Amoral, Picaro Question in the Quixote as Seen in the Perspective of Cervantes' Years with the Algerian Turks and His Readings in Those Years of the Play *Celestina* and of His Recognition of Potential Spatial-Temporal Relationships in the Picaresque Romance *Lazarillo de Tormes.*"

"Didn't it work out, Dawes?"

"No. Nobody could even show he had read those two works in those years. Or even that the Algerian Turks had libraries."

"That all?"

"No, that was only the beginning. Want to hear the rest?"

"Of course."

"Well, I had been working on that thesis for two years of my life before I found out it had already been done three hundred and sixty-seven times since 1616. Imagine that. I was heartbroken. I began at once a second-generation synthesis and codifying of all of the minor views, of course, but somehow my mind had just quit on me. I had a nervous breakdown. Somehow the real romance had all gone out of it, and all I was left with was a quixotic sham. I couldn't face it."

"Not that, huh?" she said.

"No. Anything but that. Besides, he had already wrote the damn ole book, hadn't he? Frankly, what was the point? Who would have wanted to read a second-generational synthesis and codifying of the minor critiques?"

"Who indeed?" she said.

"So there I was. Giving it up. I got into Mechanical Engineering next, dreaming of becoming a Renaissance man. I took up Compound Gearing on the Spiral Head, Gearing to Cut a Helix. That sort of thing. In my spare time I read Thomas Jefferson and Jorge Borges. Sometimes, you know, trying to get a line on the width of the field, a line on its obscurity, I'd get up early in the morning and go hang around the poolroom of the municipal library, reading the card-catalogue under 'Machines.' You know, reading things like: 622.967132 AFX: ENGINES OF DEMOCRACY: A Study Exemplar of Mature American Machines, The Builders of the Republic, by T. T. Bredaluv. . . . A watershed study, a theology really, first published in America (the author is a Yugoslavian mining engineer) in 1896. I was coming apart I tell you. I didn't know what in the fuck to make of it," he said, burying his head in his hands.

There was the longest silence. The station was cluttered with silence. Dorothy, staring at Dawes, still leaned from her window. Dawes got up to go:

"Dawes!" Dorothy said, breaking her silence. "Come in here in the shade for awhile. I'll improve your Spanish. Perhaps it'll go better."

"Can't. Gotta kiss and run this time, Dorothy. Besides, most of the source readings for my final discernment weren't even *in* Spanish. Damned ironic, I thought at the time, but they were in mirror cipher written in medieval Arabic and Latin, and inverted seven times in a cat's-eye boulder. But that wasn't so bad. What was bad was that you could only read the manuscript on Sunday mornings between eight and ten-thirty, at which time the pages, if soaked in wine seven hours on Saturday night, would bloom . . . burst into the perfect script of a Catholic scrutiny, a scorch of earth, an inquisition of flames in the vague forms of secular saints that was three foot high! Higher! Hell, Trotsky's beard itself was as high as the wall! Besides, I didn't manage to tie it all in with the decline of the Hapsburgs in the end anyway. It was a thorough waste."

"You're getting excited again, Dawes. You're losing me," she said.

"Who wouldn't get excited about something like that?"

"Stay well, Dawes."

"Love Peace Joy, Dorothy."

"Lope de Vegas, Dawes. Cervantes."

"Some of the good ones starve to death all right," Dawes said. "But then I always figured Lope de Vega sounded like only the Speedy Gonzales Frito Bandito of Spanish comedy anyway. Maybe he was his own reward after all."

"But just remember, Dawes," Dorothy said, "that *c* doesn't always equal *d*, even if *d* always equals *c*. That is. . ."

"That is," Dawes said, "it's true that *c*, just being starved, doesn't always equal being a good one. I know that! You didn't think, after all, I was really *mad*, did you?"

"I didn't know at times."

"Well, I knew. I never lost touch for a moment. I knew exactly where the heart of *reality* lay at every turning. Only I consistently refused to believe it. Not only that, I wasn't talking. I was trying to sing. And, incidentally, any ass or knight in the world could climb a mountain that is really there. But the Quixote was a radical and beautiful, because he climbed mountains that weren't even there. Honestly, Dorothy, climbing mountains that are really there is decidedly a second-rate, literal, right-wing function."

There was a pause, another silence. A vendor with a pail of apples and

Cokes passed. The station was utterly deserted now. The air was still with dust, silent rings and sun. Dorothy was still leaning on her windowsill, perhaps wound down, perhaps even thinking of taking a nap, of traveling sleeping into the south. The train, even for a Mexican goat, looked as if it might be departing at any time. Dawes thought John's face would be appearing soon, framed in the window. He got up from the platform, dusted himself off, and felt it was time to be moving.

"We'll be seeing you, Scarlett," he said, hefting his duffel, "when Johnny comes marching home again. You just sit by your window, smiling, knowing what you know, a rose of womanhood, and that way it's all worthwhile, no matter what. We who are about to die salute the virginal rose of your mind."

"Dawes," she said. "Don't be cruel to me now. Leave me my *memories.*"

Dawes Williams laughed softly on the platform. He slipped the rope tying off his Indian blanket over his head.

"All right," he said finally. "You're a real madonna of the airy, statistical grotto, Scarlett. And I'd just like to say at this juncture: I couldn't have loved you more Platonically if you'd taken the trouble to lay me."

"But Dawes," she said, "I was about to do that. I *tried.* I couldn't get you to sit still long enough."

"I'll be damned, Scarlett," Dawes said, "that's the most incredible thing I've heard all morning. Is that a fact? Why didn't you just say so?"

"I couldn't," she said. "I just didn't know *how.*"

"I'll be damned," Dawes said, "the *deus ex machina* remained off stage."

"But God damn it, Dawes, aside from that, I'm trying to get through to you. Just what *is* it you think you are doing?" she said, suddenly pointed, direct, even angry.

"Who? Me?" Dawes said humbly. "Why I'm just Broad-cast-ing/For Je-sus. Just another traveling evangelical and messianic with secular missions."

"Oh posh," she said. "I don't believe a word of it now. Not a word. All right. But, whatever else, get yourself another wild greyhound that runs on the edge of the hill, singing in the rain. Promise me that."

"I'll be damned. I didn't do my Arthur number last night—greyhounds on the left, Arthur on the right, everything else and the whole goddamn farm on the right, Gin on the right, Grandma-great on the right, Herb's shoeshop on the right, Simpson and Leone on the night, the county sheriff on the right, me in the middle, Abigail Winas on the left—did I?"

"Yes, around five-thirty, when you were out. Sounded suspiciously like Spanish too, to me."

"I'll be damned."

"You can't divide your emotions up into politics with only two sides."

"Don't I know it," Dawes Williams said. "But ideas are thicker than blood."

"You can't afford that, dividing it up, good and bad."

"Where I come from," Dawes said, "you can't afford not to. Besides, dividing it once, I call that working in free will; dividing the divisions, I call that looking for the functions of enlightenment."

"Just another absolutist, a fanatic, Dawes, that's your problem."

"Yes, well, so was Plato. That's not historically impossible, you know, Dorothy. Besides, I can afford that now. Now that I've left the land of the New Calvinist, the relativist fanatic. Like you, Dorothy. Yep, now that I've left that one-side, predetermined, multidabbling, pragmatic wasteland. That city dressed up as a country in Roman clothing. See ya, Toots," Dawes said, moving down the tracks.

"All right. But, Dawes, before you go," Dorothy said, "I have to know one thing: Which is real—your grandfather Arthur, or your uncle Tom? Are they the same thing? Was any of it real?"

"All right. Whatever. Whichever you like. I don't care," Dawes Williams said. "I forget. I think they were all real fictional characters in a novel called *Impersonations* I read as a boy, written by a man named . . . "

"I'd like to get that book, Dawes," she said.

"You should. It's a novel about growing up into absurdity in the Midwest. Writer has a fine sense for the geography of the prairie in places. Why don't you write to the publisher, Mr. John Tom Treeman in Galena, Illinois?"

"I will. Soon as I get to Mexico City," she said.

"By then it'll be too late, of course. But your interest is touching, Dorothy," Dawes Williams said. "And incidentally, Scarlett, you tell that tiny moron Joyce for me when I'm gone . . . you just tell her you met *someone* once who said her greatest-grandmother was probably a Druid whatsamacallit who ran around naked in the moonrain. You tell her that, and then you tell her she's slipped some in quality. Her social dreaming now concentrates itself only on the inferior runes of waking."

"Goodbye, Dawes. Goodbye, madman."

"Ride on, Dorothy."

He waved at her and disappeared around the corner of the station, walking west, into a slope of side streets he felt must eventually come out somewhere. He passed a pink neon sign of a running greyhound and, taking it for the only omen all afternoon, went into the bus depot to buy a ticket for riding later in the evening.

Needing a tequila suddenly, Dawes pulled up behind a pile of ropes and smoked a joint. He sat watching the market, opening, closing, breathing.

From his jeans pockets/in thin lights of the plaza turning to goat-butters, he leaned against the wall and read one of Barney Redwood's letters from Vietnam:

22 Sept. '69

Willie,

you old fucker it was damned good to hear from you. Hippie huh? Bullshit. You got about as much goddamn hippie in you as a chicken's got piss.

I'm flying Chinooks over here in the enema center of the world. As you probably heard, we lost one of our ships about a month ago with 33 aboard, only the co-pilot survived. Real bitch. I had been in to the same place the day before at least five times.

Sorry little bastards don't give a shit whether they live or die, just so when they die nobody cuts their fucking head off. We did that when I was over here with Special Forces the last time and the little cocksuckers ran from us. With the over efficient news service the way it is the fighting machine is nothing more than a political chess piece.

That's one of the main reasons I'm flying instead of on the ground where I really want to be. I enjoy flying don't get me wrong, but I also enjoyed the thoughts of having my own infantry company and able to kill more clinks than any other. It did it too year before last. I was a XO when the CO got killed and we proceeded to kick ass. All told we lost 7 killed & 15 wounded and killed 135 of NVA regulars.

Myself & five of my men got the SS for that. I wouldn't have mentioned it except when I sent the 5 in for it the Colonel wouldn't accept them without putting me in it for it too. I don't give a shit about medals for officers, but for the grunts on the ground it means a lot. I've always felt that a medal and buck might get you a beer.

In any event, if I've gotta be here I want to keep as far away from the My Lai's as possible. That told me how really sorry the news and political influence really is. People who haven't been here don't know what it's like to have to burn their own shit and smell it all day. Or use maggots to put on an open wound so gangrene won't set in—and then eat the maggots to stay alive until you get back.

That's not bullshit!! It becomes strange to look at oneself in a mirror of death and have to realize what you have to do to stay alive. The sorry cocksuckers who made this war didn't even know what it's all about other than numbers or charts and a few pictures. I'd like to take some of our decision makers into the bush with me and let them in on something. It goddamn well wouldn't be a fucking VIP trip like they've had every fucking year around. Remember—they come that month so they can stop off in Hong Kong to buy Christmas presents. Might as well make it a profitable trip huh—fuck the time!

As you can probably tell I've accumulated a real bitterness toward the whole fucking system—same as you—but in a different sort of aspect. I've still got a big mouth and I've paid for it. I've been in the service, but it's either my record or something that always keeps one in. I make pretty good money—but that's really not why I stay. I think it's because I doubt if I could ever be a good civilian again with things the way they are. In the army I can tell most people to shut the fuck up—out in the world I'd have to re-establish myself with many people with whom I'd have very little in common. The army has been damned good to me even if the higher ups haven't. And to a certain degree I can establish my own little empire each time I move. Most of my men can understand immediately how I feel about things—those who can't and don't like it either leave or get the shit kicked out of them. I'm still hard-headed and jolly well fucking crude. "That's my favorite." Keeps from wasting time—being crude.

Hey partner, enough about me. What's this fucking book about that takes so goddamn long. Jesus, I knew you had patience, but that's goddamn near ridiculous. You still looking for something?? You need some action. Get off your dead butt and don't get so fucking wrapped up in that goddamn typewriter for such an extension. Jesus Christ even I know the fucking brain can only create at certain times and only so much skill can take up the slack for only so long.

That was a mouthful but I know it's not old bullshit—I've written a little iambic pentameter about this fucking place. Long novels are for people with long memories. I stick to the short stuff and keep notes until it gets to where I can't pull my pud anymore—then I think I'll write a long novel or something. It won't be a biography because only Generals are authorized biographiles and I'll never be a General. Guaranteed by Congress so far! I'll probably retire as a fucking Captain—but at least they'll know I was here. Ha-ha.

Goddamn good to hear from you Willie—write again and I never felt you were full of shit—I just like to tell everybody that so they can get the ass—it helps sometimes.

Barney Redwood

Walking again, he felt the Tequila in his blood, like destroyed water, running through unusable piping. It was all too close, too obvious to recognize. It was easy to ignore the sign, too central and too omnipotent to be anything but deeply humorous. He had a headache in his eye. It throbbed and bloomed back, giving rhythms to the light, awareness to the sounds, meaning to the street. He ignored it. Handsaw roared with laughter, trapped deeply in a boiler below.

Moving, in the distance, to a cantina, he crossed finally into a square. There was shade there. He sat watching. Tall brown women paraded around grandiose cement fountains. They were lean, taut as something in touch with itself. They were rawly beautiful, so much more alive than the operatic stone statuary. They were life, he thought, something in touch with itself. He was death, one eye, a mask, an unreality, something out of touch with itself. He was destroying them all:

Crossing the naked, shaded womb of the square, he felt like the journeys of sleeping trains. They were watching him. He felt suddenly insecure, rotten. He was not to be watched. He had been only the watcher; that's what he had always been. That's what it was, the difference. But he didn't like it. Only he had that right, watching himself. He didn't want them to be doing that, nosing around, sniffing his edges, looking through him, piercing him with holes, with the ice blackness and orange tooth of their eyes. He didn't want a part of any of it. But he couldn't stop it. His hand was shaking; it was hard to walk. The muscles in his legs seemed to slip out from under him like stuttering clutches, destroyed impulses, impossible electricity. He didn't know if he could even make the street, the cantina, the eye like white light. He knew what it was. But not here, he thought; I can't do this here. Drop dead, yes, but not this, not here. Oh, Christ. He knew what it was. It hadn't changed. It hadn't left him. It would always be there. He knew what it was. His legs nearly buckled and his bowels knotted beneath him. He knew he just couldn't change it. The smooth, destroyed tremors ran out to the ends of his body and died blunted in stone. He knew he needed a drink. Handsaw roared with laughter. Dawes fainted. He lay swirling in a twisted rock of red sunlight, listening to a voice, Handsaw's voice, strangely the small voice of a frightened child, coming from a tiny place within him, saying:

"Damn, Dawes. She-it, Dawes. Why didn't you take the easy way out? Why didn't you join the Horse Marines?"

Dawes Williams woke, roaring with laughter. Another Mexican child, wide in the eyes again, was throwing water on him, kicking him gently in the stomach. Dawes rose finally, tipped him five pesos, and made his way into the cantina. *Cantina del Sol* was carved on the doorjamb. Going down, Dawes saw the interior was tiny, shadowed, indrawn and full of an orange tooth of smoke that refused to rise. Black forms topped in wide hats stood drinking within the green cactus plant of silent air. The desert suddenly hummed beyond, known, present, clean and full of blue sky. Dawes sat in the first chair he passed and, saying, "Tequila," with three fingers raised, drank three down and sat with his cheeks full of furiously chewed lemon until his eyes cleared. His head seemed to follow, destroyed and saved. A long horizon of a mirror and dirty yellow light, a filthy seam of smoke, ran before him the length of the interior, and, catching sight of himself, he sat watching the dark immensity of a tired shadow run through the edges of his body, shaking him like rags, cutting through him; cords of flesh. He couldn't look at it for long. The thing he had seen in the mirror, a degenerate recognition, a shadow fleeing beyond glass into the other world, had been flushed with shame, rage, disgust, embarrassment and an all-encompassing laughter. Looking away, he had instantly remembered its total impression. Not wanting to look at it again, however, even by accident, he bought three more tequilas and went to the back of the cantina.

He propped his chair against the back wall, his bare feet on his duffel working at balance, and lit a cigar. The tequila in Torreón seemed to be orange, not red, but still rough and full of destructed flesh.

Across from him a man sat reading a paper. On one side of the exposed front page was a yellowish picture of Richard M. Nixon. On the other side was a photograph of three Mexicans who had shot and murdered a priest down in Sinaloa somewhere and who were now reported as hiding in the mountains near Durango. Dawes could make nothing more out of the report. He sat for a long time, motionless, studying the drift of his tequila smoke, trying to piece together the gestalt connections in that one. He stared at the exposed page. He thought finally the whole of it could have had a slightly better symmetry only if Ronald Ray-gun had been elected president and was, therefore, staring out from the Mexican paper.

Suddenly embarrassed over his own thoughts, Dawes felt he was genuinely cracking up and losing his grip this time. Nothing was funny. He tried to shake it off. He drank another shot of tequila. Feeling better, nearly sane, he then leaned across the table with his fullest baroque extension; he winked, smiled and began whispering at the bewildered Mexican clandestinely:

"Oh ya," he said, "outlaws. The outlawed life. The world is mad, eh? Billy the Kid. Perry and Dick. The right side of this paper is fifteen years old if it's a day. That's me, if I could only find my balls. So this is where all the old newspapers go. I know I had them tied on somewhere round here. I have always wondered about that."

"*Si. Si,*" the Mexican said, staring across, taking out an old coin and flipping it for a shot of tequila. He never showed it to Dawes.

After awhile, counting out multicolored pesos onto the dry wood, he began leaving. The barman filled five unwashed, clear bottles with funnels of rum. He wrapped them in old newsprint. Dawes left one on the table and exited. It was nearly evening on the slow mule of the street.

The air was heavy, and Dawes began looking for a quiet wall to pee on. He was so drunk. He sloped with the incredible weave of the street. His bladder was bursting. A poisonous orange swirl, sweet with sickness, welled within him. Turning into the street, Dawes saw, however, that a bus was winding through the square. He saw "Mazatlán" was spun on its black, dial-a-city scroll. Making some hurried gesticulations, half-peeing quietly in his pants, he ran down the street chasing its dust. He cut it off finally at a corner, flagging it down, knocking the door. The driver stared back. Dawes waved a handful of pesos into the door glass which flew immediately open.

"*Gracias. Gracias,*" the driver said, taking his money and his ticket.

"What time does the bus leave?" Dawes Williams said, smiling. "What time does the bus fly over the mountain? What time does the bus arrive?"

The driver pointed to the back, suddenly frowning. Dawes walked back, tipping his hat, sitting finally against his duffel, propping his feet against the glass, staring out, drinking and smoking quietly. He sat listening to his heart pounding like a diseased hammer, a thin, falling wall within its own consciousness, not believing itself. The road ran out flat with a jaded mask, orange Mexican eye, the bright afternoon all evening. It rolled south with the alkaline grass, dry sun, fenceless goats chewing their way into Sinaloa and the sea all evening in the last thin light.

Once, they even all got off in heaven and pissed on the times.

He opened his eyes in Mazatlán, missing the mountains, hours later. Panicking for a moment, he saw only he couldn't recognize the air. He was a shadow. He stood behind nothingness, awake, but not able even to pronounce his genus. Nearly aware for a moment, he knew he could not sense the earth's exact place in the black universe. He knew suddenly he had always been able to do this before, not noticing it. It filled him with terror. He was shivering uncontrollably. Nameless. An orange sea-bird shrieked, waking him further. A whisper of time, place, being. He couldn't remember. Was he *something?* He must have been. Whatwasthis-Whatwasthis? Where was the earth? He couldn't place it suddenly in the precise dance of the spheroids, the exact light of the hemispheres. Then, just as suddenly saving himself, he recognized three men were sweeping out the bus, the dead sea wind from beneath him. It all came back. He recognized his kind.

He walked out into the slow Mexican sleep. The night was cold. Down at the ends of streets the white surf rolled on the stone. He stood, sighting down an alley of mud walls; he drew his blanket Indian-style around him and, rags in the winds, walked the dark sandy Mexican streets down to the beach. He was noiseless, sliding along behind himself. He saw himself everywhere, standing in the doorways, leaning behind the lamp posts, a dirty and ratlike thing, two days hungry and blurry, chewing his own eye and the yellow circles of thin, hanging light.

He wanted to move away. He thought he saw a fire burning down at the ends of the beach. He took out a quarter bottle of rum and drained it. He knew only a drink could save him now.

His eyes were not encased in the lamplight with his heart. He felt them watching him from behind hollow wooden fences, within mud walls. They were blurred. They were someone else's eyes, denying his displacement, his existence. He ignored them. Mothlike, flying within a dead insect of night, they were moving mindlessly toward the fire burning at the end of the beach.

It was a long walk. He sat down twice, smoking the weed he had smuggled into Mexico, laughing. Crossing the last sand, he saw three shadows bent within blankets, close to the fire. One he sensed was a girl. She sat under a blanket with a white boy, shivering. Slightly apart, the Negro was playing a guitar. His voice rose and fell within the mulatto crashing of the sea, the twin hemispheres of the gray islands riding like a gull's wings the dark, rainless wind. The strings slapped the slight wood and slid away into silence. They were staring at him.

"May I borrow some of your fire? I'm pretty stove in," Dawes Williams said, approaching.

"This is a social democracy, ain't it, Henry?" the Black said, staring across at the other.

"Yeah. Yeah. Right. Right," Henry said.

"No, Henry bastard," the girl said between them, "you've got it wrong again. This is damn Mexico now. Remember? This is really an honest-to-God damn feudal system now . . . but at least it's a free country."

"Well, whatever," Henry said.

The Black looked back down at his hands. He began singing again, apparently proving that even his momentary attention had not been attention at all.

Dawes wondered suddenly if he had even come, arrived on this spot. He lay down on the sand. He had never been quite awake, he thought suddenly, since he entered Mexico, perhaps before, for months, perhaps ever, but now he couldn't sleep. He lay there, turned away from the firelight, in the dark rim of the sand, listening to the girl who was huddled in the middle, speaking slowly within the ash and blooming smoke. Her voice seemed low, deeply reserved, yet forceful and exotic too. He wondered if it fitted her face, but he was somehow not able to make the effort necessary to turn himself into the fire and see her. He decided it did; it must. He decided her eyes were watching him.

"Henry bastard," she was saying, "we must go back to San Blas. I loved it in San Blas, Henry bastard. We must..."

Dawes turned and looked at her finally for a moment. Within the firelight he watched the thin bone shadows, tiny fish eyes swimming within red water, play across the lines of her face. Even sitting inside blankets she seemed angular, incredibly overbred and on the edge of a thin decline. She was staring back. Henry was not paying any attention, carrying on a conversation of his own with the Black, who was singing, and probably stoned, and also not listening to anyone, either.

". . . Did I ever tell you about the shark I killed with a knife in the surf down near Oaxaca. . ." Henry said.

". . . God, San Blas is beautiful. . ."

"Tricky as hell? Sometimes you have to dive under, ram the snout up with your left arm . . ." he said, making a sudden karate-like motion with his left arm.

". . . Well, San Blas is not exactly beautiful in a visual sense, but it's . . ."

". . . and then you've got to gut them with your right. . ."

". . . beautiful in terms of light. . ."

". . . and I mean gut the holy hell out of them. . ."

". . . especially in the afternoons, and it's beautiful in terms of people. . ."

". . . You only get one chance, one mistake; and of course you need a good shark knife, sharp as diamonds. . ."

". . . God, I want to go back to San Blas . . ."

". . . I ever show you my shark knife, Deac? And of course it helps if you let the natives show you how to pick on only rather small sharks at first. . . until you get the hang of it . . ."

". . . San *Blas,* Henry bastard, San Blas. . ."

"Yeah. Yeah. Right. Right," Henry bastard said.

"Cowshit," Dawes Williams mumbled, not even rolling over.

"Where you from, buddy?" Henry asked suddenly.

"Iowa. I live in the Midwest," Dawes Williams said.

"Man, that's got to be a fantasy," the girl said. "Nobody's lived there for ten years now. The place must be vacant."

"Whatever the hell do you do there?" Henry said.

"I'm a professional fisherman and gunfighter," Dawes said.

"You gotta be puttin' me on, man," Henry said.

"Oh ya," Dawes said. "I'm whittlin' the wood and passin' the time."

"There ain't no fish left in Iowa," Henry said, coming back.

Through the firelight Dawes could see the girl was looking incredulously at Henry.

"You'll have to forgive Henry bastard here," she said. "He's not up on too much happening east of the San Bernardino Mountains."

"Oh ya," Dawes said, "that's west all right. Reminds me some of some Eastern provincials I know. Don't know cows from raisins. I guess I was just stuck in the middle out there, you know, Aristotelian, riding the Golden Mean."

"Fuck off," Henry said.

"Anyway," Dawes said, "in my spare time, when John Wesley Hardin wasn't in town, I made my livin' skinning out freshwater sharks passing through to the coasts."

The girl laughed. Dawes rolled over, nearly sleeping. He seemed destroyed beyond feeling, lost within slow things, unreal, torn like the white paper moon within the Black's fitful song.

"Have you been to San Blas?" she said finally to Dawes, breaking the stillness.

"No," he said, sitting back up into the firelight. "Christ, I haven't even seen a windmill in this country all evening."

"Why not? You'd love it. You've got to keep moving."

"How's that? You can only be in one place at one time. You figured out a way to travel without taking yourself along, have you?"

"Sure have. You take me to San Blas and I'll show you how."

Henry shifted himself around and glared at Dawes. Dawes felt slightly embarrassed and got out what was left of his grass.

"Here," he said, "let's smoke some of this."

"Well?" she said, rolling joints. "Have you been there?"

"Don't know," Dawes said. "Haven't been able to get my eye open all afternoon for some reason. May have passed it and missed the damn thing."

"Not San Blas," she said. "It would be impossible to *be* in San Blas and not know it. It's probably because the left side of your head is swollen shut, though, that your *physical* eye doesn't work."

"Right," Dawes said suddenly feeling his head. "Who needs it? Thanks for mentioning it, though, as it 'splains a lot of things."

"Don't mention not mentioning it," Henry said, weakly sarcastic. "We like to help out where we can."

Through the firelight again Dawes could see the girl was looking at Henry, nearly peevishly this time.

"You faggot," she said finally. "Anyway, Iowa, you'd love it if you ever made it to San Blas. Henry bastard here won't take me. You're a bastard, Henry. You really are."

"Not me," Dawes said pleasantly, passing the joint. "I'm not moving. I finally made it here, and I'm not going anywhere any more."

Henry took out his shark knife. He began playing abstract, mumbletypeg games with himself in the sand.

Horseshit, the Black sang, Henry, doncha be takin' that knife out in the third act less you be plannin' to shoot it off in the fifth. . . .

Dawes couldn't believe it. He stared across the fire at the Black man, genuinely smiling, full of pleasant recognition and surprise. The Black, however, still didn't look up.

"Oh ya," the girl said, "Deac put some time in at Stanford. Some hard hard time on a scholarship. Anyway, I hate to be forward as we ain't been formally introduced yet, but how would you like to take me to San Blas?"

"Is this rote selection?" Dawes Williams said, embarrassed again.

"Into the army," Henry put in, "the great militia and national guard of Urzika's body."

"Eureka?" Dawes said.

"'Urzika,'" Henry said, "as in 'Euphrates,' the great and fertile genesis of all river valleys. Really turns you on, doesn't it? We'll get to how Mary Davis from Youngstown renamed herself Urzika later. We usually do."

"Fuck off," Urzika said.

Earthmother Earthmother flyaway home, the Black sang. Your mask's in the fire and you've nowhere to roam.

"I think you people may have been too long among yourselves," Dawes Williams said pleasantly. "Anyway, getting back to this selection thing. . ."

"Ya," Henry said, "whatever."

"Well, it's not terrifically selective in your grandmother's terms, I suppose, but what the fuck. This is a feudal system once more or, rather, I am the only vehicle left for the building of a great social democracy. Or something like that. Isn't that right, Henry bastard?"

"Ya," Henry said, "whatever."

"Henry's getting surly again," Urzika said. "Possessive despite principles."

A stillness set in. Dawes sat, watching them through the fire. Even in the blackness he could see her paleness, white as a bowl of downy owls, her eyes, pale and faded too, green as water staring back through the wood smoke. She seemed thin and drawn, wan as a space of day, a flower left hanging in a patch of ground in which only the sand was growing. He stared at her. Finally, through the parting blanket, he noticed she was perfectly nude.

"Yes," she was saying, "Henry here is good for rutting in the surf, once you can get him high enough to think of it—you really are, Henry bastard—but come to think of it, mostly you're good for nothing else." In the silence Henry glared at her.

"Urzika's like what you only read about in books," he finally said. "She's a kind of new cultural hero. Just now we're waiting for someone from a cultural-hero magazine—up this beach here, you see—to discover her. You're not from *Look*, are you?"

"Fuck off," Urzika said.

"Yeah! Yeah! Right! Right!" Henry said. "Urzika, you see, sitting right here before you, is a fiction. A kind of good copy of all of the bad women you've read about in books."

"That's right," Urzika said, "whatever you say, Henry fucker. I'm Fanny Hill, Aunt Pitty-Pat and Belle Starr."

O tell me tell me what you is I am, 'cause sometimes we's all so witty so damn damn wiiittty we kent stand it ourselves. . . .

"Only she's not even that," Henry said. "Urzika's still only Many Davis and the only problem is—she's becoming terrifically grotesque in the process of trying to recognize herself as running while sitting still."

"That's brilliant, Henry bastard. I think you love me at last. The sun is up!" Urzika said. "You great oaf of humanity you."

"Yes," Henry said, "so picture this: One day Urzika, tired like the sun, just up and left her best bed friends—Tommy Star and Willy Hero and Sally Bumblebee, the best of all—behind in Ohio. She changed her name and came west. Just like in the movies."

"That's right," Urzika said, "and things started going badly after that. I met Henry bastard here, settled down and became a whore. Finally, saving myself, I met Black Deac here, talked him into forming a tribe because he's equal and we love him for it."

"You don't have to be telling me all of this if you'd rather not," Dawes

Williams said innocently. "It's beginning to sound like Letters from Brooke Farm."

Better'n'at, better'n'at, think if I's only equal to this think I'd been thinkin' of hangin' myself with a rope. . . .

"That's not nice, Deac," Urzika said, smiling, "I'd have thought *you people* would have learned something more than superiority through your suffering by now."

"Anyway," Henry said, "in the end Urzika's about as hip as you are, man."

Dawes Williams remained silent, staring through the fire.

"Henry bastard," Urzika said, "I think you are finally losing whatever it was."

"Go to hell, woman," Henry said weakly.

"And so now, you see," Urzika said, staring at Dawes, "we sleep in the sand, not because we have to but because we *love* it, and we travel on foot across deserts and sea, not because we have to, but because we just looove it, because Henry's a warrior, a priest, a *provider,* for Christsake, aren't you, Henry bastard, you absolutely helpless sonofabitch?"

"Geeze-neat," Dawes Williams said, changing the subject. "How long do you have in Mexico, in Mazatlán?"

"Forever, honey, forever," Urzika said, drawing it out. "And you? Will you take me to San Blas? Do you have any jack?"

There was a sudden silence this time. Even the Black's guitar stopped. In the firelight they all had turned quickly into Dawes Williams, looking him over carefully for signs of jack. Even the Black's last notes died away. The sky was beginning to be streaked with the first roses of morning, an ironic, reflected red in the west, still a flat gray over the mountains to the east. Seabirds rowed soundlessly behind. They were still staring at him through the unwinding fire. Only his rags, he thought, might have saved him, now.

"Only what I got from Pap at sheep-gelding time," Dawes Williams said finally. "I didn't leave home until after the harvest, you know."

They all laughed. The Black began playing again.

"A sheep nutter by trade," Henry said. "Makes sense."

"Fantastic," Urzika said. "Let's see your rubber washers."

"I left them home with Pap. So's he'd have a way to feed the young'uns," Dawes Williams said.

"Yes, of course, but is it lucrative? You do have the bread, jack? That's what we want to know," Henry said.

"Hell, yes," Dawes Williams said, "five cents a nut. Geeze, I like this kind of talk. Besides, I bet the whole wad on a greyhound named Chihuahua's Hat."

"And she blew it for ya," Henry said.

"No. She was a sweet running bitch. She came home at ten to one."

"And that's why you are in Mexico?" Urzika said.

"Right."

Oh I, I oh, oh I slit my mama's virgin throat fo' fifty cents and quickly hit the road 'cause, 'cause I'm just a travelin' boy at heart . . .

"Can't," Dawes Williams said. "I put them in traveler's checks and mailed them home to Mother. If her rhythm's on, they roll in like baskets of cookies, on Wednesdays at noon in telegraph stations around the world."

"Really damn fantastic," Henry said. "I'm going to tell you what we are prepared to do on this one then: We are prepared to cut you out, or in, makes no difference, my friend. Full shares. You can have either six feet of ground, or Urzika. Two hundred bucks."

"I gave up on corporations and pledging ceremonies some time ago. Besides, I'm broke," Dawes Williams said within the smoke.

She-it, Henry, what you talkin' now, fool? . . .

"A hundred and fifty then. One full share on one-third of Urzika's unlimited ass. You'll never regret it."

"I told you I shouldn't have tried to meet you down here," Dawes said, deadly seriously, staring across the fire at Urzika. "I knew it wouldn't work. We're off to a bad start again already."

The Black laughed quietly.

"What's he talking about?" Henry said.

"Nothing," she said. "You were right, of course," she said, turning to Dawes.

"What's so funny? You people are always laughing at me. You mothers," Henry said, startling Dawes with his nervousness, flipping his knife in the sand. "You people are always trying to screw me over, you know."

The Black stopped his guitar and looked at Henry. He roared with laughter. He began playing again.

"You see. One hundred then," Henry said.

"You're even a bad pimp, Henry bastard," Urzika said.

"Don't you need some kind of a license to do that down here?" Dawes said. "Besides, it smells faintly bourgeois to me."

"Bullshit," Henry said. "We'll blow it all in on some good Mexican grass and stay stoned for a month. You can have all you can roll in five minutes while astride Urzika's all, over and above communal shares."

"Sounds like the high ole life all night," Dawes said.

"Stop it!" Urzika said suddenly, cupping her ears.

"You see," Henry said. "She's practically a virgin, man."

"It's not that," Urzika said. "Believe me, Henry bastard, nothing you could dream any more could make me flinch."

"What is it then?"

"It's him. Can't you see it? You're embarrassing the kid. He's straight. He is, the straight sonofabitch. How *groovy* is that?"

"God," Henry said, coming out of it, "what a hell of an idea. It's novel. I can't remember the last time I was straight. Can you?"

Ain't nobody straight, 'cause I'm just a travelin' boy at heart, nowhere, no time, or if there is, I just ain't seen'em yet real crookeds and they's hidin' themselves under cabbage tops.

"HE is! He's fucking straight as Lone Ranger's arrow, I tell you," Urzika said.

"Nobody who looks that *bad* could be all straight," Henry said. "He's a beautiful freak. He looks like emasculated Audrey Beardsley begotten by a beat-up angel on the rear of his chopper."

"Just another aesthete critic," Urzika said. "But he is well made for an asthmatic. He's kinda cute."

"I am just a purloined yeoman who has broken down," Dawes Williams said.

"Real fine," Henry said. "Let's take another tack. We're so damn broke we'll approach this thing from an honestly bourgeois point of view. We'll sell you Urzika, under the boards, for ten dollars a shot and follow you around for a couple of weeks collecting with a tin bowl. She knows wild stuff, man."

"Jesu-woopee," Dawes Williams said. "I quit. That would make her a traitor to her class and, besides, I may be simple, but I'm not virginal. That's it for me. See ya," he said, rising brokenly, walking off, reaching back for his duffel.

But Urzika was up too. He could hear her yellow shadow jumping the fire; her dark wood, dry rain, wind like faint red tubings of sky and the flowers of the sea running in the sand behind him.

"Hey, look at me!" she said, turning him, quietly attacking him, jumping him in the near dark. "I'm the goddamn naked whatsamacallit!?!"

She stood off slightly, an angle in the firelight.

"Oh wow," Dawes Williams said. "I knew it. Too much and too late."

"Whatever can you mean?" she said, pouting, coming against him, leaning within and around him.

She was suddenly silent, kissing him seriously, an unconscious vine. He thought she was a post of lean fire, something unbelieved and too suddenly touching him, something strange, and smelling of thin musk and salt rain, the sea, and the water still slightly damp in her long hair which was warm and touching him with fragile nets. He couldn't believe her. In a white epilepsy she was pushing against him, laughing against his ear with her tongue. She smelled finally of lemon and salt wind, and his hand brushed the sandy skin of her ass. He pushed her away self-consciously and she sat on the long edges of her knees, watching him curiously. In the unwinding firelight the long shadows of her breasts ran down her white belly, becoming lost in the thickened darkness between her legs.

"Aren't I wicked?" she said, cocking her head.

"It's Very Important At What Point a True Divinity Gets Down and Gets Dirty," Dawes Williams said.

They began looking at each other for a long time.

"Deal?" Henry said.

"Shut up, you pimp," Urzika said, never turning, never taking her eyes off Dawes Williams' confusion.

"I think somehow I am supposed to be just finding out I have always been the real innocent in this piece," Dawes Williams said, never taking his eyes off Urzika's.

"Com'on," she said, warming up to herself, "let's go down the beach. Let's do."

"Besides, my mother told me to never roll naked on a public beach in a Catholic country."

"Quit pontificating horseshit," she said.

"Or, if I do, especially to make sure it was not with a witch on the eve of an inquisition."

"I'd like to meet your mother," Urzika said. "I'd seduce her on the spot."

"You'd seduce my mother?" Dawes Williams said, disinterested in everything but her eyes.

"That's right. I'd take *her* straight to bed, the bourgeois floozie. I'd expose her to herself for what she is."

"Damn," Dawes Williams said.

"That's right."

"Damn," Dawes Williams said, frozen to her, not even able to believe his own disbelief.

"That's right," she said. "You're mine, honey, if I want you. I'll do and make of you what I want."

"I'll be a sonofabitch," Dawes Williams said. "I never knew all that."

"That's right," she said. "And you still don't. Not really. But you will. You still only know what I want you to know. Nothing more. By the time you do, it will be too late. That's honesty."

"I'll be a sonofabitch," Dawes Williams said. "You American women are all alike."

"You'll be less than finished, less than a sonofabitch when I get through with you," Urzika said. "You'll wish you were dead. Let's go."

"I damn well might," he said. "You've vastly misjudged my capacity and desire for death."

"You damn well will," she said. "I haven't misjudged it an inch."

Trying to move slightly off center, he found he couldn't. In the silence she was still fixing him to himself, pinning him to her falling moon, an insect helpless in dead white light, spinning in a distance of mad glass, glue and delicate polish, her eyes.

"Deal?" Henry said, more quietly this time.

"Shut up, Henry bastard. I don't do things I don't want to. We may be going to San Blas together."

"It's love," Henry said.

"You happen to possess squat for being," Urzika said, still not turning from Dawes.

The Black stopped singing again, diverting everyone's attention. The last wooden twang died away, and for the first time the Black turned the side of his head into the fire. Looking at it, Dawes nearly gaped. He saw the Black's ear had been completely cut off or torn away; it was simply missing, and a long, chainlike scar ran down that side of his face. It seemed to nearly bloom out at him, every detail, in the long, small quiet. Then Urzika turned to Henry for the first time and said:

"Henry, you happen to have the world caught between your legs, like Plato's idea of a rubber fishing pole, dragging it with one hand wherever you go. I'm leaving you. S'long."

More silence; the campfire was ringed by a wood of stone faces, with motion frozen like insects, black with light.

"You can't do it," Henry said, suddenly believing her.

"I've done it," she said.

"I won't let you."

"I've done it. Consider it done. It's done."

"It's not," he said, rising, angry. "I'll kill you if you try. I will."

Then it became so still Dawes thought he could hear ships moving miles out to sea. Urzika and Henry remained frozen against each other, yet seamed, furiously refusing to turn into light. Then slowly—just another ritual, Dawes thought—Henry got up with the knife in his hand and came toward Urzika, saying, "You're dead. I'm doing it. I'm killing you myself."

Dawes Williams felt like laughing out loud. He stood watching Henry circling Urzika with the knife. She stood calmly in the flat light. The long edge of her nakedness, an angle of shadow, was bent against him. Dawes wondered when the curtain would fall, when they would suddenly stop in the exact middle of motion, begin applauding themselves; when they would begin collecting the coins from the sand, locking up the wagon and disappearing down the road. Out of sight, he thought, they would laugh, pause to count the money, and ride burros over the end of the world plucking dulcimers and banjos.

Then the Black moved. Dawes watched him, across the shadowy line of fire, quick as a blade and as light on his feet as a dancer moving on wood. He reached Henry, feinting once and picking him off the ground with the same movement. Strangely, when the Black touched Henry, it was almost softly, tentatively, at first; then his grasp tightened on the front of Henry's neck as if he were about to rip out his throat and throw it to the wind, disgusted with its blood. He fixed him for a moment, then the Black kicked Henry's legs out from under him with an easy motion, and he pinned Henry to the ground with the coupling of his straightened arm. The knife was frozen in Henry's hand by only the stare in the Black's eyes, his undeniable quickness. And the Black's arm formed a perfect vertical shadow with the ground as if, at once, it were both growing out of and reaching under the dark line of the sand. There wasn't even a hint of motion in the Black's body, and Henry, even though the knife was still in his hand, was frozen within the wall of this motionlessness as if he were a small animal about to have his large bloom torn out by the roots.

Then the Black said: "You let her go now, Henry. She's finally done with all this crap. It's time for that now. I say so. It's over. You let her go now, Henry," the Black said so peacefully suddenly Dawes could hardly hear him. "You let her go or I'll tear out your throat."

Then he got up and turned away, and Henry still didn't move, lying out flush with the wash of the sand. Dawes stood watching, unconcerned, unrelated, safe because he truly hoped someone would slit his throat. Urzika went over and stood above Henry:

"Yes. That's right," she said. "This time I am going to take this poor, innocent kid here down the beach. Do you hear me? Hell yes, and screw out his mind for him. Hell yes, and never come back. You bastard."

"You know," Dawes Williams said, "sex is everything they ever said about it okay, but, still, it never works out so much too long."

The Black was back at the fire, head turned away, singing away. The slow guitar drifted out with the blue smoke. The morning was nearly up, wet, grotesque as flat wood in the first sun. The knife, exhausted, still lay out with the sprawl of Henry's hand.

Dawes and Urzika began walking down the beach. She took his hand. Stopping only to dress herself in the blanket, she went with him along the gray sand, under the rotting seawall. Within its black concrete umbrella they sat for awhile, smoking, braced against the stone. The sky was a deep, luminous gray, full of rain and massing clouds. It was very still.

"What happens next?" Dawes Williams said.

"Who cares?" she said. "Something always does."

"No, I mean I'm really stove in this time, I think. I don't think I could walk around corners to faint."

"I'll find some last, spawning life somewhere. I always do."

"No, I mean I'm no good for you."

She laughed.

"Let me worry about that."

"All right," he said. "It seems technically ironic I should find myself dropping dead among strangers, but I'm grateful anyway."

There was a silence. They started walking again. Urzika had to help him up, and he buckled for awhile, resting on her.

"What about that Black?" Dawes Williams said. "He's the one I couldn't figure at all."

"Don't start asking me questions now," she said.

"It's not like me, but I think I could genuinely get to like that guy."

"Do you think he could genuinely get to like you?" Urzika said.

"Don't know. Probably not. I don't seem to be too likeable lately. But it was damn good of him just the same."

"Ya," she said, "he's got a lot of love."

"'Welcome back to de raft, Huck, honey,'" Dawes said.

"What?" she said. "Fiedler's famous thing?"

"Never mind," Dawes said. "But why did *he* let you go?"

"He knows he doesn't own me. He's cooler than Henry. Anyway, he's leaving for Campeche tomorrow. He knows I don't want to go. He knows he'll see me back in San Francisco sooner or later. That's why he didn't say anything; he knows a lot of things. What the fuck? Besides, he hates Henry's guts."

"So he knew I'd be better to leave you with me than at least Henry?"

"Ya. He knew that, among other things."

"So he was just sitting there, silent, running the whole thing after all?"

"Ya. Finally. I suppose. He was running the whole goddamn thing."

"There's more sense and beauty in the mating of arrow squids, I think," Dawes said finally.

"Ya," she said, "I think you're right."

Going up on the street, they stopped at a battered coupé, and Urzika groped for awhile in the blackness. She emerged carrying a white laundry bag full of her possessions. They began walking again down the gray wash and horizon near the surf.

"What's your name?" she said finally, taking his hand.

"Dawes Williams, I think," Dawes Williams said.

"Dawes bastard," she said quietly.

They were walking north, beyond the edge of the town.

"Tell me your last name," he said.

"No," she said.

Still walking, for miles it seemed, not touching yet, the sea a float of burned lavender balsam, and then she found the shadowy, rain-heavy lean-to constructed with tropic stalks and green, naked leaves. They sat, silent, watching the white sea washing inward from the two near islands of the hanging sea. She smoked, behind him, caught up and nearly naked in his jean jacket. He stared outward until her warm hands found him and they began undressing each other. Her hands were softly pulling his clothes away; her touch was opening him everywhere, investigating his dark, probing, dissolving him, defusing his center. Her body was an inward fall, a deep spiral of musky sea lying easily within itself. Her noise was a lizard's tongue of blue ice and fire, a night wing, a reptilian noise, shuttering suddenly, shredding, breaking up and moving out from under itself into the clean and naked, rain-green hut. And he pushed against that dampness, that bloom, that wet sand running through a ring of dark, her hut of yellow eyes, her rising naked stalk, her opening house, her closing roots of sand, the sounds the wind made running on the roof of her treeless country. He didn't think he could believe her. Suddenly they were laughing, pumping against the sea wind, night, the naked skin, dark itself, her mad rain coming off whole in the air, laughing, he thought, at his sudden wholeness, nearly not ashamed, coming off within her yellow naked house, her single sweep of dark stalks, her laughing orange eye of rain pumping, still pumping, laughing at his heart still trying to move within the sand damp, the wet.

Then he turned his swollen eye against her breast and slept, a voyeur, out of his sea, trapped and drowning of air.

Still beside her, listening only out at the sea, he could only see idiots, torn from the thorn rose of the wind, trapped in the necks of glass, crying out of themselves, remembering only they are a sea of penetrated flesh, a sleeping sustained by tumors of growth. And he could think only: *I am only a dog tossed behind itself in a ditch.* I am made of a dark, unfastening light.

"Tell me your name," he said.

"No," she said.

There was only that, sleeping, and the sound the sea made halving the horizon. There was only that and her, Urzika, biting at him again like a tiny, destroyed animal, a thing loose below him in his dark.

"George," Dawes Williams said, humming above. "You may be God's Own True Girlfriend, all right . . ."

5

Dawes woke into a destroyed sleep. Urzika was gone. The night seemed to creep like bluebirds over a trellis of doors. He sat on the edge of the bed, smoking, listening to the destroyed springs, watching the old tremors like a wash of animals in the moon run out to the ends of his body. For a moment he thought he was dead. He heard the mute Michael, the jeweler of stones, moving about below him . . . absently, almost not knowing why, Dawes took Barney's last letter out and gazed through the paper:

December, 1969

Dear Willie,

I'm at the 91st evac hospital DaNang in a bed with a rubber sheet. It's 2 AM and worms are crawling out of my ass and it itches so I scratch and break them in half; my finger stinks. I stink. Everything stinks. All the staff wear masks around me when they come by. The nurse gives me a shot of 5% strychnine every 4 hours. She says it will kill the worm, but it might make me UNCOMFORTABLE! Did you know it takes at least 5 worms to push half a worm out an asshole?

All I can remember is getting shot down while peacefully flying my HUEY near the Ho Chi Minh trail and having to eat bugs and lizards for three days until we were picked up. I didn't know you could get worms from bugs or lizards.

Anyway, yesterday this officer with a mask over his face pinned a purple heart on my pillow. The citation read how my body had been wounded by hostile forces during combat. I reached down to my asshole and got half a worm on my middle-finger and— well, you know what I did then.

I hope all is well with you, and your beer is cold.

Y. friend,

Barney

It must be Easter Thursday, he thought next for no reason. He seemed disconnected, unusually out of joint even for himself. Crossing the room, he saw he cast no shadow in the mirror. Afraid, he turned on the light.

"And as for your fucking notebooks," she had said, "I was further into your head in the first five minutes than *that*."

He had heard her, sleeping. She had left. She was still in the room, hiding in the closets. He poured a wide pan of water over his head, like an open pewter eye, and stood shivering in the heat. She would never leave. He must go out and find her, tell her she would never leave, that and that her skin was made of juice, her bones the stones of blood. He could not ignore her any longer. They would die together if she wanted. He felt there may be a *NEED* to marry the bitch. She would be there, sitting before her fire on the beach, waiting. He would bury his long, destroyed cell within her and be whole again. She would acknowledge him. He was capable of being that now. Admitting his entrance, she would smile. She would know it by forgetting. She would stir her wonderful chemical pot like madness and death as thick as a laughing mask gone thin in the lips.

He crossed over to his table and wrote out:

> A day and death like any other. Nothing remarkable. But maybe, when you run through that small, peripheral bee with the sword and flattened edges of that broom, the whole hive comes alive and cries against that tiny closure of day, and you never hear it. . . . That is what haunts me the most, that tiny closure, that, and the fact that you never hear that screaming hive; that, and the fact that I have just now in time noticed the fact that Scots in dementia always seem to write poems to lice and field mice and other minuscule running forms, no one else perhaps, peculiar to the race, that, and the fact that that tiny screaming hive may not even be screaming at all . . . that, and the fact that the scholarship of these notebooks never seems to unravel their ends and may not be screaming properly either.

> Schizophrenia aside, the definitive biography of the Founding Fathers has not been written yet. At times like these I find myself worrying greatly about that and not much other.

He bowed and crossed over to the hat rack. Putting on his hat and his pants, he went out to find her. He had to sit only twice on the stairs to catch up with his blood before he entered the street, a softly spreading gold eye and stone mule of slow droppings that hurt his body like sin. He remembered that night, just before. After having come back from the fat, four-hundred-pound opal hunter's stone zoo of topaz eyes, they had lain for a long time in the blue dark above the jeweler's shop, expecting nothing spatial, making love, miming time. He had slept. She had dropped something and gone out for a walk, not caring, he supposed, for the rhythms of his air. He didn't know how she kept up with herself. She must be as delicate as a horse. He dreamed. Perhaps she would be able to bear Braun Daniel sons. In his dream the red eye of the window, fierce with the rising smoke of angels, had reflected the interior jungle of exterior forms, straw hats and ladies, through the mask of the Mexican door.

The street was a sea, swaying, caving in, a parade of freaks. He had, he knew, forgotten his name. It spent such a long time riding the wind, ignoring him. It would never return.

"Your name," he had said. "Tell me any of your names then."

"No," she had said.

"Sonofabitch," he had said, lapsing beneath her.

She had laughed.

She had gone out for a walk, and now he was following her.

She was a dream of streets, a slip of water always easing his terrible tension, his torn eye, weaving before him. She was his secret, his only possible knowledge and end, a probable beginning after all these useless years. He walked, stalking the corners. He would find her. She would be down at the beach, before her fire, waiting for him. Earlier, before sleeping, he had heard the mute, Michael, moving below them. He is the one, Dawes Williams thought, he owns it with his silence. He is the tender; and he is going about, clicking down the last whirling machines at the fair. Rings dance on his walls, bits of metal sun, fire, eyes of glass. Everything else has been sold. The last merry wheel is clicking off, spinning down, drying the air with its motored sounds, its donkeys of electrical stoppings. The world is a sea. The world is an interface of maggots and wood, springing back, a hat of streets, and he is closing it down, Dawes Williams thought; he is the one who has somehow owned it, all this time, and will take no more tickets on his amusing rides, his fantastic wheels electric with strings of lights. In fact, they, all of them, have owned it all this time. They, the Mute, the Small Daughter with the Quiet Nut of a Nun Locked Safely Within, the Fat Four-Hundred-Pound Opal Hunter Who Polishes Her Like a Semiprecious Stone, Braun Daniel, Dunken, Eddie, and Travis, the Caivisian Scholars, Arthur and Gin, Simpson and Leone, Barney Redwood, Urzika, Handsaw Williams and Boomer le Roi all own it, will sell no more amazing tickets, and are shutting it down. They will not listen. The wheel glides beyond them, selling candy, twirling plastic rings, opening for nothing its funny houses of grotesque mirrors, its boxes of lopsided freaks. A laugh welled within him. It was tiny, destroyed, a dream of dwarves without humps rising in a box of mirrors, clean, erased, nonexistent, knowing not the 43, which is sixty-four, which is sixty too many for a four-sided box, knowing instead only the four real, and one possible, sides of itself knowing only one soft reach of reflection.

"Hell!?! *THIS IS THE GREATEST STORY EVERY TOLD,*" Dawes Williams said out loud.

He had looked after her in the room:

Hump the Dwarf.

What, Dawes?

I said, *Hump the Dwarf.* The Dwarf is Humor. The Dwarf is Death. The Dwarf Separates Us from Our Possibility of Time. Possession. The Dwarf is Unserious, Unpretentious and Aimless. The Dwarf is Disbelieving Belief, Forgiving Itself, Believing again. It carries on. I say, *To Hell with Humping the Queen, Hump the Dwarf instead,* and Up with the Druid Witch, he said.

"Jesus?" Dawes Williams said. "Who wrote this mother-fucker?"

She stood in the center of the room, naked, laughing:

Ginger, man, she said.

She was only nineteen; he couldn't believe her.

Their sound went out, drifting the dark, a shadow swooning, a single blackened bind, chewing gold bugs and caving with its own weight in the doorway. It went ringing on the bits of fire, glass, metal rings, chains and crucifixes like peccadilloes lining the jeweler's walls below. He had begun laughing. He had lain for a long time, alone, watching Urzika walking in the naked candlelight. She was reading his notebooks and eating oranges.

"Don't lose me now, Dawes," she had said, nearly waking him once. "Don't lose me now, at least for awhile."

"No," he had said, nearly sleeping. "Hell no, not for a long time."

But he had. He had lost her. He seemed to misplace her somewhere within his dozing sleep. And she had walked out, her green snakeskin eyes looking for a southern hang of rain. He drifted, behind, through tumors of Mexican streets, side alleys, finding himself placed squarely within the recurring, rectangular geometry of windows, framings, and doors, the edges of houses running in long rows down into the white stuck moon and washing sea. He wandered within it, caught up in nets, following. He moved down to the beach to find her.

She would be sitting there, waiting, alone, before a tiny fire. Approaching, Dawes Williams would see the vacant footprints, like the eyes of stone creatures which had been circling around her in the sand. She would be peaceful, sitting cross-legged in that sand, staring easily into the void before her, her face and hands hooded with light.

It would be still for awhile. The thinning firelight waxing the periphery was now a great sea turtle, a fine shell smelling of gull's eggs, crawling off into the water, to bloom in the roots of the ocean again. The low breeze passed under her, between her legs, exploding her with a fiery bloom of stars, soundlessly, easily, like screaming birds without air to fly in. Dawes' eye was torn, and spread within his head, and killing him. For a moment she was afraid, looking through him. The two islands in the near sea were fearful, granite things, slipping between. She could see it so easily, and for a moment she was lonely, but his universe was tied safely within her, held like an egg, secure within her knowledge. Distracted, she stared into the fire.

"Dawes," she had said, "I'm going up so fast. Hold me," she had said.

He'd move around the fire to her. His footsteps sounded dark to her, deeply impressed with water, the thunder of a grotesque, waking pagan god raining around her. She cried out. He could say nothing.

"Stop walking," she would say, "stop circling me!"

But he reached out, leaning, touching her. She moved to him, within his arms, a circle, crushing her, hopelessly outside her, encasing her, surrounding her time with space. Her hands, outside him, moved uncontrollably; her body, inside him, was motionless, trapped, a sail caught within a net of wind. But even with her eyes closed, she could see within him, through his rhythms.

Then she'd push him away. She stood in the ring of firelight, talking in an Indian language, in a babble of broken melody. He watched her, across yards of dark sand, frozen in the universe of another star. Full of submission, he couldn't believe her. She fell silent. She stood immobile before him, cast in shadow, filling with firelight, a stone figurine with only the arms and hands detached from the body and moving. Her face, even flaring, was a white mask of moon. Her fingers drew diagrams in the light. He laughed, so bad at reading sign. His laughter, unknown to him, died quietly over the sea; it thundered in her ears, violating her.

"*Trust me,*" she said.

But he had wanted to only be himself, to call her a second-rate vampire, laugh, withdraw, wrap himself within his comedy once more and be safe again. Instead, he approached her. He found her hilarious. He laughed again. He saw himself suddenly, an eighteenth-century English academic, muttering to himself, blissful, abstracted, pacing the edges of her woods in skinny britches and cast-off knee socks that rolled up under his pantaloons like blinds. He felt embarrassed, resentful in her presence; her wisps of staring, sensual smoke weaving his stone.

She was only nineteen; he couldn't believe her. She took his hands. He stood before her. Her eyes fixed him to her like a loose, unfastened thing. They carried him up, picked him from his tree of fire and earth, the sea passing between. And her eyes were so wide, he couldn't admit to knowing. The night was sudden with the screams of birds, jeweled gold bugs ascending in beaks. Afraid, he wanted to tear himself away and run into corners. He wanted to hide in her spread, within her dead eye knowing only the mad explosion of her feathers. He was certain now she wanted to kill him, to dissolve him within only her uncertain knowledge. And she saw it, staring back. She had gotten up and run down the beach.

He found the blowing, unsmoked fire but she wasn't there.

He seemed to come to for awhile. He stood in the edge of the sea, calling easily. He would find her. They had only misplaced each other for a moment, stepping out for a walk. He remembered moving on, drinking, moving into leafy doorways, an open wooden cantina at the end of the beach. The breeze moved through, withered, twisted with the flanks of vines. The roof was straw. He sat in the narrow interior corner light for awhile, alone, drinking his eye through glasses and wheels of tequila. He was joined finally by six smiling, open-faced Mexicans who spoke in broken English and who introduced themselves, university students, by vocations. His eye throbbed terribly, fluttering delicately before him like a moth netted in veins. Without much language between them the talk was silent, but finally, nearly maddened, he tore the bandage away. The Mexicans moved in closer, shuffling their chains, inspecting it, wide-eyed and near an approving applause. The world was drifting, slipping behind. One of the Mexicans was a cartoon and had a name; the others constantly introduced him as "Meekey Moose," smiling fondly around him. He was the leader. They sat, smiling back at one another through the thickened smoke. His eye burned and he tore at it, welling, a center of pointless acknowledgment waking his sleep. He was annoyed. The Mexicans watched him abstractedly. Whenever he came close to succeeding, to plucking it out through the soft, giving-in layers of pus with his fingers, they would laugh, pound his back, stop him and hold his arms for a time. He was a great show, a funny man. They bought him tequila and beer, refusing to let him pay.

Finally all of them, Meekey Moose, the Brain Surgeon and the others, piled into the Mechanic's '48 Ford coupé and they began driving out toward the whorehouses. Dawes followed in a rumble seat with the People's Hydroelectric Engineer and Meekey Moose, who was perched on his knee, almost lovingly, a bandit with tiny designs. The streets were too close and crumbled with only pods of light. The high plants grew behind wails, whispering, hushing the corners of concrete. They were stairs, motionless and black, waiting only for a chance to drop their black seeds on the open places and chew through the brick. The city fanned out into the deserted country, and Dawes Williams sat, out of his water, drowning in foreign places, watching for Urzika, watching the road for sign. He seemed to sleep for awhile. The luminous, veining night, blooming too close to surfaces within him, seemed to reduce everything to one hum that was frightening. But the country jogged past on springs, a Ford. It was all a low-down tune, a busted-out dulcimer of Mexican wind, he thought. He nearly woke. Slowly the faces ebbed, flared back, slightly fitful, out of a flat dream of walking yellow water. He recognized his kind, easily, through layers of water. Meekey Moose was perched on his knee, smiling, talking incessantly in garbled English and flowing Spanish about his impossible virginity, that, and the fact that he was also studying to be an engineer so he might someday help build roads and bridges for the peoples. He sat, still rubbing his finger through the friction of his hand, nearly squealing with delight.

"For the Peoples, the Peoples," he said emphatically, finally coming to rest, rocking, excitedly ramming his hands within the tight pockets of his own tiny legs.

"Oh yeah," Dawes Williams said. "God, My Father Is The Distance of Molecules In Outer Space PLUS al-jabr/All Terribilitatus, All Grim Justice, A Sieve/The Evolutionist . . ."

He smiled. Meekey Moose was drunk. He swayed on his knee, staring fiercely back into Dawes Williams' eye; he took his hands out of his own pockets and began incessantly poking his ribs. He looked finally out into the night. In the distance was a neon sign.

Dawes Williams opened his eye and drifted easily behind. He felt carried along, snaked in the darkness, exploded in the blossoms of the mountains. Looking up, noticing his foot was stuck through rotten flooring, Dawes could see Meekey Moose was again staring directly in, at exactly two and one-half inches, studying him frantically with a contained delight:

"Aiiiiiieeee! Aiiiiieeee!" he said. "The American boys is up!"

"Quiet, Meekey Moose," the other one, who was studying to be an accountant for the Peoples, who was studying Meekey Moose through the broken near window, said. "Let him sleep."

It was very quiet. Dawes slumped within half an eye, watching Meekey Moose watching him back, transfixed, twinkling, never blinking the wide yellow eye as if he, Dawes Williams, might at any moment fly off with the night wind. But times had changed. Meekey Moose, the Brain Surgeon, the Agronomist, the Hydroelectric Engineer and the others had all said they came from Durango, but there weren't any gunfights to be had any more, and they all only attended the university in behalf of the Peoples. And in the darkness, bouncing the road like banjos, Meekey Moose watched Dawes Williams, the Accountant watched Meekey Moose, the Brain Surgeon watched the Accountant, who watched Meekey Moose, who watched Dawes Williams, who watched the one who said he was studying to be the People's Ché. The old Ford moved in the ruts with the grace of a tank. A single bird went off in the cactus. The car slowed. The pipes and shafts rattled the pan of the roadbed, and the People's Mechanic got out, under the air like iron plants weaving the blackness, and began wining the contraption back up like impossible leavings. Soon they were rolling again. The night was a white ring of mountains, lying off, surrounding the spaces with distance, merging the cactus bird's swoon, a single seamless blood, a wafting throat; and in the plucked strings of 2/4 time Meekey Moose was screaming excitedly:

"He fix! He fix it! He fix it again, American boys! You sit! He fix it!" His voice was peaked and squeaky. The night was trembling, opening, a vague, surreal ringing around him. And Dawes' eyes drifted before him, unfocused, lost along the slope of the road. Finally, he was almost comfortable. He would wake. He would wake because it was all an illusion and he had never been. That proved it. He smiled to himself, almost certain of something. The People's Poet gave him a beer, *"Hasta la vista con Pacifico,"* and Dawes Williams said, *"Gracias, gracias, amigo,"* drawing out the *amigo* as long as socially possible, and everyone was smiling, perhaps with design, perhaps not, he had no way to tell. But they were at least rolling again, down the deserted blue, the black-orange creepers of light under the mountains, and older Mexicans were passing in shadowy pairs. Then they rolled rattling to a stop in front of the premier whorehouse:

THE ROOSTER DE LAS NOCHES

ABANDON ALL HOPE YE WHO ENTER HERE
BUT COME IN AND BE SAVED

"Meekey Moose," Dawes Williams said finally.

"*Si. Si.*"

"Where is the girl? Urzika is . . ."

"*Si si,* American boys! *Putas,* you like Mexican *putas,* American boys!?!"

"Oh ya."

Meekey Moose's eyes flared like bright pennies, uncertain of hospitality, in a radial wind:

"No, Meekey Moose," Dawes said. "Don't think you have it down yet. Urzika is . . ."

"*Si siiii.* Niiiice girls, American boys! You liiiiike it," Meekey Moose said, again moving an extended finger quickly through the friction of his fist.

"*Siiiii,*" Dawes Williams said, "anything you say, Meekey. *Hasta la vista con Pacifico.*"

Then Meekey Moose jumped from his knee and the rumble seat, and they began filing with the others into the shadows. At the end of the street the donkey tracings were wet as noses tipped and flecked with the worms of hanging light. A shrieking whore went off in the air. Meekey Moose danced ahead. The place was dark, close in, drawn like thick air through the neck of a bottle.

A passing kid was trying to sell Dawes Williams Chiclets from a wooden box. He moved along the doorways and cantina fronts with the others.

Another, older kid broke from within the mulling crowd, running on crutches, poking at Dawes with one and calling him *American American* in a tone that rhymed with *pig.* Dawes Williams stumbled and fell in a ditch of piss and standing water. He lay there, smiling, nearly comfortable; the rhythms were easy. A crowd was gathering. They seemed to be staring through windows of water, drifting, moving within the shadows and blooms, the seams of moon on the mountain. The kid with the crutch stood extended above him like reapers. The neon bloomed the night, the seams of light like white birds on the mountain:

THE ROOSTER DE LAS NOCHES

EX IS TENT IALISTS ONLY
BE LIEV ERS BE WARE
KNOWING AN ANSWER ALLOWED ON THURSDAYS AT NOON

Sleeping then, he ignored it. He wanted only to dream, but his last yeoman's blood was up, hot in his veins like banjos and pinwheels of tequila, and he wanted somehow more to stand, to nip the crutch from the Mexican's hands and brain him with it, lapsing again, when, just as suddenly, Meekey Moose and his band of five stepped in and nothing was necessary. He lay back again, watching the others as they outcircled the upraised standard, the furious crutch, testifying in heated Spanish. Finally they began chipping in pesos to buy off the Baron of the Wood Crutches, the Keeper of the Feudal Whorehouses, and, picking Dawes Williams up, dusting him off, they carried him along. He was as disjointed and limp as the desert, as unslept as the dust waking in the beatless eyes hung in the doorways. Another shrieking whore went off in the air. Dawes Williams was smiling. Suddenly he found himself nodding politely at everyone and everything he could find to smile at, at everything that moved and walked over the horizon. Still, they were drawing a crowd. Meekey Moose's cries went out, breaking the shrill wing of the night apart and leaving nothing.

In an open sill, a doorway, a woman was kissing another woman's breasts. The smaller one was impressed on the framing. Together they draped themselves along the wood facing, lying out, passionate and whole, luxurious as unwinding smoke and the snakes of tangled, dark-eyed atmospheres.

Dawes Williams moved past, slipping behind. The Hydroelectric Engineer, who was carrying him like sacks spilling out rows of grain behind themselves, set him down finally in the wooden light. He rested against the cantina front, sloping easily with the roll of the mud wall, like an Indian. He knew he was an exhibit. Others moved nearer, staring with innocence into the ugly tear of his eye. His face on the glass, turning, was a mask okay, something whirling, a terrible, reducing hum lying within the transparent illusion of rooms. A naked woman was dancing a dog. Turning again, squinting through the street, he could see the field of naked moon, a stone of grass, the patios and nearly neat rows of dollhouses, and the baking urinals running out behind with a surprising distance behind. It was like a small city without lights caught in the shadow of the mountain. Directly before him, within the mulling sullenness, Meekey Moose was delivering a harangue, backed by his band of mechanics, brain surgeons, revolutionaries, people's poets, hydroelectric engineers, agronomists and bureaucratic functionaries, and he was calming it down again into utter silence. People drifted off in the arms of whores, a peaceful swing, and the acres of waist-high mud urinals ran out behind. Someone handed Dawes Williams another beer, *Hasta la vista con Carta Blanca,* but he found he couldn't hold it, its weight giving out below itself, slipping from his hand, breaking, and it all went suddenly still as they turned him, began carrying him to the doorway, a cementless footstep, before him a woman walking through nets and beads of unhooking light where she turned . . . Dawes Williams was following:

THE ROOSTER DE LAS NOCHES
NEVER ROLL NAKED ON   BEACHES   IN   CATHOLIC   COUNTRIES
JESUS   NEVER   LAUGHED
ABSURD EVENINGS TO ORDER OR LET

He passed under the archway, behind, but she was faster and disappeared through the throats of smoke. Meekey Moose ran ahead in the flickering light, swatting her behind. The others followed, leading Dawes Williams, seating him finally on wooden chairs like something mounted where he sat, a totem, perfectly smiling, oblivious to their staring back. A woman danced a mule in the center of the room. Looking suddenly down, he could see another, leaner woman was running her hand in his jeans and smiling too. The mule was smiling. Everyone else was smiling. In fact, looking, he could see everything in the room was only hanging suspended between smiling and killing. A small dance floor lay beyond; it sailed in blue dresses, holding up the universe with eyes, tiny design, the small and unconnected tremors running out to the ends of his body. He could feel them lying there, unanswered, alone. The electric bulbs were a water of sleep. A woman, dancing a goat, drifted by. Voluted, horrible, he shut them out. His praying shutters, burrowing tightly in his skull, disappointed by the rotten, unclenching bone. His heart was full of terrible boomings. Something was chewing the collapsing, unnatural light. Perhaps, he thought, the electric bulbs were greyhounds, orange scorpions on giant sea shrimp stinging themselves to death on the walls. He could see them, unfastening the room from his hooks, undressing it easily, ceremonies and figurations of water weeds which swayed the hill from under the wind, leaving nothing. There, below, adrift and festering like seaweed, they wove the light like nets under beams; and he could feel his eye, smearing, giving in, running without emotion over the side of his face like a hut of blue hair in the darkness. Only Meekey Moose was staring in:

"Aiiieeee! Aiiiieeeee, American boys!" he said.

His eyes were hot and childlike, huge as toads. Transfixed by grazers, Dawes Williams sat watching them swimming across inches. Soon some strippers, two lesbians, a thin woman fattened with Coke bottles, mounted a stage above him. They danced in feathers, waking him from one sleep and sealing him to another. There was uproarious applause and innocent delight. The People's Poet poured him another tequila, forcing his throat slightly, and soon, following two lesbians, a Mexican dressed exactly as Charles J. Chaplin came out, parted curtains with the tip of his cane, signaled for silence with upraised hands, and proceeded to waddle finally through the rows of dancers, for minutes on end, in the flickering, speeded light to uproarious applause. A woman with bells tied off to her ankles like swords rattled the silver light into mercy.

Dawes Williams smiled.

Slowly, without any real conviction, he began dying. A shell, withdrawing into black casing, he sat wordless. His heart tasted almost sweet. A woman, dancing with a mule, was subtly trying to attract his attention; opening her mouth, she pointed into it with her finger. They, the others filling in the room behind him, were either dancing or plotting. It was a brutal lust; the darkness murmured and was livable. Meekey Moose finally sent the one who was studying to be the People's Architect out for more tequila, refusing to let him pay. It was too perfect, too easily planted in the beginning to be real, but he was glad now that he was alive. The bees made full circuits in the electric dark. He was glad at last, he thought, because he knew he was dead. The lights like mountains, black blossoms exploding the desert, were a soft and gentle wash, swirling within him, surrounding his terrible boomings. But it was easy now; all the geese were behind him. Urzika was gone, deserting the desert with her green and silky eyes. It had been a long time since first light. Just this morning, he thought, they, everyone, had gone to the farm. The universe danced for a moment, flickered on a candle end, went out. Arthur was dead. Gin was alive. Dunker and Eddie and Travis were gone. Summer was happy, wed in strings of nylon to a plastic world, secure until the witchwood recaptured the dawn. He sat, watching it swarm, a dance of naked thieves, joyous, wood-eyed, carving worshiping stone, stringing out and swimming easily behind him. He knew, waking, they dreamed, walking forever too easily clouded in sleep: but when they slept they came alive, waking fully risen, admitting all. The rest were mummers, the flowers' stem, lost with the responsible planting. They were that, and he was the horse leech, and the Goddess, the elements of world, the horse's flesh, had gone down to the water to drink. Her face was white, upstanding, near the pond. She chalked it with moonlight; the leafy shadows moved about her eyes. He lay below her in water, safe, drifting, watching her gaze. She sighed and neighed, a mare's breath trapping the water. Finally he had passed through her on springs of water, attaching himself to the back of her throat where, swelling with blood, he drank near explosion. She ran in circles, crazy with lust. She ran finally over the ends and the cliffs of the hills, saving them both. Rousing himself, Dawes Williams said:

"I am a Celt, Meekey Moose. I find this quietly ironic enough, of course, in Catholic countries administered mainly by the Graeco-Roman Anglo-Saxon Norman heresy. Yes, ironic enough."

"Si. Si."

"*But then we are not all formalists here,*" Dawes Williams said, "*and I am not sure that mere irony is quite what we had in mind at this time.*"

"*Si. Si. American boys. Aiiiieeeeeeeee!*" Meeckey Moose said. "*You liiiike it,*" he said, *drilling his finger deeply into the friction of his palm, popping forth with a match of fire.*

The People's Architect came back with the tequila. Dawes sat, disinterested, as the People's Brain Surgeon poured a shot in his eye, anointing his pain with suffering. Soon, lulled back, he could sit only staring again within the Moose's eyes, which were wide with wonder, a horrible end. Charles J. Chaplin, just then, still prancing above Mexican horns, was twirling on the end of his perfectly pivotal cane for minutes on end to uproarious applause. He spun and tucked his hat into the crook of his elbow and stood on the exact middle of the flooring. He was prolonged, a rivet, mustachioed thinly as Prussians, jaded and flickering between curtains of movie lamps. Masqueraded in wit, slouching toward Bethlehem, about to be born, he bloomed in the mousy eyes. He painted his nose with white chalking moon. He was happy, safe in his laughter. Upkicking his cane, he propped up easily the roof of the universe with the twirling tip of his walking stick. He was Mexican, disguised. He had a mask. And out of it, still, he could feel only the reach of Summer's cold hands, pulling him along. The orange scorpion bulb was slipping the unclimbing wall. He sailed without need of answers behind. He tried to catch her once again, passing, sliding beyond her mare of flesh for the last time, wanting to touch something whole. He missed, an explosion of apple blossoms, laughing, winnowing himself in a small fire of dark, shivering, completed in her quivering hair, her body, a soft, remembered hemisphere, a light, unmembered air.

"*Dawes,*" she said, "*you goose. Honestly. You've only got one eye open now. But you've still got to make your own future, you know. I wish you the best, Dawes, but you'll never get ahead feeling sorry for yourself. It's un-American.*"

It was nonsense. He put his head down on the table trying to shut out the voice with his hands.

"*Aiiiiiieeeeeeeeeee, Meekey Moose,*" he said.

"*Aiiiiiiieeeeeeeeeeeee, American boys,*" the Moose answered easily from across the table, undressed and open with the brown jewels of passing light.

He was full of distorted features, nearly beside himself with open delight, distended, netted and woven and elongated in the beams of light, the necks and bodies of brown glass bottles. Dawes could see him there, a motion of flickering light, untied, lashed, sailing backwards into the motion of the room. His eyes remained wide. He refused to grow a tail. The light was trembling, pathetic suddenly, an illusion. The shadows behind him were excited burros kicking out the ribs of the walls. Only Meekey Moose, crowning himself, celibate, sat wide-eyed and easily surrounded. Only Dawes Williams was stone, fixed to the wood, ready for sacrifice. Cold, unblinking with wonder, he knew he had finally lost all ability to move, that he was frozen forever, stuck to red air, pinned to the zoo of his wood. Across the room a woman was dancing, a stain of blood, a flowering rouge in the air.

The People's Architect had returned again. He stood, neatly pouring tequila from another bottle. He dealt it like cards, holding finally Dawes Williams' head back, fusing his throat, corking his eye with a thimble of liquid fire. It was peaceful for a moment. He couldn't believe it. Then it flushed over him, welling, filling his center, swelling his head and bone with a fine washing pain, desire, only another king, another moment and season of life; but the music continued. The Spanish-Indian trumpets were highest, swelling too. Another woman got up to dance. She was gone in the face heels and teeth. Soon, without logical sequence, Gin's black, Methodical radio floated by, on springs and tubes and electrical hummings, speaking Greek:

"John Twenty-Twenty-nine. John Twenty-Twenty-nine, Dawes," it said. "HAPPY ARE THEY WHO HAVE NEVER SEEN ME, YET, KNOWING THE POETRY OF MY TRUER BODY, HAVE FOUND MY FORM IN THE WOOD, THE SEASONS, THE WHITE EYE AND BLOOM OF THE STONES AND THE MOON," it said. "Ezekiel saw the wheel, Dawes, the Father, the Truer Mother is Dead, buried, to be buried again, risen, six hundred B.C., a conspiracy of officers. The cities are harlots, false prophets, raising up masculine Gods."

It was nonsense. It was obvious, true. The table was cold, round, the only possible government. Sleeping bulls burned into horns, ignited the bone of his eye. There was a tiny river, winnowing the grains of the wood. The wood was a heart, beating back, a vision of speech. The air was trapped, floating on severed thorns, drifting, a tower to carry him home. He woke, behind hills, in the light dancing like the blue necks of swans. It was an old stone house. He knew he had stood here before, encircled in her grove of apple blossoms, riddling the branches, listening to the voices his arguments left, leaving the wind and mingling the roofs of the trees. Because, he knew finally, the twigs were the letters, and the vowels were the seasons, the passings of the Goddess through the rhythms of her king's year. Birth, Initiation, Death, the time forever unwinding itself in her coiling hair, a natural light; Ceremony, Order, Sacrifice. Her habit was always nakedness. She had no theories, no pretense of clothes; she was simply what was real. Creation was her body, first light. She was the clean element, her own net, whirling with ritual and order through the veins and seasons of her stone, her temples which filled with perfect light. The dawn, spring roses and autumn thorns were the equinoxes, and the curve of her naked foot a dancing ankle bell. She killed her king on Christmas Eve, wearing a hag's face. All rhythms were her mercy, her only sign.

Raising his head slightly over the wood, above the line of her table, he could see her finally, an old woman waltzing with bulls.

She disguised herself with dogs and birds and deer. She hid her secret, safely, ultimately, in a universe of knowing. He could see her dancing. She swayed in naked hair. Then, for a moment, he was caught south of her winter. She was young again, rising before him, cast perfectly, walking out of her white dream, long and pure as cuttings of water. Only her eyes were bloodstones; topaz. She was by turns a maid, a woman, a hag, a year over and beginning again. Her magic was slow. The answer was her rhythm, her ritual riddled. But he knew her. In the seasons, spitting him up easily, receiving his lust, his love and fame, she was mother, wife, temptress, sister, hag. Her year was the only Holy City. O Lady of the Wild Things, Dog Star, Barley Goddess, Temptress of the Nine Heights and Flower Fuse, once each year your chosen, your totem bird, is burned alive. . . .

The room, a ceremony of stone and alphabets, was filling behind him. He sensed their wood. But he watched her, transfixed by spinning, as she wove her boat of knowledge and claiming, a nest of hag wood now, around him. She was a ring and fire of darkness. Only the trees, like anklets and crowns that bloomed in her water, the wilderness, surrounded his name.

She was dancing before him, swaying, unfaced, old. The wry-necked, snaking bird reclaimed lay hissing in her breasts of milk . . .

Her language was the only remaining season; her letters the trees, the leafy notes. Her instruments the strings the wind left weaving the branches, calling him out. She had no opposite, no bad or good, but only form, a moving, uncir-cling design. She had armed him with exploding birth, and called him back. Her lips were berry red, a dance of bees. Her breasts, a mare's nest, entwined with tanglewood and night, enfolded her hair, which, running down, undraping twigs, unfastened her legs. There, white, a horse-lined thigh, a prophecy of birds exploding nets and rooting the ground, she was an enor-mous house, an axis and scream, an owl, hooting, lost with design, kindling a need-fire, passing through smoke, a yawn left sign-filled and gaping on her fin-gered air. She had a terrible mask. Her eyes wavered the surface of water before him. Her woods were wells to die within.

Drowning, pulled behind, he followed her design. She fled, always before him on a snow-white mare.

He remembered then: he was born to her. She was the willow then, a maid, the haze and net of birth, tail, the sense and source of dew, all moisture and life in the antlered dark. She was the secret after all, the witch of life. The untold things were nested in her swaying eyes, the windy leaves, her hair, ini-tiations; only later she was the hag and hanging water-moon, his death, all things present. She had three faces and a single, choosing aspect. She was the witch of life, the water's blood. She touched his body, igniting his wisdom. Her bark was the skin of riddles. Leaving him, she had promised to return. Her lust was final and perfect. Soft May Day was her middle. He would be an Indian, Celtic. At the end of his year she had promised herself to others.

"Aiiiiiiiiiiiiieeeeeeeeeeee," the Moose was saying.

He was openly delighted, up and dancing with an unnamed whore. He jumped high, clicking his heels, but still too wide in the face, too cute, the chin distorted, pulled down, melting. They rode a mule with ass' ears. He tried to ignore them. They rode beside, encircling, draping his limits, a southern world, mathematical structures, a wash of dooming X's.

He knew the murdered, the mad must learn to hold their breath.

He rode the north wind home to paler, deathly faces which flew like ghosts in the glass. He was hurled along, before himself, by storms of deadened leaves, into the face of the icy mountains where only the clouds were feathers and flowers of blood. Behind him, guarding his secret, flanking his rear, fled the dog, the only living thing that shared his pilgrimage. She fled, always before him, teething her mare. But strangely, arriving, it was only an Isle of Snow-White Blossoms again. The apple trees, rising, pink and white and yellow as doors, were flues and clouds of air, not sleeping, exploded by wind. Dismounting the horse, open-thighed, unfastened in nakedness, she was a woman. She chose him, burying him in the lust of blossoms, killing her yearly king by enthroning him. She untied her face in daylight and twined him to her thigh. He knew her. They walked the groves together. And there, singing in her branches, she set out her only music, the notes which played the trees. Her language was the only season. She called the sailor through the maiden's breezes, arming him, exploding his fear with birth. They listened to the river music of the evening reeds. He lay with her for a long time in the smooth, unstringing grasses fusing the woods into stones. Her face, already a chalky net, waited for nightfall. Then, dressed only in leaves, she reveled in revealing her deeper wood, a delicate, quivering heart. Secretive, a dance unweaving his fan, she moved about within him, exploding his birth and blood with apple blossoms.

She had a metaphysical eye, as blue as perfect nightmares.

Only later, then, she was the hag reclaiming his journey. She fled ahead again, unraveling only the boats and night of north wind. Behind him ran only the living things, the earthly dwarves that shared his pilgrimage. She had no words but represented herself at will. And he was silent, too, known, unknown, to be hidden once more in the universe. All masks wore space, not time, the same design of blood; and his knowledge had been neatly spun within itself, its endings known beginning, shucking him out and leaving him to be completed once more. Only she was one, eternal. Her stones, falling through an amber universe, announced her departure on diving horseflesh through the water without shape or flooring. He could not believe her. He could not contain her black, unswirling motion, her fire, much longer. Future and past, without a possible history, were present. All seconds poured out of her mildest water, blank and Un-imagined within her trance and insect of blur-ring bells.

He could see her before him, dancing easily in the mane-mounted bonfires of rooms, a dream of water and fallen timbers.

Soon, however, JHWH entered. Enter JHWH. (He was strangely unlike he'd have expected him to be, a secular, temporal parody, a projected necessity. He was overly masculine and lacked intuition. His head was made of plastic concrete, too easily styl-ized, and messed over with centuries of definition. He obviously worked in an office. His hair was shorn. In his hand nonhand he carried his swagger stick; and on his head nonhead there was a red felt cap which said, in a spinster's stitch and script, Amer-ican Legion Handfort Post Number Three. *A yellow feather was stuck in the brim.) He said nothing at all, pacing around:*

"I'll be frigged," Dawes Williams said. *"You're only a Norman Prussian after all."*

"Yes, but I am Deus Ex," *he said.*

"May I sit in the Circle of Unenlightened Pagans then?"

"No," *he said,* "I'm forgiving you."

"I'll be damned."

"That's the point," *he said.* "I'm sneakier'n you."

"I'll be good," Dawes Williams said. *"Nine times six is forty-eight. Send me away with my kind."*

"No," *he said.* "I only bloom with intimations of devils, polar things, good and bad."

"Rheo, Rheo. I flow away. There is no now. You are a foolish man."

"No," *he said.* "I've been elected to serve in your image. I am the impersonal judge. Good and Bad. Good and Bad. That's all I know. I judge your qualities and habits of life. I cannot be bothered to give elaborate opinions. I do not love you, even in the sense that I admit to possessing your elements. I get you to work in the morn-ings, ascend you into worlds of wrenches and rugs, and teach you your cast. I am Feudal, yes, your highest liege and squire to boot. I am masculine pater, spirit at least of course, but above the ongoing material creation. I build with others' tractors now. Creation is a sexual act. I am aloof in the roof. I judge only shadows now."

"I am a Methodist then," Dawes Williams said. *"My Body was a Temple. I blew it. I admit it. Damn me to my kind."*

"No," *he said,* "don't think so. You go too willingly. I think I'll damn you to Heaven. I make a good Bureau."

"That's an old joke," Dawes Williams said.

"Aiiiiiieeeeeeeee," Meekey Moose said. "Sweet Virgin Mother Protect Us the Wrath of His Thinking!"

"I am a Celt," Dawes said. *"I wish to worship at the wood's heart, the stone's eye, the language found forming forever in the swaying cranes of the trees. My lack of rid-dles is my only heresy."*

Even the whores were smiling then . . . . JHWH said nothing at all.

"Aiiiiiieeeeeeeeeeee," the Moose said again.

"Yes," Dawes Williams said, "he is an unkilling whale . . . the seasons do not know him. He is ascetic, officed in paperwork, male, above material creation. He is only the Jewish, Greek and Roman Anglo-Saxon and Norman prelude toward establishment, an excuse to rule. In his name they unfastened the land, deserted the tribe, and built the city. His secret unriddled, exposed, leaves him gaping for votes and armies and life."

JHWH said nothing at all. He paced for awhile, bereft of subtle argument and, finally, sighing with a lisp, he crossed to the front door, nakedfooted but unmoved on the backs of walking whores. Once outside, thoughtless in the wind, he entered a carriage pulled by the masses and drove away.

Suddenly bored with dying, Dawes Williams took a scrap of paper from under his shirt and wrote out:

"I don't believe I have ever encountered God, Our Father, as character, as *Deus Ex,* in second-rate modern fiction before," Dante might have said. But then neoanything has its limits and Neo-Classic is the worst. Plato was the end of everything.

The temperature in Valdosta, Georgia, incidentally, passing through, was seventy-three. This is modern disconnection, a tiny scherzo, and also bullshit.

I resign. (We are walking backwards if we are doing anything at all.)

I failed, of course. About the only undamning thing that could be said about him, Dawes Williams, is that his instincts were consistently out of control. His life was a case of nearly contained hysteria. He is tired now. His mother was a Republican. He pierced his secret wellspring, a sophomore's possible fate, and played it like trombones in the wilderness. He was a funny man. His father kept the books.

Only some of them are walking back far enough and in the right direction. Their hair is kinked and long . . . and they will reject the other, living in the fields again, talking to their ancestors, the wood, the summer solstice, the great stone eyes locked in the turning language of the grass. Ha-Ha

Ironically, tired, I am my own Greek chorus, my own suspicion.

Rheo, Sum, Esse, Fui, Futurus.

Urzika had green and unrained eyes, terrible and killing to lie beside at night, swollen and fixed with nature's design.

He tried to give her all that was impossible, beauty, belief, things past humor and forgetfulness, but there was no one, no way, to take it and fix its position for long.

He lived with Methodists in a Republic, a terrible thing.

Not Skepticism, exploding myth (the deepest blood), exploded itself beyond enlightenment. Belief . . .

He lived hunting in a haunted wood, an explosion of apples and blossoms in a particular sense bore him and slew him at lasts.

The West was full of six-guns and marshaled offices.

The East was partial, too close with forgotten solutions.

He lived in the Middlewest; but the Machine ate him with others anyway, in the end.

There was no relief in numbers.

He was swallowed, by parts, while looking for the Tribe, Matriarch, Wife; Religion in a particular sense at the finish.

He found her in a way, the Goddess, the deepest blood.

He was not sad at leaving it.

Then he died. He gave in easily. The universe was going out. For a moment, confused almost as if waking in the middle of sleep, he thought he must fight it, holding out the blackness at arm's length, holding up the beams of light. He thought he must hold up the universe, a stool for others, a play of last, important manners, dancing, dancing, only a woman now was dancing now, touch me, touch me, he thought, easily, easily a silver stork of walking bells, a song ran up her legs, touch me, touch me, there, between her legs, and ended. He tried to remember. The red light spun into fine blue points, a tiny center. He grew angry with himself. He seemed forgetful. The herons seemed to be crying out of deadened cats, a Midwestern street, the bus' horn below at the end of the block. Once, he, Dawes, he and his dog Tike, had stood amazed by the bloom and glare of the rain-sheeting window. There, standing together, he and his dog Tike and their only mother, had stood seeing light, the washing branches, feeling the cold glass rain and watching the lashing bush of the sky. The massing black clouds exploded with blossoms. There was glory in the dark, descending stalks. The hill was a living thing. They stood, staring through the glass, dumbstruck with awe. The glass was green round the edges. The orange August winds were spinners and creepers untying the cracks in the door. The houses were fortresses of wet painted lilac. Their containment had passed for civilization. Time was possible then, at that moment. And somewhere, across the state, Arthur, who was dead, was standing in his long lane leaving only low, unimpressed whispers within his cedar groves at the first outbreak of evening. The trees were waters of dusk. The jacks and dogs, dark like shadowy ships, were running along the long edge of the hill. The stones were whispering, perfect, and the dogs swooned into passion. But time was possible then, at that moment. He wanted only to move again for a moment, with Arthur, through the midst of howling dogs. He tried to remember, but, forgetting again, he could only feel them, like fine blue points, light, something uneasy with only studying itself as it slipped so effortlessly, passing away, leaving only rivers and faint whispers in the trees, leaving only Arthur's low dog howls rising in his cedar groves at the first, outbreaking evening. He tried to remember them, forgetting their face.

He set himself to wait. He tried to remember them, their face, waiting for them, setting himself, but he forgot about that suddenly. They would return soon, filling his image. He sensed their presence, their blood. They were about to conceive him again. He would be whole in a moment, remembering the future. Then he couldn't remember any of that somehow, their present blood, the thin, inner passing of a window and shadowy, faceless glass. He couldn't place them. Then, forgetting that too, that a shadow knew and remembered him, that he was, Dawes Williams tried to begin thinking of other things. The small, implosive lights, a sail and core of bells, swept by his memory, brushing his ear, a long dark cloud of water, easily bruised. The dancing woman knitted herself, going belly-up and fixed to the roof. He watched her move on a pin. There were smaller implosions, fixed blue lights wedged into dyes on his brain. She danced in a funnel. He watched. She spun it over with the dancing bells. He watched it spin in the air, fuse into a red point, light, the shadows of animals, monsters, expanding again. The sound rankled the breeze, a soft, delicate shoot of noise collapsing and ending in her legs. She danced. Then he forgot her too, becoming quietly angry with himself because he couldn't seem to think of anything at all. He knew he had forgotten her when he remembered her, saw her again, forgot her. She danced beyond him, over him. Finally he couldn't see her any more and he didn't remember that she was gone, that he couldn't. The last thing he saw before he died was Meekey Moose, who was watching, across a long table, with quiet delight, with huge, black rimless eyes, red pointed ears and yellow seas of grinning. And then he couldn't remember anything at all. For a time this made him angry, that he couldn't remember, and then that was gone, too, and he didn't even remember he was angry at not remembering.

For a long time they didn't think he was dead. He was. The Mexicans only thought he was drunk. He wasn't. He was dead. A small boy selling Chiclets passed, picking his pockets, but he didn't move. Then a woman brushed against him and he fell to the floor. It was then that Meekey Moose, a tiny cartoon expletive, a small ball forced for a moment with air, made a sound. Meekey Moose was the first to know he was dead. It was morning, early, almost light . . . the air off Mazatlán, thin as kings, spread on an easy sea. An empty bus moved in the mountains. Perhaps not. But it would be a cool day, orange, there, moving in the Mexican mountains, passing the white mud huts, the early cooking fires, the smoky horses of motion and rock all stacking the bright sierras, the places where the people painted their names on the sides of the mountains. The world rowed over him, the sea beyond. But he was away and wasn't watching. It was early, cool there in the mountains. Dawes Williams, locked in tiny, unswelling stone, roared with laughter. The sound, unheard, music untying the wind, lay off in the high, wheeling distances past Mazatlán. Alone, light drifting on the southern sea, a rising gull would pull those seeds away, lighting out north for the gulf, leaving only the silence of the bright waves to lap up his sailings, carrying only the old letters of new trees on his wings; a shudder at the end of light, a dance.

You can't get away with this stuff forever, Dawes Williams'd thought. Nobody can.

AFTERWORD

I'm not a writer of fiction. I don't do essays. Nor am I especially good at bringing literature to life in the manner of Cynthia Ozick, Leslie Fiedler, Lionel Trilling, or other writers and critics I love. I haven't written a book report since fourth grade. (It shows, I fear.) Haven't even written about books since college.

But I do read them, live with them, even disappear into them. Still, I never work to comprehend them in the manner of the essayists I admire. If a book becomes important to me, about the farthest I go is to wait for the right person to come along to show it to, saying not much more than "You gotta read this." Sometimes I have to add, "You gotta give it a chance."

For Dow Mossman's book, I'd add that.

The first time I started reading *The Stones of Summer*, in 1972, I was on a commuter train heading home from college one weekend. I didn't really read it as much as I sampled what it was I was getting into. I immediately felt the intensity of its language. I was young, and I had an appetite—in literature, in films, in music—for ambitious art and the stretching and breaking of traditional forms. More was more, and the more the merrier.

But I wasn't ready for the vast space of this book, the playfulness of its style, or the way it stretches everywhere before snapping into focus. The voice behind the pages echoed all around me, and the imaginative place it created was bigger than I had room for. It was a place I wouldn't learn how to measure until I was a generation older, watching my own children grow up in their time.

So I let the book drift away. Even without me, the story grew.

Twenty-five years later, I rediscovered it, the punched yellow commuter ticket marking my place, and read it on airplanes over the course of two months of travel and work across this country. I saved the final section for reading at home, savoring a little each night in bed before going to sleep, returning to the strange but magically familiar place Dow Mossman made. There—in the story of Dawes Williams, his town, his friends, his need to transcend the familiar, rebel against the conventional, and grab onto and ride the exceptional—I recognized experiences I knew but hadn't considered for decades. It was a place I thought had disappeared, and once I found it again, I didn't want to leave.

In my own youth, Dawes's friend Ronnie Crown was a kid named Chucky who beat up my friend walking home from school when we were seven; he was dead of drugs at nineteen. Travis, Dunker, and Eddie were my friends, too, but we risked our lives in different jams. Barney Redwood didn't ace the pool hall and ride the rails in my neighborhood, but he listened to the Beatles backwards. Summer Letch, then as now, was attainable only in one's mind. And Dawes Williams himself was lurking around, too, watching, waiting, maybe even—someday—writing.

The peculiar thing is how magical *The Stones of Summer* was to me even though I had reached the age when magic was pretty much a stranger to my life. The book had the power to send me places not just imaginatively—into my own past, into Dawes's perpetual present—but even physically. For after turning the last page, this reader at last got out of his chair and went looking for his own adventure.

Those of you who have seen my film *Stone Reader* know all about my search to understand the mysteries of this book, its author's disappearance, and how reading connects people. As I discovered after the movie came out, I wasn't the only reader who'd been touched by Dow's magic. Despite having fallen quickly out of print, the novel was still alive out there, on a few hundred library shelves, in a few dozen homes, in a few used bookshops. When the movie was released in theaters some thirty years after the book was published, in an age transformed by digital speed, readers of *The Stones of Summer* popped out from their own timelines, each clutching a single worn copy.

Some told me they had lent it to a whole circle of friends and had never been able to find another copy. Some had read it three times. One person dove deep into a lake to recover a copy fallen overboard, fearing he would never find another. A man told me he had met a woman on an airplane who carried it around everywhere she went, hoping to find someone else who had read it. And one night a woman called and told me her husband had taken her blindly to see the movie, because he hoped the film would illuminate for him her twenty-five-year obsession with the book. For these readers, as for me, *The Stones of Summer* did indeed burn with a "holy fire," as John Seelye recognized in the *New York Times* review that first brought Dow Mossman's work to my attention all those years ago. Here was a book that for all its wild fling at life, its thrash and spit and throw, had the ability to focus you right to a place you once knew, and may one day know again.

And yet up till now, *The Stones of Summer* has led a troubled life. After being submitted to many publishing houses, it was published by a heroic editor at Bobbs-Merrill and met exceptional acclaim in the *Times* and a few other venues. It was rescued for a moment by another believer, who published a mass-market paperback, but then *The Stones of Summer* dropped from sight. It failed not only to find a readership, but any sort of critical memorial. It was not even remembered as "that one book way back when," except by a few believers, like Carl Brandt, the book's agent, who told me that he and the book's editor, Betty Kelly, would for years after get together and wonder, "What could we have done differently for that book?"

But this lost book has now been found. Shortly before the galleys for the new edition of *The Stones of Summer* were complete, its author, Dow Mossman, a long generation older, told me on the phone that the book's rediscovery signals a "reaffirmation of the solid fringe." Like many of his phrases, it's an apt one. I hope you've climbed up on Dow's stone fringe and had a look around. For despite the indulgent ambition of this novel, the comical nature of it, the decades it covers, the spin-out, flare-out, flame-out of its final explosive section, and the wild originality the reader encounters all along the way, *The Stones of Summer* works as great fiction often does, inviting us in between the pages, where our hearts and souls can read their fate.

Mark Moskowitz
July 2003

THE LOST BOOKS CLUB

This edition of *The Stones of Summer* is published in association with the Lost Books Club, Inc., a not-for-profit corporation dedicated to introducing, preserving, and passing on to future generations hard-to-find, out-of-print, or otherwise forgotten works. To learn more about the Lost Books Club, visit www.lostbooksclub.com.